TURNER'S STRENGTH

JAMES SEYMOUR

To find out more about this book, please visit:
www.vividpublishing.com.au/turnersstrength

ISBN: 978-1-923078-79-6
Published by Vivid Publishing
A division of Fontaine Publishing Group
P.O. Box 948, Fremantle
Western Australia 6959
www.vividpublishing.com.au

Disclaimer
In this publication, all characters – other than the obvious historical figures – are fictitious, and any resemblance to real persons, living or dead, is purely coincidental.
This novel is set primarily in the Guildford area of the UK and spans some cities and towns of England, Scotland, the Eastern Cape Province of South Africa and the United States of America. The combination of historical information and fictional detail has been attempted, and the author has provided explanatory footnotes where possible. Some place names and sites are fictitious, and any resemblance of these fictitious names and locations to actual places is purely coincidental.

Books by James Seymour

Turner's Rage, Vivid Publishing 2020
Turner's Awakening, Vivid Publishing   2022
Turner's Strength, Vivid Publishing   2025

. . . .

Keep an eye out for the release date
for book four of the Turner Series.

Foreword

Welcome to the Turner Series! If you are starting at Turner's Strength, book number three in the series, then you will find the Prologue useful. I have included brief descriptions of the themes in the first two books, Turner's Rage and Turner's Awakening, to assist in understanding the cast of characters and their development.

For those who have read Turner's Rage and Turner's Awakening, you will be keen to continue with the characters' lives through that tumultuous time, the Industrial Revolution and the aftermath of the Napoleonic Wars, and their adventures. Some of the questions unanswered in Book Two will be developed in Book Three.

I'm sure you will enjoy Turner's Strength. There are new characters, intrigue, romance, adventure, and personal interactions between family members and the community. Those who enjoy historical fiction will find the themes addressed both fascinating and perhaps challenging.

Once again, simple English language is used, so I hope that helps with your time management. Some readers have asked for mercy and demanded a shorter book with larger print. So, I worked with my publisher to achieve a more comfortable reading experience. The cover size is the same, but the number of pages has decreased. The word count is roughly one hundred and seventy-five thousand words (including the List of Characters), representing a normal-sized book you will finish in a few days, or maybe less if you're on an ocean cruise. I hope it works for you wherever you may be in our world.

The challenge of writing about Africa, Grahamstown (Makhanda), and the aboriginal peoples and fauna has been rewarding. I sought help from various culturally experienced folks who were recommended to me and were so generous with their time. I hope you enjoy the snippets where I mention the landscape and people of the Eastern Cape Province of South Africa.

I was fortunate to visit Guildford (England) in early June this year and was again entranced by the town. So much history is found there and in its surroundings. There is never enough time for exploration. I find great inspiration in regional communities as they meld learning, achievement, joy, sorrow, compassion and forgiveness together. After all – that is village life! 'It takes a village to raise a child.'

I have said enough! It is time for that hot coffee, chocolate, or Irish liqueur. Tuck yourself away somewhere quiet and comfy, turn off the mobile, and let your mind fall back into 1827 Guildford, England. Open up the pages and find William Turner forging new friendships and gaining confidence, unaware of his father's secret plans, which will change his life forever.

I hope you enjoy this novel as much as I loved writing it.

James Seymour, May 2025

Prologue

The Turner Series is written chronologically, starting with the novel, 'Turner's Rage'. I recommend that the series be read in order; however, this may not be possible for everyone, depending on your situation and the availability of copies. In the following, I have given some notes on Turner's Rage and Turner's Awakening to assist readers who are commencing with the third book, 'Turner's Strength'.

In each novel, there is an extensive list of characters. I suggest you read (take your time and study it carefully) the List of Characters before you commence Chapter 1. It will greatly help if you are familiar with the members of the Turner Family, the main characters in the novels.

Of course, if you are keen on jumping straight in, please go for it. Many of my readers have done this and claim that the novels stand alone.

Turner's Rage – Novel No. 1

July 1826 - Guildford, Surrey, UK

The Turner family – Jonathan Turner manages a huge bakery business that supplies the Guildford community and the outlying farms. Jonathan inherited the small bakery on Quarry Street from his father, Henry, and has grown the business substantially. With the advent of steam power, Jonathan decided to build a steam-powered flour mill close to his bakery and reduce his dependence on the water-powered small mills up and down the River Wey. The high price of flour charged by the inefficient small water mills convinces Jonathan that there is much to be gained.

Jonathan's wife, Eleanora, cares for their eight children at the family home on the High Street, past the Free School. The children are as follows:

Girls – Bethany (19), Anne (17), Clementine (14), Madeline (12), Marcia (4)

Boys – Thomas (23), Simeon (9), William (6)

Jonathan is a driven business owner who understands the dangers of poverty towards the end of the Georgian period. His wife, Eleanora, is dependent on their marriage for her future and the sustenance of the children. The story begins with a frightened six-year-old, William, rushing downstairs in search of his mother for comfort. On opening the bedroom door, he sees something he should not.

The incident moves William's strained relationship with his father close to a breaking point. Anne, William's elder sister, protects him from their father's wrath. Anne, who has worked in her father's bakery for the last five years, has a chance meeting with a young man, Robert South, due to a freak accident involving Simeon. Despite knowing little about him, a romance slowly develops, which ignites Anne's dreams. Robert, a young navy officer, provides a window into a world outside Guildford that Anne has never seen.

When a mysterious Scottish brewer arrives with investment opportunities that promise to secure the family's future, William's older sister, Anne, suspects all is not what it seems.

From ruptured relationships and financial ruin to redemption and transcendent romance, this epic novel follows the fortunes and adversities of the Turner family as they wrestle with lives upended by technological and social change.

Turner's Awakening - Novel 2

November 1826 - Guildford, Surrey, UK

Worker unrest is spreading among the outlying mills, and rumours arise that the Turners' steam-powered flour mill will come under attack. Jonathan must find a way to confront the angry workers protesting the change. At home, Eleanora's health is failing. Jonathan, who has made peace with his pregnant wife, is fearful of the months ahead. Mindful of his seven-year-old son's loose tongue, he stops damaging family secrets from being revealed in their community.

Anne, flourishing in her role at the Turner businesses, is unaware that Robert's new navy assignment will bring peril to their doorstep in Guildford. Their joyful romance is tested when thrust into the middle of a political struggle for control in a volatile and changing world.

The Turner children's new friendship at Cloverdale Chase has implications that rock the family to the core. William treads carefully as his tenuous relationship with his disturbed father is cemented in place forever. Johnathan must come to terms with his wife's failing health while trying to control his rage problems that upset the balance of his family and business.

Across the Irish Sea, continuing famines and suppression by the Protestant Ascendancy increased the Irish people's misery. Struggles by any means were considered worthwhile to be free of English reign. Unknown to Anne, Robert is thrust into the middle of revolutionary violence with no guarantee of his survival.

Mystery, romance, grief and exhilaration bond the family and community in a gripping adventure as the Turners exploit technological developments and manage social change.

Turner's Strength – Novel 3

April 1827 - Guildford, Surrey, UK

Jonathan Turner's brother, Richard and his wife, Sarah, progress in establishing their station outside Grahamstown in the Eastern Cape Province. Despite the dry African weather, Richard is excited by the offer of further landholding grants. Sarah continues to have doubts about safety, understanding the Xhosa tribes' hostility towards the British, who have driven the tribes north of the mighty Fish River. Sarah worries if she will ever see her children in England again or die in this harsh new country.

Unaware of his father's plan to send him to Africa, William Turner continues to develop deeper relationships with his friends in Guildford, England. Tension remains between William and his father, and the seven-year-old searches for security outside the family. He looks forward to the planned holiday at the Isle of Wight and the prospect of more horse riding.

Fifteen-year-old Clementine misses the guidance of her mother and struggles to find her future family position. While her friendship with the housekeeper, Mrs Ethel Nibley, grows, it remains fragile. Cousin Katherine, now Clemmie's roommate, provides some comfort. Ethel Nibley, mindful of the loss of the children's mother, works hard to keep them active and gain their trust. Her devotion to the family catches the eye of Benjamin Petherton, who considers her a worthy partner for the future.

Jonathan Turner struggles to release himself from depression now that he is without his wife, Eleanora. Hamish McPherson invites Jonathan to join him in travelling the Scottish Highlands. The family prays that their father will recover soon as Anne takes on the family company's management. Events in Guildford will quickly occur, throwing the family closer together than they ever imagined.

William, Simeon, Madeline, and Katherine loved their riding trip but soon returned to Guildford. They are quickly immersed in the underlying currents of their local community. In particular, Clemmie becomes the focus of the young Rev Hotspur's regular visits, and the housekeeper questions his motives.

Soon, Anne must confront a hostile Mrs Constance, who is adamant that the Earl of Fintelton has broken their long-held agreement. There is no news from Jamaica about Robert's brother, Sir Hugh, as the bankers move to cut off credit to the Fintelton estate. While the Turner family juggle major issues, William, keen to grow up, discovers the delights of pipe smoking behind the garden shed.

We resume the saga with Richard Turner on his property, Ewell Station, near Grahamstown, in the Eastern Cape Province, making a disturbing discovery in one of the far pastures. Will Sarah's fears of native incursions come true?

Turner's Strength
List of Characters
April 1827

Note: The same character may be shown in two or more places depending on changes in status as the story continues. A character introduced in this book may not be listed depending on the dramatic impact.

SURREY, ENGLAND
GUILDFORD

The Jonathan Turner Family of Guildford

Jonathan Henry Turner	Father of William	Baker and Business Owner
Eleanora Turner	Mother of William	Wife of Jonathan Turner
Thomas Jonathan Turner	Son of Jonathan & Eleanora	Brewer
Bethany Bassington (nee Turner)	Daughter of Jonathan & Eleanora	Wife of Dr Bassington
Anne Jessica South (nee Turner)	Daughter of Jonathan & Eleanora	Director of Turner Businesses and wife of Sir Robert South
Clementine Felicity Turner	Daughter of Jonathan & Eleanora	Home help
Madeline Amber Turner	Daughter of Jonathan & Eleanora	Child
Simeon Henry Turner	Son of Jonathan & Eleanora	Child
William Earnest Turner	Son of Jonathan & Eleanora	Child
Marcia Angela Turner	Daughter of Jonathan & Eleanora	Child
Jeremy Neville David Turner	Son of Jonathan & Eleanora	Child
Katherine Turner	Niece of Jonathan Turner	Daughter of Richard Turner Residing with Turner Family

Service Staff of the Turner Family

Mrs Ethel Nibley	Housekeeper
Mrs Jennings	Cook
Miss Ivy Grey	Assistant Cook
Miss Jessica (Jess) Swamp	Scullery Maid
Miss Aggie Peters	Maid
Miss Rosalind Nibley	Mrs Nibley's daughter
Joseph Hinge	Stable Hand
Nanny Smithers	Jeremy's nanny.

The Thomas Turner Family of Guildford

Thomas Jonathan Turner	Son of Jonathan & Eleanora	Brewer
Mrs Marion Turner (nee Steele)	Wife of Thomas and Daughter of Alexander & Jennifer Steele	

Turner Business Offices, Guildford

Miss Daisy Eltham	Receptionist

Turner Family Dogs

Nosey

The Bassington Family of Guildford

Doctor Neville Bassington	Doctor – Guildford Medical Practice
Mrs Bethany Bassington (nee Turner)	Wife of Neville and first daughter of Jonathan Turner

Service Staff:

Mrs Ivy Goodhew	Housekeeper and Cook

The South Family of Guildford Residence Name: 'Porting'

Captain Sir Robert Douglas South	Second Son of the Earl of Fintelton, Sir David South
Lady Anne Jessica South (nee Turner)	Wife of Sir Robert and daughter of Jonathan Turner

Service Staff:

Mrs Norma Kirby	Housekeeper and Cook

Miss Mary Hedge	Lady's Maid to Lady South
Mr James Pocket	Carriage Driver, Footman and Stable Hand
Mr Henry Fletcher	Footman

The Local Church, Guildford

The Reverend Andrew Taggart	Rector
Mrs Laura Taggart	The Rector's wife and church worker
Mrs Dorothy Chambers	Rectory Cook and Cleaning Lady
The Reverend Philip Hotspur	Curate and Rector's Assistant
Mrs April Handle	Curate's Cook and cleaner

The Guildford Clergy

His Grace, The Very Reverend Norton Pondsdale	Bishop of Surrey
Mrs Margaret Pondsdale	Bishop Pondsdale's wife
Mr Donald Berkly	The Bishop's Assistant
The Reverend Karl Smithton	Archdeacon of Guilford
Mrs Clowance (Cloe) Smithton	Karl Smithton's wife
The Reverend Walter Moore	Rector of St Nicholas
The Reverend Christopher Crossling	Rector of St Saviours

The Turner Bakery

Mr Jeb Hiscock	Bakery Manager
Mr Peter Hammer	Senior Foreman
Mr Aaron Hall	Baker
Miss Audrey Stern	Senior Accounts Clerk

Hursts' Tailors and Seamstresses

| Mrs Fiona Smith | Seamstress and Guildford Shop Manager |
| Mr Lionel Wall | Taylor and Manager Woking, and Manager of the Store chain |

The Steam-Powered Flour Mill

Mr Terence Spencer	Mill Manager
Mrs Lydia Spencer	Wife of Terence
Master Levi Spencer	Son of Terence and Lydia
Miss Andrea Spencer	Daughter of Terence and Lydia
Mossey	The Spencer's Pony

The Sopwith Family, Guildford, Surrey

Dr David Sopwith	Local Doctor	Guildford Medical Practice
Lady Emma Sopwith	Wife of David Sopwith and daughter of the Earl of Fintelton	
Miss Victoria Sopwith	David's Sister	

Service Staff for the Sopwith Family

Mrs Molly Lane	Housekeeper
Miss Judith Malone	Victoria Sopwith's Maid
Mr Stuart Winks	Carriage Driver and Footman

The Watson Family of Guildford

Dr Bryan Watson	Local Doctor, General Practitioner
Mrs Jessica Watson	Wife of Dr Watson
Master Archie Watson	Son of Doctor Watson
Miss Sophie Watson	Daughter of Doctor Watson

The Petherton Family, Cloverdale Chase, Guildford

Mr Benjamin Petherton	Resident of Guildford
Mrs Miriam Petherton	Wife of Benjamin (Deceased)
Miss Clare Louise Petherton	Daughter of Mr Petherton
Mrs Irene Preston	Miss Clare Petherton's Governess
Mr John Steadman	Butler
Mrs Mary O'Connor	Housekeeper
Miss Coleen Doyle	House Maid
Mr Samuel Grey	Head Gardener
'Ralph'	Petherton Family Dog

The Wood Family of Guildford

Mr Blake Wood	Attorney
Mrs Mary Wood	Wife of Blake
Miss Cloe Wood	Daughter of Blake and Mary
Master Edward Wood	Son of Blake and Mary

The Webster Family of Guildford

Mervin Webster	Investor
Gwendolen Webster	Wife of Mervin
Leonard Webster	Son of Mervin and Gwendolen
Elizabeth (Betty) Webster	Daughter of Mervin and Gwendolen
Mrs Martha Pratt	Housekeeper
Miss Alice Timson	Maid

The Swamp Family of Guildford

Mr Kevin Swamp	Farmer	
Mrs Willamina Swamp	Wife of Mr Swamp	
Mr Peter Swamp	Son of Kevin and Willamina	Farmer
Mr Alfred Swamp	Son of Kevin and Willamina	Farmer
Miss Jessica Swamp	Daughter of Kevin and Willamina	

The Guilford Community

Mr Rupert Smith	Mayor & Parish Council Member
Mrs Marjorie Smith	Wife of Rupert
Mr Blake Wood	Solicitor
Mr Isaiah Linton	Blacksmith
Mr Ian Robinson	Robinson's Builders
Doctor Wilfred Chenning	Medical Practitioner, Woodbridge
Mr Jeffrey Elliot	Blacksmith
Master Caleb Elliot	Mr Elliot's son
Madame Rosie Black	Gentleman's Entertainer

Guildford Constabulary

Mr Michael Rawlins	Parish Constable

The Guildford Institute

Mr Henry Sharples	Institute Volunteer Officer

The Guildford Medical Practice

Dr Neville Bassington	Founding Partner
Dr David Sopwith	Founding Partner
Dr Brian Watson	Employed Doctor
Miss Jenny Swift	Nurse and Receptionist

EPSOM and EWELL

The Epsom Pub and Stables

Oliver Turner	Pub Manager and son of Richard Turner
Mr Thomas Baxter	Stable Manager

The Turner Family of Ewell

Richard Turner	Uncle of William, Brother of Jonathan, Pub Owner 'The Black Swan'	
Sarah Turner	Aunt of William, wife of Richard	
Oliver Turner	Son of Richard & Sarah	Pub Manager, Epsom
Harry Turner	Son of Richard & Sarah	Pub Manager, Ewell
Katherine Turner	Daughter of Richard & Sarah	Child

The Racing Horse Pub and Stables Epson

Mr Oliver Turner	Manager, Racing Horse Pub and son of Richard Turner
Mr Thomas Baxter	Stable Manager

WEST SUSSEX, ENGLAND

The South Family of Fintelton Manor

Earl Sir David South	Earl of Fintelton and Lord the Manor
Countess Lady Jane South	Wife of Sir David
Sir Hugh David South	Viscount of Leystead, Son and Entailed Heir of Sir David (Deceased)
Sir Robert Douglas South RN	Son of Sir David
Lady Anne South	Wife of Sir Robert
Lady Emma Felicity South	Daughter of Sir David, and spouse of Doctor David Sopwith

Service Staff of the South Family

Mr Thomas Pike	Butler
Mrs Cora Walsh	Housekeeper
Mr Henry Barrett	Earls Valet
Mrs Judy Wapples	Cook
Miss Margaret Lane	Lady Jane's personal maid
Miss Jane Winston	Lady Emma's maid
Mr Malcolm Stem	'Fintelton' Estate Manager
Mr Callum Fraser	Chief Hand
Mr Fred Goodger	Leader, Fields and Gardens Team
Mr Syd Mantle	Leader, Maintenance Team

Mesnil Priory, Redhill, near Reigate, Sussex

Sister Celine

HAMPSHIRE, ENGLAND

Southhampton

Wingate Line – Overseas Shipping – Sailing Ship Riptide

Mr Oscar Leahy	First Officer
Mr Maxwell Jeffries	Bosun

BEDFORDSHIRE, ENGLAND

The Green Family Bedfordshire

Sir Harrold Green	Deceased
Lady Fiona Green (nee Furness)	Widow of Sir Harrold and daughter of the Earl of Calsand

The Wendarm Family Bedfordshire

Sir Peter Wendarm	Deceased
Lady Clarissa Wendarm	Daughter of Viscount Martinhoof

LONDON, ENGLAND

'Harting' House, St James Square London Residence of the Earl and Countess of Fintelton

Mr Matthew Staines	Butler
Miss Judy Wapples	Cook

Manifold & Stout Attorneys

Mr Evan Finchley	Senior Partner, Manifold & Stout
Miss Mandy Jones	Mr Manifold's Personal Assistant
Mr Leo Hoskins	Barrister

Bow Street Magistrates Court, Covent Garden, London

Mr Justin Walker	Constable, Bow Street Runners Thief Catchers
Mr Steven Phips	Bow Street Officer

Legal Claimant Against the Earl of Fintelton's Estate

Mrs Katherine Constance	Claimant
Mr Earnest Gregson	Attorney

The McPherson Family of Greenwich

Mr Hamish McPherson	Brewer and Business Manager	
Mrs Marjorie McPherson	Spouse of Hamish	
Mr Douglas McPherson	Son of Hamish	Brewery Manager Glasgow
Mr Archie McPherson	Son of Hamish	Brewery Manager Edinburgh
Mr Lachlan McPherson	Son of Hamish	Brewery Manager Edinburgh
Mrs Taye McPherson	Wife of Lachlan	
Mr James McPherson	Son of Hamish	Brewery Manager & Business Man, Glasgow
Miss Isla O'Connor	Partner of James	

Polkinghorne Home, Mayfair, London

Mr Stephen Polkinghorne	Importer, Polkinghorne Imports Plc.

Petherton's Wines and Tobacco – Isle of Dogs, London

Mr Jerome Ilses	Manager

BRITISH NAVY

The Crew of HMS Shadow Under the Command of Captain Robert South

Captain Sir Robert South	Captain
Sargent Michael Swanton	Captain's Servant

Lieutenant Stewart Fenton	First Lieutenant
Lieutenant Samuel Peters	Third Lieutenant
Mr Kevin Trotters	Master (Sailing Master)

Diplomatic Staff:

Mr Francois Milius	French Diplomatic Staff
Mr Nikolai Volkov	Russian Diplomatic Staff

The Crew of HMS Restless

Commander Frederick Ham	Captain

Admiralty

Admiral Sir Franklin Crouch	First Naval Lord
Lady Katherine Crouch	Wife of Admiral Crouch
Admiral Walter Bird, Viscount of Stantstead and Killarney	Member Admiralty Board
Lady Patricia Bird	Wife of Admiral Bird
Commodore Wendell Wadsworth	Secretary to the First Naval Lord
Colonel Jonathan Scott	Admiralty Security Chief of Staff
Lieutenant James Harms	Security Stafff

Flagship, Commander in Chief, Blue Fleet, Portsmouth

Admiral Sir Tristan Sutherland	Commander in Chief, Portsmouth Blue Fleet
Lady Amanda Sutherland	Wife of Sir Tristan
Commodore Richard Jacobs	Secretary to Admiral Sutherland
Captain Rosco Graham	Captain of the Flagship

Royal Navy Offices, Portsmouth

Lieutenant Martin Russell	Administration Officer

BRITISH GOVERNMENT

United Kingdom Investments

Mrs Janet Stubbington	Wife of Frank Stubbington – Deceased and Director of Intelligence, the Home Office

| Mr Charles Stubbington | Son of Janet, Home Office, Intelligence Officer |
| Mr Ross Stubbington | Son of Janet, Home Office, Operative |

EASTERN CAPE PROVINCE (SOUTH AFRICA)

Grahamstown

The Richard Turner Family – Ewell Station

| Richard Turner | Uncle of William, Brother of Jonathan, Farmer and Pub Owner 'The Black Swan' (Ewell Surrey UK) |
| Sarah Turner | Aunt of William, wife of Richard Turner |

Turner's Horses

| Maisy | Richard's mare |
| Dapto | Spare horse |

Workers

| George | Senior Station Hand |

Xhosa Herdsmen, Kraal beside Ewell Station, Grahamstown

| Aviwe Mbeki | Herdsman and Senior Tribesman for Chief Nkosi |
| Dumisa Mbeki | Brother of Aviwe Mbeki |

BRITISH ARMY

Grahamstown Barracks, Eastern Cape Province

Captain John Hargrave	Officer in Charge, Grahamstown District
Mrs Thelma Hargrave	Captain Hargrave's wife
Lieutenant Frederick Sanderson	Support Officer to Colonel Hargrave
Mrs Jane Sanderson	Freddie's wife
Lieutenant Percival Gilling	Infantry Officer
Sergeant Maxwell Wallace	NCO
Sergeant Mark Attwood	Patrol Sergeant
Corporal Hugh Furness	Patrol Corporal
Private Harry Gray	Patrol Trooper
Private Raymond Henzell	Patrol Trooper
Trooper Denton Grail	Patrol Trooper

Grahamstown Community

Mr Martin Kuipers	Magistrate, Businessman, and Ironmonger
Mrs Katie Kuipers	Wife of Martin Kuipers
Mr Dirk Hoot	Hoot's Drapery Shop
Roijer Family	Roijer's Canteen
Gerrit Balma	Owner, Balma's Hotel and Boarding House

Salem Area

Mr Piet Beckhoff	Farmer

Xhosa People

Chief Nkosi	Chief of the Nkosi Tribe camped on the Gret Fish River

BOSTON, MASSACHUSETTS

Irish Community, The North End, Boston

Mr Michael Walsh	Eldest son of Seamus, Brothers' organiser, and Cobh Brothers' Commander
Mr Aiden Reid	Brother's Commander
Mrs Biddie Reid	Wife of Aiden Reid

AMERICAN WHALING SHIPS

The 'Blue Angel', Out of Nantucket, Massachusetts

Mr Charles Hart	Captain
Mrs Connie Hart	Wife of Captain Hart
Master John Hart	Son of Captain, and Mrs Hart
Miss Mae Hart	Daughter of Captain, and Mrs Hart
Mr Jack Smithton	First Mate, Sailing Ship Blue Angel, Nantucket
Mr Clarry Cutts	Helmsman, Blue Angel
Mr Samuel (Sammy) Fleming	Boatsteerer (Harpooner), Blue Angel
Mr Mervin Gates	Boat header Mate, Blue Angel

The 'Wind Catcher', Out of New Bedford, Massachusetts

Mr Paul Manson	First Mate, Sailing Ship, The 'Wind Catcher', New Bedford

PART 1

'There is no stronger bond
than a mother's love!'

April 1827

Chapter 1

Ewell Station, outside Grahamstown, Eastern Cape Province, South Africa ...

Slowing his horse to a walk, Richard Turner peered over the mound before him, smelling rotten meat. He edged his horse closer and then dismounted. Unslinging his musket, he quickly surveyed the surrounding country for any signs of wild animals, as a neighbour had spotted a leopard[1] in the early evening a few weeks ago. The breeze had dropped, and the sun was now high, glaring down on his bare arms and hands. He was glad of the shade from his wide-brimmed hat, having never experienced heat like this in England.

Tying the reins to a sturdy bush, he walked over the mound to where the remains of the steer lay. The carcass was decaying, and Richard estimated it was two or three days old. Crouching closer and brushing the flies away, the footmarks of two barefoot men and an adolescent were clearly printed in the dry clay dust. It appeared as if the three had been working together.

Despite the carcass' deterioration, Richard could still see clean knife cuts. An animal would chew the meat, but these were the marks of a quick butchering. Usually, natives would steal a couple of cattle and herd them northwards towards the safer grounds of the Great Fish River.[2] This was different! Whoever the culprits were, they needed meat

---

[1] In the early 1800's Leopards were common on the eastern escarpment of Southern Africa. Today they are almost extinct.

[2] The Great Fish River- Named by the Dutch and formally known as the Groot-vis rivier, the English added 'Great' so as not to confuse the river with the Fish River in Namibia. During the 19th century, the river formed the border of the Cape colony and was hotly contested during the Xhosa wars of 1799 to 1878 between the Xhosa nation on the one side and the Afrikaner colonists and the British Empire on the other. Wikipedia

and were hungry. He wondered if this was a one-off or signalled an escalation of tribal incursions from the north.

A sudden puff of breeze blew dust into his eyes, forcing him to rub them open. His mare suddenly stomped and snorted, trying to escape its tether. Across the gully, there was movement in the scrub about fifty yards out. Thankfully, the wide-brimmed hat sheltered his vision from the glare. The waving of the bushes ceased as soon as he raised his eyes. Perhaps it was the breeze, but his horse was becoming more agitated.

Quickly cocking his musket and keeping watch on the scrub, he ran to his horse, saying, "Easy, girl. Let's move back a bit in case the danger is close."

He patted the mare's neck and settled her down as the waving scrub across the gully continued. Richard knew if a wild animal was nearby, he needed some distance. He mounted the horse and cantered off towards a safer vantage spot. After a hundred yards, the Englishman stopped beside a clump of low bushes with a side view of the mound and the carcass. The flies buzzed around his sweaty face as he waited, with the slight north easterly breeze providing little relief.

A drop of sweat ran down his cheek, and he wiped it aside with a slow, concealed movement. The day was steamy hot. Hotter than anything experienced in his previous life in Ewell. As he sat there, thoughts of home and his daughter, Katherine, remaining in Guildford with his brother's family came to mind. He recalled the recent letter – what was it Jonathan had said? '*Katherine has settled in well, and she and Clementine are like sisters.*' Richard smiled about the comment but held the reins tight as his mare stomped and snorted as she tried to turn away. The sacrifice of leaving Katherine in England had worked well, but he could not understand the recent comment about William in Jonathan's letter.

'*I wish my relationship with William was as good as that with Katherine. The boy still aggravates me, and the distance between us grows.*' Surely Jonathan, as the boy's father, could solve this with his son at home?

'*I am sure he and I would benefit if he spent time with you in Africa. I will dispatch him by ship next year. I realise the rage problem is mine, and I can only protect him by sending him away.*'

'Sending him away!' Richard was disgusted. 'He would dispatch his seven-year-old son, depriving him of some of the most important childhood years. Surely, the loss of his mother was more than the child could bear. What was Jonathan thinking?' Richard had always been fond of William. The lad had a great sense of fairness and no lack of physical ability. He smiled as he recalled them throwing snowballs at each other last Christmas and the joyful laughter that ensued. Of course, the child would have naughty moments, but boys needed space to run! If he were sent, he would see a new world compared to Guildford and have a loving family here in Grahamstown. He would need loving care, as being dispatched might hurt his spirit greatly.

There was a movement beside the mound as two Cape hunting dogs[3] emerged from the scrub, raced across the gully, and helped themselves to the remaining meat on the carcass. Further back in the foliage, Richard could see movement. There were more dogs, but how many? His mare stomped again.

"Steady, Maisy." He gave her a gentle pat. "Hold still, girl. Till we see what is happening."

As the horse settled, the prospect of a Cape hunting dog's skin on the wall of his new farmhouse study was enticing. Having seen the wild dogs only twice, he admired the rich yellows and browns on their spotted coats. The antics of the two growling and yelping dogs were entertaining as they wrestled for scarce portions and nipped at each other between chewing. He was surprised they would fight over such old beef. Perhaps this dry spell had made it more difficult in the hills. He must ask his neighbours if their coming down the escarpment was normal.

As he clasped the musket hard and aimed, he lifted the barrel to allow for the range. Richard's instruction in shooting was limited, and since arriving in Grahamstown, there had been no time to join a gun club and find a mentor. He understood the basics, but the theory was never as good as practical knowledge. Focusing on the larger dog, he saw he had a clear shot. Before he could squeeze the trigger, four more small dogs jumped out from the side and joined the meal. Then, another larger dog stood high on the mound, smelling the air and looking directly at him. Richard knew this was the pack leader.

---

[3] The Cape hunting dog: The African wild dog (Lycaon pictus), also called the painted dog or Cape hunting dog, is a wild canine which is a native species to sub-Saharan Africa. It is the largest wild canine in Africa. Wikipedia

Richard smiled, enjoying the pups jumping and fighting over various portions of their feast.

'Your family appear hungry, Mister Cape Dog. Enjoy what's left of the steer.'

Richard uncocked the musket, slung it over his back and turned his horse for home.

As he moved off, the pack of dogs stood tall, continuing to smell the air, watching the lone rider move away to the east.

Fintelton Manor, Outside Petersfield, Sussex, England ...
The butler, Mr Pike, rubbed his eyes as he entered the candle-lit servants' dining room where the staff waited for him.

"Good morning, everyone! Please be seated and enjoy your breakfast."

Immediately, conversations started as the staff took their places and served themselves.

"Mrs Walsh, we won't need the morning candles in a few weeks. The sun is rising earlier. I must go out and watch the daybreak this morning."

The housekeeper laughed, "You may have no choice, Mr Pike. I am sure that young Master William will wake early and have them down here within the next few minutes. He is an active child, that one! I wonder where he will end up."

Pike frowned, took a spoonful of his porridge, and said, "The Earl and Countess have been very kind to the children. I hope they appreciate it."

"I am sure they do, Mr Pike. It was a blessing that Sir Robert married Miss Turner. She is introducing new life into the family. With Lady Anne stirring the pot, the future looks brighter."

"If you say so, Mrs Walsh. I will not disagree with you."

"Young Katherine appreciates being here. She is a cousin and has lovely manners. In the kitchen yesterday, she offered to help. I thanked her but explained how it would be inappropriate. She is a sweet child."

"I had forgotten what it was like to have children in the manor, Mrs Walsh! It certainly livens up the place."

As he enjoyed his first spoonful of porridge, a young lad appeared beside the seated butler, tapping his shoulder.

Turning his head, Pike found William Turner's pleading brown eyes looking directly at him.

"Excuse me, Mr Pike. Would you allow us outside to go to the stables and do our chores?"

Simeon, Madeline, and Katherine arrived as Pike took another spoonful of porridge.

Mrs Walsh laughed, "It certainly does liven up the place, Mr Pike!"

The old butler placed his hands on the table and stood.

"Well, Master William. If I don't, Mr Stem will reprimand me for detaining his students. But make sure you are back in time to clean yourselves before breakfast. Take this lantern as it is not light yet."

Mrs Walsh gave each child an apple to ease any hunger pains before they ventured off into the cold. With a protective touch, she ensured their coat buttons were all done up. "Stay together, children. There is a fog outside, and it is a fair distance, so you boys look after the girls."

"Yes, Mrs Walsh."

The children thanked the butler as he unlocked and opened the back door. He held them back until he had checked the fog. It was still misty, but there were signs of it clearing.

"The fog will soon be gone. Make sure you tell Mr Stem you have arrived before tending the horses, please."

His voice trailed off into the distance as the children ran hard along the lane, searching for the dim light ahead of the Estate Manager's office. The lantern bobbed up and down as they disappeared into the misty half-light.

Pike peered after them and then looked east, searching for light on the horizon. Only a slight glow was present, and he knew he had twenty minutes before sunrise. He closed the door and returned to his porridge.

Mr Malcolm Stem took a swig of his half-warm coffee, stood and stretched his arms straight. The sudden knocking surprised him as he was not expecting anyone this early. He came around his desk and moved towards the door.

"Morning, Mr Stem. Are we on time?"

"Morning, William!" Looking at all the eager young faces, he said, "You are earlier than I expected, children! It will be a fine day for our picnic."

Simeon asked, "Will the Earl and Countess be joining us?"

"You mean at the creek?"

"Yes, Sir."

"I am unsure about the Earl, but I know the Countess is keen on attending. Sir Robert arrived home last night and will also be riding with us. The Countess will bring Lady Anne and Miss Victoria in a carriage."

"Is there a road down to the creek?"

"No, but a track will accommodate a carriage if they take it slowly. Now, children, off quickly, please, and do your chores. Then, you should return to the manor for breakfast. We shall head off around ten after an early morning tea. So, make sure you are back here by nine-thirty! Off you go!"

Mr Stem could see the excitement growing on the children's faces. They had mastered the basics and were ready for a ride down through the fields to the creek at the bottom of the valley.

He called after them, "We will saddle up your horses when you come back."

Later in the morning, Anne and Victoria found themselves alone in the large breakfast room overlooking the gentle valley extending down to a creek around a mile away.

"What a pretty outlook, Anne. Perhaps you should have married Robert's brother! You would have become the mistress of this household in time."

In a low voice, Anne quickly replied, "Marrying Sir Hugh would not have been a bed of roses. I will tell you about this some other time. It's best if we do not mention him, Victoria. The news from Jamaica is that he contracted some terrible illness and struggles to survive. The Earl and Countess are most worried about their eldest son."

"Sorry, Anne. That was thoughtless of me. My apologies."

"You were not to know, Victoria! But the less said, the better, as the countess is sensitive about the matter."

The clatter of young footsteps interrupted their conversation. As Robert and the children entered, he said, "You must have been up before dawn if you were down at the stables this morning."

William rushed around the serving trays, inspecting what was on offer. He then found a bowl, filled it with porridge, sat beside Anne, and ate eagerly. As all the children enjoyed breakfast, quiet descended over the table.

Taking the opportunity, Anne asked Robert, "At the creek, we will need some protection from the mud. Are there any dry flat areas further up the bank?"

Robert swallowed a mouthful of bacon and wiped his mouth before speaking, "No need. Stem has carefully chosen the spot. Many years ago, my father had a special platform constructed with shaded and sunny areas. It is quite civilised and offers a grand view along the babbling brook. It is a pretty spot – you will love it."

Anne and Victoria were relieved they would not be struggling through mud.

"How thoughtful, Robert. I should have known you would have something like this prepared!"

The young ladies grinned at each other and began to giggle.

The countess, entering, asked, "Will you include me in your humour, girls?"

Anne blushed and replied, "Good morning, Lady Jane. I was surprised when Robert advised of the platform near the creek."

"Yes, it is a pretty spot, but over time, I became fed up with the mud, so I asked the Earl for some improvements. I have not been down there for nearly ten years. Are you aware of the condition of the platform, Pike?"

"I believe, Milady, that Mr Stem has taken action to ensure you will be comfortable."

"Excellent. I hope the mail is here before we arrive back. I am keen to hear about Sir Hugh's recovery."

Commencing on some bacon and eggs, William looked up and asked, "Robert, will you be taking a crossbow or a musket?"

"I had not planned on doing so, William. Why do you ask?"

The other children looked up with interest.

"I thought there might be some rabbits or hares down there, given it is close to the water."

"You are right, William, but it is hardly likely they will show themselves at this time of day. However, I will bring some fishing rods and tackle, and we will see if there are any trout in the stream. There is a good pool near the platform."

Rectory, Guildford, Surrey, England …

"Philip, thank you for joining me for morning tea. It is always best to consider sermons a day before discussing their merit and issues. So, we should talk today about your sermon delivered last Sunday and perhaps some areas where it could be improved."

The young curate, Philip Hotspur, complained, "I was unhappy about being forced to preach, and it appears that some in the congregation are spreading lies about me severely beating Edward Wood in the classroom."

The Reverend Andrew Taggart sat back in his chair, finding it hard to fathom why this young man continued fantasising about his calling to the clergy and that the truth of his classroom actions would not emerge.

"Philip, I find myself in a difficult position. On the one hand, I have you denying that you hit the child hard; on the other, I have twelve children, including Edward, confirming that you hit him with enough force to cause the injuries he sustained. I also note that it has been four years since you were ordained, and last Sunday was the first time you ever preached. It is no wonder the congregation are questioning your competence."

"I shall not change my story from the truth!"

The Rector could see the young curate's determined face. It was clear that Philip feared his reputation being ruined, and if Blake Wood, the father of the injured child, acted against him, it might lead to this. Reverend Taggart decided he would need a different approach if this issue were to be solved.

"Philip, may I remind you that we are facing a serious situation here? I must solve this and want the best outcome for you and our congregation. I am offering my help and friendship, but I need you to respond. We can work together and possibly find a solution or agree to disagree, which might lead to your departure."

After these words, Andrew could see the fire in Philip's eyes.

"Reverend Taggart, I am not sure if you are aware, but I am the bishop's nephew. I can assure you I will not be leaving this parish. If anyone leaves, it will be you. I suggest you find a way to solve your problems to my satisfaction, or you may suffer the consequences!"

Andrew sat there in disbelief. He had offered his friendship and help and found this rebuffed by a threat. Did this young man have no moral conscience? Was the bishop also of a similar character? Was Philip bluffing, or should he believe what he was saying?

A long silence followed as Andrew pondered his next move. Philip avoided eye contact and gazed around the room. What the Reverend Charles Upton had advised was correct. He should have listened more carefully. The problem was that Andrew did not trust his bishop; if Philip had the Bishop's backing, there was nothing to be gained in arguing this stalemate.

"Very well. I think you may leave now."

"And what duties do you wish me to perform in the future?"

"You may continue with your present duties, Philip. I will expect a draft of your next sermon by Thursday."

Philip Hotspur's expression changed to anger as he picked up his case and hat and left without saying a word. The young clergyman was annoyed that the Rector and Wardens had not covered up his recent outburst against a child in the parish school. As he trudged towards the Institute, he thought, 'The sooner Uncle Norton dispenses with Taggart, the better. The Rector is a fool for being too close to the parishioners and has no idea of a career. Why, surely, Taggart, at his age, should be an archdeacon or a dean by now? To think he expects me to preach so often to this rabble. The sooner I take over, the sooner I can delegate these boring pursuits he forces on me.'

With his head down and his frame bent forward against the strong breeze, he mumbled as he made his way down an alley from the High Street to North Street, hurrying towards a coffee house.

Ewell Station, outside Grahamstown, South Africa ...

"Sarah, I found a carcass on the western field close to the boundary fence this morning. On closer inspection, it was clear that men had butchered the steer. Probably natives, as there were many footprints of bare feet in the dust. The prints were still clear as the breeze was light."

"What were you doing up there without someone with you, Richard? It is too far from the homestead – anything could have happened."

Richard could hear the annoyance in Sarah's voice. He tried to calm her. "I was careful and kept my distance."

"That is not good enough! I don't want to become a widow in this foreign land. Make sure you have one of the men with you and with a gun." She asked, "Don't the natives herd the cattle off towards their land when they steal them?"

"Yes, that's what worries me. It appears the natives are becoming bolder and moving closer. Usually, they would herd them to their camp near the Great Fish[4]. But if they are butchering the meat here, they must be camped far closer than I realised. I wonder if Lieutenant Sanderson knows this is happening?"

"You can ask him tomorrow in town."

Richard was far away, recalling the history of the natives as it had been explained to him. The Khoikhoi were not the problem as they had easily adapted to Dutch and English rule. It was the Xhosa[5] tribes who had put up a fight over the land. The last uprising was in 1819 at Grahamstown when the army had forced them further north across the Great Fish. Since then, the Xhosa had steadily drifted back south of the river, some coming as far as Grahamstown. As the years passed, they grew in confidence. It was time that the army cleared them out again.

Snapping out of his thoughts, Richard replied, "Yes, I will ask him. I might also ask Captain Hargrave. I must admit this was one issue I did not research. I thought the natives out here were under control."

"What do you mean under control?"

"Well, the natives should all be north of the Great Fish. If the Xhosa are here butchering our cattle, they are becoming brave enough to come down as far as Grahamstown or perhaps even further. If they butcher animals, they can butcher people!"

Sarah looked up in surprise, and when she saw the worry on Richard's face, she understood what he was thinking.

"Richard! It might be wise to advise Jonathan not to send William out here. We don't want him in danger."

"He won't be in any danger. I will remind the army they are respon-

---

[4] The Great Fish River – Often the English locals abbreviated the name to Great Fish for ease of conversation. Author comment.

[5] The Xhosa are a Nguni ethnic group whose traditional homeland is primarily the Eastern Cape Province, South Africa. They are the second largest race group in Southern Africa and are native speakers of the IsiXhosa language. Some notable Xhosa people are Makhanda (also known as Nxele) who in 1819 led an abortive assault on the town of Grahamstown. He was imprisoned on Robben Island and drowned while attempting escape. Nelson Mandela was also a Xhosa and jailed on Robben Island spending 18 of his 27 years of imprisonment there. Wikipedia

sible for keeping the natives under control. But what kind of a father is Jonathan, thinking he cannot keep his rage under control? I think it is an excuse to rid himself of the child. I cannot understand my brother."

They sat silently for several minutes, pondering Jonathan Turner's desire to send his third son to Africa.

Sarah finally said, "We should be thankful they look after Katherine. I miss her so much!"

"I miss her happy little smile." Richard was annoyed with his brother in England. "Well, if he does send William, we will do our best for him!"

Turner Residence, Guildford, Surrey, England …
Mrs Ethel Nibley, the Turners' housekeeper, sat at the shiny desk now installed in her room along the hallway in the servant quarters. It was a luxury she remembered from her days with her husband at Sandhurst. She had written many letters to her dear Andrew while he was in Portugal during the war. Then he was home, and the future looked bright until the doctor advised that his cough was a sign of the consumption[6].

Their life had never been the same since that day.

Her daughter Rosalind reminded her so much of Andrew, but now she found it hard to remember the details of his face. She shuddered and gritted her teeth, unable to forgive herself for forgetting the man who had been the love of her life. She admitted that her memories had grown dull, and her service life had been so hard that there was little time left by the day's end to recall her cherished moments with Andrew.

She was ashamed as she sat back and wrestled to picture her husband's face. They had bought a cottage in Sandhurst and spent a wonderful six months there before his cough developed and the consumption set in. His army colleagues had been kind and helped pay down most of the bank loan before he died. But even moving in with her mother and assisting in the sewing business was not enough for their meagre existence and covering the cottage payments. She decided to leave Rosalind with her mother and enter service. This had stabilised her situation, and then the job with the Turners was like a

---

[6] Tuberculosis (TB), also know as the 'White Death', or historically as consumption. Wikipedia

dream coming true.

It was nine years since Andrew's death, and Ethel had resolved to make the best of her life while remaining in service. But the events of the last month had changed her prospects significantly. Two marriage proposals in one month, and now she thought she had accepted the wrong one. She must talk with Mr Turner again tonight.

A knock came on the door. "Yes, Jess!"

"Mrs Nibley! How did you know it was me?"

"I recognised your footsteps."

The scullery maid, Jessica Swamp, was amazed that Ethel knew the sound of her steps. She admired the housekeeper greatly and treasured Mrs Nibley's support since she entered service with the Turner family.

"My kitchen duties with Mrs Jennings are complete, and she asked me to see you. Are there any other jobs for me today?"

"Yes, Jess. Have a look at the kitchen noticeboard. You will find your duties there. Next time, please check there first. I renew them every day."

The sixteen-year-old seemed frightened as she said, "Sorry, Mrs Nibley. I did not intend to disturb you."

Ethel suddenly realised she may have been too abrupt and hurt the maid's feelings.

"Jess!"

"Yes, Ma'am."

"You are a good worker, Jess. We are all so pleased that you are here. If I was too abrupt, please forgive me. I was far away in my thoughts. Let me know if you need clarification of the jobs on the board."

Jess seemed puzzled and asked, "Sorry, Ma'am, but what does 'clarification' mean?"

"It is a big word, so I am glad you asked. It means if you need anything explained."

"Thank you, Ma'am."

Ethel smiled as a happy Jess set off to find her next chore. The new routine was beginning to settle down, and everything was working smoothly except for Clemmie, who continually needed attention. It was time Ethel settled this, too. She decided to visit Doctor Bassington and ask for an explanation of what specific care was required. Surely, a little more exercise and fresh air would benefit the girl.

Jess stood near the noticeboard in the kitchen and studied her list. She could recognise the name at the top but could not make out the jobs below. As Aggie passed, carrying a pail of water, she noticed the maid struggling.

"May I help you, Jess?"

Not hearing the maid's approach, Jess turned in fright until she recognised Aggie.

"You can't read, can you, Jess? I know your eyesight is good, so that can't be it."

Jess looked at Aggie in horror and said, "Please don't tell Mrs Jennings or Mrs Nibley."

Aggie smiled, "Certainly. But you will need to learn soon. The days of being unable to read and write are gone, young lass. How about I give you a hand after lunch? We get an hour off then, so we would have time to visit the Institute."

"What is the institute, Aggie?"

"That's where people like us learn how to read and write!"

Jess smiled, but Aggie could see the fear on her face.

"It won't hurt, Jess. You will be safe with me."

"But if my father finds out, he will beat me!"

Aggie had suspected for some time that Jess's home situation was difficult. Now, she could clearly understand the fear in the young girl's eyes.

"Then, we will make sure your father does not find out! Now, the unfinished jobs on the list for today are taking the clean linen upstairs and making a start on changing sheets before Ivy joins you. That will keep you going until lunch. Off you go, and I will be ready for our trip to the Institute when you are finished."

Fintelton Manor, Outside Petersfield, Sussex, England ...

Anne and Victoria sat with the countess while Madeline and Katherine perched themselves further along the bank, watching Robert teach Simeon and William how to cast a trout line. The sun was growing warm, and Katherine was keen on some wading. Anne was impressed at how the Earl's location for the platform was protected from the wind. It also allowed a generous amount of sunshine to warm them up.

"Come on, Maddie! Let's take off our shoes and stockings and do some paddling. It looks so beautiful in the water."

Madeline was reluctant but quickly followed when she saw Katherine removing her shoes.

"This is a beautiful spot, Lady Jane. A good place for reflection or reading a book in the summer sun."

"I had forgotten the tranquillity here, Anne. I remember sitting here watching the Earl, Hugh, and Robert fishing. Emma found it hard standing still and was always wading behind them, inspecting whatever interested her. Of course, the odd rude comment from the boys about Emma disturbing the water and scaring the fish would come, but Emma always ignored them."

Anne looked towards the river and saw Madeline and Katherine delicately dipping their toes into the stream.

Lady Jane sighed before continuing, "We spent many a pleasant time here, and now I wait for news if Hugh will ever return."

The countess looked away and closed her eyes as the bright, early afternoon sun warmed her face.

"It is a pity that there is only one ship a month from Jamaica; otherwise, communication might not be so difficult. Surely some of the navy ships could carry mail?"

Anne considered Victoria's remark, "It does seem strange as there is much trade - so many plantations and a naval base. I must ask Robert when he is finished teaching the children. Perhaps he knows!"

"Ouch!"

They all glanced toward the creek and smiled as Simeon hooked his clothes while trying to cast.

"Lady Jane, I am sure you will receive a message about Hugh's return soon. Have you considered when you will visit Harting next?"

"I am not sure I am up to it, Anne, with all this worry over Sir Hugh. Why do you ask?"

"Robert must attend a meeting with Admiral Crouch, and the attorneys have asked for a meeting before the end of the month. I am sure some of these matters will require your and the Earl's attention. Father asked me to meet with the builders of the London bakery and check their progress. We intend to open in September, and that is approaching rapidly. Spending a few weeks there in early May would be quite helpful. Of course, Robert may be gone by then, so I need to arrive earlier and be with him."

Victoria stood up and made her way to the side of the platform. "I will take a little stroll and join the girls. They will be riding back soon, so I will take the opportunity for some discussion."

"Would you like your hat, Victoria?"

"No, thank you, Anne. I need some sun while it is out."

The countess smiled as Victoria walked along the bank slowly. Anne could see that Lady Jane was thinking deeply.

"I also received a letter from the solicitors, Anne. I assume it was the same as yours?"

"I would expect so."

"Robert has stirred the hornet's nest by stopping the payments. The solicitors are concerned that we are breaking the agreement signed long ago."

"Have you ever read the agreement, Lady Jane?"

"No, I never asked or thought about it until we needed to review the Estate's finances. Only the Earl fully understands the agreement as it is a codicil to his will."

"Would the Earl permit you to see it and share it with Robert and me?"

"I am not sure, Anne. I am afraid to open this can of worms. You understand my fears."

"Lady Jane, I think Mrs Constance has been fully compensated for any loss she suffered. In fact, I would say she has been over-remunerated. The Earl was very generous! Giving her a lifelong tenancy of the property was more than enough. She has funded the construction of a second building out of the monthly cash flow, and who knows what income she receives from her tenants. Having seen the property and some rooms, I would say the boarding house brings in a handsome income. The lady has no financial worries; strangely, she still holds a position at a bank, allowing her additional income."

"You have seen the property and inspected it?"

"Yes, after Robert's injury at the charity ball for the Irish, we visited Wimbledon and posed as prospective tenants. David was Doctor Boswell, and I pretended to be his wife. We asked Robert and Emma to remain on the coach. Mrs Constance was not at home, and the disguise worked well. We did meet the son. His Christian name was

David. He was the spitting image of Sir Hugh."

The countess drew in a quick breath and sat there in silence. Anne listened to the babbling brook as the water rushed over the creek stones, allowing her mother-in-law time to consider this information.

The countess asked, "What does the son do?"

"The maid told us he is indentured to a builder and is doing well. I think he and the maid, Fanny, may be a couple. She seems to have the run of the place."

The countess sat there for a long time thinking about Anne's comment. As it was approaching half past two, Mr Stem prepared the horses for the children, and Robert waded out and commenced packing the fishing gear with the assistance of a footman.

"Anne, it may be best if you discuss this with the Earl when an opportunity arises. A question coming from me may not be advisable. I think he may take a softer line with his daughter-in-law. But should we wait until we hear if Hugh has survived?"

"From the solicitor's letter, I am not sure we have that long. But I will write tonight and see if they might stall her a few weeks longer. If you decide to join us in London, it will be important that Lord Fintelton also comes."

Anne saw that Victoria and the children were now approaching. She stood and said, "Lady Jane, I think I have a plan for solving this situation, but it will depend very much on how the circumstances unravel."

The countess stood, smiled, and hugged Anne.

"Lady Anne South, you never cease to amaze me. I could not have asked for a better daughter-in-law!"

The Institute, Guildford, Surrey, England …
Mr Henry Sharples, the Institute Librarian, raised his head as he heard someone entering the reading room.

"Why, Miss Aggie Peters. I have not seen you here for some time. Welcome back, and who is this young lady with you?"

"Thank you, Mr Sharples. Let me introduce Miss Jessica Swamp. Jess is keen on improving her reading and writing, and I was wondering if you had any books that might assist."

"Certainly, Miss Peters. There are quite a few that I can point out.

What level of reading are you at, Miss Swamp?"

Jessica stood there in awe of this refined gentleman who asked, as far as she felt, an embarrassing question. Aggie could see the tears swelling in her eyes and quickly said, "Basic, Mr Sharples. Basic, please!"

Having been at the institute for years, Henry Sharples had seen this before and realised how momentous this occasion was for the young lass. With a kind voice, he gently said, "You are being very brave coming here today, Jessica. I am sure you will be reading before you know it. If you need any help, please ask. Follow me, please, and I will show you where the books are kept."

Reassured by the man's kind remarks, Jessica followed Aggie as they moved towards the bookshelves.

Unseen by the two maids, the Reverend Philip Hotspur, sitting at a reading desk on the other side of a bookshelf, turned as he listened to the conversation. He raised his head and watched as Aggie Peters and Henry Sharples walked past, followed by a blushing Jessica Swamp.

"Here, Miss Peters. An excellent book for beginners! Perhaps you might sit down with Jessica and look at it. There is a table here, out of the way! Please borrow and use it at home if you find it helpful."

Aggie noted where the book had come from, sat at the table, and asked Jess to join her. Unfortunately, neither girl noticed Philip Hotspur seated on the other side of the bookshelf, preparing his sermon.

"Look at this, Jess! It has all the letters of the alphabet, their sounds and how to use them. We can work on it together, and you can take it home each night and practice."

"Aggie, I could not take it home! My father would beat me. He hates girls learning. Only my brothers get learning."

Aggie could hear the fear in Jessica's voice. It was hard to believe that a father would have such a view, given the changes that were going on in society. "Well, perhaps I could explain to him that you need basic reading skills for your job?"

"No, no, Aggie! You don't understand. He is a violent man. He will also beat my mother for allowing this, even when she is unaware. We must keep this a secret and do it at the Turners."

The tears reappeared on Jessica's face, and Aggie clasped her hands. "It's alright, Jess! We will practice at lunch times. You will read before you know it, and you can tell your father you taught yourself."

Aggie handed across a handkerchief, and Jess wiped her eyes. It was clear that the home situation was not safe at all. 'Perhaps,' Aggie surmised, 'Jess should move in with her at the Turner's house.'

As the two girls thanked Mr Sharples and left, Philp Hotspur peered between the books and noted what an attractive little lass Jessica Swamp was. He smiled to himself and said quietly, "Interesting! Interesting, indeed."

Chapter 2

Turner Residence, Guildford, Surrey, England ...

All was quiet, with baby Jeremy finally sleeping and the children in bed. The housekeeper yawned and approached Mr Turner's study. She knocked and half opened the door, "Mr Turner, might I have a word, please?"

"Yes, Ethel. Come in."

Ethel entered and closed the door. Jonathan came across to hug her, but she pushed him back softly.

"Jonathan, it is only in this study that I may call you by your first name. We must maintain our distance until we decide how Benjamin should be told. I feel guilty already and must find an honourable settlement with him."

"Ethel, you are constantly in my thoughts. Each night, I wrestle long and hard over your engagement to Benjamin and struggle to find a solution besides declaring the truth. The situation has become complex, and we must find a way to slow down his plans. It may be best if you plead with him for more time."

"I agree, but I cannot suddenly break my word to him. I think asking for more time before making an announcement may be prudent. I must explain that with you deeply mourning the loss of your wife and Clementine requiring daily care, it would be too hard on the family if I left now. Perhaps a three-month delay would be reasonable, and then another month for you to recruit a housekeeper."

"Ethel, Benjamin will ask when he can announce the engagement. You must advise him that you are unsure and need more time. It must be done soon so he understands your doubts; otherwise, he may assume you are only delaying because of the problems here. With your acceptance of his proposal, he already assumes you are in love with him!"

"I understand, but I am unsure I can move that quickly."

Jonathan moved closer to Ethel and said, "Ethel, you will marry me, won't you?"

"Yes, Jonathan. I will, and I wish this complex situation had never developed. But we will marry in the end. You understand I highly regard Benjamin and his daughter, Clare. I would never betray them, so Benjamin must fully understand the circumstances and agree with them before you and I marry. I could not bear having him think I broke his trust. We must ensure he remains a good friend."

"I agree!"

Jonathan moved closer and hugged her. He revelled in the scent she wore and the softness of her touch. She wrapped her arms around his neck and held him tight as they kissed. Then slowly moved away and said goodnight.

Before she opened the door, he came and stood beside her and said, "I love you, Ethel! More than anything in this world."

"I know, Jonathan, and I love you too."

Smiling at him, she opened the door and walked down the hallway towards the kitchen.

The Rectory, Guildford, Surrey, England ...
"Good morning, Benjamin. Come in, please."

"Thank you, Laura, for showing me in. Good morning, Andrew. I apologise for this being short notice, but I must discuss some important issues with you."

Laura Taggart smiled and carefully closed the study door behind her as she continued her Wednesday commitments.

"Benjamin, would you care for some refreshments before we start?"

"No, thank you! Perhaps after we finish, please."

Andrew knew Benjamin Petherton as a careful and considerate man, but this morning, he seemed tense.

"Perhaps you should sit back and relax for a minute or two before we proceed. You seem a little stressed!"

"Yes, a good idea. I feel nervous about this matter and must ask that it remain confidential between you and me. It is a matter of deep concern and prudence. Let me explain."

The Reverend Andrew Taggart, now most interested, was honoured that this man would confide in him.

"Andrew! It may be best if I outline my medical situation first. Doctor Sopwith has been treating me for a heart condition for several years. I am over fifty and realise that many men die at this age, particularly people in business. I am now reaping the rewards of many long years of hard work, but my failing health dictates my lifestyle.

I am concerned for my daughter, Clare, as she will inevitably be left alone. I have no close relatives, and with the size of her inheritance, she will probably be the target of fortune hunters. So, I have appointed some trustees for her protection. I believe these trustees are all people of integrity who will have Clare's best interests at heart."

The two men continued their discussion until Benjamin knew that Andrew understood what he had planned for his daughter.

"Andrew, I have discussed my affairs with my solicitors. They have advised me that in my situation, there will always be some long-lost relative who will challenge the will, a fake business partner will declare an interest or one of the trustees may fail in their duties."

Andrew had similar thoughts: "Yes, when money is involved, often there is a dispute that leaves the most vulnerable destitute. It is a sad reflection on our society."

"I have some documents that will solve that situation, and I ask that you sign them so I am sure Clare cannot be swindled out of her inheritance."

"It would be a pleasure, Benjamin."

"Thank you, Andrew. You are a friend indeed. But please keep copies of these documents in your files so they will accompany you wherever you go. I pray it may be many years before you might be needed."

"I sincerely hope that is the case, Benjamin."

"I must explain about appointing Mrs Ethel Nibley as one of the trustees for Clare."

Surprised by this comment, Andrew said, "You mean Jonathan Turner's housekeeper?"

"Yes, indeed. Mrs Nibley is a wonderful woman, and her integrity is beyond reproach. She has also shown a great interest in Clare, which has convinced me she is more suitable than the other trustees I have appointed.

I have legally arranged to gift Mrs Nibley a significant endowment to ensure she is a woman of means and freed from service. My solicitors have already completed the details, and she remains in Jonathan Turner's employment by her choice. Ethel is dedicated to that family and their welfare, which is truly inspiring."

"Yes, Benjamin. Ethel is a fine woman who is very caring. I have not had that much contact with her. However, I will make a point of becoming more familiar."

"I must tell you, Andrew, and please keep this confidential, that I have asked Ethel to become my wife, and she has accepted."

"Congratulations, Benjamin. Your news is welcome."

"Andrew, until the engagement announcement is made, please say nothing. While I am keen to marry soon, it may be some time before our engagement becomes public! It will be hard for Ethel to extricate herself from the Turner family. Of course, as she is an Anglican, we will be married in your church."

Andrew noticed Benjamin's frown. "Are there some doubts in her mind?"

"I am unsure, but you understand how important an engagement is. It gives time for reflection, and who knows what the outcome might be? I think it is best kept confidential. Particularly from that young curate of yours! I am sad to mention this, but I do not trust that young man. I do not trust him at all!"

Andrew was about to agree but held back, knowing he must keep his opinions of Philip Hotspur private.

"Andrew! The next task is to find a reliable person to witness these documents as we sign them. Once that is done, I will leave you with your copies and rush the others off to my solicitors in London."

Fintelton Manor, Outside Petersfield, Sussex, England ...
William attempted to loosen the tight blindfold around his eyes. It was strongly tied, and he could see no light at all. He was still afraid of the dark, a feeling that never left him despite his brother and sisters being present.

Lady Jane sternly said, "William, do not loosen the blindfold! That would be cheating. Walk forward, and you will find the donkey!"

The young lad enjoyed playing Blind Man's Bluff but felt a little insecure at the manor. Robert jumped up and led him a bit closer.

"Walk forward, Will!"

The seven-year-old reached out, crept further forward, and felt the donkey.

"Here it is." He remembered watching Simeon the last time they had played at Cloverdale Chase with Clare's family. Without Clare, it was not the same, but he must concentrate. He felt around the edges, imagining how the donkey would appear and decided where the tail should go.

There was silence as he pinned the tail onto the pillow supporting the donkey drawing. Then a large cheer went up as everybody, except William, knew who had won.

"Sim, help me with this blindfold!"

His brother loosened the knot, letting the cloth slip over his nose. He saw everyone congratulating Madeline, who had pinned her donkey tail roughly at the correct spot. The other tails were either on the donkey's back or belly.

William gave a long breath of disappointment but then hugged Maddie, "Well done, Maddie! But I will beat you in the next game."

Before the children could start another round, Anne said, "That is enough for tonight, everyone. It's time for bed. I will check in ten minutes, so off you go!"

As the children reluctantly left the room, Robert asked, "Pike, I am sure you have seen many a game of Blind Man's Bluff over your time here."

"Sir Robert. As I recall, you and Sir Hugh were most competitive. But it was Lady Emma who usually won."

Robert laughed, "Yes, Emma had a unique way of navigating the dark. She always knew when a game was coming, checking the room first and memorising the furniture positions. It worked well for her."

With a rare smile, Pike asked, "Lady Fintelton! Would you care for coffee or tea?"

"Yes, Pike. Tea, thank you."

Once Pike was out of the room, Robert quietly said to Anne, "Pike was here long before we were born and must have seen the family's complete history. I cannot remember him ever missing a family occasion. He would be a great asset if we ever wrote a family history."

Anne nodded as she considered Robert's comment, "For our family, I think it would have to be my father if such a task was undertaken."

The Earl, who had enjoyed the evening's entertainment, asked, "Robert, when do you sail again? I understand the Blue departed some time ago. Emma and David will return on the Friday after next. If you and Anne are here, you might help us welcome them."

"I am sorry, Father, but Anne and I must travel to London next Wednesday. There is a meeting I must attend at the Admiralty. I expect to be off soon to the East following that meeting."

Anne quickly said, "Lord Fintelton, you must give them our warmest regards, and I will visit soon after returning from London. I have missed Emma so much!"

The countess added, "Me too, Anne! They may not remain here long as David will be needed at his practice."

Anne asked, "Lord Fintelton, will you and Lady Fintelton join us at Harting? It would give you more time with Robert at St James' Square before he departs."

"I am not sure, my Dear. The roses are starting to bloom, so I must not miss them. Robert may drop in here on his way back to the ship. Have you planted any roses at Porting yet?"

The Earl's comment did not amuse Lady Jane, and Anne could see that the Earl and Countess would probably join them in London.

The conversation continued, and Anne excused herself to check on the children.

Later in the evening, after the others had retired, Anne sat next to Robert but seemed distant.

"Anne, what are you thinking? You are usually deep in thought when you are not talking, probably about your father's business."

"It is my business also, Robert, and I agree with you. But tonight, I am considering the plight of your father's estate. We still do not know if Hugh will return or if he has found any further information on the Jamaican plantations. From what you have told me, the Irish and Scottish estates are also unknown quantities, and Finteldown[7] may need a capital injection to bring it back to running order. There are problems, Robert, and we must address them."

---

[7] Finteldown – The Earl of Fintelton's Irish estate in County Down. Recovered from derelict land agents and in a state of disrepair due to the Earl losing his capacity to manage the estate and Sir Hugh ignoring the situation. Refer to 'Turner's Awakening', Chapter 24, Page 526.

Robert frowned, "I had put the estate's finances out of my mind. I was enjoying our time together!"

She leaned over and kissed him, "I know, Darling, but we must confront the issue of Mrs Constance in London, and we are still without an understanding of the estate's health!"

Anne sat there momentarily thinking and said, "Earlier, when the children had finished their games, you said that Pike must have an excellent knowledge of the estate's history. I know this is a long shot, but would he know about your father's activities with Mrs Constance?"

"I am not sure. Possibly! He worked with my father right through that period. But what is the significance of Pike's knowledge."

Anne turned and checked that no one was listening. Victoria had retired, but Anne was unsure about Sir David and Lady Jane. The coast seemed clear, so she quietly said, "Hear me out, as I think this is important. We know now that your father was in an affair with Mrs Constance, not that it seems she was ever married. They had a child together whom they called David. The child was born almost at the same time as Emma. Your father made generous provisions for the woman and the child. We are uncertain why he did this, but the first thing that comes to mind is that he made it clear that the child would never be formally recognised as his son.

If we understood more about the relationship, it might explain why such a significant gift was made. It seems strange unless there was a very close bond between them, which seems unlikely, or perhaps the lady threatened your father with exposure if he did not comply with her wishes. I would like to know the details of the events before we confront her."

"Anne! Please, do not continue." Robert turned with a serious frown, "I have no intention of confronting this woman. The attorneys may take care of that. I am only interested in stopping the cash outflow."

"But, Robert, what if she decided to expose your father? There is much to consider here. All sorts of scenarios could be played out. Knowing what happened would be a significant advantage for us if negotiations are required. If Pike can provide some information, that would be a great help".

Robert looked at the fire, and Anne saw he was uncomfortable with her suggestion.

"Please, Robert?"

"No, Anne, I would rather not!"

Anne was not to be put off, as she knew they were running short of time.

"May I speak to Pike then?"

"If you must!"

"Thank you, Darling. Now show me the way to Pike's office downstairs."

"Now?"

"Yes, there is no time to be lost."

Robert turned away towards the fire again, and Anne noticed the frown. He was angry for the first time in their marriage. She wanted his anger gone before she met with Pike.

"Robert, there is much at stake here for your parents. They need our help, and time is running out. We are here, and these things must be done. Your mother has already agreed that I can talk with the Earl about Mrs Constance's agreement."

"She has? I was not aware of that."

"Yes, we talked at length this afternoon while at the creek. She wants it all sorted out, Robert. Will you help me?"

Robert walked to the fireplace and placed his hands on the mantle. He gazed down into the golden reddish flames that darted one way and then another. What would the outcome of these conversations be? Was digging up all these old secrets right, or could they let them die? Would it go away? No! It would not, and he was the one who proposed they stop the monthly payments to Mrs Constance.

"You are right, Anne. Come on. We shall visit Pike."

Anne smiled and followed Robert along the passageway, where he opened a door revealing a staircase down to the servant quarters. As they reached the bottom step, Mrs Walsh greeted them.

"May I be of assistance, Sir Robert?"

"Thank you, but no, Mrs Walsh. We need Mr Pike as I plan a small surprise for his Lordship."

"Oh, I see. You will find Mr Pike in his office." She indicated along the passageway.

Robert smiled, took Anne's hand, and led her to Pike's door. He gently knocked.

"Come!"

When Anne and Robert entered, the butler stood with a look of surprise.

"Please be seated, Pike. We come in search of information. May we each take a chair?"

"Certainly, Sir Robert. Lady South, welcome to my office. I believe it is your first time."

Anne nodded and said, "Yes, Pike."

"Now, how may I be of assistance?"

The old butler sat there, waiting to hear what was required of him. There was neither a smile nor a frown, and Robert could see that Pike maintained his neutral position, always ready to serve the family without question but guarded in his comments.

"I am sorry to intrude, Pike, but Lady South and I need your assistance. You confided in me some time ago of your concern for the estate's finances. Our investigations have been ongoing for several months, and the issues you raised have merit. One relationship of the Earl's may become problematic, and we need some background information. The matter occurred some years ago. I will let Lady South explain. By the way, Pike, we hold you in high esteem, and everything said here will be confidential."

"I understand, Sir, and I will assist where I may!"

Anne quietly led Pike through what she and Robert had discussed upstairs. However, she did not name the lady until the last statement.

"Mr Pike, we understand the lady's name was Miss Katherine Constance. Would you recall that name, and can you help fill in some of the details?"

The butler sat with a straight back and a troubled frown.

"Sir Robert and Lady Anne, you ask me to reveal his Lordship's confidential information. Such disclosure would place me in a difficult position with my employer, who has complete confidence in my discretion."

Robert could see that Pike was reluctant to proceed any further. The butler demonstrated great allegiance to his master, and Robert was proud that their butler would not divulge family secrets.

"I understand, Pike and I apologise for putting you in that position."

"Thank you, Sir!"

Pike stood to usher them out, but Anne quickly asked another question.

"If we were to ask a question about Lord Fintelton's trips in the past, would you be able to answer that question?"

"Lady Anne. I recall the previous conversation with Mr Stem, where similar questions were asked. I would not be able to add anything further."

"Might you tell us the name of the hotel where his Lordship usually stayed?"

Pike said nothing, and Anne could see his annoyance. Perhaps she had overstepped the mark with this man, but as the frown dissipated, it was clear he was of two minds. While he would rather avoid this conversation, he considered whether giving the hotel's name breached trust. Since Mr Stem had confirmed that the Earl had resided at a particular hotel on many occasions, withholding this information would not be a breach of duty. However, he was still most concerned about betraying his employer.

"Sir Robert and Lady Anne! I understand that you are trying to solve the estate's financial troubles. I am only too happy to assist where I can, but I must draw the line on divulging the Earl's personal information. It would be none of my business if the Earl stayed in a particular hotel. However, if these events took place regularly, as you assert, I would imagine the hotel would be easily identified from receipts in the estate's financial records. I am sure you have thought of this already, so there is nothing further that I can add. Is there anything else I may assist with, Sir Robert?"

Pike looked directly at Robert, who recognised the man was pleading for a release.

"Thank you, Pike. You are a loyal staff member of this estate, and I thank you for this. We will now leave you. My apologies if we have upset your night."

"Not at all, Sir Robert. I believe we all want what is best for the estate."

"Well said, Pike. Thank you."

As Anne and Robert departed Pike's office, the staff still present nodded or said goodnight before they found the stairs leading to the ground floor.

As they walked towards the drawing room, Robert said, "I am glad that is over!"

Deep in thought, Anne asked, "Robert, where are the archives kept?"

"In some locked sheds beside the Estate Manager's office."

"We must go there now, Robert!"

"But Anne, it is nine-thirty and pitch dark outside. Mr Stem will be asleep as he has a big day tomorrow."

"Robert, don't you understand? Pike wanted to tell us something, but he could not. If he had betrayed his master, he would have risked his position. The man is so intelligent and a fount of wisdom on this estate. I should have realised when I was interviewing Stem that I was talking to the wrong person. Pike has given us the key to understanding this matter. Not only will we find the hotel's name, but there may be far more information than we expect."

"I see! You are correct, Anne. He told us something that we should already know. So, he did not break anyone's confidence. That man is a gem! There is much more to Pike than meets the eye."

"Robert, we need our coats and some lanterns."

"No, Anne. It can wait until the morning. I need some sleep."

"I won't sleep until we solve this, Robert, and we have just been given a clue that I think will be of invaluable help. We will need Victoria's help with this task. Many hands make light work! It would be best if we keep Mr Stem out of this. Also, it is good that Emma is not here. She must not be involved."

Robert wondered why Emma could not be involved. He put the thought aside, looked down at Anne, and could see the determination on her face. There was no stopping her now.

Soon, Anne, Robert and Victoria walked along the lane to the estate manager's cottage. They carried two lanterns, and Victoria walked between them. It was a chilly night; the clouds had cleared with the stars shining brilliantly above.

Victoria said, "What a beautiful night sky! Look at the stars up there."

Robert yawned and agreed, "It reminds me of camping out on a hunt. The clear night sky is always a marvel. I expect there will be a fog soon! This time of year is renowned for them. If the fog thickens, we must hold hands on our return to avoid becoming separated."

Robert knocked gently on the door when they reached Mr Stem's office. Malcolm Stem was still up and appeared concerned as he opened the door.

"Is there an emergency, Sir Robert?"

"No, Mr Stem, but we have an urgent task that we must finish before tomorrow. Would you have the keys to the Archive sheds, please?"

"Certainly." Stem rushed off and quickly returned with two keys.

Robert turned and asked Anne, "Which years are we searching for?"

Anne was surprised and quickly calculated the dates, "It was twenty years ago, so 1807 going back to 1797."

Stem quickly said, "That will be in Shed number two, Sir."

"Thanks, Mr Stem. Would you have another lantern?"

"Yes, Sir, one is in each shed beside the door." Stem then pointed to a deposit box mounted beside his cottage's door. "When you are finished, leave the keys in this box. I will collect them in the morning."

Robert nodded, and they were off around the house and found the sheds.

Several hours later, sitting on chairs and sorting through wooden boxes, they became frustrated as no related correspondence was found.

"Robert! Is there another place that the Earl might store confidential information?"

"Not sure, but once, as a child, I saw him place a document in a space at the top of his wardrobe. I was ushered out of his room quickly once he saw me there. That would have been fifteen to twenty years ago. But surely not! That would not be secure at all."

"True, but I think we have exhausted our search here. Time, we retreated!"

Victoria readily agreed and, following a long yawn, packed up the box she held.

Grahamstown, Eastern Cape Province, South Africa ...
Richard Turner guided his cart down the High Street towards the town square, where a small crowd had gathered outside the courthouse. Three tall Xhosa tribesmen waited patiently but nervously outside the magistrates' office. Some in the crowd raised their voices, discussing what must be happening inside.

"Looks like trouble, Sarah!" Richard slowed his horse with a gentle pull on the reins.

His wife quietly suggested, "We should avoid this!"

Nodding, Richard tugged the horse left into the next street and made a discrete detour. Pulling up near the ironmonger's building, he hopped down and dusted his coat after the ride from their property. Before helping Sarah from the cart, he fastened his coat buttons against the cold westerly wind.

"The weather is surprising, Sarah! Yesterday was hot, and now today is turning chilly. Did you bring your coat?"

"Yes, of course! I will need half an hour in Mr Hoot's shop, and then I will meet you at Roijers' Canteen for lunch."

"Careful, Sarah, the dust is thick here! Thankfully, the wind is not strong yet. I need some supplies from the ironmonger's shop but that can wait until after lunch. First, I will pick up the mail from the barracks' office and meet you at Roijers."

Sarah pointed over Richard's shoulder, "Oh, look, there is Lieutenant Sanderson's wife. I must talk with her before shopping."

She quickly rushed off, waving to Jane Sanderson. Richard was glad Sarah was developing friendships here as there was little chance of it near their property. Meetings like this would divert her mind from their daughter, Katherine, who remained in England with his brother's family. Thoughts of Ewell, their English hometown, made him smile as he walked off towards the military barracks.

He stopped across the street from the courthouse, noticing a tall, well-built African man exiting the magistrate's office in a magnificent robe. Wrapping the colourful material around him and standing at full height, he looked down with a sneer at the crowd. A sudden silence came over the settlers, and a few took steps backwards. Magistrate Martin Kuipers emerged from the front door and stood beside the Chief.

"Gentlemen, Chief Nkosi and I have agreed on a plan for restitution of all stolen cattle. I will announce it this afternoon at the Guild committee meeting, and I hope you will all attend. It is a good settlement for all concerned."

There were slight murmurings from the nearly fifty men standing in the street. Richard watched as the Chief and his men ignored the crowd and crossed towards his side of the road. He admired the swagger in their step and proud posture as they approached silently. Each was over six feet tall, muscular and healthy, a presence that demanded respect. He took a few steps backwards, ensuring they had plenty of room. The Chief gave Richard a neutral glance as he passed.

Later, at Roijers' canteen, Richard Turner waved to his wife as he entered and walked towards her. Sarah sat at a table for four on the far side of the noisy room, with Jane Sanderson sitting opposite.

"Mrs Sanderson. A pleasure seeing you here. Are you joining us for lunch?"

"Yes, Mr Turner. I hope you don't mind, but today's canteen is full. My husband should be here soon. How is the house building progressing?"

"We have the kitchen operating now, but there is still much to do. We came in today for the Guild meeting and a few more bits and pieces of hardware. I hope Mr Kuipers has plenty of stock. The last time we came, we needed to place orders as they were short of many items. I believe a shipment has arrived via Port Alfred since then."

"At last! As I told Sarah, I have been waiting for some dress material. If only Freddie had been posted to India, we could have avoided these delays. Still, it is like Christmas when a shipment arrives."

Sarah suggested, "That must explain the number of settlers in town today!"

Richard quickly replied, "I am not sure, but it may involve the Magistrate meeting with Chief Nkosi. I saw the Chief and his men leaving earlier."

Jane mentioned, "Freddie has been out with a patrol gathering information on how many cattle have disappeared. I hope it is finished and no more cattle are taken."

Richard smiled, humouring Jane's naive suggestion, and then took out the mail, "Sarah, a letter from Katherine!"

His wife hurriedly took the envelope and smiled as she opened it, "Please excuse me, Jane, but I must read this. It has been so long since I heard from her."

Richard quickly reread the menu and then signalled the waitress. Jane smiled and looked up as Lieutenant Sanderson joined their table.

"Richard! What a pleasure finding you and Sarah with Jane. How are you both?"

"We are fine, Frederick. Sarah is enjoying her day in town. Jane's company is welcome, and receiving a letter from Katherine, our daughter, is like Christmas. You will remember we left her with my brother in Guildford?"

"Of course! How is she finding living with the other family?"

Sarah, tearing herself away from the letter, said with a laugh, "From this letter, it seems she is not missing us at all. Jonathan has enrolled her in finishing school lessons three days a week, the same school his daughter Clementine attended, and she is making plenty of friends in the community and at church."

"Oh, the lucky girl!" Jane smiled, "I made some lovely friends at my finishing school. I may not have met Freddie without meeting his sister! Look at us, married with our first child on the way." She looked lovingly at her husband.

"Yes, thank the Lord for Elsbeth!"

Sarah looked up again and put the letter down.

"I am sorry, Jane. I should have asked about your coming confinement. You look so well today in your beautiful dress."

"Thank you, Sarah. With the morning sickness over, I am feeling far better."

The ladies continued quietly talking as Richard placed his lunch order and asked Freddie about the meeting with Chief Nkosi.

"Freddie, I heard the magistrate announcing an agreement had been reached. Can you tell me the details and save me the time of attending the Guild meeting?"

"The Xhosa[8] will return all the stolen cattle. The Chief is keen that no hostilities develop like last time. The sticking point will be agreeing on how many cattle have been taken. Over the last two weeks, I have spent considerable time with settlers to ascertain the numbers. Of course, I think the Dutch included cattle lost to leopards, lions and cape-hunting dogs in addition to the rustling. These little extras do not assist the credibility of their claims. Have you lost any cattle, Richard?"

"I wanted to discuss that with you. Yesterday, I found a slaughtered

---

[8] The British Government commenced allocating property to settlers around the town of Grahamstown in 1820. The government policy of forcefully moving the Xhosa tribes north of the Fish River (Groot-visrivier), creating a buffer zone, was not well received by the tribes. This dispossessed the Xhosa people of their land increasing the hostile feelings between the Xhosa and the settlers.

animal in the western paddock. It appears that natives were the culprits, as several footprints were in the dust. The steer was butchered with knives as the cuts were clean and not from chewing teeth."

Freddie frowned, "That is a worry as I have not heard of slaughtering before. It would not have been Nkosi's tribe as they herd the cattle back to their enclosures. When they slaughter, they do it close to home. Your discovery sounds more like a new raiding party. I would say Nkosi has competition."

"I thought the Xhosa had been told to stay beyond the Great Fish?"

"Richard, that is fine in theory, but there are not enough settlers to cover all the land to the north. The Xhosa know where the unoccupied land is and keep sneaking back to use the grazing land. It is almost impossible to keep them out. There is no need for alarm, though, as we keep a good watch on them. But this is a new development, and I would say their camp is near if they are butchering meat."

"My thoughts exactly! What about Chief Nkosi? Why is he allowed to stay?'

"He has been helpful to the military in the last few years. The Captain allowed them to use an old Xhosa campsite five miles north of Fort Brown along the Great Fish. He provides information on other Xhosa tribes and where they are grazing cattle."

"I thought you used the Khoikhoi[9] for that?"

"We do, but another friend does not hurt."

Richard Turner nodded as he thought about the difficulties with the natives. He now held title over more than five thousand acres, but it was impossible to finance the fencing of all that land. At least having his property close to Grahamstown, he could count on help from the military if relations heated up.

"Freddie, I hope you don't mind me asking, but how many troops do you have here?"

"Two hundred and fifty plus another fifty ancillary staff."

"What about at Fort Brown?"

"About one hundred and fifty. But don't worry! There are nearly a thousand troops at Fort Beauford. Some will soon be coming our way en route to Port Elizabeth."

---

[9] The Khoikhoi, also known as Hottentots, are the traditionally nomadic pastoralist indigenous population of southwestern Africa. With European expansion in the cape colony many Khoikhois became farm workers. Wikipedia

"Fort Brown is on the Great Fish. How far is that from here?"

"About twenty miles. If there is trouble, Nkosi and our other helpers will inform us of tribal movements."

"But you were unaware of these natives who butchered my steer?"

"It may be a one-off. I would not worry too much if I were you. The natives know we will not tolerate cattle rustling or slaughtering."

Richard knew the infantry would take at least a day to get through the rough country between Fort Brown and Grahamstown. He decided on stocking up on powder and shot, just in case.

"Don't worry, Richard. We thrashed ten thousand of them last time with three hundred troops[10]. There won't be any more trouble. The Xhosa wars[11] are over."

"Freddie, if they butchered my steer and you have not heard of them being close by, I think we should be worried!"

Lieutenant Sanderson realised that Richard's comments correctly described the situation.

"I will discuss it with Captain Hargrave and probably take out a patrol tomorrow and scout north of your property. If there are any natives, we will send them back to the river."

"That would be most helpful, Freddie."

Richard looked away. He could not stop thinking of the proud swagger of those huge natives as they walked away from the meeting.

Turner Business Offices, Guildford, England ...

Daisy Eltham knocked on Jonathan Turner's office door and quietly entered, carrying the morning mail.

"Your mail, Mr Turner!"

"Thank you, Daisy."

"Mr Turner, a Mr Petherton is downstairs and asks if he could see you. He said he is your personal friend but has no appointment. Would you have time for a quick word with him?"

On hearing this, dread spread across Jonathan's face, and he refrained from looking up. He continued staring at the document he was previously reading. Gaining control over his feelings, he said, "Yes, Daisy. I can spare him the time. Please ask if he might wait a few

---

[10] The Fifth Xhosa War comprises the Battle of Amalinde (1818) and the Battle of Grahamstown (1819).

[11] The Xhosa Wars (or Cape Frontier Wars) was a series of nine wars extending from 1779 to 1879 between the Xhosa Kingdom, the British Empire and the Trekboers. Wikipedia

moments, and I will come down and fetch him. I need the exercise! Ask if he cares for any refreshments."

Daisy smiled, "Yes, Mr Turner."

She quickly left Jonathan in a somewhat stressed state. He stood up, walked across and placed his hands on the window ledge. He gazed out but did not see the view or the rain approaching, terrified that Benjamin might be aware of his proposal to Ethel. What would he say if he asked – he should have thought of this before. A drop of sweat ran down his face as his mind stirred into a panic. He must not lose this man's friendship. He must reinforce it. But how? He was not ready for this meeting. He always made mistakes when he was not prepared. The meeting could become a disaster.

Damn! Why had he agreed to meet Benjamin? It was now too late; he must meet with the man — his rival for the woman he loved.

Jonathan picked up a letter and carried it with him as he went downstairs to the reception.

"Daisy – would you have this posted today."

He looked up to find Benjamin rising from the reception lounge.

"Benjamin, welcome. Come upstairs, please. Did Daisy offer you a cup of tea or coffee?"

"Morning Jonathan, so good of you to see me. Yes, I have asked for a coffee."

"Daisy, a coffee for me as well."

Daisy nodded and quickly moved away.

"Come, Benjamin. We have much to catch up on. I have not told you about my trip with Hamish McPherson. I am a better man for it."

"Good Jonathan, we all hoped it would lift your spirits. I will take my time up these stairs if that is acceptable. I'm not as young as I used to be."

Jonathan noticed that Benjamin was moving slowly and finding the stairs a strain.

"Are you well, Benjamin? May I assist?"

"No, no! I find stairs more difficult these days - my knees can sometimes be painful."

Jonathan waited as Benjamin slowly navigated the stairs to the landing.

"Ah, well, here we are! Please come in and take a seat. The coffee and biscuits will refresh you."

Benjamin smiled as he sat down and gave a breath of relief. He sat there familiarising himself with Jonathan's office and cleared his mind before speaking.

"Thank you for seeing me, Jonathan. I come on a delicate matter, and I am quite nervous about how I will explain this. But firstly, I must ask another question that will help me put this in context."

Jonathan sat and did not speak. His interest was now rising, and he was surprised how Benjamin was still puffing from coming up the stairs. Jonathan's stress had subsided, and he felt sympathy for this man he considered a good friend.

"Let me pour you a glass of water, Benjamin. I can see you are still breathless."

Jonathan went to a side table and returned with the water. He placed it on the desk beside his guest.

Benjamin took a sip and said, "Thank you, that helps. I must admit my throat was dry."

He took another sip and said, "Jonathan, what I am about to say must be kept in complete confidence. It is a personal matter, and you are a good friend. I wanted your support on this before it proceeded too far."

"I will maintain your confidence with pleasure and provide my support. But, tell me, Benjamin, what is the issue?"

"This concerns your housekeeper, Mrs Ethel Nibley."

"Ah!"

Benjamin explained the situation with his daughter, Clare, and how he had provided for her future. He then explained how he had appointed Ethel Nibley as a trustee and his reasons for this. With some hesitancy, he talked of his gift to Ethel, ensuring she was now financially independent, but asked that it remain confidential.

"Of Course! You mean she no longer needs to work for me?"

"That is correct, Jonathan. She is now financially independent, and to my shame, I have advised her that she should now live independently and have servants. I apologise for this, as I overlooked the family atmosphere she works in and how close your family is to her. Please forgive me, but what I am about to explain will help you understand my going behind your back."

"Benjamin, I am not her father or brother. You are free to talk or discuss whatever you wish with Mrs Nibley. I think she is an independent lady who works her contract with us as agreed."

"That is most kind of you, Jonathan. It is a great relief, and I thank you for being open with me."

Daisy arrived with the coffee and some pastries. She filled the cups, asked about milk, and then placed the cups beside both gentlemen. She then put a plate of pastries on the desk and left.

"Thank you, Daisy. A pastry, Benjamin?"

"They look delicious, but I must decline. Doctor's orders – you understand, I am sure."

"Yes, yes. These doctors take all the fun out of our lives but keep us alive. I am thankful for Neville, David, and Bryan. Good doctors, indeed!"

"Yes, David Sopwith has been treating me for three years, and I could not ask for better care. Now, Jonathan, I must complete my task and finish this meeting with you. Your time is valuable, and I must not waste it."

"Feel at ease, Benjamin. I have no other appointments this morning."

Benjamin took another sip of coffee, surprisingly broke a small portion of a pastry, and ate it.

"The sugar will do me some good!"

Jonathan smiled and waited for him to recommence.

"Over the last three months since meeting your housekeeper, Mrs Nibley, I have heard her troubled story. I also know your kind recommendations about her integrity and love for your family. These are qualities that you do not often find. In fact, on several occasions, I met with Mrs Nibley over lunch and enjoyed developing our friendship.

Jonathan! I must not delay any further. I have proposed to Ethel, and she has accepted me."

Jonathan Turner tried hard to show surprise and happiness about the announcement. Despite his disappointment, he smiled and shook Benjamin's hand.

"Congratulations on your engagement, Benjamin. That is wonderful news, and I wish you both well."

Relieved that he had made his announcement, Benjamin sat back, looking far more relaxed and breathing easier.

"Jonathan, I have been mulling over Ethel's relationship with your family. I understand you recently lost your wife and have suffered terribly. I also know you greatly depend on Ethel and would be lost without her. Tell me, please! Can you find a replacement housekeeper in the next month or two? I ask because I desire an early date for our marriage. You will understand that I yearn for a loving wife and a mother for Clare."

"Certainly, Benjamin. If that is Mrs Nibley's wish, I will not stand in your way. But I recommend an engagement that allows more time together before marrying. I only suggest this as your decision seems hasty, and engagements allow both parties time for reflection before entering matrimony."

"You are right, Jonathan, but I love Ethel with all my heart, and she is the one for me. It has been so long since I had a woman in my life. I certainly would appreciate it if you could replace her soon. Once I know that is done, I can make the final arrangements for the wedding."

"Of course, my friend. I would not stand in your way. You have a busy time in front of you."

They both sat there nodding and sipping their coffees. Jonathan could not help thinking that Benjamin seemed set on satisfying his requirements more than considering Ethel's feelings.

"Jonathan, I have not said this to anybody else as it concerns your family! But Ethel's handling of the bottle stealing convinced me of her integrity and character. I would have been greatly disappointed if she had not gently dealt with your child and returned the bottles."

Jonathan was suddenly brought out of his sorrowful thoughts of losing Ethel. The hairs on the back of his neck were suddenly tense. Surely, William would know better than to steal from a friend.

"She confronted the child, and a few days later, the error was confessed. We even had a quiet chat at Cloverdale Chase and settled everything. Ethel handled it so well –this confirms why I care for her. She is such a loving person!"

"Yes, yes! She has some marvellous qualities."

Jonathan tried to hide his anger as he thought about how William's actions would destroy his life. This child might also ruin his relationship with Ethel. The boy must go to Africa as soon as Jonathan might manage it. Damn him! Damn! Damn!

"You seem far away, Jonathan? I am sure you have other appointments, so I must be off. If you would keep our conversation confidential, that would be most charitable of you. Thank you for this time together. I will expect you and your family at our wedding."

"Thank you, Benjamin. I would not miss it for the world."

Benjamin stood and shook Jonathan's hand before moving towards the door. Jonathan felt the weakness in Benjamin's handshake and wondered what the actual state of his health was. As they entered the passageway, Audrey Stern passed. Jonathan quickly asked, "Audrey, would you please assist Mr Petherton to the front door? Good day, Benjamin, and take care on the steps now."

"Thank you, Jonathan. I shall be in contact."

Jonathan Turner smiled, returned to his office, and closed his door. He moved to the window again, his knuckles turning white from his strong clasp on the ledge.

How could this happen? Why was it happening to him again? What had he done to deserve this? That boy had interfered again and ruined his life with Ethel. Was this fair? No, it was not. It was time he solved this problem. But he had written to Richard saying the child would come in the African spring. No, it must be sooner before anything else was ruined.

William would destroy him, Ethel, and their family if he did not act soon.

Chapter 3

Fintelton Manor, Outside Petersfield, Sussex ...

In the morning, Lady Anne's maid, carrying a tray, made her way up the servants' stairs and approached Sir Robert and Lady Anne's room. Mary knocked, entered, placed the tray near Anne's side of the bed and quietly opened the curtains. Bright sunlight flowed into the room, announcing a beautiful country morning.

Robert remained fast asleep after a late night, but Anne opened her eyes, stretched, yawned and asked, "What time is it, Mary?"

"About nine, Milady. Here is some breakfast for you." She picked up the tray and placed it on the bed. "There is no need to worry about the children – they are already off riding with Mr Stem."

"Thank you, Mary. Come back in half an hour and help me dress."

The maid discretely left, leaving Anne to survey her breakfast. She sat there first, looking out the French doors and then at the beautiful food in front of her. She pinched herself, wondering if this was all real, and then looked down on a sleeping Robert, the man she had made love with late last night. She smiled as she gently swept Robert's hair back over his brow and said, "Robert, time to wake, Darling. We have much to do today."

The Earl's youngest son stirred and then opened an eye, looking up at his wife beside him.

"What time is it, Anne?"

"Around nine!" She giggled, "If we hurry, we might make morning tea today."

Robert sat up and looked at Anne's breakfast tray, "Why don't they bring me a tray as well?"

"Because gentlemen have breakfast downstairs, Darling! I need a little time to organise myself for the day."

Robert reached across and stole a piece of toast, and crunched it. Looking satisfied, he moved closer and kissed Anne's shoulder.

"Can we stay in bed all day and make love?"

"You can wait until tonight. You had your fair share yesterday evening! Today, I must find a way to talk with your father. If we are to find the documents in his room, we will need his help or gain his agreement to search. We cannot invade his room and start without permission."

"Do you think you can convince him?"

"It is worth a try, Robert. It will be our last chance before leaving for Porting on Monday. I talked with the butler yesterday and briefed him. Pike will have your father in the rose garden this morning, and I will join him. It is time the subject was broached, and I am sure he will assist."

"Should I also come?"

"No. It is best if I do this myself! I will also let your mother know what is happening. Perhaps you could help Mt Stem with the children, please."

Robert gently kissed his wife's cheek, "Thank you, Anne. Let's hope he is rational this morning."

High Street, Guildford, Surrey ...

Having finished his appointment with Doctor Bassington, the Reverend Andrew Taggart walked up the High Street towards the Guild Hall. Two men approached from the other direction: an older distinguished gentleman and the other young, tall and well-attired. There was something familiar about the men, and Andrew searched his memory for a name – but it would not come. Still worried about his young curate, Andrew found concentration difficult.

"Mr Taggart! It is I, Mervin Webster. We have returned to Guildford, Sir!"

Andrew stopped before the men and peered at them, searching for recognition. Suddenly, his mind recalled a previous parish member from long ago.

"Mervin! My dear old friend, how are you? Is it twenty years since we last met? And who is this with you? Surely it is not Leonard?"

"It is Reverend! My son, Leonard, has grown."

Reverend Taggart raised his eyes, "He has indeed! Hello, Leonard, what a tall, fine young man you have become."

"Reverend Taggart! It is a pleasure."

"Mervin, what brings you here from Cornwall?"

"Medicine and retirement, Andrew. When you have time, I will explain, but it is enough to say I have made my fortune in Cornwall, and now I have moved the family back to Guildford."

"You are very welcome. When did you arrive?"

"We came in a rented coach on Monday. The family will reside at the Fox and Hound until we can find a rental or a house to buy. I will also need a good doctor, Andrew. Who would you recommend?"

"Why? Is your health faltering, Mervin?"

"Unfortunately, yes. We moved back due to my ailments and wanted more opportunities for the children. Cornwall is somewhat limited, and a broader community will suit us well. Guildford is far enough out of London to enjoy the delights of the country but close enough for good medical services."

"True, true, Mervin. I certainly can recommend some good doctors. Why not bring the family to lunch on Sunday after church? Laura will be keen to catch up with Gwendolen and Betty. I assume they are with you."

"Yes, Andrew. They are here. Gwennie has already taken Betty to Hursts for some new clothes. She is so happy to be in Guildford. Being so close to London, the shopping is wonderful. It was a bit sparse in Truro. We will join you for Sunday lunch. Thank you for the invitation."

"Wonderful, Mervin. I must be off now – I have a full round of visits this morning and preparations for the Sunday services this afternoon, including reviewing Mr Hotspur's progress on his sermon. Please ask Gwendolen to call on Laura for afternoon tea. She will be finished at school by three-thirty. I will let her know so she is expecting them."

"I will, Andrew. I will!" Mervin Webster murmured, "Did you say, Phi.... No, it can wait! We will look forward to Sunday."

"Good day, Mervin! Good day, Leonard!"

Andrew walked briskly up the High Street, happy that the Websters had returned. He would first take some morning tea with Laura, then visit the Turner residence and check Clementine's recovery. Andrew knew Philip Hotspur regularly saw Clementine and would quietly ask Mrs Nibley if his young curate was making a nuisance of himself. An unknowing fourteen-year-old led astray by his curate was not what he wished for in this parish.

Turner Household, Guildford, Surrey ...
During the morning, Jonathan Turner spent time in his study working through various issues with the new bakery in London. He gathered his papers, placing them in a leather case before departing for the office. Straightening his jacket, he opened the study door and found Aggie dusting the furniture.

"Morning, Aggie."

"Morning, Mr Turner, will you stay home for morning tea?"

"No, I am off to the office."

"Yes, Sir. By the way, Mr Turner, how was your trip to Scotland? I have not had the chance to ask since you returned. The house has been so busy."

"It was a lovely time, Aggie. Especially the sea voyages."

"You were not seasick?"

"No, I find I must have been born with sea legs. I enjoyed it immensely."

Jonathan always had his plans for William in the back of his mind. This conversation was his opportunity. He needed someone to accompany William, and Aggie got on well with the lad. If she could cope with sea travel, she may be a good companion for the voyage.

"How about you, Aggie? Can you stomach the sea?"

"Oh yes, Mr Turner. I love the sea. My father took me to the Isle of Wight several times, and we sometimes rented a small sailing boat there and went fishing. The movement never affected me. I always wished I could sail off somewhere overseas one day."

"Well, you never know. The opportunity may happen. Perhaps in time, you might marry a sea captain, Aggie?"

Aggie smiled and then said, "Using a pun, Mr Turner. There are none on the horizon at the moment!"

Jonathan laughed, "Well said. You are young, Aggie. There is still plenty of time."

"Thank you, Mr Turner."

As Jonathan Turner walked down the High Street, he realised that Aggie would be perfect for the job if he could convince her. She would travel with William to Port Elizabeth, accompany the lad by coach to Grahamstown, and stay with Richard and Sarah at their property. Once William was settled in, she would return by sea to Guildford and give them a first-hand account of what was happening out there.

He thought to himself, 'A perfect plan. What could go wrong!'

Jonathan started whistling as he walked on.

A knock came on the front door of the Turner residence. Aggie answered the knock and found the Reverend Philip Hotspur holding some flowers.

"Good morning, maid! I call on Miss Clementine Turner!"

"Mr Hotspur. Good morning! Please come in."

Aggie opened the door wide, allowing Philip in. Knowing the house, he approached the stairs, expecting access to Clementine's bedroom. Aggie quickly ran ahead of him and blocked his path.

"Please, Sir. If you would wait in the drawing room. I will inform Miss Turner that you have arrived. She is well enough to entertain in the drawing room now."

"There is no bother, maid! I am a clergyman and will see her in her bedroom. She must not be disturbed out of bed for me."

A strong voice came from behind Philip, "There is no need, Mr Hotspur. We thank you for your consideration, but given Miss Clementine's speedy recovery, it would be improper for you to visit her bedroom. The drawing room will be appropriate."

Philip Hotspur spun around and found a glaring Mrs Ethel Nibley behind him. The young curate smiled and realised this was an exchange he would not win.

"I see. Thank you, Mrs Nibley. Your feminine consideration of etiquette does you credit. I will be happy to wait in the drawing room."

Philip walked off, making a statement and plopped himself uncomfortably down on the settee.

Another knock came at the front door, and the young, discontent curate soon found himself in the presence of the Reverend Taggart as they waited on Clementine. Andrew Taggart conversed politely with Mrs Nibley while Philip's spirit lifted at the sight of Ivy and Jess bringing the morning tea.

"Mrs Nibley, you never told me the family had such handsome young ladies on your staff."

"You never asked me, Mr Hotspur!"

"Please, would you introduce them?"

Ethel was immediately suspicious of this young man but remained calm and made the introductions.

"Thank you, Ivy and Jess. It was a lovely spread indeed, especially the hot scones. Now, who made these delicious morsels?"

"Mrs Jennings, Mr Hotspur, but I helped her!"

Ivy quietly whispered to Jess, "Quiet, Jess."

Seeing Ivy's embarrassment, Ethel ushered the girls back into the kitchen as Clementine arrived. The housekeeper was disturbed. She noted Hotspur's eyes were lingering on Jess as she left with Ivy.

Andrew Taggart stood and welcomed the injured young lass, "Clementine, I am glad to see you up and about. That must be a great relief."

Clementine, never at a loss for words, responded in detail, monopolising the conversation for ten minutes. She commented, "Father feels he will be able to bring me to church this Sunday."

"That is wonderful news, Clementine. Your friends have missed you, and the company will help you recover. I think your absence has been discussed a lot."

Clementine smiled at the Reverend Taggart and then glanced at Mr Hotspur, looking down the hall curiously towards the kitchen.

"Mr Hotspur, will you have another scone and jam?"

"No, thank you, Clementine. I am glad that you have made such a speedy recovery. Now, I must be off as I still have much to do on my Sunday sermon."

He stood, thanked Mrs Nibley and then left.

Following morning tea, Andrew Taggart asked Ethel if he could speak with her.

"I, too, must be off. Thank you, Clementine, for receiving us this morning. I am cheered to see you so well, and I will tell Mrs Taggart about our visit."

Ethel walked Reverend Taggart to the front door.

"Mrs Nibley. If I could speak confidentially?"

"Yes, Reverend Taggart." Ethel wondered what this could involve. She led him outside the entrance, where they would be out of earshot.

"I wanted to check that young Hotspur was not making a nuisance of himself. I understand he comes here nearly every second day and visits Clementine."

Ethel smiled, "Yes, he does come here often. However, I feel he somewhat lacks purpose these days. I hope I am not speaking out of turn?"

"No, no! Please speak freely as this is a confidential enquiry."

"Reverend Taggart. Since the school incident with Edward Blake, I think the congregation have lost faith in the young man. His mistake will take many years for the congregation to forgive. I assure you that I maintain a careful watch when he is in the house. Clementine is safe. However, he has never left so quickly as today. Perhaps Reverend, you should visit more often."

As Philip Hotspur walked down the busy High Street towards his lodgings, the memory of the two pretty lasses serving morning tea was much on his mind. He smiled at the prospect of some company with these girls.

Fintelton Manor, Outside Petersfield, Sussex …

William led the horse with the reins and carried a worried expression. His walk had changed to a wide-legged gate. Every third or fourth step, he would stop, grip his pants, murmuring, 'Ow!" Then, he would proceed again.

Mr Stem and the other children were now some five hundred yards ahead, but there was no way William was getting back on his horse today.

The young boy stopped as he saw a rider galloping past Mr Stem and the children and headed straight in his direction. He would be here within a minute, and William stopped and wondered what he would say.

Robert had watched William for some time and recognised the problem. A new rider not riding was a signal.

Slowing his horse from a gallop to a canter, he slowed her down and trotted up to him, "A bit of a sore behind, William?"

With a pained expression, William looked up and said, "I felt a little sore last night, but it went away. Today, it is far worse on the inside of my thighs and behind. I love riding but I can't now. It is too sore."

Robert grinned, "That is normal. I was wondering when this would happen. I think Mr Stem may have been a bit ambitious with the horse riding. A little bit each day is usually better. I think we shall organise some other activities for this afternoon. Come on, let me pull you up here. You can sit behind me. Put your arms around my waist, and we will walk the horses home."

With that, Robert leaned down and pulled him up. There were a few grunts of pain from the young lad, but he quickly took his position. Robert edged his mount over to William's horse and said, "Here, girl!"

The horse swung its head up to look at him, and he quickly grabbed the reins and led her forward.

"Don't worry, William. It happens to everyone. If the others keep up this pace, they will share your predicament. It takes time for your body to adjust to saddles and rubbing. Some people never achieve it. I prefer sailing rather than riding."

"Me too. Water doesn't hurt, but it can be cold."

"Well, if you don't fall in, William, you don't get cold. You learn that quickly in the navy."

"I want to be a sailor one day when I am taller."

The Earl was settled in the rose garden, and Anne wandered down. The sun was bright, and the colour of the roses was magnificent. Under a wide-brimmed hat with her fair hair flowing out in the gentle breeze, Anne strolled along a line of roses, snipped off a deep red one, and smelt the fragrance. She sat beside the Earl with a smile, showing him her choice.

Pike appeared, set up a table and called a maid to bring some tea and pastries.

"That rose you have there, Anne[12], is called the 'Crimson Surprise'. It has a beautiful flower with a magnificent fragrance and is common in this part of England. That is the one most ladies pick when they tour my rose garden."

"The colour is deep and amazing!"

---

[12] The 'Crimson Surprise' rose is fictitious and modelled on the 'Crimson Glory' rose which was developed in Germany in 1935. JS

Anne conversed with the Earl for nearly fifteen minutes before focusing on what was needed.

"My Lord, there is a matter that we need to discuss, and I would be most honoured if you would help."

"What could that be, Anne?"

"Robert is most concerned about the finances of the estate."

"Ah, I have told him that Sir Hugh will apply himself to that when he returns."

"Yes, I understand, but we all fear for Sir Hugh's health."

Anne said no more for a minute as the Earl considered this.

Before she spoke again, he said, "I understand! The countess is beside herself and fears the worst."

Anne could see that the Earl's conversation was lucid, and he had not diverted from the topic. She had his attention, and this may be the opportunity they needed.

"My Lord, Robert confided in me that the estate was out of money the other month, and he found emergency monies to ensure the bank understood the estate was liquid. The servants' wages are now paid up to date, but the funds are languishing again. Mr Stem advises that the estate will soon be out of cash."

The Earl sat there and said nothing. He looked out on the rose garden and frowned as he decided on the right words, "Anne, I am far too old to run this estate now. I am beyond it. I have put all my trust in Hugh, but he is far away, and we are unaware if he is alive."

There was a short silence, and then, with a faltering voice, he said, "I no longer know what to do!"

Anne rested her hand on his and gently said, "You are not alone, Sir David. You still have a loving son here who wishes to help you. I, too, wish to assist."

"This estate has been my life, Anne. But my mind is going. I find it hard to concentrate now and address the problems you describe! I had no idea the situation was so serious."

Anne squeezed his hand, and he held her hand tightly.

"My Lord, I have married your son, and I intend that we have children. We will ensure you do not lose your home. Your line will continue."

The Earl opened his mouth but then hesitated. He pulled a handkerchief out of his pocket and dabbed his eyes.

"But what of Hugh, Anne? What of Hugh?"

"If Hugh returns and needs nursing, we will nurse him. We will do everything we can to support him. You should have no fear about that."

"If he is dead, Anne, you understand you will be the next Countess of Fintelton. Are you ready for that, Anne?"

"I pray that Hugh is alive and well, but if not, I will do everything I can to make you proud, my Lord. Robert and I will always care for you, Lady Jane and Emma."

Anne could see that her elderly father-in-law was becoming emotional. As he sat himself up, he cleared his throat, took the rose from Anne, and said, "A beautiful rose, almost perfect, Anne. But not as perfect as you."

He lifted his teary eyes and looked her straight in the face.

"When I asked the countess who this girl was, marrying our Robert, she told me that you were the perfect match for him and would make us all proud. I took her word then but wondered how a commoner could do that. But Anne, I was wrong. You are the perfect woman for my son. We have been blessed by having you as our daughter-in-law. Thank you, daughter, for your love and devotion to my son."

Anne sat back but kept hold of her father-in-law's hand.

"I have struggled, your Lordship!" A tear ran down her cheek as she looked at him again. "It has been like a dream come true. I have become a princess compared to my old life. But I must keep it in perspective. So, you, the Countess, Robert and I must save your estate, my Lord. Will you help us?"

The Earl sat there smiling as he looked into her beautiful blue eyes. Then he released her hand and sat back.

"I will help, Anne. But you may not get another sensible word out of me for a long time after this."

Anne smiled. She now understood that the Earl used his absent-mindedness to protect himself from worry and stress. It was his way of coping and staying alive. He knew he could no longer manage the estate's affairs but was proud and would not admit this to others.

"We need some important information, my Lord."

"Ask, and you shall receive, Anne."

"We have received a question from the attorneys about Mrs Constance, complaining about not receiving money from the estate. We need to understand this woman's background and the details of the estate agreement with her so we can sort it out."

The Earl sat there staring out at his rose garden. Anne could see the look of concentration on his face. What she had said would have brought back difficult memories for him and may have turned him away from their open conversation. She prayed that he would confide in her before his memory shut this conversation down.

"I see! I had forgotten about Kathy."

He made to stand up but then reclined again.

"It was long ago, and I thought it was all complete. How much do you know, Anne?" The Earl continued to gaze out through the rose garden to the horizon.

"Enough to know that Mrs Constance is a dangerous woman."

The Earl considered Anne's reply and then closed his eyes before he spoke.

"The details you need are in an adjoining room to my walk-in dressing room. It is locked for safekeeping."

Anne nodded, indicating she understood.

The Earl then called the butler, "Pike!"

The butler near the patio's doorway came out and down the steps to the Earl.

"My Lord!"

"Pike, when Robert and Anne are ready, please go with them and unlock the storage cupboard door where my files are kept. Give them access whenever needed, and you may assist if asked. Do you understand, Pike?"

"Yes, my Lord."

"That will be all."

Pike walked back to the patio and remained ready to serve his master.

Anne smiled and said, "Thank you, my Lord. We will do our best for you and the estate."

"I know you will, Anne. You are one of our family now and understand what is required." The Earl turned and gazed at her again. "Since we first met, Anne, I could see the strength in your eyes. I think you will do well with your beauty and warm personality."

"If it happens, my Lord, and I hope it does not, I will do my best."

"Oh, I am afraid it will happen, Anne. Hugh should have sent news by now. It has been too long. One thing, Anne! Promise me you will not desert young David. David Constance! None of this is his fault. He is an innocent bystander caught up in a very difficult situation. Make sure he is cared for, please."

"I promise, my Lord. And Mrs Constance?"

"She has been generously looked after. We have no other duty towards her. But the boy must have a future."

"I will personally make sure of this, my Lord."

"Thank you, Anne. Now, you must be off on your business, eh?"

"Very soon, my Lord."

"Well, off you go. After I finish this tea and scone, I must walk around the rose garden."

Portsmouth, England ...

Ross Stubbington watched from the second-floor window of an empty apartment across the road from the coffee house. He had arranged a significant payment for access and the silence of the landlord. For two weeks, he surveyed the comings and goings of the navy personnel. Now that he was sure of the faces of each of the regulars, he would concentrate on his target, Lieutenant Martin Russell.

He aimed to identify the man who was the navy contact in the Irish message chain between Ireland and England. A bold confrontation with the man would have alerted the courier that his cover was blown and ruined the security services plan. Stubbington knew it suited his superiors that Russell continued believing he was undetected. The English would set a trap for him, revealing who was manipulating the navy and any other connections he had with the Irish.

Leaving the apartment, he crossed the road, dodging a cart and entered by the front door of the coffee house. He took the first cubicle with a good interior view and waited to place his order. Avoiding being too obvious, he picked up a broadsheet and commenced reading it.

"What will it be, Mr?"

"Bacon, eggs and some toast! Thanks!"

"Coffee?"

"Yes, thanks."

"Be about five minutes. There are a lot in the house today!"

"Right, mate!"

Ross detected the slightest hint of an accent in the waiter's voice. If the noise level in the coffee house had been lower, he might have identified it. The navy men were the culprits making a jolly racquet. As four officers left, Ross dropped a saltshaker and leaned down, putting his head in front of the group.

One in the group yelled to warn of the impending collision, "Watch out, Russell!"

The lead man, walking fast and shouting over his shoulder, missed seeing Ross and struck his head with his knee.

"Ow!" Ross howled as he hit the floor.

Almost falling over Stubbington, the navy man grabbed the cubicle wall.

"Sorry, Mate! I did not see you there."

"Fine, fine. It was my fault."

Russell gave Stubbington a hand up.

Ross smiled and looked him in the face, "Thanks. I lost my grip on that saltshaker. My apologies!"

Russell half smiled, "You're new here. Watch out for us navy blokes! Always looking in the wrong direction. Have a good breakfast, mate!" The navy lieutenant left, catching his friends and joining their boisterous comments.

Ross, a man with experience in interrogating suspects, detected slight signs of suspicion on Martin Russell's face. Smiling, he waved his thanks and commenced reading his broadsheet again.

Soon, a large plate of bacon and eggs was placed before him. The waiter stood there and asked, "New in town, Mister?"

"Rafferty, Mate. Samuel Rafferty. We supply canons to the navy. Work with Steele's Foundry in Woolwich. I will be here for a few days. By the look of this breakfast, I will have to come back. Thanks, Mate."

"We always serve a good spread. It keeps the navy men coming back. Watch out for them blokes, Mate! Always being the joker and having accidents! Particularly that Russell. A bit accident-prone if you ask me!"

"Is Russell his surname?"

"Say, mate! Why do you want to know that, eh? You're not going to cause trouble, are ye?"

"No, Mate. I'll be here for a few days and might want someone to talk with."

The waiter looked hard at Ross and then said, "Russell! The navy men are like private schoolboys. They use the surname. He doesn't come in every day. Now, I'll fetch your coffee and toast!"

"Thanks, Mate! What's his Christian name then?"

The waiter scratched his head. "Can't remember." But as he walked away, he turned and said, "Martin, I think!"

Ross started devouring the food before him as the waiter disappeared into the kitchen. Stubbington could not help but think he may have stumbled onto more than he had bargained for. Waitpersons were usually easy to talk with and friendly. This one was quickly suspicious. What was his relationship with Russell? Was this coffee shop also a front, or was the waiter just a suspicious person? Time would tell, but he had now singled out the courier. The lieutenant was still here, so he must believe his cover was not blown, or perhaps he was just after money and unaware of what was in the messages. Whatever his role was, it appeared the news from Dublin had not arrived yet.

Turner Household, Guildford, England ...
After church, Jonathan Turner sat with Thomas and Marion, discussing their departure for Glasgow.

"Is everything ready for tomorrow, Thomas?"

"Yes, Father! We have packed all our belongings, except our travelling gear, into boxes, and all is ready for the removalists. Seeing we remain here tonight, the men could have started packing today, but, as it is Easter Sunday. They can start tomorrow."

"How long will it take to reach Glasgow?"

"Mr McPherson will accommodate our items on one of his ships from Woolwich. It should leave by Thursday and be there in a couple of weeks. He has already left for Glasgow and wants the restructure finalised before we arrive. Mrs McPherson remained in Greenwich as she had business in London."

"Why not travel with your luggage? The sea voyage is fascinating."

"I thought Marion would enjoy the journey up through Derbyshire and Lancashire. The country is stunning, and there are many beautiful lakes. While we are without children, we thought it may be an ideal time for some sightseeing as we travel."

Marion nudged Thomas and whispered, "It is time you made the announcement, Thomas!"

He looked back at Marion and smiled. Ethel could see that Marion was excited, and she wondered if …!

"It is time we made our announcement, Father. We should tell you and the family now before we leave. I am proud to announce that Marion bears our first child."

Ethel and Clementine rushed across to Marion and hugged her. Jonathan shook hands with his son, "This is wonderful news. When is the baby due?"

"In late October, Mr Turner. As it is early, we have not told my father or Mr and Mrs McPherson yet. But we thought we should tell you before we left. I will write to them tonight now we have announced the good news."

"Wonderful, Marion. Now, Thomas, you must take good care of your wife on this trip."

Marion laughed, and Thomas said, "I will, Father. We will take the trip slowly, enjoy the countryside, and visit all the towns like Oxford and Derby before we make a long stop in Ullswater, where I have booked three days' accommodation. Marion will be treated like a Princess on vacation."

Marcia nudged between Ethel and Clemmie and asked Marion, "Where is the baby, Marion?"

Thomas's wife patted her tummy and said, "In here, little one. You must wait until October before you meet your new niece or nephew."

"How long before October?"

"A lot of sleeps, Marcia, but I am sure it will go quickly! You can visit us in Greenwich once the baby has arrived. I am sure your father and Ethel will bring you."

Marion suddenly realised what she had said and blushed as Ethel retook her seat and Jonathan had a quick drink of water. There was a pause in the conversation for a few moments as Clemmie directed Marcia back onto the seat beside her.

Marion quietly said, "I am sorry I …!"

"What will you do with the house, Father?" Thomas was keen on keeping the conversation flowing.

"I have not considered that yet."

Thomas suggested, "As Robert is back, perhaps Victoria Sopwith might wish to rent it until she finds a suitable house to purchase."

Marion quickly added, "Now that Victoria works for Hursts, I think her thoughts are of London. But I am sure she would not be torn away from her brother, David. Perhaps the rental might suit her well, and she will purchase a London townhouse. I hear that money is not an object."

"I would keep that quiet, Marion. Victoria is keen on her privacy." Thomas was aware of how carefully they guarded their private affairs.

Jonathan agreed with Thomas' suggestion, "You are right, Thomas. I should mention this to Victoria before I act on the house. She might be interested. Excuse me while I duck into my study and put a note in my diary for when she returns with Anne. Thomas! Come with me, please, as I have some documents you should take with you."

As Jonathan and his eldest son walked off, Ethel asked, "How many months are you, Marion? You look so well."

"About two, Ethel. I think I am nearly over the morning troubles. I am feeling comfortable, which is a blessing."

In the study, Jonathan closed the door and pointed Thomas to a chair beside his desk.

"Thomas, I have not told you this before, but I have agreed to help the government with some enquiries. This letter explains it all, but please keep it confidential and keep it somewhere safe. Thank you for the information you provided on the McPherson Brewing Company. It seems everything is above board. However, I wonder about this sudden need to send James to Ireland as General Manager. Hamish has never mentioned any interest in Ireland before. See if you can find out what is happening, and let me know as soon as you can?"

"Yes, it does seem sudden, but I assumed it relates to the girl. Perhaps there is more to it. Leave it with me for a month. We won't be there for another three weeks, so I shall write soon after that."

"Good lad! I won't keep you any longer. You have much to do, and I have some issues to solve."

Later in the afternoon, as Marion found time to speak with Ethel alone, she said, "Please forgive me, Ethel, for my comment before lunch. It was not meant the way it came out. I am sorry if I hurt your feelings or embarrassed you."

Ethel smiled, took Marion's hands, and confided, "There is no damage done, Marion. And if I should find myself in a position where I might persuade Mr Turner to visit Greenwich with the children, then it will be done."

They both smiled, and Ethel hugged Marion.

"I am so happy for you. Take good care of yourself on the trip."

Marion hugged Ethel and whispered, "Make sure you come to Greenwich. It would not be complete without you now!"

Rectory, The High Street, Guildford, Surrey …

"Thank you, Laura. That was a magnificent lunch. Your cook presented it beautifully, and the delicate tastes were exquisite."

"To finish the meal, Mervin, we have some chocolate pastries I procured from the Turner's High Street bakery shop. I think you will enjoy them with your tea or coffee."

As they watched the plates being cleared, a thankful murmur came from the guests.

Gwendolen Webster, a short but strongly built woman in her fifties, was careful to keep her hair in place and her new crimson dress protected from food accidents. She was keen to hear about the church society and which of her old acquaintances still attended.

When Laura mentioned the Turner bakery shop, she remembered a past acquaintance.

"Are the Turners still here in Guildford, Laura? I remember Eleanora Turner and her children. She was a genteel person with all the airs and graces you would expect from an upper-class lady. I would be keen to make her acquaintance again."

Laura smiled, "Yes, the Turners have a house along the High Street near the Free School. Unfortunately, Eleanora passed away in February. It was a tragedy for the family, especially the younger children. Jonathan took it very hard and is still recovering."

Mervin added, "That is a tragedy, indeed! I recall they had the bakery on Quarry Street east of St Mary's church before we left. Is that still operational?"

"No, soon after you left for Cornwall, Jonathan moved the family into the home on the High Street. The business outgrew the Quarry Street bakery, and Jonathan purchased a bigger site near the wharf. His business has expanded greatly over the last two decades."

Betty Webster asked, "Mr Taggart, I remember being at school with Anne Turner. Is she still here in town?"

"Yes, Betty, how could I forget? She recently married and lives at a property called Porting, up past the castle on the high side of the street! It is a lovely house. She married Sir Robert South from Fintelton Manor."

Laura Taggart mentioned, "The Turner family often visit the riverbank for afternoon tea on a Sunday afternoon. Anne might be there, although she was not in church this morning. I heard they visited Petersfield for horse riding lessons for the children, so they may not have returned yet. Perhaps, Betty, you and Leonard might walk down to the riverside this afternoon and check."

Betty was keen, "Yes, Leonard will escort me. I want to meet with Anne again. She was a dear friend when I was previously at school here."

Andrew Taggart found it hard to recall any great relationship between Betty and Anne, but perhaps he was unaware. From the corner of his eye, he could see the Reverend Philip Hotspur approaching the front door from the High Street. Andrew's heart sank as he could not turn the young man away.

"Mervin and Gwendolen, please excuse me while I invite our young curate in."

The knock came, and Andrew quickly opened the door and explained his guests to Philip.

Entering the dining room, the Rector made the introductions.

"Mr Mervin Webster and Mrs Gwendolen Webster, may I introduce the Reverend Philip Hotspur. Philip has been with us for six months and is settling well. The Websters have moved here from Cornwall."

Mervin Webster looked confused but said, "Good day, Mr Hotspur."

"Thank you, Mr Webster and Mrs Webster!" Philip glanced around the room, noticing Betty and Leonard at the table.

"Mr Webster, this must be your son and daughter?"

"Yes, my son, Leonard, and my daughter, Betty."

Philip moved around the table, shook Leonard's hand, and then took Betty's and kissed it.

"Enchanted, Betty!"

Laura Taggart immediately recognised Philip Hotspur had found another possible conquest in Betty. She was interested to see if he attempted extracting financial information from Mr Webster.

"So, Mr Webster, what brings you and your family to Guildford?"

"Retirement and good medical services, Mr Hotspur."

"Surely, London would be the place for medical services."

"Mr Hotspur, London is near these days due to the good roads. I hear many make the trip in one day by carriage, granted they usually arrive late at night. Given the pollution and the crowds who also live there, I have no desire to live in London."

"I see. You will be looking for a gentleman's estate, then?"

"Yes, somewhere close to town but with some land. I may be retired, but I will plant roses. There is nothing better than a country rose garden."

"My sentiments exactly, Mr Webster."

Later in the afternoon, Philip, hearing that Betty was keen on contacting Lady Anne South, offered his services, and they set out for the riverside. With some urgency, as soon as the young people left, Gwendolen asked, "Mr Taggart, I must ask, and I should explain why first. My sister, Felicity, and her husband attend church in the parish of Deptford. I often contact Felicity, and she keeps me well-informed. Would Mr Hotspur be the same curate who lately served there?"

"Yes, Gwendolen. I believe he is. Is there a problem?"

Gwendolen became most distressed, took out her fan, and waved it madly, trying to cool herself.

"Mr Taggart, are you aware of the details of the curate's departure from his last parish?"

"I have not been made acquainted with them, Gwendolen. The curate came as a gift. The bishop's privy trust pays for all Mr Hotspur's expenses for the first year of his curacy. We, as a parish, are thankful for this assistance."

Gwendolen looked at her husband and sucked her bottom lip. Mervin, slowly realising what Gwendolen was leading to, said, "Gwennie, now you have come this far; you should tell Andrew and

Laura the complete story."

Mervin's wife took a deep breath and continued, "Andrew, I take no pleasure in passing on this information. Mr Hotspur left the parish of Deptford in disgrace. On arriving at the parish, the young man became engaged quickly to Miss Mary Rochedale, who came from a delightful family. Mary was young, around seventeen, and easily fell under his spell. I will not go into details, but her parents, on finding that Mary was with child, acted quickly against Philip, banning him from ever seeing their daughter again. After meeting with the parents, I believe he was thrown out the front door of their home. Mrs Rochedale and Mary were on the channel ferry the next week, and I understand they are still in Italy. For Mary's sake, it was kept quiet. However, there was no explanation from the parish when Philp suddenly left. Felicity only heard of it some months later and has kept it confidential.

I only mention the matter as we find him here in your parish acting as if nothing ever happened. I strongly suggest you rid the parish of that curate as quickly as possible."

Mervin Webster added, "Andrew, this will not affect us attending your parish as we are well-versed in this young man's despicable character. However, the mothers of young ladies should be made aware of his antics. It would be a tragedy if he led another innocent young lass astray. I am uncertain how you should advise your parishioners, but I feel it is necessary."

Gwendolen then spoke, "Now, if you would excuse us, we shall follow our son and daughter and end this young man's association with them. Thank you for a wonderful lunch, and we look forward to next Sunday."

The Wey Riverbank, Guildford, England ...
"Clemmie, will you be a pirate and chase me?"

Clementine looked up from where she sat comfortably on a rug and explained, "I can't, Marcia. I am still recovering from my injury. The others will be home tomorrow. They will chase you around then."

Ethel, who was unpacking the picnic basket, called Marcia, "Come here, little one, and help me with this. There are some chocolate pastries in here."

Marcia was immediately distracted and rushed to the basket,

"Where are they?"

"Here! And look, there is one for you right now! You sit down beside me here, and you can eat it."

"Wowee!"

Seeing Marcia was now distracted, Ethel quickly unpacked the basket as Nanny Smithers and Mr Turner arrived with Jeremy. The baby was fast asleep and soon placed in a portable basket cot Jonathan had purchased for family picnics. Marion was quickly sitting beside the cot, cooing over the baby.

The days were now becoming slightly warmer, and there was a definite hint of spring in the air. Under the clear blue sky, some daffodils were flowering along the riverside, and the weeping willows dipped their long leaves in the water. Ducks and swans started to paddle towards the party assembling on the riverbank, and Marcia ran towards them, throwing part of her pastry as they scattered into the water.

Ethel called, "Marcia, there is some bread here for you to feed the ducks and swans. The pastry is for you to eat!"

The little one, delighted with the crowd of birds fighting for the pastry, ran back to the housekeeper for the bread.

"Good afternoon, Mrs Nibley and Clementine."

Ethel turned around and found Philip Hotspur, a young lady and a gentleman approaching. Philip beckoned his guest to come forward.

"Mrs Nibley, might I ask if Lady Anne is with you this afternoon? Miss Betty Webster and her brother Leonard have arrived from Truro, and Betty is keen to become reacquainted with Lady Anne."

Ethel quickly stood, "Good afternoon, Mr Hotspur. Sorry, but we do not expect Sir Robert and Lady Anne to be home until tomorrow. Please introduce your guests and join us. Mr Turner is walking along the bank. I am sure he will soon return and would be keen to meet your guests."

"Thank you. Mrs Nibley, please may I introduce Miss Betty Webster and her brother Leonard. Mrs Nibley is the Turner family's house-keeper."

Betty and Leonard courteously nodded to Mrs Nibley.

Philip continued, "This handsome young lady is Miss Clementine Turner."

Leonard walked across and took Clementine's hand, "A pleasure, Miss Turner. May I introduce my sister, Miss Betty Webster."

Miss Webster bowed and sat on a cushion beside Clemmie. "Miss Clementine, Mr Hotspur informs me of your recent accident. I hope you are recovering well."

"Yes, the injury heals well, but it will be some time before it mends. The doctors tell me at least another two months, so I am being careful."

At that moment, Marcia raced up and threw herself onto Clemmie's lap, clambering against her. She asked, "Who is this, Clemmie?"

Clementine cried, "Ow, Marcia! Please be gentle. As you can see, my recovery has had its ups and downs."

Betty and Clementine giggled and fell into conversation. Soon, Neville and Bethany arrived to join the party. Marcia was off attacking Neville with a stick as he ran along the bank, pretending to retreat. Leonard, interested in the game, watched as he inspected the riverbank. Bethany took a cushion and sat beside the girls.

Clemmie introduced Bethany and asked, "Beth, do you recall Betty Webster from the church school? Betty was a friend of Anne's before they moved to Cornwall."

"Hello, Betty. I am now Mrs Bethany Bassington. That is my husband being chased by Marcia. She loves playing pirates with the other children, but they are away today." Bethany looked hard at Betty and said, "I remember you. That must have been nearly twenty years ago. Yes, I remember you coming home with Anne on a few occasions at Quarry Street. My, how time flies. What brings you back to Guildford?"

"My father has made his fortune in Cornwall and suffers from declining health. He decided to retire in Guildford, where he could find good medical attention and be close to London, where his investments are managed. Leonard will commence his second year at Oxford in August. I will be living here with my parents and visiting Leonard occasionally. I hope to make new friends here."

Philip Hotspur could not believe his luck as he overheard Betty's comments and was about to add to the girl's conversation when a determined Mervin Webster placed an iron fist on his shoulder, looking him directly in the eye.

In a low voice, he demanded, "Mr Hotspur, I need a word with you!"

"I am sorry, Mr Webster, but I was about to converse with the ladies here. Might it wait ten minutes?"

Raising his voice, Mervyn said, "No, Sir! It may not!"

As Philip stood and followed Mr Webster down to the water's edge, Neville, holding Marcia's hands, introduced himself to Leonard. Marcia, pulling free, rushed to Ethel.

"I believe you are Leonard Webster, Sir? I am Bethany's husband, Neville Bassington. Good to meet you."

Leonard smiled and replied with his hand held out, "Honoured, Sir. Guildford is a pleasant town. I am staying here with my parents while they settle in. I will be away in early August to Oxford."

"Ah, what do you study?"

"Mathematics! I am keen to become an engineer."

Neville was impressed, "You will need plenty of energy for that. It is a demanding career."

"I run every day, trying to stay fit. The hospitality here is very warm, and I eat too much. Running helps to keep the weight down."

Neville was impressed with this young fellow, "Where do you run?"

"Mostly to the west of town. I charge out into the country, searching for paths and hills. We live near the intersection of London and Epson Roads. Do you know of any steep climbs where I could do short-distance sprints uphill?"

Neville grinned and said, "The road I live on is steep indeed. Come off the High Street at the Tunsgate market and up South Hill Road. The incline will provide you with a good workout."

Ethel quietly passed Marcia a plate with a slice of cake on it, "Here, Marcia. Take this cake down to Leonard, and please be careful!"

Carefully, she balanced the plate as she walked down to Leonard, still conversing with Neville by the river's edge.

Offering the cake, she said, "Ethel wants you to have some cake, Leonard."

Raising his eyebrows at Neville, he said, "Oh, thanks, Marcia. You have been a very good little girl today – how would you like to share my cake?"

Marcia was not going to say no, and Leonard, with a smile, sat beside her and passed half the cake.

The men looked up as they heard the raised voices of Mr Webster and Philip Hotspur further along the riverbank.

Philip asked, "How may I be of assistance, Mr Webster?"

"Mr Hotspur! I must be direct on this subject. I know why you departed from the Deptford Parish and concur with the decision taken by the parish council. I believe you are an unsuitable young man for the clergy. Your only ambition as a cleric is to be placed in a society where you can prey upon wealthy young women, select and court one and finally live off her inheritance for the rest of your life. Am I incorrect, Sir?"

Philip appeared insulted and strongly replied, "You certainly are, Sir. Please lower your voice, as we are in public. I must be excused from these vile accusations and disagree with them all."

Mervin, not to be trifled with, raised his voice loud enough for the riverbank party to overhear, "Then tell me, Mr Hotspur, why Mr and Mrs Rochedale ended your engagement to their daughter Mary?"

Mervin Webster had called Hotspur's bluff, and the young curate stood with his mouth open.

Mervin continued, "Mr Hotspur, I will not interfere with your occupation here as I hope you have mended your ways. But, Sir, if you trifle with my daughter, you will suffer greatly. Keep your conversation civil and with no indication whatsoever of a future relationship. Do you understand me, Sir?"

Philip said nothing but slightly nodded and then slowly walked away from the afternoon tea party along the riverbank. Leonard, who had been listening, turned back to Neville and said, "Dear me!"

Neville was unsure what was happening but now knew Mr Webster was not a man to be trifled with. Ethel heard the raised voices and noticed Philip's hasty retreat. Jonathan Turner, returning from his walk along the riverbank, plopped himself down on the picnic rug and, with a smile, said, "Well, what a jolly party we have here. Is everyone having fun?"

Chapter 4

Fintelton Manor, Outside Petersfield, Sussex ...

As Sunday lunch finished, William moved between Lady Jane and Anne and asked, "Can we ride this afternoon, please? We leave tomorrow, so this will be our last chance."

"Not yet, William!" Lady Jane raised her voice, saying, "Children, we are having the easter egg dance now. Your housekeeper carefully arranged it. What is her name again, Anne?"

"Mrs Nibley."

'Yes, Mrs Nibley and all of you did such a wonderful job preparing the eggs, and she will be most disappointed if she finds out we forgot it last Sunday. Also, I am looking forward to seeing you all dance."

Madeline was excited and rushed over to where the boxes of eggs stood, "Where shall we set up, Lady Jane?"

"Out in the drawing room near the piano, dear. I have arranged for Mrs Walsh to play for us. Madeline and Katherine, you may set up the eggs. Perhaps Anne and Victoria might assist you."

Each girl carried a box and rushed into the drawing room. William slowly followed, a little disappointed they were not riding again. Raising himself from the table, the Earl noticed William's downhearted slouch as he ambled past. The Earl touched William's shoulder, saying, "Cheer up, William. I am keen to see who breaks the least eggs. You can go riding after that and say goodbye to your horse. Perhaps come a week early in July before we go to the seaside. That is not far off, and you shall have more riding then. Ask your father when you return home. I am sure he will agree."

"Yes, your Lordship. That is an excellent plan. I shall ask him."

With that, he was off shouting at Simeon and the girls about how he would break the least eggs. Mrs Walsh took her position at the piano and commenced a spritely jig, with Madeline awarded the honour of starting the dance. She immediately squashed an egg with her first step and caused an uproar of laughs from everyone.

That night, as Lady Jane was making herself comfortable in bed, the Earl entered her room and sat beside her.

"Jane, what a wonderful Sunday. I am tired but feel more alert than I have been for some time. It must be the children visiting. It is a pity Hugh never married. He would have had children now the same age as the Turners. We have been blessed this week."

"Yes, we have David. I pray that Hugh is alive each morning, but my hopes are fading. It has been so long since he left."

Lady Jane sat there looking towards the window. She had nothing left to say after such an active day.

"You are tired, but before I say goodnight, I must tell you I had a long talk with Anne today. She is assisting Robert with our financial affairs. I permitted them to access the old files in my bedroom closet. You know the closet, don't you?"

"No, David. I don't know of it!"

"There is a door at the back of the dressing area, and I keep it locked. It leads into a large storage space where I have filed many of our financial records."

'Well, I am glad you have told me about it. What would have happened if you had died, and I was unaware?"

"Pike was aware, and he would have told you. I asked Pike to assist Robert and Anne. You know, Robert chose a good girl there. She is intelligent and with a kind heart. But you can see the strength in her eyes. She is a fine partner for Robert."

"She is, David. She is!"

"Sleep well, Jane."

As Lord Fintelton made his way out and gently closed the door, the countess sat back against her pillows with a pleasant smile.

In their room, Robert and Anne poured over the documents they had found in the Earl's safekeeping cupboard.

"Robert, this agreement that your father has as a codicil to his will is not what I expected. The life tenancy for the mother to occupy the house is as we expected, but the granting of cash was to be monitored and is only required until the son, David, could support himself. The monthly cash income was designed more for David Constance's support than his mother's. We need to ask the attorneys how they are assessing that."

Robert looked up, "That may explain why she is still working. Does it say anything about the property?"

"Yes! If Mrs Constance vacates the property of her own accord or dies, the property immediately returns to the Fintelton estate. Your father let the lawyers set this up, and he agreed to it."

Robert was still confused, "Probably. So why is Mrs Constance complaining?"

"She counted on the money and forgot the cash flow was only available while David was dependent."

Anne could see her husband drifting away in his thoughts, so she questioned, "Robert! What are you thinking about?"

"I was considering that now Father has instructed Pike to open his secret room for us and given us access to all his documents; perhaps Pike will provide us with more information."

Anne jumped at this suggestion, "You're right. Instructing him to open that room indicates to Pike that he may assist us."

Robert walked to the wall and pulled the sash cord.

Within a minute, a footman was at the door.

"'Sir Robert. May I be of assistance?"

"Yes, Peter. Would you ask Pike if he could join us, please?"

"Certainly, Sir."

After the footman had departed, Robert said, "This may help us avoid a trip to Portsmouth."

Soon, there was a knock on the door, and Pike entered with a box under his arm.

"May I be of assistance, Sir Robert?"

"Yes, Pike. Lady Anne and I were wondering now that the Earl has allowed us access to his secure files whether it would be possible for you to provide more information to us on Mrs Constance."

Pike stood there with a vacant expression as he considered his reply and said, "Sir Robert, I will assist, but on one condition: that every-thing I reveal in this room remains confidential. Of course, the information given may be used in any negotiations with Mrs Constance for the good of the estate."

"That is agreed, Pike, and Lady Anne and I will keep your confidence."

Pike then turned his gaze to Lady Anne.

"I also agree, Pike."

"Thank you, Lady Anne. You will understand that when a butler is appointed, he must maintain far more integrity than any other staff member. To break this confidence would mean I would have no choice but to resign. It would be hard for me to live with myself if I failed this family."

"Thank you, Pike. Now, what can you tell us about Mrs Constance?"

"Might we sit around this occasional table, Sir? The details may take some time, and I have some documents in this box I must show you."

"Certainly, Pike." Robert was impressed again. Pike had come prepared.

They all pulled up a chair, and Robert and Anne waited in suspense.

"The Earl became restless around 1797, and his visits to Portsmouth started in the summer. During that year, he visited Portsmouth three times. On his London trips, he always took his valet, but for Portsmouth, he insisted on the Butler. It was difficult for me to refuse."

Robert and Anne both smiled.

"The Earl explained to me, on our trip to Portsmouth, that a friend had told him of a club called 'The Groom's Club' that supplied exclusive company. This document was the brochure the Earl provided to me."

Pike passed across a brochure showing the rear view of an attractive lady on the cover, drink in one hand and a rose in the other. The lady was well dressed, and there seemed nothing obscene about the drawing. The caption read, 'Exclusive high-class ladies to provide amiable company for the respectable lonely gentlemen'.

Robert lifted his eyebrows, and Anne sneered and said, "Respectable gentlemen, what rot!"

Pike continued, "My sentiments exactly, Lady Anne. The Earl and I had our first argument that night as I tried to dissuade him from his course of action. I could only go so far, and the Earl would not take my advice. So, I obeyed his instructions.

My role was to visit the Groom's Club and pick out a member of their staff that would fit the Earl's requirements. I was to organise the timing and pay the bills. The Earl never appeared at the Groom's club. I would assume this was standard practice as I met numerous other butlers and valets at the club. I think it is safe to say that there would have been many similar clubs for gentlemen at that time in Portsmouth."

Robert commented, "Yes, due to the navy, it is a hotspot. Unfortunately, the place is riddled with disease."

"Yes, Sir. When we visited Portsmouth, the Earl would rent a two-bedroom gentleman's apartment with servant quarters. He would normally invite the lady for dinner and entertainment, and the lady would stay the night. The young woman would often be in the second bedroom by the morning."

Anne asked, "Did he not show some remorse given that Lady Jane was with child."

"Yes, Lady Anne, he did show remorse and realised the error of his ways. But that occurred later. Here is an invoice for one of the ladies. I have them all here."

Pike passed over an invoice and receipt from the 'Groom's Club'.

"Pike, you have kept all the records all these years. What for?"

"Sir Robert, before taking up the position of Butler for the Fintelton Estate, I was in another gentleman's employ. I shall not give details; however, the gentleman demonstrated similar behaviour and was caught out. His footman gave him away for a bribe, and the consequences were extreme. Enough to say I saw the machinations of what happened and made sure I would be prepared if I ever found myself in that situation again."

"But surely you would have been acting under orders?"

"That is not the question, Sir Robert. A butler is only as good as the trust put in him. If trust is lost, then he must resign. There is no room for mistakes."

Robert nodded and said, "Point taken. Pike."

"If I may continue, Sir."

Anne nodded for Pike to continue.

"The Earl was unhappy with the choice of women, so several were tried over the visits. On one occasion, Miss Constance appeared when I was at the club. She was most attractive and caught my eye. I enquired about this woman and was told she was exclusive and only serviced the wealthiest clients. I was not to be put off and said she would be supplied for my employer, and we would meet the cost."

Pike handed over an invoice and receipt, and Robert stuttered, "My goodness! That was four times what the others charged."

Anne was disgusted by this time and did not even attempt to look at the invoice. Pike noticed how uncomfortable she was becoming.

"Lady Anne. I am telling you this as it is necessary to explain Mrs Constance, as she is now known. I can assure you she is in no way innocent."

"Perhaps we could quickly finish this, Pike, as I am disgusted with all this detail."

"Certainly, my Lady. When the Earl met Miss Constance, he was entranced. With the other women, it was pure lust. It was far more than this with Miss Constance, as she communicated well and could provide the companionship these men thought they were missing. I am sure that if the Earl had tried, he would have found his wife far better company.

However, I could see that he would insist on seeing Miss Constance from then on. As the resident butler, I heard most of their conversations, and it was clear that Miss Constance had a game plan. She wanted out of her occupation and sought a title. Ridiculous as it was, she lined the Earl up as her man for the future. Over time, her demands increased, and the Earl became aware he was in trouble. He could not find ways to be there often enough to keep this young woman happy. She demanded he divorce his wife and marry her.

The clincher came when she announced that she was pregnant. The Earl was in a terrible state but still felt he loved this woman. He was unsure what he should do. However, it was then that the countess confronted him about his extramarital relationship. Lady Anne, you are aware of the rest of the story."

Anne nodded in agreement, but there was no smile.

Pike took a sip of water and continued, "As you would imagine, being the organiser of these goings on, I met many people at the club and often conversed with these butlers and valets. Through these discussions, I noticed that Miss Constance used the same game plan on several wealthy gentlemen."

Anne sat up straight and became intently interested.

Pike continued, "I thought you would be interested here, Lady Anne. I am sorry you have been subjected to the sordid details, but you must understand the degree of deceit involved. I am sure two other wealthy gentlemen felt love for Miss Constance and set her up for life. As I said, this must remain confidential, but I can supply you with names if needed."

"Pike, you are a gem!" Anne knew now that Pike was so intelligent. He had been sitting on this information for half a lifetime, ensuring it was at hand in case it was needed to defend his master. Now, it could be released without it being seen as a betrayal.

Anne was thinking quickly, "Tell me, Pike, was Miss Constance consorting with these other men when she saw the Earl?"

"I believe so, Lady Anne. I have kept records of enquiries I made. I also have other documents whose source must remain confidential."

"So, David Constance may not be the son of the Earl?"

"Precisely, Lady Anne. I tried my best to reason with his Lordship as he negotiated his separation from Miss Constance; however, he would not have a bar of it. He felt the child was his, but there is no proof of who the father was."

"Robert. We have her. I can deal with this now. Thank you, Pike. That is sufficient for tonight."

Pike handed a letter to Anne, "Lady Anne. You will find the information you require in this letter. Please keep it confidential. It is a letter from no one and is not signed in case of ramifications. However, it provides enough information for the attorneys and the searches they should conduct."

Anne stood, "Thank you, Pike."

With that, Pike nodded to Sir Robert and left the room.

Anne looked at her tired but happy husband and said, "Next stop, London!"

With a grin, Robert said, "It was a fascinating story, Anne."

With a stern look, Anne replied, "Don't even consider it, Robert!"

Portsmouth, England ...
In the twilight, Ross Stubbington slowly walked along the neat avenue of detached double-storied townhouses. The gardens were

neatly trimmed with freshly planted flower beds ready for spring. He wondered how a Navy lieutenant could afford a house in this affluent area. It seemed a little out of place, but he was unaware of Martin Russell's financial situation.

Quickly gazing around, he checked that no one else was on the street. Seeing the coast was clear, he opened the gate and approached the front door. All was quiet, so he knocked and waited to see who answered. To his surprise, the front door was unlocked and slightly opened on his touch. Stubbington gently pushed it further and entered, closing the door behind him.

He called, "Mr Russell! Are you at home?"

There was no answer, so Ross called again louder, "Martin Russell! Are you home?"

A scratching at the kitchen door attracted his attention. Stubbington's senses were now on full alert, and he ventured down the hallway in silence and gently opened the door. A small cat tip-toed through the space and rubbed itself against his ankles, giving a high-pitched but soft meow.

Looking up from the cat, Ross entered the kitchen and found the room in disarray. At the end of the bench, Martin Russell was lying on the floor with his throat cut, blood still oozing from the wound.

Ross knelt and checked for a pulse, but the man was dead. The struggle had occurred recently and had been violent as several bruises on Russell's arms and cheeks became obvious. His eyes blankly stared upwards at the ceiling, with the skin on his face turning white.

The cat reappeared and rubbed itself against Ross's thigh. He stood and noticed three half-full cups of coffee on the kitchen table. They were still warm. He looked up and stood silently, listening for the faintest noise. There was nothing. Finding a half-full pitcher on the counter, Ross poured milk into a saucer. He placed the milk on the floor and said, "Enjoy your last drink here, Puss! I think the news from Dublin has arrived."

From the implements strewn over the floor and smashed plates and broken containers on the shelves and counter, it was clear the struggle had occurred in the kitchen. What had the intruders or perhaps guests wanted?

As quickly as possible and in silence, he searched the flat, gathering anything of interest. As he reached the top stair, he heard the voices of the police arriving outside. Ross thought, 'How were they aware an incident had occurred here?'

He scrambled down the staircase and flew through the house and out the open back door, disappearing along the back alley.

Ten metres away, standing behind the head-high alleyway fence, a lone man, completely still, holding a long, bloodstained knife, watched through a thin crack in the paling wall as Stubbington passed and off into the deepening twilight.

'You have not left for Woolwich yet, have you, Mr Samuel Rafferty? I wonder if you are Mr Rafferty or someone else?'

Turner Household, Guildford, Surrey ...
That evening, Ethel waited until the house was quiet and then ventured into Jonathan's study.

"I would have waited until tomorrow, Jonathan, but I decided we should talk before then. Benjamin has requested a meeting for lunch tomorrow. I think he will pressure me to announce the engagement. I must delay this, but I want your advice on what I should say."

Jonathan approached Ethel, but she held her hand up, "Jonathan, stay at your desk. We have guests here tonight, and the children might stir. Anyone might venture in."

"Yes, I was alarmed by Marion's comment at breakfast. It was almost as if she had guessed we were fond of each other. I am not sure how!"

"Women have a unique way of discovering things, Jonathan. It is called intuition."

"I see."

"Now, this is what I propose to tell, Benjamin."

Ethel spoke for some time, and Jonathan suggested some small changes but agreed with her approach.

"He will understand, and it is an excellent way of starting the process so no anger develops. Given his health problems, my only worry is whether he will agree to wait that long. I think he is becoming anxious. The delay will also mean we must wait far longer before we can marry. Are you prepared to wait, Ethel?"

"Yes, Jonathan. I cannot walk away from Benjamin and marry you the next day. This process must be done gently, and that will take time.

We must ensure everyone remains friends and keep our community together. Also, Jonathan, I think you should go up and sit with Clemmie for a while. She is starting to feel isolated while she recovers. I will be discussing her exercise routine with Doctor Bassington tomorrow afternoon. She needs more time outside in the fresh air."

"I will go up now. I hope tomorrow goes well for you, Ethel. I will pray about it tonight."

Ethel stood and slowly opened the door. No one was outside, so she waved and left. Jonathan waited a few minutes before climbing the stairs to Clementine's room.

Opening the bedroom door, he said, "I thought I might come up and say goodnight, Clemmie."

Clementine raised her eyes from a book and smiled as her father entered, "Thank you, Father! I am recovering, but I have become lonely. My shoulder is slow to mend."

"At least it is not hurting."

"Yes, but I cannot lie on that side. Most nights, I end up on my back, and I think I am beginning to snore as I wake with a dry throat."

Jonathan laughed, "Don't tell the young men that. It might put them off."

"Father, why does Mr Hotspur continually visit me? He is very boring and stays far too long. I am becoming uncomfortable with his intrusions."

"I would assume, Clemmie, that it is part of his role at the church. Pastoral care is what I think they call it. If you are disturbed by his visits, seeing him is unnecessary. I will have a word with Reverend Taggart."

"Thank you, Father. I would prefer that. He makes me uncomfortable, and I don't particularly appreciate how he looks at me. He is always asking questions about Victoria Sopwith and now is asking about Katherine. He seems to have no other interests than the young ladies in the church."

Jonathan sat back and considered Clemmie's comment. He had not noticed this before, but certainly, the ladies would. He had been too preoccupied with his problems.

"Your description paints an unhealthy picture of this young man. I will also talk with Ethel. She will keep him under control."

Clemmie looked at her father and could see the concern on his face. She decided the time was right to ask where his feelings lay.

"Father, are you still missing Mother?"

"Yes, Clemmie. Very much! I expect to see her beside me every morning, but she is not. I sometimes feel bereft and struggle with my thoughts."

There was a short silence as they both thought about Eleanora. The loss of a wife and a mother had affected them greatly, and only now could they talk about it.

"Father, after Mother died, I felt so alone. I was worried that you would marry someone else and that mother would be replaced. I think I was jealous of anyone who came close to you. But I was selfish. I only thought of myself and wanted to talk with you, but you shut yourself off from us."

"I am sorry about that, Clemmie. I was confused and unsure what to do. The depression made me helpless for many weeks. I think the trip with Hamish McPherson assisted my recovery."

"It did, Father. You are far more relaxed now, and we can talk."

Jonathan smiled as he thought about the relief that Ethel's company brought him. His life was changing, but he still felt guilty, as if he had a wife. But she was gone – never to be here again. He felt the pain again, and a tear ran down his cheek.

Clementine saw the tear, and she held her hands out to him. He moved over, and they hugged each other.

"I did not know or understand, Father, the pain you must have felt."

"It was all I could think about, and I disregarded my children. I am sorry for that, Clemmie. It is time we dwelt on happier times ahead, such as your recovery."

"Yes, Maddie has been sad and misses Anne as much as our mother. The incident of bottle stealing did not help. I think Mr Petherton has been most generous to our family."

"William is not learning from his mistakes, but I will remedy that soon."

Clementine wondered why her father was suddenly talking about William but put it out of her mind.

"I can walk around freely now, Father. The shoulder still hurts a little, but I can exercise now, which is a joy. I am doing some drawings for Victoria, which have filled up some of my days."

"Good for you, Clemmie. I have an idea. How about we walk together tomorrow and put flowers on your mother's grave? Just you and me."

"Should we not focus on positive things, Father?"

"Yes, we should, but there is no reason why we cannot cherish your mother's life. There are so many good things to remember and build on. We should honour her in that way. The children will return in the afternoon, so we should use the opportunity in the morning."

Clementine yawned and stretched.

"You are right! I would like that."

"Good. After breakfast, we shall set off. It is not far, and I am sure you can manage it."

Jonathan stood, bent down and kissed Clementine on the forehead, "Good night, Clemmie."

"Thank you, Father. I will sleep well now."

Jonathan smiled as he softly closed the door.

Ewell Station, outside Grahamstown, Eastern Cape Province …
Richard Turner sat at his desk, considering the loss of his steer to the natives. He was not worried about the financial loss but concerned that the natives were butchering an animal on his land. He had no idea how the Xhosa could be stopped and what dangers it could cause if he were to defend his cattle. It was safer for the military to act rather than him.

He remembered the catchphrase, 'It takes a thief to catch a thief!' Perhaps he should approach the Xhosa chief and ask for help guarding his livestock. He could make it worth their while by letting them set up a camp on his property, and they would be paid. He wondered if this approach might be acceptable. It would require a visit, and he would need assistance as it would be foolish to go alone.

Over dinner, Richard and Sarah discussed his plan to visit the chief. He could not find the Xhosa camp alone as it was twenty miles distant and near the Great Fish. He needed guides and possibly some protection. The man who could provide both was Lieutenant Sanderson. Perhaps Freddie would agree to be his guide.

Sarah suggested, "Why not wait till he comes to town again?"

"I thought of that, but that might be some time away. We may lose many more cattle before then. If I try to befriend this man, he may help us."

"But what about Freddie and the military? Are they not protecting us from these natives."

"Yes, but they only have so many men to cover a vast area. Freddie has already told me they can't patrol all the land between here and the Great Fish. The natives are hidden everywhere, grazing their cattle. The land must be hilly and covered in scrub for them to be so well concealed."

"What makes you think this chief will help, Richard?"

"If I offer his men some remuneration or trade, it may work."

Sarah nodded to herself and sat in a comfortable chair beside the fire.

"Richard, if you are going away for two or three days, I am staying in town. I have never felt safe here, and I am certainly not being left alone on this station with the house only partly built."

"I understand your concern, so I will hitch my horse behind our cart and take you to town tomorrow. I need to see Freddie, so it is on the way. Will you stay at Roijers for a few days?"

Sarah nodded in agreement but said no more. She had followed her husband to Africa, but there was a limit. She would not be left alone with only the Hottentot girls for company. This land was hot and dry during the day and freezing at night. The cold wind whistled down from the escarpment on the western horizon, and the stream that ran through their property was dry. She was unsure how the cattle and sheep survived, but Richard seemed confident that this place would be a success. She nodded her head again and restarted her knitting.

On the Road to London ...

Thomas and Marion had set off around ten thirty, giving Marion's body as much time as was needed to ensure the morning sickness did not interrupt their travel. The day was fine, with some clouds building to the west. Thomas was thankful for the smooth road, meaning they would reach London at a civilised time. He sat back, relaxed, pondering the three weeks ahead as they headed for Scotland.

"We are off, Darling. Soon, you will see your father and brothers in

Woolwich, and your uncle and aunt may visit Glasgow. Are you happy, Mrs Turner?"

"A little sad we are leaving Guildford. I made every effort to make it our home. But now we have a new adventure in front of us. Yes, I am excited. But I am not sure I will enjoy the temperatures in Glasgow."

"Me either! But it will give us an excuse to snuggle up."

Thomas enjoyed the thought of them cuddling in front of a raging fireplace.

"Until little Miss Marion or Master Thomas arrives. Imagine that, Darling. We will be parents!"

Thomas smiled, "I can imagine Mrs McPherson's face now. She will be delighted."

"We should return to Greenwich for the birth so I can spend some time with her planning. You do not mind us returning to Greenwich, Thomas?"

"Not at all. I would not have the grandparents and close relatives missing out. It will be a time of much celebration."

Marion smiled and then sat back as she considered something on her mind for some days.

"Thomas, do you think your father will marry again?"

Her husband, who was thinking about breaking their good news to Marion's auntie, Mrs Marjorie McPherson, was surprised by the question.

"Why, I have not considered that at all. Why would this be on your mind, Marion?"

"While we stayed at your father's house, I noticed a close relation-ship between Ethel and your father. She attends meals with the family, her daughter Rosalind is often there, and she and Jonathan often confer on many issues. I am sure there is a strong relationship, and I would be happy if it developed further."

Thomas was not convinced, "No, there is nothing to it. She is a hard-working lady and has kept the family together since my mother died. I think you are mistaking appreciation for devotion and concluding that there is an attachment. I would be surprised if he married again!"

Marion snuggled up against Thomas and kissed him on the cheek.

"Darling, there is more than appreciation in their relationship. Have you ever looked closely at Ethel? Behind the work clothes and servant posture is a beautiful woman. There are many similarities between Ethel and your mother. Your father has noticed her beauty and charming personality. I think you may be surprised very soon, Thomas."

"How do you discern this, Marion? I am unaware and see no evidence of any attachment."

"Women have an inbuilt intuition about these things, Darling. We will see them together by the time little Master Thomas Turner arrives in October."

With a frown on his face, Thomas glanced out the window and then turned and gazed down into the beautiful smiling face of his glowing pregnant wife. With a laugh, he relaxed and said, "Well, I never would have thought that!"

Cloverdale Chase, Guildford, England …

As he rode along the lengthy driveway, the Reverend Philip Hotspur could not have been more impressed. He saw a small team of men working on the carefully placed gardens, which enhanced the house's aspect. Small but elegant conifers were planted about twenty metres apart, lining the driveway from the entry gate to the mansion's courtyard. He enjoyed the crunch of the crushed granite under his horse's hooves and imagined himself being driven in a gleaming carriage and arriving home.

With a smile, Philip dismounted near the front door, where a servant took his horse. He strode up and tapped his whip handle on the door. Soon, the butler appeared and greeted him.

"May I be of assistance, Sir?"

"The Reverend Philip Hotspur for Mr Benjamin Petherton."

"Yes, Sir. Please come in and make yourself comfortable in the drawing room. Let me show you the way."

Philip took a seat and admired the rich décor.

Benjamin Petherton was hard at work in his study, and the only visitor he expected today was Ethel Nibley at one o'clock. A knock came on his study door.

"Come!"

"Mr Petherton! A Reverend Philip Hotspur has arrived to see you. I have him seated in the drawing room."

"Oh!"

Benjamin sat back in his chair and took a deep breath. Philip Hotspur was the last person he wanted in his house, but he must show good manners and at least greet the young curate. He looked at his timepiece and found it was slightly past ten forty-five.

"Hm! Steadman, it is nearly morning tea. Ask him if he would care for a cup and inform him I will be along presently."

"Yes, Sir."

Through the window across from his desk, he could see the gardeners making good progress on the shrub planting along the driveway. It would be perfect by the time Ethel arrived. He must rid himself of this gentleman long before she came. Who knows what rumours Philip would start if he saw Ethel in her carriage entering the property?

Benjamin stretched and closed the top of his desk. As he walked to the drawing room, he thought some information might be gleaned from this young man.

"Mr Hotspur! Welcome to Cloverdale Chase."

"Thank you, Mr Petherton. Forgive me for disturbing you, but as it was morning teatime, I thought my timing might be opportune. My, this is a splendid house. I have not had the pleasure before."

"My late wife decorated the house, and I miss her greatly. The house is quiet as I only have Clare with me now. My son, Mark, died several years ago. You were correct about morning tea – I am looking forward to a cup. I take it you will join me."

"Yes, Mr Petherton. The butler has taken my order."

"Of course!"

"Please accept my condolences on the loss of your wife and son. I was not aware."

"Thank you, Mr Hotspur. I understand that you are a recent arrival and would not have known. How are you settling into the parish?"

"It has been difficult. Coming from London, I am used to higher standards, and settling into the country lifestyle is somewhat disturbing."

"In what way, Sir!"

"Well, I am used to the refinements of London, like your fine house here, Sir. I am sure you would agree that Guildford is limited in society."

"I understand your concern, Sir, but in time, I hope you will find that the society here is quite adequate. I moved from London to the country for its fresh air and genuine people. I find Guildford a charming place to live."

"Given the right opportunities, I will soon agree with you, Sir."

As they shared morning tea, Benjamin tried his best but struggled to achieve civil conversation with young Hotspur. The young man appeared to have an elevated view of his station in life and had radical beliefs.

Philip Hotspur, keen to impress, thought it might help if he dropped a name or two.

"I understand you know the Turners, Mr Petherton? Mr Jonathan Turner."

"Yes, I know him well and have done business with him through the Guild."

"Good. I call on Miss Clementine Turner nearly every second day. She is recovering from a serious injury to her shoulder. Dr Bassington and Dr Watson performed miracles when they operated. She is making good progress."

"I see. There is no infection?"

"No. There has been no mention! Clementine improves each day. A fine young lady. She will be eligible within a few years, and I am sure many men will call on her."

"Do I detect a personal interest, Mr Hotspur?"

"I am not sure at this stage, Sir. I am new to town and must tread carefully. The Turner housekeeper is a handful. She pushes me out as soon as she can. Still, with the death of Mrs Turner, there is no one to control her."

"I see. Do you feel Mrs Nibley oversteps the mark?"

"I do, Sir. Yet, I must not be uncharitable. The family has shown me great friendship, and I am sure Mrs Nibley is competent. Her dedication to that family is unmatched. Mr Turner gives her far more leeway than any other housekeeper I have known. I sometimes feel she is the honorary mother now that Mrs Turner is gone. Of course, this is a blessing for the children. There is no substitute for a mother's love. Mrs Nibley protects her cubs like a lioness. I understand Mr Turner admires the services she provides the family and insists that Mrs Nibley's daughter, Rosalind, joins them often."

"She must be very close to the children?"

"Like a mother, Mr Petherton. Are you aware that she joins the family for dinner each night? I understand it has assisted the family in recovering from the mother's loss. Yes, she is an admirable woman indeed and a stabilising influence."

Benjamin considered the comments this young man made about the Turner family. He was thankful the curate's opinion was charitable, but Philip took a little more liberty than he was entitled to with their relationship. He must not let this continue.

"Now, Mr Hotspur, I have recently heard why you no longer teach in the church school. Might I enquire about the cause and hear your first-hand account?"

Philip Hotspur looked up from his tea with a start.

Later, as the Reverend Hotspur left, Benjamin Petherton sighed in relief and closed the front door. The young curate's comments about Ethel revealed a closer relationship with the family than he had anticipated. The deeper this relationship became, the harder it would be for him to pry her away. He decided it was in their interest that she left the Turner household's service as soon as possible.

He quickly glanced at his timepiece. It was now midday. There was only an hour to prepare before he expected Ethel.

Dashing upstairs to his study, he opened the desk and recommenced working on a document.

Gibb Field, Guilford, England ...
"Thank you, Isaiah!"

"That be no trouble, Terry. It be least I do, given all your orders for bits and pieces from shop."

"It will be a great surprise for Levi and Andrea when they find the pony in the stable shed."

"It will, indeed! Now, you know how keep horse. There be plenty work. Keep the youngins busy – for sure."

"That is part of the plan, Isaiah. They should be capable of handling a gentle little pony like Mossy. Thank you for the extra feed in the shed. It will give us a fine start."

"That's my pleasure, Terry. I be going! Lot to do back at the furnace this afternoon."

Terry Spencer waved as Isaiah Linton returned to the blacksmith's shop further along the riverbank. Finding a spare piece of land with a shed took time. Isiah Linton had been most helpful with the Turners' new flour mill, and whenever Terry needed a new part, the blacksmith produced quality work quickly. The two men had become good friends, and when Terry mentioned purchasing a pony, Isaiah offered some of his land and a shed further along the river. Terry could not believe his luck.

Making sure the gate was securely locked, Terry returned to the mill. Walking along the riverbank path, he noticed movement on the other side of the river. It appeared like young Jess Swamp from the Turner kitchen entering a room at the boarding house. That seemed strange as he understood the proprietor only accepted men. Terry realised he must be mistaken; it could not be Jess as she would be working at the Turner's house.

Terry Spencer smiled as he thought of Levi and Andrea's excitement when they found out they owned a pony.

Near Cloverdale Chase, Guildford, England ...

Philip Hotspur had visited another parishioner near Cloverdale Chase and was returning to town when he saw a carriage coming in the other direction. He noticed Mrs Ethel Nibley sitting alone as it passed.

Before he could raise his hat, the carriage was speeding away. Philip wondered why a housekeeper would be travelling in that comfort by herself. The sight aroused his interest, and he turned his horse and followed, curious about who she was visiting.

Digging in his spurs, he galloped off in pursuit. Keeping the carriage in sight, which was now two hundred yards ahead, it slowed and turned into the main gates of the property he had visited earlier in the morning. His interest heightened as he stopped behind a tall poplar tree hiding him from view and watched the coach's arrival.

Mr Petherton exited the house as if he were expecting Mrs Nibley. He opened the carriage door and took her hand, escorting her inside. The door was closed behind them.

The curate wondered why a gentleman would hold a servant by the hand and escort her inside. The more he considered this incident, the more he searched for explanations.

Cloverdale Chase, Guildford, England ...

Benjamin Petherton moved forward to give Ethel a welcome kiss on the cheek, but Ethel held him back and quietly said, "Benjamin, the servants might see."

"I can give my guest a welcome kiss. They will think nothing of it."

"I am not a guest but the Turner's housekeeper!"

"Ethel, if you would declare your financial independence, you would be free. It is time we made our announcement and acted like an engaged couple."

The pleading on Benjamin's face was evident, and she felt some pain knowing what she must tell him.

"Let us sit down and have some lunch and discuss this. I am worried for the Turner family, Benjamin. Much is going on, and I am an integral part of it. I cannot walk out and sever all my ties. If I am to live in this town, it must be done with mutual agreement and in good faith."

Benjamin saw the butler coming and held his tongue.

The footmen served the soup and then retreated.

"Ethel, I visited Jonathan Turner last week and discussed our relationship with him."

"You told him without my knowing?"

"Yes, Ethel. He needs to know so he can plan to replace you. It is only fair."

"But Benjamin, I thought we had agreed to keep it a secret until we were both ready."

"Ethel, I feel older by the day. With my medical condition, there is much uncertainty about my lifespan. Can you not understand that you would have custody of Clare as my wife? I want you, Rosalind and Clare to be financially secure and in a family unit for the future. You would make the perfect mother for Clare."

"And what of my feelings, Benjamin?"

"I have asked for your hand in marriage, and you have accepted, Ethel. I have assumed you love me, and we shall be married soon. I want to tell the world of our betrothal."

Ethel sat there, amazed that this man could compartmentalise marriage so well. She had mentioned romance to him when he first raised the offer. But there had been no romance in their courtship. It was more like a business proposition. She was now gaining a clearer picture of what she could expect from their marriage. It was not what she wanted.

Ethel was determined to delay this marriage; if she could not, she would run. The financial advantages had swayed Ethel, and her decision was wrong.

"Benjamin……Benjamin!" How could she put this and not offend the man?

Benjamin Petherton sat there waiting for her to speak.

"Benjamin, I am very fond of you and appreciate what you have done for me. I am happy to be a trustee for Clare and will do all I can to protect her in the future if there is a need for this.

But Benjamin, there must be some romance when it comes to marriage. There must be a meeting of minds and a commitment to become a family. All I hear from you is your arrangements and the financial benefits. I know you mean well, but I am in two minds, and I am unsure that we are matched for each other."

"I assure you, Ethel, that we are the perfect match for each other."

"If that is so, Benjamin, why am I in two minds?"

"It is nerves, Ethel. The loss of your Andrew put you in a terrible position, and you have struggled to keep your family out of poverty. I admire your strength and the way you have handled adversity. I could not admire you more for what you have achieved. You and I are equal, and in the short life I have left, I am convinced we can succeed in many more ways."

"Benjamin, please do not say anything more about your lifespan expectations. It is most depressing."

"Sorry……!"

The butler appeared and asked, "Mr Petherton. Are you ready for the second course?"

"Certainly, Steadman. Let the footmen serve us, please."

Ethel took another spoonful of soup before a footman whisked her plate away, leaving her with a spoon in her hand. Carefully placing her spoon on her side plate, she wondered if the footman was making a point. Sitting there quietly gazing around the beautiful room lined with mahogany walls and strong furniture, she noticed the many portraits, probably of relatives, and several crystal vases filled with roses.

"The room looks magnificent today, Benjamin. Are the roses from the garden?"

"Yes, I asked the head gardener for a special selection. I wanted to impress you."

"That is very kind, and I am impressed. I hear from Anne, that is, I should say, Lady Anne, that the Earl of Fintelton is deeply interested in roses. You should invite him to see your collection."

"I doubt he would come, given my denomination."

"But Benjamin, you are attending the Anglican church now. Surely mentioning this would be enough."

"Perhaps, but we are not here to discuss the Earl of Fintelton, Ethel. We must settle the date to announce our engagement."

Ethel bit her lip and wished she could explain that she had decided to marry Jonathan Turner. But she knew this would be a great mistake.

"We must delay it, Benjamin. I am unsure if I have made the right decision. I need time. Please allow me another three months, and then we will discuss it again."

"But why are you unsure, Ethel? I have offered to share all that I have with you. You are restored to being a Lady in our society. Clare is so happy with you, and I love you most dearly."

"Benjamin, I tried before to explain, and you did not hear what I said. This engagement is a time to acquaint ourselves with each other and ensure we have found true love. It is the meeting of two minds and far more than finances and freedom. If you are to be my soulmate, I must be sure you are right for me. I am not sure of that yet."

Benjamin was disappointed and took a deep breath. "So, you ask that our engagement be extended for three months? The condition being that you would marry me after that?"

Ethel sat there dumbfounded that Benjamin could not grasp the meaning of love. What had he felt for his first wife? Was that just a financial transaction? She was becoming desperate to give him a hint that this marriage would not come about. But the harder she tried, the less he heard her voice. The man was determined to marry, regardless of her view or the cost.

"I must go, Benjamin. I am not feeling well."

"My poor, Dear! Have I upset you?"

"No, I am genuinely unwell. Please order the carriage. We shall talk again soon."

Chapter 5

Porting, Guildford, England …

After dropping off the children at the Turner household, Robert and Anne were glad to head for Porting.

"I am ready for bed tonight, Anne. It has been a long day."

Anne had her head against Robert's shoulder with her eyes closed. She moved her hand across and held his.

"I hope Mrs Kirby has some supper ready for us. I think I will eat and then go to bed. It was a wonderful week, but I am glad to see home again."

Robert squeezed her hand and smiled, "It is our home now. It has become our home! How things change, Anne. We are home in Guildford."

Anne smiled and said, "I am glad you consider it home. I thought you may always consider Fintelton your home."

"No, my love. Home is where you are and where you and I live together. Porting is our home and where we shall have our children."

Anne settled back against his shoulder and gazed out the window. As they approached Porting, she noticed men in the driveway.

"Robert, what is happening on our driveway?"

He looked up and saw several navy men standing beside a coach parked near Porting's front entrance.

"I am not sure."

The men watched as Robert & Anne's coach came to a stop beside them. A young Lieutenant standing in front of the guards moved forward and opened the coach's door, giving Robert a salute as he jumped out.

"To what do I owe the honour of this welcome, Lieutenant?"

With a stern face and standing tall in a neatly pressed uniform, the young officer quickly replied, "Captain South, Lieutenant Harms at your service, Sir. I report directly to Colonel Scott, an acquaintance of yours. Admiral Bird requires you at the Admiralty for a meeting by three tomorrow afternoon. Here is a message from the Admiral, Sir."

Harms passed across a sealed envelope.

"We must leave here within the hour to reach Westminster on time. I apologise for the late notice, but the decision was made yesterday, so we came immediately knowing you would be here on Monday."

"How long since you arrived, Lieutenant Harms?"

"Around three-quarters of an hour, Sir. Your housekeeper seems a little distressed by all the commotion."

"Mrs Kirby is somewhat excitable. Have your men eaten?"

"No, Sir. Not since Ewell."

"Well, I will have Mrs Kirby provide some supper as we have a long night ahead. Have them go around to the back door and into the kitchen. I will speak with her now and then pack. We will be on our way quickly."

"Sir. You will need to change into your uniform, please, as we will go directly to the Admiralty. It appears there is some emergency. HMS Shadow is waiting for you at Woolwich. I am unsure of this, Sir, but I have heard you will sail tomorrow on the evening tide."

"Tomorrow! The meeting must be urgent. Move your men to the back entrance and enter the kitchen, Lieutenant. I will join you there soon for some food."

Standing beside Robert, Anne heard the full conversation, and she was off in a flash to instruct Mrs Kirby and give her whatever help she needed.

Robert opened the message and read:

Sir Robert South
Captain HMS Shadow
Royal Navy
C/- Porting
Guildford

22 April 1827

Captain South

I must sadly inform you that Admiral Crouch fell ill the Thursday before last and has suffered a stroke since that time. He is being given the best care; however, the doctors have advised that it will be at least six months before he recovers. The Board of Admiralty met in the interim, and I was appointed Chairman of the Commissioners.

My great hope is that our Admiral will make a quick recovery and return soon. However, as with all predicaments, things tend to happen simultaneously.

The situation in the Eastern Mediterranean has deteriorated and requires immediate attention. I will brief you on Tuesday afternoon on a mission requiring your departure no later than Wednesday morning. Lieutenant Fenton brought Shadow to Woolwich, and you will depart with additional guests onboard.

I cannot emphasise how urgent this request is, Robert. I need you here as soon as possible.

My apologies for interrupting your leave again. Please pass on my apologies to Lady Anne.

I expect you here at 3 pm on Tuesday.

Admiral Sir Walter Bird
Chairman of the Commissioners, Acting
Admiralty House
Westminster

Robert now understood the emergency. Thank goodness he had Lieutenant Fenton on *Shadow*. The frigate would be ready to sail, but who were these guests that Admiral Bird mentioned? Enough of this. He needed some food, and then they must be off.

As he entered the kitchen, he found six men eagerly eating a generous spread that Mrs Kirby and Anne had prepared. Robert grabbed a chicken leg, took a bite, and gently guided Anne into the hallway.

"Admiral Crouch has had a stroke. Admiral Bird has replaced him."

"Oh no! Robert, poor Lady Katherine must be beside herself. The Admiral is such a nice man."

"I know, Anne. When you reach London, please call on Admiral Crouch and Lady Katherine. I think she will need your support in the months ahead. I must leave in a few minutes. I am going up to change. Anne, I may not see you again for some time. Take care, Darling."

Anne realised this was more serious than she had expected. As Robert pulled her close, she began to shake with fear. He could feel her trembling in his arms.

"I will be safe, Darling. Just distant for a while. I need you to be strong, Anne. Be strong for me, Darling. You know I love you more than anything else in this world. I promise to improve my letter writing. I will write before we sail tomorrow."

Holding her close, he kissed her and enjoyed her warm body against his. He would cherish the scent of her perfume while they were apart. Then releasing her and rushing off upstairs.

Suddenly, he returned and asked the Lieutenant, "Harms! When did you change the horses last?"

"At Ewell, Sir."

"There are fresh horses in the stable. James, the groomsman, will help. Get some of your men out there and change them. We will need another team at Ewell. Mrs Kirby, if you would pack some food for the men, they will need it." Then he was off upstairs again.

Anne knew that Robert was already in fighting mode.

Swan Lane, Guildford, England …

As he reached the halfway point of his late-night run, Leonard Webster emerged from the lane onto North Street. He enjoyed exercising in the evening as it made him tired before bed, and he found the weariness helped him sleep. After a late start due to his parents entertaining guests at dinner, he had hurriedly changed before heading off.

The streets around Guildford were surprisingly clear in the evenings, and he relaxed as he powered up the slight incline. Bounding past some secured carts, he missed seeing a couple and collided with them, tripping and falling on the dirt road.

Staggering and dusting himself off, he rushed back to help. Leonard found a young lady struggling to her feet, rearranging her clothes, and a moaning man lying still on the roadway.

"Sorry! I could not see you for the carts!"

"You knocked Phili out, you fool! Now that is going to spoil my night's takings. You need to pay me my dues, lovey!"

Leonard looked at the woman in horror and realised he had collided with a whore. He backed away, not wanting to associate, when Philip Hotspur yelled in agony, "Damn, I've cut my lip, you scoundrel!"

Recognising the voice, he changed direction and knelt beside the prostrate curate, who was trying to lift himself off the ground.

"Here, Mr Hotspur, let me give you a hand. Where do you live? I'll take you there and clean you up."

"Leonard Webster. What were you doing here at this time of night? You hit us like a steamtrain!" Philip groaned as he was helped to his feet. Webster noticed multiple scratches on the pained face.

"I am glad you are alright. Point out the way to your residence, please."

"I'll do that, lovey. Now I know Phili is alright, we might still make a night of it. Grab him and bring him along this way. He lives along Martyr Road. I know the way. I've been here plenty before." She laughed and stepped off in front of them.

Leonard obediently followed, holding up a smelly and tipsy Philip Hotspur, unsteady on his feet. After getting the couple inside, he hauled Philip up the stairs and into the bedroom, where the young lady, who introduced herself as Rosie, pointed towards the bed. As Leonard lay the curate down, Philip laughed and pulled Rosie over him.

"You naughty boy, Phili! And here's me thinking you were dead to the world." She hugged him tight, laughing.

Leonard Webster quietly backed off and closed the front door on his way out. He wiped the sweat off his face and recommenced his run slightly slower, trying to take in the revelation he had just witnessed.

Rector's Office, Guildford, England ...

"Thank you, Philip, for bringing your sermon this morning. I must say it is short!"

The Reverend Hotspur, somewhat annoyed, curtly replied, "I do not care for long sermons. It provides too much opportunity for the older members of our congregation to fall asleep. Short and punchy, I prefer."

The Rector, attempting to keep the conversation positive, ignored his curate's terse response and said, "Well said, Philip. I concur, but I would encourage you to insert something about our beliefs in the text. The fox hunt will catch their attention, but the sermon should be based on some scripture with a little exposition. Perhaps something from 1 Corinthians 9, where Paul talks about the race and our eternal prize. You may be able to relate that to the fox hunt."

"Yes, I missed that. What reference is it, Mr Taggart?"

"Hold on, and I will find it." Andrew Taggart quickly grabbed his bible and turned to 1 Corinthians. As he searched for the passage, Philip noticed the striking painting of his wife, Laura.

"That is a wonderful painting of Mrs Taggart. Was it a commission?"

Andrew looked up with a confused smile on his face. He could not make out this young man. For the first time, he had said something friendly to Andrew.

"Yes, many years ago, I asked my cousin, who had a great yearning to be a portrait artist. I think he did a good job of it. Laura does not like it, but what lady ever appreciated a portrait of herself."

"I would not be sure, Rector. But it does catch the wonderful character of your wife. She is a fine lady, and you can see that in the painting."

Andrew wondered why Philip had made a point of Laura being a fine lady. Perhaps he was being genuine. Andrew took it as a kind compliment.

"Thank you, Philip. The reference is 1 Corinthians 9, verses 24 to 27. See if you can slot that in at the beginning and the end. Perhaps I should bring a bugle to church on Sunday?"

As Andrew chuckled, Philip sat there blankly and said, "Whatever for?"

"The fox hunt, Philip. I thought I would enter the spirit of the hunt."

"Oh!"

Andrew could see the humour was lost on the young curate and resumed their conversation.

"Now, have another go and see how it develops. I will be here late this afternoon till around five if it is ready by then; otherwise, tomorrow morning. I am encouraged by your early preparation. Full credit to you, Philip."

"I thought I should try to improve on last week. That was a bit of a disaster."

"You tried, Philip. I do not ask for anymore, and I will be here to help you as you progress."

Andrew noticed several deep grazes on Philip's face, "Are you injured? You have several scratches on your face."

"I fell over running last night. I needed some exercise. A darn cat ran out at the wrong moment."

"Good for you, Philip. Exercise is a wise occupation for a young man."

"Rector! Might I ask your opinion on an incident I witnessed?"

"Yes."

"Yesterday, I was concerned by something I saw. It involves one of our parishioners. I was passing Cloverdale Chase and noticed Mrs Ethel Nibley arriving by carriage."

"Mrs Nibley, the Turner's housekeeper?"

"Yes. It was strange as Mr Petherton greeted her in person. He took her hand as if she were a lady and helped her down from the carriage but continued with her hand into the house. He appeared most attracted to the servant."

"I see. And what did you deduce from this?"

"Well, it is strange for her to travel in a carriage and be greeted that way. I think it reasonable to assume there may be a relationship."

Knowing he had agreed to keep Benjamin's proposal to Ethel secret, Andrew was keen that Philip carried this conversation no further.

"Possibly and possibly not. Benjamin Petherton is a very kind man. He may have been showing courtesy."

"That is possible, Sir. But I felt it was more. It is possible that Mrs Nibley is being led astray by that man. After all, Mr Petherton is a recusant[13]."

"Philip, I would be careful what you say. You may stir up a difficult situation based on nothing but a gentleman welcoming a lady."

"She is not a lady, Mr Taggart, but a servant. She would not be the first servant to aspire to a higher station by whatever means possible."

Andrew ignored the slur against Ethel Nibley and advised, "Philip,

---

[13] Recusancy: was the state of those who remained loyal to the Roman Catholic Church and refused to attend Church of England services after the English Reformation. Wikipedia. Despite the Catholic Emancipation Act 1829 discrimination against Catholics continued. JS.

if you are so worried about this, why not go directly to Mr Petherton and ask him? Better to know the truth than acting on idle gossip that might defame the man or the lady."

Andrew could see that Philip was unsatisfied, but at least he was thinking about his options. Once he latched onto an idea, the young curate found it hard to let go. His reckless nature would need to be watched carefully. However, Andrew was sure Philip would not rest until he was convinced it was an innocent meeting. It might be best if he alerted Benjamin about Philip's suspicion.

Philip stood and made his way to the door.

"Thank you for your help, Mr Taggart."

"A pleasure. I will see you this afternoon or tomorrow, and we will continue."

After the curate left, Andrew returned to his study desk and sat back, considering the portrait of his wife. 'Yes', he thought, 'the character did come through. Cousin Ralph had captured her essence beautifully.' Then he thought of Ethel Nibley and the good character of that woman.

Suddenly raising himself in his chair, the rector realised Philip Hotspur had linked the picture to what he had witnessed. He used the example of the strong character shown in the portrait to plant the seeds of doubt. For some reason, Philip wanted Andrew to believe that a devious situation was developing at Cloverdale Chase.

What was his purpose? Was this a trap?

Andrew scribbled a quick note to Benjamin Petherton. He sealed it in an envelope, hopped up, and walked to the kitchen, where Laura discussed dinner with the cook.

"Laura, would you please have this sent by a rider immediately?"

"It must be urgent, Andrew?"

"Indeed, I am afraid it is!"

Turner Household, Guildford, England ...
William looked up at his father with pleading eyes.

"Father, if we left a week earlier, we could ride our horses at Fintelton for several days. The Earl invited us. He told me!"

"We have already planned to be at the Isle of Wight on the twenty-first of July, William. The Earl and Countess will be at Luccombe Bay by then and will not want us at Fintelton. They would be at 'Eastleigh' before we leave for Fintelton."

Simeon and Madelaine complained, "But with an invitation, Father, surely Mr Stem could look after us."

"I do not think so. Mr Stem will have enough to handle with the Earl and Countess being away. It was very generous of the Earl to invite you, but I am sure we should not push the friendship too hard!"

Madeline was confused, "What do you mean by 'push the friend-ship', Father?"

"The Earl and the Countess have more to do than entertain children before leaving for their summer holiday. Perhaps they might invite you back to Fintelton after their break at the Isle of Wight. Now let that be an end to it!"

The children became quiet, disappointed and tired, Ethel watching the body language as they climbed the stairs.

"Mr Turner, a farm or stable near 'Eastleigh' may rent out horses. The Earl must source his coach from somewhere. He might advise us on a suitable riding place."

Jonathan was uninterested but saw that Ethel wished to help, "Ethel, our visit is for swimming lessons. I, too, would like lessons. Perhaps you and Rosalind, too! Excursions to a riding farm will make things too complicated!"

"But the children will not swim all the time. Remember, we are going for two weeks, and the novelty will wear off. They will need other amusements. If they have no alternatives, they will make mischief at 'Eastleigh.'"

Ethel was making a good point that Jonathan had not considered. He hoped that by July, he would have announced his engagement. Having screaming children everywhere was not his idea of a relaxing holiday. His housekeeper's suggestion had merit.

"You are correct, Ethel. They will need more than one outlet. We will find a farm and keep them entertained. You may let them know when you go up."

Ethel moved closer and, in a soft voice, said, "Thank you, Jonathan." She then kissed him on the cheek. Jonathan wanted more but knew he must restrain himself. He did not notice William watching from above.

"I will go up and tell them now. The children will sleep better with this news."

A short time later, Jonathan heard a muffled cheer from the boys and girls. He smiled, realising that he needed Ethel's advice more than ever. Walking into his study, Jonathan sat at his desk, pulled out a folder, and opened it. The folder contained details of the passage to Africa he was planning for William.

The ship would leave on Sunday, the fifth of August 1827, with passengers needing to be on board by nine p.m. on the fourth. The nine-week voyage would stop at Santa Cruz or the Canary Islands and on to Cape Town. From there, a local barque would take them to Port Elizabeth, where Jonathan planned for Richard to meet them.

It was time to swear Aggie Peters to secrecy and see if she would agree to accompany the boy to Grahamstown. Once Aggie decided, he would book the tickets and write to Richard, advising him they were coming.

Ethel had finished wishing the children good night in the bedrooms upstairs. She felt a tug on her dress as she left the boy's room. William stood there with his finger raised to his lips.

She whispered, "What is it, William?"

The young lad leading her to the balcony rail asked, "Why did you kiss my father on the cheek before?"

Ethel said, "You were not supposed to see that. It may be best if you don't mention what you saw, or there may be trouble, William."

"I know, but why did you kiss him?"

Ethel took a deep breath and said, "To thank him for something he did."

"Do you like my father, Ethel?"

"Yes, I like him."

"Like my mother liked him?"

Ethel blushed, and William could see her apprehension.

"Well, let us say I like him as a friend."

William looked at her hard, and Ethel knew he was testing her. She said, "Time for bed now, William!"

The boy was about to ask something else, but she turned him around and firmly pushed him back through the door.

"Good night!"

Cloverdale Chase, Guildford, England …

The rider arrived shortly after eight o'clock in the evening, and the butler, Steadman, paid the tip and took the message upstairs.

Still working in his study, Benjamin Petherton heard the soft knock on his door.

"Come!"

Steadman entered, "A message for you, Sir. The rider apologised for the delay – evidently, the message should have been delivered far earlier. There was a mix-up."

Benjamin was not expecting an urgent message and was curious about the author.

"Thank you, Steadman."

He opened the envelope and commenced reading.

Mr Benjamin Petherton
Cloverdale Chase
Guildford.

Dear Benjamin
Earlier today, I heard some information of concern.

The Reverend Philip Hotspur reported a carriage visit by Mrs Ethel Nibley to your abode today and suggested a relationship between yourself and that lady. I challenged his accusation, asking what proof he had. Philip agreed he had no evidence but suggested that he saw you and Mrs Nibley in a compromising situation. I spoke sternly to the young man, asking him not to spread his thoughts further. I am not sure if I succeeded.

Benjamin, I have not broken your confidence. At present, Philip only has a suspicion. However, I fear he may try to use this information to his advantage. I know not how.

I was keen to alert you to his mischief before anything could eventuate.

Best wishes
Rev Andrew Taggart

Benjamin screwed up the letter as he put it down.

'That damned man!' It was clear that Andrew was sure Hotspur would make the information public. But when and why?

Rumours of inappropriate behaviour would soon surface if his relationship with Ethel became known before an official announcement. There was little tolerance between religions, and advantages would be taken at any opportunity. Both their good characters could be destroyed. Benjamin stood and paced backwards and forwards, trying to solve this situation.

'There is only one way to solve this! The engagement must be announced formally tomorrow morning. I will place it in the Guildford Gazette, and I hope I can notify Ethel in time.'

He scribbled the announcement out quickly and placed it in an envelope. Pulling the servant cord, he waited for the butler.

A soft knock came on the door. Opening it, Mr Petherton placed the envelope in the butler's hand.

"Steadman. Place this announcement with the Guildford Gazette early tomorrow! By early, I mean very early before they go to print. The notice must be in the broadsheet tomorrow morning!"

"Thank you, Sir. I shall attend to it myself. I know the staff there and the cut-off times. It shall be done."

Benjamin's head was now spinning. He knew he had made this decision without notifying Ethel, but their reputations were at stake. She would understand and thank him for his action. After all, it was an engagement notice. There would be no shame if the engagement did not lead to marriage. He felt his action would protect them from any evil lies the young curate might spread. Satisfied that he had acted properly, he closed his desk and retired to his bedroom. Sitting on the bed, he felt his forehead and wiped away the sweat. He was feeling giddy and knew that he was over-excited. Grasping a small green bottle, he took a swig of his medicine and lay back against the pillow.

Admiralty, Whitehall, London ...

Sir Robert South sat across the desk from Admiral Bird and could see the anxiety on the Chairman of Commissioners' face.

"Things are hotting up in the East, Robert! Some diplomatic staff await you on 'Shadow' who must speak with Admiral Sutherland in Malta. Now that the remainder of the Blue is refitted and returned to Malta, Sutherland will return here as I need him in London while Admiral Crouch is indisposed. Admiral Codrington[14] will continue as Commander-in-Chief, and you will report to him.

The Prince has requested your return as soon as possible to replace Colonel Scott as head of security. It appears your heroic actions at the Irish charity ball will be rewarded. So, whatever happens out there, you are expected in London by the first of January 1828."

Robert was surprised that the Prince would be involved, "I am honoured by the Prince's request, and I will serve him with pleasure. However, Sir, the Prince's appointment as First Sea Lord seems odd. I assumed you, the senior admiralty commissioner, would take the position next year?"

"Apparently not! It appears the title of Lord High Admiral is to be reinstated, and the Duke of Clarence will be soon appointed. I struggle to understand how the Prime minister expects the Board of Admiralty and the Navy Board to work under these arrangements. Given our troubles in the eastern Mediterranean, Canning[15] could not have decided on this at a more inappropriate time. It seems his decisions are as bad as his aim! Robert, keep your head down and make sure you come back."

"Yes, Sir. I will do my best."

Admiral Bird smiled as he knew Captain South had a history of always ending up in the hot spots.

"I assume you might have been involved in the Dublin excitement a month or so ago. Admiral Crouch did not brief me on that."

"You are correct, Admiral."

"Well, that may be why you are requested to visit the Home Office[16] this afternoon. A Mrs Stubbington requires your presence. Here are the details."

---

[14] Sir Edward Codrington (1779-1851) was a British admiral, who took part in the Battle of Trafalgar and the Battle of Navarino. In December 1826 Codrington was appointed Commander-in-Chief, Mediterranean Fleet and sailed on 1 February 1827. Wikipedia. Captain South's and Admiral Sutherland's involvements are purely fictional. J.S.

[15] The Right Honourable George Canning, Prime Minister of the United Kingdom, 10 April 1827 to 8 August 1827. Wikipedia

[16] The Home Office – On 27 March 1782, the Home Office was formed by renaming the existing Southern Department, with all existing staff transferring. On the same day, the Northern Department was renamed the Foreign Office. All domestic responsibilities (including colonies) were moved to the Home Office, and all foreign matters became the concern of the Foreign Office. One of the initial responsibilities of the Home Office was the operation of the secret service within the UK. Ireland at that time was part of the UK. Wikipedia with an addition by JS.

The Admiral passed across an envelope.

"Thank you, Sir. Would you be aware of Mrs Stubbington's role?"

"It appears she is highly placed in security at The Home Office. I would say it relates to Ireland."

"I see."

"Lieutenant Fenton brought *Shadow* up from Portsmouth to save time. The diplomats are already on board and waiting. There is a rush to reach the French and Russian governments and hasten their ambassadors to London. With this new Tzar, the whole landscape of foreign policy has changed. It would be best if you sailed first thing tomorrow morning. I am sure you will need to write some letters tonight. Here are your orders. Get to Malta as fast as possible and hand the diplomats over to Codrington and Sutherland. They need extra help as it is a highly complex situation over there.

Once you are in the Med, keep lookouts up at all times. The Egyptians teamed up with the Ottomans and, by joining their assets, have a significant fleet. Codrington has been ordered to use every bit of diplomacy he can and needs the extra diplomats. He aims to keep channels open with Mahmud II, the Ottoman Sultan. While this is happening, we will bring the French and Russians here for talks on a treaty. The Tzar is agitating for war, but we must keep him out of Greece. The Ottomans should stay in control until we can negotiate independence for the Greeks. This will be a busy time for all of us. Codrington may ask you to return with the diplomats if this is required.

Whatever happens, Captain South, the diplomats must be kept safe and delivered to fleet headquarters in Malta as soon as possible. You have my authority to use whatever means are necessary. We have provided extra powder and shot as our intelligence indicates Egyptian and Ottoman frigates may be operating off Tunis.

The Lord be with you, Robert. Good sailing!"

"Thank you, Sir."

Robert tucked the orders under his arm, saluted the Admiral, and headed for the Home Office.

Rector's Office, Guildford, England ...

"Thank you for coming, Jonathan and Blake. I am sorry to call you unexpectedly on a Tuesday afternoon, but there is an issue, and I need your advice. As my parish wardens, I felt that we should discuss this carefully before I proceeded any further."

"This sounds serious, Andrew."

"That is the problem, Jonathan! It involves young Hotspur, and I am unsure what action I should take or if any action is needed."

Blake Wood was keen to hear the details, "If this involves Philip Hotspur, I suggest you start at the beginning and explain carefully. We will ask questions as you proceed if that is acceptable."

"Certainly, Blake. It will also assist me if I start at the beginning. As you know, I had requested an assistant in our parish for many years, but the bishop always knocked me back. We could not afford an additional curate, so it was a great surprise when the bishop granted my request in January this year, and Philip Hotspur took up the position."

The Reverend Taggart carefully explained his difficulties with Mr Hotspur and his reasons for hesitating to discuss this with the bishop.

"You mean he is the bishop's nephew?"

"Yes, Blake. I learned this from a fellow clergyman by chance and felt it somewhat complicated the matter. Now Philip has threatened me with the connection."

Jonathan, who had been silent up to this stage, said, "I think if you give this young chap time, he will commit some mistake that will be sufficient for him to either move on or be convinced to leave the ministry."

Andrew questioned, "Has he not done enough already for this?"

Before his wardens could answer, Andrew recounted to them the details disclosed by the Websters and their wish that the curate should move on to another parish.

Blake Wood, being an attorney, advised, "At this stage, there is not enough evidence to prove he is unfit for his duties. I did not proceed in pressing charges when he injured Edward. It would have been his words against the children. A court would not allow the children's testimony."

The Reverend Taggart frowned and took a sip of water.

Jonathan added, "Andrew, let this play out for a while. Keep good records of his activities and see where they lead. We will catch him and then let the bishop decide. That way, you will be out of the firing line."

"Well, Jonathan! I am in the firing line, and it is becoming very tiring. It may be that I need a vacation."

Blake Wood agreed, "That is an excellent idea, Andrew, but your vacation must wait. I would plan for six months in advance, say October or November. If you are absent now, the bishop may suggest Philip is put in charge without adequate experience. That would not help your position at all."

Turner Business Offices, Guildford …
Jonathan Turner was delayed longer than he intended at the rectory and was in a mood as he entered the office foyer. Peter Hammer and Terry Spencer were waiting for their Tuesday meeting, and they smiled as he arrived.

"Sorry, chaps. Some troubles along the way. Come on up, and we will start."

As they neared Jonathan's office, he saw Anne working hard next door and said, "Welcome back, daughter! We must talk after I meet with Terry and Peter."

Anne waved to the three of them and said, "We shall!"

The meeting with Peter and Terry continued for some time, and as they finished, Jonathan asked Peter, "Are you ready to replace Jeb in London? You must leave within two weeks as Jeb will need time here before his wedding. A couple of weeks with Audrey for the final arrangements should be sufficient."

"All in hand, Mr Turner. I will be leaving this Saturday, the twenty-eight of April. Jeb will have a week to show me the ropes, and he should be back by Sunday, the sixth of May. That will give him three weeks with Audrey before the wedding."

"Good, Peter. That should be plenty of time."

Terry added, "And enough time for us to give him a good send-off."

Jonathan smiled, "I will let you fellows arrange that. Let me know the details when it is decided, and I will have the bills paid. Now, gentlemen, I must meet with Anne. Thank you for waiting for me this afternoon."

Gathering the required documents, he followed Peter and Terry and rushed to Anne's office. There, he found Victoria Sopwith with Anne, discussing patterns.

"My apologies, Victoria. I was not aware you were here."

"Not a bother at all, Mr Turner. We are finished!"

As Victoria gathered the patterns, Jonathan realised this would be the perfect opportunity.

"Victoria, I previously meant to ask if you had found accommodation yet?"

"Yes, Mr Turner. I have leased an apartment on Quarry Street, overlooking the river. It is large enough for me, a maid, a housekeeper/cook, and a guest room. It will suffice until I find something I like. With our work in London, I am not in a hurry."

"I see! As Thomas and Marion have embarked for Glasgow, I thought I should offer you their house."

"Thank you so much, but it would have been too large for me. It was a kind thought indeed. Now, I must be on my way and leave you with Anne."

The Home Office, London …

A young woman came from the door behind the receptionist and approached Robert.

"Captain South, if you would follow me, please."

Robert followed her up the stairs and along the corridor into a waiting area. She knocked on a door, entered, and ushered him through.

"Captain South. Thank you for coming. I understand you are short of time with your imminent departure for the East."

"You are correct, Mrs Stubbington. It seems there is some urgency in my orders."

Janet Stubbington's expression did not change, and she indicated that the captain should take a seat.

"I have not had the chance to interview you since the Dublin incident. You will be pleased to know that Aiden Reid safely left for Boston."

"I am unsure if I should be relieved or more worried!"

"I would be relieved if I were you. But of course, you are the only person on our side who can identify him. None of us have ever met the gentleman."

"Mrs Stubbington. Might I ask, please, whose side you are on?"

"Certainly, Captain South. As you will work more with us in the future, I should give you a briefing.

Concerning the Irish mission, I understand that your concern has been that persons within the British establishment have been manipulating the Irish people to give longevity to the upper class's land holdings in Ireland. Is that correct?"

Robert was still unsure what answer he should give this woman. She saw his hesitancy and continued.

"Our company here is an unseen part of the Home Office. If you were to enquire about us, you would find no information. We must remain secret because we do undercover work for His Majesty's government. As you are a serving officer in the Royal Navy, I know you will keep this confidential."

"So, you are saying you are some type of secret establishment used by the government. Are you spies?"

"I think that over dramatises our function. Let us say we collect information."

"Where, exactly, are you placed in this organisation?"

Janet Stubbington sat back and smiled again, "I am your direct contact with our Investment Company. I report to the board of directors."

"Which Director would that be?"

"The Prime Minister of His Majesty's government."

"I see!"

Robert was, at last, starting to understand how Mrs Stubbington fitted into the murky picture that had been developing in his mind. Perhaps he could now find out who had been manipulating the Irish.

"Robert, I know you will want to ask questions, but hear me out, please, and perhaps some of your questions will be answered."

Captain South nodded in agreement and let Janet Stubbington continue.

"When Lady South passed on Aiden Reid's letter, we were astounded. We had no idea the Irish had such a network under our noses. However, it makes sense, as many Irish men serve in the Royal Navy. We should have investigated this earlier.

The letter was the first step in establishing a link with the Irish. No one had previously suggested that there was a Republican network directly linked to the House of Lords or the Commons. Our assumption had always been that the Irish were working on their own. I understand you have discussed this with Admiral Crouch, who requested that we investigate your concerns. I am unsure if Admiral Bird is aware of this."

Robert did not comment but continued listening.

"As we are in the very early stages of our investigation, the first task was to uncover those involved in the network in Portsmouth. You are acquainted with Mr Ross Stubbington?"

"Yes. Ross worked with us in Ireland."

"He has been in Portsmouth investigating Lieutenant Martin Russell. Unfortunately, Russell died on Sunday evening by misadventure. I only received the message today after lunch. Whoever he was working for was not keen on his being investigated."

Robert breathed in. He had stumbled onto a network far more dangerous than he had imagined.

"The problem for my company is the person who may have assisted with our enquiries is no longer available. The elimination of Martin Russell puts us at a dead end."

Robert would not agree, "But the man was a navy lieutenant working in the Portsmouth offices. He must have had contacts. Otherwise, the network would not have functioned!"

"We agree." Janet sat back as if she was deciding what to say next. "There must be a network, but we need them alive for interrogation. My people will quietly investigate and see what can be found. But Robert, there are more pressing issues. I understand you have discussed some of your suspicions with others. I need you to tell me in whom you confided."

"Surely that would be a breach of trust?"

Janet Stubbington sat there waiting for Robert to answer. The captain said nothing.

"Robert! Let me make this clearer. You have voiced a suspicion that some members of the House of Lords are using the Irish Republicans to create attacks on the British to sway British opinion against the Irish people. It is possible that whoever you confided in has shared this information. Martin Russell is dead! Someone was making sure he could not talk. So, we must assume there may be hostile reactions towards you. Do you understand what I am saying?"

"You are implying that they may wish me silenced in one way or another."

"Precisely. If we are to protect you, we must know who you have informed."

"How do I know that I can trust you?"

"At some point in time, you will need to trust someone. Let me guess! I assume you talked with Admirals Crouch, Sutherland, and Commodore Jacobs."

Robert sat there, considering his options. Mrs Stubbington was correct; he needed an ally as it was far bigger than he could handle. There were no other options. His decision would be a step of faith, but he needed help.

"You are correct except for Admiral Sutherland. I also discussed it with Major Coombes and my wife, Lady Anne."

"Thank you." Stubbington made some notes and then looked up.

"You will be sailing tomorrow, Robert. We cannot protect you while you are at sea. However, you are the captain and must ensure your safety. I assume you will have Swanton, Peters, and Trotters with you?"

"Your information is accurate."

"It is our business."

Robert's concern grew, "Do you expect I will encounter trouble on *Shadow*?"

"We are not sure. A delicate investigation such as this takes time, and our prime suspect was deceased before we could question him. The urgency of your departure might suggest various scenarios. My advice is that you protect yourself by whatever means possible. Also, we have checked Lieutenant Fenton's history, and he appears free of any influence, so he should be trustworthy. You will need to make your own decision on this."

Robert sat there wondering if he would ever escape this cat-and-mouse situation.

"Mrs Stubbington, might I ask that you take action to protect my wife?"

"Already done, Robert. We consider Lady Anne as not at risk, but we will provide protection."

"Thank you."

"Now Admiral Bird is releasing you to the control of Admiral Codrington in the East. Do not be surprised if you are recalled before that mission is over; as I said, you are the only person who can identify

Aiden Reid. We consider him the most important contact we have ever made with the Irish Republicans. There is a power struggle gaining momentum as we speak, and we will need to keep in contact with Reid if he can be persuaded. We have information he is headed for Boston."

"But Boston is a large city. How would you find a man there who is an expert on becoming invisible?"

"That is correct. However, every operative always has a support system. We will find the details on Reid for when we are ready."

Robert considered the briefing Janet Stubbington had provided him and the fact that she would protect Anne. It appeared that he was now working with her.

"Mrs Stubbington! Would it be fair to say that you and your people are now my support system?"

"Outside the navy, that would be correct. Now please read and sign this letter. It will provide some protection for your wife."

As Robert read the letter, it became clear how they would protect Anne. It was probably unnecessary, but he was not going to argue.

"What is the name of the man who will be placed on my home staff?"

"Fletcher! Mr Henry Fletcher."

"May I inform Lady Anne that he will be coming?"

"Yes, please do. I understand Lady Anne arrives in London next Tuesday. I will visit her soon after that. Your briefing her in advance will be helpful."

Robert frowned, signed the request section at the base of the letter and passed it across to Mrs Stubbington.

"Thank you, Captain South. You will understand that in the Home Office, our focus is on the internal affairs of the British Isles. Our government is paranoid about stopping a similar revolution from breaking out here, as in France. The Irish Republicans are our highest priority. As I mentioned, do not be surprised if you receive orders to return home early. As the hour is late and I understand you have letters to write, I suggest you be on your way, young man. Keep safe, and we will talk again on your return."

Steele's Foundry, Woolwich ...
Late in the morning, a tall, thickset man in a long overcoat approached the entrance of the main foundry building. He politely stopped a

passing employee and enquired where the office was. Tipping his cap, he walked towards the office building near the river bank.

Carefully opening the front door, he approached the receptionist and asked for the manager. Mark Steele, who was present, came over.

"I am Mark Steele, Assistant Manager, Mr ...?"

The tall man gazed at Mr Steele briefly and asked, "I was after the manager. I believe that is Mr Aleaxander Steele?"

"Yes. My father is in Greenwich for a lunch appointment. He will return later in the afternoon. May I be of assistance?"

Mark could see that the stranger was considering his options. The man was not nervous but hesitant and asked, "Would Mr Samuel Rafferty be in then?"

Having been fully briefed by his father about Mr Rafferty, Mark replied, "No. He is in Birmingham for the week, visiting some foundries about forging equipment. He should return in two weeks."

"I see."

"If you give me your name, I could pass on a message."

"No, there is no need. I will call again."

The stranger turned and left.

Mark watched as the man carefully surveyed the establishment before leaving. Once the stranger was out of sight, he quickly entered his father's office and jotted down his description. He would brief his father later in the afternoon.

Chapter 6

Mayfair, London ...

Knowing that time was desperately short, Robert rushed from the Admiralty to his carriage and shouted to the driver, "To Admiral Crouch's home in Mayfair, please and as quickly as you can."

The carriage darted away, and Robert sat back, wondering about Mrs Stubbington's advice that he and his wife may be in danger. If the Republican leader in Dublin was dead, who was after him now? Aiden Reid was in Boston, so it was none of his tribe. But who? Then the thought struck him – perhaps she was referring to the Lords. Surely not. They would never stoop to those lengths.

He sighed. Being a ship's captain was hard enough without all this added intrigue. He would be glad to be on his way but then thought of Admiral Bird's comment. 'We have reports of Ottoman and Egyptian frigates cruising off Tunis.' Was this a slip of the tongue, or was Bird warning him of a far more present danger than he had thought? Whose side was Sir Walter on, if any?

Where would this stop if they thought his wife Anne was in danger? Surely, they would not? He recalled talking with William at Fintelton. The boy wanted to become a sailor. Why not enjoy his childhood before the worries of this complex world confronted him? Robert sighed. He must write to Anne tonight and warn her of the possible dangers.

The carriage stopped outside the Admiral's house, and the security guard came to meet the unexpected visitor.

"Captain Sir Robert South for Admiral Crouch, please."

"Do you have an appointment, Sir Robert?"

"No, I am a close friend of the Admiral's and wish to pay my respects."

Taking account of the captain's uniform, the Guard was hesitant and was about to speak when Lady Crouch opened the front door and came out.

"Please let him enter, as he is a dear friend of our family."

"Certainly, Lady Crouch."

Robert rushed forward and took Lady Crouch's hands. He could see how tired she looked and the anguish on her face.

"Lady Crouch, I arrived in London at lunch and have been in meetings since then. I came as soon as I could. How is the Admiral?"

"Thank you, Robert. Come inside, and I will explain."

Robert followed as Katherine Crouch hurriedly led him inside. As they climbed the stairs to the first floor, she continued, "It is like living in prison. They will not let him go home to our estate in Hampshire. I am sure he would be far more comfortable there and more likely to recover. The doctors refuse my requests, insisting he may not be moved."

"I am so sorry that you feel this way. I will write to Admiral Bird, explain the situation, and ask that you might take your husband home."

"Thank you, Robert. That would be most kind. Perhaps you could see Sir Walter tomorrow?"

"Unfortunately, we sail on the early morning tide. I will write and post it tonight."

"Thank you."

Lady Crouch spent the next ten minutes explaining the Admiral's condition. The further she explained, the more Robert understood how desperate the situation was.

"He is so short of breath he can hardly talk. There seems to be no cure. I am desperately afraid he will not recover." She started crying into her handkerchief.

"There, there, Lady Katherine. I understand it is a dire situation, but you must face this with strength. Admiral Crouch would wish you to be strong. Lady Anne will be coming to London next week, and I have asked her to call. She will be some company for you."

"That would be wonderful, Robert. Your wife is such a treasure."

"Lady Katherine, is there any chance I might see the Admiral?"

"Certainly, Robert." She lowered her voice to a whisper and said, "He dictated a letter to you. I have tried to write as legibly as possible.

We have done it secretly as his secretary must now check all his correspondence. I shall give it to you as you leave. Now follow me, and you shall have your opportunity. But remember, he is very weak."

"I will, Lady Katherine."

She led him up another flight of stairs along the hallway to the main bedroom. Lady Crouch opened the door, and Robert saw a large, comfortable room with beautiful windows facing the east. The Admiral rested on his back with several blankets over him, eyes closed.

Lady Crouch bent down and quietly said, "Franklin, it is Robert. He has come to see you, Dear. Open your eyes and give him a wave."

The Admiral slowly moved his arm across and took Lady Franklin's hand. He raised himself slightly so she could place a pillow under his head. Opening his eyes, he gazed around the room until his eyes focused on Robert. Admiral Crouch smiled and waved him closer.

Robert could see the mouth moving but could not hear.

Lady Franklin said, "Come closer, Robert."

The captain kneeled beside the bed and placed his face close to the Admiral's head.

Faintly, he heard, "There is a letter for you. Written before my stroke."

Robert replied, "Lady Katherine has advised me, Sir. She will give it to me."

The Admiral took a deep breath and then spluttered, "You were right, Robert. Protect yourself!"

Then he collapsed back onto the pillows and closed his eyes.

Robert could see this little exertion had exhausted the man. He was wasting away. At least he could still communicate.

Lady Katherine stood at the door with tears in her eyes. She held the letter in her hand.

Robert stood and leaned over the Admiral and gently took both his hands, "God's speed, Sir. You have been one of my best friends. We will meet again."

He stood momentarily, smiling at the man who had made him a captain. He felt helpless but wished to do more for his friend, who drifted back into sleep. Reluctantly, he turned and walked across to Lady Katherine. It appeared to them both that the admiral would be gone very soon.

She passed across the letter as she cried. Robert took her in his arms and comforted her. As she clung to him, she said, "Robert, place the letter in your inside coat pocket. They inspect any documentation going out of this house. Thank you so much for coming."

He followed her instructions, making sure the letter was carefully hidden.

"I will write to Admiral Bird tonight, Ma'am! I will see myself out."

As he started to leave, a thought came to him. He stopped and turned, "Lady Crouch, when were the doctors here last?"

Lady Crouch stood there trying to recall, "It was yesterday morning, Robert. They bled him again to lower his temperature. Why do you ask?"

Robert was immediately concerned. The Admiral was desperately ill, close to death. The doctors should be beside his bedside daily.

"Might I ask a relation of mine to visit the Admiral? He is a specialist on Harley Street and deals with major trauma. He may be of some assistance."

"Thank you, Robert. But we have the best doctors supplied by the navy."

"I thought he may persuade your doctors to allow the Admiral to return home."

Lady Crouch suddenly realised what Robert was suggesting. She rushed over and held his hands, "Yes! Yes, Robert. Send him as soon as you can."

"His name is Doctor Neville Bassington. You may have met him at our wedding. I believe he is travelling to London with Anne on Friday. I am sure he will come as soon as requested. Please advise your staff that he is expected so the security will let him through."

As he descended the stairs to the front door, security confronted him and asked if the Admiral had passed across any documents.

"No, no documents."

"Thank you, Sir."

Robert walked past, out the front door, and as he boarded his carriage, he shouted to the driver, "Navy wharf, Woolwich, and hurry, please."

Guildford, England …

William walked across, stood near the pony, and waited for it to lift its head and smell his hand before returning to a good feed of oats. He patted the horse and turned to Levi, "She is a beautiful pony. Have you taken her for a ride yet?"

"Yes. A couple of rides, but nothing long yet. I hope my father will take us out into the fields soon, and we can follow a track."

Simeon, Madeline, and Clare also voiced their approval of the lovely little pony.

"She is so cute and just the right size for you, Levi."

"Would you like a ride around the paddock, Clare? You will have to wait until Will has his turn. I promised him yesterday."

"I will think about it while William rides."

There was no hesitation on William's part, and as soon as Levi had checked the saddle, he mounted her. Gently coaxing the pony, he let her walk quietly around the fencing until he returned to where the children stood.

"She is very gentle but responsive. I think you will be fine, Clare."

"I am not sure. I have never been on a horse before."

William was surprised, "I thought your brother rode all the time."

"He did, but I was never given the opportunity. But I would like to try."

Levi could see she was keen but slightly timid. "Here, Clare, come over, and I will help you. You understand a woman rides side saddle, don't you."

"Yes. If I come again, I will wear some pants. Side saddle is a stupid way of riding a horse."

Simeon and Levi carefully helped Clare onto the saddle while William held the horse.

"Would you like me to lead him around, Clare?"

"Yes! Thanks, William."

They started at a slow walking pace towards the far fence. William looked up and found Clare smiling.

"This is fun, Will. I think I will ask my father for some lessons."

She looked around and waved to the others. As she did, William lost his footing and fell before the pony, who jerked to a stop. Clare, looking in the other direction, lost her hold and fell from the pony onto William.

"Ah! Sorry, Will. What happened!" Clare began to giggle as she noticed the mud on William's face. He spat some out, saying, "I tripped on my feet. I should have been looking down."

By this time, Levi and Simeon were beside them, and Sim held the pony steady as Levi helped Clare. As she put weight on her left foot, she screamed and fell to the ground again.

"I think I must have sprained my ankle. I can't walk on it."

The children looked at each other, and Simeon said, "We can't carry her all that way! Clare, you can ride the pony to the doctor's surgery. We best move fast, as your carriage will soon arrive at our house."

Madeline said, "I will run home and tell them you have been delayed. Should I send your coach to the doctor's surgery?"

"No, don't run home. Let us see what the doctors say."

Sitting on the pony and watching the small crowd of children protecting her, Clare said, "I feel like Joan of Ark. We are going into battle." Clare raised her hand and pointed forward with a giggle.

Madeline said, "Careful, Clare. Don't fall off again."

"I won't. I am getting good at this except for my ankle."

As they arrived, the boys carefully lifted Clare and took the limping girl into the surgery while Madeline held the pony. Levi returned with a worried look on his face.

'I hope we don't get into trouble over this. I don't know Mr Petherton. Is he a nice man?"

"Yes, he is! He will be very forgiving."

Turner Household, Guildford …

Mrs Jennings, coming down the stairs carrying various trays and mugs, heard the knocking at the front door. She hurried through to the kitchen.

"Someone is at the front door!"

The housekeeper raised her head and said, "It will be the footman from Clare's carriage. They must have arrived early. I will answer it."

On opening the front door, Ethel found Benjamin Petherton standing there with a broadsheet in his hand.

"Mrs Nibley. Excuse me for being early, but I must talk to you urgently. Is there anywhere private where we may talk?"

Ethel was surprised as she had not spoken with Benjamin since their lunch discussions a few days earlier. Becoming embarrassed, she said, "Not here, Mr Petherton. Could it wait until lunch tomorrow?"

"I am afraid not. Here! Let me show you this announcement in the Guildford Gazette. I need some time with you to explain."

Ethel took the broadsheet and said, "What are you talking about, Benjamin? Show me this announcement."

He pointed to the bottom of the page, where marriage notices and engagements were announced.

She read:

'Mr Benjamin Petherton of Cloverdale Chase, Guildford, is happy to announce that Mrs Ethel Nibley of High Street, Guildford, has accepted his marriage proposal, and the couple announce their engagement.'

Ethel looked up at Benjamin in shock. As she tried to gather her thoughts, she said, "You best come in, Benjamin. Come through to Mr Turner's study."

She led him down the hall, through the parlour, and into the study. Quietly, she closed the door and waited for Benjamin's explanation.

Benjamin spoke unusually quickly in a highly animated way. Ethel could hear the trepidation in his voice.

"I can explain, Ethel. I had no choice. I was protecting your reputation and mine."

"What do you mean, Benjamin? Did you place this announcement in the Gazette?"

"Yes. I had no choice. I would have called on you last night, but it was too late. Then there were appointments this morning that could not be broken, so I came as soon as possible. Let me explain, please?"

Ethel was starting to fume. Her name was in the Gazette connected to Benjamin's. It was public, and she was not prepared for this. He had broken his word and announced their engagement. For Mrs Nibley, this was the last straw.

Benjamin could see the anger brewing in Ethel's normally loving face. He knew a sound explanation must be provided quickly.

"It was because of Philip Hotspur. He saw you visiting Cloverdale Chase recently and put two and two together. He voiced his concern to the Reverend Andrew Taggart that I might be leading you astray.

Andrew sent a note last night advising me that he felt the man might make trouble for us. I felt that announcing our proposed marriage, … , sorry engagement, would solve the whole problem. No one could accuse us of impropriety if they knew we were engaged."

Ethel stood there in disbelief. The Guildford community was now aware of their relationship without her approval. The embarrassment was too much for her, and she wanted to hide. But there was a growing anger within herself that she had let this go on for too long.

Gathering all her strength, she looked up and said to him, "Thank you for telling me, Benjamin. Now, if you would please leave. I have some housework that must be completed before dinner."

"But can we not talk this through, Ethel? I was trying to protect you. You know how people talk. I had to stop Hotspur's mischief. The man is a nuisance, to say the least."

"I agree, Benjamin, but I must go now. I will let you show yourself out. Goodbye."

Ethel walked out of the study, leaving Benjamin with his mouth open. She passed through the kitchen down the hall to the servant quarters and closed and locked the door of her room as she entered. Sitting on her bed, she put her head in her hands and wept.

Most upset that there was such tension between himself and the woman he loved, Benjamin started to breathe quickly. He was beginning to feel giddy. As Aggie went past in the hallway, she asked, "Mr Petherton, have you seen Mrs Nibley?"

Benjamin did not reply. Noticing he was swaying back and forth, she enquired, "Mr Petherton, are you well?"

"Yes, I think so! Mrs Nibley went to the kitchen."

As he stood there, Madeline came beside him and said, "I am sorry to tell you this, Mr Petherton, but Clare fell off her horse and sprained an ankle!"

In alarm, Benjamin shouted, "What horse? Where is she?"

Frightened by his shout, Madeline whimpered, "Coming from the doctor's surgery."

"I must go to her!"

Benjamin rushed down the hall and through the front door, where he found Simeon and William helping Clare up the front stairs.

"Father, I am so glad you are here. I have sprained my ankle – I cannot walk!"

Benjamin, rapidly gasping, kneeled beside her, "Huh…how did you do this, my Dear?"

"We were all riding Levi's pony, and I fell off. It was so funny as William was leading the pony, and he missed his footing and fell over. The pony stopped suddenly, and I fell on top of William."

Already highly emotional, Benjamin suddenly recalled his son Mark dropping from a horse to the ground and dying. The fact that his daughter was riding a horse and had accidentally fallen on William tipped Benjamin's balance.

As he stood, he screamed, "You what! You should never go near a horse. You know what happened to your brother. Mark is dead, and now you have had a similar accident. What were you thinking, Clare?"

All the children stood motionless in fear as they had never seen Mr Petherton in a rage before. Fortunately, Doctor Bryan Watson, who had brought the children in the medical practice's carriage, was close and moved towards Benjamin.

"It was an accident, Benjamin. The children were careful. She will recover quickly."

But Benjamin Petherton was somewhere else, back in the depths of his mind, dealing with the horror of losing his wife and then their son. The memories were still raw, and the moment's emotion became vivid. He found himself dizzy, short of breath, and his chest under great pressure.

"What were you thinking ……" Benjamin had lost control as his vision blurred, and his voice trailed off, "I can't …. see!"

Grasping Bryan's coat to steady himself, he found his knees weakening as he fell. His heart was pounding, and then there was darkness.

"Children, take Clare inside and sit her down. Please call Mrs Nibley and Aggie."

Dr Watson assumed Benjamin had fainted, so he knelt beside him, feeling for a pulse. It was extremely weak, which was strange. If anything, the heart should be beating quickly with high blood pressure. Not being aware of the heart condition David Sopwith had been treating him for, Bryan struggled to understand why this was occurring.

Suddenly, Ethel arrived and knelt beside a prostrate Benjamin.

"What happened, Dr Watson?"

"He was in a rage at the children because Clare had fallen off a pony, and then he fainted. I am waiting for him to come around. But his pulse is very weak."

"You know Doctor Sopwith has been treating him for a heart condition?"

"No, I was not aware!"

As Bryan said this, Jonathan Turner came up the stairs with Anne. When they saw the man prostrate on the floor, they rushed over. Ethel, becoming tearful, stood and explained the situation.

Dr Watson was becoming alarmed as Benjamin was not recovering but showing signs of deterioration.

"I must move him onto a bed. There is something very wrong here. I left my bag at the surgery. Could someone please retrieve it for me? I need some water for him, quickly!"

Jonathan could see the worry on Bryan's face and immediately took the carriage, speeding towards the surgery. Aggie, who was moving the children inside, rushed for the water. Bryan was now opening Benjamin's shirt and placed his ear on the chest, searching for a heartbeat.

Anne noticed that Ethel was shaking, so she moved over and put her arm around her. Ethel began crying and hugged Anne tight. The situation was desperate, and Anne realised that Ethel would be better off in the kitchen.

"Come with me, Ethel. Dr Watson has the situation under control." She led her away down the hallway.

Bryan was now alone with Benjamin. He wanted his patient on a bed in the house where he could be kept warm and rest.

Suddenly, Benjamin opened his eyes and gasped in pain. He held his hands to his chest and tried to call out but could not speak. Then he gripped Bryan, looking him straight in the eyes, and the doctor was sure he was trying to say 'Please...'.

Then he collapsed again. Dr Watson felt the pulse, but there was nothing. He started firmly massaging Benjamin's heart. After nearly two minutes, he felt for a pulse. Nothing!

Slowly, he straightened his back and sat back. There was nothing more he could do. The man was dead.

Banks of the Fish River, North of Fort Brown, Eastern Cape Province …
Having been close to the Great Fish River for most of the afternoon, the small travelling party continued searching for Chief Nkosi's camp. Richard Turner shouted to Lieutenant Sanderson as the light faded, "It will be dark soon. Time, we set up camp. We can find the chief in the morning."

"More likely, he knows we are here." Freddie laughed, "His lookouts have probably been watching us for the last few miles. I would guess he will come tomorrow morning before we break camp. They always know when someone approaches. It is like going back to feudal times, clan versus clan."

"I thought he was chief of all the tribes?"

"No, just a few! There are many tribes, and they compete for ascendancy. But Nkosi has a good scouting system. He knows where all the tribes are and keeps them under control. If this party who slaughtered cattle on your land are around, he will know where they are. If not, he will be interested."

Richard was tired and ready for sustenance and sleep, "Let's make camp."

There was no argument from the Lieutenant, "Sergeant Preston! We make camp here for the night."

"Yes, Sir."

The sergeant had the small scouting party of ten troopers dismount and set up the tents. Soon, a fire was crackling, and one of the men was assembling the ingredients for soup. Richard carefully unpacked his small tent and ensured he was within the perimeter set up by the soldiers. When a trooper offered some assistance with his tent, he was thankful.

"I had not thought much about camping when I applied for land here in Africa, Mr Grail. I am a bit of a beginner at camping. Why do we not camp beside the river bank?"

Trooper Grail smiled, "At dusk, animals gather at the water's edge. Best if we keep our distance at night. As for camping, the infantry travels light Mr Turner, and can raise a tent in five minutes. Bradley, over there, is a master at soup. Once the tent is up, you can take it easy for the night. We know Chief Nkosi is close. You can rest easy, as they will know we are here."

"Thanks, Mr Grail."

"Call me Grail, Mr Turner. We save words around here. In action, it is surname only."

Richard nodded his agreement. The trooper was right, and soon Richard joined an interesting conversation with the men around the campfire and a bowl of soup. Some more experienced soldiers recalled tales of the Battle of Grahamstown with first-hand accounts. Some listened as they cleaned their muskets and checked their kit. He found a new understanding of these men who had explored this part of the country and fought to extend the territory. The question in his mind was how the original inhabitants would appreciate the English taking possession. There must still be much resentment, given the natives were required north of the Great Fish.

In his weary state, it was all too much for Richard. He said good night to the men and retired into his tent. Soon, he was fast asleep after a long day in the saddle.

Cloverton Chase, Guildford, England ...
Ethel sat on the bed, hugging a sobbing Clare.

"What will happen to me now, Mrs Nibley." The child hugged her hard, refusing to let her go.

Ethel knew the most important issue for Clare was security for the future. She would be feeling alone and vulnerable.

"I will be with you, Clare. I will stay here tonight, and tomorrow, we will pack your bag for a stay at the Turners' house for a few days. Some time with Madeline and the family will do you some good."

"Don't leave me, please. I am so scared. I will not live with Mrs Preston. She makes me so depressed with all her rules."

"Well, I must talk with her soon. Now, take this powder that Doctor Watson left for you. It will help you sleep."

Ethel emptied the powder into a full glass of water and mixed it with a spoon. She passed it across to Clare.

"What will it do to me?"

"It will relax you so you can sleep. I am keen for you to rest that soar ankle in bed. In the morning, we can talk, but right now, you need sleep. I will be in the next room if you call, but first I must go downstairs and talk with Mrs Preston. Now, drink this up, please, and

I will sit with you for ten minutes and let you settle down."

Clare looked into Ethel's eyes and smiled slightly, "Thank you for looking after me, Mrs Nibley."

"It is a pleasure, Clare. You understand that I am one of your trustees and would have been your stepmother if your father had lived. Did your father explain these arrangements to you?"

"Yes, he did, and I hope we remain together always!"

She drank the mixture and passed the glass back. Ethel was thankful that Clare was so obedient and well-mannered.

"Now it is time to settle down and say your prayers."

"I am not sure what to say. I think God has forgotten me and taken my father away as a punishment."

"Why would God punish you?"

"For riding that pony, falling off and spraining my ankle. Father was so angry, and then he collapsed. It is my fault."

The tears started again, and Ethel hugged Clare. She whispered in her ear, "No, Clare. God has not forgotten you at all. Your father was a very good man who loved the Lord and His ways. Mr Petherton has provided for your future. I will be with you always, Darling, and we will have many happy times together. So, God is good and has looked after you, especially today. The pony accident was not what made your father angry. He loved you but was tired and lost his temper for a few moments. We all have times like that. It was not your fault. We have much to do tomorrow, so it will be a long day. You need a good sleep tonight."

Clare was unconvinced but lay down and took Ethel's hands as she started saying the Lord's prayer.

"Our Father..."

Ethel joined her in the prayer.

"Who art in heaven..."

As they finished, Ethel bent down, softly kissed Clare on the cheek, and settled into a chair beside the bed. She sat back and watched as Clare closed her eyes. So much was running through Ethel's mind that she jumped when she heard Clare whisper.

"Thank you, Mrs Nibley. My father quite often sat beside my bed as I went to sleep. He would become lonely at night and needed to be beside me."

Ethel calmly whispered, "Hush now, little one."

What might tomorrow bring? Whatever it was, Ethel knew she must be strong for Clare, Rosalind, and the Turner family. She gently breathed in and sighed. Life had just become far more complicated than ever before. Looking across at the still child, she could hear the relaxed breathing as the young girl drifted off to sleep. Dr Watson's powder must have been strong as it had taken effect in a few minutes. Ethel wished he had given her one.

She looked down at the peacefully sleeping child. She was a beautiful girl, much like her daughter, Rosalind. She could understand how much Benjamin must have loved her and how he would do anything to protect her. In her heart, Ethel knew she would keep her promise to Benjamin. Clare was now in her care, and she would protect this little one with all her might. 'Rest peacefully, Benjamin. Clare is safe!'

After Clare was fast asleep, Ethel went down to talk with Mrs Preston and the butler. What was the butler's name? She had forgotten. Ethel was exhausted. The one thing she craved was to curl up in bed and sleep.

The London Road, North of Guildford, England …

Sheltering under a small shop awning, Philip Hotspur positioned himself on the High Street and Epson Road corner. He patiently waited for Jessica Swamp to appear on her walk home along the High Street. The Reverend would offer her the protection of his umbrella as the rain became heavier.

The curate knew that Jessica was young and impressionable, and with encouragement, she would trust him completely. Soon, he would meet with her father and convince the man that he, Philip, should be her tutor. Hotspur smiled as he considered how easy it was to pull a young lady into his clutches.

It was ten minutes past the hour, and the curate was becoming impatient. He decided to cross the road to the east. As the clergyman raised his umbrella, he saw the lone girl walking up the High Street and approaching the corner. He strode out in great confidence, presenting a handsome profile.

As she neared, Philip could see the smile of recognition on her face. Behind his smile, Philip thought, 'Here comes a little bird into my trap.'

"Miss Jessica Swamp, what a coincidence to meet you here. I was only recently thinking of the beautiful cakes provided for morning tea when I last visited the Turners."

Miss Swamp gave a welcoming nod and beamed up at the young clergyman.

"My, you are walking without an umbrella and becoming wet!"

"It is no bother, Mr Hotspur, as I am nearly home."

"In that case, I will provide shelter till you reach home. Fortunately, I have a large umbrella that will cover us both."

Jessica was a little overwhelmed by the kind offer and found it hard to believe that a notable man like Mr Hotspur would show concern for her. She felt wet and knew the rain was becoming heavier, so she accepted his offer. With a smile, she allowed him to cover her with the umbrella, and they walked towards the Swamp's home.

"Do you walk at this time each day, Jessica?"

"Yes, Mr Hotspur. They offered me accommodation at the house, but I prefer living with my family. Sometimes, my mother can't cope, and I cook and do housework. She is not well, and my brothers don't help much as they are tired after a hard day's work on the farm."

"I see, but it would be pitch dark in the middle of winter."

"Guildford is a very safe place, Reverend. I cannot remember any trouble here except for Mr Turner's mill when the men tried to burn it down. Anyway, it is a short distance. You see the group of cottages coming up! That is where I live."

"Not on the farm?"

"No, my father and the boys walk there each day. He remains home sometimes, doing the paperwork requiring attention. I don't mind the walk as it keeps me fit, and I have a good raincoat for the weather."

"Then where is your raincoat today, Jessica?"

"You sound like my mother, Mr Hotspur. I left it at home as I thought it would not rain today."

"A good answer! I will leave you here as it is only a short distance for you to run. I will see you either at the Turners' house or church. Take care, now!"

As she ran off into the growing twilight, she called over her shoulder, "Thank you, Sir!"

Philip heard a large dog barking and whining a welcome from the cottages.

He could not help thinking what a lovely girl she was, speaking well and with excellent manners. How could someone from such a home be so refined? It must be the mother. He would welcome the meeting when he visited the father in the next few days.

Turner Household, Guildford, England ...

Johnathan sat in his study, considering the momentous events that had occurred today. Benjamin Petherton was dead, and he felt he should feel more sorrow, but it would not come. Perhaps it was because Benjamin was a competitor for Ethel's love. He felt ashamed of himself, although he realised the man's death was convenient. But he must not act in haste. People would be suspicious if any new attachments were announced at present. Surely, two months would suffice. He must delay until after their July visit to the Isle of Wight.

Aggie knocked on his office door, "Mr Turner, all the children are in bed, and the duties are done. Is there anything else before I retire, Sir?"

"Thank you, Aggie, for stepping in for Ethel today. It has been a sad day, and your help has made it easier."

"Yes, Mr Turner. I did not know Mr Petherton well, but from what I saw, he appeared kind. Poor little Clare! What will become of her, Sir?"

"We must wait for Benjamin's will to be read. The Petherton estate is large, so a judge must decide. As she is without any other family, the trustees are responsible for where she lives. It may take some time before Clare's future becomes clear."

"The poor child – she will miss her father greatly."

"Yes, I agree, and we must do our best to support her, depending on where she resides next. There is nothing else I require of you tonight; however, there was a question I needed to ask you, and this seems to be the perfect opportunity when there is some quiet in this house."

"Yes, Sir."

"In August, I will need someone to escort one of our family overseas. It is confidential, but let me advise you that I will need someone trustworthy as a carer for the family member. Would you be interested in a trip overseas?"

"I certainly would, Mr Turner. I assume it would involve returning as well?"

"Yes, of course. Would you be prepared to keep it a secret? The trip details will be made known to the family closer to the time. If you feel hesitant about this, please say so, as I can easily find another person for the job."

Aggie was becoming suspicious as she detected an underlying scheme.

"Mr Turner, who would be the person I would escort?"

"Firstly, Aggie, you must be prepared to keep this confidential until the trip is announced?"

Aggie felt reluctant but also thrilled at the chance of a lifetime. She had always wanted to travel, and here was a free opportunity. She decided to take the chance.

"Yes, I would, Mr Turner."

"Good, then I will include you in my plans for the mission. In the past few months, I have arranged for William to join my brother overseas for a spell. The young man needs some experience on a farm, and Richard will be able to provide that in a safe environment. It will benefit William greatly and help him in his future schooling here."

"Then I understand he will be returning. Would I be escorting him back?"

"No, Aggie. He will be there for around two years."

Aggie had heard of other young boys being sent off to faraway places, but not a seven-year-old. Usually, the boys were between twelve and fourteen, past when sickness might do them great damage. She knew she had no right to question Mr Turner's judgement but thought she might comment. She feared for the boy's welfare.

"Mr Turner, I have heard of older boys being sent out, but William is only seven. Surely it could wait a few years?"

"I am afraid not, Aggie. However, that is my business, and it shall be done."

"Mr Turner, I have become close to William since I arrived here. I would feel more comfortable if you took Lady Anne into your confidence and discussed this with her. I would gladly accept your offer if she were content with the mission. I could never forgive myself if anything happened to William."

Johnathan could see that Aggie meant well and was protective of the boy. Her concern was commendable, but she was unaware of all the circumstances and needed her mind put at rest. Her request was not unreasonable.

"I understand your concern, Aggie. I will have Lady Anne discuss this with you in good time. You have my word."

"Thank you, Sir. I will accept your kind offer and look forward to travelling with William."

"Remember, Aggie! Not a word to anyone, as it must be kept confidential. I will advise Anne soon but must wait for the best time. I am sure you understand."

"Yes, Mr Turner. I bid you a good night, Sir."

Jonathan sat there for some time, working through how he would first convince Anne and then how she would talk with Aggie. He felt confident he could manage the first, but the second may prove more difficult. It had been a long day. He closed his desk and headed upstairs for bed.

Cloverdale Chase, Guildford, England ...

Ethel woke in a strange room. Then she remembered she was at Cloverdale Chase. Benjamin and Clare's home. The home she might have had if she had married Benjamin Petherton. She stood and stretched and then peered out the window. A roof gable blocked most of the view, but she could make out the head gardener's building and some trees towards the property boundary. Many of the outdoor staff were already at work. The sky was overcast, and a stiff breeze blew from the north.

Sitting back on the bed, Ethel Nibley considered her new status as a lady of means and a trustee to Benjamin's child. Mr Petherton had freed her from service, but she had decided to continue at the Turners. She would need to make many difficult decisions today, but before that, she must face the hostile staff she had found here last night. On arriving yesterday evening, Mrs Preston refused to speak with her and demanded that Clare come to her room. When Ethel intervened, a heated exchange resulted in Mrs Preston rushing away crying. Later in the evening, the butler, Mr John Steadman, seemed more approachable but hesitant to accept her authority as Clare's trustee.

She decided to dress and check on Clare before going downstairs for an early breakfast. It would be best if many of the matters with staff were cleared up this morning before Clare came down. As she carried very little luggage, dressing was quick, and she ventured out of her room and knocked before entering Clare's.

The unmade bed was empty, and the girl was nowhere to be seen. Ethel quickly left, descended the stairs, and entered the breakfast room. Glancing around, she could see the table was set, ready for breakfast, but there were no aromas or choices of prepared food.

She became deeply worried and commenced searching for the staff quarters. In the kitchen, she found four female staff casually having breakfast.

"Excuse me. I am Mrs Ethel Nibley, one of Clare's trustees. Would any of you be the housekeeper?"

One of the ladies stood, "I am Mrs Mary O'Connor, the housekeeper. How did you get into the house? Are you the lady who is engaged to Mr Petherton?"

Ethel realised these women were unaware she had slept here last night and was with Clare.

"Yes, I am. I arrived with Clare last night and slept in the room beside her. She was very upset about her father's death yesterday, and I was comforting her. But this morning, I have checked her room, and she is missing."

Mrs O'Connor put her hand up to her mouth in surprise when Ethel mentioned the death of Mr Petherton.

"What do you mean Mr Petherton is dead? We have not heard that!"

The other maids stood up and gathered around.

"Yes, yesterday, in the late afternoon, he collapsed on the front verandah at the Turner household. He passed away as Doctor Watson was trying to assist him. Clare was inside with the other children and was distraught at the time. We settled her down, and she had dinner there. Mr Turner sent a rider with a note for Mr Steadman, the butler. I thought you all were aware. Has no one told you?"

"No, Ma'am! We have not been told."

The other staff commenced talking among themselves. Their concerns were genuine, and Ethel could see that the news had not been passed on to them.

"Mrs O'Connor, might I have breakfast while your staff search the house and find Clare? Also, I would like to meet with Mr Steadman and Mrs Preston. Please find them and ask that they attend me here."

"Yes, Mrs Nibley. Jenny and Beth, please go and find Miss Clare. She may be up at the fort. If she is not inside, please check up there. Beth, please find Mr Grey before you start and send him here. The garden and stable staff must be told."

The housekeeper turned to Ethel and said, "Now the maids have gone, I can tell you. Last night, Mr Steadman came to me very late and said Mrs Preston had some terrible news – her sister had died, and she must go to London at once. Given Mrs Preston's sad state, Mr Steadman volunteered to accompany her. He told me that Mr Petherton asked him to go with Mrs Preston. They took one of the estate's carriages and a driver."

"What time was that?"

"He told me that around eleven last night."

"Mrs O'Connor, Mr Petherton died around five thirty in the afternoon at the Turner's house. So, Mr Steadman was lying. I think they have taken Clare with them. For what reason, I am not sure. Let us hope she is safe. Now I need a pencil and some slips of paper. I must send urgent notes to Mr Turner and the Parish Constable."

Turner Household, Guildford, England ...

Jonathan Turner enjoyed a hearty breakfast as Simeon and William joined him.

"Father! You know how Mr Petherton died here yesterday?"

"Yes, Simeon." Jonathan continued eating his bacon and eggs.

"Well, now that they have taken him away somewhere, what will happen with the body?"

"It will be the same as when your mother died. The undertaker will prepare the body for the funeral and build a coffin. The body is placed in the coffin and then taken to the funeral. After the funeral service, the coffin is taken outside the church and buried somewhere on the grounds."

"Mr Petherton was a Catholic, so will the funeral be at the Catholic Church?"

"I am not sure. Simeon. Why do you ask?"

"Well, we attend the Church of England. As we are not Catholic, will we be able to attend the funeral?"

"Yes. Just because we are Church of England does not mean we cannot attend the funeral. I am sure Mr Petherton and particularly Clare would want us there. We will attend!"

Aggie came into the kitchen with a note in her hand.

"A message for you, Mr Turner. A rider delivered it and said it was urgent."

"Ah!" Jonathan took the message and opened it. As he read the note, the children could see the alarm on his face.

"What is it, Father?"

"A note from Ethel. I must go to Cloverdale Chase immediately!"

The Mayor's Home, Guildford, England …
The Reverend Philip Hotspur mounted the step onto the landing and knocked on the front door. Philip was enjoying the fact that he had news that would rock the Guildford society. But better still, the fact that he provided the information to the mayor rather than it coming from the rector would be another triumph on his path to dislodging the Reverend Taggart.

The front door opened.

"May I help you, Sir?" The young maid was courteous.

"Yes. Good morning, I am The Reverend Philip Hotspur!"

"Yes, I am aware of who you are!"

This comment slightly took Philip aback as it was not given in a friendly manner.

"Would the Mayor and Mrs Smith be in? I visit our mayor and his wife on a pastoral care visit." Philip knew the mayor would still be home this early in the morning.

"Please remain here, Sir. I will ask!" With that, the maid closed the front door.

Philip was somewhat surprised at being left outside as he was a friend of the household and expected immediate entry. However, he was happy to sacrifice the lost time, keen that the mayor's wife was included. Philip knew from previous conversations the speed with which information divulged to Marjorie would return to him from another source. She was one of Guildford's main gossips. The news would spread like wildfire, with the mayor's wife rallying for his cause.

Soon, the door opened again, and a smiling Mayor, still in his dressing gown, welcomed the young Hotspur.

"Come in, Philip. Please join us at the dining table. We breakfast late, and you caught us unawares. Now, will you have a tea or coffee?"

"Thank you, Mr Mayor. I always find such kindness at your home. A coffee, if I may, as I have dreadful news! I thought before it became public, you should be advised."

Marjorie Smith suddenly became alert and focused on Philip. She said, "Morning, Mr Hotspur. Now, this does sound serious. Please feel free to speak with us confidentially."

"Thank you, Mrs Smith. As you know, I regularly visit the Turner household to call on poor young Clementine, the daughter of Mr Jonathan Turner. As part of my pastoral care ministry, I am helping her through the calamity she has suffered."

Mrs Smith could not hold back, "Of course, Philip. Mrs Nibley has told us you have been a tower of strength."

On the other hand, Rupert was unsure if Philip's commentary was correct but held his tongue, wondering where this conversation was leading.

"Yes, Mrs Nibley has been most efficient in her care of Clementine, perhaps a little officious at times. But we have navigated through to my satisfaction. But the news I bring is distressing. I am sure that we have always held Mrs Ethel Nibley in high esteem. She has been a pillar of our society in Guildford. Yet I must inform you that our opinions may have been misled."

"Oh, no!" Marjorie held her hand across her mouth, fearing what Mr Hotspur might say next.

Rupert was becoming uncomfortable with this conversation. He advised, "Mr Hotspur, I am sure you have researched what you are about to say, but I would caution you to take care when talking about others."

"That is precisely my point, Mr Mayor. I am afraid I have seen evidence with my own eyes! I felt a duty to brief you urgently so you are not shocked when others confront you with this news."

Eager for the punch line, Marjorie encouraged him, "You are so good, Mr Hotspur. Protecting us with advanced information allows us to counsel others."

Rupert lifted his eyes, not enjoying this early morning melodrama, but said nothing.

Feeling he had the situation completely in control, Philip decided now was the time to deliver the clincher.

"Mr Mayor and Mrs Mayor. Wednesday morning last, I was returning from a pastoral care visit when I spied Mrs Ethel Nibley, the Turner's housekeeper, in a carriage alone entering Mr Benjamin Petherton's driveway."

Rupert was now aware of where this was leading but felt he should let the young curate deliver his punchline.

"She was welcomed by Mr Petherton, who took her hand in his and kissed it." Philip thought a little exaggeration would not hurt. "He held her hand as he walked her from the coach to the front door, and they entered together. It was clear that there was deep feeling between the parties. I am afraid that Mr Petherton may be leading Mrs Nibley astray!"

The Reverend Hotspur watched carefully for the mayor and his wife's reactions.

Then, adding to the drama, he said with some spite, "As you know, he is a recusant!"

Marjorie was now beside herself, not having heard of this before, "No! No! What terrible news. The shame it will bring on the Turner family."

"Mr Mayor! It was my duty to brief you before anyone else broke the news. We must protect the poor, misled Mrs Nibley. Who knows how far this relationship has gone and what damage is done?"

Rupert knew Philip had not checked his facts and let the young man voluntarily hang himself. With some empathy for the curate, he decided he could not let this continue.

The mayor calmly sipped his tea and said, "Now, Marjorie. I think there is an explanation."

Sitting straight and aghast, Philip said, "Surely not, Mr Mayor. I have seen this with my own eyes!"

Marjorie cried out in distress but also with accusation, "Oh dear! The poor woman being led astray by a recusant!"

Rupert frowned, stood, and retrieved yesterday's broadsheet from the sideboard. He placed it in front of Philip Hotspur and pointed to the Marriages and Engagements notices at the bottom of the page.

"Perhaps before you enlighten us any more about this news, Philip.

You should read this!"

A confused Philip took the broadsheet from the mayor and then read the engagement notice of Mr Benjamin Petherton and Mrs Ethel Nibley.

Completely crushed, the curate said, "Oh no! Oh, my goodness!"

Chapter 7

Turner Household, Guildford, England …

Early Thursday morning, Constable Michael Rawling and attorney Blake Wood sat with Jonathan Turner and Ethel Nibley in the Turner's drawing room.

"What do you mean there is no sign of them, Constable? Where have you searched?"

"Mr Turner, we have searched the whole town and questioned many people. If they are here, they are well hidden. I would presume they would not have stopped halfway but continued straight to London. If that is the case, they could be anywhere."

Jonathan looked at Ethel in case she had a further question.

"Constable, if they tried for London, they must have changed horses near Ewell or Epsom. Have you considered this?"

"Yes, Mrs Nibley. I sent watchmen to both towns to search for information."

"Thank you."

Blake Wood interrupted, "Constable, the penalty for kidnapping is death. There is no alternative or commutation for this crime. We must send out information on this couple as soon as the posters can be printed, noting Preston and Steadman are wanted for kidnapping, and a reward is offered for their discovery."

"We do not know if it is kidnapping, Mr Wood. I understand that Mrs Nibley is one of the three trustees for Clare Petherton. But before we act, I should discuss Clare's removal with the other trustees. This case is strange, and neither the butler nor the governess seems likely to harm the girl."

Blake Wood was becoming impatient, "Constable Rawlins, there was no possibility the other trustees knew of Mr Petherton's death before the butler and governess acted. So, what authority could Steadman and Preston have for these actions?"

"Mr Wood, do we know who the other trustees are?"

"No, I am afraid not."

The Constable explained his hesitancy, "Without the butler present, I am not sure who Mr Petherton's attorneys were. The remaining staff have no idea. The keys to Mr Petherton's desk are gone, and I am unwilling to break into furniture at this early stage."

Jonathan interrupted, "The butler and governess probably took the keys and decided they could get away and disappear before anyone could hope to find them. For all we know, Steadman may be fully informed of who the other Trustees are and may have already made a ransom demand for the girl. We must discover who Benjamin's attorneys are and contact them. I know he had offices at the Isle of Dogs. If we could find his premises, the staff there would know."

"Mr Turner, London is out of my jurisdiction. Someone must go to London and hunt them down. I suggest you visit the local Constable in the Isle of Dogs and mount a search."

Blake said, "Better than that, Mr Turner, I will go as I have drafted some letters for Mr Petherton's attorneys and Clare's trustees. We will find them, and if I may, Mr Turner, I will request the assistance of your attorneys in London."

"Your offer is accepted, Blake, and we will pay the regular fee for your services. I don't want you out of pocket on this mission. Anne is heading off to London on Friday morning. I will arrange transport for you with her."

"Thank you, Mr Turner."

Porting, Guildford, England ...

Anne slept as Mary Hedge, her lady's maid, came into the room with a tray, put it beside the bed, and began opening the curtains. Her mistress rolled over away from the light and continued enjoying her sleep.

"Milady! It is Thursday morning and seven o'clock." Mary could see that Anne was drowsy.

"Milady!"

There was a slight movement from Anne, but then she lapsed back into sleep.

"Milady!"

Suddenly, Anne's eyes were open. She continued lying there for a few seconds and then comfortably sat up against some pillows, rubbing her eyes.

"Mary, what time is it?"

"Seven in the morning, Ma'am. It is a beautiful morning outside."

"My goodness! I have overslept. Quickly, my clothes, Mary!"

"Lady Anne!"

Anne ignored the maid and hurriedly jumped out of bed and raced to the wardrobe.

"Lady Anne! I have sent a message to the office advising you will not be in until ten. Your father has asked if he could meet you here at nine o'clock. Miss Aggie Peters came and notified us. He asked if you would remain home until you and he had spoken."

Anne rubbed her eyes, "My, I wonder what that could be about?"

"Milady, you have plenty of time to enjoy breakfast and rise later. I will have your clothes ready by eight. Should I return then?"

"Yes, Mary. Thank you for sending the message. I am sure Daisy will reorganise my appointments. It is a bit of a bother, as we leave for London tomorrow, and I need to finish much work today before we set off."

Mary was sure Lady South was considering ignoring her father's request. The maid beckoned Anne back to bed and lifted the tray, ready to place it before her mistress.

"Lady Anne. You have worked so hard this week. I can't recall you being home before eight o'clock every night. Remember you are the Managing Director. You can have some late starts. No one will mind, and you need some time for yourself."

"Do you think so, Mary?"

"Yes, my Lady. Now, hop back into bed and have a relaxed breakfast. I will fix your clothes and organise a bath for you. That will be refreshing."

"I knew I chose the right maid when I recruited you, Mary. Thank you. Is there any news of Clare Petherton?"

"No, Ma'am. Not that I have heard."

Anne could hear two horses galloping up the driveway as she sat back in bed.

"I wonder who that could be."

Mary walked over to the window and looked down. There were two men, one dressed in a groomsman's uniform.

"It appears that one of the riders is a messenger. I am not sure who the other man is."

Anne's interest increased as she had been expecting Robert's promised letter all week.

"Please go down and find out, Mary."

"Yes, my Lady."

The maid rushed off on her mission, and Anne leaned back, ignoring breakfast. It must be the news she expected. But who was the other gentleman in a groom's uniform? She looked down at the tray and was pleased with the delicious spread in front of her. Mrs Kirby continued to improve in her choice of fruits and cereal. Anne started with the fruit while she waited for Mary's return.

The day outside was sunny, with the temperature warm and pleasant. She felt spring had finally arrived, and they could expect a fine summer. That would be pleasant for their planned vacation at the Isle of Wight. They could go together if only Robert were back, but he would be far away now and probably in danger. She prayed for his safety and that he would soon return.

Mary burst into the room and reported, "It was a messenger, Milady. There are two messages, and the rider advised that no replies are required. He has left. The gentleman in the groomsman's suit is a Mr Henry Fletcher, and he arrives with a letter of introduction from Mrs Janet Stubbington, from the Home Office."

Mary passed the messages and letter across.

"Thank you, Mary. Please come back in half an hour, and you may help me dress."

She put the messages aside and opened the letter:

The Home Office
Investments Department
Post Office Box 792
Whitehall

Dear Lady Anne

I am writing to advise that Robert has safely departed for the eastern Mediterranean via Malta. Before he left, I was fortunate to meet with him.

Part of our discussions focused on your safety. Please do not be alarmed, but as a precaution, and at Sir Robert's request, we are assigning a security man to your staff. Mr Henry Fletcher will serve as an ostler and, when required, is skilled as a footman. His main role will be to advise you on security.

There will be no cost, and he will reside with the other staff.

I understand you are travelling to London on Friday. I have set aside Wednesday, the second of May, for a lunch meeting with you and would ask you to join me. At lunch, I will explain the reasons for our precautions in more detail.

I will pick you up from Harting at midday.

Yours sincerely
Mrs Janet Stubbington

Anne read the letter twice and realised that the situation in England must have deteriorated for this man to be assigned to her staff. Janet would have given Robert more information, making the appointment necessary. She shuddered as she remembered the Irishman who had invaded her bedroom during Robert's last mission. Perhaps this precaution was for the best. But she would be under scrutiny by this security man who would add another difficulty to her busy life.

She shrugged and resigned herself to the situation. Then she opened Robert's letter:

HMS Shadow
Woolwich Navy docks
London

My Dearest Anne

By now, you will know we are long gone from Woolwich. The mission takes us to the eastern Mediterranean off Greece. I fear it will be some months before I return. Unfortunately, I cannot tell you more, but I will be safe and return as soon as possible.

The ship is fully victualed, and we have a complete crew. The men enjoy the prospect of a long voyage, and morale is high. Shadow is in excellent condition, and I expect she will be a good fighting ship.

We will be out of contact until we reach Malta. I will send letters then.

I miss you greatly already, but we both must be strong and keep to our tasks with vigour. Please continue to consult with my mother and sister on the plight of the estate. You will probably have it sorted out by the time I return.

With all my love
Robert.

P.S. I met with Mrs Janet Stubbington at the Home Office, and we have agreed to place a security officer on your staff for the next few months. Please take into consideration Mr Henry Fletcher's recommendations.

A tear ran down one of Anne's cheeks as she hugged the letter to her chest. She missed him greatly already and wanted him home now. But she knew this would not happen for months. She must make herself busy with the different businesses and her friends. It was time to finish breakfast, dress and meet Henry Fletcher. She wondered what complications would be added to her life.

Turner Household, Guildford, England ...
Ethel Nibley pinned the staff duties for the day to the notice board, walked out onto the back verandah, and gazed across towards the castle. The spring night had been unexpectedly cold, and the morning was still chilly, but the day was warming with a clear blue sky and bright sunshine lifting the temperature.

Ethel murmured, 'If only my thoughts were as clear as this day.'

With Clare missing, she found it hard to relax and prayed for the girl's safety. The meeting confirmed that the Constable knew nothing further than was ascertained on Wednesday. It was a day since the girl went missing, and they were still trying to find Benjamin's solicitors.

The situation was hopeless, and Ethel housed uncharitable thoughts towards Mrs Preston and the butler, Steadman. They lied through their teeth to her and disappeared during the night. What would they achieve by stealing the girl? When they are caught, the penalty would be harsh. Why would anyone risk their lives by kidnapping?

They could not access any money while they were in hiding. So, that was not the motive. It must be some other reason, but what? Ethel had wondered what Clare's mother would have made of all this. Then she realised the lady was a Roman Catholic. But surely, it could not be as simple as that!

Simeon, Madeline, and William entered the kitchen for breakfast and joined Marcia. Despite the hint in the air of warmth, Mrs Jennings was cooking a hearty meal.

"Mm, Mrs Jennings! That smells good."

"Eat your porridge first, William, before I serve these."

Mr Turner then arrived and sat with the children, "Has Clemmie come down yet?"

"No, Father."

"Mrs Jennings! I have a meeting with Anne soon, so could I have some bacon and eggs and a sausage or two, please? I will skip my porridge."

William looked up from his bowl and frowned as his father started enjoying the piping hot second course. He dared not comment as he knew from long experience how his father would react. The boy looked down again and shovelled the warm oats and milk into his mouth faster.

Simeon said, "Father, the days are becoming warmer. Do we need to cut so much wood as the pile is still high in the woodshed?"

Jonathan took a break from chewing his sausage and looked at Simeon.

"Do we still need hot water, Sim? Do we still need to clean the house and use hot water? Do we need to be warm at night? The nights are still cold, and we often have baths. Mrs Jennings, do we still need to wash clothes and sheets?"

"Yes, Mr Turner!"

"Thank you, Mrs Jennings." The cook smiled to herself.

"Now, Simeon! Can you answer your question?"

"Yes, Sir! We will continue."

Jonathan smiled and then started chewing on another sausage.

William asked, "Father, you said that when Beth and Anne left, you would employ either a man or a lad to chop the wood and do the hard work outside. When will you be recruiting the man?"

Mrs Jennings turned and went 'Shush!' to William.

Mr Turner slowly raised his eyes and stared directly at the boy.

"What do you mean by that, Son?"

Simeon could see the rage beginning on his father's face and decided it might be better for William if he had some support.

"You did, Father." He spoke most respectfully. "We knew it was on your mind and wondered when it might happen."

Jonathan, now focused on Simeon, thought hard about the question. He sat there chewing his sausage and frowning.

"I remember now. I did say that. I will let you know. But keep chopping the wood, boys."

Simeon gently kicked William's leg under the table and cast his eyes on his porridge bowl. William, who was street smart, quickly understood the message and continued with his head down, spooning the last bits of porridge into his mouth. As Mrs Jennings moved around the kitchen, she gave Simeon a little thank you rub on the shoulder without Mr Turner noticing. She could see both boys smiling as they finished their porridge.

After the children finished and left to dress for school, Ethel came in and asked, "Mr Turner, excuse me."

"Yes, Ethel. This is not about the wood chopping, is it?"

Ethel smiled and explained, "Mr Turner, I am not sure what you are talking about, so please excuse my interruption. I know you are in a hurry, so I will be quick. I wonder if I might borrow the carriage today. I want to check something at Cloverdale Chase."

"Certainly, Ethel. I must make a short visit to 'Porting' to speak with Anne, but I will send the carriage here as soon as they drop me off at the office."

"Thank you."

London Road, Guildford, England …

The Reverend Hotspur wiped his brow after trotting his horse along the London Road north of the town and stopped at a group of old setback cottages slightly down the hillside. He checked the address in his notebook and vaguely recalled the building outlines from when he walked Jess home the other night. There was no number or any sign of identification.

'Might as well ask which cottage the Swamps lived in!'

He approached the first cottage and was confronted by a large, snarling black dog of no particular breed. Observing a healthy caution, he took a few steps backwards and waited for someone to stir from the derelict-looking building. As the minutes passed and the dog sat watching him, he decided that a safer action plan was trying the next cottage. Hearing the snarling dog through a feeble-looking side fence, he felt somewhat exposed as he approached the front door.

It swung open, and a short, thick-set man with greying hair came out and shouted, "Shut up, Barney, you mongrel!"

Turning and raising his eyes onto Hotspur, he asked, "A Reverend, eh? Who might ye be, eh?"

"The Reverend Philip Hotspur, Mr Swamp. I have come on a pastoral care visit."

"None here be sick, Reverend! You be mistaken, eh? Mistaken, eh?"

"No, no, Mr Swamp. Pastoral care is about well-being and covers many areas, such as spiritual advice and support in times of need."

"Ah! Spiritual advice it is, eh? Support in times of need, eh? We not be in any need, Mr Reverend Hotspur. Not any, eh! Thank ye very much."

"Perhaps, Mr Swamp, we could discuss this over some tea?"

"Tea, did ye say, then? Eh! Wife don't make tea. How bout water, then?"

"Yes, Mr Swamp. Water will be satisfactory."

They stood there for nearly a minute in silence, gazing around and considering each other, then Mr Swamp finally said, "Well, ye better come then! Eh!"

"Thank you."

The Reverend crouched as he entered through the lower-than-usual doorway. The house inside was surprisingly neat and offered a reasonable amount of comfort.

"Willie! A glass of water for the Reverend Hotspur, eh! Have seat over here."

Kevin Swamp indicated a seat and sat down opposite. As his wife came in wondering who the visitor was, he made the introduction.

"This man be Reverend Mr Hotspur, Willie! Mr Reverend, this be my wife, Willamina."

Hotspur quickly stood and gave Mrs Swamp a short bow, "A pleasure, Mrs Swamp. Thank you for your hospitality."

"Ooh, Reverend. You are welcome. We don't get many visitors. I will make you a cup of tea!"

Mrs Swamp rushed out of the room in a bit of a dither, and to Kevin Swamp's annoyance, Philip gave him a forgiving smile. Mr Swamp wanted this visit over as he had little time for the clergy and was suspicious of this haughty man.

"Now, eh! What ye be wanting, Mr Reverend? I must get out to farm and check lads soon!"

Philip Hotspur was well prepared for the discussion and wasted no time commencing.

"Mr Swamp, there are two issues we should discuss. The first issue concerns your daughter, Jessica. I understand she works several hours a day for the Turners in the High Street."

"Jess, eh! That be right. Good girl, that one, eh! Good girl."

"Yes. I have regular contact with the Turner family and have made the acquaintance of your daughter – a fine young girl with many qualities. But I understand that she cannot read or write. Of course, I have kept this confidential as it would not be advisable that the Turners learn of this."

Kevin Swamp scratched his ear and squirmed in his seat, "Why that be, Mr Reverend, eh? Me boys can read and write as they take over farm soon. But girls need no writing and reading, eh? They be having babies, eh? Suckling babies when married! Washing and cleaning, Eh! No need of reading, Mr Reverend!"

"Yes and no, Mr Swamp."

Mrs Willamina Swamp came in with the cup of tea in an elegant ceramic cup and saucer and placed it on a table in front of Philip. The curate was surprised by the lovely cup.

"I leave you two alone, then."

Philip smiled and nodded his thanks. He waited for Mrs Swamp to exit before he drove his point home.

"Girls need to read and write today, Mr Swamp. They need it for their work. There is much to read so they can understand their household duties. How can they shop if they cannot read numbers and make additions? She may lose her job if the Turners find out."

"No, no, Mr Reverend. Jess doing fine job there, eh? The Turners much happy with her. She no need reading and writing! The boys need a bit for farm. But girls, no. Not at all, eh?"

Philip knew that Kevin Swamp would react in this way. He was now ready to clinch the deal.

"Mr Swamp, the second issue is your tithe[17]."

"Tithe, eh? It be twenty-five pounds a year, it be, eh!"

"Yes, Mr Swamp. We have been reviewing the parish records and understand it was commuted[18] in your father's time. That was some thirty years ago, and we agree that twenty-five pounds was fair then. Our current assessment is that the value of your farm produce is far higher. I have made a list of your produce registered with the parish overseer and calculated the full value of your crop. Your tithe should now be fifty-eight pounds a year. It seems you have been underpaying for some time."

Kevin Swamp blurted out, "No, not at all, eh? Not at all, Mr Reverend, Sir! That amount was settled upon with Father long ago. The tithe always been paid, and it be twenty-five pounds, and that be it. Twenty-five pounds, eh?"

Philip Hotspur knew he now had the man where he wanted him.

"I am afraid, Mr Swamp, that the tithe must be paid under British law and represent a tenth of your produce. Now, the conversion of the production value to money is quite straightforward. Nothing in the regulation states a commutation made many years ago must remain unchanged. The new tithe will be fifty-eight pounds, and the Parish Constable advises me you have not paid your tithe for last year."

Philip took a sip of his tea and regarded the fine porcelain cup. He then looked up at Mr Swamp, raising his eyebrows and smiling. Kevin Swamp stood and glared at him. Why had his wife used the best

---

[17] Tithe – A tithe is a one-tenth part of something, paid as a contribution to a religious organisation or compulsory tax to government. Tithes were originally paid as one-tenth of the produce of the land (crops, eggs, cattle, timber, fishing, etc) to the rector, as alms and as payment for his services. Wikipedia. In Great Britain in the early nineteen century, the tithe system was compulsory. JS

[18] Tithe commutation – An agreement between the church and the landowner to pay the tithe in monetary value rather than produce. JS

crockery instead of a dirty old mug, advertising the meagre wealth they had built over the years? The tithe was a hot topic among farmers who found the requirements too harsh. Every year, the task of making ends meet was becoming more difficult. At least having his two sons working on the farm reduced his costs. Without this assistance, it would become impossible. Having the existing tithe agreement changed by this churchman was most disagreeable. He would not stand for it.

"Mr Reverend Hotspur! We not afford that increase. Agreement is for twenty-five pounds a year – it remains that! Eh?"

"I understand your circumstances, Mr Swamp, but the law is the law, and we must abide by it."

As the curate sat there thinking, Kevin Swamp felt they had reached a stalemate.

Then, in a far more conciliatory tone, Philip said, "Mr Swamp. There may be something I can do to help you!"

The farmer was immediately interested as he knew the church could force the increase if they wished.

"Help, eh?"

"As I mentioned when we commenced our little chat – I highly regard your daughter, Jessica. If you allowed me to teach her how to read and write, I might be able to ensure your increased tithe is delayed for many years. What do you say to that."

Swamp looked hard at the Reverend, trying to understand why he would waste time on his daughter. Education for girls was not necessary. Their place was in the home.

"Where you teach her? Eh!"

Philip knew he had him.

"At the Institute or the church. There would be no cost to you. But our agreement must be secret so the Turners do not find out. Jessica needs that job!"

"Aye, the money good, eh? The money!"

Swamp smiled and held out his hand. Philip Hotspur clasped his hand and confirmed the deal.

"You can talk with Jessica and advise her it is a secret. I will contact her and schedule our first meeting when the time is right. Please ensure she understands the tithe and that she tells no one. Thank you, Mr Swamp."

As he walked out to his horse, the Reverend Philip Hotspur whistled as he thought about how beautiful Jessica was. Better than that, she would now be under his control.

Mr and Mrs Swamp stood by the cottage's front door and waved goodbye.

"Kevin! What that Reverend man want?"

"Ah, Willie! Me thinks he has an eye for Jessica, eh? Jess, Ha Ha! He may be our son-in-law one day!"

'Porting', Guildford, Surrey, England …

Mary Hedge popped her head around the door and announced, "Mr Turner is here, my Lady."

Anne was soon in the drawing room with her father.

"Good morning, Anne. I must be quick as there is much going on. Clare Petherton was missing on Wednesday morning when Mrs Nibley visited her room at Cloverdale Chase. A search was mounted, but there was no sign of her. Late on Tuesday night, the governess told the staff that her sister was desperately ill, and Mr Petherton, worried for Preston's safety, asked the butler to accompany her to London. I am sure it was a lie, as Benjamin was already dead in the afternoon. It appears the governess and the butler took Clare with them."

"Oh, dear! That sounds very suspicious. What of Clare?"

"There is no sign of her anywhere. I suspect she is with the governess and probably near London now. If we knew the names of his attorneys, we could notify them of his death. They would then instruct the executors to order an official search for Clare. It seems ludicrous that these servants could snatch her away without notice."

"Why can't the servants at Cloverdale Chase tell you who Benjamin's attorneys are?"

"Ethel asked, but they were unaware. It seems only the butler knew about Benjamin's business."

"Where was his business, Father?"

"The Isle of Dogs. I believe he imported spirits from all over the world."

The name rang a bell for Anne. She was trying to link it back to a person she had met. She said out aloud, "Stephen Polkinghorne!"

"Who?"

"Remember, Father—the lady who pretended to be Sir Hugh's wife. Lady Clarissa Wendarm was also involved with this man. He assisted us with unravelling the truth about her. His business is in the Isle of Dogs!"

"Do you think he would assist us, Anne?"

"I am sure he would. He was most embarrassed about Lady Wendarm and went out of his way to set things straight. I have his address somewhere. I will find it tonight and advise you."

"Anne, I know you are leaving for London tomorrow, and I would join you, but I can't leave the family now when Ethel, I mean Mrs Nibley, is so upset. Would you find him and seek his assistance, please?"

"Certainly, Father. Is there anyone else who requires transport to London?"

"Yes. I have engaged Mr Wood's service, and he has requested the assistance of our London attorneys. He has all the documentation attesting to Mrs Nibley being a trustee for Clare. He will also ask them to seek out Benjamin's attorneys. If we can find Mr Polkinghorne, that will shorten the search considerably."

"I will message Mr Wood this morning and invite him to join me in my carriage. Neville is also coming with us. He received a note from Robert asking him to attend on Admiral Crouch, who is most unwell."

"When you say 'us', who else is travelling with you?"

"My maid, Mary Hedge."

"Of course! Thank you, Anne. I think we may be making progress at last. I am afraid for Mrs Nibley. I have never seen her so worried."

"She will handle it, Father. I have great respect for Ethel's abilities. I think her struggles in the past have prepared her to face anything. Now, Father. What was it you wished to discuss with me this morning?"

"Ah, yes. You will recall your recommendation that we appoint a General Manager. I have considered this carefully and agree that we proceed with this appointment. The London and Bristol bakeries will distract us, so the time is right. We need someone who is concentrating on our markets and our future growth. You and Victoria will need time for Hursts' new London venture. There is so much to do, Anne. We must move fast on this appointment."

"Thank you, Father. That is a relief as I wondered how I would cope. Please, if you would involve me in the interviews."

"Yes, By the time you return, I will have more information. The other issue is a bit more delicate. As you know, I have struggled greatly over the years with my rage problem. I think I am now controlling it better than at any other time in the past. But I still have moments when I nearly fail. It is usually directed at William, and I am terrified I will damage the boy beyond repair if it occurs again."

Anne became silent and concerned as she listened to her father's soul-searching. She feared the conclusion he may reach and was not sure she would agree.

"I am William's father and have decided what to do. Everyone will disagree with me, but it must be done. I do not ask your permission, Anne, but I ask for your confidentiality and assistance. My decision is that William will spend two years with his Uncle Richard in South Africa. He will leave in August, and Aggie will travel with the boy to ensure he arrives safely. Of course, all this must be kept confidential until he leaves."

Jonathan hesitated as he could see Anne was in shock.

"But he is only seven, Father!"

"He will be closer to eight by the time he travels, and Aggie will be with him. He will be safe."

"Father, I am honoured that you advise me of this, but what assistance do you expect from me? I can see that you have struggled to make this decision, and you have also considered the reasons for it, which are valid. Surely, William will see your decision as a betrayal and feel he is being cast aside from the family. Losing his mother has been bad enough! This will only further his worries. I am at a loss as to what assistance I can render?"

"I need you to talk with Aggie and assure her that the family will support William in this decision. She has similar fears to yours, but I have specified the time frame as two years. She has agreed to escort William to Africa on one condition. She insisted that you be told of my decision and satisfied that he will be safe. Given the distance involved, I do not think this is unreasonable. He will have his Auntie Sarah to care for him like a mother in Africa. I understand it is different, but it is better than here. For a child such as William, it will be the making of him!"

Anne looked away and thought for a moment. She was eager to

stand up for William but knew this would create division with her father. She decided it would be better for her to consider this while she was in London and then give her father an answer.

"Father, let me consider your request while I am in London. We can discuss this further when I return. Be assured I will always support you, but it may not be in the way you desire. Let us both think on this for a few weeks."

Jonathan smiled, "A few weeks it is! Certainly, we currently have enough pressing issues to settle. As Mrs Nibley requires the coach this morning, I must be heading off."

"Why does she require the coach, Father?"

"She feels there are clues to Clare's whereabouts at Cloverdale Chase that Constable Rawlins has not considered. She will ask the staff more questions."

Balma's Hotel and Boarding House, Grahamstown, Eastern Cape Province, South Africa ...

The small patrol of troopers and Richard Turner returned on Friday afternoon, nearly a week after setting out. Sarah watched from the raised footpath beside the boarding house as the sun started setting. She could see the tired but happy faces of the men as they made their way towards the army barracks.

Richard waved to Lieutenant Sanderson, saying, "I will see you tomorrow when we talk with the Captain."

Freddie waved and led his party on.

Richard stopped outside the boarding house, dismounted, climbed onto the footpath, and kissed his wife.

"It took far longer than I expected, Sarah. The natives take their time making decisions. But we have been successful. I must speak with Captain Hargrave tomorrow and finalise the arrangements. But first, the horse needs stabling, and I need a good bath before we talk at dinner.

The sun was setting in the west, and the native parrots and other bird life created a cacophony of squawks, screeches, and whistles from the trees beside the town. It was as if they were entertaining the town's inhabitants, but it was the stress of nightfall and the native birds readying themselves for the dangers of the dark.

As the Turners enjoyed their meal, Richard admitted, "That was a tough ride. I am too old for that sort of exercise again."

"You look tired, Richard. A few days' rest will set you right. But did the chief agree?"

"Yes, he did. But there were conditions. He insisted that the men could bring their wives and children with them and set up a permanent camp at the edge of our property. We must give them one steer every six months for their services. I thought that was fair, especially if it stops the cattle thieves. I would rather trade cattle for protection than have them stolen."

"Yes, I agree, but having the natives living on our property may create other problems. We employ many Khoi Khoi! How will they get along with them?"

"I will keep them separated. The Xhosa can watch for the invaders and graze their cattle on the government land next door. I will tell them where the boundaries are."

"Were there any other conditions?"

"Not from the chief, but Freddie advised that the Captain must approve this agreement. He must be aware of any agreements with the natives so his men don't make mistakes."

"What do you mean by mistakes?"

"Shooting them, Sarah! How else do you think the British have conquered this country."

Turner Business Offices, Guildford, England ...
As Anne arrived at the office, Daisy stood and passed her a message.

"Lady Emma Sopwith left a message for you, Lady Anne."

Anne was excited by the news, "She is back, Daisy?"

"Yes, she was here earlier and said the ship from Ireland was early, and they came directly to Guildford. They remain here for a week and then visit Fintelton."

"Wonderful!" Anne took the note and read that Lady Emma requested her company for lunch at the Fox and Hound at one o'clock.

Before climbing the stairs, she turned and said, "Daisy, I will be working hard upstairs. Please remind me at twelve forty-five that I am due at the Fox and Hound for lunch. Also, send a boy out to find Victoria, as I would like her to attend."

"Yes, Lady Anne. I think Miss Sopwith already knows. She was with Lady Emma when they called earlier."

"Good, thank you, Daisy."

Daisy quickly noted the appointment in the diary.

Cloverdale Chase, Guildford, England …

Ethel was assisted out of the coach and found the front door firmly locked. There was no answer after pulling the doorbell several times.

"Arthur, I will go around the back. I think it may be best if you come with me."

"Yes, Mrs Nibley. I will tie up the horses first."

They slowly moved around to the rear of the house and found the back door to the kitchen. Ethel tentatively entered first, followed by the tall groomsman, Arthur.

The housekeep and maids were having a late cup of morning tea, and Mrs O'Connor stood in fright as they entered.

"Oh! You surprised me, Mrs Nibley. Have they found the young girl yet?"

"Unfortunately, not, Mrs O'Connor. But I was wondering if I could have a private chat with you. It would only take a few minutes. Perhaps one of the maids could provide Arthur with a cup of tea?"

"Certainly, Mrs Nibley."

Mary O'Connor led Ethel away from the kitchen and into the drawing-room, offering Ethel a chair beside a small table. Sighing as she sat, the housekeeper said, "The longer it is, the more worried I am about Clare."

"I share your worry, Mrs O'Connor. I won't keep you long, but I cannot understand why the butler and governess would have taken such a chance to take Clare away without notice or authority. The penalties are harsh – Constable Rawlins told me it is hanging, and they don't commute for kidnapping."

"They deserve it for taking away that poor girl the day after her father died. She did not even have time to say goodbye to the servants." Ethel noticed the anger in Mrs O'Connor's voice.

"Mrs O'Connor! Would you know if Mr Steadman or Mrs Preston were religious?"

"Oh, yes! They never missed a Sunday and would accompany Mr

Petherton and Clare. They were disappointed when Clare asked to attend the Church of England, but Mr Steadman and Mrs Preston continued at the Catholic church. They would always attend together."

"Which church did they attend?'

"The one out at Batton Place! I am unsure of the name as I never went, but Mr Petherton's wife and son are buried there. I think it is called 'Star of the Sea'. I am not sure."

"Were Mr Steadman and Mrs Preston close?"

"In what way, Mrs Nibley?"

"Were they a couple?"

"I am not sure. If they were, it was well hidden, but when Mr Petherton was away, they often disappeared for a day or two at the same time. They always had reasons, but it did seem more than a co-incidence."

"As they have disappeared mysteriously, would I be able to see their rooms?"

"Certainly. But there is not much to see. I am sure Mr Steadman and Mrs Preston were not planning on returning."

Ethel followed Mrs O'Connor through to the servants' quarters, and after the housekeeper had unlocked the rooms, she quickly checked. There was very little left except for liveries and old clothes. The personal possessions in each room were gone.

"I agree with you, Mrs O'Connor. It appears they had no intention of returning. I appreciate your help."

"You are welcome, Mrs Nibley, and I hope we see Clare back soon."

Ethel smiled, called Arthur, and headed back to the coach.

Once on board, she asked, "Arthur, we need to visit the 'Star of the Sea' church at Batton Place. Do you know where it is?"

"Yes, Ma'am"

Soon, the carriage pulled up outside the church.

"Arthur, would you please see if you can find the priest? I will remain in the carriage."

The groomsmen quickly found the priest, and he soon stood beside the carriage, facing Ethel.

Arthur said, "Father Sullivan, Ma'am!"

"Father Sullivan, I assume you have heard that young Clare Petherton was kidnapped by the butler and governess soon after Mr

Petherton died on Tuesday?"

"Yes, but I thought she was missing. I have heard no mention of kidnapping."

"Well, call it what you will, but when they are caught, they and anyone who has helped them will hang."

The priest became uncomfortable as he heard the penalty and coughed into one of his hands.

"I am sure she will be found soon, Mrs Nibley! Mr Steadman and Mrs Preston are good people. They would never harm Clare."

Ethel was immediately suspicious, "Why do you say they would never harm her, Father Sullivan? Are you aware that she is with them?"

The priest seemed to shrink back from the carriage and spoke loudly enough for Ethel to hear, "I could not say as that would be a breach of confidence, Mrs Nibley. I know that Mr Steadman and Mrs Preston are good people."

"Were they upset when Clare started attending the Anglican church?"

"We were all upset – it was difficult for the congregation."

"Father Sullivan, if you can help me find them, that would not be a sin or a breach of confidence. Clare has been taken away by people with no legal authority over her. They have stolen this child from her home. No matter the child's religion, we are duty-bound to save her. If it were found that you concealed information that could have saved the child, I would hate to think what repercussions there could be for your church in this community. We must all support each other and do what is right under the law."

Ethel could see that the priest was struggling with his conscience. Sweat was appearing on his brow.

"Please, let me stand aside for a few seconds and pray about this?"

"Very well, Father Sullivan."

The priest moved a few steps away from the carriage, held his rosary, and closed his eyes as he swayed back and forth and contemplated. The minutes became ten and then fifteen.

Ethel asked, "Father Sullivan, every second may be important in saving the child's life. You must tell me what you know."

Sullivan returned to the carriage crying and wiping his tears with a handkerchief, "I have done a disservice. I was carried away by parochialism. I have sinned!"

"Tell that to your bishop, Father Sullivan. But please tell me where they are?"

"There is a small monastery near Redhill in Sussex. It is called Rosefield. You will find them there."

"Thank you, Father! But tell me, why would you allow such a thing?"

"We all wanted her to be brought up in her mother's true faith. Miriam Petherton is buried out there." He pointed towards the graveyard. "Mr Steadman pleaded with me for somewhere for the child to be safe. He told me she was in danger. I never doubted him as he was a regular worshiper here. Mr Steadman said there was no time left - they must be on their way. It was all done too quickly. I am so sorry! Please forgive me?"

"But what was the danger that Steadman was referring to?"

"Of losing her mother's faith. They want her to remain in the true church."

"As I said before, Father! Take your confession to your bishop; I hope the community does not find out. Your secret is safe, but you should publicly set it right before you are found out!"

HMS Shadow, off the East Coast of France, North Atlantic Ocean ...
Captain Sir Robert South stood on the poop deck talking with the two diplomatic staff travelling with him.

"My apologies, gentlemen, I cannot provide better accommodation, but you will understand this is a fighting ship. However, we have beautiful fine weather, a calm sea, and a fair wind. We are making good progress, and by this time tomorrow, I hope we have rounded Sagres Point in Portugal and headed for Gibraltar. If the wind holds, we may pass Gibraltar by Sunday night."

"We do not stop in Gibraltar, Captain?"

"No, Monsieur Milius. I have clear orders to arrive in Malta as soon as possible and keep you and Mr Volkov safe. We are to avoid contact and cruise unharmed to Malta. The British Commander in Chief is expecting you."

"Das, Captain. Speed is urgent. We hope the Admiral has representatives of the Sultan there and from the Greeks. We need a cease-fire[19]

---

[19] Greek Independence: Great Britain, France and Russia had called upon Greece and the Ottoman Empire to cease hostilities that had been going on since the Greeks revolted against the Ottoman rule on March 1821. The Allies wanted a treaty that caused the Ottoman Empire to create an independent Greek state but with the Ottoman Sultan as its supreme leader. Wikipedia The Greeks were not keen on any Ottoman leader taking charge of their country. JS

to have time to settle this war for independence."

"Well, gentlemen. That is out of my control. I will leave that to you. If you would excuse me, I must talk with my officers. I will join you for lunch at one o'clock in the great cabin. Oh, gentlemen, please! We will be commencing battle practice in ten minutes, so you are welcome to watch, but for your safety, please remain on the poop deck. The deck on which you are standing. Here!"

Robert pointed at his feet. The gentlemen immediately stood on either side of him.

Robert smiled and understood their translation was literal, "Good. Thank you, gentlemen."

Robert moved away and joined Fenton at the stern.

"I think a squall is coming. Sir. The clouds in the west are building rapidly."

"I agree, Mr Fenton. Best we finish our broadsides quickly. You may call battle stations and practice as you see fit."

"Thank you, Sir."

Fenton walked forward to the poop deck rail and called Lieutenant Peters over.

"Is your timepiece ready, Peters?"

"Yes, Sir."

Fenton lifted a megaphone to his lips and yelled, "Battle Stations, all hands to Battle Stations!"

He smiled as he told Peters, "Let us see if they can do it in one minute ninety-five seconds this time."

The Fox and Hound, Guildford, Surrey, England ...
Anne, Emma and Victoria had so much to catch up on at lunch that the conversation was endless.

"I thought you travelled to Fintelton before returning to Guildford?"

Emma excitedly replied, "The ship was early, so we came here first. David wanted to carry me over the threshold and into the house. He is such a romantic. I think it was better this way. Appearing at the manor straight away would have been taking me home again. I need to make my parents understand my home is here now. We shall go down next Friday and stay until Monday. David is keen to return to his practice before we visit."

Anne nodded in agreement. "I thought the same about Robert, but he is committed to Guildford now as his home. I pray that Hugh will return soon; otherwise, the home front may become complicated."

Emma eagerly asked, "Has there been any news of Hugh?"

"Yes, the last letter your mother received indicated that he was recovering well. It came from Lady Fiona Green. She was the lady who remained in Kingston and looked after him. Who knows, Emma, you may have another sister-in-law soon."

"That would be wonderful. Do you know any more of Lady Fiona?"

"Only the scant amount Mr Polkinghorne told us in London, but he praised her highly. We shall have to wait and see."

"That would be amazing if Hugh finally married and was content. What a blessing that would be for my parents."

Emma sipped her tea and finished her sandwich before asking in a low voice, "What about the estate? Have you made any progress?"

"Yes, quite a bit, but perhaps we should discuss that privately."

Emma suggested, "Tomorrow morning?"

"Sorry, Emma. I am travelling to London tomorrow. Would you and David join me for dinner tonight?"

"Unfortunately, we are dining with the Reverend Taggart and his wife. When do you return from London?"

"I am not sure yet, but probably in two weeks. I will call on you once I have returned. That will allow you plenty of time with Victoria to catch up."

Emma said, "Victoria! I have missed you so much, and David could not find you yesterday. He searched but without luck. Where were you?"

"Did not Molly Lane advise of my new address? Forgive me! I must have forgotten to have here drop a note to your house that I have moved to a small rental off Quarry Street overlooking the Wey."

Emma was surprised, "That sounds interesting. I shall visit you tomorrow, but before we say anymore, we should all order."

"Yes. But while I am reading the menu, please, Anne, what news of Clare Petherton?"

Emma questioned, "Who is Clare Petherton?"

Turner Business Offices, Guildford, England …

Ethel ran through the front door of the building, past Daisy, up the stairs and into Jonathan's office.

"Jonathan, I have found her. I know where she is!"

Jonathan stood with a great smile, "How...?"

Daisy appeared in the doorway and interrupted, "Sorry, Mr Turner! Is everything alright?"

"Yes, Daisy. Please excuse Mrs Nibley, but she is excited. Now, Daisy, I want you to send someone to fetch Constable Rawlins immediately."

"Yes, Mr Turner."

As Daisy left the office, Jonathan quickly closed the door. He sat beside Ethel.

"Tell me how you found her."

"She is at Rosefield Priory near Redhill in Sussex." Ethel gasped, "A glass of water, Jonathan. I am so excited, and my throat is dry!"

As Jonathan passed across the water, Ethel recounted the story of her visiting Cloverdale Chase and then the meeting with Father Sullivan.

"It was all about religion. Preston and Steadman must be strict Catholics. They could not stand seeing Clare become a protestant. So, they planned on hiding her in a monastery for the rest of her life. They must be simple people not understanding that they would be found out sooner or later."

"You are being kind by saying 'simple'. Steadman and Preston have been very devious and should be charged, but if we can solve this without the courts, it would occur far faster. Clare must be terrified by what has happened. First, we must discuss this with Constable Rawlins and decide what action to take."

"Jonathan, I do not trust the priest. He may even now be sending a message telling them they are discovered. We must act quickly, or they will disappear again."

A knock came on the door, and a puffing Constable Rawlins walked into the office.

"Mr Turner! I ran as Daisy told me it was urgent."

"Have a seat, Michael. We need your help, particularly your uniform. We must travel to Rosefield monastery near Redhill, Sussex."

"Is that where the girl is?"

"Yes, and we need you with us. There is not a minute to spare, Michael."

"Mr Turner, I cannot just up and leave. It is out of my jurisdiction."

"Michael, if you come with us, your family will have free bread for a year. Pastries as well! Of course, it will be confidential between you and me."

Constable Rawlins considered and then looked at Mrs Nibley and then Jonathan.

"And Mrs Nibley as well?"

Jonathan nodded, and Ethel said, "Please, Michael!"

The Constable said, "Could Daisy pass a message to my wife, please."

Jonathan stood and said, "Of course, Michael. Now, Ethel, let us bring our little girl home!"

With tears running down her cheeks, Ethel hugged Jonathan and said, "Oh, thank you, Jonathan! Thank you, thank you, thank you."

The Country Squire Pub, Guildford, England ...

Aaron Hall and Ralph Fenn were waiting for the others to arrive for their Thursday evening darts game. It was five o'clock, and the pub was filling up.

"We can't keep this board much longer if they don't turn up soon."

"Here is Terry, Aaron. But where is Peter?"

Aaron Hall shrugged, "He can sometimes be a bit unreliable."

Terry went over and joined the two young men, "Sorry about being late! There is a bit of a problem with the mill crusher. All fixed now, thanks to our friendly blacksmith, Mr Linton. He's a good man, that one. Where is Swampy?"

"Not here yet – we need a practice round to keep the wolves away." Aaron smiled, saying, "He won't be long as Merryn is at the bar tonight. I think something might be brewing there."

Ralph agreed, "Half his luck – she's a cutie."

Terry asked, "Anyone for a pint!"

They all chipped in, and Terry ventured off, dodging between patrons and smiling at Merryn as he approached the bar.

Aaron was becoming concerned, "If Swampy is not here by now, I would say something has come up at the farm. We must start the game, so we need another partner."

Ralph started looking around, "Take your pick, Aaron. There are plenty of blokes to choose from."

Aaron knew that Ralph, with his height, perfectly complemented

Terry, a shorter chap. They were a hard team to beat. So, being of medium height, Aaron looked around for someone who could match Ralph's size. There was a young man around their age sitting two tables away alone. He looked athletic, so Aaron plucked up the courage, walked over and asked, "Excuse me, mate, but we are short a dart team member. Would you be interested in a game?"

The tall young man raised his eyes and smiled, "Why not! I haven't had a game since Oxford."

Aaron watched as he took his glass, pushed his chair back, and stood four inches above him.

'Perfect!' He said to himself, enjoying the sight of Leonard's long arms.

"Let me introduce myself. I am Aaron Hall, a baker from Turner's Bakeries. And you?"

"Leonard Webster! I am studying at Oxford but presently assisting my parents to move into Guildford."

"Where are they from?"

"Truro! My father had several businesses there but has retired due to ill health. They were originally from Guildford, so they decided to retire here."

"Good decision. It is a growing country town. Come over to the darts, and I will introduce you."

Terry and Ralph gasped when they saw the tall stranger returning with Aaron.

After the introductions, the chaps got into the game. To Aaron's relief, Leonard was a reasonable dart player. As each round ended, the competition grew, and before they realised it, the last round started. In the end, Terry and Ralph won by a point, with a disappointed Aaron thanking Leonard for helping them out.

"What's this, eh? You boys played without me?" Swampy had arrived and joined the conversation.

Aaron quickly said, "Leonard Webster, Peter Swamp, our missing team member. You can call him Swampy."

"Glad to meet you, Peter. Thanks for being late. I enjoyed the game with my new friends here."

"That's good! Sorry, fellas, but we had a lot of tasks this afternoon, so I had to keep working. Alf is a bit off-colour, so Dad and I kept on.

Are you from around here, Leonard?"

"Till the end of July, and then I am due back in Oxford. My parents have moved here from Truro, and I am helping them settle in."

Peter opened his mouth to make a smart comment about education but thought better of it. Leonard, the tallest of the group and somewhat athletic, seemed to deserve respect.

Aaron added, "He's not bad at darts, Swampy. How about another game before we call it a night."

Terry apologised, pushed off for home, and left the younger lads to the second game.

Chapter 8

Reigate, Surrey, England …

Mrs Nibley and Constable Rawlins curled up in opposite pillowed corners of the coach and slept as they approached Reigate. Jonathan watched as the savage lightning flashed through the rain, giving glimpses of the countryside passing by. They had not let the terrible weather deter them and fortunately reached Reigate by midnight. Jonathan opened the window and called to the driver, "Find a pub! We must stop and rest the horses."

"Yes, Mr Turner."

Both Ethel and Michael Rawlins stirred.

"Are we at Redhill, Mr Turner?"

"No, but we all need sleep before tomorrow. The horses must be fed and rested; a good breakfast will help us clear our minds and give us the energy to carry on. Redhill is only three miles away. We cannot hope to get much sense from a monastery at midnight. With this weather, we have been lucky to make it this far. Best if we stopped now and found some shelter for the night."

Michael Rawlins readily agreed, but Ethel was keen to continue. Jonathan finally persuaded her it would be safer to break the journey here.

After such a long night, they missed breakfast and woke late. Constable Rawlins set out to find the local parish constable with whom he claimed an acquaintance. Jonathan and Ethel enjoyed a sizeable morning tea as they waited.

By the time Michael Rawlings fetched Constable Swan, Jonathan was impatient and had decided to board the coach. Both constables climbed onboard, and Michael made the introductions.

Jonathan explained the previous events before Ethel continued, "The butler, Mr Steadman and the governess, Mrs Preston, must have bundled the girl into a carriage in the middle of the night and disappeared without permission. The child must be terrified!"

"Mrs Nibley, would you have any documentation proving you are the child's trustee?"

Jonathan realised the constable needed some verification before proceeding any further.

"Yes! Here are all the documents."

"Thank you, Mrs Nibley."

Constable Archie Swan quickly read through the trustee documents and recognised the magistrate's signature, witnessing the instructions.

"You are lucky. I know Magistrate Bussell's signature. These documents are fine. The one thing I can't understand is why this priest told you they were in Redhill. There is no convent there!"

Ethel blurted out in surprise, "But the priest admitted they were there!"

"I am sure he did, but he might not be aware of the changes. There was a convent there many years before the dissolution. But that was sold off to a London family. There have been no Catholic nuns since then. We also have two nunneries in the area. Reigate Priory was sold off by good old King Henry, and some rich folk live there now, but there is a nunnery at Mesnil Manor behind Redhill towards the hills. We understood it was the Church of England, but since the Catholic Relief Act and the nuns taking the oath of allegiance[20], rumour has it they celebrate the Catholic mass."

Ethel questioned, "So you are saying that is the only place they could be?"

"Yes. If villains came to a convent here, that would be the only one available to Catholics."

Jonathan was conscious of time passing and asked, "Constable, would you sit with the driver and direct him."

Swan climbed out of the cabin and said, "It is on a side road and

---

[20] Oath of Allegiance: The Catholic Relief Act 1791 provided further freedoms on condition of swearing an additional oath of allegiance of the Protestant succession in the United Kingdom of Great Britain and Ireland. This allowed Catholic Schooling and clergy to operate openly and thus allowed permanent missions to be set up in the largest towns. JS

hard to find in the heavily wooded area up near the hills."

Within ten minutes, the coach turned off the main road, down a lane, heavily wooded on either side, passing the manor house, and proceeded through the woods to some low-set buildings that must be the convent. As the coach stopped, a dog came out barking, but Constable Swan quickly jumped down, patting and calming him.

An elderly nun wearing a black habit, veil and brown scapula appeared from the other side of the coach and smiled at the visitors, saying, "May I be of assistance? I am Sister Mary."

Constable Swan replied, "Sister, might we see the nun in charge, please? We come on urgent police business."

"Certainly. Please follow me."

Jonathan noticed the nun's slight limp as she walked before them but decided it may be prudent not to offer assistance. They followed a long path through the buildings until they came to a hall with an office to one side. She spoke kindly, "Please wait here."

Walking off, she knocked on the door and entered. After several minutes, a younger nun with the same habit and veil but no scapular greeted them.

"Good morning, Constable. God bless you. May I be of assistance?"

"Yes.....!" The constable was unsure of her name.

The nun quickly said, "Call me Mother Celine, please."

"Mother Celine, we come on urgent business. A young girl by the name of Miss Clare Petherton has been kidnapped, and we have reliable information that she has been placed here for protection. The persons involved in the kidnapping may have misled you into thinking she was either their daughter or perhaps a child in desperate need."

The nun said nothing, but the constable could see from her uncomfortable expression that she knew something.

"Mother, it is vital that we find the child, as she must be terrified. Her mother passed away many years ago, and her father collapsed and died last Tuesday. We have been searching for her ever since. It appears there is a sinister plot against her, and we must consider it kidnapping. I am sure you understand that the penalty for this crime is death. There is no commutation."

The mother still stood in silence.

Ethel could bear this no longer and cried out, "Please, Mother, tell us. We have great concerns for the child and travelled all last night, arriving as quickly as possible! Not only has the child been subject to kidnapping, but she is injured and requires assistance."

Mother Celine listened carefully to what Ethel said.

"You came in all that bad weather. My, my! Now, who are you, daughter?"

"I am Mrs Ethel Nibley, Clare's Trustee. There are two other trustees, but given Mr Petherton only died last Tuesday, the attorneys are still trying to contact them. Clare is an only child and has no one else. Those who took her were the butler and Clare's governess from Mr Petherton's estate and had no authority or permission."

Mother Celine could hear the desperation in Mrs Nibley's speech and recognised it came from the heart. She also was aware of who Constable Archibald Swan was."

"You say the child was injured. In what way?"

Ethel said, "She sprained her left ankle falling from a pony and is in much pain."

Mother Celine was now convinced. She had heard enough!

"We have no child by the name of Clare Petherton with us. But we have a young girl called Angela Smith who was delivered here for her protection. There was some trouble at home. Mr and Mrs Steadman, who delivered her, advised us of a doctor who prescribed a powder to make her sleep. The man and woman are expected here again this afternoon. I thought you were them. Perhaps, Mrs Nibley, you might meet Angela with me."

"Yes, please!"

"Gentlemen, if you would wait here, as we do not encourage outsiders to enter our buildings."

The mother prioress led Ethel away. Jonathan, Michael and Archie were surprised when the elderly nun appeared with a tray of three cups of water and some cakes.

"Some refreshments always help!"

"Thank you, Sister."

As they were walking, Mother Celine spoke in a friendly voice, "Angela could hardly walk when she arrived yesterday. She was in much pain. We did what we could to assist her."

Ethel's emotions overcame her, and she sobbed while taking the nun's hand and kissing it.

"Oh, Mother! It must be her! I pray it is."

The nun led Ethel into a small building with several separate rooms. She opened the first door, revealing a bed with a fast-asleep young girl. Ethel approached, carefully lifted the blanket and immediately recognised Clare.

"Clare! Clare, thank God!"

Turner Household, Guildford, Surrey ...

Clementine entered the kitchen and found Simeon, William, Madeline and Marcia all eating porridge under the watchful eye of Mrs Jennings.

The cook asked, "Where is Katherine?"

"She is coming! I think she must have overslept, but she is dressing now. Is there any news of Clare Petherton?"

The children waited for the cook to answer. Mrs Jennings, noticing the children peering her way, said, "Nothing yet. We may hear some news tonight, but I doubt it. Probably Sunday at the earliest."

Clementine frowned and joined the children for some breakfast. Simeon and William finished quickly and rushed out to the woodshed.

"They are in a hurry!" Clementine was always suspicious when the boys were eager to do their chores. Madeline looked up and explained, "Simeon, William and I are going to the river. We will meet Levi, Archie and Sophie at Mossy's shed for some riding."

Marcia was excited, "Maddie, Maddie, can Buster and I come?"

"No, little one. We can't even take Nosey for fear it will scare the pony. Mr Spencer will only let us come."

Marcia stamped her foot and screamed, "That's not fair. I want to see Mossy."

"What's not fair, Marcia?" Katherine rushed in and sat at the table.

Mrs Jennings explained that the little one was not invited for some horse riding.

As a kind young girl, Katherine said, "You can play with me this morning, Marcy. I am not keen on horses, and Rosalind is coming up, so we might take you on a walk and do some Saturday shopping. Perhaps even buy you some sweets."

When Marcia heard the mention of sweets, she suddenly said, "I want to go shopping! So does Buster."

The girls all smiled, and Madeline asked, "Would you buy a sweetmeat for me too, Katherine?"

After an hour, the boys were satisfied enough wood was ready for the next few days. They collected Madeline and set off for the shed. The weather had been horrible on Thursday and Friday nights and was now patchy, the low clouds signalling more rain coming. With this in mind, they jogged along, hoping Madeline would keep up with them. It was raining when they reached the shed, and they ducked inside, finding Mossy and the others.

Simeon asked, "Where is your father?"

Levi said, "He's gone. He said it was too wet! So we will give Mossy a rub down and a feed, and that will be it. Sorry about the riding."

Simeon and William were disappointed, but Madeline asked if she could help rub down the pony. The boys agreed, and Sophie decided to assist from the other side.

As the girls worked, Levi sat back, pulled a few pipes out of his bag, and lit one up.

Simeon asked, "Aren't you too young to smoke a pipe?"

Archie answered, "No, you can smoke at any age as long as your parents don't find out!" Archie grinned at Levi, and they both started laughing.

Simeon curtly replied, "Well, isn't that the point?" Simeon was not interested in having smoke in his lungs.

Levi stood and menacingly asked, "You're not going to tell, are you, Sim?"

Simeon quietly thought about the question and answered, "Only if they ask me?"

"Well, they won't, will they? No one is going to blab, are they?" Levi looked around menacingly at his friends. They all nodded in agreement. As the children were leaving, William told Simeon he would stay for a while.

"Don't smoke a pipe, Will! If Father finds out, you will be in big trouble." William shrugged and started rubbing the pony again.

After the others left, Levi asked William, "Do you want to try, Will?"

"Yep."

Levi lit another pipe and handed it to him. With a big smile, William asked, "What do I do with it?"

Levi grinned at Archie and said, "You suck in and swallow the smoke. Suck hard like this. It tastes nice."

Archie covered his mouth as he laughed, knowing where this was leading.

William asked, "Like sugar?"

"Not quite." Levi demonstrated and sucked in and turned to blow the smoke out without William seeing. There was no need as William was already sucking on the pipe, and smoke was filling his mouth and nostrils. He blew it out and coughed slightly.

Levi encouraged him, "That's good, Will, but you need to swallow the smoke. Then you will be a man!"

"Wow! Will I?"

Levi and Archie, both grinning, said, "Yep!"

William immediately sucked hard on his pipe and swallowed the smoke. It felt unpleasant, but he wanted to be a man, so he continued.

They all laughed, and Archie patted Will on the back, "That's my man!"

William sucked on and swallowed far more smoke than Archie and Levi could believe. Archie said quietly to Levi, "Should we tell him to stop? He will be sick. He is already going green!"

"Nah, let him suffer. He will remember it for the rest of his life. His first smoke."

Archie smiled but became uncomfortable as William lost the colour on his face.

The seven-year-old took a large suck and swallowed it quickly. William's head spun, and he rubbed his soar eyes from the smoke. Then he started coughing and gasping for breath. Levi was rolling around laughing as Will's nausea kept increasing, and then he fell on the ground and crawled out of the shed. From inside, the boys could hear him vomiting. Archie came out with a watering can, bent beside the boy and said, "Have some water, Will. It will help."

The boy grabbed the can, drank the water quickly, and then vomited again. Archie sat him against the shed wall to get some breath down his windpipe. The young lad looked deadly white; from inside, Archie could still hear Levi laughing.

"Come on, Will. I will take you home."

Archie helped him, put an arm under his armpit, and pulled him up against his side. Walking through the rain seemed to help, and the coughing stopped, but he occasionally felt like vomiting. By the time they passed the doctor's surgery, William was ready to drop again, and a curious Doctor Sopwith saw them from his window as they struggled on.

David Sopwith rushed outside and picked up William in his arms.

"Follow me, Archie. Your father is not in today, so it is safe for you to tell me what happened!"

Bachelor's Quarters, near the River Wey, Guildford, England ...
Jessica Swamp knocked on the door and opened it. Her brother sat at a small table eating cooked fish and potatoes. Peter lifted his eyes and smiled, "Come and join me, Jess. There is enough for two!" Jess was not impressed with the messy state of the room.

"No, Peter, I am not here for lunch. I wanted some advice from you."

"It must be serious, as you should be at work."

"No, we are given around an hour and a half for lunch. Are you enjoying your day off?"

"I am bored stiff. I don't know why I must take a day off, but Father insists. He says I will kill myself if I work seven days a week. But I like working on the farm."

"Every so often, your body needs a rest. Why don't you visit the Institute with me and read some books? Oh! ...." Jess suddenly realised her mistake in what she said.

"Since when could you read?"

Blushing, Jess admitted, "A friend at work is teaching me. I love it, and I want to read so much, Peter. It opens a new world for me."

Her brother sat there thinking about her reply. Their father had always denied Jess's education at home, but her mother secretly taught her. When Kevin Swamp accidentally discovered a lesson taking place, he belted his wife and demanded it stopped, but Willamina found other ways to teach her daughter. Bless Mother, as she had suffered greatly for her children.

"Make the most of it, little sister and make sure Father does not find out."

Jess smiled and sat at the table. Gazing around, she said, "I will help you clean up before I go. You can't go on living in a mess, Peter. You need the place clean."

"Thanks, Jess. Now, what advice do you need."

"This is very personal, so don't tell Mother, Father, or Alf. Promise?"

"Yes."

"Peter! When I walk home at night, the Reverend Hotspur meets me near the shops and walks me home. He has done it twice now. He is very nice and acts like a gentleman. I must admit I like him and enjoy his company."

"A Reverend!"

"Yes. I am sure he has a good future in the church. They usually receive a stipend far more than our father's income. The church tithe pays for it."

"That's true."

"Do you think he likes me, Peter?"

Peter smiled and said, "Well, I am sure he enjoys your company as he has made it happen twice. That says something! You would not be in his class, Jess. Farmers are not highly regarded."

Jess was not ashamed of who she was and felt slightly insulted, "Why not, Peter? Without farmers like you, Father and Alfie, people would starve in England."

Peter scratched his head and wondered why Jess could be bothered with a clergyman. They had never attended Sunday services and felt hostility towards the church due to the tithe. Why should they pay a tithe for these useless ministers to laud it over them? He was sure he should dissuade Jess from this young curate.

"I think you should stay clear of him, Jess. He is probably up to no good. Why would he want to know us? We are not in his class, and he will not stoop to ours."

"But I think I like him, Peter. He is so nice, and I don't want to stay a servant forever."

Peter was now worried about his little sister. He could see no good coming of this relationship. Also, he did not trust churchmen. They always portrayed themselves as upright citizens, but underneath, they were just as bad as ordinary men.

"Why not find a good farm boy? There are plenty around. I can introduce you to some."

"Peter, I want more than that. I have worked for the Turners for months and seen their wonderful lives. Reading and learning will take me there. I don't care how I get there but I want more."

"Don't tell father and mother that. You might get a beating. Let me see what I can find out about Hotspur. Merryn works in the pub, and she hears a lot of gossip. I will ask her to see what she can uncover."

Jess knew of her older brother's attraction to Merryn and wondered if anything had developed.

"Will you marry Merryn, Peter?"

"I hope so, but she may be like you and want more!"

"Sorry, Brother. I did not want to insult you, but I am ambitious and want a good life. Times are changing, and people with learning can do anything."

"Jess, be careful. Most people around here don't think that way. They are still comfortable with country life. But if you want change, then perhaps you should start attending church. It may introduce you to others besides Hotspur. I don't trust clergymen."

Jess considered what her brother said and gave a smile. He was right; perhaps it was best to keep her ambition quiet. The last thing she wanted was to be the centre of attention.

"Do you think it would hurt if I attended church tomorrow? It would look better if you came with me. I would feel more comfortable if I had some support. I have never been to church before and would not know what to do."

Jessica's brother had no intention of attending church. He could think of nothing worse.

"But I will be working tomorrow!"

"Peter, Father can replace you, and perhaps instead of taking off Saturdays, you could change it to Sundays? Father won't mind, especially if Mother backs us up. You could come early to dinner tonight and talk with Mother. Please!"

Her brother had always had a soft spot for his sister. When she was younger, he often stood between Jess and his father, defending her. Jessica could now care for herself, but Peter knew things were still not right at home. He had moved out as he could not stand his father's standover tactics. But Peter could see that this clergyman was already affecting Jess's heart. He would not stand in the way of her happiness.

"Jess, I can't go tomorrow as I have had today off. If Father agrees to change my day, I will go the Sunday after. I can make the excuse that it is Merryn's only day off. He will believe that."

Jessica was overjoyed, "Thank you, Peter. You will need a coat. I know where I can find one."

"They will get a surprise when we both turn up at church. I will go on one condition: we sit in the back seat and don't go up for communion. I am nowhere as good as all the other people who attend church."

Jess jumped and hugged her brother tight, who slightly blushed, not accustomed to this treatment.

"You will not regret this. Thank you, Peter! Now, if you want to marry Merryn, let's clean this place up!"

"You know I would not bring her here, Jess! That would not be proper!"

Doctor's Surgery, Guildford, England, ...

"Why were you boys smoking, Archie? If your parents find out, you will be in hot water. As it is, I am not sure how William will explain this. Perhaps it is better if he doesn't."

Holding a bucket under his chin, William retched again but could bring nothing up. The doctor gave him some more water.

"It was just some fun, Doctor. We meant him no harm."

"No harm! Swallowing the smoke would have done him no good at all. You are fortunate he did not fall unconscious. He may have stopped breathing altogether. Sometimes, the body does the opposite of what you expect. Never do this again, please, Archie?"

"Yes, Sir."

Archie sat there petrified, knowing what a mistake he had made. The doctor could see the sorrow on his face and knew the boy was now fearful of the consequences. He was also worried, wondering how Mr Turner would react if he learned about this. William must be kept safe until he recovers. He would need at least three more hours before he was well again.

"Archie, you are not the first to make mistakes with smoking. It's best if nothing is said about this at all! But we need to keep William out of sight while he suffers. The best solution is for you and William to come home with me, join us for lunch, and wait for Will to recover.

I will send a message to both families advising that you are having lunch with Lady Emma and me and discussing sailing boats."

Archie was not slow and agreed with the proposal straight away. William continued retching.

"Thanks, Doctor Sopwith."

"Well, I can't let my swimming students get into trouble, can I?"

They both grinned like little boys who had escaped from an angry giant.

Harting House, St James's Square, London …

The weather had turned miserable on Friday evening, with fast-moving storms raging across southern England, trees down and some roads blocked. Lady Anne South decided it would be safer to shelter at Ewell than press on further at night, and they agreed on rooms in her uncle's pub. The weather cleared on Saturday morning, and the coach arrived at Harting around three in the afternoon.

"Welcome, Lady South. I understand you were delayed due to bad weather. I hope the journey was not too trying?"

"Thank you, Staines. It was safer taking rooms at Ewell than continuing in that terrible weather. We had a good run today, apart from several trees being moved off the road."

"Will Doctor Bassington be staying, Milady?"

"No, Staines! Doctor Bassington is due at his accommodation in Harley Street following afternoon tea. Mr Wood will be with us for three days while various legal problems are sorted out. Mary Hedge, my maid, will require a room in the servants' quarters, please. Would you arrange some refreshments while the staff unload our luggage? We skipped lunch, so we are all hungry."

"Certainly, Milady. I have left mail in your room. Dinner is planned for seven if that is suitable."

"Yes, thank you."

"If you and Mr Wood follow me, please, I will show you to your rooms."

"Thank you, Staines. Oh, Staines! Sorry, I forgot. Miss Victoria Sopwith and her maid will arrive on Tuesday afternoon. You will need to arrange rooms for them, please."

After Blake Wood was settled in, Staines led Lady Anne to her room on the second floor. He gave a slight cough after he opened the door for Anne.

"Is there a question, Staines?"

"I am sorry to bother you after a long trip, Milady. However, might I enquire if there has been any progress on the estate's financial position?"

Anne knew that the cash shortages had seriously inconvenienced Staines and felt pity for him, as the butler was probably concerned about his job security.

"Yes, Staines. Significant progress has been made, and my trip here partly involves meetings to continue resolving the situation. There is no word on Sir Hugh, but we expect a letter within days advising of his health and possibly financial information from Jamaica."

"Thank you, Milady. You will understand my concern?"

"Yes. Mr Stem has been briefed on the monthly payments, so those should now be regular. I am sure we are through the worst of it, Staines. There is no need to worry."

"That is a great relief, Lady Anne. Thank you."

Anne smiled, "Monday morning, Mr Wood and I will require the carriage ready at nine fifteen. I have an appointment with the attorneys at nine-thirty. Mr Wood is a Guildford attorney who will also assist the family."

"Very good, Milady. Refreshments will be ready in fifteen minutes. As Mrs Wapples is at Fintelton, I have employed a temporary cook. I can assure you Mrs Falconer is up to the task."

"Thank you, Staines."

With that, the butler was gone, and Anne closed the door, threw her hat on the bed, wandered across to the window and looked out on St James Square. She did not see the view or the strange weather with the rain falling hard again. Her first thoughts were of Robert and his safety. She had no idea where he was except that he was in the Mediterranean. Then she thought of Clare Petherton. Would her father and Ethel have reached Redhill yet?

The rain pelted against the window. Anne was tired. She turned and walked across to the bed and lay down, but suddenly remembering the urgent information they needed from Stephen Polkinghorne, she rushed to her desk. Quickly writing and addressing a note, she pulled the servant cord and sat back, waiting.

"Yes, Milady!"

"Stuart, would you please have this sent immediately by a rider to a Mr Stephen Polkinghorne in Mayfair? Thank you."

"Yes, Milady."

She passed the letter across and watched the footman race off for the servants' stairwell. Satisfied she was free of commitments, Anne closed the door and lay down on the bed again. Soon, she was fast asleep.

Downstairs, Staines approached Dr Bassington, who was taking some afternoon tea.

"Dr Bassington! This message arrived for you yesterday. I believe it is an urgent message from Sir Robert South."

Neville thanked the butler and took the message from the tray. He frowned as he read the news about Admiral Crouch.

"Staines, is the coach unpacked yet?"

"I believe so, Doctor."

"When Lady South comes down, would you explain that I have an urgent request to attend on Admiral Crouch? He is near death, and Sir Robert has requested my help. I will take the coach there, and then they can deliver me to my lodgings. I will send it back here then."

"Thank you, doctor. Should I advise Lady South that you will return for dinner?"

"No, I will have some supper at my lodgings. My wife arrives on Tuesday with Victoria Sopwith, so I must ready the rooms for her. Thank you for the offer, Staines. When do you set up camp at the Isle of Wight? I understand the staff here go down for the summer?"

"We usually pack up in the last week of May and finish setting up the residence there for the Earl by mid-June. I am unsure how long Lady South remains in London, so I will leave a temporary housekeeper and a few other staff in case Harting is required over the summer. Will we see you at Luccombe Bay this summer?"

"We have been invited, Staines, but I doubt we will make it. If we do, it will be a short visit indeed. Now I must be off."

"Yes, Doctor. I will advise Lady South at dinner. If your lodgings are unsuitable for your lady, plenty of vacant rooms are available here. I am sure the Earl and Countess would be honoured now your sister-in-law is here."

"That is kind, Staines. I will keep it in mind."

Neville gathered his coat and bag and gave Staines a parting smile as he headed through the front entrance.

Mayfair, London, England …

Doctor Neville Bassington arrived at Admiral Crouch's residence around five o'clock in the afternoon. Despite being tired from the long coach journey from Guildford, he was prepared for a difficult task ahead. The message from Robert painted a solemn picture, and Neville was unsure he would add anything to what the doctors had already prescribed.

Surprised by the security, he explained that he was expected and that Lady Crouch would vouch for him. As security sorted out the situation, he admired the substantial three-storied house before him.

Following Lady Crouch up the stairs, she said, "Thank you for coming, Neville. Why …? Was it only last Tuesday night that I saw Robert? I believe they sailed on Wednesday for the East. Are you related?"

"Yes, Lady Crouch. Given what has been on your mind, you may not recall, but I married Beth, the sister of Robert's wife, Anne."

Lady Crouch stopped on the stairs and turned around, "Of course. I remember you were one of the Doctors at Robert and Anne's wedding."

"That is correct, but please let us continue to the Admiral. I understand that he is very weak."

As they entered the Admiral's bedroom, Lady Crouch explained how the Admiral had fallen ill and suffered a stroke soon after.

"The Navy doctors have been treating him ever since."

Neville asked if she would light more candles and then wake the Admiral. He placed his medical bag beside the bed and looked at the sleeping man. He noticed the room was warm from the fireplace, but the Admiral had several blankets over him.

Removing two blankets, he asked, "Why does he have so many blankets, Milady?"

"The doctors told me to always keep three blankets over him."

"I see."

"Franklin! The doctor is here to examine you. Wake up, dear!"

Neville saw that the Admiral was groggy but awake and slowly opened his eyes.

As Neville leaned over him, the Admiral asked, "Who the devil are you?"

"Doctor Neville Bassington, a Harley Street specialist in Major Trauma. I am also the brother-in-law of Sir Robert South."

"Oh!"

After thoroughly examining the Admiral, Neville sat back and considered what he had found. He yawned and then addressed the wide-awake Navy man.

"Admiral Crouch, I understand you are very tired, but I want you to listen carefully, please. Ma'am!" He indicated that Lady Crouch should join them. "Admiral, I am not sure who your treating doctors are, but I wish to change their instructions, and I will explain why.

I am confused by what originally caused the onset of your troubles. But, Sir, if it had been a stroke, there would be some paralysis or other symptoms such as slurring of speech or difficulty understanding what folks are saying. You have no paralysis, no problems with communication or other apparent symptoms. It is more likely that you have not suffered a stroke as you are quite lucid, and all your bodily functions are working as expected, which would not be the case after a stroke.

Regarding your tiredness, I would say, yes, you have suffered a severe cold or infection. But that has passed."

Lady Crouch protested, "But Doctor, he has been near death! He is so tired and has no energy."

"Ma'am, the fireplace keeps the room at a comfortable temperature. By keeping three blankets on the Admiral, his body has been trying to cope with excess heat for a lengthy period. The heat would have forced a temperature. He appears dehydrated, and I assume the doctors have been bleeding him?"

"Yes, every day in the mornings."

"That would have further weakened him. From what you have told me, he has not kept up his liquids and is dehydrated. Another week of the same treatment would probably have resulted in a serious failure of the organs and death.

We must change his situation immediately. Firstly, please only use one blanket when he complains of being cold. He must immediately drink a glass of water and continue this every two hours for twelve hours. After that, he may drink as he requires, but please ensure he remains hydrated. The Admiral must continue resting for three days as he is weak. Make sure they give him no more powders, and there is to be no more bleeding. This practice of taking blood is not required for his condition and may risk infection. I believe the powders prescribed have drugged him and been partly responsible for his tired state. Admiral, I want you up and walking around the house within three days. You should start gradually but try to build up your strength."

Lady Crouch asked, "Doctor Bassington, you are saying the Admiral is far better than we had imagined, and the blankets and powders are making him so tired."

"Yes, Milady. I will return tomorrow night and expect a significant improvement in the Admiral. If the Navy doctors wish to contact me, refer them to this letterhead."

Neville passed a printed sheet of paper showing his contact details. He then passed the Admiral a glass of water and, with a smile, said, "Time to make a full recovery, Sir. Within a week, you should be ready to travel to your estate in Hampshire."

Harting, St James' Square, London ...
"Milady. It is Mary. Dinner will be served in fifteen minutes. Will you come down, or would you like something brought up here?"

Anne felt the warmth of a blanket over her and opened her eyes. Several candles now lit the room, and it was dark outside.

"My, I must have drifted off. I will come down, Mary. There are several issues Mr Wood and I must discuss. Perhaps if you would assist me for a few minutes."

"Yes, Milady. I have not unpacked your luggage yet. I will do that while you have dinner."

"Thank you, Mary. Is your accommodation suitable?"

"Oh, yes, Milady. Very comfortable, indeed." The maid passed across an envelope and said, "Milady, This message was delivered by a Mr Stephen Polkinghorne."

Anne quickly opened the envelope and read the message.

"He says he can find the information we require about Mr Petherton's details. He apologises, but due to appointments, he cannot deliver this until tomorrow at half past five in the afternoon. Well, we must be ready for him, Mary."

"We are making excellent time, Gentlemen. On our port side is Gibraltar, and the eastern Mediterranean lies ahead. We will be in Malta by next Sunday morning if this wind holds. However, a more reliable estimate is probably Tuesday week."

The Diplomats seemed happy with their progress and adjourned to the great cabin for recreation.

"Mr Fenton!"

"Yes, Captain."

Robert walked to the stern of the poop deck out of hearing distance from the other crew members.

Watching the wake of the frigate trail off in the distance, the captain said, "Mr Fenton, you are making good progress with the crew, but I fear they are not yet in battle readiness. We approach Algeria and then Tunisia; we know these countries are not friendly! As we have already discussed, the Admiralty intelligence is that Ottoman frigates and schooners are exercising near Tunis. My orders are to deliver these diplomats safely, no matter the cost."

Fenton was beginning to understand there was trouble ahead.

"If our crew were more battle-ready, I would have no hesitation in following the shortest route. But we are not, and I would like more time so you can bring the crew up to speed. I was impressed when you achieved a battle station's time of one minute fifty-nine seconds. That is a good improvement. Now, I require you to bring that down to one minute and thirty seconds."

Fenton's eyes opened wide. After swallowing, he said, "Captain, that is not possible! I have never heard of that time for a frigate."

"Mr Fenton, my old crew on *Restless* achieved that."

"Yes, Sir. But that was a schooner."

"Yes, but a large schooner! Mr Fenton, we are sailing without any support. If we were to meet four Ottoman fighting ships, we would not stand a chance despite our ability. We would either be sunk or need to surrender. Now, I want you to assemble your officers and mid-shipmen and discuss how you can achieve the time for battle stations I require. I suggest you consider where the sailors are stationed so they are always near their gun crew positions. After tonight, we might call battle stations at any time. Bring the officers up to the poop deck here and discuss the requirement. I will stand watch for the next hour as you make your plans. Once this is complete, you have the rest of the day to achieve your objective. Do I make myself clear, Mr Fenton?"

"Yes, Sir!"

"You may proceed, Mr Fenton."

"Aye, Sir."

Captain South could see Fenton was disturbed and not confident he would achieve his captain's wishes. Robert was unconcerned as it was time for this crew to feel battle stress. There was no better way to learn than through mistakes. Robert was encouraged as he heard the command.

"Mr Peters spread the word. All officers and midshipmen meet on the poop in five minutes. Hurry man! We have little time."

Lieutenant Peters was off in a second, and quickly, officers appeared enquiring what the meeting was about.

The captain, satisfied that Fenton would work hard at achieving an impossible goal, approached Mr Trotters, the master, and called, "Trotters!"

"Aye, Captain."

"Plot me a course just south of Mallorca and then on to the Strait of Bonifacio at the top of Sardinia. From there, across to the Messina Strait at the top of Sicily and onto Malta. I must know how long it will take if this wind holds."

Trotters stood momentarily and asked, "I thought we were hurrying to Malta, Captain. Are we trying to keep out of sight?"

With a confident look and a low voice, South replied, "Yes, Trotters. You know we are not battle-ready yet. I do not fancy being captured by the Ottomans. But keep it to yourself."

Trotters smiled and replied, "Aye, Sir."

Harting, St James's Square, London …

Shortly after half past five in the afternoon, Mr Stephen Polkinghorne arrived at Harting. Anne had finished welcoming Victoria Sopwith and her maid, who were now using the time before dinner to unpack.

"Milady! Mr Stephen Polkinghorne has arrived and is in the drawing room."

"Thank you, Mary. Please have Staines advise him. I will be there in a few minutes."

Anne had been feeling overly tired for the last few days. She found that she required rest by this time of day, which was beginning to worry her. There was no time now for resting, and she must ready herself to meet Mr Polkinghorne.

As she entered the drawing room, Stephen Polkinghorne immediately stood.

"Mr Polkinghorne. Thank you for waiting. I am pleased to make your acquaintance again. I apologise for disturbing your Sunday, but Mr Petherton's death and the circumstances have left Guilford in turmoil. We are desperate to locate his business and find his attorneys."

"Lady South. I understand, and please do not fret, as I have only been waiting a few minutes. I received your message and have compiled the information you required." He passed the envelope across to her. "Mr Petherton is an old friend of mine, and I have attended many functions with him over the years. A very pleasant man! It is a tragedy that he has passed away, particularly for his daughter, Clare, who will be orphaned. Here are his details, business address, name of the manager and his secretary, and the name of his attorneys and their address. You will find Green & Green Attorneys very accommodating. They are one of London's best firms."

Anne took the details with pleasure, "Thank you, Mr Polkinghorne, that is most kind of you. I hope we have not caused you too much trouble. This information will solve the puzzle for us regarding his attorneys. You are probably unaware of the circumstances, but he died on Tuesday afternoon at my father's house in Guildford. Late that night, the butler and governess kidnapped the daughter."

"Clare?" Stephen was taken aback and most concerned. He stood and paced to and fro, repeatedly saying, "I should have been there!"

Ane was surprised by the extent of Stephen's concern. Trying to calm him, she said, "Mr Polkinghorne, the death was sudden and unexpected. There was nothing you could have done from here in London. But you may assist us now. It is a complicated story, but my father and the police are trying to find the girl. The problem has been that we do not know the details of his attorneys or Clare's trustees. Mr Polkinghorne, may I invite you to dinner with us tonight? We have taken up much of your time."

"Thank you, Lady South, that is most generous, but unfortunately,

I have another engagement, perhaps another time. However, given what you told me, I can further assist you. I am one of Clare's trustees. Benjamin made me a trustee over ten years ago. I am unaware of the other trustee, but I am sure I could find one of the partners of Green's Attorneys tonight and acquire that information for you. I am also familiar with his business and the manager there. Let me write down the details for you while I am here. His building is in the same street as mine at the Isle of Dogs."

Anne was astonished as Stephen commenced writing. She wanted clarification and asked, "Are you telling me you are one of Clare Petherton's trustees?'

"Yes. Benjamin and I were close friends many years ago while we developed our businesses. We often met for lunch or dinner. When Benjamin married Miriam, we saw less of each other, and then he moved the family to Guildford. Being located in the country made it difficult to catch up regularly, and when Miriam died in childbirth with Clare, Benjamin was a lost soul. That year, Benjamin asked me to be a trustee for Mark and Clare in case he passed away before they came of age. He was a very caring man and planned for his children. When Mark died in a riding accident, Benjamin once again was devastated. All his progress since Miriam's passing was lost, and it has taken him years to gain confidence again. It is a sad story."

"Mr Polkinghorne, I had no idea of the connection. Now, are you sure you would not stay for dinner?"

"No, thank you, Lady South. But if I might ask one other question. Since we last met at the Bath Hotel, I have had no word about Lady Clarissa Wendarm. I had done my best for her, but when she disappeared from my home, I decided it may be best if I resisted continuing the search. Might I ask if she did invade the Fintelton Estate, and do you know her whereabouts now?"

Anne stood there ashamed, realising no word about Lady Clarissa had been sent to Mr Polkinghorne. Surely, the Countess would have written.

"Mr Polkinghorne! What can I say? I must apologise as I thought the Countess would have written to you. I am sorry to advise you that she did try to invade the Fintelton Estate, but soon after that, she died and was buried in the Petersfield graveyard of the Church of England.

I am very sorry that no one advised you."

Anne could see the grief on this gentleman's face, and for a second or two, he could not speak.

"Thank you. I have often wondered about the outcome, and I should have written, but I …….. Well, it is done now. I must be off and find this attorney. I will have the information delivered, Lady Anne."

"Thank you, Mr Polkinghorne, for your assistance. I am sure we will meet again soon about Clare."

"Yes! Yes, Lady South."

A downcast, Stephen Polkinghorne left Harting, and once the coach was far enough away, Stephen pulled out his handkerchief and wiped the tears from his eyes.

"Clarissa, you poor thing. Godspeed!"

Offices of Manifold & Stout, Attorneys, London, …

It was a rush on Monday morning, but Lady Anne and Mr Blake Wood arrived on time for their appointment with the senior partner, Mr Evan Finchley. Mr Wood was unexpected, but this was soon remedied.

Lady Anne finished her explanation, "At this stage, I am unaware if Clare Petherton has been recovered. If she has not been found, the information from Mr Polkinghorne should be of assistance."

Mr Finchley was still wrestling with the full story and needed further clarification, "So, what you are saying is that Mrs Nibley, your father's housekeeper, is one of Clare Petherton's trustees. Mr Stephen Polkinghorne is also a trustee, and we have no information on the third."

"That is correct, Mr Finchley."

"Well, I think the critical issue here is protecting young Clare. The details of Mr Petherton's estate will be solved in time. I will introduce Mr Wood to our partner, Mr Hadley, who deals with international clients. He will accompany you to Greens, and you may follow up on the third trustee. They will ask for written permission from the other trustees to release the name you require. The process may take some weeks. However, it must be commenced. I have a feeling that custody will be the next battle. But if we have two trustees onside, we should win."

Blake Wood appreciated the assistance, "Thank you, Mr Finchley."

"Mr Wood, I suggest that while Greens start the wheels turning this afternoon, you visit Mr Petherton's business and brief the manager. There is every possibility that Steadman may turn up there to create mischief. It would be best if Mr Ilses is aware of the full situation! But don't mention this to Greens, or they will think you are interfering with their client. Just tell Mr Iles to meet with Greens tomorrow to clarify the situation."

"I will do that, Mr Finchley."

Mr Finchley smiled, "Let us hope Clare Petherton is found soon. Lady Anne, if you would excuse us for five minutes, I will introduce Mr Woods to Mr Hadley. Would you care for some tea or coffee while you wait?"

"A coffee would be appreciated, Mr Finchley."

The coffee was soon served, and the senior partner returned within ten minutes.

"Lady Anne, I think Mr Wood will be busy for some time now, so might we move on to Mrs Constance? The lady has repeatedly been in contact and requests a meeting with a family representative to recommence the financial agreement set up with the Earl. I have booked a time for the following Monday, the seventh of May, and would ask if you will be the family representative."

"Yes, I will, Mr Finchley and I have authorisations here from the Earl and Countess."

Anne passed these across, and Mr Finchley carefully read them.

"I see that the Earl and Countess, while giving you authority to negotiate, have asked that I be present to advise you. Is that acceptable to you, Lady Anne?"

"It is, indeed! I will value your advice most highly, Mr Finchley. Now, there is much to explain about the enquiries that Sir Robert and I have made."

"I would appreciate that, and I will take notes."

"Yes, but before we start, as there is no time to lose, I must present you with this document that has been uncovered. A party closely involved in the events over twenty years ago has provided names and details of other gentlemen benefiting from Mrs Constance's company. It is reliably believed that these gentlemen also settled with Mrs Constance, providing her with a lifetime income in each case."

Mr Finchley smiled as he took the document and said, "I have a feeling I know who provided this document, but I will not ask."

Anne smiled, "Do you have contacts who can verify these details, Mr Finchley?"

The attorney quickly scanned the letter and looked up, "In answer to your question, Lady Anne, I believe so! One of the gentlemen mentioned here is also a client of Manifold & Stout."

Anne suddenly enjoyed a great feeling of relief and confidence. She sat back in her chair and smiled.

Turner Household, Guildford, England, …
The coach arrived mid-morning, and Aggie called the other staff, "Come quickly. Clare is with them!"

Remembering Clare was injured, Jessica ran down the steps and helped the injured lass out of the coach. Hoisting Clare's arm over her shoulders, Jess assisted her as she limped up the stairs to meet Clementine and a squealing Marcia. Jonathan and an excited Ethel Nibley followed into the house.

Clemmie embraced Clare, "You are safe, Clare. We were all so worried."

Clare smiled and said, "I was worried myself, Clemmie!"

They all laughed freely, relieving the tension in the air.

Mrs Jennings said, "You should have sent a message, Mr Turner. Clare, it is wonderful having you back in the house!"

"Thank you, Mrs Jennings. I wish it were under different circumstances, but it would be good to be settled now and catch my breath."

Ethel Nibley agreed, "So you shall, Clare. We shall place you in the guest room until all the legal issues are settled. Would you like to visit home and pick up some things before you settle down, or will we do that later?"

"Perhaps tomorrow, Mrs Nibley. If I might borrow a night dress from one of the girls, that will be sufficient. I am afraid of visiting home now. I will have more courage tomorrow. Do you know where my father lies?"

"Yes. Your father's body will be at the funeral director's premises."

"Might we visit later?"

"Certainly, Dear."

Jonathan left Clare with Ethel and the others and went to his study. He called in Aggie.

"Has there been any word from Lady Anne or Mr Wood?"

"No, Mr Turner. I was hoping you would have news."

"No, Aggie. We are still in the dark. All we know is that Ethel is a rightful trustee. No more than that! I hope the others in London are making headway."

Isle of Dogs, London, England, ...

Blake Wood juggled through the noisy crowd as he checked each warehouse on either side of the dingy street, hoping to find Mr Petherton's business. Traffic was everywhere as traders bought and sold, carts being loaded or unloaded, and a steady stream of people, to and from the dock at the end of the street, passed. There were so many discussions, shouting, and yelling on the road that it would be hard to hear if a conversation was necessary. The buildings were old, and many had no names or street numbers.

Searching for number forty-one, he knew he had the correct side of the road as the numbers he could find were odd. He decided to enter one and ask.

The building was shabby outside but reasonably clean and quiet inside. A clerk sat at the reception desk, and a man stood behind him.

"Excuse me, but is this number forty-one?"

"No, mate. We are number thirty-nine. You need the building next door! Petherton's Wines and Tobacco!"

"Thank you."

The man standing added, "Mate, they usually open and close early. It is three now; if you are lucky, someone might be there."

"Thanks!"

Blake left quickly and walked along the front of the property next door. It was a far larger building with two barn-type doors allowing carts to enter and depart from different areas. The building was in good repair, with the front entrance between the barn doors. He breathed in relief as an 'OPEN' sign was still inside the window. He quickly entered.

The latticework walls of the hallway gave a direct view of the storehouses on either side. Blake saw at least thirty men opening and closing large boxes filled with racks of wine bottles and straw in each storehouse. Some men had journals and were writing as each bottle was checked. Moving along the passageway to the steps that led to the next floor, he found a sign. It read 'All Visitors Proceed Upstairs'.

Blake smiled and thought this was more like an establishment that Benjamin would run.

A reception desk was at the top of the stairs, but it was empty. However, a bell graced the front of the desk. Picking up the bell, he gave it a shake.

The sound of approaching footsteps preceded a suited middle-aged man opening the door and, in a polished voice, asking, "May I be of assistance."

"Yes, I am Mr Blake Wood, an attorney from Guildford. I am looking for the manager, Mr Iles, please."

The man smiled and said, "Mr Jerome Iles at your service, Sir."

"Mr Iles, I wonder if there is somewhere confidential where we can talk."

Mr Iles became suspicious, "You will understand that in a suburb such as this, we do not let strangers enter our offices. Would you have any identification, Sir?"

"Certainly, Mr Iles."

Blake put his briefcase on the desk, and at once, Jerome Iles took a step backwards, ensuring the door behind him was open if he needed to retreat quickly.

"I did not intend to scare you, Mr Iles, but it is easier with my briefcase on the desk. Ah, here it is, my practice certificate. I also have some papers signed by Mr Petherton."

Iles seemed more relaxed, "You should have said so, Mr Wood. I was not aware you had an association with Mr Petherton."

"Is there somewhere we can talk?"

"Yes, follow me, please."

Jerome Iles led Blake into a conference room lit by candles. He offered a chair at the long table and sat down himself.

"I would offer you tea or coffee, but the receptionist has gone home. We usually close at three, but you are lucky today as we undertake our end-of-month stocktake. I should take the open sign down soon."

"There is no need for refreshments, Mr Iles. Is this room sound-proof?"

"Well, I don't know. Why do you ask."

"I am about to give you some rather bad news, so I thought it might be best if you hear it first before any of your employees."

Mr Ilse was now looking concerned, "Everyone else is downstairs."

Blake Wood nodded and commenced in a low but steady voice, "I must advise you that Mr Benjamin Petherton died last Tuesday in Guildford."

"My goodness! Why has it taken so long for us to be advised? Surely, the butler would have given you the details."

"The butler and the governess that night kidnapped Mr Petherton's daughter, and we have search parties looking for them. The police are involved."

Jerome Iles said, "I never trusted Steadman. He was a shifty character and rude at times."

"Mr Iles! Mr Steadman may turn up here and claim some benefit or property. He is a cagey operator and will be looking for money. I advise you to have your assistant manager briefed on the kidnapping and made aware of Steadman. If he does turn up, someone should contact the police immediately. Of course, this is only if the assistant can be trusted."

"I will do what I can, but you can appreciate there are not many police around here. But we have trustworthy staff."

"Good. Now, are you familiar with Mr Petherton's attorneys? We need the Executors in Guildford to start clearing up many matters."

"Yes, Greens in Chancery Lane."

"You mean Green and Green?"

"Yes. You have heard of the firm?"

"They are one of the best firms in town. I assume, Mr Iles, that Greens will be closed before you can reach them tonight."

"Yes, they usually close at five." Glancing at a clock, he said, "With the traffic now, it would not be possible tonight."

"Then I will meet you there in the morning, say ten o'clock. There will be many instructions given in terms of the business here. It is quite fortunate that you are doing a stocktake. I must talk further with them on the trustees for Miss Petherton."

"But!" Blake could see that Jerome Iles was struggling to cope. "What do I tell the staff."

"At this stage, it would be best to tell them nothing. When employees hear that an owner has died, all types of strange things happen. Stock disappears first, then other unusual events. Do you have an assistant manager?"

"Yes, he is leading the stocktake tonight."

"Good! There is no need to inform him now of Mr Petherton's demise. Wait until tomorrow. Let him know you have an appointment first thing in the morning and will return here as quickly as possible after our meeting. The attorneys will tell you what steps you must take tomorrow and probably send someone to assist you. I am afraid you will be very busy in the months ahead."

Mr Iles sat there stunned.

"Remember, Mr Iles, ten in the morning at Greens."

"Of course! I will be there."

Fintelton Manor, Outside Petersfield, Sussex ...

Around four in the afternoon, a knock came at the door of Lady Jane's study, and the Earl and the countess's maid, Miss Margaret Lane, entered. Margaret remained near the door as the Earl slowly came across and sat opposite his wife.

Lady Jane, becoming impatient, asked, "Well, David. What is it?"

"Jane, a sad letter delivered by a navy rider from Portsmouth has arrived." The Earl paused as he looked out the window, gathering his strength.

"David, not Robert? I could not bear it!"

"No, it is not Robert. The Governor of Jamaica writes to us. The Governor confirms that despite Hugh's best efforts, he passed away on the twenty-ninth of March. I am sorry, my Dear. I am so sorry!"

Lord Fintelton sat there still in disbelief at the news. Lady Fintelton grasped the letter from the Earl's shaking hand and opened it.

> *The Office of the Governor of Jamaica*
> *The Right Hon. Sir William Wade, BT.*

The Right Honble, The Earl and Countess
of Fintelton.
My Lord and Lady

I have the sad duty to inform you of the unfortunate passing of your son, Sir Hugh South, on the twenty-ninth of March 1827.

Please accept my sincere condolences and prayers.

I met with Sir Hugh earlier in the year and found him recovering but still struggling with the disease he had contracted. At that time, we all had high hopes for his full recovery. Doctor Cowper advised me that his illness was incurable and only a matter of time. He went for an early evening walk on Thursday and overexerted himself. The doctor confirmed that he died peacefully, and the cause of death was his enthusiasm for recovery.

Hugh, being so far from home, we decided that his body be cremated and his ashes returned to England. Lady Fiona Green will deliver his ashes and carry extensive details of his affairs in Jamaica. She will brief you on her return. Dr Cowper travels on the same ship and will answer any questions on Sir Hugh's condition.

My staff have ensured that all travel arrangements have been made, and the ship should arrive in Southampton by Tuesday, 15 May, if not before. Lady Fiona Green and Dr Cowper will travel directly to Petersfield and take lodgings. They will contact you once they arrive.

Once again, please accept my condolences.

Yours sincerely
Sir William Wade, Bt.
His Majesty's Governor, Jamaica

Lady Jane stood, rushed to a sobbing Sir David, knelt and wrapped her arms around him. They both shed tears and stayed close long into the afternoon.

As the sun set, Lady Jane's maid came in with a wrap for her mistress and a rug for Sir David. She quietly asked if they would care for some tea.

"Yes, Margaret. That would help, now."

Margaret felt the cold air coming in, and asked, "Should I close the doors, Milady?"

"Not yet, thank you."

The countess sat beside her husband and watched with him as the sunlight faded in the late afternoon and the creek at the bottom of the valley slowly disappeared into the twilight. She turned and said with enough strength, ensuring the Earl heard.

"David, you understand that this now changes everything?"

Lord Fintelton, at first, did not reply but then said, "Yes, Jane. It changes everything, forever!"

PART 2

'In time, my son!
In time, you will understand.
And then we shall talk again!'

May 1827

Chapter 9

'Harting', St James's Square, London ...

Alone at the dining table, while enjoying a delicious lunch and quiet time, Anne breathed deeply and sat back, wondering if Clare Petherton had been rescued. Earlier in the morning, she could not finish her breakfast and retired upstairs for another hour and a half, delaying her planned visit to the new bakery. By mid-morning, Anne had recovered and set off under the watchful eye of her security man, Mr Henry Fletcher. Now back at Harting, she would enjoy a few quiet hours before Victoria and her maid arrived.

"Lady Anne! Some messages for you."

The butler passed across a tray where Anne saw the familiar seal of Fintelton manor on the first message.

"Thank you, Staines."

The butler assisted her as she rose from the table. Anne walked down the hallway, made herself comfortable on a settee in the drawing room, and opened the first message from the countess.

Fintelton Manor
Harting, Sussex.

My Dearest Anne

I hope this message finds you well and that your duties in London are not too taxing. The Earl and I often discuss the London bakery and your new business with Victoria at Hursts. You can be assured of my patronage when we visit Harting again.

I look forward to seeing the new fashions with the change in season.

Also, we are keen to hear the outcome of your discussions with the senior partner at the offices of Manifold and Stout. I needed to write to ensure you held the most current information on the family.

A sad letter from the Governor of Jamaica arrived around four in the afternoon today.

Anne sat up straight and said aloud, "Oh, no!"

Sir William Wade advised us that Sir Hugh passed away on the twenty-ninth of March. The Governor had visited Hugh earlier in the year and found him recovering. He also notes that he received regular updates from Doctor Cowper indicating that Sir Hugh had contracted an incurable disease, and it was only a matter of time. One evening, Hugh, excited by his recovery, over-extended himself on a walk in the park and died soon after. Lady Fiona Green cared for Hugh and was with him at the end. The Governor advises that he suffered no pain and was at peace with the world.

Lady Fiona and Doctor Cowper's vessel is due in at Southampton on the fifteenth of May, and they will then visit Fintelton and deliver Sir Hugh's ashes and personal belongings.

The Earl and I are devastated at the loss of Hugh and will be in mourning for some time. We hope you will visit Fintelton and stay with us after you complete your business in London. I have sent a message to Admiral Bird and a letter to Robert informing him of Hugh's passing, and the Earl will advise the Privileges Committee of the changes in our family and your new status.

I would also ask that you inform Mr Stephen Polkinghorne of these events and inform him that his acquaintance, Lady Fiona Green, will be staying with us. I will send an invitation for Mr Polkinghorne to join us where he may renew his acquaintance with Lady Fiona. If you would please pass it on.

Please take care while you are in London. Lady Emma and possibly David will join us this coming Saturday. I will send details of when the memorial service will be held once the arrangements are complete.

With our love
Jane Fintelton

Tears came to Anne as the butler entered.

"I am sorry, Milady, as I did not intend to disturb you."

Anne blew her nose and wiped her eyes.

"Sir Hugh has passed away!"

Staines stood there like a statue, understanding Lady Anne's tears. The significance of her comment was not lost on him, who had a quick mind and understood that the line of succession in his employer's family would now change.

With great care, he said, "Please accept my condolences, Milady. Unfortunately, I did not have the pleasure of meeting Sir Hugh. I will advise the staff, who I am sure will wish to support you as best they can. Please also convey our support to the Earl and Countess at this sad time. Would you care for some coffee or tea, Milady?"

"Thank you, Staines. I appreciate your kind words. Yes, some coffee would be much appreciated."

"Milady, Mrs Stubbington has arrived! Shall I tell her that the time is inconvenient?"

"No, Staines! Please, show her in and some tea as well."

"Yes, Milady."

Anne sat there, now wondering what Janet Stubbington would want with her. The peaceful time she craved at home was fast disappearing. 'Home', she thought. 'This will soon become one of my homes. My world is changing, and I am not prepared. I need Robert here to help me.'

"Lady South. Please accept my condolences on the passing of your brother-in-law. It must be a sad time for the Earl and Countess."

Anne thought, 'Of course, she would know!' She stood and tried as best she could to remain calm. Gritting her teeth, she welcomed the lady.

"Mrs Stubbington. Please come in and have a seat. I have ordered some refreshments."

"Anne! Remember, we agreed to use first names."

"My apologies, Janet. A few moments ago, I received some distressing news about the death of my brother-in-law, Sir Hugh South. You find me slightly melancholy."

"Please accept my condolences. Was it expected?"

"Yes. Hugh had been severely ill for some time, but there was hope of a recovery and return to England." She took a deep breath and gathered herself, "It appears he overexerted himself and paid a heavy price."

Janet could hear the true distress in Anne's voice. She wondered if it were due to Hugh's death or the implications this death would cause for Anne's future. She thought it might be the latter.

"You will make a fine viscountess, Anne. You have the strength and temperament and will make your husband proud."

Anne looked up and realised Janet knew exactly what she was thinking.

"Do you believe that? I am not sure I wish to become a countess." Anne sniffled, and a tear ran down from her left eye. She dabbed it gently. "Sorry, Janet. I never sought the position, and I had hoped for Hugh's recovery. He should have married and had a son. But now it is forced upon me!"

"Life is strange, Anne. Thousands would love to be in your place, and here you are, miserable because you have no desire for wealth and title. I am sure you will succeed, and your King and government will be grateful for your service. In time, you will become accustomed to your new position. But you do not become a countess until the Earl passes on. Sir Hugh held the title of Viscount Leystead, passed down from his father. Robert will inherit this. You are now the Viscountess of Leystead."

Janet Stubbington could see Anne's astonishment.

"Were you aware of this, Anne?"

"No, I was not. Do you mean I already have a title? I thought it would not come until the Earl's passing."

"I spoke to the Duke this morning before coming. He is head of the privileges committee and advised the title may be used immediately. Robert will be sad for Hugh but glad you have a title."

Janet noticed the fear in Anne's eyes before lowering her gaze and commencing to sob again. She could see her attempts to cheer the young lady were inadequate, and a more compassionate approach was needed. Moving closer, she sat beside Anne, putting her arm around her shoulders as the young lady shed tears.

"Now, now. You will overcome this. Soon, Robert will be home, and you will visit Fintelton again. This time of sadness will pass. Life can be hard at times, but believe me, it will pass."

Anne rested her head on Janet's shoulder and cried her heart out.

"I see I have come at the wrong time, Anne. I am sorry." Janet held her close as the loss of composure slowly passed.

Anne, sobbing, whimpered, "No, no, Janet. You have come at exactly the right time. I needed someone confidential to talk with. I am usually better than this, but the news is depressing."

It was long since Janet had held a young woman on her shoulder. She felt a deep connection developing with this new bride. A girl young enough to be her daughter. Mrs Stubbington had predicted how difficult it would be for Anne and felt guilty that she had not prepared the young lady for what would confront her. Anne needed hope.

"Anne, I tell you this confidentially, so please keep it to yourself. An order has been sent to Admiral Sutherland to return to England. Robert will convey him home on Shadow. You will see him again within a month or two."

Anne sat up, wiped her face, and looked straight at Janet.

"That is wonderful news. I have missed Robert greatly. His being here would make all the difference."

"Well, there is other news too. I have invitations for you and Victoria to a soirée at the Russian Embassy this Saturday. You will be my guests and travel with me. Now that you are here in London, it is time for you to be introduced into society. I understand Admiral Bird will be there, and you might talk with him about Robert."

Anne looked up at Janet and took the two tickets.

"Would it be proper to attend when I should be in mourning for my late brother-in-law?"

"Certainly. I am sure you will show the proper amount of decorum and find a dress with a little black in it. Not too much, or it will be obvious. You will be among friends, and Lachlan and Taye McPherson are joining our party."

Anne was still unsure. "Leave the tickets with me, and I will discuss the dinner with Victoria tonight. Our lunch engagement tomorrow is still on, isn't it? Perhaps I could let you know then?"

"Yes! The business I was to discuss with you can wait until then. It is best if I make my way to my next appointment so you can recover from your bad news. If you need anything, Anne, don't hesitate to send a message. You, Robert, and I are all on the same team. Ensure you always keep Henry Fletcher with you and listen to his advice. Call me if you need help."

"Thank you, Janet. That is most comforting to know."

Janet Stubbington stood, said her goodbye, and made her way out. As she walked down the hallway, she was deep in thought. At the front door, she found the butler waiting for her.

"Staines, thank you." She lowered her voice and moved closer. "During the rest of the Viscountess's stay in London, ensure Henry Fletcher is always with her. I expect there will be callers to pay their respects. When they come, it would be best if they met with Miss Sopwith. I am sure Lady Anne's friend will be capable of handling them. Your mistress needs some time to recover from the news of Sir Hugh's sad passing. She will be involved in some difficult negotiations in the coming week and must be fully refreshed before she attends. I expect you to protect her Staines, and I will hold you to that!"

As the butler listened to Mrs Stubbington's advice, he was confused about this lady's relationship with his mistress. It appeared there was a closer connection than he was aware of. Given her concern, he was tempted to advise that Lady South was unwell but decided against the move.

"Mrs Stubbington, I assume by the Viscountess you mean Lady Anne South?"

"Yes! Sir Robert inherits the title from his late brother. Your mistress is now the Viscountess of Leystead."

"I see! I will do the best I can, Mrs Stubbington. Miss Sopwith will be briefed on her arrival."

"Thank you, Staines. I shall return later in the week. I think the viscountess needs her coffee now."

Janet raised her eyebrows and made her way out.

Staines soon knocked and opened the drawing-room door, providing the coffee Anne had asked for. The butler poured a cup and offered milk and sugar.

"Milk only! Thank you, Staines. What do you make of Mrs Stub-bington?"

"Milady. If I may take the liberty of expressing my opinion?"

Anne nodded that he might.

With the greatest respect, Staines said, "I would hate to be on the wrong side of her, Ma'am. Rumour has it that she is a most powerful person. Today, Ma'am, you may have seen a compassion in her character that is rarely displayed. While I am sure the Lady uses people for her purposes, I think she may be most protective of you. I could not comment further. Milady."

"I agree with you entirely. Thank you, Staines."

After the butler left, Anne continued sipping her coffee, considering what Janet had said. Perhaps Janet was becoming more of a friend than Anne had ever imagined she could be. The thought of Victoria's company within a few hours cheered Anne, and she settled again on the sofa and opened her other messages.

Turner Household, Guildford, England ...
Ethel had returned with Clare from Cloverdale Chase, and the children were home from school.

"Before you chop the wood, boys, you may have afternoon tea." Mrs Jennings had prepared some quiches for their special guest, Clare, and knew the other children would be disappointed if they ran short of food.

"There are plenty for everyone!"

The children eagerly assembled around the table, knowing how tasty Mrs Jennings's quiches were. As they ate, there was silence.

Clare asked, "Are you boys taking the dogs for a walk today?"

Simeon looked up, "Yes. After we chop the wood."

Pleased with the answer, Clare suggested, "If I come with Ralph, can we go up to the fort at Cloverdale Chase?"

"No, we are going towards the river and to Mr Linton's blacksmith shop. We want to make some swords. If you come with us, you can make one too!"

Clare was surprised, "Why do you want to make swords?"

"Mr Taggart told us about pirates at school today. In the early part of the last century, there were pirates around. They still exist today, but they are a different type of pirate. Smugglers! We must ask Father at dinner if he can tell us about smugglers."

Clemmie asked, "What has that got to do with you making swords."

Simeon explained, "We are the King's men, like Robert. The swords will help us defeat the pirates. The plan is that when we go to the riverbank for Sunday afternoon tea, we will be armed and ready to fight them."

Clare was confused and asked, "Do you expect smugglers to arrive on Sunday afternoon?"

Simeon continued, "No, no! When our mother was alive, we would go every Sunday. Often, we divided into two teams, the pirates and the King's men."

William excitedly said, "We always beat the pirates and sent them packing!"

Mrs Jennings added, "It was more than that, Clare. Mrs Turner enjoyed the open air. She felt it was good for the family to exercise and enjoy the company of others in the community. Usually, there were guests invited. Since her death, we have only been down there once or twice."

"Probably!" Simeon laughed, "Because William always injured someone with a large branch. Father was not keen on going! Will is an excellent fighter. Mother was often bandaging someone."

All the children laughed as William cried out, "I did not!"

Clemmie was about to comment but held back as Mrs Nibley entered the kitchen and poured herself a cup of tea. Madeline asked, "Ethel! Are we going for a picnic this Sunday down beside the river? The boys are making swords and want a pirate fight."

"If your father agrees, then we could. You need to ask him tonight at dinner."

Clemmie answered, "We will! It is time we had a good picnic at the river. Perhaps Neville and Beth could come."

William called out, "What about Doctor Sopwith and Lady Emma?"

Clemmie agreed, "Yes and Victoria!"

Ethel advised, "I think Victoria left yesterday for London. She will stay with Anne."

William called out, "Could we invite Leonard and Betty? Perhaps Mr. and Mrs. Webster will come and Reverend Taggart."

Ethel said, "My, this will be a big picnic. Before you invite anyone, we must seek your father's permission."

The boys were soon off with Nosey to the blacksmith's shop. The girls decided to exercise Ralph and Nosey on a walk to Porting and see

Mrs Kirby. Mrs Nibley considered if it was safe and decided they could not keep Clare wrapped in cotton wool forever. Then she remembered Clare's sprained ankle.

"Clare – what about your ankle? Will you be able to walk that far?"

"Yes, thank you, Mrs Nibley. It feels far better today. I will be careful."

Katherine said, "We will help if it is a problem."

Ethel thanked Katherine and waved them goodbye.

Mrs Nibley realised Clare needed to be outside and talking with the girls. After being closed away for all those years by Mr Petherton, having friends the same age to walk with her would be a new beginning for the girl. Then, remembering they were unsure what had happened to Steadman and Preston, she decided that Aggie should deliver some bread to Mrs Kirby, and she could walk after the girls. There was no harm in having some help close at hand.

HMS Shadow, Strait of Bonifacio, Sardinia ...

Captain South climbed onto the quarter-deck, followed by the two diplomatic staff. He gestured towards the ladder leading up onto the poop deck[21] and said, "Mr Volkov! Please climb up here, and Monsieur Milius, if you would follow, Sir. I will join you in a few minutes."

Robert watched as the two men carefully climbed the ladder. He then turned and walked to the main, where Lieutenant Peters was watching the coxswain and some sailors checking the flag box.

"Peters!"

Lieutenant Peters came to attention and answered, "Sir!"

"Any sign of larger ships?"

"No, Sir. Multiple smaller ships are in sight, but none the size of a frigate. It seems we have evaded the foreign forces."

"Well, the Sardinians are involved with the French, but since Boney was beaten, they are far friendlier with us. I would be surprised if we saw Ottoman warships up here. Still, keep a good lookout up each mast as we work our way down the coast. I am wary of what we might find as we near the southern end and venture back into the Med."

"Yes, Sir. There is a lookout on the main and fore. I will put one up the mizen following lunch."

---

[21] For those unfamiliar with old sailing ship decking a frigate usually had a raised deck at the aft of the ship where the senior officers stood with the helmsman and navigator. This deck was called the 'poop' deck. JS.

Robert returned Lieutenant Peters' salute and continued, finding Master Trotters working with a team mending sails.

Saluting, Trotters said, "The winds have been good to us, Captain!"

"Yes, Trotters. If they hold, we should be at the bottom of Sardinia by Wednesday evening. Then we race to Malta. Let's hope they hold till we reach our destination."

"A good storm once we pass the southern tip would be handy. It would give us plenty of cover."

"Aye, Mr Trotters. Ensure you have your best sails up, as we may need to sprint."

"Aye, Sir."

Robert rounded the main mast and made his way back to the poop deck.

"Mr Fenton. It appears we may have dodged any unfriendly ships. We will be in Malta by Friday if the weather permits. I am keen to arrive as we have taken a week longer than planned."

The diplomats at the rear of the poop deck missed what Robert was saying due to the noise of the wind. As they conversed about the Greek situation, the Captain and First Officer were free to talk privately.

Fenton, glancing at their guests, asked, "Captain! Do we leave the diplomats in Malta?"

"Yes, Mr Fenton. I would assume we will be assigned to a frigate group for duty. Who knows, we might see some action."

"The men are ready, Sir!"

"I agree, Fenton. You have trained them well."

As Fenton smiled from the compliment, a strong voice called from above, "Sails on the port bow!"

Both Fenton and the Captain grabbed their telescopes and scanned the horizon.

"I can't see them from here. I am going above Mr Fenton. You have the ship."

"Aye, Sir."

Robert had dreaded this moment. He was sure he had taken the safest route to avoid detection. There were only two possibilities. Either this was a chance meeting of naval forces, or the Ottomans had realised he had not passed their way and were searching for him. Reaching the main tops, the captain rested and pulled out his telescope. He thought he had found a sail but lost it. There was still no clear view. Quickly, he pulled himself up and launched himself for the crosstrees some fifteen yards above. Still, without a good view, he grabbed the ratlines and pulled himself up to the topgallant yard.

The royal was still unfurled, so he had a clear view of the sea ahead. Taking his telescope from his belt and extending it, he focused on the white specs far to the south. The details of the ships were still below the horizon, but the topgallants were above – his lookout had a good eye. As the topsails started appearing, Robert was sure there were four ships, and two were large enough to be frigates. Closing his telescope, he clambered down to the crosstrees.

"Well done, Jacktar. You have a good eye. Keep an eye on them and pick out their course if you can. It appears they are sailing southeast, but it is not clear yet. Call down when you are sure."

"Aye, Captain."

Robert descended the ratlines as fast as he dared and then jumped onto the deck. Running from the main, he was quickly on the poop deck.

"Fenton! Turn her to starboard ninety degrees and make a course for the coast while I talk with Trotters. Call the Master, please."

"Aye, Sir."

The First Officer sent a midshipman to find Trotters and then commenced shouting orders. Shadow soon turned towards Sardinia.

Trotters appeared beside the captain. Robert looked him in the eye and said, "Master[22], I am not sure, but I think they have found us. They must have a larger fleet than I realised."

Deep in concentration, Robert looked to the port bow. Trotters waited in silence.

Robert knew that every eye on the poop deck was now watching him. The morale of the ship was dependent on his next move. The next order was a critical moment. He must evade the Ottomans at all costs and keep the diplomats safe.

"The charts, Master Trotters. Let us plot a new course."

"Aye, Sir. But who are we avoiding?"

"A squadron from the Ottoman navy, Mr Trotters. I assure you they

---

[22] The Master on a sailing ship was the senior petty officer in charge of sails. He often also took responsibility for navigation.

have been searching for us and will turn towards us within minutes."

A call came from the lookout overhead, "Four ships turning our way."

The first officer had been searching the south-west for more ships but jerked his head around and nodded an acknowledgement to the captain.

"How long before dark, Fenton?"

"Two hours, Sir!"

"Gentlemen, it appears we are outnumbered. We must find a friendly port and quickly!"

South, Fenton and Trotters moved to the chart table and studied their position.

Trotters suggested, "We are fifty miles southeast of Olba, Sir. I recommend we head for the coast there. We will need to tack with this westerly, but the squadron chasing us will have the same task. We will maintain our distance."

Fenton agreed. He was still unsure if the Ottomans would challenge them. But it was concerning they had changed course towards *Shadow*. The first officer spoke, "I concur, Sir. We will not make the port before nightfall, but the harbour is long and deep. It will be well-lit due to the many buildings fronting onto either side of the harbour."

Robert asked, "Trotters, this westerly was blowing yesterday. Did it blow well into the night?"

"Aye, Sir. It was strong until about four bells of the first watch. After that, it subsided slightly, but not much. We were still making eight knots for the other watches."

Robert took onboard Trotter's reply and studied the southern horizon. The group of ships had changed course and were now heading directly for them. Given they had some smaller ships – probably schooners or ketches – they could send them into the port while the frigates stood off waiting for *Shadow* to come out. They would be trapped there until the Ottomans decided to retire.

"Fenton, plot your course for Olba and put up every sail you can to make haste. I want the Ottomans to think we are scared and retreating for Olba. Trotter's advice is that it will be dark within two hours. If the westerly holds once it is dark, we will change course and head halfway to Naples and then down to Messina. We will take a chance and hope the Ottoman squadron heads to Olba. We will be halfway across the

Tyrrhenian Sea when they search the port and find us gone. Let's pray this westerly holds."

Trotters smiled and said, "I have been watching the clouds since morning. The weather has been building in the west all day. We could be in for a storm tonight or tomorrow morning just at the right time."

"I will hold you to that, Trotters! Now, I must brief our diplomats on why we are changing course."

Robert looked again over the port bow down to the south. The sails were gaining height, and any good lookout would report they were moving towards *Shadow's* position. He considered, 'Is it a chance incident, or were the Ottomans somehow given information?' He feared the latter was true, and once again, he questioned if the Admiralty was in safe hands.

Turner Household, Guildford, Surrey, England ...

The children had all returned and were readying themselves for dinner. The house was a hive of activity as Mrs Jennings and Ivy Grey, the assistant cook, worked hard preparing dinner for the large family gathering at six-thirty. Upstairs, Marcia was being difficult, hesitating over which dress she would wear to dinner, and Madeline uneasily contained herself, impatient that the five-year-old should hurry up.

Jessica Swamp had finished her duties downstairs and tapped a busy Aggie on the shoulder, asking, "Could I see you outside on the back verandah for a minute, Aggie."

"Have you got time, Jess? You should be on your way home."

"Please, I need to ask you a question."

Aggie swung around, checking on progress in the kitchen. She could see there was time to duck out if she was quick.

"Mrs Jennings! I need to show Jessica where the spare buckets are kept. It won't take long."

The cook looked up, nodded with a frown and resumed preparing soup.

"Come on, Jess. We must be quick."

On the back verandah, Aggie put her finger to her lips and signalled, "Shoosh!"

Backing away, she beckoned Jess to follow her to the side of the woodshed.

"Now, what is it, Jess?"

Jessica Swamp took a deep breath and opened her mouth, but nothing came out. She was pent up with emotion and wondered if she should return inside.

"Come on, Jess. They need me in there to help!"

"It is about reading and writing. I enjoy working with you and have learned so much, but now my father has told me that Mr Hotspur will teach me reading and writing."

"You mean Mr Philip Hotspur?"

"Yes. My father told me I had to do whatever he asked as it was important for my future job here. Father has never allowed me to have learning before, and now he insists on it, and I don't understand why."

"Have you asked your mother about it?"

"No. Father told me I must not tell anybody what he said and to obey Mr Hotspur."

Aggie was becoming suspicious. She asked, "Has Mr Hotspur asked you or told you about this yet?"

"No, but he does walk me home often."

"Since when has he been walking you home?"

Jess bit her lip but decided she could trust Aggie, "Don't tell anyone, but I think he likes me. He started walking with me on a rainy day two weeks ago. I told my brother, Peter, but he was not impressed. Peter does not like clergymen. But he has agreed to attend church with me as I have never been there. I thought that might make a good impression on Mr Hotspur."

Aggie could see a pattern growing in Jess's story, but then she was distracted by a familiar smell.

"Can you smell smoke, Jess?"

"What do you mean?"

"I mean smoke from the shed."

"No! But Aggie, why does Mr Hotspur want to teach me reading and writing? Do you think he likes me?"

Aggie noticed the smell becoming stronger but needed to concentrate on what Jess said. She had never trusted Philip Hotspur as the young curate had always had agendas. The visitations to Clemmie had slowed as Hotspur found his advances always blocked. Perhaps he had a new target, but the girl had little to offer a man like Hotspur.

If anything, he would not settle for anyone with less than a ten-thousand-pound dowry. She was confused by what Jess said but knew that with Philip, there was always an ulterior motive.

"I am unsure, Jess. I would advise you to take any relationship he proposes very slowly and always have someone with you when you meet him. I have heard tales but will not repeat them. I think you should tread carefully."

"So, you don't think he likes me?"

"I am sure he likes you, but it may be for other reasons unknown to me. Perhaps he wants you to become a church member."

"What would that involve?"

Aggie could now see that the smoke was coming from the woodshed. It must be someone smoking a pipe in there.

A sharp call from Mrs Jennings asking Aggie to return made her jump. There would be no more time with Jessica.

"I must go, and you should be off home. We can talk again tomorrow morning."

Jess understood, smiled and said, "Thank you, Aggie. You are the only one I can talk with here. See you in the morning."

As Aggie rushed into the kitchen, Ethel asked, "Aggie. Have you seen William? I can't find him anywhere."

"Perhaps you should try the woodshed."

A confused Ethel raised her voice, saying, "The woodshed......!"

"I must go, Mrs Nibley. Mrs Jennings needs me for dinner preparations."

The housekeeper thanked Aggie and watched her go before walking onto the back verandah and looking out to the woodshed. An occasional mist of smoke arose from the back of the shed. She walked across and peered around the corner.

On top of a pile of wood with his back to her sat William, oblivious to the world and puffing away on a pipe.

Ethel moved silently up behind him and shouted, "Well, who is this old man smoking his pipe!"

William, taken completely by surprise, fell off the pile, losing his grip on the pipe and hitting the soggy ground with a thud. Looking up, the young lad said, "Mrs Nibley, I wasn't smoking – just trying it out."

"I'm sure you were smoking, William!"

"Please don't tell, Father. It will give him an excuse to beat me. Please!"

Ethel smiled and said, "On one condition! You give me the pipe, and we see no more of you smoking until you are sixteen and working."

"But…. It was a gift from Levi, and I am doing no harm."

"Then, Mr Turner must be told."

William could see he had been caught red-handed, but a way out was offered. He picked up the leather pouch, tobacco and the still-warm pipe and handed them to Ethel.

"Thank you. Now go and wash before dinner, please. Hurry up!"

The fact that William had been naïve and mentioned Levi in his excuse indicated to her that William's friend was becoming a bad influence. He was the right age, fourteen, to become a bit cocky and full of himself. Not that she had that much experience with young lads, but it would be better if this boy learned his lesson before he led someone else astray. She would need a strategy so William would not be caught up in the process.

'Harting' House, St James's Square, London …

There was a soft knock on Anne's door, and Victoria softly tip-toed in and found Anne fast asleep. She closed the door and settled on a comfy seat beside the bed. After a while, Anne opened her eyes, feeling the presence of someone beside her.

"Victoria, you are here. I am so glad to see you."

"I find you in bed at five thirty in the afternoon, Lady Anne," Victoria said in surprise. "That is not the busy Anne South I know. Are you well?"

A sleepy Anne sat up and rubbed her eyes, "It has been hectic since I have been here and will continue like this for the next week. Now you are here, Victoria, I have an excuse for relaxation and enjoyment. As soon as we can, we must disappear to Piccadilly and have a morning coffee."

"We shall indeed, and you can join me as I hunt for a place in Belgravia[23]. I have been advised of a project in Cadogan Place beside a central garden along the street. Of course, they are not built yet, so

---

[23] The author is aware that the first homes in Belgravia were not available until 1830. Using poetic licence, I have had them built slightly earlier. However, I have indicated that Victoria will have to wait for the building of her new home. JS

I will rent while I wait, but I think it is best to buy early as the value should increase over the years. From what the builder, Mr Cubitt[24], described, the homes sound perfect for what I want."

"I think they might be expensive, Victoria. Are you sure?"

"Not yet, but money is not a problem, and I need a place of my own. I don't want to sponge off David for too long. And I will be close by and can easily keep in contact and visit."

"That would be nice, especially while the Admiralty sends Robert on missions." Anne looked out the window and fell silent. Victoria knew Anne longed for Robert and attempted to take her mind to more pressing matters.

"I am sure he will return soon. Until then, we will have much to do with setting up Hursts in London. Next week, we must decide on the sites identified. From what I hear of your friend Mr McPherson, he should be able to guide us."

"He will. I am glad you are here, Victoria. I need a friend to lift my spirits. Is there any news from Emma?"

It was Victoria's turn to remain silent. Anne could see that she was holding back something important.

"Don't worry, Victoria. Lady Jane has written to me and advised about Sir Hugh. It is a shame indeed."

Victoria raised her eyes and looked directly at Anne, "She must have received the news only hours before I left on Monday. I called on her, but everything was in confusion, with the staff rushing to pack her things. She greeted me but begged to be excused as she was to join her mother at Fintelton. The coach left later in the morning. I expect she would be there by now."

Anne sat up straight, "We both need to be there within two weeks. Lady Fiona Green arrives around the fifteenth of May, and I expect the memorial service will be held the following week. It is a pity Robert will miss this, but it cannot be helped. Give me ten minutes, and I will join you in the drawing room before dinner."

Victoria smiled and made her way to the door.

"Wait!" Anne rushed over and hugged her warmly, "Thank you for coming, Victoria. You are so dear to me! I have missed you."

---

[24] Belgravia was developed in the early 19th century by Richard Grosvenor, 2nd Marquess of Westminster under the direction of Thomas Cubitt. Wikipedia

Victoria smiled and hugged her back before leaving the room. She was still surprised to see Anne appearing so weak. It was not usual at all.

Jonathan Turner's Study, Guildford, Surrey, England ...
Jonathan took a deep breath, gathered all the documents, and placed them neatly within the file before closing it. The organisation of William's dispatch to Africa was taking far more time than he had expected. He sat back and wondered if there was an easier way. The thought struck him that perhaps the boy should remain at home. He recalled the small face peeping from behind the ajar bedroom door, witnessing his treatment of Eleanora. He flinched, knowing it was himself who was guilty, not the child. And the boy, despite his devotion to his mother, had never given him away. Surely, that was enough not to send him away.

His mind wrestled with his conscience as he considered the prospect of an interfering William beside him as he settled into life with his new wife-to-be. But it was custom for difficult children to be sent away. After all, the youngster would be with his Uncle Richard and have all kinds of adventures. He would be safe, and Auntie Sarah would take care of his schooling. If the boy stayed, it was likely that William would ruin Jonathan's happiness with Ethel in the weeks to come. No, the boy must go! It was the only way.

Jonathan patted the file with a smile, enjoying the warmer evening temperature and hoping the cold spell of the last few days had ended. It was time for bed, and he would sleep well tonight, knowing his plans for William were now shipshape. Then Jonathan remembered the contracts for several new clients Peter Hammer had left for him. Frowning, he placed William's file in his second desk drawer and pulled across the pile of contracts. They must be checked and signed tonight and ready for tomorrow.

A soft knock came on the study door, and Ethel entered and asked, "Jonathan. May I have a word, please?"

"Of course, my Dear. These contracts can wait until we have talked."

He took her in his arms and kissed her gently on the lips. She responded and hugged him tight.

Ethel looked into his eyes and said, "It would be good if we could marry soon. This keeping of secrets is becoming waring. How long before we can announce our engagement."

"Ethel, I would do it tonight if I could. Benjamin died here in this house. If we were to announce our engagement now, it would create all sorts of rumours. We must wait until we arrive at the Isle of Wight. That will be an appropriate time, and the gossip chains will be kept at bay for another two months. We must manage this process carefully. I am sure you will hear from Benjamin's attorneys in London soon. They will require you to hear the will reading. The fact that Benjamin publicly announced your engagement to him in the Gazette will work in our favour. There will be no suspicion."

Ethel looked at Jonathan, and he saw a tear in her eye, "Jonathan, I was so angry with him for doing that, but his actions helped us. I am ashamed of what I felt."

He held her close as she rested her head on his shoulder and gently cried.

"Shush, now! You have been through a great deal in the last few days. No one could ever accuse you of not treating him fairly. I will accompany you to London, and we can stay with Anne at Harting. Hopefully, the recruiting consultants will have some applicants for me to interview in London by then."

"What position are you filling?"

"We have decided to lighten Anne's load by employing a General Manager for our developing bakery network. He will also be responsible for flour sales nationally."

Ethel thought about this and asked, "Is it not too early? There is only one bakery at present."

"Yes, but a huge Guildford bakery for him to manage and the London bakery's set up and staffing. The Bristol building is ready for development, and the sooner both bakeries are operational, the better. I need a man who can get these things happening. I am also considering a bakery in Reading as Hamish has opened his second pub there, and the bakery here is having trouble filling the London and Reading orders."

"But London will soon be supplied by your new bakery. You will have spare capacity."

"Yes, the London bakery will help, but Hamish plans four pubs in

Reading and at least two in Bristol. There will be a lot of expansion in the next year."

Ethel had not been aware of how large Jonathan's interests were becoming.

"You are right. Anne concentrating on Hursts will be enough for her in the future. But there is something else I must tell you. I want you to take some deep breaths and not become angry."

Ethel understood that Jonathan easily became enraged when the children stepped out of line. If her strategy for correcting William's smoking was to work, she needed Jonathan's support. She could see the worry in his face already.

"This does not involve William, does it?"

Ethel was ready for this and held him close again, kissing him. Enjoying the passionate kiss, Jonathan relaxed and became more interested in this beautiful woman embracing him. He was becoming aroused.

"Deep breaths, Jonathan."

He kissed her again and then took a deep breath. Ethel could see that he had settled down.

"I have a strategy for this situation, and it needs your involvement to be complete. It involves William, and we will work together for his benefit."

Jonathan was confused. What difficulty had William now created, and what would his involvement be?

"Ethel, the best way to solve this is if I have words with him and, if needed, punish him accordingly."

"I agree, Jonathan, but this time in a different way."

She spent fifteen minutes talking with him and outlining the plan. When Jonathan heard that she had found William sitting beside the woodshed smoking a pipe, he said, "He what!"

"Calm down, Jonathan. There is a way we can solve this, but it must be done carefully. If we follow our strategy, then William will realise the error of his ways, the bad influence of Levi will be stopped, and your relationship with William will grow rather than deteriorate. Also, your relationship with the Spencer family will be enhanced by involving Terry. We live in a village, Jonathan. We are all connected, and we must work together."

Jonathan sat back down at his desk chair and rubbed his chin. "Perhaps you are right."

"I am sure I am right, and now you should finish up. Go to your bedroom, change into your pyjamas and dressing gown, and come to my room in half an hour."

She moved across, lifted his chin and gently kissed him. Jonathan suddenly knew his wait was over. She was ready to commit herself fully to him. He kissed her back and stood.

"Are you sure, Ethel? There will be no turning back after this."

"I do not wish to turn back, Jonathan. We are in love and soon will be husband and wife."

She backed away, smiling at him and closed the door behind her. Jonathan looked at the contracts on the desk, needing his attention. He piled them up and said, 'Blow this!" He was quickly away to his bedroom.

Ewell Station, Outside Grahamstown, South Africa ...

Richard Turner looked up from the letter and called out as he entered the partly constructed homestead, "Sarah, the next shipment of materials has arrived from London."

"It is about time! The builders might return and finish the job. We must have this farmhouse complete before the cold sets in."

Richard scratched his head, "I am not sure that is possible unless this good weather extends through to next summer. Anyway, I must travel to Port Elizabeth and take charge of the shipment. I want it here quickly. Will you come or stay in town?"

Sarah smiled, "I will not miss a chance to visit the ocean again."

"Good! We leave tomorrow, and we can pack tonight. I must ride to the western boundary and see how Nkosi's people are settling in. I will take George with me as he is calm and a good negotiator. He can handle our new friends while we are away."

Closing the door behind him, Richard walked across the partly finished verandah, down the steps and over to the small barn with a primitive-looking lean-to attached large enough to accommodate three or four horses. He grabbed a saddle, tossed it onto Maisy's back, and fitted the bridal. He did the same to one of the farm's other horses, Dapto, and then led them down towards the farm gang completing the dam.

"George!"

A tall Khoikhoi man raised his head and looked straight at Richard.

"Come, George! We must visit our new friends on the western boundary. I need your help translating. You ride Dapto." Richard offered the reins.

"Yes, baas."

The man came running and quickly mounted the freshly saddled horse. George was a well-built, muscly Khoikhoi man of about forty, with a large smile and a bald head. He dressed in daggy old overalls supplied by the station and preferred barefoot even when riding. George took his name after learning that the chief of the English was called King George. Rumour had it that he had changed his name after the British won their Eastern Cape victory and took control from the Dutch. Richard had never asked what his previous name was for fear of insulting the native.

George had worked hard at improving his English over many years and was now a useful translator for Richard. The Khoikhoi had as-similated well with Cape settlers from all countries and could see the advantages of working for the English. In Grahamstown, the Khoikhoi tribe lived together around a mile northeast of town, and those who worked for Richard made their way on foot each day, heading off before dawn.

As the two riders approached the property's western border, they could see some fifteen Xhosa men working on the outer kraal fence and the mud walls of three huts.

"They nearly finished, baas!"

"You're right, George. But where are their cattle?"

"No come, till the kraal fence finished. Women and children come then, too."

Richard dismounted and indicated that George should do the same.

"George, I and my wife must go to the coast. I may not be back for two weeks. The materials for the house have arrived at Port Elizabeth. We will bring it all back here. You must check on the Xhosa each day. See, they are settling well. Also, ask about any unknown tribesmen passing through. Do you remember the carcass here?"

The black man nodded his head in agreement.

"I will introduce you to the Mbeki brothers. They are in charge.

Aviwe speaks good English. I understand he learnt from a German missionary at the Cape. His brother is not so fluent."

"What does fluent mean, baas?"

"Dumisa does not speak English well."

Richard noticed that Geroge was suddenly reluctant.

"Are you coming, George?"

"I must stay here, baas. I am not invited in. I only go when they beckon me. It is the way things are done."

Richard was unsure if he should force George forward or comply with what the Khoikhoi had advised. He could see Aviwe and Dumisa looking their way. Smiling, Richard said, "Stay here, but come when I beckon."

He set off and walked the fifty yards across to the Xhosa men. George stood silently with the horses, watching the proceedings.

"Molweni[25], Mebki brothers." Richard said their first names as they shook hands.

The men stood tall and peered down at Richard but smiled as they exchanged greetings. Richard then explained that he would be away for many nights and that George Southby would assist them while he was away. As he mentioned George's name, he pointed to the Khoikhoi man.

The native leaders appeared to understand, but they asked, "Why is a Khoikhoi called George Southby? Why not his tribe's name?"

Richard explained, "He names himself after the King of England, and I cannot pronounce his surname, so I gave him the name 'Southby'."

Aviwe appeared to understand and explained to his brother.

"Ah!" The brothers smiled, and Aviwe said, "You chief here! Southby it is!"

The native moved forward towards George and beckoned him to come over with a smile and a hand movement. George responded by walking very slowly with his head down.

Dumisa looked pleased as he could see George understood the traditions of the Xhosa. He nodded his approval to his brother. The Khoikhoi tribesman stopped short of the brothers, gave a short bow, and said in Xhosa, "Molweni." George said in English, "It is a great honour to meet the Mbeki! My name is George."

---

[25] 'Molweni' is translated to Good Day or Greetings – a Xhosa greeting for more than one person.

Aviwe and Dumisa slowly stepped forward and said, "*Ewe*[26]." Aviwe said in English, "Welcome, George, to Mbeki *kraal*."

The Xhosa men also gave a short bow and then moved closer and talked in Xhosa with George. Richard could see the proceedings were friendly, and the men were relaxed in each other's company. Richard picked up the word '*unjani*' and knew they were enquiring about his health.

After the natives had finished their introductions, Richard explained. "George will come each morning to see you before working on the dam. He will show you the dam if you wish. George, would you translate that, please?"

After Southby translated, the natives nodded in agreement and pointed towards the dam.

Richard said, "That is correct, George. Ask them if they have seen any other tribes passing through?"

George nodded and started another conversation with the men. There was much pointing, but it appeared nothing definite.

"Baas! They say there are tracks, but hard to tell who comes and goes. They will keep looking each day and tell us if they find anything. They say their wives and children will be here soon."

Richard said, "Good!". He smiled at the men and waved goodbye.

At the homestead, George dismounted and stood there scratching his head.

"Baas, Xhosa will bring many cattle. They build a big kraal. You clear more land for them? You no want them on your fields."

Richard could see Southby's concern, "How many cattle?"

"Maybe two hundred!"

Richard shouted in surprise, "Two hundred!"

"Yeah, Baas! Big kraal."

"I see. You are right, George. After we finish the dam, we will clear more land. We will clear a lot more land and build a few fences!"

Rectory, Guildford, England ...

Around eleven o'clock, Tuesday night, there was a loud knocking on the front door, which woke Laura Taggart with a shock. She shook Andrew's shoulder, and he slowly woke, asking, "What is it, Laura?"

---

[26] 'Ewe' in Xhosa means 'Yes – We acknowledge your greeting.'

Then he heard the loud knocking again.

"I will go!"

He rose, pulled on his dressing gown and slippers, and rushed down the stairs to find out who was making this row. There in front of him was a fully dressed Archdeacon Smithton.

"Archdeacon! What can the matter be at this time of night?"

"My apologies, Reverend Taggart, but I must come in and talk with you. I have bad news, and you and I must make some decisions quickly."

Andrew issued the shaking priest to his drawing room and sat him down. In her dressing gown, Laura joined them and asked, "Some tea, Archdeacon Smithton."

"Oh yes, Laura. That would steady my nerves greatly. Thank you, you are so kind."

Laura rushed off for the kitchen.

"Andrew, the bishop ......" Karl was overcome with emotion, drew his hands up over his eyes and could not speak. Taggart had known Karl Smithton long before he took the position in Guildford twenty years ago. Karl was a lecturer and mentor for theological students at the seminary at Oxford. He was a kind man and had great empathy for the students. Andrew knew Karl was now in his seventies and should have retired long ago. But his financial position was a little above destitute, and the bishop had overlooked his age and kept him on as an Archdeacon in the diocese. Karl was distraught, and Andrew waited for him to regain his composure.

"My apologies, Andrew. It has been an awful night. Cloe and I were at a dinner with the Bishop, where he entertained several friends from London. During the second course, he lost some colour and then complained of chest pains. We got him upstairs to bed while Doctor Sopwith was called. By the time Sopwith arrived, he was unconscious. I stayed with them during the whole process. The doctor tried everything he could think of, but the bishop kept breathing lighter and lighter, remaining asleep. Then, after an hour, he stopped breathing. Sopwith tried to revive him for nearly half an hour, but it was useless. He was gone."

Karl burst into tears remembering a fine man who had provided a financial lifeline for him. Andrew wondered if Karl was upset for the bishop or more worried about where his next meal would come from.

"You have had a terrible night, Karl. In the morning, things will become clearer."

Laura returned and passed a cup of tea across to Karl.

"Thank you, Laura. I need this."

"Karl, you look so upset."

"It has been a bad night, Laura. I'm afraid that our Bishop passed away unexpectedly."

"Oh dear!"

Taggart sat thinking about the implications. He asked, "What has been done since the bishop died, Karl? Has a message been sent to London?"

"No. That is why I came here. I wanted to discuss what should be done. You are the most senior minister in town, and I trust your guidance. I have not had a bishop die in front of me before!"

"I understand, Karl. Let us discuss the issues now and then reconvene tomorrow morning at nine at the diocesan office, where we can sort all the matters out in detail."

"Thank you, Andrew, but there is one other matter we must discuss: the Reverend Philip Hotspur. He is the bishop's nephew and must be informed."

"Oh, of course. I had forgotten Philip! He will be most upset when he hears the news. Karl, I think we should go and tell him now so he can be with Margaret at this sad time."

"Yes, yes. Hotspur should be with the bishop's wife. That will comfort her. Do you know where he lives?"

"Yes. Philip has a place at the back of North Street in Martyr Lane. It's difficult to find, but I'll take you there once we finish here."

"Thank you, Andrew."

"Now, Karl. Who is with Margaret?"

"Sopwith, I would expect. And, of course, the servants!"

"Your wife did not remain with her?"

"No, no. Clowance is a bit old now for stressful situations. I took her home to bed and then came here."

"What about the visitors?"

"They all hurriedly left once the doctor came."

"So, she has no one there to comfort her?"

Karl did not answer but took another mouthful of tea. Andrew looked up at Laura with a pained expression.

She smiled and said, "I will be ready in a few minutes, Andrew. You should come up and change as well. There are some biscuits on the table, Karl. Have some and finish your tea while we change."

Within ten minutes, they set off and cut through a lane to North Street. Andrew led the way, heading straight for Philip Hotspur's residence down Martyr Lane towards the cricket field. It was strange being out in the streets at this time of night, with only the occasional person passing quickly on their way home. Fortunately, it was spring and not as cold as they would experience on a winter's evening, but Laura kept a strong grip on Andrew's arm, not enjoying the night air and some mist as they neared the river.

Andrew said, "I am not sure if he is a deep sleeper, Karl, but I'm sure we can wake him!"

Andrew pointed to a lane leading to the west. They quickly entered the narrow roadway and stopped outside a small two-storied townhouse where candlelight illuminated the upstairs front window.

As Andrew knocked loudly on the front door, Laura noticed the shadows of not one person but two on the first-floor blind. They could hear raised voices upstairs, and suddenly, the candlelight was snuffed out. It took some minutes before Philip appeared at the front door.

Clothed in his dressing gown and rubbing his eyes, the curate half opened the door, "Reverend Taggart. I was asleep!"

"Good evening, Philip. I am sorry to wake you, but we have some bad news. Your uncle, the bishop, passed away tonight, and you are needed at the bishop's residence to comfort his wife. We are going there now to assist."

Philip was suddenly fully awake, "But there must be some mistake! I saw him this afternoon, and he was cheerful."

The young curate stood there with his mouth open, apparently dumbfounded. As they talked, Andrew and Laura noticed a young lady in a cloak quietly move down the internal staircase and disappear down the hallway towards the residence's rear.

Chapter 10

High Street, Guildford, Surrey ...

William and Simeon noticed Leonard Webster coming out of a lane as they walked Nosey towards the River Wey. As he approached, Leonard was deep in thought.

William called out, "Good morning, Mr Webster."

"Good morning, William and Simeon. Remember, you can call me Leonard. So, what are you boys doing here so early in the morning?"

Simeon replied, "We take Nosey for a walk each morning before breakfast. It is one of our chores. Father does not like dogs much, and the girls are not allowed outside until it is time for school, so we must do it."

William added, "We enjoy being with Nosey. It is good fun."

"I agree. I had a dog in Truro when I was younger. We did everything together. Unfortunately, he was crushed by a bullock team. His name was Spence. I have great memories of him. Enjoy your walk with Nosey."

Leonard was about to walk off, but Simeon said, "We had a dog before Nosey. His name was Snups. He was killed when burglars broke into our house!"

Leonard was surprised by that, "That is a tragedy. I bet you miss him."

"Yes, we do!" Simeon was thinking about Snups, but William wanted to ask about running.

"Could we come running with you one afternoon?"

"I am not sure you could keep up, but we could run after school sometime. How about Friday afternoon? We must be back by five thirty as I play darts with a few mates on Friday evening at the pub. You will need permission from your father if we are to run together. Who should I ask at your house if I call in there?"

"Probably Mrs Nibley, the housekeeper. She makes the decisions now. Can Nosey come?"

"Of course! It would be good having Nosey running with us."

The boys waved as Leonard ran off. Simeon started to run towards the river, imitating Leonard's style. William caught up and asked, "You are running like Leonard! Does it help?"

"I'm not sure, but it feels good. We need to ask Leonard what the best running style is. If we can learn that and practice, we might win some of the races at the church picnic. I am sick of always coming last."

William was excited, "Yeah. I am sick of being beaten by Levi and Archie. If we could grow a bit taller, we would have longer legs. We could run faster."

Simeon thought about that, "Maybe we don't need longer legs. Maybe we need to move our legs quicker."

William listened to Simeon's suggestion, "We can ask Leonard on Friday. But our training must be a secret so the other boys don't find out."

The Church Rectory, High Street, Guildford ...

Andrew Taggart rubbed his eyes and peered out from under the sheet. He could hear some boys running past and a dog occasionally barking. The light was slowly growing in the east, and the clock on the drawers at the end of his bed showed the time as just after six. He noticed it was a chilly morning for early May.

Rolling over, pulling the blanket and sheet off, he rose, moved to the window, and closed it. Sinking back into bed, Andrew slightly shuddered as he pulled the blanket up, wondering how Laura had spent the night consoling the bishop's wife. Margaret was beside herself when they arrived around eleven thirty. Doctor Sopwith gave her some powders, but there had been no effect when Andrew walked Karl Smithton home. Seeing the bishop's wife in such a state, Laura volunteered to stay the night. Mr Hotspur had strangely vanished as soon as he had given his condolences. His sudden absence did not reflect well on Philip's pastoral care skills.

Andrew moaned as he realised he would spend the day with Karl sorting out what must be done at the bishop's office. It was time he could ill afford, but it must be done. Karl would be a nervous wreck and not capable of any decision-making. Andrew sat up, puffed up the pillows behind him and then lay back down, gazing out the window.

He had served here for nearly twenty-five years and enjoyed the ministry. But Guildford was growing, and the church was large indeed. He was tired of the increasing demands placed upon him every day. Now in his early fifties, he had no desire to burn himself out in Guildford. Perhaps he should look for a smaller church with a smaller workload. That would allow him time to try the lessons he had learnt from the Reverend Simeon's seminars. The inspiring leader had made Andrew think long and hard about his theology and churchmanship.

Perhaps a smaller country church would be good. He must discuss it with Laura today at morning tea. It was time for a change. He dreaded the thought of the Archbishop arriving for the funeral. Perhaps someone would be sent down from London to organise the event. Surely, it would not be this week or the next. Following the funeral, the bishop's duties would be spread among the local clergy, and he would be sure to receive a heavy load. Andrew sighed.

'I need a cup of tea.'

He rose from his bed, pulled on his dressing gown and shuffled downstairs, where he found Mrs Chambers already stoking the oven fire.

"There is a cup of tea ready for you here, Rector. Did you hear that the bishop died last night?"

"Yes. Someone did mention it!"

Mrs Chambers looked up in surprise.

Harting House, St James's Square, St James, London …
Once again, Anne could not face breakfast and rushed back to her bedroom. On entering the breakfast room, Victoria asked Staines, "Has Lady Anne been down yet?"

"Yes, my Lady, but she retreated to her bedroom, asking not to be disturbed."

"I see. Did Lady Anne have any breakfast?"

"No, my Lady."

Victoria's upbringing was sheltered, but she did know what morning sickness meant. One morning of sickness could be anything, but two mornings in a row was the start of a pattern. She sat there wondering if Anne was pregnant.

Turner Household, Guildford, ...

Leonard Webster knocked on the front door of the Turner residence and stood back, glancing down the street as he waited.

"Aggie, the front door!"

A reply from the scullery came, "Yes, Mrs Jennings. I am still washing dishes. Can Jess answer it?"

"Jess. See who is at the front door, please!"

"Yes, Mrs Jennings."

Leonard turned as the front door opened, finding a young lady with a white mob cap and dust coat covering her servant's uniform.

Jess had to raise her head to see the face of the tall gentleman, "Yes, May I help you, Sir?"

"Good morning. I am Leonard Webster, a friend of the family. I wonder if I might speak with Mrs Ethel Nibley, please."

"Certainly, Sir." Jess stood there trying to decide if she should ask him in. She was not sure who this gentleman was.

Leonard, recognising her anxiety, said, "My father, Mr Mervin Webster, is a good friend of Mr Jonathan Turner, and my sister, Betty, is a good friend of Lady Anne. They went to school together. Mrs Nibley will recognise me."

That was enough for Jess, "Come in, Sir. Please follow me." She directed Leonard to the drawing room.

"Please have a seat. I will call Mrs Nibley. Would you care for a cup of tea?"

"Yes, thank you."

Jess smiled and walked away on her mission to find Ethel.

"Mrs Jennings! Is Mrs Nibley in her room?"

"Yes, I think so."

"Thank you."

Jess walked down the hallway towards the servant rooms. She knocked on Ethel's door. Soon, Ethel poked her head out.

"Yes, Jess."

Miss Swamp had never seen Ethel's hair when it was let down and stood back admiring it, "Oh, Mrs Nibley, you have beautiful long hair. I have never seen it before."

"Thank you, Jess. Now, what was it that you wanted."

Jess blushed, "Sorry! Mr Leonard Webster is waiting to see you in the parlour."

Ethel wondered why Mr Webster's son would call, "I see. Please give him a cup of tea, and I will be there in a couple of minutes."

Jess nodded and was off. She was surprised to find Ethel with her hair down and not sitting at her desk fully dressed. It was most unlike Ethel. She put it out of her mind and took Mr Webster's cup of tea from the kitchen.

"Mrs Nibley will be with you in a few minutes. You took her by surprise, and she must finish something before she can come. Here is a cup of tea and biscuit while you wait, Sir."

Leonard focused on Jess this time and noticed her longish dark brown hair with a hint of red. She had bright, ruby-coloured lips and long eyelashes that matched her hair with fair skin that was most attractive.

"Yes, Miss….! Sorry, but I do not know your name."

"Miss Jessica Swamp, Sir!"

"Yes, Miss Swamp."

Jess smiled and went to walk away when Leonard asked, "Are you a relation of Peter Swamp?"

"Yes, he is one of my brothers." Jess always felt it was safer to mention her brothers when a man asked about her family.

"I know him. I play darts with him at the Country Squire, down the Shalford Road."

"You mean near the bachelor quarters!"

"Yes, the Country Squire pub."

"Thank you, Mr Webster. I will tell Peter I have met you. You must excuse me as I have a lot of jobs to finish this morning."

Leonard was impressed by the young lady and watched as she rushed down the hallway.

Ethel was now in the kitchen but still tying her hair up. Aggie was giving her a hand.

"Thank you, Aggie. I ran out of time this morning. I woke up late.

Dear me!" She was embarrassed as she normally rose before the others and had the daily jobs list up by staff breakfast. Pinning the lists to the notice board, she straightened her uniform and proceeded to the parlour.

"Mr Webster, I have not seen you since the afternoon tea at the riverbank."

"Ah, yes. A very pleasant time. I must apologise for my father's outburst at the Reverend Philip Hotspur. I hope it did not spoil your afternoon."

Ethel smiled, "It certainly livened up the event. But we should not dwell on other people's issues. What can I help you with, Mr Webster?"

"Simeon and William have asked if they could run with me on Friday afternoon after school. I told them I would check with you for permission before agreeing. I will only run slowly and ensure they don't overexert themselves. I think they have something in mind for the church picnic."

"Oh, is that coming up?"

"Yes. The Sunday in two weeks."

"Did I hear someone mentioning the church picnic?"

Clementine happened to be coming down the stairs for a late breakfast.

"Yes, Clementine. Mr Webster is here asking for permission for Simeon and William to run with him."

Clementine nodded to Leonard, "My apologies, Leonard. I was not aware you were here." She sat down and made herself comfortable in the chair opposite. Leonard smiled but then refocused on Ethel Nibley.

"So, would that be permissible, Mrs Nibley?"

"I am sure Mr Turner would approve. Thank you for your interest in the boys."

"As I said, I think they have something in mind. They will return before five o'clock as I must be at the Country Squire pub for darts at five thirty."

After Leonard had left, Ethel said, "He is a nice young man, Clemmie."

"Yes, he is. Could I go to the pub and watch them play darts?"

"I'm not sure it is the best place for a young lady. Perhaps when you are a few years older and decide what you will do with your life."

"Oh, I know that. I will be a fashion designer and work with Anne and Victoria in London. Perhaps I will be old enough to meet boys in the pub then!"

"Perhaps! The pub is not the place for a young lady. Church is a far more acceptable place, and Leonard goes to church."

"I am not interested in church!"

"I see. Well, we can talk about it when we discuss dresses after lunch. Now breakfast is waiting for you. Run along."

Clemmie smiled and walked off to the kitchen. Ethel tidied the cushions in the parlour and thought about young Miss Turner's request to go to the pub. Surely, her finishing school would have taught her about acceptable places to meet. Perhaps she never completed her course. She must ask Mr Turner.

British Army Barracks, Grahamstown, Eastern Cape Province ...
By nine in the morning, the Turners reached Grahamstown and stopped at the Army barracks to look for Lieutenant Freddie Sanderson. The grounds seemed quieter than usual, and Richard and Sarah headed straight to the headquarters.

"Good morning, Sergeant. Would Lieutenant Sanderson be in?"

The sergeant stood and explained, "Unfortunately, Lieutenant Sanderson departed with a patrol yesterday. He will be away until next Sunday. Captain Hargrave is here – I could enquire if he were available."

"Thank you, Sergeant. If you would please."

The sergeant smiled, "Take a seat here, please. I won't be long."

Within a few minutes, he returned, "If you would both follow me." He led them down the hall and into the captain's office.

"Morning, Richard and Sarah. How can I be of help?"

Richard apologised as they had not wished to disturb him and had asked for Freddie. They also explained how they were headed for Port Elizabeth to pick up the next shipment of building materials.

Captain Hargrave seemed concerned, "Do you have others travelling with you? I mean some security."

"No. We thought that between here and Port Elizabeth was safe."

Captain Hargrave stood and walked over to a district map on the wall. "So did we until last Sunday. There was an incident between Salem and Bellcrest last week." He pointed out the area. "We only heard on

Saturday, and I sent Lieutenant Sanderson with ten troopers on patrol to find what is happening down there."

"What kind of incident?"

"Same as yours but with a slight difference. Cattle were butchered! A farmer found the carcasses. It seems the natives needed a substantial amount of fresh meat. Altogether, there were two heifers and three steers taken. The farmer was Mr Piet Beckhoff, a Dutch descendant of many generations and as stubborn as they come. He took three Khoikhoi with him and tried to track down the thieves. He has not been heard from since."

Richard leaned back in his chair, clasping his hands, "That is far worse than our experience."

Sarah asked, "With that amount of meat, there could be up to thirty or forty natives. What is being done to stop them?"

"As I said before, Freddie took a section with him on his patrol, but we don't have enough men to confront a hunting party of that size. We are only slightly larger than four platoons here. I have sent a request to Port Elizabeth for another fifty soldiers. In the meantime, I am waiting for Freddie to report back. It may be advisable if you are travelling to Port Elizabeth to have some security with you."

Richard was relieved to hear this suggestion, "What do you suggest?"

"I have a section patrol leaving tomorrow, which usually scouts and checks farms from the Assegaai River down to Paterson. But I can direct them to accompany you as far as Nanaga. You will be safe from there to Port Elizabeth, and the patrol can head back through Paterson. On one condition, though."

Richard and Sarah were more than willing to give whatever help they could in exchange for protection.

"That you deliver these dispatches to Army headquarters in Port Elizabeth."

Sarah quickly replied, "It would be our pleasure, Captain."

"Oh! One other condition as well. Since you will probably stay overnight at Balmas' Inn, I insist you grace us with your company at dinner at my residence. Sarah, have you met my wife, Thelma? She would love to meet you and hear any news from her home country."

"Certainly, Captain. I would be honoured."

"Shall we say seven, then?"

Anne was completely better by morning tea and rushed downstairs to join Victoria. She was already in the library, and Anne joined her. Anne loved that room with its deep leather chairs and the bookshelves that lined three of the walls. There was a settee, two chairs with coffee tables, and a soft, beige carpet—a place to lock yourself away from the world.

Victoria said, "Welcome, Anne. Are you recovered?"

"Yes, Victoria. I think I am recovering. It must be a tummy upset or something. I am not sure, but it is nothing. I am back to my usual self."

Victoria glanced at her friend and noticed Anne was pale and did not appear lively. Something was wrong, but she refrained from further commenting on her health.

"While we have morning tea, perhaps we can talk about Hursts?"

"I had the same idea, Victoria. Have you all the documents we used in Guildford?"

"Yes, they are here. I brought them and some new dress designs for you to consider."

Anne was interested and reached out, "Oh! Let me see the designs, please."

Victoria passed some papers across and sipped her coffee as Anne leafed through them.

"They are beautiful. Mostly for young women. Who did these designs?"

"This will surprise you, Anne. It was Clemmie."

"No!"

"Yes, she is a very talented young designer. She has been learning from Ethel Nibley and sewing with Rosalind. Ethel spent some years working with her mother, who is a seamstress. It seems we have a lot of homegrown talent to help us."

Anne looked up from the designs and said, "I am amazed. I knew she was not interested in accounting. It is no wonder. She has a creative mind and probably will enjoy art far more."

"Yes, she has a good eye for colour. Notice how the scarves and hats match the dress colouring. For her age, she has some wonderful insights with colour."

Staines entered and asked, "Might I provide anything else for your morning tea, ladies?"

"No, thank you, Staines. We have all we need here."

"If I might remind you, Lady Anne. Mrs Stubbington will be picking you up at twelve."

"Thank you, Staines. I have an hour before I must change."

The butler nodded and left the room.

HMS Shadow, Tyrrhenian Sea, Heading East ...

As the sun climbed above the main[27], the captain came on deck and headed towards the poop deck.

"Where are we now, Mr Trotters?"

"My calculations put us two hundred and thirty-two miles off Sorrento, Sir."

"Excellent. That strong wind helped us make good time. If this weather holds, we might pass Sorrento before dawn tomorrow."

"Yes, Sir. We have been using the chip log[28] every half hour during the night. Despite the rougher conditions, the readings have been consistent. *Shadow* has been flying, Sir."

"Any sign of the Ottomans?"

"Yes, Sir. We picked up a schooner to the southwest as dawn broke. When they lost sight of us, they must have realised that we might try to run to the Italian coast."

"Well, they won't catch us now. Not at this speed. Where is that schooner?"

Trotters pointed. "She be southwest, Sir. Trying to cut the angle and keep us in sight."

Robert could see the small sail on the horizon. Otherwise, the sea was empty. The Ottoman ship would have every sail up, trying to close the gap. But even if their courses coincided, a schooner could never hope to engage a frigate successfully. So, the Ottomans had something else in mind. It would be best if *Shadow* changed course and headed directly towards Messina. With this westerly wind, they could make another knot in speed if they put up the royals.

"Master, do you have a course for Messina ready?"

"Aye. Sir."

---

[27] The main is the middle and tallest mast on a square rigged three masted frigate.

[28] A chip log is a navigation tool mariners use to estimate the speed of vessels through the water.

Robert beckoned to Lieutenant Peters, officer of the watch. Peters quickly moved across, ready for the captain's orders.

"Gentlemen. I want to make more speed. We can catch up on some lost time as we run south. That Ottoman schooner will watch us but not attack. So, we have a clear run now down past Messina and onto Malta. In fifteen minutes, we will change course to Messina. Lieutenant Peters, Mr Fenton is at lunch, and I will join him. He will be on deck before you change course. Make your preparations, gentlemen. Master! After we change course, I want every sail up she can hold."

Peters and Trotters said, "Aye. Sir."

Robert surveyed the horizon and noticed one slight flash from the southwest as he scanned to starboard. Usually, that represented the sun reflecting on a telescope. He peered hard at it but could see nothing further.

"Peters, keep an eye on that horizon to the southwest. I thought I saw a flash or a reflection. It is becoming darker, Trotters!"

"Aye, Sir. That storm I predicted is coming."

The captain took another look and then decided on lunch. He must brief Fenton and then update the diplomats on his plan. *Shadow* was a week overdue, and Admiral Sutherland would be asking why. Robert would not be surprised if an English frigate were cruising off the bottom of Sicily, expecting them.

Diocesan Offices, Guildford ...
Archdeacon Smithton had taken the bishop's chair at the head of the table, and Andrew sat a few seats along from him. The diocesan meeting room provided the furniture and workspace they needed to start on the pressing issues.

"Karl, have you written a message to the Archbishop yet?"

"No, I thought we should go through his diary first."

"It may be prudent to send a message immediately; otherwise, word will arrive before you inform them. That would not go well for you, Karl."

Smithton looked up, and Andrew could see the stress on his face.

"Thank you, thank you. I had not thought of that. But what should I say?"

Andrew breathed in and wondered how simple this man was. Then he saw Karl start to shake, and a tear ran down his cheek. The Reverend Taggart understood that Karl would be terrified of losing his position now that his benefactor in the bishop was gone.

"Let me pen some words; you can adjust as you see fit."

"Yes, yes, Andrew. Please hurry, as I must get it away."

Andrew set to work, knowing this would be a long day. After some adjustments, he rewrote the letter and passed it to Karl. The Archdeacon read it in full, signed it and took it to the bishop's assistant, who would arrange a messenger.

Reverend Taggart heard Mr Berkly say, "I will go now."

With that done, Karl returned and concentrated on the bishop's diary. He started thumbing through the pages, which were heavily filled with appointments, meetings, and Sunday parish visits. Karl was not coping with the level of detail requiring attention. He started shaking again. Andrew stood, moved over and sat beside him.

"We can work through it together. You make a list of appointments and meetings that can be put off. I will work through the parish visits. We must let the parishes know these will not occur."

Karl stood up and moved across to the sideboard, took two glasses and the decanter of Sherry, and returned, pouring them a glass each.

He whispered, "I need this. ..."

Just as he took a sip, the door flew open, and a wild-eyed Philip Hotspur rushed in, thumping his hands flat on the table and yelling, "What are you doing in here, Taggart and Smithton? I see – you think you are taking over! You are vying for the bishop's position. You vermin! Where is Moore from St Nicholas and Crossling from St Saviours? Get out of his office, I say! I tell you, get out. The Archbishop will ask me to take over."

Karl stood and adamantly replied, "The Reverend Moore and the Reverend Crossling are on their way."

Mr Berkly, the bishop's assistant, entered and apologised, "Archdeacon, I tried to stop him. He would not listen."

Hotspur was raging, "You have no authority. I will talk to the Archbishop about this. Consider yourselves dismissed. I take the authority of the bishop. I am his nephew. You are not family. Get out. Get out of here."

Andrew Taggart remained seated and smiled at Philip, but Karl

Smithton was most offended and shouted, "We are not in his office but in the diocesan meeting room."

In a rage, Philip spat back, "You have taken his chair, Smithton. You have no right. Get out!"

As the curate shouted, the Reverend Crossling and Constable Michael Rawlins entered. Christopher Crossling asked, "Philip, have you been drinking?"

Hotspur spun angrily and shouted, "Who dares ask that?"

Archdeacon Smithton called out and beckoned, "Philip! We all know that you are upset at your uncle's passing, and we understand that you may have had a wee bit too much to drink while consoling yourself. But you need to leave now and let us continue our work."

"I will not! You fraudsters are Sadducees! You are an embarrassment to the church. You get out of my uncle's office. You leave things alone. You hear me! Get out."

Hotspur grabbed the Archdeacon and harshly pulled Karl towards the door. Unseen to him, the Reverend Moore was entering. He put his arms around Philip and said, "Now, Philip, I advise you to calm down and let Archdeacon Smithton go."

Hotspur turned his head, recognising Reverend Moore's face against his. Seeing the stern look, he jerked his head back, needing support to remain standing.

"Let Archdeacon Smithton go, Philip!"

Constable Rawlins approached and calmly repeated, "Let him go now, Mr Hotspur."

Walter Moore moved so the Constable could take hold of Hotspur's arms and unfold them.

Philip resisted and yelled, "But they should not be here, Constable. This office is mine now that the Bishop is dead. My office!"

Michael Rawlins was a big man and towered over the assistant curate. He grabbed Philip by the scruff of the neck and manhandled him out of the room.

"I don't want any more words from you now, Mr Hotspur. You come with me and spend a few hours sleeping off whatever you drank, my lad."

As the door closed, the clergy took their places around the table and sat.

Andrew said, "My, Walter. That was convenient, you turning up with the Constable when you did."

Walter Moore smiled. He answered, "Coincidence. I met him out on the street. He was going to give us an update on the bishop. I think he also needs Sopwith to complete the record of death. A couple of hours' sleep in a cell will do Philip good."

A relieved Karl Smithton sat at the table, taking a deep breath and said, "My goodness, that was a performance if I have ever seen one."

Andrew Taggart added, "Nearly as good as his normal performances. As one of my parishioners once said – it is a plain case of the vulgarities!"

Mr Berkly, who had come back in, started to laugh.

Karl looked at Andrew in amazement as the good Reverend began to chuckle. Moore and Crossling also began to laugh, and it became an uproar. With a growing smirk, Karl Smithton giggled and broke out in the loudest laugh Andrew had ever heard from a clergyman.

When they regained their composure, Karl, who seemed to have found some strength from the fellowship, said, "I think we should get this meeting going. Thank you for coming, gentlemen. Mr Berkly, would you take notes? We have drafted a letter to the archbishop that has been approved and sent off. We must go through Bishop Ponsdale's diary, cancel anything we can for the next few months, and take on the jobs that can't be undone."

Pleased to see Smithton becoming composed and more business-like, Andrew asked, "Karl, I noticed the archbishop was preaching at Petersfield on Sunday, the twentieth of May. The South family has asked me to take a memorial service at Petersfield near that date. I would happily do that parish visit for you if no one else wishes to take the service."

There were no objections, and Karl nodded to Andrew.

"Thank you, Andrew! That would be a relief as I am becoming too old for diocesan trips. Should Mr Berkly visit with you? He usually attends with the bishop."

"No. That will not be necessary."

"Good, as he will be needed here!" Karl was keen to finish this meeting as he was already becoming hungry. "Now, we should go through the rest and allocate jobs where necessary."

Andrew was happy with that result and would gladly consider Petersfield his next church home. But it would also depend on the Earl of Fintelton, who owned the living[29].

'Harting', St James's Square, London …

After picking up Anne, Mrs Stubbington's carriage left St James's Square, turned the corner onto Pall Mall, and soon stopped outside a large building. Alighting, Janet led the way through the foyer and up one set of stairs and stopped at a doorway.

"Here we are. As I said, the club is close and convenient. Come in, Lady Anne. We have a private dining room, and I am sure Henry will have your coach here as soon as we finish."

Anne entered and saw the marvellous view up and down Pall Mall from a bay window at the front.

"What a view. I can see up to Trafalgar Square from here. There are so many people in London, and it is so busy!"

"You are missing Porting and Guildford already, Anne?"

"Well, it is my hometown, and Robert and I are so happy there. But this might change in the future. London has its attractions, so I will enjoy them while I have the opportunity. I have a friend staying with me, and I am keen she sees the Piccadilly arcades."

"And who might your friend be?"

"Victoria Sopwith. She is the younger sister of Doctor David Sopwith, who married Lady Emma South, the Earl of Fintelton's daughter."

"Ah, yes! I recall the name now. I sense you will feel more positive once you and Victoria enjoy some shopping, Anne."

"Janet, I have been blessed with what we are given. To think I can visit Piccadilly so easily and afford to purchase items is something I would never have believed a year and a half ago. My challenge in life is to be prepared to give things up as our circumstances change. I have a habit of holding on too tight."

"It is a common problem, but I must brief you on the purpose of our meeting today."

---

[29] A Living during the Regency period (1795 to 1837) was a benefice agreed between the local bishop and the Lord of the Manor for the stipend of a minister. Usually, the Lord of the Manor was responsible for finding the applicant (often a younger brother in the family) and for funding of the stipend. Usually it was a tithe (ten percent) of the agricultural production of the parish.

Anne looked away from the window and concentrated on Janet.

"You will recall the contract you signed with us on providing information. Well, as you progress in society, we would ask that you attend functions that we strategically choose so your contacts will feed information to us. We have several persons of note who provide the same services to us. It is a way for the British government to gain insights into trade, politics, church, and security issues. We see your area of expertise as trade and business contacts."

Anne questioned, "You will send me to business conferences?"

"No, more like individual meetings that come from your trade. In your case, farming, food, and technology will be the particular focus. We will also assist in the development of Hursts' clientele. Your contacts there will be most helpful. The government department I work for is the Home Office in King Charles Street. We are particularly interested in home insurrection and the Irish republicans."

"I am unsure how to help, but I will do my best. I, too, would prefer our country to remain stable."

"Thank you. Before we proceed, I must advise you that I have invited Lachlan McPherson to join us this morning. He and his wife, Taye, will attend the function on Saturday night. You will find Taye a delightful person."

"Tell me, do the McPhersons have an agreement with you as well?"

"Yes, Hamish is a long-time associate, and his friendship with your father led us to you and Robert. Lachlan, like you, is only new to this game. The same as you. So the briefing today over lunch will benefit you both."

"I see."

Anne was finally assembling all the puzzle pieces that had confounded her for so long. They were all on the same side and working for the British government. No wonder her father had kept the agreement hidden in his study and refrained from discussing it with her. He would have understood the need for confidentiality.

Janet waved to the waiter, and he briskly moved to the table and said, "Ladies, here is the wine list. Please call me when you are ready."

Once he had moved away, Anne said, "Thank you, Janet, for being so forthright today. The details you gave me have explained much about the past few years. I now understand what has been happening.

But why the secrecy? Surely, it would be better to tell people from the start what your background is."

Janet smiled, "We make considerable investments in security. We need to be sure the people we contract are trustworthy and maintain confidentiality before we tell them too much. I am sure you understand that all I tell you is confidential."

"Yes, of course."

Soon, Lachlan McPherson arrived, and Janet stood to greet him, "Lachlan, how are you? I understand you know Lady Anne."

"Good day, Janet, and hello again, Lady Leystead."

The lunch went well, with Janet briefing them on who would attend the evening function and who would be of the greatest interest. She even explained the political situation in the Eastern Mediterranean and the delicacy of keeping the allies together, particularly the Russians.

By the end of lunch, Anne was tired and finding it hard to hold her concentration. She was glad when Janet called an end to the proceedings.

Janet said, "I took the liberty of organising your coach for your return journey, Anne. Henry Fletcher is standing by to receive you."

Anne was surprised by this, "Thank you, Janet. Do you mind me asking how long Henry will be on my staff?"

"For some months yet. We are being careful with the Irish situation at present. I should be able to tell you more next week. I take it that Victoria Sopwith will join us on Saturday night?"

"Yes, she is keen to come along. Thank you for lunch, and I look forward to Saturday evening."

Anne found her coach at the front entrance, and Henry Fletcher was ready to escort her. She noted that Henry was becoming a necessary part of her support team, for which she was thankful. She entered the coach and sank into the seat, taking a deep breath of relief.

Church School, High Street, Guildford ...
It was approaching two-thirty, and the children were becoming restless, thinking about home and probably afternoon tea. Mrs Laura Taggart rose from her desk and announced, "Children, we have a special guest this afternoon who is going to continue the conversation Mr Taggart started with you on Monday."

The children sat up straight with interest written all over them, and whispers about smugglers could be heard from the back of the room.

"Yes, that is correct! Who said, smugglers?"

Several hands went straight up, and there was a feeling of excitement in the classroom. A small voice from the middle of the room sang out, "Is it Blackbeard the pirate, Mrs Taggart?"

Laura laughed and said, "Almost as good. Now put away your slates and chalk and tidy your desks because we will all go home after our special guest finishes."

There was a quick commotion as desks were tidied, and the small talk subsided.

"Children, welcome, Mr Mervyn Webster."

Mr Webster burst through the door, dressed in what looked like a monk's robe and hood, which only extended to about five inches below a robust belt studded with diamonds and a sword hanging from it. Beneath the robe, he wore black sailor pants and black shoes with wood buckles. He had blackened two teeth and donned a false moustache and beard.

"Ah, Ha! Ah, Ha, me Hearties! Ha, ha, ha!"

The children all sat back in fright, thinking Mr Webster was real. The sudden quiet from the shrinking children, punctuated by a few little screams, made Mervyn realise he might appear too realistic. Halting his advance and standing close to the teacher's desk, he removed his hood, pulled out his sword and placed it on the desk.

"It is alright, children! It is only me, Mr Webster. Now you can come out and see my costume, belt and sword. This sword is real and belonged to a pirate who was captured long ago. I was fortunate to purchase it in 1806 from a shop in Cornwall. If you look at the butt, you will see many notches cut out of it. Do you know what that means?"

Dawn Luckett shouted out, "They used it for counting."

"That is right, young lady. But also, for the number of …"

Mrs Taggart interrupted and said, "To count their prisoners, please, Mr Webster."

Mervyn twigged quickly and agreed, "Oh, I see – Yes, prisoners! Today, you can all be the prisoners. How many prisoners do we have."

Everyone quickly counted, and Simeon was first to shout out, "Sixteen, Mr Webster."

"That's right, young man! And how did the prisoners escape?"

They all looked up silently, and one voice said, "They ran away!"

"No, no, no! You can't run away when you're a prisoner on a pirate ship. Someone had to save them! Who would that be?"

William, who worshipped the Royal Navy, quickly said, "Admiral Nelson of the King's navy!"

"Yes, young man. Now we have a special surprise for you. You, the prisoners, will all be saved by the Royal Navy. Come in, Captain Nelson."

Through the door came Leonard Webster, dressed in a naval officer's uniform and a captain's hat. He looked splendid, and the children screamed in delight and ran around him, touching his coat, sword, telescope, and brass buttons. Leonard certainly looked the part and grinned as he enjoyed playing the role.

Mrs Taggart said, "Now, children, all sit at your desks, please, so Mr Webster can tell you about smugglers in Cornwall."

Mervyn made it short so the children would not lose interest, and bang on three o'clock, they finished the story with some smugglers thrown into jail. It was a presentation the children would not forget, and William, Simeon and Edward accompanied Mr Webster and Leonard as they walked home, bombarding them with other questions.

Mervyn Webster said, "As you are all so interested in pirates and smugglers, I will show you a little display."

He invited the children inside the Webster house and had them sit in the parlour with Leonard. Mr Webster retreated from the room but re-emerged with what looked like a small treasure chest. He placed it on a table surrounded by their chairs and slowly opened the lid. Inside, it was packed to the rim with gold doubloons.

"Treasure!" he said in a voice that lingered happily over the room.

The children were amazed and asked, "Is it real?"

"Of course, me hearties! Doubloons a-plenty! Now, you each may have one."

The children stepped forward and took a doubloon. Simeon was the first to ask, "Are they real, as gold should weigh more than this?"

"Oh, yes. They are real." Mervyn took one, peeled the gold-coloured paper from the chocolate, and put the round morsel in his mouth.

"You see!" he said with a smile. I never said they were gold, did I!"

The children saw the fun in the antics and laughed as they munched their chocolate doubloons.

"You can all have one more, and then it is off home."

"Thank you, Mr Webster."

William tugged Mervyn Webster's arm, "Mr Webster! We are going to the riverbank on Sunday afternoon for a picnic. You must come and join us. We can play Pirates and smugglers."

Mervyn smiled and said, "William, that is a kind invitation, but we have not been invited. If your father invites us, we will be there. Now Leonard will walk you all home."

Leonard took a doubloon, carefully looked at it, peeled it and placed the chocolate in his mouth. Smiling, he said, "Not bad at all!"

He then took three more and gave one to each of the children as they exited the front door.

The London Road, North of Guildford, England ...

Jessica Swamp could see the Reverend Hotspur waiting for her at the corner. She smiled at him as she approached and said, "I was wondering if you would be here today, Mr Hotspur."

"Why would I not be Miss Swamp? It is a pleasure to walk you home some afternoons, and I have something important to tell you."

Jessica looked up in surprise, "What could that be?"

Hotspur had considered how he would carefully break this news to Jessica. It must appear that he was doing her a favour, and she would be in his debt. The fact that he had coerced her father's agreement to tutor his daughter would be kept from the girl. It was enough that the father had sworn her to secrecy.

"I had the pleasure of visiting with your father the previous week. He informed me that your education was lacking and you needed further learning to prosper in your work at the Turners. He asked if I could provide you with some free private tuition. Of course, it will mean I must take some time out of my busy day to do this, but I had no choice but to agree as I am aware of your great desire for learning."

Despite still being young at sixteen, Jessica Swamp was street-smart, and from what her father had instructed, she knew that Hotspur was framing this in an entirely different way. The man acted like he was belittling himself to stoop down and help a poor girl such as herself.

Peter was right – this man was devious, and she now agreed with Aggie – there was an agenda here. She decided that if he had such a low opinion of her abilities, she would play dumb and act it out.

She stopped in amazement and looked directly into his face, asking, "You mean he asked if you would give me lessons?"

Philip, playing the role of benefactor, said, "Yes! He was keen on the proposal and felt it would benefit you greatly. I hope you are willing to undertake this study?"

Jessica knew the Reverend Hotspur had misrepresented her father and was using the situation to his advantage. But why? She was sure now that Philip's proposition might have ulterior motives. But why pick her? He must be attracted to her. She had never considered herself beautiful. Why would he be attracted to a plain farmer's daughter who had little prospects in life but to marry a farm labourer who might one day gain a farm of his own? What did he hold over her father, allowing him this private access to her?

She decided to accept his proposal and find out what she could gain from this situation. Jessica was keen to benefit from more tuition, given her limited schooling. She was interested in knowing what Mr Hotspur's intentions were. Jess knew she could walk away from this agreement whenever she wanted to.

Philip, feeling confident, said with a smile, "What say you, Jessica Swamp?"

'Harting', St James's Square, St James, London …
On Wednesday evening, Anne was extremely tired and craved an early night.

"I am sorry, Victoria, no cards tonight. I hope I am not sick, but I am fatigued. I must retire. Please ask Mary to bring my dinner upstairs as I think I might have a light meal, do some reading and then go to bed."

Victoria was surprised as normally she found it hard to keep up with her friend.

"Anne, if you are indisposed, why not call Doctor Bassington? They are not far away, and Beth might come as well."

Anne was too tired for this and quickly replied, "No! Perhaps tomorrow, I must retire now. Staines!"

The butler quickly stood beside Anne, "Yes, Milady."

"Staines, help me up these stairs, please. I feel giddy. I must rest."

Victoria rushed to assist as Staines gently held her left arm. Victoria took the right, and they slowly took an unsteady Anne up the stairs. Mary Hedge soon joined them, and Staines let the two women take charge and exited as Lady Anne struggled to her bed.

In a quivering voice, she said softly, "I must rest!"

Mary carefully lowered Anne onto the bed and watched as her mistress' eyes closed, and she fell fast asleep.

Victoria softly said, "This is strange indeed, Mary."

Mary felt Anne's brow and said, "There is no temperature. Perhaps she is exhausted."

"No, Mary. There is something wrong here. I will have Staines call Doctor Bassington."

Victoria quickly left the room and found Staines waiting outside.

"Is she ill, Milady?"

"Yes, I believe so. Staines, would you call for Doctor Bassington, please? Tomorrow, we must move her to the first floor. There are too many steps for her on the second floor."

"I will have the room made up tonight. It will be ready for tomorrow. Please excuse me, and I will call Doctor Bassington."

"Thank you, Staines."

The butler rushed off, and Victoria moved back inside Anne's room.

"She is sleeping deeply, Miss Victoria. I have never seen her like this before."

"Nor I, Mary. Have you had your dinner?"

"No, Milady."

"You go, and I will stay here and watch over her. Come back in an hour, and you can take over. I feel we must keep a careful watch until the doctor comes."

Victoria sat beside the fireplace and relaxed for ten minutes until a knock came. The door opened slightly, and Staines poked his head around the corner with a finger to his lips. He beckoned Victoria to follow him out into the hallway.

"Yes, Staines!"

"I have sent for the doctor. However, Mrs Stubbington has arrived and asks for Lady Anne. She delivers tickets for the Russian Soiree on

Saturday night."

Victoria looked away as she considered what must be done.

"Staines! Call my maid Judith, please. She can relieve me while I come down and talk with Mrs Stubbington."

"Yes, Milady!"

Victoria knew Janet Stubbington was a forthright lady; sickness would not put her off. She would shield Anne from this disturbance. Her friend desperately needed rest.

The visitor turned as Victoria entered, "Mrs Stubbington, excuse me as we have not been introduced. I am Victoria Sopwith, a friend of Lady Anne. I am afraid the Viscountess is fast asleep."

"Miss Sopwith, it is a pleasure to meet you. Excuse my inquiry, but your lovely Irish accent makes me wonder if you are the daughter of the late Sir James David Sopwith and Lady Marguerite Felicity Sopwith of Bellcanon Estate, Coleraine?"

Victoria was surprised by the question, "Yes, I am. You are very well informed, Mrs Stubbington."

Janet smiled and said, "This is a pretty room, Miss Sopwith. Lush furnishings and a warm fire! It is very relaxing indeed. My apologies for coming unannounced, but I deliver invitations to the Soiree at the Russian Embassy. I had wished to talk with Lady Anne and thought her illness had passed."

"Thank you, Mrs Stubbington. It may be illness or exhaustion! She has had a long day. I believe you saw her at lunch?"

"Yes, a short working lunch. The Viscountess was good company."

"I am afraid she is fast asleep. May I be of assistance?"

Janet considered the well-spoken and considerate young lady.

"Victoria, It was a tragedy that your parents and brother passed away. I am glad you have another brother in Guildford. I imagine you will settle there?"

"Not quite! I reside now in Guildford and will soon acquire a residence in London."

"You will move to London?"

"In small doses, Mrs Stubbington. Being brought up in Coleraine by guardians, I am unaccustomed to large cities, but I support Lady Anne in setting up Hursts' first fashion house here."

"I see! Miss Sopwith, I came with an invitation for Lady Anne to attend the Soiree at the Russian Embassy on Saturday night next. I hoped to introduce Sir Robert's wife to some of the London community. I was unaware you were in London, but Lady Anne advised me you would be keen to attend. Given Lady South's state of health, it may be advisable if you attended with her. We will be in the British Government party. Would you be willing to come with us?"

Victoria's eyes sparkled, "Yes, indeed! But only if I am with Lady Anne."

"You would be with Lady Anne and myself!"

"Then we shall come. I am sure Lady Anne will recover by Saturday. Perhaps your business might wait until then. If Lady Anne does not recover, I shall accompany you, Mrs Stubbington."

Victoria surprised herself by making such a quick and bold decision. She had found that the move to London and her position working with Anne on establishing Hursts' London premises had given her a new confidence she had never felt before. Victoria now had a mission in life outside her family ties. The feeling was exciting; she wanted to meet people and expand her horizons.

Janet stood back in surprise, impressed by Victoria's confidence.

"Good, I will pick you and Anne up here at seven-thirty. Given your friend has been unwell, we will not make it a late night, but it will be long enough for several introductions and some fellowship. During our carriage ride to Mayfair, I shall brief you about the other guests."

As Staines watched Mrs Stubbington's carriage depart, a messenger arrived. The butler took the mail and paid the rider with a half crown.

Closing the front door, he found a seat in the foyer and hoped it would not be long before Doctor Bassington arrived. As he sorted the mail, he noticed a letter for Sir Robert South marked 'Private & Confidential'. Turning it over, he read the sender was Sir Hugh South, with the sender's address of The Grand Hotel, Kingston, Jamacia. But Sir Hugh was dead! The letter must have been written before the Earl's son and heir died.

Staines thumbed the letter as he considered the situation. Sir Robert was far away on a navy mission, so it would be months before he read it. Given his wife was here, it was probably fitting that she received the letter. There may be information on the estate's affairs. He would give it to Lady Anne when she was recovered in the morning.

Rectory, High Street, Guildford, Surrey ...

Andrew Taggart sat in the lounge chair sipping a sherry as his wife read by candlelight across from him. His day had been long, and he was now considering how he would fulfil all the new tasks the meeting at the diocesan office had brought him. Then he recalled the scene at Philip Hotspur's residence the previous night.

"Laura, might I interrupt your reading?"

His wife looked up and smiled. She waited for his next comment.

Andrew rubbed his forehead and took a deep breath.

"Did you see the young woman coming down the stairwell last night?"

"You mean inside Philip's house."

Andrew said, "Yes."

"I was wondering when you were going to ask me. I assume the front bedroom upstairs is Philip's?"

Andrew thought momentarily and said, "I am not sure, as he has never invited me in. But I would agree."

"Even if it was not, she certainly was not stopping to be introduced."

"I would say she had been instructed what to do."

"I know what you are thinking, Andrew. We should not jump to a conclusion. But it was twelve-thirty in the morning. She appeared to be completely dressed and was leaving. There may be an explanation, but it is not a time when a respectable girl would be venturing off home from the back door of a gentleman's house."

"If I ask him, he will deny it as he does everything else."

"Well, I saw the young woman, and I assume Karl did as well. It would be best if you asked Karl. You have every right to do so. If he agreed, three of us could confirm there was a young woman present and that she was upstairs in the front room when we knocked. The moving shadows from the candlelight made it obvious there were two upstairs."

"Yes, if it were only you and me, he would argue we were conspiring. But if Karl also agreed, then we would have him."

"Even if there are three of us, do you want the stress of challenging him? Surely a good talking to would be sufficient. Then you could take it up with the new bishop if he is discovered again."

"Johnathan said if we gave him enough time, he would trap himself.

He was right. I see no improvement in the young man's behaviour."

"Keep notes and ask Karl to confirm it in writing. He is seventy now, and who knows how long he will last."

"It is strange that you say that. I have been thinking deeply, Laura. I think I am wearing myself out here in Guildford. The challenges are too great for me, and I have been toying with the idea of moving to a smaller church."

Laura was not surprised, but she wanted to be sure this was not just a reaction to all the trouble this new assistant curate was causing.

"I hope Philip is not the cause of these thoughts. Anyway, if we do move on, it should not be until the problems with Philip are resolved. It would be inappropriate to leave this for the next Rector."

"I know. You are correct, and I agree. But I am feeling tired and need a change. It has been a good twenty years here. We should put it to prayer. Will you pray with me, Laura?"

"With all my heart, Darling."

Fintelton Manor, Outside Petersfield, Sussex ...
The butler, Thomas Pike, entered the parlour where Lady Jane was reading.

"Excuse me, Milady. A message has arrived from Guildford."

Lady Jane took the message and opened it.

The Rectory
High Street
Guildford, Surrey

May 2027

The Right Honble. The Earl of Fintelton, and
The Right Honble. The Countess of Fintelton

My Lord and Madam,

We continue to pray for you both at this sad time. Please let us know if there is anything we can assist you with to help you through this terrible loss.

I was honoured to receive your invitation to be the celebrant conducting the memorial service for Sir Hugh and the committal of his ashes on Thursday, 17 May 1827. It gives me great pleasure to accept this invitation.

I understand you will advise me of the arrangements in due course.

Please remember that Laura and I hold you dearly in our prayers, and we look forward to renewing our acquaintance on that day.

Your servant
The Reverend Andre Taggart

Lady Jane smiled and said to herself, 'You will not be staying in town as I insist you and Laura stay here at Fintelton. I will write and tell you.' She rose from her chair, took a candle, and walked to her writing room. In a few minutes, she was finished, folded the message, and sealed it.

Coming back to the parlour, she pulled the cord for the butler.

On his arrival, she said, "Pike, have this sent tomorrow morning, please."

Sitting there thinking about her son, she realised that the Reverend Andrew Taggart had become closer to Hugh than anyone she knew. Then again, perhaps that was not the case. This Lady Fiona Green may also fit the category. She mused on this and wondered about the relationship between Lady Fiona and her son. Lady Jane South looked forward to meeting Hugh's friend and seeing Laura and Andrew again. As she and the earl aged, it became more difficult for them to travel and meet their friends. How she felt at present might mean this may be her last meeting with the good Reverend.

Chapter 11

'Harting', St James's Square, London ...

In the quiet of the evening, Matthew Staines could faintly hear the arrival of a carriage outside. The butler must have drifted off to sleep and shook himself as he heard at least two passengers climbing down and waiting for their bags. Glancing at the hallway clock, the butler raised his eyebrows, noticing it was one o'clock in the morning. Standing and covering his mouth, he yawned, straightened his livery and pulled the cord for some footmen to assist. Unlocking the front door, Staines found Dr Bassington and his heavily pregnant wife, Bethany, approaching.

"Ah, Staines! Thank you for waiting. I apologise for the delay, but I was operating at the hospital. I came as soon as I could. As it is so late, I thought we might stay overnight. Lady South must be fast asleep by now. I will look in but probably examine her in the morning if that is acceptable. Mrs Bassington accompanies me. Being Anne's sister, she was concerned!"

Staines smiled, "Thank you for coming, Doctor and Mrs Bassington. You are welcome, and there is plenty of accommodation. We are worried about the Viscountess. She seemed almost unconscious earlier in the evening. We could not wake her."

Bethany put her hand over her mouth in fear, "Oh, my goodness!"

A yawning Victoria Sopwith in a dressing gown appeared beside Staines, "Neville and Beth, thank you for coming. Anne wanted to retire without dinner. She was dizzy and needed help getting up the stairs. Once she was asleep, we could not wake her. It is most unlike her to be so lethargic."

Neville, hearing the initial symptoms, frowned, "I better have a look at her first. Which room, Staines?"

"The blue room on floor two, Doctor. We will move her to the first floor in the morning."

Neville nodded and rushed off.

"Mrs Bassington, if you follow me, I will show you to your room. Please leave the cases. I will have a footman bring them up directly. Let me take one of those light bags you are holding."

Victoria said, "Let me take the other bag, Beth."

Bethany had packed in a hurry and carried several small carry-cases. As the footmen appeared, the Bassingtons left the other luggage for them in the doorway and followed Staines up the stairs.

Neville opened the door, finding several candles lighting the room, and Anne was fast asleep on her bed. He noticed she was covered in several blankets and sweating heavily.

'What is wrong with these London people always piling on the blankets? No wonder she is weak!'

Putting his medical bag down, he removed the blankets carefully, but Anne did not stir. Lady South was fast asleep and oblivious to all going on around her. Neville agreed this was most unlike Anne.

He quickly checked for the essential signs and found them normal. Anne appeared relaxed and comfortable, but she was deeply asleep. He considered if he should wake her or let her rest. Deciding on the latter, Neville placed a blanket bedside her on the sheet in case she became cold. Then, extinguishing the candle, he let himself out of the room and found Staines, Victoria and Bethany in the hallway.

"Why did she have all those blankets over her, Staines?"

Victoria spoke up, "That was my doing, Neville! Staines has been most helpful and concerned. I was making sure she did not gain a chill."

"Well, given the mild night, she was struggling with heat from the blankets. That would have tired her considerably. All the signs are normal, and she seems to be resting comfortably. You may see her Beth if you wish, but I have put the candle out. It is probably best to let her rest until morning. I am confident she is safe tonight, and the sleep will assist her recovery. I will carry out a full examination in the morning."

Two footmen passed them in the hallway with the Bassington's luggage and took them to a room down the hall. Staines apologised, "Doctor Bassington, I apologise for giving you a room on the second floor. I had forgotten your good wife was pregnant. Would you like a room prepared on the first floor?"

"Thank you, Staines. This floor will do. We are here now, and she has a doctor with her."

Both men smiled.

Bethany asked, "Staines. You mentioned Lady Anne as the Viscountess when we arrived. Has her circumstances changed?"

The butler moved closer and quietly spoke as if the matter was confidential, "Yes, Mrs Bassington. I am unsure if this information is public, but the last few days have been eventful."

Neville pricked his ears up as he heard this statement.

Staines continued, "As you are family, I feel it is safe to advise you. We received news from Lady Fintelton of Sir Hugh's passing away. Lady Anne was most upset by the news, compounded when Mrs Stubbington arrived. The meeting caused our lady some concern. I am not aware of the details. Lady Anne was also indisposed this morning after breakfast but regained her strength mid-morning and completed an appointment at the new bakery. She spent several hours there and was exhausted when she returned before lunch."

Bethany said, "That is our Anne. She never stops. It appears she is suffering from an extremely tiring day. But Staines, you did not explain the title."

"My apologies, Mrs Bassington. On Sir Hugh's death, Sir Robert became the Earl's heir and was granted Sir Hugh's title of Viscount Leystead. Lady Anne, being Sir Robert's wife, becomes the Viscountess of Leystead."

Bethany said, "I see."

Neville interrupted, "It is late, and we are all tired." He smiled and said, "Doctor's orders. Everyone to bed, as we all need rest. I am sure we can sort this out in the morning. Thank you, Staines, for all your efforts today and Victoria for being here with Anne."

Later in their room, Bethany asked, "Neville, if Anne was indisposed after breakfast, that may be significant."

"You're right, Beth. Those are my thoughts exactly! I think Anne's life is about to change forever. We shall discuss this tomorrow as I am exhausted! We need clear heads in the morning. Please, let's turn in for the night."

"But Neville!"

"Beth, I don't know yet! Tomorrow, we will know. Then we can discuss it. I am exhausted as well. I need sleep."

The High Street, Guildford ...

The Reverend Andrew Taggart had not slept well and took an early morning walk down the High Street to clear his mind. Following Laura's comments last night, he decided to settle Reverend Hotspur's situation before even considering moving to a new parish. She was correct! He must end his daily worry about what nightmare Philip would cause next.

There was no time like the present, so he would visit his curate for breakfast. He knew Philip employed a cook each morning; another place at breakfast would be no trouble. By now, Philip should have shaken off the drink from yesterday, resulting in the terrible scene at the diocesan offices.

By the time he decided to visit, he was near the bottom of the High Street. Taggart turned right, walking along Swan Lane, up North Street to Hayden Place. From there, he headed for Philip's house on Martyr Road and knocked on the front door. Mrs April Handle heard the knock, rushed from the kitchen and opened the door.

"Good morning, Rector. I am just starting Mr Hotspur's breakfast. Will you be joining him? I was not aware."

"Yes, thank you, April. I had not planned on breakfast, but yes, I will join him."

"Come in, Rector. You sit in the kitchen, and I will let Mr Hotspur know you are here."

"There is no need. Philip is expecting me. I will go up! You keep cooking the breakfast. It smells enticing."

"You men can always smell the bacon and herbs!" She laughed as she turned and rushed back to her cooking.

Andrew looked around and made himself familiar with the home. As this was his first time inside, he was especially keen to explore the upstairs. In particular, he wanted to know if the front room over-looking the street was Philips's bedroom.

Walking softly up the stairs, he was keen not to wake the sleeping curate. On the landing, he looked around and saw three rooms with closed doors and what he suspected was a bathroom door at the rear of the hallway. He turned towards the street and proceeded to the entrance of what he thought was the front bedroom. Gently opening the door, he found the young curate still fast asleep in a large double bed. The bed looked as if two people had been sharing it for the night, and he noticed a lady's dress and underclothes hanging over a chair.

Andrew raised his eyebrows, wondering where the woman must be. He turned and walked back along the landing, checking the doors. There were two bedrooms with the beds made before he opened the last door at the far end.

Peeping in, he came face to face with a young lady lounging in a bath.

As she screamed, he said, "My apologies!" Quickly, he closed the door and descended the stairs to the kitchen.

Mrs Handle was coming along the hallway as he reached the ground floor.

"Is there a woman up there, Rector?"

"Yes, it appears so! Philip is awake, so I will join you in the kitchen."

"Yes." Mrs Handle looked up the stairs and sighed. She turned and led the Rector to a large kitchen table, where a lovely plate of bacon and eggs awaited him.

Andrew Taggart sat and dug into his serving.

"Exquisite, Mrs Handle! These eggs and bacon are delicious."

"Here, Rector, have some toast and tea. That will wash it down."

A young woman in a dressing gown threw open the door and complained, "Mrs Handle, Phili never told me there was a meeting here today. Who are you, Mister, barging into my bathroom?"

Mrs Handle quickly replied, "This is the Reverend Andrew Taggart, and he is the Reverend Hotspur's boss!"

The young woman instantly changed her tone, "Oh, nice to meet you, Mr. Reverend. Phili….Philip didn't tell me you would be here early."

Andrew smiled and said, "Philip didn't know I was coming so early! I was concerned, as yesterday would have been a hard day for him. I wanted to check on his welfare."

The young lady was confused and about to ask another question when Philip Hotspur entered in a loose-fitting blue dressing gown and asked, "What! What are you doing sitting at my kitchen table and taking breakfast, Rector?"

"I needed to see you, Philip. Mrs Handle invited me to breakfast when I knocked."

"What …Mrs Handel, why …!"

Suddenly talking over Philip's gasps, "Rector Man, you know Philip's uncle died the day before yesterday, and he has been so upset. I came to settle him down. So upset he was!"

Andrew cut across the conversation and said, "Thank goodness Philip has a friend like you, my dear! You might introduce your young lady friend to me, Philip."

Hotspur stood there in shock. It was all becoming too much for him.

"Mr Rector Man! My name is Rosie Jones, and I am a friend of Phili's. I have been helping him manage his stress. His uncle's death was quite a shock for him. You know!"

Taggart smiled and said, "Yes, I can imagine. Thank You, Rosie. I am glad to meet you."

Philip, who had calmed himself, suddenly said, "Best if you go now, Rosie."

"What about breakfast, Lovely? I always get breakfast."

"Not today, Dearie!" He gave her a one-pound note. "Get yourself dressed and have breakfast at the local. Off you go."

He pushed her through the door to the staircase, and then he came and sat at the table.

"What can I assist you with, Reverend Taggart?"

The Reverend Taggart smiled, "Philip, we must meet soon, but I will let you know when. There are some issues we should discuss."

'Harting' House, St James's Square, London …
Neville found Anne sitting in bed with a cup of tea. She appeared quite well and ready to talk.

"I am sorry that Victoria called you last night, Neville. I was extremely tired. That is all."

"I don't think so, Anne. We will find out after breakfast. I brought all my medical gear as Admiral and Lady Crouch expected me mid-morning. I don't recall examining a woman so far under as you were last night. You did not stir or sense I was in the room. That is not normal at all. But I am glad to find you looking so well this morning."

Anne shared with him, "I have been feeling tired lately. But I put it down to my present heavy workload. Father is in the process of hiring a general manager for the bakery and mill operations. That will ease my load considerably."

Neville listened carefully, but Anne did not address the issue he felt was the cause.

"We can talk soon after breakfast. Beth is here and looking forward to seeing you."

On the mention of breakfast, Neville noticed Anne carrying a concerned expression. She said, "Yes, come back after breakfast, Neville. Thank you."

Neville returned around nine and, within a half hour, had completed the examination. Sitting near the bed, he said, "Congratulations, Anne. I find you are around two months pregnant. The child and your busy work schedule would have caused your exhaustion. From what you have told me, the morning sickness has begun, and you may be susceptible to it. It would be best to rearrange your work program for the next few months as it may not improve until June."

Anne sat there stunned, "You mean I am going to have a baby?"

"Yes, around the fourth of December. Congratulations again, and if you excuse me, I must be on my way. Admiral Crouch and his wife are expecting me. You will be glad to know he will make a full recovery."

"Please pass on my best wishes to them and explain that I had intended to visit, but my condition and appointments prevented me. If they travel to Hampshire, I may visit them there."

Anne smiled but became quiet, and Neville saw his sister-in-law grappling with the news of her pregnancy.

"Anne, remember how tired you have become in the last few days. If you keep up your current activities, this may increase and lead to other issues. You must ensure plenty of rest time, less work and healthy food. We can talk about this further when I return for Bethany. Now I must go."

"Thank you, Neville. Please, if you would call Beth and Vicky."

Victoria and Bethany were outside the room when Neville emerged after examining Anne.

"Well, Neville. Is she in good health?"

"Yes, Beth. In good health indeed. Anne asked for you both."

Beth was impatient, "Can you tell us any more than that?"

Victoria asked, "I don't understand. She was in such poor health last night."

Neville said, "I think you will find she was exhausted, and there are good reasons for that."

The door opened, with Anne appearing in a white dressing gown. She said, "Come in and talk, girls".

Neville laughed and said, "I will leave you three together as I am off to Admiral Crouch's home. I am hoping he can leave for Hampshire tomorrow."

His comments were lost in the conversation between Anne and her friends. He could hear the excitement as he walked away.

Bethany asked, "You're not, Anne?"

"Yes, I am. Neville thinks around two months."

Mayfair, London ...

"Good morning, Lady Katherine. I hope you and the Admiral are well?"

"Neville, I cannot believe the improvement in Sir Franklin's health. He is walking freely, and the naval doctors have agreed we may return to Hampshire for his recovery."

"Excellent, Lady Katherine. By the way, Lady Anne South sends her best wishes and apologises for not visiting yet. She has had a busy schedule and is now unwell. She wondered if you would be open to her visiting when you return to Hampshire."

"Oh, yes, Neville. Please tell her she would be more than welcome. I am sure it would be good for the Admiral as well. Give her my best wishes."

"I will, Lady Katherine. Perhaps you might excuse us as I complete the final examination."

"Certainly."

As she left the room, the admiral stood, and Neville noticed he remained unsteady.

"Please remain seated, Admiral Crouch. There is no need to stand. I would prefer you to relax. At your age, the less stress you put on your heart, the better."

"Come, come, Neville. I am one hundred per cent better than when you first called. My returning to Hampshire for a few months seems overprotective. I prefer a return to work."

Nevile smiled and commenced the examination. One of the tests he tried was feeling the artery in the admiral's neck for around fifteen seconds. He noticed the heart was beating fast and recorded the rate.

"What are you doing, Neville? No doctor has felt my neck before."

"I was checking your blood pressure. I have been reading some papers from Stephen Hales[30] and Thomas Young[31], both English scientists who made great progress in explaining how blood pressure relates to disease. Simply put, blood pressure can affect your heart's behaviour. The top of your neck below the jaw is a good place to feel your pulse. I notice your heart is beating a little fast."

"Probably because I am nervous about all this medical care."

Neville thought about the Admiral's comments.

"Admiral Crouch. You will recall when I first came and changed your treatment. I must say that I found the treatment prescribed to be quite ill-informed. I understand your doctors were of the highest integrity, but their methods seemed contrary to what you required. If we had not changed the treatment, you may have died."

The admiral considered Neville's words and asked, "What are you alluding to, Neville?"

Doctor Bassington realised he had ventured into dangerous territory by criticising doctors who were specialists in their fields.

"I am not suggesting anything, my Lord. My concern is that you receive care appropriate to your condition. My mentioning your previous state is that I cannot understand why your doctors did not diagnose your condition correctly and why they treated you for a stroke."

Sir Franklin Crouch did not comment.

---

[30] 'Stephen Hales was the first, in 1727, to determine arterial blood pressure, when he measured the rise in a column of blood in a glass tube bound into an artery.' From Werner Forssmann's 1956 acceptance speech for the Nobel Prize in Medicine. Wikipedia.

[31] Thomas Young: In physiology, Young made an important contribution in haemodynamics in the Croonian lecture of 1808 on the "Functions of the Heart and Arteries," where he derived a formula for the wave speed of the pulse. Wikipedia.

Neville continued, "I now find from your wife that these doctors are content for you to return to Hampshire. When I first visited, I understood the doctors had refused your return and introduced strict security arrangements. It seems a contradiction."

"Yes, they were surprised when they came earlier this morning." The admiral smiled as Neville finished the examination.

"There, we are done. I advise you to have at least two weeks at home resting before you even consider returning to work. I prefer a month, but you can decide after the first two weeks. Not many visitors, please, and no stressful situations. With the weather warming, keep blankets to a minimum and ensure you are hydrated. That is, drink plenty of water. Each day, you should go for an easy walk around the garden, both in the morning and afternoon, and each day extend the walk. If you have no further issues, the decision to return to work is yours. I will write a letter containing these recommendations and leave it with you. I am in London every second week from Tuesday to Thursday evening. You have the address, so contact me there, and I will give you a final examination. It is not my place to make further comment, Admiral, but I would advise you to take care."

Neville moved to a seat beside a table and scribbled his advice.

As he passed the letter, the admiral asked, "Any news on Robert yet?"

"No, Sir. Anne has not received any letters since 'Shadow' departed Woolwich."

The admiral frowned, "He should be in Malta by now."

Neville was curious, "Excuse me for enquiring, my Lord, but I thought you would be kept up to date by your office?"

"Unfortunately, news travels slowly by ship. I am sure Robert is safe and well in Malta. My greatest fear is the Navy has shut me out. I fear I may be put out to pasture. That is why I am keen to return."

The surprising admission caught Neville by surprise. He understood that the admiral had now taken him into his confidence. He must respect this and support this man.

"Sir, all I can say is that if you have at least two weeks rest, you will be far more able to handle the great pressures of your vocation. Better to rest now and fight again another day."

Admiral Crouch knew of Neville's history as a navy surgeon and appreciated his unique understanding of the stress on naval leaders. He must not share too much with Bassington, but he was thankful for his support and the rescue from the navy doctors.

"Any chance of you visiting Hampshire if I need you, Neville?"

"At your estate?"

"Yes, it is fifteen miles to the west of Petersfield."

"It would depend on whether I am in London or not. Here is my practice address in Guildford." Neville passed across a card. "Send me a message if you need me. I will see what I can do."

"I will not forget what you have done for me, Neville. Thank you. Where do you practice in London?"

"Harley Street, Sir. The Sloan Specialist Practice on Harley Street. Lady Crouch has the details."

"When I return to London, I shall call on you for a check-up. We shall meet then and compare notes on where Robert is."

They shook hands, and Neville left, thanking Lady Katherine on the way out.

'Harting', St James's Square, London ...

Following morning tea, Anne returned to her room for more rest. All kinds of thoughts were going through her mind about being confirmed pregnant. She had not even considered this, although she now realised it all made sense. Inside her, a new life had started, and she must protect the baby at all costs. Suddenly, nothing else seemed to be so important.

She knew Victoria had left for Hursts' new rented premises and would not return until this evening. Beth would be off with Neville for lunch, and she had no appointments until Saturday night's soiree and Monday's meeting with the solicitors and Mrs Constance. Having had a cup of tea and some scones, she felt well but knew she needed rest if her appointments were to be kept on Saturday and Monday.

Placing some cushions up at the head of the bed, she sat and gazed out the window. Then she noticed the mail still on the dresser. Hopping out of bed, she retrieved the letters and sorted them. A letter addressed to Robert caught her notice. Turning it over, she noticed the Fintelton seal and the sender's name, Sir Hugh South. Opening the envelope, she removed the letter and returned to bed.

25 March 1827

Sir Robert South
Harting House
St James's Square
St James, London
United Kingdom

My Dear Brother

I am writing about my great adventure in Kingston town and my pending return to Fintelton.

It has been nearly four and a half months since I left England's green shores, and I long to see them again. It is only due to the grace of our Good Lord that I will sail from Kingston in early May 1827. But first I must tell you of my adventures.

After Neville Bassington's buck's party in Guildford and making a complete ass of myself, I recognised that I had chosen a way that only led to destruction. You could liken me to the prodigal son who worshipped wine, women and song. I had been visiting Doctor Sopwith for several months before that time and was aware of his diagnosis that I suffered from a terminal disease. I chose to ignore his advice. You might recall I suffered a severe illness around the time of our father's minor stroke. The attack laid me up for a week and made me question myself as to my actions in ignoring Sopwith.

As chance would have it, I confided in old Taggart and gained valuable insights from him. You will recall my change of heart and apology to Neville the day after the wedding. Soon after, I took our father's advice and decided to visit the estates in Jamacia.

I came to realise that Taggart is an amazing man. I could not have wished for a better confidant, and we had several talks before I departed for overseas. We must talk more about him when I return.

It took nearly a week of the voyage before I found my sea legs. I relapsed into heavy drinking for comfort and then fell under the spell of Lady Clarissa Wendarm. By the time we reached New York, I thought she might be a suitable partner for marriage. A letter was posted to our mother asking for information on Lady Clarissa's suitability. Sadly, I never received a reply.

On arriving in Kingston, the governor accepted my credentials and welcomed me. I then visited the plantations to assess their operations and financial viability. The miserable conditions our workers suffer and their family's run-down shanty houses came as a shock to me. I understand it is business, but I was dismayed that we could be associated with such establishments. We must make changes in the future even if it means less profits. Our employees should be treated with respect and given the same opportunities we provide our tenants in England.

I also discovered that our agents in Jamacia had not acted with integrity toward us. On returning to Kingston, I studied the plantation figures and found alarming discrepancies. It was then that I was struck down by this terrible disease, which I continue to suffer from. The doctor told me I was unconscious for three weeks, and the expectation from Doctor Cowper was I would pass away within a day! But as you know, we, Turners, are made of hardy stuff, and some weeks later, I regained consciousness in the presence of Doctor Cowper and Mrs Fiona Green.

I have not told you of Fiona. She was Lady Clarissa's travelling companion on the ship out from England. At one stage during the voyage, she tried to warn me about Clarissa and that lady's back-ground. Under Clarissa's trance, I ignored Fiona's advice to my detriment. On regaining consciousness, three weeks later, I found that Clarissa had deserted me, and Fiona had arranged my care and remained my friend and protector until now. I am unsure what would have happened to me without Fiona's loving care. She is an amazing woman whom I wish I had met earlier in my life.

My recovery has been long and slow. I have often taken one step forward and two steps back. It has taken over two months for me to gain the confidence to walk again, but with the help of Fiona, I am now walking freely. My passage to England should arrive at Southampton on the twenty-sixth of May 1827. I will also have the bonus of Lady Fiona Green and Doctor Ronald Cowper as my travelling companions and carers.

After four months of severe illness, you will find me a changed man physically and spiritually. But I yearn for England and family. I have ventured outside twice in the last few days and walked slowly with Fiona. Doctor Cowper has warned me not to over-exert myself, and I am training carefully for the trip home.

Often, dear Robert, I find myself running with you as a boy through the wheat fields, our hands skimming across the wheat and our chests gulping in the crystal clear air of Fintelton. I see the golden sun setting and the joy on our faces as you, Emma, and I sit around the open garden fireplace, laughing and singing with our parents. I even long to hug old Thomas Pike and thank him for keeping me out of danger in the many scrapes I fell into as a lad. How I long for home and to see you all again.

Yet, as Doctor Cowper rightly warned, I must be mindful of my frailties. If I do not survive the voyage, I have enclosed a bank draft from the Imperial Bank of London (the bank we work through here in Kingston). Please bank this into the estate's account. More will come as the government solicitor recovers the monies owed to the estate.

In the case of my demise, Lady Fiona Green has been appointed as one of my executors, and she will carry my last will, along with all the other legal documents assembled here. Let us hope this is not needed, and I will return soon.

Please pass on my best regards to your loving wife Anne, my dear sister Emma and her husband David, and my beloved mother and father.

Your loving brother
Hugh

PS – I am pleased for you to pass on this letter to Anne, Emma and mother and father.
PSS – Tell Andrew Taggart I have received the blessing he requested. He will understand.

The tears ran down Anne's face as she tightly hugged the letter. Poor

Hugh! He only found the right way days before he was taken. Mary Hedge opened the door and saw her mistress sobbing. She put the tray beside the bed and gathered some handkerchiefs from the dressing table drawers.

Mary passed across the handkerchiefs and said, "There, there, my Lady! You will recover soon. Here is a nice cup of tea and some biscuits for you. There, there."

Anne shuddered as she took Mary's hands and said, "Our life together has changed, Mary. Sir Hugh is dead and forces upon me consequences I never asked for. I find myself pregnant, and my husband is thousands of miles away. I will need you very much to keep me strong. I do not know what I am going to do, Mary. I need Robert so much."

Anne started sobbing even more violently, and Mary sat beside her and cradled her in her arms.

"There, there, my Lady. Do not be upset. It is a time to be happy and look forward to the birth of a son or daughter. Life is like this. If it were not for we women, there would not be a human race."

Anne smiled as she cried and hugged Mary tight. They sat there for a few minutes until Anne started gathering herself again. She noticed another document under Hugh's letter that she had not read.

Asking Mary if she would bring her a cup of coffee and waiting for her maid to leave, she thought it might be the information they needed about the estate's finances. As the door closed, she held the second document up. It was the bank draft that Hugh had mentioned in his letter. She gasped in astonishment and covered her mouth. The draft was for fifty thousand pounds!

Before he died, Hugh had solved the estate's problems. Suddenly, Anne felt strength sapping back into her body. There was hope now for the estate and new opportunities for the future. She must write to Robert today and leave London after the meeting with Mrs Constance. The countess must be told that her son's death was not in vain.

Approaching Seven Rivers, Eastern Cape Province ...
The troop led the way as the small party left Grahamstown midmorning and took the road southeast towards Port Elizabeth. There was an officer, nine troopers, and five dogs. Richard and Sarah felt far more secure being part of the army patrol.

The first part of the journey was easy until they met the mountains two miles south of the township. It was slow for the next four hours as they wound around corners, mounting summits and descending deep valleys.

"I am starting to have second thoughts, Richard. I had forgotten how hard this road was and the cold easterly wind."

"Once we reach Seven Rivers, it flattens out a bit. We should be there by late afternoon. Enough time to set up camp before dark."

Sarah shivered as she pulled her coat around her. In the valleys, there was some protection from the wind, but as they rose to another summit, the easterly wind gained strength, swirling up from the Southern Ocean and around onto the coast.

Nearing four in the afternoon, Lieutenant Gilling pointed out the way into the small township of Seven Rivers, and the troop commenced setting up camp.

"Mr & Mrs Turner, we will camp here and be away in the morning by ten. I will send Sergeant Attwood and three troopers to check on Piet Beckhoff's farm and see if there is any news. It is only fifteen miles across to Salem from here and then another three to the farm. Lieutenant Sanderson or someone from the family will be there and let us know what has happened. Please join us for dinner around the campfire tonight."

"Lieutenant Gilling! What is the situation here with wild animals?"

"It is a fertile area with an abundance of game. That's why we brought the dogs. They will let us know if any big cats come prowling. If I get a chance, we will procure you a lion's skin for your new house."

"Might I go on the morning patrol? I would like to see the country."

Sarah was a little alarmed by this as she was not keen on being left alone with the soldiers.

"Mr Turner, they will leave before dawn and move fast. I want them back here by nine-thirty and our party on the road by ten. We could be in Port Elizabeth by tomorrow night if we make good time. Are you sure you will keep up with the troopers?"

"Certainly, Lieutenant. I will enjoy the experience."

The Lieutenant looked doubtful but felt it should be safe enough, "Please be ready by five thirty. Atwood will ask for you then."

Sarah enjoyed the dinner with the soldiers as she heard about the lives they had made here with their families in the eastern cape. She was surprised that most were middle-aged and had settled in Grahamstown.

"Corporal Furness, how long have you been stationed here?"

"Why we came with Colonel Wiltshire in sixteen. So did Davey over there!" He pointed out a similar aged trooper laughing at a joke. "We were all together when the Xhosa attacked Grahamstown."

Sarah asked, "I have heard of the battle. But tell me, are you married with children?"

"Yes, I met my wife here, and we have two girls, three and one. Soon, we will need to return to England. I would like them to have schooling there. It is too remote here."

"What about the other men? Do they have families? Yes, all the men here have families back at the fort. There are plenty of single men also. They are the more recent recruits."

"Do you miss England?"

"No, not that much! But now I have a family I must think about when we return. I have already served two terms, so soon I must decide."

"What about your wife – was she born here?"

"No, Colleen was eighteen when the family immigrated. Her father gained grants of land from the government in twenty. Since then, they have expanded that, like your husband, Ma'am. They live in town but have a large farm south of Grahamstown. I guess that is why we are still here."

Sarah smiled and thought about the life of an army trooper. It would be a dangerous job in these parts.

"I hope there are no natives close by tonight, Corporal."

"The natives will stay away, Mrs Turner. They don't fight at night. It is the big cats and cape hunting dogs you need to worry about. We keep the fires burning to keep the animals away and the guards awake." Corporal Furness rubbed the ears of the dog sitting at his feet and said, "Rusty and the other dogs will give us plenty of warning if anything comes near."

Sarah was growing tired. She stood and patted Rusty, "I am afraid my tiredness is calling me to bed. Thank you for the conversation. Good night, Corporal."

She turned and faced her husband, "Come on, Richard. You need to be up early in the morning!"

The Turners took another look at the brilliant night sky and then disappeared into their tent.

In the early morning, the small patrol approached Salem an hour after leaving camp. Sergeant Attwood turned in the saddle and said, "We will drop in on Mrs Hertzog's shop. I will tell her we are in the neighbourhood. It is always best to leave a trail behind you, just in case."

"What do you mean, 'just in case', Sergeant?"

"I have seen many times what the Xhosa are capable of, Mr Turner. We have not heard from Lieutenant Sanderson since he left nor from Piet Beckhoff." The Sergeant gazed around the plains ahead and said, "If you ask me, it is all too quiet."

"I see."

The sergeant quickly returned from the shop and explained, "Mrs Hertzog sent a man up yesterday, but he is not back yet! We will go on another ten miles but return if there is no sign of them. The Lieutenant would have sent a rider to the Port Elizabeth barracks if there was trouble. But let's hope we find the patrol soon."

Richard was also becoming alarmed despite being so close to Port Elizabeth. The Eastern Cape Province was vast, with plains running away for miles covered in low scrub. It would be easy for natives to hide and for a small party to be ambushed and killed.

"Sergeant!"

"Yes, Mr Turner."

"It is seven now. If we don't find anyone by eight, we should turn back. We have split our party in two. I'm not sure we should linger here much longer. We have no idea what we are up against."

"We shall talk about that at eight, Mr Turner. Now, follow me, please!"

Pony Shed on the River Wey, Guildford, UK ...

"Mossy must eat a lot of feed to make all this pony poo!" William shovelled another load of manure into a bucket, and Madeline carried it out and dumped it near the river.

The children had agreed with Levi Spencer to do afternoon chores around the shed in exchange for pony rides. Levi was most pleased with this as it meant he could sit back and smoke a pipe as the children worked. The one thorn in his side was his sister, Andrea, who did not agree with the arrangements and said it was their pony, so they should also do chores. She loved rubbing down the pony and continued with Clare, sharing the duty on the other side.

"Steady, little Mossy! You will soon be done."

The pony shook its head, and the girls stood back until Mossy settled.

Clare said, "You have a beautiful thick forelock, Mossy", as she brushed it down. "I wonder why all horses don't have thick forelocks."

Simeon said, "Perhaps it depends on the breed. I read somewhere that different breeds have different characteristics. Ponies have better forelocks than horses."

Clare asked, "What is the difference between a pony and a horse?"

Andrea said, "Horses are bigger."

Dawn Luckett ran in as they talked and asked, "Am I in time for a ride?"

Levi chuckled and said, "Sorry, Dawn. They are rubbing him down. All over for today."

Clare asked, "Dawn! You live on a dairy farm, so why don't you ride horses there?"

"My father won't let me. He says they are too big, and I am too small. I must wait until I grow a bit. But Mossy is the right size."

"Perhaps, Dawn, you could ask your father to buy a pony. We could come and ride with you on the farm."

"I suggested that, but my father says it will disturb the cows. Hey, guess what I saw last night?"

Madeline, raising her eyes, asked, "What?"

"Well, I had to remain with my aunt in town last night until around six. But my father picked me up on the horse and cart. On the way home near the York Road corner, guess who I saw?"

All the children stopped and looked at Dawn. Madeline said, "Well! Who was it?"

"I saw Mr Hotspur walking with Jessica Swamp, and they were alone. It was nearly dark, and she was walking close to him and having a big conversation."

Simeon said, "Jess, the girl who works in our scullery?"

Dawn smiled and continued, "Um! She was smiling and laughing. Do you think they will marry?"

Clare frowned, "Does she know what a bad man he is?"

Dawn, keen on keeping the conversation going, added, "She must have heard about what happened to Edward. At least he does not teach us anymore!"

They all agreed, but Simeon was deep in thought. If Jess was close to the Reverend Hotspur, she may be telling him about their family. After all, Mr Hotspur regularly visited their home to see Clemmie. He must talk with Ethel about this.

Levi pulled out his pipe and coughed, "Perhaps he was doing his pastoral duty thing. You know, looking after people. Cough, cough! Jess had a long walk home, and he was protecting her. But she should not marry that clergyman. They don't have much money. Cough!"

Dawn was upset with that comment, "Levi! Yes, they do. The church gets our tithe each year, and that pays them heaps. My father is always complaining about it. She would be very well off if she married him."

William, keen to add to the conversation, said, "If she wants money, she should marry Leonard Webster. His father has a treasure chest. We saw it yesterday."

Levi sat up, interested in hearing William's comment.

Simeon started to say, "Yes, but it was…."

Madeline cut across him, saying, "Have you seen the beautiful dresses his sister Betty wears? I wish I had some like that. I think they are rich!"

Clare was still worried about Mr Hotspur, "Someone should warn Jessica about Mr Hotspur."

Sharing Clare's concern, Simeon said, "I will ask Mrs Nibley about it. She might know more; if she doesn't, she might talk with Jessica."

Madeline was not convinced. "It may be better if we don't say anything at all. But Mrs Nibley is trustworthy and will keep it to herself."

Levi continued puffing on his pipe, sitting back and enjoying watching the children doing his chores. William was keen to try pipe smoking again and edged closer as Levi blew out a circle of smoke.

"How did you do that?" William was fascinated.

"It takes a lot of practice, Will. You will pick it up after you learn how to smoke properly."

Dawn shouted over their conversation, "Wasn't Leonard Webster handsome yesterday dressed as a ship's captain? I bet he will join the Navy!"

Simeon added, "I don't think so. Mr Webster has a lot of money, and I think Leonard is going to Oxford, so he knows how to manage his father's money. I think Mr Webster is older than he looks."

On hearing this, Levi looked up and put his pipe down.

Madeline asked, "What do you mean, Simeon, about his looks? He is old!"

"I meant he looks younger than he is. They moved here because Mr Webster is sick."

Madeline said, "He looked happy yesterday when he was being the smuggler. He is a nice old man."

"How do you know he is rich?" Levi asked.

William, keen to be in the conversation, said, "After school yesterday, Mr Webster invited us into his house and showed us his treasure chest. It was full of gold doubloons. There were lots of other treasures in it as well."

Simeon thought he should explain that the doubloons were chocolate, "The doubloons were ..."

Levi shouted across Sim and cut him off, "How big was the chest?"

"As big as this box here." William was feeling proud to reveal such information.

Mr Spencer suddenly appeared and asked, "Are we all done here? I can smell pipe smoke! Levi! Have you been smoking again?"

He walked over to his son and found the warm pipe beside him.

"I told you no smoking here. It could start a fire."

"I am always careful."

Mr Spencer was not impressed, "We will talk about this at home. Now, children! Grab your things and go home, please. Your parents will be expecting you."

'Harting', St James's Square, London ...
The butler entered the library where Lady Anne was comfortably resting and waiting for Victoria Sopwith to return from Hursts' London shop.

"Excuse me, Lady Anne."

"Yes, Staines."

"Mr Evan Finchley has arrived and asked if he could see you urgently. He understands he is not expected but claims his visit will only take a few minutes."

Anne put her book down and realised it must be important if the senior partner of Manifold and Stout, Attorneys, was here in person.

"Yes, please show him in, and Staines, please send in a maid with some refreshments."

Anne was curious why Mr Finchley had come.

"Lady Anne, my apologies for interrupting your afternoon; however, developments have necessitated this meeting. There has been a change in plans. But first, let me bring you up to date. My staff have been working on the details in your letter, whose source is unknown, for the previous week." Finchley smiled, "As a result of these inquiries, we have made some helpful discoveries. Let me explain!"

Anne sat forward and asked, "Please do, Mr Finchley."

Mr Finchley opened his case and removed several documents and files. He passed across one file to Anne and said, "Please keep this file confidential as it contains a summary of what we have found. As you know, originally, we intended to meet with Mrs Constance and her lawyer at our offices on Friday week. Mrs Constance complained about the delay, and we agreed to move the meeting to Monday next. This morning, we received a request from Mrs Constance to bring forward the meeting to tomorrow, Friday morning, at eleven. She apologised and said she could not meet with us on Monday due to unforeseen circumstances beyond her control."

"Did she explain what the unforeseen circumstances were?"

"No, she has not. But we have made enquiries and found some interesting information. It appears there is a serious medical condition."

Anne was becoming impatient.

"Well?"

"It appears Mrs Constance suffers from some long-term disease. She is undergoing treatment and has sought an important appointment on Monday. Generally, we agree to a postponement if a medical condition is involved, although I am fed up with her date changes. However, we have no choice; if we meet on Monday, she and her solicitor will not turn up. I recommend that you agree to her request, and I hope it is convenient for you, Lady Anne?"

Anne answered, "It is convenient, Mr Finchley. I have no appointments for tomorrow. Now, what else have you found?"

Mr Finchley noted Lady Anne's agreement to the postponement on his file. Taking a deep breath, he continued, "The details contained in the letter of the other gentlemen who Mrs Constance entertained have proven reliable. Over the years, Mrs Constance has made a fortune and owns a townhouse in Mayfair provided by one of her previous suitors. She is a lady of means."

"So, her claims of being short of funds are all nonsense?"

"Precisely."

Anne was pleased by this news and knew that they could now proceed to rebuff the madame's claims.

"So, Mr Finchley. How do we proceed from here?"

"Come tomorrow morning, we go in hard. Leave it with me for the strategy. Mrs Constance will fight for every penny, but we may have a significant advantage if she suffers from a serious disease. I will have my people making further enquiries over the next three days. It would greatly assist if we knew what her medical condition was."

"Why not ask her tomorrow?"

"She will be aware that it may affect her bargaining position. I am surprised she mentioned it because her Attorney should have advised her not to divulge any medical condition. Which makes me believe it is a serious condition indeed."

Being aware of Sir Hugh's medical complaint, Anne wondered if the disease was related.

"Lady Anne. Thank you for agreeing to the change, and we shall see you at our offices at ten thirty tomorrow morning. I will not take any more of your time and take my leave, please."

"Certainly, Mr Finchley. Staines will show you out."

The butler appeared and assisted Mr Finchley to the front door.

Anne was satisfied with the information the attorneys had gathered, and the delay was most convenient as it allowed her more time to rest. The one thing that bothered her was the promise she had made to the Earl to protect David Constance. She would have to consider this again after the meeting on Monday.

Simeon and William walked down the church steps onto the High Street and suddenly found Levi Spencer behind them, saying, "Walk down to Churchyard laneway and turn in there. I need a word with you both."

William complained, "But we don't go that way!"

"You will today, or you won't ride Mossy again!"

As they walked beside the church, Simeon asked, "What do you want, Levi?"

"Just walk, and I will tell you in the laneway."

The boys walked in silence and turned into the lane. Stopping within a few steps of the entrance, they turned and faced him.

"Here, Will. I have a pipe and some tobacco for you. You should have fun with this."

He passed it across, and William had no hesitation in grabbing it.

"Gee! Thanks. Please show me how to blow smoke rings. They are terrific, and I want to show my sisters."

Simeon said, "I think you need to keep it a secret, William or you will be in trouble."

"You better help Will, Sim. Make sure he is not found out. You said Mr Webster, the smuggler, was rich. Can you show me where he lives?"

Simeon asked, "Why do you want to know?"

"I don't believe he is rich. I think you two were telling title tales. If he were rich, we would know about it."

William was annoyed that Levi said they were lying about Mr Webster. Simeon said, "Maybe we were – you're right! He isn't rich; he acts like he has a lot of money."

"Why would he do that, Sim." Levi was confused as he did not expect them to agree with him.

Not understanding what Sim was doing, William cut in, "They are rich. He has a treasure chest and lots of money. They came from Cornwall, where the smugglers live."

"Well, if he is rich, show me where he lives. Otherwise, I will know you are lying."

"He lives along the street here. Follow me." William dashed off up the High Street with Levi in hot pursuit.

Simeon frowned, knowing something was suspicious, and William was falling for it as usual. He jogged behind Will as he led them to the top end of the High Street past the Free School. Stopping outside the rented house, William pointed and said, "There!"

Levi smiled and said, "Thanks, Will! I will see you down at the Pony Hut on Saturday. Must go now."

He darted off past Sim, who was following.

"See you, Sim!"

Simeon glared at Levi and watched as he rushed back towards the church.

"Quick Will! Come with me."

Levi was now well ahead of them, but Simeon noticed when the older boy turned left into the Town Path beside Holy Trinity church. As Simeon ran after Levi, William was on his heels. They reached the church entrance, ran through, and entered the graveyard. Still running, they climbed the sloped graveyard and quietly approached the stone back fence. Simeon signalled for silence with a finger to his mouth.

William whispered, "What are we doing, Sim?"

"Be quiet! I want to see where Levi was going." He placed one foot on a stone protruding from the fence and pulled himself up to see over the wall and across the road. William, with a bit more difficulty, did the same.

They could see Levi walking off with another lad down Sydenham Road, a shortcut past the castle and down to the river. The two lads were laughing and talking at length. William said, "Isn't that Caleb Elliot?"

"Shush!"

William could not hold himself up any longer and fell back into the long grass. He looked up and found himself staring into the eyes of the Reverend Andrew Taggart. A nervous Simeon climbed down and joined William.

With a smile, the Reverend asked, "Well, boys! Are you playing hide and seek?"

Simeon answered, "A bit like that, Mr Taggart. Can we tell you about it? I think there is going to be some trouble."

"Yes, you can tell me. Let's make a pact, like we did once before. It will be between us and no one else unless we need to help someone. If so, you might need to tell a few more people."

Simeon breathed out in despair, "Caleb Elliot is involved!"

Andrew Taggart, immediately wary, said, "I think you need to tell me the whole story."

Turner Household, High Street, Guildford ...

Ethel Nibley closed the letter and reinserted it into the envelope. She placed it on her desk and went into the kitchen to assist Mrs Jennings with the dinner preparations.

"Anything wrong, Ethel." The cook noticed Ethel's concerned expression.

"Not a word to anybody, Mrs Jennings, but I think we will have trouble with one of Clare's Trustees."

Mrs Jenning nodded and softly said, "Poor Clare!"

Suddenly, William and Simeon ran in through the scullery and grabbed what was left of afternoon tea.

"Where have you boys been? The girls have been home for ages."

Ethel noticed William's eyes enlarged as she asked her question, and he downed a biscuit and then some milk.

Simeon said, "We were talking with the Reverend Taggart after school. He was telling us more about smugglers. He might come to the Sunday picnic if he is invited."

William, catching on, said, "And Mrs Taggart, too!"

"Come on, Will. We need to change and do our chores."

The boys put down their glasses and rushed upstairs, soon returning to the woodshed to cut wood.

At dinner, Ethel mentioned how the boys had been learning more about smugglers today. Jonathan was interested and asked, "What did Mr Taggart tell you?"

William looked down at his plate and was lost for words. Ethel noticed how out of character this was for him, and a slight suspicion arose.

Simeon said, "He told us there are no smugglers around here, but they are mostly along the south coast near Cornwall. The smuggled goods come in from France and Spain, and sometimes the smugglers are caught and taken to London to be hanged."

Will looked up and said, "Yes and put in prison."

Jonathan smiled and said, "Not much use putting them in prison if they are dead, Will!"

"I meant before they are hanged."

The boys then concentrated on their meals. Once again, Ethel noticed this as odd. Usually, they were talkative and joined the conversation.

Once all the children were in bed, Ethel visited Jonathan's study to discuss the letter she had received from Clare's Attorneys in London.

"Jonathan, I will not disturb you for long, but I wanted you to see the letter I received today from Green & Green Attorneys in London."

"I was wondering when that would arrive. It seems Benjamin's attorneys have been at work."

He slowly read the letter, then gestured to bring her chair over.

Green & Green
Attorneys and Notaries
Chancery Lane, London.

Mrs Ethel Nibley
C/- of The Turner Household
The High Street
Guildford

Dear Mrs Nibley
Re: The Estate of Mr Benjamin Simon Petherton – Deceased, Tuesday, 24 April 1827.

We apologise for the length of time taken to contact you. Our firm first became aware of Mr Petherton's passing on Monday, 30 April 1827. Since then, we have briefed the Trustees for Miss Clare Petherton. I understand you witnessed Mr Petherton's passing away, and we offer our condolences.

The Trustees of Clare Petherton have advised that Lady Gwendoline McDermott will soon arrive in Guildford and care for Miss Petherton at Cloverdale Chase.

We have also sent Mr Daniel Pither to organise with the undertaker the funeral service, which the Executors of Mr Petherton's estate have asked to be held on Tuesday, 8 May 1827, at the Star of the Sea, Catholic Church, Batton Place.

It has come to our attention that Miss Petherton was travelling with Mr Petherton's Butler, Mr John Steadman, and Miss Clare Petherton's governess, Mrs Irene Preston, at the time of Mr Petherton's death. We have also been advised that the child was forcibly removed from their care and brought back to the Turner residence. At this stage, the full circumstances are unavailable to us, and we thank you for caring for Miss Petherton until Lady McDermott arrives.

A letter has been sent to Mr Jonathan Turner, Businessman of Guildford, notifying him of the serious consequences of forcibly removing a child from her legal guardians or carers. We have asked Mr Turner to ensure Clare remains with his family and yourself until Lady McDermott arrives in Guildford.

Yours faithfully
Mr Patrick Regan
Attorney
Green & Green Attorneys.

"Have a seat, Ethel, as we must discuss this. What did you make of the letter?"

"No, Jonathan! Before I speak, I want to know how you interpret the letter."

Jonathan smiled, "It appears Preston and Steadman have surfaced at Greens and are trying to convince the Attorney of their innocence by accusing us of abducting Clare. It is preposterous!"

"My thoughts exactly. But what do we do?"

Chapter 12

Turner Household, The High Street, Guildford ...

On Friday morning, Jonathan Turner sent most of the children, including Clare, off to Fintelton Manor for Saturday and Sunday, returning by Monday evening. Due to their age, Marcia and Jeremy remained at home. A rider with a message had been sent to the Earl and Countess explaining the situation, requesting their assistance and advising them of their arrival.

Ethel Nibley had asked to go, but Jonathan advised her to remain as she would need to fend off Lady Gwendoline McDermott, who Johnathon felt would arrive imminently. Following the departure of some very excited boys and girls accompanied by Mrs Jennings and the stable hand, Joseph Hinge, Jonathan packed his bags for London, determined to straighten out this situation.

Attorney Blake Wood, whom Jonathan contacted late Thursday evening, was pleased to assist and would join the coach trip. When the London Attorneys intimated that Mr Turner and Mrs Nibley had forcefully taken Clare from her carers, Jonathan felt that this situation must be immediately resolved.

He spoke with Ethel at a rushed breakfast, "I have a meeting with Andrew Taggart here at eight-thirty, after which the coach will take me to the office. Blake will join me after lunch, and then we will speed away to Harting. It is good of Blake to drop everything and accompany me. Unfortunately, Michael Rawlins has other commitments, but he provided me with some documents concerning the incident and the search for Clare. Ethel, would you please keep Lady McDermott at bay? I have a bad feeling about that letter, as it appears Geen's attorneys are unaware that you are a trustee. I cannot believe that Benjamin would not have informed them and must ask if the correspondence arrived. Hopefully, I will be back in time for the funeral. Take care, Ethel."

After Mr Turner had rushed to his study to prepare his London papers and pack, Aggie asked, "What will you say when this Lady Gwendoline arrives and asks for Clare."

Ethel frowned, "The truth – that she is away on a riding trip and will return by Tuesday morning!"

"But she will ask where they are."

"Yes, and we don't know where they are, do we?"

Aggie smiled, "I see. It is keeping her at bay until the funeral."

"Yes, and hopefully, Mr Turner will return with the legal powers we require to protect Clare. Let's pray he is successful."

Offices of Manifold and Stout, Attorneys, London ...
The senior partner of Manifold and Stout sat at his desk quietly reading as Lady Anne South made one last review of Mrs Constance's letter of complaint. After stalling Catherine Constance for nearly two months and several meeting date changes, the wait was over. The lady would arrive in the next few minutes, and the conference would begin. Anne was sure that today's morning sickness was over as it was eleven o'clock in the morning. She felt some energy in her body but was unsure if she was well enough to handle this situation. Her maid Mary and her security man were stationed in the firm's junior staff room and ready if her mistress fell ill again.

"It is nearly eleven, Lady South! Are you sure you are well enough for the conference?"

Anne looked up with a smile, "Certainly, Mr Finchley. I appreciate your concern, but this must be done. We need a settlement to this situation. I would like that to happen today, but I fear Mrs Constance will be more difficult to handle than I have assumed. We have delayed her requests long enough. Today, we will fire our opening shots and make a start."

"Perhaps, Lady South, we should not raise our battle standard at first but seek negotiation. I always aim for an earnest meeting where all parties are not placed in an aggressive position. Do you have any further questions on the agreement before Mrs Constance arrives?"

"I am fully across the agreement now and feel confident our approach is correct. I am ready!"

Mr Finchley frowned and looked at her, "I am not keen on your suggestion of me stepping outside the conference room once the initial negotiations are done. Surely you can talk with her while I am present. Depending on her negotiating skills, she may take advantage of you."

"I can assure you, Mr Finchley, I can handle Mrs Constance. We have completed our research and have all the information we need on this woman. Sometimes, an intimate meeting between two women can allow deeper conversations than a legal negotiation allows. She may relax and become more compliant."

Finchley nervously smiled, leaned backwards as he scratched the back of his neck and said, "Let us see how the meeting proceeds. If you decide I should leave the room, I will be close if you need help. She does not come from the same station in life as you, and her manners may become aggressive."

"You forget where I have come from, Mr Finchley. My father has climbed from an indentured baker to a business owner. I have worked for him since I was thirteen. I know how to deal with all classes of society!"

"My apologies, Lady South. I was not inferring ......"

A knock came at the door, and Mandy Jones, Mr Finchley's private secretary, half opened the door, popped her head around the corner and announced, "She is here, Mr Finchley. But she has a solicitor with her. A Mr Gregson!"

"Thank you, Mandy. Show them into the conference room and offer them refreshments, please."

"Yes, Mr Finchley."

Michael Finchley contemplated this development. Anne could see his mind working overtime, assessing the options. Soon, his steely brown eyes focussed on her again.

"Lady South!" There was a slight delay before he continued.

Anne added, "It may be that Mrs Constance feels there is more legal merit in her agreement than what we have ascertained. The solicitor will run an argument that relies on breach of contract. We can handle that."

"It might also indicate that Mrs Constance is clutching at every straw! Perhaps there is some compounding circumstance that has made her feel vulnerable. Did your staff discover the nature of her illness?"

"No. I am afraid the doctors would not release any information. But my people will continue to make enquiries."

Anne asked, "Would you please ask Mandy back in for a moment?"

The attorney rose and called his secretary, who quickly came in. As Lady Anne addressed her, she turned and listened.

"Mandy, would you advise me on Mrs Constance's demeanour and complexion?"

Surprised by this request, the secretary quickly answered, "She moves gracefully but a little slowly. She is well-dressed and polite. Her dress is full, with a scarf up to her chin. I am sure her powders are very thick, perhaps overdone."

Anne asked, "She did not remove the scarf when she sat at the conference table?"

"No, Milady."

"Thank you."

As Mandy left, Anne thought about the description. An idea floated into her mind, and she found herself feeling stronger.

"I am ready, Mr Finchley!"

The attorney could see Anne suspected something but was not confident enough to share it with him. He stood and gestured for her to follow.

Turner Household, Guildford, England ...

Jessica Swamp commenced changing the bed sheets on the first floor but was far away in her thoughts. The Reverend Hotspur had informed her that she would have her first lesson at his house at half past five that evening. Her father would pick her up at seven o'clock.

At first, she thought little of it, but now she was unsure if she wished to attend. Her work at the Turner residence commenced at seven in the morning, and even with an hour and a half for lunch, she was exhausted by the time she finished at six. All she wanted to do was go home, have dinner, and talk with her mother till bedtime. The extra hour and a half with Hotspur would mean finishing her work here early, arriving home late, and dinner left in the oven. Yet her father insisted that she attend.

The more she thought about it, the more problems she imagined. Being alone in his house with Philip Hotspur was undesirable, and he had not mentioned whether the cook would be present. She wrestled with how she could avoid the meeting without punishment from her father. She stood at the window gazing out but seeing nothing, wondering what to do.

"Jess! How are those sheets going?"

As Aggie waited for an answer, Jessica continued her thoughts, withdrawn from the world around her. The maid knew this was unlike Jess, who was usually a happy girl, full of conversation and keen to learn.

Moving across, Aggie took her hand and asked, "What's wrong, little one? You are miles away in your thoughts."

The scullery maid focused and saw Aggie standing there. She thought, 'Why not ask?'

"Sorry, Aggie. It is because Mr Hotspur wants me to be at his place tonight for my first lesson. I don't want to go. I am happy having you teach me during our lunch hours."

Aggie was immediately suspicious, "You should not attend a lesson at that time and at his house. It would not be proper."

"But what will my father do? He said I must attend, and if I don't, he will beat me."

The housemaid could see that Jess was terrified. There was no way that Aggie would let her go to the lesson. It was inappropriate for a young lass to be alone with this evil man Hotspur at night without a chaperone. Darkness would fall before she finished – which could ruin her good name.

"Here is what you are going to do. You will stay here tonight in my room, and we will talk to Mrs Nibley. Your father and Mr Hotspur must be confronted, and the situation explained. If you don't want the lessons, that is your decision. No one can force you."

"Yes, they can! Father beats Mother, and he beats me. If I don't go to the lesson and stay here, father will probably blame mother and beat her."

Aggie stood back and sat on the bed. She patted the bed and said, "Come and sit beside me, Jess."

She could see the young lass was terrified, and this problem needed fixing.

"You are not going to that lesson, and we are talking with Mrs Nibley and probably the Reverend Taggart. Perhaps we can ask him to call tonight. It is time this was all sorted. We will visit your home and discuss this with your mother and father tomorrow. If your father so much as lays one hand on you or your mother, then he will be in big trouble. We need to find out why he is so eager for you to be tutored by the Reverend Hotspur. Come on. Let's go down and talk with Ethel."

Offices of Manifold and Stout, London …
As they entered the conference room, Mrs Constance's solicitor stood, but the lady remained seated. During the introductions, Anne quickly glanced at Mrs Constance, noticing her light grey and well-fashioned dress, perfect for a business occasion. The lady had taste and money as the dress was made of an expensive, fine, light muslin and a bluish-grey woollen scarf that hid the neck completely. She showed no signs of anger but a calm expression, waiting to see what would develop. Katherine Constance was a handsome woman indeed and matched the age Anne expected. However, the scarf and the heavy powders did seem out of place, and Anne remembered how her mother had used the same method to disguise injuries.

"Good morning, Mr Gregson. I am Mr Finchley, Senior Partner here at Manifold and Stout. I understand that this is Mrs Constance?"

"Yes, Mr Finchley. May I introduce my client, Mrs Katherine Constance."

"Good morning, Mrs Constance."

The lady sat there and gave the Earl's attorney a small nod.

Evan Finchley bowed slightly and said, "Mr Gregson and Mrs Contance, may I introduce Lady South, who attends as the family representative."

Mr Gregson smiled and said, "Delighted, Lady South. Thank you for seeing us."

Mrs Constance calmly nodded but again said nothing.

Anne glanced across, and the two women's eyes met. In that instant, Anne saw the beauty of the woman fully revealed. She understood how this lady could easily seduce and manipulate a man. Highly skilled at focusing on her clients' weaknesses, Katherine Constance immediately recognised Anne's steely eyes and wondered if she had underestimated her opponent. Katherine looked away, considering how best this battle might be won.

Despite the tension in the room, Anne was determined to follow Mr Finchley's instructions and let him lead the discussions. "Good morning, Mr Gregson and Mrs Constance."

The attorney quickly engaged Mr Gregson, asking, "I understand Mrs Constance requires clarification on some matters. I wonder if you could give us a summary of your requirements, Mr Gregson?"

"Certainly. I have a copy of the agreement between Mrs Constance and the Earl of Fintelton's Estate. I believe The Earl and Mrs Constance hold the originals?"

"That is correct, Mr Gregson, except that there were three originals. I have the third original, which is held at our office."

Finchley courteously handed over the document, and Gregson quickly scrutinised it with Mrs Constance. She nodded her agreement, and passed it back, saying, "Agreed."

From the one word issued by Mrs Constance, Anne noticed that the lady spoke in a fine voice. Strong enough to be heard but with an intensity and tone that encouraged interest. She had been trained well, and if it had not been for their knowledge of her, you would assume she was from the upper class. Anne could see the woman was intelligent and probably cunning.

Gregson continued, "You will notice that the regular monthly payments for subsistence are due on the last day of the month. These payments have not been made for three months. The Earl's Estate has made some decisions without notifying Mrs Constance. We ask that the payments be recommenced immediately, and the amount owing be paid. The lack of payments significantly affects my client's finances."

Mrs Constance's solicitor paused, allowing Mr Finchley the opportunity to respond.

"And this is the only question you raise, Mr Gregson?"

"No, we have other concerns, and I would ask that you respond to the first issue before I continue."

"I see. Before answering, we need to hear any other issues you raise so I can withdraw and discuss them with my client. You will understand our belief that the agreement has been fully complied with. If there are other issues, we will consider them quickly and give you our preliminary comments. Depending on the complexity, making a final decision today may not be possible."

Mrs Constance suddenly intervened, "We expected this and will give you time to consider, but the issues must be raised today and conveyed to the Earl."

Anne could now hear the tension in Mrs Constance's voice.

Mr Finchley looked up and calmly asked, "If you would please inform us of the other issues?"

Gregson smiled and said, "Certainly, Mr Finchley. As you know, the house was bought for Mrs Constance in 1812, and she has lived there ever since. It is her only home, and the property is the only home that her son, David, has ever known."

Anne smiled to herself, given that she was aware of the other residence built on the property.

Michael Finchley said, "I see. Please continue."

"Mrs Contance understands that the property reverts to the Earl's Estate on her death. As the home holds considerable memories for her, she asks that the property be sold to her for the sum of two thousand and seventy-five pounds so her son may inherit the home and continue to live there."

Gregson stopped there, giving Mr Finchley time to complete his notes and consider the proposal.

Anne was not surprised by this development, and it answered her question about what would become of the second house constructed on the property. This woman had a game plan, and it must be driven by some cause relating to her mortality as the property reverted to the Estate on her death.

Gregson continued, "As Mrs Constance has maintained the house for some fifteen years at her own expense, we believe the sum offered is reasonable, considering wear and tear. We believe this is a soundly based settlement and ask you to consider it and advise your decision.

Concerning David Constance, Sir David's son, or should I say the Earl of Fintelton's son, we understand that the son's relationship with the Earl has never been recognised. We believe he is entitled to some inheritance from the Earl and recognition. To compensate him for what he has lost due to his lack of recognition as a legitimate son and heir of the Earl, we suggest an annuity of three hundred pounds a month be paid for the remainder of his life. This settlement should be easily achieved given the annual income of the Earl's large estate and investments.

We ask that the Earl consider these requests and advise us of his decision. Once again, we believe the claims are soundly based on law and do not wish to revert to litigation to ensure these requests are fulfilled."

Mr Gregson smiled and retook his seat. Mr Finchley put down his pen and assembled the notes he had taken.

"Thank you, Mr Gregson and Mrs Constance, for being so summarised in your claims, which I believe I must discuss with Lady South in private for some minutes before we respond. I will arrange a light lunch for you, or if you prefer, we could resume, say, at two pm again here."

Mrs Constance replied, "Given the time is twelve, Mr Finchley, we will dine elsewhere and return at two. Thank you for your offer. Until two, then."

Anne watched as Katherine Constance and her solicitor left. The woman walked with poise, and there was no sign of any affliction. Perhaps her presentation was all show, but Anne suspected there may be a health problem.

After Mr Finchley closed the door, Anne asked, "What was your opinion of their requests, Mr Finchley?"

"I must admit I was surprised by the tack they are taking. They request far more than they are confident of winning and hope to scare us with the veiled threat of litigation. Their plan is based on the Earl and Countess not wanting this publicity. I am afraid to say it is a common strategy and often works."

"I see! Mr Finchley, I only had a slight breakfast and need some sustenance. Would we be able to have lunch here as I have many questions from this interview we must discuss?"

"Yes, I had planned on this. I will have the refreshments brought in."

Anne quickly reviewed her notes while the attorney was absent to organise the lunch. It was clear to Anne that the information now assembled against Miss Constance was soundly based and would hold up in court. The one issue that Anne was concerned about was fulfilling the Earl's wish for the protection of David Constance. How would she achieve this, and was there a need to discuss it with the boy's mother?

Turner Household, Guildford, England ...

The Reverend Andrew Taggart arrived early for the meeting with Jonathan Turner. Ethel took the opportunity to talk with him.

"Reverend Taggart. I am sure you have much to discuss with Mr Turner, but I wonder if you could spare me some time after your meeting. We have a difficult situation with one of our staff, and your assistance would greatly benefit. I cannot tell you more now as there is little time before you meet with Mr Turner. But it would be greatly appreciated if you could spare us half an hour."

"Certainly, Mrs Nibley. I will help if I can. The meeting with Mr Turner will not be long – no more than fifteen minutes. So, after that, where should I find you?"

"In the kitchen, please. Here is Mr Turner for your meeting!"

Mrs Nibley stepped back and left the Reverend with Mr Turner.

"Andrew! You beat me here. Sorry! I was not ready to greet you. Now, what is this urgent matter?'

"Morning, Jonathan. We need somewhere private, please."

"I see. Come along this way, and we shall talk in my study."

Jonathan led him into the study, gestured to a chair and closed the door.

"I am sorry to be so secretive, but we must call an urgent meeting with the wardens. You were right to suggest that Hotspur would disgrace himself if we gave him enough time. Well, he has, and now we must confront him. We shall also need Archdeacon Smithton at the meeting. He can corroborate the evidence I now have. This unacceptable behaviour must be stopped before he goes any further. I am afraid he will soon cause someone some significant harm."

Jonathan could see Andrew's anguish. He, too, had heard confidentially from Rupert Smith about Mr Hotspur's attempt to darken the names of Benjamin Petherton and Mrs Nibley.

"Certainly, Andrew. But it must wait a few days, please, as I must rush off to London and set out the facts of Clare Petherton's abduction to her attorneys. They are now indirectly accusing me of abducting her. I hope to return quickly. Can we delay the meeting until, say, Tuesday? Why not three in the afternoon, here?"

As Jonathan wrote the meeting time into his diary, Andrew asked, "What is happening with Clare?"

Jonathan explained as he tidied his desk. Andrew was amazed that the attorneys in London would take that approach.

"Let me know if they try to wrench her away with this Trustee Lady. Benjamin Petherton and I signed papers stating that if anything ever happened to him, I should ensure that Clare remained in the care of Mrs Nibley. He was careful, always ensuring he planned for any eventuality."

Jonathan stopped tidying and said, "Is that so? I was not aware of that. Thank you for telling me. It may be needed, Andrew."

Offices of Manifold and Stout, London …
"Welcome back, Mrs Constance and Mr Gregson. Sorry for the slight delay, but we needed time to finalise our response to your request. I will detail our responses in a letter, but summarise them now."

Gregson smiled and quickly said, "Thank you, Mr Finchley."

"Mrs Constance! I am sure you are familiar with the details of the agreement between yourself and the Earl of Fintelton. The provision of the property at Wimbledon was a lifetime tenancy, but the property remained in the ownership of the Estate. On your death, the property continues to be part of the Fintelton estate, and your son will need to find lodgings elsewhere."

Mrs Constance looked directly at Mr Finchley, showing no emotion, and waited for him to continue.

"The allowance of three hundred pounds a month was paid for the sustenance of your son, with you as trustee until he became financially independent. We understand he completed his indenture with a builder in February of this year and can now contract building work in his own right."

Mrs Constance immediately called out, "That is not correct. He has entered an indenture for another three years. He took that up in February and plans on developing his skills."

Finchley smiled, "Yes, we are aware of that. However, his first indenture allows him to contract for building work on his own, and so he is now independent. There is no further need for the allowance in terms of the agreement."

Katherine Constance retorted, "Well, that is incorrect, and we will fight it in court!"

Gregson then turned to his client with concern and said, "Please, Mrs Constance! Let us hear what Mr Finchley has to say."

"Thank you, Mr Gregson. Mrs Constance, we understand that you use the property at Wimbledon as a respectable boarding house. The income received from the property affords you a fair income, and you are by no means destitute. We also understand Mr Gregson's statement that the Wimbledon house is your only residence is incorrect. From our enquiries, we discovered that not only the Earl of Fintelton but two other gentlemen of your acquaintance made provisions for the support of you and your son."

Mr Finchley stopped there to let this information sink in.

"We understand that from these settlements, you acquired a residence in Chelsea, a three-floored building comprised of units and that several are used for dubious purposes."

The attorney stopped and took a sip of water.

"I can explain the other properties…"

"Mr Gregson, please. We listened to you this morning. I would ask that you allow us to give a full reply."

Gregson sat back in his chair and indicated that Mr Finchley should continue.

"Concerning the question of Mrs Constance's son, David. We know that when Mrs Constance became pregnant, she was contracted for services by three gentlemen of means and received a generous settlement from each. Regarding the paternity question, it seems unclear who the father was and if any further clients were consulting Mrs Constance at that time, casting further doubt on the circumstances.

The question of paternity is therefore put aside, and there will be no recognition of a relationship between David Constance and the Earl of Fintelton."

Katherine Constance calmly said, "We did not ask for recognition but a fair settlement given the circumstances. You have no proof of these other so-called gentlemen and settlements. There was only one gentleman I was involved with, and that was the Earl of Fintelton. I would deny any other liaisons."

Anne could see some colour developing on Mrs Constance's face, and she felt that Katherine's hostility was growing. Mr Finchley was backing her into a corner, and it was clear that Gregson, her attorney, was surprised by some of the facts being revealed.

"I am sorry, Mrs Constance, to …"

"You should be sorry for the slanders you are making!"

"As I was saying! I am sorry to raise these issues, but the facts must be clarified here and now. Mrs Constance, I suggest that you may not have disclosed these issues to your attorney, Mr Gregson, who may now see this case differently."

Gregson was sitting back in his chair, thinking deeply.

"You say you have proof of the issues you have raised, Mr Finchley?"

"Yes, Mr Gregson. I am authorised to show you the names of the gentlemen involved."

Finchley passed across a page with some notes on it. Gregson took it and shared it with Mrs Constance. He passed the page back and waited for Mr Finchley to finish.

"Mr Gregson and Mrs Constance. The Earl of Fintelton has complied with the agreement with Mrs Constance. The Wimbledon house will remain available for Mrs Constance until her death. Mrs Constance will stay responsible for all the running expenses of that house and must reside there. If she does not live there, then the agreement stipulates the property must be returned to the Earl's estate immediately.

There is also the issue of the additional house built on the property. The Earl has no objection to that house being removed to another site and deems the structure to be the property of Mrs Constance. However, if Mrs Contance vacates and does not remove the home within a reasonable time, it will be deemed the Earl's property."

Anne could see that Mrs Constance was fuming.

"Mr Gregson and Mrs Constance, I assure you that the Earl has considerable evidence that may be used against you if you bring your matters to court. It may also be found that Mrs Constance has been actively committing fraud against the gentlemen concerned, and they would proceed to act against you if these matters came to light. I would advise you to withdraw all your claims and abide by the agreement that is still in operation. If you do not have any further questions, we will wish you a good day."

Mr Finchley stood and indicated the door out.

Gregson whispered to his client, "We shall discuss this at my office."

Aware of the exasperation on Katherine Constance's face, Anne turned to Mr Finchley and said, "I must speak with her before she leaves!" Before he could reply, Anne was out into the vestibule and after her.

"Mrs Constance, if I might have a word." She drew the lady away from her counsel.

It was clear from her face that Mrs Contance was in no mood for discussion.

Anne knew she was taking a risk but asked, "I was wondering if you would be willing for me to contact you. I must be in Guildford and Fintelton shortly, but I will return to London before the month ends. Would you be agreeable to a meeting? Just the two of us – no attorneys."

Mrs Constance faced Anne with hate in her eyes but then composed herself and said, "After today, I must admit I would prefer never to see you again. However, I assume you have something to offer based on your request. Here is my card and contact details. I shall consider your request when it arrives."

Ensuring she held her composure, Anne replied, "I cannot talk now, but I will send a note later in the month when I return. Good day, Mrs Constance."

Turner Household, The High Street, Guildford …
The Reverend Taggart sat in the drawing room waiting on Mrs Ethel Nibley and Miss Jessica Swamp. Andrew and Ethel had talked at length yesterday about Mr Hotspur's English lessons with Jessica. The Rector was unaware of this situation and found it inappropriate for Philip to host this young lady at his home.

"Ah, Ethel and Jessica. How are you both this morning?"

Ethel smiled, but Jessica immediately burst into tears and hugged the housekeeper.

"She fears her father and what he will do to them privately. By them, I mean Jess and her mother. Beatings have often happened before. Jess remained here last night for safety. Mr Swamp requires some stern words, please, Mr Taggart."

Andrew Taggart said, "I see." He was ashamed that Hotspur once again seemed involved with pursuing a young lady and somehow trapping her father into an agreement where he had control over her.

"Jessica, we will ensure you and your mother are not harmed. Today, we will free you from these worries. I have a carriage outside, and Mrs Nibley, Miss Peters, and you will accompany me to your father's house. There, we will settle this once and for all. I am afraid it must be done so all your family can live peacefully and enjoy life. It will not take long. So, let us go."

Aggie had given Ivy last-minute instructions and rushed into the room, "Sorry, some last-minute preparations for dinner."

Andrew laughed, "It is the same at our house. There is not enough time in the day."

They all left the house, boarded the Reverend Taggart's carriage and soon were outside the Swamp's home. As they descended, the usual warm welcome from Barney, the dog next door, started with loud barking, then some angry snarling through the wall. Jessica walked to the fence and patted the dog.

"Shush, Barney! It is only me and some friends. Good boy."

The dog gave a little high-pitched friendly yelp and a yawn and lay beside the fence. When Jessica returned, Kevin Swamp was standing outside the front door scowling.

"What you want, Mr Rector Head Man, Sir? We no need help here and got no money for ye. Ah, Jess, me girl! Where you been? The Hotspur man been looking for you. You get inside to your mother, girl!"

Andrew Taggart breathed in deeply and, stepping forward with his hand extended, said, "Mr Swamp. It is good to see you again. We need to discuss a significant problem with you and Mrs Swamp. It affects Jessica's welfare and future. May we come inside and discuss it with you?"

Jessica had returned to the party and stood close to Aggie.

"Welfare, eh! Whose welfare be that Mr Head man, Rector Man?"

"Jessica's welfare, Mr Swamp. She is most distressed about some issues, and we must sort these out. Could we come in and discuss this over some morning tea?"

Mrs Willamina Swamp emerged from the front door and stood beside Kevin, who was silent and thinking.

"You better bring them in, Kevin. They be welcome. It is an honour that you visit us, Mr Taggart and you ladies."

Kevin, not pleased about this at all, gestured them in through the low front door, opening into an expansive and well-furnished parlour. They also found Peter Swamp inside, and he quickly stood and introduced himself.

Willamina said, "Please have a seat, and Jess, would you help me make the tea?"

Jessica was willing to assist her mother, letting her explain what was happening privately.

The Reverend Taggart wasted no time and explained, "Mr Swamp, may I call you Kevin? If you wish, please call me Andrew."

"Yes, Mr Headman Rector! Kevin and Andrew, I like that better. I spose, Andrew, you are here to negotiate the marriage of my daughter Jess to that young fella, Hotspur? I thought that was what he had in mind. Ah ha, he he!"

"I am afraid not, Kevin. We are here to advise you about Mr Hotspur's behaviour and to understand the details of your agreement that Jessica should submit herself to him to learn reading and writing."

"You not get any more money from me, Andrew, man! We have an agreement for that tithe, and it stays the same. We no afford pay any more, or we go broke!"

When his father mentioned the tithe, Peter Swamp looked up and became most interested.

Looking around at the comfortable, well-furnished room, Andrew said, "I am sure that is the fact. However, I am not aware of how the tithe affects our discussion. I understood that Mr Hotspur would provide his services free of charge, and you would ensure Jessica followed Mr Hotspur's instructions."

Mrs Swamp and Jessica came in with the morning tea and started distributing cups and plates.

"No, no! Hotspur man interested in my little girl, Jess. I can tell you as you his boss. But you ladies must keep this a secret."

Ethel and Aggie agreed.

"We think that he marries her and be happy. He told me the tithe was to increase for last year and this year, but he could fix it with you that it stay same if Jess come him for lessons."

Andrew Taggart now understood what was going on. Hotspur had threatened Swamp with an increase in the tithe but sweetened the deal by saying he could ensure it did not increase if Kevin complied with his wishes. Taggart was ashamed of the young curate. Philip's deliberate manipulation of Swamp was the last straw. It was high time he was gone from this parish and the church. The man was a womaniser and a thief with no morals or understanding of the Gospel. He did not care who he manipulated for his gain.

"I see. Thank you, Kevin. I understand now what has happened. I must apologise on behalf of the church. Mr Hotspur has far exceeded his authority. He has lied to you; I am ashamed and sorry for that.

The churchwardens review the tithe in the latter part of the year. There has been no consideration of it to date this year. No one has planned to increase your tithe. It remains the same until the wardens assess it closer to Christmas. Mr Hotspur has no authority over this; therefore, his agreement with you was false. He tried to defraud you to gain access to your daughter for ulterior motives."

Peter Swamp said, "I thought as much, but I did not suggest this to Jess because I was afraid of upsetting her."

"Rightly so, Peter. Mr Swamp, Jess already is being assisted in her wish to read and write by Miss Aggie Peter's here." He pointed to Aggie, who smiled at Kevin.

"There is no need for this agreement with Mr Hotspur, and I will release you from it immediately. There is no shame for your family as Jessica did not attend the first lesson last night."

"I know that Mr Rector, Headman, Sir. He been here this morning looking for Jess. I told him I would send along once I find her. I not do that now!" Kevin turned to Jess and said, "You stick with Miss Aggie, you do."

Jess ran over to her father and hugged him. It was an emotional scene for them all, and Willamina joined in the hug.

"Kevin, there is one more thing. Perhaps we could leave everyone inside here, and you and I might talk outside."

Kevin stood up and led Andrew outside. Barney began to snarl and then bark loudly as if defending the king.

Kevin bawled at him, "Shut up, Barney. Ya, stupid thing. Git away!"

The dog gave a low snarl, walked away from the fence and sat at the neighbouring house's front door, snorting uncomfortably.

They stood together, Andrew looking at Kevin and Kevin looking at the farm.

Andrew was keen for this to be finished and said, "Kevin. Have you seen the parish stocks[32] near the Tunsgate market?"

"Fixes those thieves, don't it?"

"Yes, it does. But, more to the point, I have been told by reliable sources that you beat your wife, Willamina, and your daughter, Jessica. You also maltreat both Peter and Alfred to get your way."

Andrew stopped to gauge the man's reaction before he continued. Kevin started to shake his head and was about to speak, but Andrew continued.

"Kevin, let me advise you as a friend. Never beat your wife, daughter, son or anyone else again. There is no use denying it, as I have witnesses who are prepared to stand up in court if you do. The next time you lift a finger against your family, you will find yourself in front of the magistrates and then in the stocks in front of our entire community. Do I make myself clear?"

Swamp was looking at the ground and spat. He was annoyed, but Andrew knew he understood and was ashamed.

"I expect to see you and your family at church at ten thirty on Sunday. As a respected citizen of Guildford, it is time for you to clean up your act and become friendly to our community. It won't hurt, and you may find that you will enjoy the companionship after some time. Now, do I have your agreement that you will never again beat any member of your family?"

Kevin stood there silently.

"I need a verbal answer from you, Kevin."

The man looked up, and Andrew could see tears in his eyes.

"It was how I was brung up. It not my fault."

"Yes, it is, Kevin, and you can stop it now, this day forever. You cannot gain love by beating people. Do I have your agreement?"

---

[32] Stocks are feet restraining devices that were used as a form of corporal punishment and public humiliation. The stocks consist of placing boards around the ankles or wrists. Wikipedia

"Yes!"

"Good, now let us finish that cup of tea inside."

Later, as they were climbing into the carriage, Peter Swamp ran out of the front door and stopped Andrew Taggart, who was about to climb in.

He stuck out his hand and clasped Andrew's, "Thank you, Reverend Taggart!"

He smiled and then scampered back inside.

Turner Household, The High Street, Guildford …

As Ethel, Aggie and Jess entered through the front door, Ivy rushed out and said, "Ethel! A Lady McDermott is here, asking for Clare. She is seated in the parlour."

"Oh, I see. Thank you, Ivy. Off you go, girls, back to work."

Ethel swallowed and took a deep breath. She was sure this would be a difficult meeting. The lady had wasted no time in coming from London. The one relief was that Clare and the other children were well on their way to Fintelton.

Before Ivy left, Ethel asked, "Do we have sufficient lunch to entertain this lady?"

"Yes, Mrs Nibley. When would you like it served?"

"Perhaps in half an hour."

Ivy nodded and sped away.

Ethel gathered herself and walked to the parlour.

"Lady McDermott! Good morning, and welcome to Guildford."

The Lady sat there and questioned, "And who are you - making yourself so familiar?"

Ethel was shocked by this response and answered, "I am Mrs Ethel Nibley, the housekeeper, and represent Mr Turner."

The Lady sat there and looked away, "Well, call your employer, please. I must see him immediately."

"I am afraid Mr Turner is on his way to London. He will return next Tuesday. May I be of help?"

Lady McDermott, showing signs of annoyance, ranted, "Well, this is rude indeed. A letter has been sent by Green's Attorneys advising your employer that I would be coming. I expected him to be here. I know nothing about a letter to you, Nibley, and I have no time to waste on you, little people of no consequence! Now, where is young Clare?"

Ethel tried to contain her anger and answered, "I understand she is on a trip to the country with the other children on a riding expedition."

"A riding expedition. What do you mean? She was to be kept here so I could take custody of her. Who do you people think you are?"

"I am sorry, Lady McDermott, but the letters from Greens came after the children left."

The visitor nearly exploded at this comment, "You mean your employer let the child out of the house in this disgusting small town? Don't you people have any idea of etiquette? Letting her run wild in this town and sending her away without proper chaperones to who knows where. But where is this riding expedition?"

"My apologies, but Mr Turner takes care of that information."

"So, you tell me she is not here, and now you advise me that you do not know where they are!"

Realising this Lady was overstaying her welcome and insulting the household as best she could, Ethel decided to move her on.

"Lady McDermott, it appears there is nothing else I may assist you with. I am sure Mrs O'Connor will have a comfortable room ready for you at Cloverdale Chase and some refreshments."

"Oh, so you know the staff at Cloverdale Chase, do you? I would expect that you people of the lower class would know each other."

Ethel bit her tongue and smiled at the lady. She understood the conversation would be difficult, but this woman's rudeness was beyond belief.

"Mrs McDermott, we cannot help you any further. Now, I would encourage you to leave."

Lady McDermott sat straight as if insulted, "I have no intention of leaving until you produce Clare Petherton for me here and now."

Ethel was trying hard to control her emotions, "We have discussed Clare already, and I am advised that she will return on Tuesday next. There is nothing else I can do for you, so please leave this house."

Ethel called Ivy and glared at the lady as the maid entered.

"Ivy, please show Lady McDermott out."

"Nibley, you can call me a coach!"

"My apologies, but we do not call coaches. It is a short walk to the nearest stables. Good day, Lady McDermott."

Ethel turned her back and exited the room.

Ivy indicated, "If you would come this way, my Lady."

"Well, I am glad someone in this house has some manners."

She lifted herself slowly out of the chair, took her walking stick and strolled along the hallway to the front door.

"What a poky little house this is. My, my! Help me down the stairs, girl!"

Ivy carefully assisted the lady down the four steps to the road. Lady McDermott walked away without thanking the maid, shaking her head and mumbling.

Coming back into the kitchen and not seeing Ethel standing behind Aggie and Jess, Ivy said, "Now, there is one who needs to be in Abbots Hospital." When Ivy saw Ethel there, she put her hand over her mouth and whispered, "Sorry, Ethel." With a giggle, Jess said, "I'd hate to be her neighbour."

Ethel started to giggle, and so did Aggie, as they hugged each other and had a good laugh to relieve the tension.

Ivy innocently commented, "I understand she will not join us for luncheon!" They all burst out laughing again.

Three Miles North of Piet Beckhoff's farm, Near Salem, Eastern Cape Province ...

Trooper Henzel called, "Sarge, over there about a hundred yards. A trooper's horse!"

"Right, let's go."

The small party of troopers and Richard Turner cantered their horses through the scrub and slowed as they neared the stray. Sergeant Attwood held his hand up and signalled for them to approach slowly. Soon, he dismounted and walked to the horse as it chewed grass.

"Hey, girl!" He let her smell his hand and patted her softly on the mane. The others approached and stopped around Attwood.

"That's Harry Gray's horse. There is no way he would leave her like this. He must be here, somewhere close."

Sergeant Attwood said, "Mr Turner, please dismount and hold these reins. We will spread out around you and see if Harry is somewhere close. It will only take ten minutes."

Richard followed the direction and took the reins of Harry's horse.

He let both horses chew on some juicy grass nearby.

Soon, he heard a trooper call out, "Found him."

There was silence for a few minutes and then a call from Attwood, "Mr Turner! Would you mount, please, and bring the horses over here."

Richard quickly led the horses to where the trooper's body lay. He was on his side with a spear through his chest and protruding from the back. It appeared that wild animals had mauled his neck, and a leg and arm were missing. His neck was torn apart as if the animal was making sure of the kill. Richard had to look away, having never seen anything like this before.

He said, "I hope he was dead before that animal attacked."

"No doubt about that, Mr Turner. The spear went straight through his heart."

The troopers took his bedroll from behind the saddle, wrapped his body, and tied the roll around him. Carefully lifting his body onto the horse, they secured it and mounted.

Richard noted this was all done in silence as if it were normal. He knew that all these troopers were long-timers and had probably performed this ritual many times before. There was no need for words; they knew what to do and kept their feelings under wraps lest they affect morale.

Sergeant Attwood said, "The others must be close by. Lieutenant Sanderson would not leave a trooper to fend for himself. The question is, which way do we go?"

Henzell suggested, "North, Sarge. The natives will be heading north."

Attwood surveyed the country ahead of them. The plain to the north was vast and extended west to the escarpment and east towards the sea. The low scrub extended north for a few miles to some forested hills.

"We head for those hills. If I were a native, I would head for cover. Mr Turner, please keep your horse behind mine if you would. We must be ready to retreat if we come upon the natives. Please make sure you keep close. These natives could be anywhere. Is your musket and pistol loaded?"

"Yes, I loaded them this morning."

"Good. If you see anything, let us know – we are all scouts now and know there is danger ahead."

Richard was not keen on joining a war and protested, "Sergeant Attwood, surely we should head back to camp. We would be safer if the complete party stays together."

Attwood turned, rubbing his eyes, and replacing his hat, "Mr Turner, Lieutenant Gilling advised that if we were not back by ten, they should proceed to Port Elizabeth. The party will be safe and reach the port before dark. We have seven troopers and a lieutenant out here, and they are in trouble. Now we have found one of our men dead, I must complete a search. I have no choice. I can't return and say we did nothing."

He waited for Richard to answer. Richard understood his predicament and nodded in agreement.

Attwood signalled to follow him, and the small party headed north.

Fintelton Manor, Outside Petersfield, Sussex ...
As the Earl entered the parlour after a refreshing nap, he looked at the clock and saw it was three-thirty in the afternoon.

"Did I miss afternoon tea, Jane?"

"No, Dear. Pike has taken our orders for scones and tea. I ordered your regular. Emma and I have been discussing this message I received from Anne's father. I am afraid your peace is about to be interrupted."

"Thank you. What message was that?"

The Earl walked to the window and gazed over the patio and down the valley. There was a slight breeze and a brilliantly clear blue sky. The temperature was mild, and the Earl enjoyed the hints of summer coming.

Lady Jane announced, "Jonathan Turner has asked for a special favour. You can read the letter, but it seems there is a legal argument over a young girl they have been protecting. Her name is Clare Petherton. She was abducted after her father's death but was recovered by Mr Turner. Now, the London attorneys are accusing him of abducting the girl. It is complicated, so you should read the letter."

"And how will this disturb my peace?"

"As I said, David. You should read the letter. He has asked if we could have the children here for a few days for some riding. He must attend London and straighten out this situation."

The Earl turned and lifted his eyebrows, "Why not? I enjoyed my discussions with young William. He is a spirited boy. I wonder if the girls enjoy roses. As I recall, Madeline did."

Lady Jane was pleased as she saw the Earl becoming more alert as soon as he heard the children were coming.

Emma smiled, enjoying the favourable reaction from her father, and asked, "When do they arrive, Mother?"

"I am expecting them around six this evening."

Emma breathed in, "My goodness. That is soon. Why the rush?"

"You too can read the letter, but it seems some Trustee is being sent from London to collect the child."

Emma thought about the comment and said, "I remember discussing this with Victoria Sopwith before she left for London. I was packing to come here, so I paid scant attention. She told me about the kidnapping. It was the butler and the governess who took the girl. There were great fears for her safety and the possibility of a ransom. It was horrible to think that such a thing could happen to a child straight after witnessing her father's death. The butler and governess must have been heartless people."

"Here, Emma! Read the letter. There is far more."

Emma took the letter, and the Earl asked, "Does Pike know of our unexpected guests?"

"Yes, my Dear. Mr Stem has also been advised. He will supervise their riding. I am not sure if the Petherton girl is a rider. We will wait and find out this evening. Also, Clementine did not attend last time due to an injury, so she must be with Clare and start afresh."

Emma looked up and explained, "The housekeeper, Mrs Nibley, discovered where she had been taken, and they rescued her. But the butler and governess escaped."

The Earl, who hated the idea of any child coming to harm, said, "The penalty for kidnapping is death. If they are found, the courts will have no sympathy for them."

Emma whispered, "The fools, they should have stayed and confessed."

The Webster's Household, The High Street, Guildford …
The maid answered the door and found the Reverend Andrew Taggart standing outside.

"May I help, Reverend?"

"Good evening, Alice. Would Mr Webster be in? I need a few minutes with him if possible."

"Certainly, Reverend Taggart. Please come in."

Alice Timson showed the reverend into the drawing room and said, "I will let him know you are here. Would you like some refreshments?"

"No, Alice. Thank you for the offer."

Soon, Mr Webster entered the room, "Andrew, good to see you. How can I be of assistance?"

"Mervin, I need to talk to you about a delicate issue, and I should have come before this, but it has been a busy few days. You will recall your recent appearance as a pirate or smuggler at the church school."

"Yes"

"Afterwards, you entertained the Turner boys and Edward Wood. Being impressionable young boys, William inadvertently spoke about your treasure chest, and it seems some boys of possible ill repute became aware of it. I know of one of these boys, and I feel your house may be a target for a burglary."

"Surely not! Let me show you the chest. The doubloons are filled with chocolate."

Andrew explained, "Even so, some easily led lads, due to envy, may attempt a burglary. It is not the Turner boys or Edward. These children are from good families; I can attest to their honesty. It was Simeon and William who alerted me to the fact. They claim to have heard some older boys discussing the possibilities. Unfortunately, I know one of the boys and would not put it past him. I would advise you to lock your doors and windows at night and brief your staff on the problem."

Mervin rubbed his chin and said, "I see what you mean, but I do not wish to frighten my family by this. Let us keep it between you and me, and I will brief some of the staff and Gwendolen in time. She is quite highly strung, and I might delay, hoping nothing happens."

"It would be best to inform the staff to be on the lookout."

"I will, Andrew and I will thank William and Simeon for the information. I agree with you; they are fine young men."

High Street, Guildford, Towards the London Road …
Leonard Webster slowed his running pace as he entered the town, still

breathing fast after a refreshing run out past some farms and back towards the commercial district. He was looking forward to a pint and a game of darts with his new friends at the Country Squire pub.

As he walked along the High Street, he jolted to a stop as he heard a young woman cry in alarm from a laneway.

"Let me go. You have no right!"

Then he heard a sharp slap, and the girl fell silent except for her sobbing, "Leave me alone! Please…!"

As it was nearly dark, Leonard could only see the entrance to the lane, but there was the faint outline of a man and a woman close to the entrance, with the young lady struggling to be free.

"You will do as I say, or your father will hear of this."

Leonard Webster thought the voice sounded familiar.

The young woman continued crying and struggling to be released.

Leonard approached, calling out, "I say! Is everything alright there?"

He could see the man look up at once and mumble something as he threw her to the ground. His white collar attracted the light as he turned and retreated into the darkness. Leonard rushed over and assisted the young woman to her feet.

"Are you all right, there?" Leonard could see the girl was around sixteen or seventeen and refrained from calling her Madam. She was still crying, pulled her long hair away from her face and clutched the cheek where she had been struck. He immediately recognised Jessica Swamp.

"Jessica. What happened?"

Leonard nearly had her standing before she fainted and fell heavily on the pavement, knocking her head. He knelt beside her and noticed a bad bruise starting on her cheekbone and blood dripping from her nose. He gently tapped her hand.

"Can you hear me, Jessica? Can you hear me?"

There was no response.

Lifting her with both arms, he carried her along the street towards his parents' home, which was close by. As he turned the corner and approached the house, her eyes opened, and she said, "Where am I?" Feeling her cheek, she whimpered, "Oh, that hurts."

"Hold on, Jess – you have been badly beaten. I am taking you to my parents' house. Mr and Mrs Webster. You will be safe there, and I will fetch the doctor."

As Leonard carried the injured girl up the stairs, she passed out again. Opening the front door, he entered the hallway's bright candle-light, calling, "Mother, Father, I need some help here, please!"

Gwendolen Webster appeared at the end of the hall. Seeing her son with an unconscious young lady in his arms, she rushed down the hallway and said, "Bring her in here. My goodness – what happened?".

"She was attacked in a laneway. The man rushed away when I arrived. Then she collapsed. By the look of her, she was savagely attacked."

"My goodness!"

The housekeeper, now standing beside her mistress, asked, "Should I fetch a doctor, Ma'am?"

"Yes, Mrs Pratt. Send Alice. As quick as you can, please!"

As Leonard gently laid the girl on a sofa, Gwendolen said, "Watch her while I get some hot water and towels. That nose is possibly broken, and I must stop the blood. Betty! Betty, come quick."

As Mrs Webster rushed off, Betty came into the parlour and found a prostrate young lady on the sofa and a kneeling Leonard holding a handkerchief to her nose.

"What has happened?"

As Leonard explained, Betty looked closely at the girl's face.

"My goodness, that is Jessica Swamp from the Turner house. She is one of the servant girls. We must alert the Turners."

Chapter 13

Fintelton Manor, Outside Petersfield, Sussex ...

William half opened his eyes and noticed a faint light in the large window. He closed his eyes again, snuggling up under the blanket. Suddenly realising it was Saturday and they were at Fintelton, he sat up, threw the blanket off, moved beside Simeon's bed and gently shook his shoulder.

"We are at Fintelton, Sim. Time to go riding."

"Go away!" Simeon turned over and faced the other way.

Not to be disappointed, William pulled on his clothes, left the door open, walked along the hall, and silently entered the girls' room. He knelt between Madeline and Clare's beds and shook Madeline's shoulder.

Maddie snorted and opened her eyes, "What are you doing here, William? It is still dark."

"Come with me, and we can saddle up the horses."

"After breakfast, William! You know the plans." Maddie rolled over and pulled the pillow over her head.

The children had travelled all day and reached the Manor around six in the evening. Although tired, they were all in high spirits, given this unexpected visit. Lady Jane had invited Mr Stem, the estate manager, to explain the riding program during dinner. Clementine and Clare would start from scratch, and the others would concentrate on improving their skills. Mr Ben Chipping, an ostler in the stables, would be helping the riders, and Mr Stem would train Clementine and Clare.

Clare sat up and yawned.

"I have never been on a farm before! I will come with you, William. Give me a few minutes to get dressed. You go and put your shoes on." She pointed down at his bare feet.

William smiled, "I forgot." The seven-year-old was off in a second. He darted back into the boys' room and found his shoes and socks.

In the staff quarters, maids were setting the table for breakfast, and the smell of scrambled eggs and bacon was already filling the room. Mr Pike, the butler, was at work in his office and Mrs Walsh, the house-keeper, was talking with the cooks.

A clatter came from the steps to the ground floor, and William and Clare ran into the kitchen and straight to Mrs Walsh.

William asked, "Mrs Walsh, can we go to the Estate Office and saddle up our horses?"

"Not without some breakfast first, young Master William. Who is this young lady with you?"

"This is Clare Petherton, who lives with us in Guildford." William was going to continue but thought better of it as Clare would not wish to be thinking of her father. "We are going riding today. Can we have some breakfast now and then go? We want to help with the horses."

"Hello, Clare. Welcome to Fintelton. I have not seen you here before."

With excitement, Clare said, "No, Mrs Walsh. It is my first visit, and I greatly enjoy staying at the manor house. I am going to learn to ride."

"Well, Clare and William. I am sure Mr Stem will be up and about, but not expecting you this early. You can have breakfast here with the staff, and then I think Mr Pike will let you go. It is still dark outside, and there is some fog, so Mr Pike will be worried about that."

William was eager and confident and said, "I know the way, Mrs Walsh."

"Yes, but Clare does not, and if you became separated, then it will be frightening for her."

The children followed Mrs Walsh's instructions and sat at the end of the servants' breakfast table.

Mrs Wash asked a maid, "Molly, please bring two plates of scrambled eggs and bacon."

"Yes, Mrs Walsh."

By the time the children had nearly finished their servings, the other staff assembled for breakfast. The children stood with the others as Mr Pike led them in Grace. As they sat and began breakfast, Mr Pike approached William and Clare.

"Master William, the fog is clearing outside, and the sun will soon rise, but it is still a bit uneven and bumpy for a young lady to walk on. I understand, Clare, that you recently injured your ankle. It may be best, William, if you walk slowly and hold Clare's hand until she can see the ground. If you agree, you may go to the Estate Office."

William, nodding in agreement, woofed down his last piece of bacon, and Clare put her plate aside.

The eleven-year-old girl said, "Thank you, Mr Pike. Thank you, Mrs Walsh." Clare nodded to the lady at the far end of the table.

Pike led them to the back entrance, which he unlocked and opened. The soft wind rushed in and gave the children a slight chill. Clare put on her coat before going outside.

Mr Pike handed William a lantern and ushered them off. They had not gone more than three steps when Mr Pike shouted, "William! Take Clare's hand, please."

The boy was concentrating on walking slowly and had already forgotten that instruction. He took Clare's hand in his, and they walked together.

"You have a nice warm hand, William. I like your hand."

William, at first, was not sure what to say. But as they walked on, he enjoyed the feel of Clare's hand. There was something comforting about it. He smiled.

"Your hands are soft and warm, too."

HMS Shadow Off Cape Passero, Ionian Sea, Sicily ...
Since Messina, *Shadow* had every possible sail up as they struggled to shake off the Ottoman schooner five miles behind. The winds favoured them, leaving their frigate sixty-five miles from Malta.

"She is still there, Mr Trotters, but not gaining. We should be safe as British ships will be exercising in the waters ahead. If we can maintain nine knots, we should be in Malta by mid-afternoon."

Mr Trotters, as he looked back at the following schooner, hesitated but then said, "Captain, I think she is gaining on us. Perhaps there is a wind change coming from the north."

Robert extended his telescope and focused on the ship.

"She has more sail up. Why would she do that, given we are in safe waters?"

Robert looked up at the lookouts. They were all focused on the following schooner.

"Damn," he said. "They must be tired and not alert. Trotters change the lookouts, now!"

"Aye, Sir."

Robert peered to the south-west and wondered. 'Surely not!'

"Trotters! Call Mr Fenton. I am going aloft."

Tucking the telescope into his belt and racing for the main mast's rigging, he scrambled quickly up, making for the tops. From there, he wasted no time and climbed for the cross trees. Passing a lookout who was descending, he asked, "Did you see anything from the south-west?"

"No, Sir. It was clear."

Robert climbed on and hauled himself onto the cross trees. As he settled himself there, he found the light of the sunrise from the east almost blinded him. Rubbing his eyes, the captain could still not find a good south-west view. He must move above the sails, so he hauled himself up to the topsail spar, hanging on for dear life until he could find a firm foothold. Stabilising himself, he pulled out his telescope and gazed south. Immediately, a single sail bobbing up over the horizon came into view. 'It must be a topsail, but what navy?' He could not distinguish what ship it was, but it was tacking this way.

Lowering the scope, he turned and took another look at the schooner. It was gaining faster than he realised and was now only two miles behind them. 'She must be making thirteen knots, maybe fifteen. Her sails are full, so she has far more wind than us.' The ripple effect on the water in front of the Ottoman ship indicated the wind change as it ran towards them.

'Why are they working so hard to catch us after all this time? There must be a reason.'

Robert was confused. It made no sense – a schooner could not take on a frigate. He gritted his teeth and did a full sweep of the ocean. As he pulled his telescope towards the east, he noticed a black spot flash past his eye before it was blinded due to the sun's glare. 'What was that?' He rubbed his eyes again and repointed the scope to the east. The glare was blinding, but as he opened his eyes, a small cloud band on the horizon blocked the sun.

What the Captain saw was not welcome. Two frigates and a schooner were not more than five miles to the east, heading on a collision course with 'Shadow'. From their markings, they were Ottomans. He lowered his scope and thought. Five miles and a diagonal course. Time until interception, possibly half an hour. They were travelling slower due to their wind position. *With the wind change, Shadow* would beat them, but only just. If he changed course, he would lose speed. It would be close – very close. Whoever was the captain of that leading frigate had planned this perfectly.

He secured the scope and started down the rigging. Reaching the cross trees, he could see the replacement lookout coming up. As he passed him, he said, "Two frigates and a schooner coming from the east. Keep an eye on them. Should be easier as the sun rises."

Robert raced down the rigging and back to the poop deck.

"Mr Fenton, we have company!"

Rectory, The High Street, Guildford ...
The Reverend Andrew Taggart tossed and turned during the night, unable to free his mind from the issues with Philip Hotspur. Finally, at four in the morning, he quietly dragged himself out of bed, attempting not to disturb Laura. She stirred, rolled over and settled again. He lit a candle, descended to the kitchen, and boiled the kettle for some tea. Walking back to his study, he noticed a slip of paper under the front door.

'What is that?'

Diverting his course, he picked up the paper, finding the message addressed to himself. The handwriting was that of his young assistant curate.

Taking the letter into his study, he placed it on his desk and lit more candles. After sipping the hot tea, he sighed and sat at his desk. Quickly glancing out the window, he wondered when the sun would rise. He pulled his dressing gown tight as he felt the cold morning air and decided to start the fire.

As the fire crackled, Andrew put his hands close to the flames and warmed them. He stretched and wiggled his fingers, wondering what difficulty his curate would complain about now. Placing two candles on his desk, he moved his study chair closer to the fire, yawned and opened the letter.

The Reverend Philip Hotspur
Martyr Road
Guildford, England

The Reverend Andrew Taggart
The Rectory
The High Street
Guildford, England.

4 May 1827

Dear Reverend Taggart

By the time you read this letter, I will have left Guildford and be travelling north to a new beginning. I believe the cities of Manchester and Birmingham are looking for bright, young, educated men to work in their manufacturing establishments.

After much contemplation, I have concluded that there is no future for me in the clergy. Despite my earnest endeavours during my time here, it seems my skills have not been appreciated, and to a certain extent, I remain friendless. I have done my best, but I must say that I have lost interest in spiritual matters and feel I can use my talents better in administration or business.

Since the unexpected death of my uncle, there is nothing to hold me here in Guildford.

I thought I would write and let you know about my decision. I have appreciated your mentoring and the hospitality from you and your good wife, Laura. I certainly wish you both the best for the future.

The Diocese funds my position here until November of this year. I have a rental agreement for my Martyr Road townhouse and an agreement with my housekeeper and cook, Mrs April Handle. I would be greatly obliged if you would be so kind as to clear these debts utilising the monies owed to me.

There is one issue that I must explain before leaving.

I had previously offered my services to Miss Jessica Swamp as an English teacher, and she had accepted my kind offer. She was due for her first lesson at five but did not arrive. I waited near the Turner's residence to ascertain why she was absent, and we met on her walk home. During the walk, we stopped outside Bakers Lane and discussed future lessons.

Unfortunately, as it was nearly dark, she tripped on a loose cobblestone and fell to the ground, suffering some injury. She cried out as some stranger was passing by and attracted attention. Considering this might have left me in a compromising position, I was frightened and decided to withdraw from the young lady. I am sure the passer-by helped young Jessica up and saw her on her way safely.

I vacated the scene because of the reputation of Mr Kevin Swamp and his sons. They are known to have severe tempers, and I feared retribution from them before the incident could be explained. You will understand my state of mind at that time, my hesitancy, and being keen that no slurs were cast upon the church.

I must say that I have not found Guildford a friendly place. Despite my best efforts to support the community, there has been little reciprocation from the residents. So, I have no misgivings in giving up my curacy. The one exception, of course, is your friendship and mentoring and the kind hospitality from your good wife.

I will advise you of my forwarding address once known and ask that you send any mail there. If any inquiries come from my family in London, I ask that you keep the news in this letter confidential. I will inform them in my own good time.

Thank you for your mentoring here as a Guildford curate, and I wish you and your wife my best wishes in the future.

Yours faithfully
Philip Hotspur

Harting, St James's Square, London …

It was early as Anne's eyes opened wide, and she took a gasp of air. Her throat was dry, and throwing off the quilt, she reached for a glass of water. She was sweating and felt exhausted again. 'It must be the quilt and blanket. I was too hot.' Then she recalled the dream where she was sheltering from the sun. William was offering her cups of water as the herds of wildebeests and zebras passed by.

"They are not a problem, Anne."

"Yes, they are! Look out, there is a Lion!"

William clapped his hands at it, shouting, "Go away! Go away!"

The lion charged.

Now wide awake, Anne raised herself as she rearranged the pillows and lay back again, considering the dark and cold room. The fire still had red embers, but no light came through the curtains. She lay there remembering the dream. Then she felt her tummy, thinking about the new life inside her. What a miracle that a new child was developing in her womb. Would it be a boy or a girl? She hoped a boy as this would please Lady Jane and the Earl. But it did not matter as she would love either. It would be their child, hers and Robert's. The first of many, she hoped. It was funny that now she was with child, nothing else seemed to matter. She must protect this child with her life if that was required. She knew she would, but what about her other duties?

Then Anne remembered her father discussing sending William to Africa. She knew if her mother were alive, she would never allow it. How could she stop him? What was wrong with her father that he would send his flesh and blood away to the other side of the world? Yet many fathers did this as if it were a rite of passage to manhood. What effect would it have on a sensitive child like William?

At least she could protect this little one inside her.

She hopped out of bed, pulled on a dressing gown and rekindled the fire. Soon, yellowy gold flames started dancing upwards, and the room grew warm. She took two more candles and placed them on the desk. It was time to write to Robert before the demands of this day. This letter would be special as she would tell him they would have a baby near the last week of November or the first week in December. Anne knew Robert would be excited when he heard. What a pity he was so far away.

Smiling at the thought of her husband's joy, she dabbed the nib in the inkwell and began penning her letter.

The Webster Residence, The High Street, Guildford ...
Mrs Gwendolen Webster, Leonard and Betty enjoyed breakfast, discussing the day's planned events and commenting on the colder-than-usual night for this time of the year.

Gwen said, "Leonard, we must start considering your packing for Oxford soon. When does the next term start?"

"No, mother. The first term has already started. I will return in August as I need more time to consider a change to engineering. I have discussed it with Father."

Mervin Webster rushed in, crying out, "We have been robbed! The Reverend Taggart told me there were rumours, and it has happened. I should have taken more notice!"

Seeing her husband in such a panic, Gwendoline gave a slight scream, "What do you mean, Mervin?"

"My study! The strong box has been prized open, and the treasure chest has been taken."

Leonard, trying to calm his father, said, "The treasure chest is no great loss, Father, as it only contained chocolates."

"It cost a pretty penny, Leonard and three thousand pounds is missing from the strong box."

Gwendoline was becoming angry, "Why did you have all that money in the house, Mervin? It should have been in a bank."

Mr Webster held the side of his head and swayed back and forth, then collapsed into a chair.

"Are you alright, Father!" Betty cried out and moved beside her sobbing father, slumped in a chair, with his head cradled in his arms.

His wife moved close and carefully moved his head back so she could see him. Mervin's face was flushed, and Gwennie knew he was having one of his turns.

"Quick, Betty! A glass of water. Leonard, would you fetch the doctor, please."

The son was quickly off and put his running practice to good use. Doctor Watson arrived within minutes, accompanied by the Reverend Taggart. Mervin was now relaxing, and the stress on his face had disappeared, but the tension of the burglary remained.

With Leonard and Doctor Watson's help, Gwendoline guided Mervin to the guest bedroom at the rear of the ground floor.

As the doctor commenced examining the patient, Andrew Taggart led Betty Webster back to the parlour and asked what had caused the health scare.

"He discovered we had been robbed. Father finds stress hard to cope with at his age. He took one of his turns where he must stop everything and relax, letting his body calm down. It has something to do with his sicknesses. The difficulties with Jessica Swamp here last night had already upset him. We hoped he had calmed down by this morning, but it seems he has not."

The Reverend had not heard this news, "Jessica Swamp?"

"Yes, Leonard found her injured in a laneway. He brought her here for help. We did the best we could and called the doctor. It appears she was struggling with a stranger."

"Was she injured?"

"Yes. Jessica had a bad bruise on her cheek and her arm. Her nose appeared broken, but Doctor Watson thought it was a nasty bump from when she fell. After that, we took her to the Turner's house, where she spent the night. Leonard let the Swamps know. He is a friend of Peter Swamp. They play darts at the pub on the same team."

Doctor Watson emerged from the bedroom with Mrs Webster.

"The signs are all good. Mr Webster should be fine by tomorrow morning after a good rest today. Mrs Webster, if you would ensure he takes those powders, they will help him sleep. I will come back this evening and check on him."

Doctor Watson nodded to them all and rushed off for his next appointment.

Betty said, "I am glad that is over. We all need some rest."

Reverend Taggart added, "We should be thankful he is recovering. Can you tell me what was stolen?"

"Three thousand pounds from the strongbox and a replica pirate chest full of gold doubloons. The gold was just paper but filled with chocolate."

Andrew smiled and asked, "Might I see the scene of the burglary?"

"Yes, of course, Rector. I have not seen it yet either."

Andrew followed Betty to Mervin's study, and they were shocked by the mess they found. Papers were strewn over the floor, the window in front of the desk was wide open, and a frame and window lock were broken. The strong box had been dragged out of a cupboard and remained open with the lock jemmied away.

Leonard came through the doorway and asked, "Anything I can help with, Rector?"

"I would suggest you have someone send for Michael Rawlins, the parish constable."

Leonard agreed, "Already done, Rector. I have sent a maid." He looked at the mess on the floor and said, "We should start cleaning up."

Andrew Taggart frowned, "I think it best to wait until the constable arrives. He will want to see what happened. Let me know when your father recovers, and I will pay him a call."

As Reverend Taggart walked away from the Webster's house, he thought about the coincidence of Mervin and Leonard entertaining the children at school about smugglers, and the next night, his house was robbed. Remembering what William and Simeon had told him, he wondered if his warning to Mervin had proved true. It would be hard to establish the connection, but if the constable knew, they could make enquiries.

Over his shoulder, Andrew heard someone behind him as he walked down the High Street. He turned and found Leonard Webster catching up with him.

"Reverend Taggart, there is something you should know."

"What is that, Leonard?"

"It is about Jessica Swamp."

The Reverend was embarrassed as he had forgotten about Jessica due to his concern for the Webster's burglary, "My goodness! I forgot. I must visit the Turners now."

"Rector, I did not say anything at home or to anyone else, but I need to tell you."

Andrew, impatient to move off to the Turners, said, "What is it, Leonard? You seem reluctant."

"I don't like becoming involved in these things, but I heard the girl cry out from the laneway. I am sure she was slapped hard on the face and then thrown to the footpath. It was quite violent. The man was in the dark laneway, but I recognised his voice."

"Who was it?"

"When I saw the flash of his white collar, I knew it was the Reverend Philip Hotspur!"

Turner Household, the High Street, Guildford ...

"Mr and Mrs Swamp. Please come in." Ethel could see the horse and dray at the foot of the front steps.

"We come to get our Jess, Mrs Nibley. We thank ye for your care last night, but Willamina not sleep a wink worrying. She a worrier, she is! Oh, she worry – you understand. She close to Jess, she is. Much more en meself."

"I understand, Mr Webster. Come in, both of you and have a cup of tea. Your daughter is still asleep, but we will check on her. She had a nasty fright last night."

Aggie quickly left the room and went to the servant's quarters. Jessica was still fast asleep, but some blankets had been thrown off. It would not be long before she woke.

Ethel nodded as Aggie mouthed, "Soon!"

Thinking about the best way to wake the young lass, Ethel suggested, "Mrs Swamp, perhaps you could go with Aggie and wake Jessica. The best place for her now would be a few days at home resting after that dreadful scare."

Willamina Swamp was happy to go with Aggie and followed her to the maid's room.

Ethel thought she would reinforce the words they had with Kevin yesterday. She wanted to make sure Jessica's learning continued.

"Mr Swamp, once Jess has recovered, please send her back here so she can continue her work. She is a fine girl and a hard worker. The lessons on reading and writing with Aggie Peters are helping her immensely. She will have a fine career one day."

"Ah, Redin and Write! My day, women, no need it. They be mothers and do suckling, eh! But if you needen her that way, then, she must Redin and Write! Eh!"

Ethel nearly broke out in a laugh but managed to contain it. She said, most sincerely, "Oh, yes! She needs it."

Ivy passed Mr Swamp a cup of tea as they waited for Jessica. Ethel decided to keep the stalled conversation flowing, "Mr Swamp. Do the police know who it was that attacked, Jessica?"

"Aee, Ye, Ha. Cough, Cough, Oops! Cough, Cough." He swallowed. "Ah, few. Ye caught me swallowing me tea! Sorry! Cough, Cough. Wait, ple, OH! No, no. None yet, but we get em! When we find em, they be sorry! Ooo, be sorry! Cough, cough."

"Mr Swamp, perhaps you should let the police handle this."

"Oh, Mrs Nibble – we prefer old way. We give em smart persuasion, Eh! They learn real fast. Ha, ha! Oh, yes. Real fast!"

Ethel thought she would discover what was delaying Jessica. As she entered the servant hallway, she could hear the young lass sobbing and crying out that she wanted to remain at the Turners. Willamina gently talked with Jess about coming home and said her father would not beat her when she returned, but Jess would have none of it.

Ethel entered the room and suggested that Jessica stay, as the doctor would call this afternoon.

"Mrs Swamp, given her state of mind, it might be better if Jess remained here."

As for Mr Swamp beating her, Ethel explained that Reverend Taggart had spoken to her father on this subject, and it would not happen again.

Jess calmed and hugged her mother. Soft words were spoken, and Willamina came out and explained to Mr Swamp that the doctor would see Jess here that afternoon and then Mrs Nibley would bring Jess home.

"No, I want see my daughter now! I be sure she want stay here, please!"

Ethel understood the man's concern and thought it best if Jessica joined them, "Aggie, would you please ask Jessica to come out."

When Jess emerged with a badly bruised cheek and some gravel rash on her nose, Kevin Swamp was shocked, and Willamina held Kevin's arm, trying to calm him.

Kevin shouted, "Who did en ye?" Then, putting his hand over his mouth and in a softer voice, said, "Scuse me, all. Jess, who done this!"

Without hesitation, Jess said, "The Reverend Philip Hotspur!"

Mr Swamp stood there almost growling and slowly said, "He be a dead man, he be! No-un touch me daughter, like that!"

Willamina whispered, "Thank them, Kevin, and we will see Jess later."

"Thank ye all. Thank ye, Mrs Nibble, for tea." Ethel smiled.

"We see ye tonight, Jess."

Harting, St James's Square London ...

Before lunch was served, Staines entered the parlour and said, "Lady Anne, an urgent message for you."

He passed the message on a tray, and Anne picked it up and quickly read the message.

"Staines! My father will arrive here either late afternoon or early evening. It involves Clare Petherton's kidnapping case. The attorneys are meeting after lunch tomorrow to identify the facts that vary in the witness statements. I wonder why, as it seemed clear-cut to me. Well, we shall find out when he arrives. He brings Attorney Blake Wood with him, Staines. Do we have rooms ready?"

"I will have them made up now. As you are attending the Russian embassy reception tonight, will you have dinner with your father here before leaving, Milady?"

"No, Staines. I will eat at the Russian Embassy."

Elliot's Blacksmith Shop, Guilford, Surrey ...

Constable Michael Rawlins and the Reverend Andrew Taggart, accompanied by Levi Spencer and his father, Terry Spencer, approached the Blacksmith's shop.

Michael told those accompanying him, "Let me do the talking, please. If we all start making accusations, Jeff will become angry and make this far more difficult."

As they stood at the entrance, Jeff Elliot came over, shook hands with Michael Rawlins, and asked why the others had accompanied him.

"Jeff, there was a burglary at the Webster's house last night, and we are doing some preliminary enquiries gathering information. We are not aware of who carried out the burglary, but we have some information concerning Caleb."

Immediately, Jeff's friendliness disappeared, and he stood straight, ready to defend his son.

"There is no need to worry as I am sure Caleb is not involved, but we must ask him some questions. Would you ask him over, please?"

Jeffrey Elliot stood there and asked, "What information do you have?"

"It would be better if you and he heard it together."

Jeff was not convinced but agreed to bring his son over. Once Caleb was present, Michael explained the situation and asked, "We have information that you were seen with Levi Spencer," Rawlins pointed to Levi, "at around three o'clock, Thursday on Oxford Terrace. Is that correct?"

Caleb looked nervous and said, "Yes, Constable."

"Would you please tell me why you met him and what you talked about?"

Caleb nervously swallowed and said, "We met by chance. I happened to be going that way, and I ran into Levi. We talked about playing darts."

"Caleb. Did Levi say anything about Mr Mervin Webster's house?"

"Yes. Levi mentioned talking with William and Simeon Turner, who said Mr Webster was the richest man in town. He said they showed him where the house was."

"Did Levi show you where the house was?"

"No, there was no need, as I have made some deliveries there for Father. I know where it is."

"Where were you last night?"

"I was at home."

"Jeff, can you confirm that?"

"Yes, we worked late last night. We were both tired and in bed by ten."

Constable Rawlins was convinced, "Thank you. It appears neither Caleb or Levi were involved. That is all we need to know."

Port Elizabeth Road, Past Nanaga, Eastern Cape Province ...
The small party of troopers had searched for a day out past Salem and then back around Seven Rivers. Without any conclusive result, they camped overnight and set off early, hoping to move fast and reach Port Elizabeth by midday. Richard Turner was glad to be moving into safer grounds. It was two in the afternoon when they entered the fort compound, finding the other troopers and Lieutenant Sanderson

waiting for them.

Freddie Sanderson rushed over and called to Sergeant Attwood, "You found poor Harry? Well done, Sergeant! We searched for two days without finding him. I say the corpse smells a bit high!"

"Yes, Lieutenant. We need him in a box quickly! What happened with your patrol? We could not find any trace of you except for Harry."

"We were ambushed west of Salem. Harry took the first hit and screamed after realising he had a spear in his chest. He slumped in the saddle but miraculously stayed upright. His horse bolted off. That was the last we saw of him as we were so busy fighting off the natives. Two of my troopers had serious injuries, so we could not spend much time searching."

"I thought you might have sent a few men out to find him!"

"I would have liked to, but there were over fifty natives. It was a large group, all Xhosa hunting men, and we had to keep moving to outrun them. They were a tribe I had never seen before, all young, healthy, and angry. We were lucky not to lose more troopers."

Sergeant Attwood noticed Mrs Turner greeting her husband with a hug.

"Mr Turner went with our patrol. I think he was shocked when he saw Harry's body. It is always hard the first time."

Sanderson said, "I see. I will have a word with Richard tonight. They will need an escort home with their shipment. This group of natives is a real problem. They showed no sign of retreating, so I fear for the settlers out there. The Major is discussing the despatch of a company for a hunt and driving them back across the Fish."

"Has a message been sent to Captain Hargrave?"

"Yes, I sent two of our troopers off yesterday. They will be there by tonight. We must keep the settlers safe until we can drive this raiding party away. The Major is making plans, including us escorting the Turners back to Grahamstown. I will see Mr Turner now and make the arrangements. If you would attend on the Major, you can brief him on your patrol."

Turner Household, the High Street, Guildford ...
There was a knock on the front door, and Aggie answered. She found Lady McDermott standing there.

"May I help you?"

"Call Nibley! I shall not come in – I have no desire to enter this house again. I must inform the housekeeper of the action I am taking. Hurry up, young maid! I do not have time to stand around waiting for you people."

"Whom may I say is calling, Ma'am?"

"Lady McDermott, of course. What is wrong with you, country people? Have you no memory whatever? Hurry up."

"If you would take a seat on the verandah, Ma'am. I will see if she is available." Aggie gestured to the double chair near the verandah wall.

"You what! I will not be treated this ...."

Aggie tried to hide her grin as she slowly closed the front door and headed to the kitchen.

"I am afraid the battleaxe is back, and she is angrier than ever. She asked for Nibley this time. No Mrs or any other title. I mean, who does she think she is?"

Ethel sighed, "I would say she is quite well off, badgered her husband to death and is used to getting her way. Well, into the bear pit again."

Opening the front door, Ethel said, "Welcome, Lady McDermott. Would you like to come in and take a seat?"

"I would not think of entering a house with you, Nibley. After the way I have been treated."

"I would remind you, Lady McDermott, it is Mrs Nibley!"

"How dare you! I shall call you servants what I like. You have too high an opinion of yourself, Nibley."

"I apologise, Lady McDermott, but if you cannot converse civilly and respectfully, I must end this conversation."

Ethel closed the door in her face.

There was a tirade of insults from outside and some silence before another more sedate knock was heard.

A red-faced Lady McDermott stood before Ethel and said, "Mrs Nibley, I must warn you that I, as Clare's guardian, have reported you to the police as having forcefully taken the young girl from my care and hidden her away. Your crime amounts to kidnapping, and you will soon be arrested. If you do not bring Miss Petherton to Cloverdale Chase by ten o'clock tomorrow morning, then I will have no other option than to have you arrested. Do I make myself clear?"

"Lady McDermott, you seem to think you can take the law into your own hands."

"I certainly do when dealing with obstinate persons such as yourself. You are a disgrace to this household. Why I ..."

Ethel cut off the woman's next tirade.

"It may be preferable if you thought first before you come out with your outrageous statements and make a fool of yourself."

"Why, I have never..."

Ethel cut her off again, "Lady McDermott, at present, I am not convinced you are the guardian of Clare Petherton. You have provided no identification or letter of introduction, and there must be doubt of the veracity of your claim due to your preposterous publicly aired comments and continuing vulgar insults.

I should also inform you that we are in contact with Green & Green Attorneys of Chancery Lane, London, and will continue discussions with them about Clare Petherton's situation."

"I can't believe such lying statements. They would have told me if..."

"Madam, if you would close your mouth and listen for a moment, you might spare us all from this unpleasant conversation."

Lady McDermott stood there with her mouth open, "Well, I ...!"

"Clare Petherton has three guardians, of which I am one. The attorneys have not yet arranged a meeting to discuss the custody arrangements. That will occur in the coming weeks.

You will also find that Mr Benjamin Petherton and I were engaged to be married at the time of his untimely death. If you doubt this, you should check the Guildford Bulletin dated Tuesday, April the twentieth. Check under the notices of engagements! So, it would be charitable to show some respect as I am his grieving fiancé."

"You show no signs of grieving to me, Mrs Nibley."

"How dare you, you old noisy windbag! I will repeat my message that Clare Petherton will be present at Mr Petherton's funeral; however, you will have no access to her. If you wish to converse with her after the funeral, it will be made possible, but only under strict supervision, as we do not want Clare forcibly abducted again.

Let me say this very clearly. Clare Petherton will remain part of the Turner household until a formal meeting of Guardians is held in London and the guardians make a mutually agreed-upon decision on custody. But I can assure you that I would never consent to Clare ever coming under the control of such a miserable lady as you, Lady McDermott."

Lady McDermott stood there with her mouth open.

Ethel continued, "I suggest, Lady McDermott, that unless you have plans to attend the funeral, your trip to Guildford has been wasted. I would ask that you do not visit this household again, or I will have the police remove you for trespass. Good day, Lady McDermott."

Ethel closed the front door and leaned back against it, sighing. She opened her eyes and found Aggie, Ivy, Jess, and Nanny Smithers clapping around her. Then Aggie gave her a big hug.

Ivy said, "Would you like a glass of sherry, Ethel?"

"Would I! Definitely!"

They all walked into the kitchen laughing and talking about Ethel's defence of Clare.

Ethel noticed a letter in her pigeonhole, which was not present this morning.

"Where did that come from."

Ivy said, "I found it on Mr Turner's desk this morning when I collected his cups and glasses. I popped it in your pigeonhole."

"Thank you, Ivy."

The housekeeper read the letter and looked up with a smile, "It appears that I am travelling to Fintelton Manor tomorrow!"

The others looked up, "What for?"

The Russian Embassy Reception, Kensington, London ...
Mrs Stubbington picked up Anne and Victoria around seven thirty, and the carriage ride to Kensington took fifteen minutes. Victoria was surprised by the queue of guests outside.

"It will take a little while to enter as the Russians process their guest carefully before letting you through."

Victoria nodded as she wondered what it would be like inside.

Janet said, "Crowded!" As if she could read Victoria's mind.

Vicky laughed, "How did you know what I was thinking?"

"Victoria, whenever I take anyone to a reception, they always wonder this. You will see soon enough. We must wait for this queue of carriages first. It may take ten minutes."

Anne was thinking about Robert and the mission he was on. She knew it involved the Ottomans but wondered if the Russians were involved.

"Janet. I know there is trouble brewing in the eastern Mediterranean. Robert advised me of this before he set off on his latest mission. Does it involve the Russians?"

Janet thought before she spoke, "It would be best not to discuss the Greek's quest for independence. The British Government is keen to keep the Russians from entering a war with the Ottomans in Greece. It will be a touchy subject here tonight, so I would steer clear of it."

The coach was at the entrance within ten minutes, and the ladies were delivered to the front door. As they entered, Anne heard her title announced for the first time.

"The Right Honourable, The Viscountess of Leystead, Mrs Janet Stubbington of the Home Office, and Miss Victoria Sopwith."

Anne felt it was strange not to hear her real name. However, she would need to adapt to this process. Victoria grinned at her, proud to be beside Anne as the announcement was made.

As they stood at the entrance for all to see, Janet whispered, "Congratulations, Anne, you outrank me now!" After the introductions, Mrs Stubbington led them off towards the closest group of guests. Anne suddenly recognised Lachlan MacPherson, his mother, Marjorie, and a younger lady who stood close beside him.

Janet did the introductions, "Lachlan, you know the Viscountess of Leystead."

"Lady Leystead. It is an honour to meet you again. May I introduce my wife, Taye? She has been keen to meet you for some time."

"Thank you, Lachlan. Hello Taye – I am so glad to meet you. We are still meeting members of your family. Forgive me if I forget some names. Now, I believe you have three children. What are their names?"

"Lady Leystead. It is a pleasure – you look radiant tonight, Ma'am. The children are called Elsie, Finley and Rory. Ten, eight and five."

Majorie could no longer contain herself and said, "Beautiful children and two boys to carry on the family ancestry."

Anne raised her eyes and smiled, "Mrs McPherson, so good that you are here." She moved forward and kissed her cheek, and Mrs McPherson was delighted to respond.

As Lachlan made further introductions, Anne noticed Victoria in another group beside them, being introduced to several young gentlemen.

"Where is Mr McPherson? I hope he is well."

"He is still in Glasgow sorting out the situation with James and settling in Thomas and Marion. He writes often but also says he is tired and often takes a couple of days to rest. I worry about him, but he has good doctors in Glasgow. The university there trains them well."

"Will you be joining him there, Mrs McPherson?"

"I would like to, but he has forbidden me, saying he will soon return to Greenwich. I suspect he is waiting for one of the company ships to sail this way. They have many ships in the line and are most comfortable for travel. Ask your father, he took a delightful trip with him. They are such good friends. I …."

Anne could see Taye and Lachlan's worried expressions as Mrs Marjorie McPherson continued speaking without taking a breath.

Taye interrupted her by saying, "Mother, Dear. Lady Chester has been calling for several minutes. It would be rude to leave her alone if my Lady would excuse us?"

"Certainly, but we must speak again later, Mrs McPherson."

Before Marjorie could start again, Taye whisked her away, allowing Anne and Lachlan to speak.

Lachlan said, "I do apologise, my Lady. I am sure you understand how excited my mother becomes."

"She is a sweet lady, Lachlan. I believe she is doing wonders for the Irish Charity."

"Yes, she has found a new home there. How is your recruitment of a new General Manager coming along?"

"My father should arrive in London tonight. I hope he returns with details of the shortlisted applicants. I am keen to have someone in the position as soon as possible. I have too many responsibilities; if Robert were home, I would hardly have time for him. Not a good recipe for a newly married couple."

"I agree. Finding time for the children as the business grows becomes more difficult. I think we will be expanding our executive structure soon."

Anne was inspired, "I like the sound of 'Executive Structure'. Do you mind if I use it as well?"

Before Lachlan could answer, a gong rang, and an introduction was given, "Ladies and Gentlemen, His Royal Highness, The Duke of Clarence and St Andrews."

Lachlan said, "Certainly. It is not of my making. I found it in an article somewhere, so why not."

Anne was surprised by the announcement and said, "I was not aware the Prince would be here tonight."

"He usually turns up to these Embassy Receptions. The problem is it is difficult to get away before he does."

Anne watched the prince as he was introduced to a group of men on the far side of the room.

She said, "I see."

She was sure that one of the men was Stephen Polkinghorne. As she watched, there was hilarity among the prince's group, and then, giving a wave goodbye, he moved on to the next group. As Anne watched, Taye rejoined them and commented to Lachlan, "She will be busy for some time. Lady Chester is from the Irish Charity's committee and has captured her attention!"

Still focusing on the previous group the prince had conversed with, Anne asked, "Lachlan, do you know that fellow over there, Mr Stephen Polkinghorne, in the greyish suit." She pointed him out.

"Yes, I think so. Stephen runs an import business for tobacco, wines and other goods. I believe he has been very successful and influential in several trades."

"Would you do me a favour and ask him over here? You might tell him an acquaintance of his, the Viscountess of Leystead, requests his presence." She giggled, "That should do the trick! I will talk with Taye while you arrange it."

"Certainly."

Taye was most apologetic and said, "My apologies for mother, Marjorie. She goes on and on. It is hard to get a word in. She means well."

"I understand, Taye. It is not a problem, and I have a fond spot for Mrs McPherson despite her enthusiasm." They laughed, and Taye became far more comfortable in Anne's presence.

Some minutes later, Lachlan led Stephen over and made the introduction.

"My Lady, I believe you know Mr Stephen Polkinghorne."

"Yes. Hello, Mr Polkinghorne."

Stephen gulped and realised this was Lady South. He said, "Ma'am, I mean, Lady Leystead. I was confused about who you were, but I apologise. I should have known. You are a friend of Lachlan and Mrs McPherson." He nodded to Taye and smiled.

Lachlan quickly noted the lack of introduction and said, "Sorry! Stephen Polkinghorne, may I present my wife, Taye."

"Hello, Taye, that is a very traditional Scottish name."

They enjoyed the conversation until Anne asked if she and Stephen might be excused as they talked privately.

"Stephen, are you attending Benjamin Petherton's Guildford funeral?"

"Yes, I certainly am. I leave on Tuesday and should arrive on Wednesday before lunch."

"Good! Would you join us for dinner at my father's house on Wednesday? There are issues we need to discuss about Clare Petherton. She resides at present at my father's and blends in well with the children. It would be a great favour if you would do this for me, Mr Polkinghorne."

Stephen looked perplexed, "I had intended to return to London by Saturday for business commitments, but Wednesday should not interfere with those plans. If it is that important, I will be there for you, my Lady!"

"I greatly appreciate this, not only for myself but for young Clare, who I am sure will be glad to see you."

"Lady Anne, I understand that Clarissa Wendarm is buried at the Petersfield cemetery. If I am to spend some time in Guildford, I might venture down there and pay my respects. Perhaps someone could guide me to the grave the day following Benjamin's funeral."

"I will arrange for the Fintelton Estate Manager, Mr Stem, to do that. He is a fine man and made the funeral arrangements. That may delay you from returning to London by Saturday."

"I will change my arrangements. The business can wait. I wish to pay my respects as I was close to the Lady."

"Are you aware that Lady Jane, the Countess of Fintelton, expects Fiona Green to arrive soon? I would be pleased to arrange a meeting for you if that is helpful."

"If she is present, that would be marvellous."

Anne was keen to develop this friendship for Clare Petherton's sake.

"I shall send a rider tonight and advise you at the funeral."

"Thank you…"

"Polkinghorne, you are monopolising the Viscountess, my good man. Give me some time with her, please."

Anne turned and found herself gazing up into the eyes of a smiling Prince William.

She curtsied and blushed at the same time.

"My, you are a beautiful young wife, my Lady. Robert is a lucky man. I have been wondering how his trip to the East progresses."

"I am not sure, your Grace. I mean, your Highness, my apologies. I hope he is safe and sound in Malta and delivered his precious cargo."

The prince was delighted and laughed, "I am sure he is. You understand he will be my head of security when he returns. That would be good for you as he will serve with me in London for two years. There will be time for you two to become reacquainted. I am a true believer that a husband should be near his wife. This navy life is most punishing on any marriage."

"I agree, your Highness. I will be glad to see him arrive home safely."

"Well, that should be soon. I heard there will be a conference in London of the British, French, and Russians and that Robert will bring Admiral Sutherland back from Malta. I understand they leave Malta any day, so you may see him within a month and a half. If you see Birdee! Oh, sorry, I meant Admiral Bird. You can ask him."

"That is wonderful news, your Highness. Thank you so much."

"As soon as he is home from sea, I insist we entertain you at Clarence House. Adelaide loves entertaining and would be delighted to meet you. I will have my private secretary note it down. You will receive an invitation." The prince sighed, "My apologies, but I must leave your beautiful company as there are many others to meet tonight."

He took her hand, kissed it, and turned to the next party, guided by his aides.

Anne stood back and closed her eyes, breathing deeply. She had not expected that. Opening her eyes, she found the prince standing before her again, admiring her blue eyes.

"My dear, do you understand that your husband saved my life at the

Irish Charity Ball?"

Anne was so surprised by his presence again that she could only nod.

"I shall not forget that ever, young lady! Your husband is a hero, and you will see what I shall do for him once I am King."

With that, the prince was off again. Suddenly, Janet and Victoria were beside her, and Vicky said, "My, aren't you the popular one tonight?"

"Oh, Victoria. I am so tired. Might we go now?"

Janet put her arm around her waist and supported her as they made their way to the entrance.

HMS Shadow, Forty-Five Miles off Malta ...

The lookout shouted down, "Three ships to the South. Two frigates and a schooner. They carry a British Flag."

Robert looked up and waved to the lookout.

"We are safe, gentlemen. Without firing a shot! These Ottomans would not dare attack us now. Trotters, change course towards the British frigates, please."

"Aye, Sir."

Fenton said, "They were after us, Sir! No question about it." He looked over *Shadow's* stern at the two Ottoman frigates less than half a mile behind them.

Robert also regarded the ships that continued gaining on them but were slightly changing course.

Fenton laughed, "They are veering away now, Sir!"

Robert pulled his telescope out and focused on the poop deck of the leading frigate. Several officers stood together discussing the British ships heading their way. A tall officer who appeared to be the captain walked across to the gunwale. He turned and shouted an order and then looked back at Shadow. Robert knew the Ottoman Captain was looking directly at him. The man stood at attention and raised his hat in a sign of respect as the frigate turned away to the north. Robert immediately returned the compliment and raised his hat towards the Ottomans.

He stood there briefly as the enemy frigates headed towards Sicily.

Fenton came across and said, "They nearly overtook us, Sir. But we outsmarted them."

Robert smiled, "We did, Mr Fenton. I was relieved to see those British frigates. Now, we must deliver our precious cargo to the Admiral. We shall salute the British Frigates as we pass and be in Malta by early afternoon. I must go below and finish my report. Let me know before we pass them. I must acknowledge their assistance. You have the ship, Mr Fenton."

"Aye, Sir."

On the Southampton Road, Past Winchester ...

The Reverend Philip Hotspur glanced across at the young lady who sat beside him in the rented carriage as they sped towards Southampton.

"You look sophisticated when scrubbed up and have some nice clothes on, Rosie. I think you will carry off being my wife quite well. The young English gentleman and his new bride, Rosemary! What a proper couple we make."

Rosie smiled at the compliment, giggled and said, "You will need to give me some speech training. I must get rid of the slang I use if I am to pass the test."

"That can be arranged. We will start tonight in bed. I will teach you how to 'Ooo!' and 'Ah'!"

She giggled and said, "I already know how to do that, Phili!"

"Rosie, from now on, you are Mrs Philip Hotspur, and everyone will call you Rosemary or Rose. Remember that!"

"I will, Dearie. But how will we pay for the tickets and set ourselves up in Sydney Cove?"

Philip moved closer, put his hand behind her back and held her waist tight, "Before he died, my uncle wrote a letter of introduction for me. What could be better than a Bishop's introduction? I had an inkling that his health was declining, so I arranged it just in time."

"But what about money, Phili? I mean Philip, Dear."

He squeezed her waist again and moved his mouth close to her ear. Philip whispered, "There is plenty of money, Rose. Plenty! I kept it quiet as a clergyman, but I bet some money on the horses. I won three thousand pounds, Rose, my Dear! That will be plenty for us to set up in the penal colony. I also have another thousand pounds from my previous parish in London and some savings from Guildford."

"Oh, Philip, Dear! You are so clever."

She turned and kissed him several times as they embraced.

Sitting back, Philip Hotspur pondered on the recent events in Guildford. He knew he could have found more money but decided to disappear before old Swamp and his sons came after him. They would never catch him now. And how stupid was Mervin Webster taking some pleasure each week with Rosie? No wonder the old man had blood pressure problems. As he rested each night before sneaking home, his little confidences with her in bed revealed much about the location of his treasures. Once Philip was through the study window, opening the strong box took slightly longer than expected, but finding the treasure chest was easy. Some antique dealer in Southampton would provide a good sum for such an ornate box.

Rosie looked up at Philip's happy face, "What are you thinking about Philip, Dear?"

"How fortunate we are!"

The one regret he had was not being able to have Jessica Swamp in his bed. He could not explain it but was deeply attracted to the pretty young lass. He sighed, but before Rosie could ask, he reached into his pocket, pulled out a gold doubloon and placed it in her delicate hand.

"Here! Tear the paper off this and taste it. Why, I might also treat myself to one!"

Chapter 14

Harting, St James's Square, London ...

Late on Saturday, Jonathan Turner climbed down from the coach and stretched, relieved to have arrived after a long, rushed trip to London. Long waits at turnpikes due to the Saturday traffic and dropping Blake Wood at the Swan Hotel near Chancery Lane had resulted in a later arrival than planned.

"Mr Turner, Welcome."

"Thank you, Staines. It is good to be out of the coach and stretch again."

Jonathan allowed the coachman to pass his bag to Staines, "Is this your only bag, Mr Turner?"

"Yes, travelling light this time."

"Lady Leystead will be glad to see you. There is much news!"

Jonathan was confused and asked, "Who is Lady Leystead?"

"My apologies, Mr Turner. You will not have heard yet, but with the unfortunate passing of Sir Hugh, his title has now been transferred to Sir Robert. Lady Anne is now the Viscountess of Leystead."

As Staines was explaining, Anne and Victoria rushed through the front door.

"Father, I am so relieved you have arrived."

"Anne ...!" Jonathan hugged his daughter but was concerned by the weariness on her face.

"Mr Turner. We are glad you are here. You can guide us on some business decisions for Hursts."

"I will do my best, Victoria. But I know very little about fashion. How are you?" He hugged Victoria and walked with them inside, chatting about the trip.

As they entered the drawing room, Anne asked, "Father, where is Mr Wood? I thought he was staying with us."

"I asked him to, but he declined. He has taken lodgings at The Swan Hotel close to Green & Greens in Chancery Lane. He is setting up a meeting for Monday morning due to the urgency of clearing up the confusion over Clare Petherton."

Anne asked, "What confusion, Father?"

The conversation over Clare Petherton and the vague accusations from Green & Green attorneys lasted until after dinner. Only then did Anne take Mr Turner aside to the countess's study.

"Father, I must tell you something in confidence. Please keep this to yourself for the next month or two, as it is very early, and Robert is unaware."

"Jonathan sat comfortably in the study beside his daughter, "You have my interest, Anne."

"Neville examined me a few days ago. It is confirmed now that I am with child. Please keep it confidential as I will tell the Earl and Countess when I join them next week. Victoria, Mrs Stubbington, and the staff know and are sworn to secrecy."

Jonathan smiled and hugged his daughter, "Daughter! Ethel and I could not be happier for you. That is wonderful news. It explains a lot. But why Mrs Stubbington?"

"She happened to be here soon after I became aware. She was most supportive. But, Father, have you noticed how tired I seem?"

Jonathan nodded.

"It appears I have late morning sickness. I am two months pregnant, and it has hit me hard and later than usual. I must spend time resting each day. Victoria has been a tower of strength and has done so much for me in the last week. I could not have coped without her."

Her father smiled, "I am here now, and perhaps I may assist as well."

Anne became emotional and hugged him tight. She cried, "I need Robert so much, Father, but he is months away from home. I have felt so alone."

"Now, now, Anne. I think this news will greatly uplift both families. It has been a difficult few weeks, but your news is exciting. With Bethany soon due and Marion with child, I look forward to becoming a grandfather."

He passed Anne a handkerchief. She smiled and asked, "Father, you said Ethel and I before. Why did you include Ethel?"

Jonathan realised he had made a mistake and paused before speaking, "You have a quick mind, Anne. I made a mistake, so I should tell you, but this also must remain confidential."

Anne nodded, and Victoria sat up and asked, "Should I go, Mr Turner?"

"No, Victoria. You have already heard my slip of the tongue. You should hear this as well. I have asked Ethel Nibley to become my wife."

Anne sat there in amazement, "But she was engaged to Benjamin Petherton, and he only died last week."

Jonathan took some time to explain the situation. As he finished, he finally said, "You will see now why it must be kept confidential for the time being."

Victoria asked, "Has she accepted, Mr Turner."

"Yes, she has, and I am a happy man."

With a smile and a warm voice, Victoria said, "That is wonderful. Congratulations, Mr Turner."

Fintelton Manor, Outside Petersfield, Sussex ...
On Sunday morning, the Earl and Countess led their visitors to the eastern end of the manor to a delightful small internal chapel brilliantly lit by the sunlight shining through the southern windows.

As the guests took their seats with the servants sitting at the rear, Lady Jane said, "We thought, children, as your visit includes Sunday, that we should have a short time of contemplation and prayer before breakfast. The Earl and I will visit our Petersfield church and leave you with Mr Stem for your activities. I think he intends to take a trail ride this morning. If any of you would like to attend church with us, you are more than welcome to do so."

Clementine and Katherine shot up their hands. Clare had difficulty deciding but, to Mrs Jennings' relief, chose to remain for riding.

Mr Stem, sitting beside Mrs Jennings, noted this and softly asked, "Why would Clemmie and Katherine decide for church?"

She whispered back, "I think their rears are soar from yesterday."

Malcom Stem smiled and nodded back as if to say, 'I understand.'

Lady Fintelton continued, "The Earl will lead us in a short form of morning prayer, and then we shall have breakfast."

Simeon, William and Madeline looked at each other, sighing with relief. They were all keen to go riding as this trip may be the last chance before the holiday in July.

At breakfast, William was seated beside the Earl. The young lad was curious about this old fellow and asked, "When you were young, Lord Fintelton, did you ride a horse?"

"Yes, William. I was a good rider in those days. I can't now because it jolts my back too much. Nothing is better than jumping the hedges and racing across the fields after the fox and hounds. I immensely enjoyed riding with my friends in the old days!"

The Earl grinned as if he recalled the thrill of riding in the pack. William had heard of fox hunts but had never seen one.

"What happens on a fox hunt, my Lord?"

"What Happens! Have you never seen one?"

"No, Sir!"

"It is a magnificent gathering of family and acquaintances from the district. They ride over, and we gather at the front of the manor and have some hot wine and sandwiches before heading out. The men wear red tunics, and the women are dressed in black. Usually, only the younger women come."

The countess could not resist interjecting, "That is rubbish, my Lord. What about Lady Sinclair and Lady Frost? They were both in their fifties and keen on the hunt."

"You are quite correct, my Dear. Good horsewomen as well! I withdraw that comment. Anyway, there is much fellowship and laughter before the hunt starts."

William asked, "What is fellowship, my Lord?"

"Talking and enjoying each other's company. The fun starts when the dogs arrive. I am sure you have seen an English hunting dog. We usually field a pack of around forty dogs; however, we have not hunted for some time, so the number of dogs in our pack may have decreased."

"Where are your dogs, my Lord? I have never seen them."

"We keep them down at Templeton farm. They do not disturb us there as they bark a lot."

William was more than interested, "Could we see them today, my Lord?"

Sir David could see the excitement in William and the other children, who loved dogs.

"Not this morning, William, as you are riding, and the Countess and I are attending church. But I will arrange it with Mr Stem, and you can ride down there after lunch. Why, I may come myself in the carriage. I would like to see the dogs again."

Madeline asked, "Is it not cruel to hunt the foxes, my Lord? Surely, they would stand no chance with forty dogs chasing them."

"No, Madeline. The fox will often escape, which is why it is such a challenge. But don't feel sorry for them. You should see what a fox does to newborn lambs. Why they..."

Lady Fintelton interrupted, "That is sufficient, my Lord. We do not need the gory details at breakfast."

"Of course, my Dear. You are quite right – not appropriate at all!"

William asked, "Did your father hunt, too, my Lord?"

"Yes, a painting at the top of the staircase shows him leading a hunt. He taught me much about riding and hunting."

William, sounding slightly sad, said, "My father can't even ride a horse. He works all the time. But Mr McPherson taught us how to train our dog. He is a smart man and has two beautiful dogs."

The Earl considered William's comments about his father and said, "I am sure your father is a very intelligent man. He has built a huge business and constructed the new flour mill."

All William could remember about his father was the beatings he received. He forced a smile and continued with his breakfast. The Earl noted his insincere smile and realised there may be an issue. He decided to talk with William more privately as the boy seemed to be trying to tell him something.

Pike entered and went to the countess, "A message from a Lady Fiona Green, my Lady."

Lady Jane took the message and eagerly read it, saying, "At last!"

Everyone looked up at her comment, wondering who Lady Fiona was.

"My Lord! It appears Lady Fiona Green and Doctor Cowper have arrived in Petersfield. They ask for Monday and Tuesday to regain their land balance and will arrive at Fintelton on Wednesday. That timing will work well for us. They carry Hugh's ashes and will enlighten us on his time in Jamaica."

Then, she paused, and the Earl could see the emotion welling up in Lady Jane.

"If I may, my Dear. Let me respond to them this morning, and we shall leave the message at the hotel before we return from church."

"Thank you, my Lord. Now, children, it is time for riding. Clementine and Katherine! If you would dress for church and be ready for the coach. We shall leave at nine."

There was silence among the children as they finished breakfast before rushing off to change.

Lady Jane came from her place at the other end of the table and sat beside Lord Fintelton.

She whispered, "David, I forgot about Clare and the loss of her father. I hope I did not upset her."

"She seems quite settled here. I think she is mature for her age. Perhaps being an only child for the last few years has shaped her character. I have been impressed by her maturity. A lovely child!"

"I should have waited until the children were gone before I told you. It was the emotion of hearing Hugh's ashes are so close."

The Earl stood and helped his wife out of the chair. He could see the tears on her cheeks.

"My Dear. Hugh would want you to remember the good things in his life. He was a fine young man. Certainly, he went astray, but he made a fine effort to correct that in his last year. Let us celebrate his life next Thursday and give him the respect he now deserves."

"I know you are right, but I miss my boy so much!"

The Earl took Lady Jane in his arms and cuddled her as she held him tight.

Local Anglican Church, Petersfield, Hampshire ...
After receiving communion, the Earl, the Countess, Clementine and Katherine returned to their seats, and the Countess continued to watch proceedings at the communion rail. Lady Jane noticed a well-dressed, unaccompanied lady who steadied herself after rising from the rail and carefully navigating back to her seat several rows behind. As she passed their pew, there was a meeting of eyes, and the woman smiled pleasantly.

The Countess immediately thought this must be Lady Fiona and would have gone to her except for the next hymn starting. After the service concluded, Lady Jane quickly rose and approached the lady.

"Excuse me, Madam, but would you be Lady Fiona Green?"

"Yes, my Lady. I would presume you are Lady Fintelton. I am very pleased to meet you in person. Forgive me for not being introduced, but I am alone. I felt a little rested this morning and decided to attend church."

"I am so glad you did. We have finally met. Thank you for caring for my son for such a long time. You have been in my prayers for months."

"Lady Fintelton, I only saw the best of your son. He was a fighter and wanted so badly to come home. Alas, he lost his battle, but I also bring you a lot of good news. We will need much time to talk so I can tell you everything."

Lady Jane wiped a tear away as she said, "You and Doctor Cowper will have that. Please stay as long as you like. We will talk at length in the coming days."

"Perhaps it is best if you talk with Doctor Cowper first. He is keen to visit his parents in Truro before leaving for Sydney Cove. He has signed a three-year contract there."

"Certainly. But you will stay for a week or two, Lady Fiona."

"Yes, I will, as I must also visit Guildford and meet with certain people. I understand you have a son and daughter-in-law there, so perhaps we could travel together. It will only take a few days, then we might return to Fintelton."

"Yes, my son Robert and his wife Anne live there. I am sure Anne would demand we stay. I also have a daughter, Emma, who married Doctor David Sopwith. They also live in Guildford. You must meet them."

"My, Guildford sounds like a popular spot, Lady Fintelton. Would you join me for some morning tea before you venture home? I am just across the square at the Red Dear Hotel."

"I would love to, but I am here with my husband and two young guests. We also have the Turner children visiting, and they are riding at Fintelton this morning. Unfortunately, the Earl has promised to take the children to see the dog pack this afternoon, so we must return to Fintelton immediately. But thank you for the offer." Lady Jane paused and then asked, "Lady Fiona, there is a burning question I must ask before leaving."

"Yes, my Lady."

Lady Jane tried to hold a straight face as tears came. Half crying, she asked, "Did he suffer at the end?"

Fiona smiled, holding the sobbing countess close, "No, my Lady. He was strong and a fighter. I was sitting beside Hugh at the time. Your son was relaxing after a walk. It happened in an instant, and he felt no pain. I know he is with the Lord now."

The countess could not contain her sobbing and held Fiona tight.

The Earl could see the moment's emotion and gave his wife a minute to recover, "Jane, come now —my Dear. We must return to Fintelton. Thank you, Lady Green. I am keen for you and Doctor Cowper to come. I am sorry I must pull the countess away."

"I understand, my Lord."

The Earl led a teary countess away as Clementine and Katherine curtsied and spoke quickly to Lady Fiona before rushing after the Earl and Countess.

British Navy, Eastern Mediterranean Base, Malta …
Captain South, Lieutenant Fenton and Lieutenant Peters followed the Admiral as he led them to his house along a path that curved around a hill leading to a significant mansion.

"It is a magnificent view of the fleet from your house, Admiral," Robert commented.

Admiral Sutherland replied, "The navy chose a good spot for this mansion. I enjoy having morning tea at the front of the house overlooking the harbour. There must be some benefits to the job! Pity my wife is not here to share it with me."

They climbed the steps onto a wide verandah, and the Admiral pointed out some chairs near the far end, which held a magnificent view and comfort while they discussed their mission.

"Gentlemen, below you see our mighty fleet that keeps these Ottomans in Greece under control. Our intelligence indicates that the Sultan will completely control Greece within months. The sheer size of the Ottoman armies is beating the Greeks. The problem is that we now have Russia threatening to invade from the north. At present, it is a stalemate as the Sultan concentrates on assembling a fleet at Navarino, on the Greek west coast, and the Russians are slowly building up their army in the north."

Lieutenant Peters asked, "Why do the Russians want to invade?"

"Good question, Lieutenant." The Admiral spoke quietly, "It appears the Czar sees an opportunity. Perhaps he feels the Greek instability should be exploited. The Russians find it hard to resist any opportunity for territorial gain."

"But what is our role then? We don't want to fight either of them."

"Correct, Peters. We prefer the Greeks rule their land with the Sultan as the supreme head. This combination would allow peace in this part of the world. However, the Greeks were not keen on an Ottoman being head of state, which might give Russia an excuse to invade. Gentlemen, a drinks cabinet is inside, and the staff will serve you. Perhaps you could give Sir Robert and me ten minutes before rejoining us. Take a walk around the garden."

Fenton and Peters were happy to find a spot on the hill and enjoy some cold refreshments.

"Robert, good to see you. I was worried when you became overdue."

"Given the importance of my passengers and the order to protect them at all costs, I decided to head up around Sardinia and down the east side of Sicily to avoid the Ottomans. It worked well until we entered the Ionian. We were fortunate to meet some British frigates; otherwise, there may have been trouble."

"Well done. I think those diplomats are in for a busy time. I won't say much in front of the others, but London has a new plan—a conference between the Russians, French and us to sort this out. The Foreign Office wants a joint treaty to settle the matter and keep the Russians from invading. I am afraid you may miss the action, Robert. Codrington believes we should attack and destroy the Ottoman fleet; however, his orders are to use diplomatic measures and take a calm approach. He can see the Ottomans are thumbing their noses at us. I think it will come to a battle in the end – but that is my opinion, which differs to the politicians and the Admiralty."

"Why should I miss the action, Sir? My ship is battle-ready, and we have joined the fleet here."

"Correct, but I am ordered home by Admiral Bird to assist him in these treaty matters. I shall be travelling on 'Shadow' with 'Restless' and a French frigate, '*Solange*', joining our company. The French and Russian diplomats will travel on 'Solange'. We must be away in three days and head for Portsmouth. Sorry about missing the action, but there will be other opportunities."

Robert was concerned, "Admiral, Ottoman ships are everywhere along the south coast. Fortunately, we escaped them by the route I chose. But as we headed across to Malta, they appeared again. They would have proved hostile if it were not for some British ships exercising nearby."

"I think you overestimate the situation, Robert. We know they are training and becoming quite a navy, but they would not dare attack us. Our force is too strong, and remember, we have the French and the Russians with us. On Wednesday, we return home quickly. The treaty must be negotiated before this new Czar decides to invade. We leave the blue fleet with Admiral Codrington and head for Portsmouth. You will need to find room for Commodore Jacobs as well. Now let us find the others and have some morning tea."

Rectory, Guildford, Surrey ...
Andrew Taggart raised a glass of sherry to his lips and considered his long day of church services and the past week's events. Leaning back into his study chair, he found Philip Hotspur's letter and reflected on the date. The letter had been written and dated the night of the burglary at the Webster's house.

'Strange!' he thought. Surely, that must be a coincidence. He knew Philip had a base character, but as a clergyman, he was sure the curate would not break into a parishioner's house.

Andrew sat there, finished his sherry, placed the glass on his desk and leaned back again. He decided to put this to prayer. As he prayed, it occurred to him that if it was Philip, he must have gained information somehow on where the money was stored.

Hearing a loud knock at the front door, Andrew jumped up, hoping to open it before it disturbed his wife, who had retired for the evening. Swinging the door open, he found a depressed Mervin Webster eager to talk with him.

"Mervin, I was not expecting you!"

"I am sorry to bother you, Andrew. There is a pressing matter I must clear up, and I need your help."

"Come in and take a seat in my study."

Closing the door behind him, Andrew followed the slow-moving man.

"Sorry again. As you know, I have the sugar sickness[33] and lack energy greatly these days. I walk as much as possible, and it has been a long day."

He sighed while taking off his coat and sank into the chair.

"How can I assist, Mervin?"

"This burglary has greatly disturbed me. I have thought deeply about it and believe I know who the culprit is! However, revealing all the facts may result in deep embarrassment for my family and me and a backlash from the community."

"I am surprised to hear this. We have the greatest respect for you here, Mervin."

"Alas, Andrew, I am a sinner like every other man."

Andrew nodded and let him continue.

"I have considered the burglary several times and wondered who would commit such a crime. It is not so much the money but the fact that they violated my home. I think I understand what has happened. I have sometimes made foolish comments to friends outside my home. I may have mentioned the money I stored at home more than once."

"I see. Is it that these friends may have also talked in the wrong places?"

"Well, yes!" Mervin stumbled over his words, but Andrew let him finish. "You see… it is not easy for me … I need … damn it – how do I say this?" Mervin was turning red with embarrassment.

"Please, Andrew! Keep this confidential."

"All you say here is confidential."

"I have a mistress, Andrew, and often see her late on a Saturday night when my wife thinks I am at the club. Her name is Rosie Black, and she lives down towards the river. A comfortable abode but quite out of the way for obvious reasons with a dark entrance at night."

Andrew was amazed that this sick old gentleman would get up to these tricks; however, he maintained his calm expression.

"I have told her about the money and its location several times. It

---

[33] Diabetes. JS

is the relief you feel after the act. You understand, don't you? The relief allows you to share confidences and talk. Sometimes, when you relax, you speak freely about issues you shouldn't."

"I see. Does Clowie know about this?"

"Of course not, Andrew. She must not! It would destroy her. That is why I cannot tell the police."

Andrew Taggart sat there, understanding what was coming next. He felt sick in his stomach, not wanting to hear anymore. But he listened and would do his best to help Mervin.

"So, Mervin, how can I assist?"

Mervin rubbed his eyes, knowing he was close to tears. "Andrew, firstly, I am ashamed of myself for being in a position where I cannot tell the truth. That is not me. I am an honest man. I have not told anyone, but following the burglary, I scoured the room and found a handkerchief behind the open safe door. It is grey and would have been easily missed in the darkness. It is the clue the police need, but I can never tell or give it to them. If they find this handkerchief, my marriage will be ruined."

He passed across the item, and Andrew unfolded it and noticed the initials 'P.H.' embroidered on a corner. He recalled seeing similar handkerchiefs in the hands of Mr Philip Hotspur.

"What do you wish me to do with this, Mervin?"

"I cannot keep it. If my wife finds it, I am a dead man. You know how Clowie is – she would provide it to the police, and the whole story would come out. My marriage would be ruined. I would be the subject of gossip for years to come."

Andrew sat there looking at the handkerchief. He recalled visiting Philip's house and meeting the young, attractive Rosie. She must have a reasonably sized clientele here in Guildford. She may have even had Sir Hugh South as a client. That could be bad for Mervin, given the disease that Sir Hugh carried.

"Mervin, you know you have behaved stupidly. I will say no more on this subject. But have you confronted this Rosie girl about the robbery?"

"I tried several times, but the house is empty. It appears she is gone!"

Andrew nodded, now realising that Rosie and Philip were deeply involved in this burglary. They had escaped and were moving north.

Philip had the money, and when it ran out, he could send Rosie to work again so he had an income. He could not fathom the depths the man had sunk to.

"Andrew!"

Mr Taggart shook his head and refocused on Mervin.

"Andrew. May I pass this handkerchief to you? If anyone asks, you can say he left it here long ago and that you forgot to return it to him. No one will suspect anything."

Taggart looked at Mervin, disappointed that this man expected Andrew to lie for him. Surely, he knew there was a limit to how much he could do.

"Mervin, leave it here, and I will consider your request. I know you will keep this confidential, and so shall I. Please do one thing for me. No two things. Firstly, see Doctor Sopwith and have him check you for any disease you may have picked up."

Mervin spluttered, "I had not thought of …."

"Secondly. Tell the police not to continue the investigation as you do not wish to press charges against anyone."

"But what if they ask me why?"

"Tell them about your sickness and your turns. You need a peaceful existence here in Guildford."

Mervin momentarily contemplated then smiled and replied, "That is true! I will have no difficulty in doing this." He wiped the sweat off his forehead with a handkerchief and said, "Thank you, Andrew, from the bottom of my heart. I will sleep well tonight."

Mervin rose quickly from the chair, nodded to Andrew, grabbed his coat, was out the front door, and rushed home.

Andrew Taggart remained seated at his desk, gazing at the handkerchief.

'I am sorry, Lord, for this. But you are a God so full of forgiveness and mercy. Forgive me for my sins. In Jesus name, I pray. Amen.'

He took the handkerchief, moved to a chair beside the fireplace, and sat. Handling the handkerchief, he gazed at the initials 'P.H'. He mused, 'Philip Hotspur – what a fool you have become.'

Slowly unfolding the handkerchief, he placed it into the burning fire. As the garment burned and turned to ash, he said, "Good Riddance!"

Before leaving Harting on Monday morning, Mr Turner handed Anne the shortlist for the General Manager's position and the applicant's resumes.

He also asked, "Have you picked out some wedding presents for Jeb and Audry – the wedding is close."

"No. I will do that today. If you can clear up this matter by Tuesday evening, we can leave together for Guildford on Wednesday."

Jonathan said confidently, "It will be cleared up today!"

Before Anne could reply, she placed her hand across her mouth and ran off, giving him a wave. Jonathan was concerned as he watched her run up the staircase. But there was no time; he must meet Blake Wood at Greens, and time was short.

As the coach arrived in Chancery Lane, he noticed a black police wagon and several officers at the corner. He wondered if there had been a burglary. Rushing from the carriage, he met his attorney in the foyer, who quickly ushered him down a corridor into a waiting room with a receptionist seated at a desk.

"Miss Clarke, this is Mr Turner. Could we please see Mr Regan now?"

"Certainly, I will inform him you have arrived, Mr Wood."

"Thank you."

Miss Clarke disappeared into the office and then reappeared, gesturing for them to enter. As Blake was entering, he noticed over his shoulder the receptionist making a rushed exit through the front door. He thought this was strange but refocused on Mr Regan.

At a large desk sat a small man in a large chair. He stood and said, "Welcome, Mr Turner and Mr Wood. Please have a seat."

"Thank you for seeing us, Mr Regan. We were keen to clear up this matter mentioned in your letter about Steadman and Preston claiming that Clare Petherton was forcibly removed from their care. You see the young g….."

"Mr Turner, please. Before you commence, I should inform you that we have sworn statements from both Mr Steadman and Miss Preston, whom I have known for many years and know they are trustworthy and reliable persons."

"That may be so, Mr Regan, but the facts are…."

"Yes, I would like to gain a fact from you, please, Mr Turner. I understand that Lady Gwendoline McDermott has arrived in Guildford, and your housekeeper, Mrs Nibley, has been rude to her and refused to hand over Clare Petherton into her care. Also, the housekeeper refuses to advise Lady McDermott of the girl's whereabouts."

Jonathan Turner was taken aback by the hostile reception he received. It was as if he was being accused of a crime. At that moment, the door to the office opened, and a tall man in an ill-fitting suit entered.

Mr Regan announced, "This is Detective Inspector Sullivan from the London police force. He has been informed of this case and will listen to your answers. I am sure you won't mind."

Blake Wood interjected, "Detective Sullivan, this is a private interview, not a police station. If you would be so kind as to leave this office."

The policeman answered, "I am sorry, Mr Wood, but I must be present for an accused kidnapping. Mr Regan has briefed me on the case and provided me with Steadman and Preston's statements. They have laid a charge that you have kidnapped this young lady. Mr Turner, please advise me of the whereabouts of Miss Clare Petherton."

"But no one has accused Mr Turner of kidnapping. You do not understand the facts of the case!"

Sullivan spoke up, saying, "On the contrary, Mr Wood. Mr John Steadman and Miss Preston have both accused Mr Turner of kidnapping the girl. We have written complaints from them."

This intrusion flustered Jonathan. He had expected a reasonable conversation with this attorney but found he had entered a trap.

"If you would advise me of Clare Petherton's whereabouts, Mr Turner."

Jonathan looked at the detective and then at Blake Wood.

Blake said, "Mr Turner, it is clear that Steadman and Preston have committed perjury, and this will be revealed once we have the facts established. It may be best to reveal Clare's location to satisfy this policeman."

Regan shouted, "Answer the policeman, Mr Turner."

"She is on a riding trip."

The detective became annoyed and shouted, "But where?"

"I am afraid I cannot release that information to you, Detective, for some very good reasons. Clare Petherton will arrive at my house on Thursday morning in time for the funeral. Do you understand I am a Magistrate in Guildford?"

Once again, the detective asked, "Your final chance, Mr Turner."

Jonathan said, "This is all a huge mistake. The facts are entirely different to what you understand. I must protect Clare from what is happening here."

The detective looked at Regan, who nodded to him.

He said, "Mr Jonthan Turner, I am arresting you for the kidnapping of Miss Clare Petherton from Mesnil Priory on Saturday, 28 April 1827. You will be remanded to the Bow Street Magistrate's Court until a magistrate can hear the charges against you."

He opened the office door and issued in two police officers, each taking one of Jonathan's arms and manhandling him out of the room. Jonathan shouted, "Blake, get Finchley from Manifold & Stout as quickly as possible. Also, brief Reverend Taggart and get him here soon. You won't get away with this, Regan!"

Regan stood there with a pleasant smile on his face.

Blake Wood asked, "I would like to talk to the senior partner here, Mr Regan."

"That will not be possible, Mr Wood. Mr Green is on leave until next Monday. I think that is the end of our meeting here today. Good day."

"No, I think not. I am unsure how you are involved in this, but I fear you have no idea what trouble you are causing yourself. Now show me to the managing partner's secretary so I can book an urgent appointment before I leave. If you refuse, I will find the lady myself."

Regan did not move, so Blake gathered his things and left the office, slamming the door.

Port Elizabeth, Eastern Cape Province, South Africa ...
Richard climbed the steps to the reception foyer of their hotel and walked across to the dining room.

"Sarah, I have secured a contract for the bullock team to cart our materials to the property. It should be loaded by next Thursday, and we can set off home. We will also have an army escort. Lieutenant

Sanderson has arranged that for us."

Sarah sat at the lunch table and looked up at him with red eyes. She wiped away a tear and softly said, "Richard, sit down. We must talk."

Richard was concerned and said no more. Once seated, he asked, "Have you ordered anything?"

"Not yet, but I have asked for a wine for both of us. We need to talk before eating."

Richard could sense this was serious and gave Sarah his full attention. He said, "Are you well?"

"Yes, Richard. Physically, I am well, but mentally I am struggling. Let me explain. You saw the state of the dead trooper they brought in from the plains. Killed by natives and mauled by wild animals. You know how hard this country is to farm. We must build dams for water. We must bring Xhosa tribes onto our property to protect us from scavengers. We live in a community where the next neighbour may be miles away. We are not settlers but explorers. Our position here is so difficult. We have taken over a country where the existing population don't want us. We drove them out of their farmland and told them where they could live. When we move them to another area, they invade the people already living there. No wonder there are tensions among the natives."

Richard had heard enough, "But Sarah…...!"

Sarah would have none of his interruptions. She was intent on finishing before he made any comments.

"Listen, Richard. We are building a nicely designed home like the manors in England. But you have seen the settlers' homes. They are like forts with small windows that a native cannot climb through. They use the windows to defend their family's lives if they are attacked. Our new home, if attacked, will last all of five minutes before the natives are inside and kill us. South Africa is not a place for us. If you wish to stay, that is up to you. I have come out here and done my best but have decided it is not for me. I am going home to England."

Richard sat there wondering how he could convince her to stay. But Sarah took some papers from her bag and placed them before him.

"Here is my ticket for a ship leaving on Wednesday for Portsmouth. I have paid for it out of my own money. I will wait for you in England, Richard, but not here. If we stay here, we will never see our children again. I would rather be poor and have my children than be here chasing a golden dream that will not eventuate. I have followed you in every decision you have made. I am here and have tried, but I will not stay in this country. I am not a settler, Richard. I am growing old, and all this is too hard for me. I will sail on Wednesday and hope you come too. If not, I will wait for you in England."

Richard could not believe his wife would leave him here alone.

He said, "There is nothing to return to in England besides the children. Our future is here and is already developing. We have free land. We have workers. We have cattle and sheep. We will have crops. There is a wonderful future here."

Richard looked into Sarah's eyes and saw the tears running down her cheeks.

She said, "Then make your future here, but don't ask me to stay here as I must leave for home. Can't you see that this country is killing me? I am fifty-one years old, Richard. I cannot do the work of a twenty-year-old. Katherine and I will live with Harry at the Ewell pub. We will write and keep in contact. You come home when you are ready, Richard. If your dream comes true, we will celebrate it when you return. If it does not, you will have a place when you return home."

Richard nodded in agreement. He could not believe this was happening.

"I cannot leave, Sarah! You know how much I have invested in this place. It will pay dividends in the future. I will come home for a visit in a couple of years. You go. Katherine will be pleased to see you. Jonathan will make sure you are looked after. I will write to him tonight and tell him what is happening. It may prevent him from sending William."

The tears continued to roll down Sarah's cheeks.

"You know I still love you, my Darling. It is just that I cannot live here anymore. It is too wild and untamed. I want a quiet life with our children and hopefully some grandchildren in time."

Richard could not say anything. He was shattered at the thought of his wife leaving.

She said, "Shall we order now?"

James McPherson's Residence, High Street, Glasgow …
It was a fine morning in Glasgow as Thomas Turner's coach arrived at

James McPherson's house in the High Street.

"Marion, I know this house brings bad memories for you, but think about our new life and what we can achieve. James and Isla will want us to have a happy time here."

Thomas's wife sat there with a confused look on her face. She remembered how they had arrived on their honeymoon to spend a few days with James and see Glasgow. It was here that the news came that her mother had died. A tear came to her eye, remembering that terrible day, but she wiped it away and, with gleaming eyes, turned to Thomas and said, "My mother would be thrilled that we bring our child to this house, Darling. If it is a girl, I am sure she will have my mother's nose. We will make the best of this time."

Feeling disturbed, Thomas leaned across in relief and lightly kissed her cheek.

From outside the carriage, they heard, "Come on, you two love birds. Welcome to Scotland and Glasgow."

James McPherson stood with an umbrella in his hand, and Hamish McPherson, with a wide smile, waved his greeting.

As James opened the carriage door, he said, "Looks like rain, so I came prepared."

They quickly exited the coach, and welcome hugs were shared before entering the house.

"Beautiful home you have here, James."

"Thank you. Isla and I chose it after my mother and father moved to Greenwich. We were keen to be close to the company offices at George Square. The house is also close to the London Road for trips south. As you know, I often travel south to meet with my father."

"What about the brewery?"

"Well, we have two here in Glasgow. The main brewery is just past Braehead on the south bank of the Clyde River. It is a bit of a hike by carriage, but if you leave early, it does not take long. The small brewery is similar to what we shall build in Guildford and is closer to Fairfield. I could show you that one tomorrow if you like."

Mr MacPherson interrupted, "Thomas, James was keen to welcome you before heading to Ireland. Perhaps you can catch up tonight at dinner. It may be best to show Marion your rooms here and commence unpacking. We have a lot to talk about in the coming days. I must leave for London soon, so the sooner we start, the more familiar you will be with your duties before I leave. I also must introduce you to Douglas tomorrow, who will work with you until Lachlan arrives."

"Thank you, Mr MacPherson. That sounds excellent. Perhaps, James, we might meet at dinner tonight."

Late that night, there was a knock on Thomas and Marion's door.

"Sorry to disturb you, but I wondered if I could borrow Thomas for a few minutes, Marion?"

"Certainly, James. After all, this is your house."

James smiled and indicated to Thomas to follow.

They climbed an internal staircase and reached an open area on the next floor. It was sparsely furnished but seemed comfortable. James pointed to a couple of lounge chairs and indicated they should sit.

"This all sounds a bit hush-hush, James. What is on your mind?"

"Sorry about my father at dinner. I could not say much. They are transferring me to Ireland because of Isla. It seems our partnership and religion does not fit the mould, and the best way to sideline me is to send me to the rebellious country."

"Has your father said that?"

"No. The official story is I am being made General Manager Ireland so I can be close to Isla."

"I'm sure your father has the best intentions for you."

"I wish I could agree. Look, Thomas! You and I are friends, and we need to keep in contact. Events have happened here of which you are not aware. It would be best if you were prepared for similar future events. I know I can trust you, and you will understand. Let me explain."

Over the next hour, James talked with Thomas and gave him a history of the shipping line and various Irish cargos. He seemed to indicate that he had no choice due to his financial debt to a gentleman at the docks. But it must remain a secret from Mr McPherson."

Thomas asked, "Why?"

"I do not wish to ruin my close relationship with Father."

Thomas was not sure James was being truthful but said, "I will do the best I can for you, but there is a limit on what I can do. You understand I can't involve myself in anything unlawful. I would be dishonouring the trust your father has put in me."

James replied, "What I have mentioned is all I ask. There is nothing unlawful. I appreciate your friendship."

Harting, St James's Square, London …
Blake Wood arrived around six in the evening, worn out from an exhausting day. There was slight rain outside, and he removed his wet coat, quickly passing it across to a footman.

"Thank you. Where will I find Lady Anne, please?"

"This way. Sir."

The footman issued Mr Wood into the parlour, where Anne and Victoria sat on a comfortable settee before the fire.

"Mr Wood, we expected you and Father long ago. Where is my father?"

"Lady Anne. It has been a disastrous day. I have been at Manifold & Stout working with Mr Finchley. We have prepared a defence for the Magistrate's hearing tomorrow morning. I have sent a message to Reverend Andrew Taggart asking him to come to London immediately with his documents."

"Mr Wood – you have not answered my question. Where is my father?"

"Of course – you would not have heard. Excuse my thoughtlessness. Mr Turner was arrested this morning by the Bow Street Officers for kidnapping. He has been remanded at the Bow Street[34] police station and will be placed in front of a magistrate tomorrow morning."

Anne stood in shock, and Victoria said, "My goodness!"

---

[34] The Metropolitan Police Service was founded in 1829 by Home Secretary Sir Robert Peel under the Metropolitan Police Act 1829 and on 29 September of that year, when the first constables of the service appeared on the streets of London. Prior to the Metropolitan Police, the enforcement of the law was mostly up to private citizens, and parish constables and watchmen who had the right and duty to prosecute crimes in which they were involved. Wikipedia. In this novel I have used artistic licence relating law enforcement to the 'Bow Street Runners' and the 'Bow Street Magistrates Court' for dramatic purposes. JS

Chapter 15

Fintelton Manor, Outside Petersfield, Sussex ...

Walking outside onto the verandah, Lady Jane South felt the hints of warmth still lingering in the late afternoon. A north-easterly breeze stirred, cooling the pleasant spring day and giving a slight chill across her back. She pulled a shawl around her shoulders and sighed as she viewed the inheritance that her eldest son should have had.

In the west, the sun was nearly down, and darkness would soon creep over the manor and then rush away towards the horizon, blanking out the day. She hated the night as it was when the pain of losing Hugh was the worst. Having the Turner children here again had thankfully diverted her mind from the depression. Their constant chatter and laughter had cheered her immensely. But the pain always lurked in the background and would remain forever.

Gathering herself, she turned and said, "Pike! It is time Sir David was brought inside, please."

"Yes, Lady Fintelton."

The Earl, who had already stirred, welcomed the footmen's help and joined Lady Jane in the drawing room.

Lord Fintelton said, "A beautiful afternoon out there, but I agree it is becoming a bit chilly. I will be sad to see the children leave tomorrow. But Lady Fiona and Doctor Cowper will be welcome on Wednesday. It will be a busy week, my Dear."

Pike excused himself and announced, "A carriage has arrived, my Lady. A Mrs Nibley from the Turner household carries a message from Mr Jonathan Turner for you. I have brought the message, and Mrs Nibley is comfortable in the servants' quarters."

"Thank you, Pike."

She took the letter and commenced reading:

Turner Residence
High Street
Guildford

The Right Honble. The Countess of Fintelton.

Dear Madam

My apologies for this rushed letter. It is Friday morning, and I must leave for London immediately. We hope to clarify with the attorneys acting for Mr Benjamin Petherton's estate the facts of Miss Clare Petherton's kidnapping by the Butler, Steadman, and her Governess.

Thank you for hosting the children and for the riding lessons. I pray we can repay your kindness in the future.

I have sent Mrs Nibley, our housekeeper and a trustee of Clare Petherton, to accompany Clare in a separate carriage to my children. You may not be aware of this, but Mrs Ethel Nibley was engaged to marry Mr Benjamin Petherton, Clare's father. Her close relationship with Mr Petherton gives her a vital interest in Clare's safety. She will use an alternate route to Guildford, as Clare Petherton is best to remain absent until the trustees meet and discuss the custody arrangements. We expect that to happen on the day of her father's funeral, Thursday, 10 May 1827.

The reason for my letter is that you may receive a visit from either Lady McDermott, who claims to be one of Clare's trustees, or her representative, demanding custody of the young girl. No meeting of Miss Petherton's three trustees has occurred, which is required before custody arrangements may be made.

My attorney and I believe there is some mischief in Lady Mc-Dermott's claims, given the confusing letter from Green & Green Attorneys, which provides untruths about Clare's forced removal from Cloverdale Chase in Guildford.

I expect this situation to be rectified before the funeral on Thursday.

My advice would be not to entertain Lady McDermott and her representatives as we are unsure of her actual identity, and given the size of the inheritance, it may be possible that these people are imposters. I hope to have the issues clarified in London this coming Monday and Tuesday.

Thank you again for hosting Clare and our children. Knowing young Clare is safe at Fintelton is a great comfort during this stressful time.

Kindest Regards
Jonathan Turner

Lady Jane was most concerned and passed the letter to her husband. The Earl quickly scanned the letter and said, "Turner is quite right in saying the trustees must meet and determine the custody arrangements for the girl. She appeared relaxed in the company of the children, so it seems suspicious that some person arrived demanding custody and intending to remove her to London. Given the size of the inheritance, I also concur with his protection of the child until that meeting occurs. We should talk with Mrs Nibley, my Dear. I am sure she can provide more information."

The countess wasted no time and called the butler.

"Pike, please escort Mrs Nibley to us at once."

Fintelton Manor, Outside Petersfield, Sussex ...

William was standing with Robert on the poop deck, watching the huge swell coming from the west. The noise of the westerly was deafening as the captain shouted, "Lieutenant Turner, go to the middle deck and tell that man to get below."

"Aye, sir"

As William climbed down the ladder from the quarter, the ship rolled violently, and he fell from the ladder into a wave crashing over the guard rail. Gasping and screaming for help, he raised himself and rubbed his eyes.

"Will, you're dreaming again!"

Madeline and Clare were kneeling beside his bed.

"Quick Will! Get your clothes on and come. We are going to the stables before breakfast to say goodbye to our horses." Madeline moved away and tried to stir Simeon, but he rolled over and moaned, "Leave me alone. I want to sleep."

As they waited outside the door, Clare smiled as Madeline said, "Simeon has always been a sleepy head, but he reads books late into the night."

William was ready quickly, pulling his old clothes over his pyjamas. Coming with the girls, they headed for the servants' breakfast room.

Mr Pike looked outside from the servants' exit, closed the door and turned to face them.

"The fog is too thick, children. Have some breakfast as you wait. I will check again in ten minutes."

William objected, "But Mr Pike, we know the way backwards and the path is marked clearly to the stables."

"Does Mr Stem know you are coming?"

Madeline said, "I am afraid not."

Clare suggested, "We will hold hands all the way. If we don't go now, we will be late for breakfast!"

Pike was not persuaded, "No children! Ten minutes, so have some breakfast here."

Somewhat sad and his head bent down, William walked to the table and sat at the end closest to the exit. Madeline sat beside him, and Clare on the other side. Mrs Walsh approached with some bowls for porridge and said, "Children, why the sad faces? You can say goodbye to your horses soon, and then you will have a pleasant ride back to Guildford. I am sure Mrs Jennings has many stops planned for refreshments."

Clare replied, "Thank you, Mrs Walsh. I will miss Fintelton. It has been a pleasure being here. Thank you for all your help. Will you be at the Isle of Wight when the Turners visit?"

"Yes - we usually pack up and go the last week in June. It takes a lot of organisation, but we all enjoy being beside the sea, and the Earl ensures everyone has plenty of extra time for a holiday. He even brings in extra staff from London to help. Will you be with the Turners when they come?"

"I hope so very much! Mrs Nibley is one of my trustees, and she said that I can come, but it depends on the other trustees."

"I see! Well, I hope we see you there."

A maid approached with three plates of bacon and eggs and said, "The porridge is coming but not ready yet, so this will keep you going."

The children had not realised how hungry they were and immediately commenced eating. William watched the clock as he devoured his meal.

After ten minutes, Mr Pike raised himself from his chair and walked past them towards the exit.

"Come, children, we shall have another look."

They all stood and quickly followed him. On opening the door, Pike found the fog had slightly cleared, although small, patchy puffs of mist were moving across the field.

"I am in two minds, children. I understand you are familiar with the path, but you may become lost if some fog blocks your way. However, it should start to clear soon, so against my better judgment, I will allow you out. But as Clare suggested, you will hold hands and not let go. William, you are in the middle, please."

Mrs Walsh stood alongside the children and checked that their coat buttons were all done up.

Within a minute of leaving, Mr Pike noticed the fog closing in and appearing thicker. The butler frowned, realising it would be difficult to find them now they were out of sight.

"Mrs Walsh. I will fetch my coat and go after them. I have a bad feeling about this morning."

The housekeeper nodded and could not believe how quickly the mist had thickened. Mr Pike was soon out the door and heading after them.

At the stables, Mr Stem and his teams of labourers waited for the fog to clear. His plans for drainage work in a lower field must change if this weather continued. The mist's thickness reminded him of a few years ago when the fog had not lifted until midday. The men had run out of conversation, remaining quiet, but were becoming restless. Suddenly, Syd Mantle waved and put a finger to his lips, signalling everyone to be silent.

Syd whispered, "We are all here, aren't we, Mr Stem?"

Malcolm Stem whispered back, "Yes, Syd. Everyone is here. All twenty-three of us."

"Well, I just heard some people walking nearby in the grass. Not on the path but towards the house."

Realising they must be strangers, Stem whispered, "Can't be too far if you can hear them. Everyone quiet and listen for them!"

Stem knew that people spoke louder when walking through thick fog. As there was no breeze, the sound could carry easily. Suddenly, a crystal-clear conversation, as near as ten to twenty yards away, could be heard by all.

"Where the hell are we, Justin? How will we ever find the horses again in this fog?"

"I know where we are! We are behind the house and near the stables. This fog is good as no one can see or hear us."

"Well, what do we do now?"

"Sit tight, Steve, and wait! The children will come this way if they are going horse riding."

Close by, Sydney Mantle whispered to Malcolm Stem, "They are looking for the children. Strangers! What are they up to?"

A sudden chill came over the Estate Manager. He knew the reason why the Turner children had arrived so suddenly. It was because of Clare Petherton. Something about keeping her away from Guildford for her protection: perhaps these strangers were about to snatch her. Well, that wasn't going to happen on his watch.

Stem said, whispering to his team leaders, "Callum, Frank, Syd! Tell the others to grab a spade each and come back here. Quiet like, and hurry!"

The Estate Manager would protect these children with his life if needed. He was also keen to preserve the good reputation of Fintelton Manor.

As the others gathered around the Estate Manager, they listened in complete silence. Malcolm whispered loud enough for them to hear, "Listen, lads! I don't like strangers trespassing on our property without permission. I also don't like strangers attacking children!"

There were murmurs of agreement.

"Let's circle these blokes so they can't escape. When I give three short whistles, we close in. Hopefully, the fog will lift enough to see them. We take them by surprise and lock them up."

Each man nodded, showing that he understood the plan.

"Callum, you take seven with you and head that way – no more than twenty paces! Frank, you take eight men around to the manor side, so you come in behind them. Syd, you are with me, so spread your men out from here at about twenty paces."

They could hear the men talking as the Fintelton men formed a circle.

"I'm cold, Justin. We need to keep moving."

"Look, Steve, if we stay here, the children will come past. As we see them, we grab the girl! Hold her tight so the young'un can't wiggle free. Just stay still for a few minutes, and you will get your exercise. That will warm you up. But for the time being, stay still and listen. Now, be quiet!"

There was no more talking, and Stem prayed his men would take up their positions silently. Syd Mantle had just completed positioning his men when he heard the children talking and laughing as they approached from the Manor House.

Syd thought, 'Surely, Mr Stem could hear them coming. Why doesn't his whistle blow?'

The children felt increasingly confident as they walked hand in hand through the fog.

Clare said, "I wonder if we will see some rabbits?"

"Probably," replied Madeline. "The fog protects them from view, like at night. They would like that. But they can hear noise, so we should be quiet and not scare them."

Justin Walker assumed from the noise levels that Clare was the closest to them. Through the clearing fog, he nudged Steve, ensuring he was ready. Steve Phips rose from his crouching position and wiggled his fingers, readying himself for action.

Madeline and Clare each held one of William's hands. Clare said, "Your hands are warm again, William. I feel much safer with you here."

Madeline complained, "What about me, Clare? Don't you feel safe with me?"

"Yes, of course, but ..."

The children heard three loud whistles. At the same time, someone grabbed Clare from behind, "Got you – you little brat!"

A man had jumped out from behind Clare and grabbed her arm hard. Another man appeared, pushing her into a cloud of mist. Finding herself alone, Madeline screamed, hoping someone would see her. William could hear Clare yelling, "Let me go. Please, somebody help me." Several large slaps cracked out, and then there was silence. The young boy instantly had visions of his father's treatment of him. He ground his teeth and stood taller as he ran harder, searching for his friend.

Mr Stem shouted, "Close in fast, boys!"

Suddenly, a man shouted to William's left, "Stop, you thief!" Followed by a large thud and the sound of a man collapsing on the ground. Mr Stem was close and found Callum Fraser kneeling beside one of the strangers, unconscious on the ground.

"Where is the other?"

Callum pointed, shouting, "He went that way with the girl."

"Lock this one up, Callum. Come on, boys – time to run and get her."

After blindly running through the fog for fifty yards, there was a voice from perhaps fifteen or twenty steps ahead. Walker shouted, "Stop where you are, or I will hurt the girl, you hear!"

There was silence, but soon he said, "We are thief-takers[35] from London acting for Mrs McDermott - let us go, or the child will suffer!"

Justin Walker, totally surprised by the presence of the men, was becoming desperate. He knew how tough farm workers could be. If they caught him stealing a child, they might hang him. With this thick fog, he was sure he could escape. He and Syd Mantle had spent much time planning this exercise and would receive large fees for presenting the child to Lady McDermott. Walker must escape this trap as the money was desperately needed. There was no way he would release her, and it was too bad if she copped a beating in the process.

Stem signalled to Syd to go one way and Frank the other. Their teams moved silently through the grass so they could surround the man. The Estate Manager noticed that the fog here was lifting. He could see nearly ten yards ahead, but the stranger was still hidden.

"Let her go, man! You are trespassing, and you have stolen and beaten a child." Stem wanted the man to know they were around him. He yelled, "I have twenty men here. If you don't let her go, you will

---

[35] In 1805 the Bow Street Horse Patrol, the first form of uniformed policing seen in the capital, was established alongside the Runners, later amalgamating into the Metropolitan Police in 1837. Unofficial 'thief-takers' operated independently from the Bow Street Runners, being employed by fee-paying members of the public to catch criminals and present them before a magistrate.

hang! Walk back and show yourself and hand over the girl."

Clare regained consciousness from her beating and realised what was happening. Feeling the man's tight grip on her arm, she screamed and begged to be released. Stem then heard a wallop and the girl crying out before she was hit again. Then there was silence.

Walker, grabbing her hair and covering her mouth, quietly muttered, "Keep quiet, you little brat, or I will really hurt you!"

Syd, now standing beside Michael Stem, nudged him and whispered, "I am going to kill that bastard. That poor little girl!"

Michael also hated this kind of man, but he knew keeping calm and in control was the only way to save Clare's life. He grabbed Syd's arm, held him close and whispered in his ear, "For God's sake, keep calm. We need to convince him to let her go."

The stranger yelled, "Stay away, or I will break her arm." Then Stem heard another scream of pain from Clare.

"Stranger, you are surrounded by my men. There is no escape. Show yourself now, or you will hang!" Stem was hopeful that this would bring the man to his senses, but he was also worried about the number of times Clare had been beaten.

William grabbed a spade from the ground and followed the sounds of voices ahead of him. When he heard Stem's men had surrounded the stranger, he moved forward and soon saw the Estate Manager crouching with Syd. Being well coordinated, they never heard him rushing sideways into the fog, trying to move behind the stranger but not too close. When William thought he was in position, he stopped and stood dead still. He hoped his navigation was better than when playing blind man's bluff.

Walker considered negotiating with a threat that might frighten them away, "You men, this is your last chance! If you do not go back one hundred yards now, I will kill the girl."

Hearing the man was close, William was sure the stranger was only a few yards ahead.

There was another scream of agony, and Stem could hear Clare wailing her eyes out. William could not bear the sound of Clare being tortured. Grinding his teeth, he would wait no longer. Having plenty of practice at pirate picnics beside the river Wey, the lad started whirling the shovel around his head. Lurching towards the voice, he gathered momentum. The boy burst through the fog, appearing behind the man, who turned in surprise. But it was too late, as Will let him have the full force of the shovel blade slightly angled against his head. The blade cracked the man's head hard, with blood spurting everywhere as he first fell on his knees and then rolled down across Clare's legs.

Will ran forward and yelled, "Clare, are you alright?"

There was no answer as the girl lay there in shock with the man's blood pouring onto her. Mr Stem suddenly appeared and stopped at the sight of William kneeling beside Clare, trying to pull the stranger off her. The man was still alive but weak, and Stem had his men remove him to one of the rooms behind the estate office.

"Patch up his wounds and tie him to the bed! Syd, you better ride for the doctor and get him as soon as possible. I want this stranger alive to face the full force of the law."

"Why, Mr Stem? Let the bastard die! You heard what he did to that little girl. He is an animal. Let him die and save everyone a lot of trouble. They will never prosecute a small boy for saving the girl's life."

"No, Syd. I understand what you are saying, but we must see justice done. Get the doctor and let the magistrate make the moral decisions. We have all had enough for this morning."

Pike came out of the fog, carrying a crying Madeline. He stood beside the estate manager as Stem lifted a shaking Clare into his arms and cradled her head against his shoulder.

"Shoosh now, Clare. It is all over. You are safe forever. We are taking you back to the Manor."

The child was whimpering, and tears still streamed down her face. William stood beside the old butler and held onto his trousers' pocket while rubbing his eye with his other hand.

Pike looked down at the boy, who was still shaking and noted the expression of rage on William's face. The butler gently said, "You did well today, William! You did damn well!" Stem broke into a smile as he heard the butler's comment.

As the group slowly headed across the grass towards the manor house, the sun broke through the mist, and the manor ahead glistened in the morning sunlight.

Anne and Victoria sat in the gallery waiting for Mr Turner to appear in the dock. She could not believe that her father was arrested and held overnight at the police station before appearing before a Magistrate this morning. It was a miscarriage of justice as it should have been the butler and governess standing in the dock.

Victoria noticed Anne's worry and said, "I am sure this will be dealt with quickly, and your father will be free to return to Harting after the hearing. The Magistrate must realise that your father has been protecting Clare."

Anne smiled but said nothing as she watched her father being led into the dock. He looked around and saw her sitting there and smiled at them. Then, he took a seat and waited for the Magistrate to arrive. Anne had hoped this might have been a reasonably private matter, but the gallery was full, so there must have been much interest. Suddenly, a gentleman squeezed into the seat beside her and said, "Good morning, Lady Leystead. You may remember me from the wedding. I am your sister's father-in-law, David Bassington. How are you this morning."

"Mr Bassington! Sorry, I did not recognise you. I am well, except that my father is facing a magistrate for a crime he did not commit."

"I thought that was the case, so it will be interesting to see what transpires. I am unsure if you are aware, but due to the seriousness of the charge, it will not be the three magistrates but the district judge who hears the pleadings. This should be in your father's favour. Judge Kirby is no fool. I am sure your father will be released."

The Clerk announced, "All stand for Judge Kirby."

Everyone stood as the judge entered and took his place on the bench.

The Clerk read in a loud voice, "Your honour, a preliminary hearing between The Crown vs Turner where the accused, Mr Jonathan Henry Turner, stands accused of the kidnapping of one Clare Louise Petherton on the twenty-eight of April, eighteen hundred and twenty-seven."

The judge shuffled a bunch of papers into order and addressed the defendant, "Mr Turner! The charge against you is most serious, and I have before me two sworn statements from one, Mr John Steadman, and from one, Miss Irene Preston, which support the veracity of the charge. I also understand that you refuse to reveal the location where

Miss Petherton is held.

Mr Turner, you are a reputable businessman from Guildford and have never had an offence, so a criminal act such as this is unusual. Soon, I will ask how you plead, either guilty or not guilty. However, before I ask that question, I must explain that before I commit you to trial either in this court or the Old Bailey, I have agreed to hear submissions from the Crown's barrister and your barrister. In such a case as kidnapping, this procedure is not unusual due to the seriousness of the offence. The Clerk has confirmed to me that you have had access to your barrister and discussed the case with him, and he will make various submissions, as I am sure the Crown will, about the crime involved.

As this case is considered a serious criminal act, after the submissions are made, I may need to consider them for an hour or two and speak with the barristers involved in my chambers. Once that is done, I will make my decision as to whether a case against you is justified or if it should be dismissed. If I find a legitimate case against you, I will decide if it should be heard here or at the Old Bailey.

Do you understand the process, Mr Turner?

"Yes, Your Honour."

"Thank you, Mr Turner." The judge looked down at his papers and made some notes.

Raising his eyes again, he said, "Jonathan Henry Turner, you have been accused of kidnapping one, Clare Louise Petherton, of Cloverdale Chase, Guildford. How do you plead to this charge? Guilty or not guilty?"

Jonathan answered, "Not Guilty, your honour!"

"Thank you, Mr Turner."

"Mr Crombie. Please."

The barrister for the Crown stood and commenced his case against Mr Turner, "Your Honour, in front of you, there are two sworn statements that set out the facts of this case. It is a clear account by individual parties of the events on 28 April 1827. On being advised of Mr Petherton's sudden death, the butler, Mr John Steadman and the governess, Miss Irene Preston, decided to take the young Lady to her trustees in London. As the sole beneficiary of Mr Petherton's estate, Miss Petherton stood to inherit a fortune, and Steadman and Preston were concerned about the young lady's safety.

Mr Turner and his party arrived at Mesnil Priory early on Saturday morning and forced their way in. They discovered where Miss Petherton was housed and took her from the convent. Mr Turner threatened force against the nuns if they did not cooperate.

The child was injured due to a horse-riding accident and was also suffering from witnessing the death of her father some days earlier. Displaying a callous disregard for the child, they took her away and returned her to Guildford, where they forced her to reside with the Turner family. Mr Turner must have realised that Miss Petherton was not friendless and decided to hide the child somewhere so she could not be found. The trustees acting for Miss Petherton sent one Lady McDermott, trustee of Miss Petherton, to Guildford to recover the child. On attending the Turner household, we understand that the lady was advised that Miss Petherton was on a riding trip with the Turner children, and the housekeeper was unaware of where the child was. However, after questioning the housekeeper, Lady McDermott was advised that Mr Turner knew the location.

Your Honour, it appears this is a callous act of hiding the child with intent to profit from Miss Petherton's inheritance, which we understand is considerable."

Judge Kirby sat forward and asked, "Mr Crombie. I am aware of your client's allegations and the sound reputation of Green & Green Attorneys, who have briefed you on this matter. However, I must ask if you have any other facts to present. My question relates to the allegations being short and lacking in detail."

"The case details with interviews and witnesses have been provided to you, your Honour."

"Mr Crombie. Are Mr Steadman and Miss Preston present?"

"No, your Honour. They fear for their lives and have gone into hiding."

"And why do they fear for their lives?"

"Because of Mr Turner's threats against the nuns at Mesnil Priory, your Honour."

"I see. So, the threats were not against them but against the nuns at the priory?"

"Yes, Your Honour."

"Mr Crombie. Were there any threats from Mr Turner directly against Mr Steadman and Miss Preston, verbally or in writing or by any other means at any other time."

Mr Crombie hesitated as he thought about the reply he should make.

"Well, Mr Crombie?"

"Not that the plaintiffs have advised me of, your Honour. However, given the recent events, I am sure further evidence will be provided before the trial."

"Thank you, Mr Crombie. I will note you have more evidence to add to your submission?"

"Yes, Your Honour."

"Mr Crombie, please answer this question with either a yes or no."

Crombie answered, "I will, your Honour."

"Have you explained to your clients that if their statements are false, they will be charged with perjury?"

"Yes, your Honour. I understand that they firmly believe in the truth of their statements."

"Mr Crombie. If this case goes to trial, I will require Mr Steadman and Miss Preston to present themselves in court and take an oath that their statements are true and correct. Are your clients prepared to do this?"

"Most definitely, Your Honour."

The judge appeared unsatisfied as he gazed at Mr Crombie and then made more notes.

"Mr Hoskins. Please provide your defence."

Hoskins stood and looked around the courtroom. He smiled, recognising an elderly lady sitting in the gallery. He then turned towards the court and gathered himself before commencing.

"Your Honour, we have provided you with three written, factual statements relating to what occurred at Mesnil Priory on Friday, 27 April 1827. I understand that Mr Crombie's witness statements date the happenings on Saturday, but that is incorrect. The events at the Priory happened on the Friday. The statements I have provided come from Attorney Mr Blake Wood of Guildford, Parish Constable Michael Rawlins of Guildford, and the Parish Constable of Reigate, Constable Archibald Swan. Your Honour, I would point out that all three statements describe a far different account of what happened on Friday at Mesnil Priory to what the prosecution suggests.

The events that led to the disappearance of Miss Clare Petherton commenced on the day of her father's untimely death at around three in the afternoon on Tuesday, 24 April 1827. Mr Benjamin Petherton, while visiting the Turner home, had a heart attack and died at the front entrance. Mr Turner and Mr Petherton were good friends. It is not unusual for Mr Petherton to visit as his engagement to Mrs Ethel Nibley, the Turner's housekeeper, was announced in the Guilford Gazette that morning.

That night, at seven in the evening, on Tuesday, 24 April 1827, Mrs Nibley returned with Miss Petherton to the Petherton home, Cloverdale Chase, Guildford. Mrs Nibley slept in the room next to Miss Petherton's bedroom for the night. She attended at Miss Petherton's request. Understandably, the child did not wish to be alone that night.

Mrs Nibley, at around eight in the evening, explained the situation to the butler and the governess, who were at Cloverdale Chase and unaware of Mr Petherton's death earlier in the afternoon. It is noted that the governess, in particular, objected to Mrs Nibley's presence at the house; however, she abided by Mrs Nibley's instruction after hearing of Mrs Nibley's appointment as a trustee for Miss Petherton.

In the morning, Mrs Nibley discovered Miss Clare Petherton's bed empty. She was advised by the housekeeper that Mr Petherton was asleep upstairs and was not to be disturbed and that Miss Preston had needed to visit a sick aunt in London urgently. The butler, Mr Steadman, claimed he had discussed this with Mr Petherton before he retired that night and had permission to accompany Miss Preston, given her poor state of mind. We can provide sworn statements to verify these events.

It has been confirmed that the house staff were not aware of Mr Petherton's death until Mrs Nibley advised them on Wednesday morning. Mrs Nibley's presence at the house surprised them, as they were unaware she had spent the night at Cloverdale Chase.

Mr Petherton died at around three o'clock on Tuesday afternoon, so it was clear that he never returned to the house, Cloverton Chase, or gave any instructions to Steadman, the butler.

It was unclear if Steadman and Preston knew that Mrs Nibley was a trustee. However, the butler had close dealings with his employer and was likely aware. Mrs Nibley's arrival on Tuesday at around seven in the evening with Miss Petherton was when the butler and governess first learned of Mr Petherton's death. Mrs Nibley explained to the butler and governess she would stay the night and care for Miss Petherton. She asked the butler to advise the staff. On Wednesday morning, Mrs Nibley asked the staff where Miss Petherton was and asked for the butler. The staff were unaware of Mr Petherton's death or that Mrs Nibley had stayed the night. At that time, Mrs Nibley discovered that the butler and governess, without any approval of the trustees, had fled, taking Miss Petherton with them.

Your Honour, it was late on Tuesday night, the twenty-fourth of April 1827, that the kidnapping took place. Without any authority, Mr Steadman, the butler, and Miss Preston, the governess, removed Miss Clare Petherton from her house in secrecy.

It was not until the Thursday afternoon that Mrs Nibley, after discussing with the priest at the Star of the Sea Catholic Church, Guildford, discovered where Miss Petherton had been taken. We will provide a statement from the Catholic Priest at Guildford that he advised Steadman and Preston of a convent near Reigate where the child would be safe. On enquiring, Mrs Nibley found that the priory had long been sold, and the Parish Constable, Mr Archibald Swann, led them to Mesnil Priory, the only operating priory near Redhill.

Mr Jonathan Turner, Mrs Ethel Nibley and Parish Constable Rawlins set off on Thursday afternoon, the twenty-sixth of April 1827, to reach Reigate and recover Miss Petherton. Due to bad weather, the late hour, and confusion about the property's exact location, they decided to book accommodation for the night in Reigate. On Friday morning, the twenty-seventh of April 1827, they were joined by the local Parish Constable Archibald Swan, who checked Mrs Nibley's trustee documentation and travelled with them, directing them to Mesnil Priory at Redhill. After discussions with the head sister of the priory, Mother Celine, Mrs Ethel Nibley was escorted to identify the young girl, who had been left there by Steadman and Preston under the false name of Miss Angela Smith.

These events took place, and we will provide witness statements verifying each step in the process."

Judge Kirby asked, "Mr Hoskins, would you advise me if Mr Turner made any threats against the nuns?"

"None whatsoever, Your Honour. I will say that the Parish Constable,

Mr Archibald Swan, reminded Mother Celine of the penalty for assisting kidnappers. There was no reluctance on Mother Celine's part to assist Mr Turner and Mrs Nibley at that time."

"Thank you, Mr Hoskins. Does that conclude your defence?"

"Your Honour. I wonder if you would clarify a point in the prosecution's initial comments. As you advised Mr Crombie, we rely on their statements being truthful. If I am not mistaken, Mr Crombie indicated that Mrs McDermott, one of Miss Petherton's trustees, is presently in Guildford trying to protect the alleged kidnapped child. Would that be correct?"

Judge Kirby frowned and thought about the request. He said, "Mr Hoskins, this is highly irregular as you are entitled to state your defence only, but I will allow the question in this case to clarify the prosecution's statement of fact. Mr Crombie, is Lady McDermott presently in Guildford?"

Crombie stood, appearing worried, and said, "My clients advise me that she is Your Honour."

The Magistrate raised his eyes towards Mr Hoskins and asked, "Is that clear enough, Mr Hoskins."

The barrister smiled and politely answered, "Yes, thank you, your Honour. It appears we have a significant issue at law before this case proceeds very far at all."

"And what might that be, Mr Hoskins?"

Leo Hoskins, a barrister with a reputation for much theatrical presentation, turned and pointed to an elderly lady in the gallery.

"Your Honour, might I introduce you to Lady Isabella McDermott, wife of Sir John McDermott and a trustee of Miss Clare Petherton. Would you please stand, Lady McDermott?"

There were murmurs throughout the courtroom as Lady Isabella stood and smiled at the judge.

Judge Kirby asked for quiet and said, "Mr Hoskins, I take it you have a signed statement from this lady and documented papers of identity." He looked up and acknowledged Mrs McDermott. "That she has confirmed her identity as Mrs McDermott and a trustee for Miss Clare Petherton?"

"I do, your Honour, and I will file these with the Clerk." Hoskins held up some papers and indicated to the Clerk, who rushed over and accepted the document. Rushing back to the bench, the clerk handed the documents to the judge. Kirby read through the papers and then raised his eyes towards the defence barrister.

Mr Hoskins addressed the judge, asking, "Your Honour, I suggest that the plaintiffs are committing perjury and false representations to this court."

The court went from silence to uproar, and Anne joined the melee with a loud cheer.

The judge raised his hand and asked for quiet, "Mr Crombie, I would ask that your clients attend this court next week to be examined for perjury charges. If you so desire, you may amend your case papers with the court and resubmit them for next week. I will leave that to you."

There was another small cheer from the gallery.

"Mr Turner, I am still concerned about the whereabouts of Miss Clare Petherton. Would you please advise me of her whereabouts?"

Jonathan stood still, feeling the tension of being in the criminal court dock.

He swallowed and said, "Your Honour, she is in the care of Magistrate Sir David South, Earl of Fintelton. She will be returned to my house in Guildford tomorrow to ready herself for her father's funeral. She is safe and well cared for, your Honour."

While Jonathan spoke, the judge nodded in agreement. He made some notes, then looked up and said, "Mr Turner, further legal issues may arise from this case, which may require your attendance. However, I am satisfied that you are an honest man and that the charges against you have been contrived. This case is dismissed." With a smile, he said, "Mr Turner. You are free to go!"

Judge Kirby smiled at Jonathan and closed his papers before leaving.

The Clerk called out, "All rise!"

With that, the judge left the courtroom. An emotional Jonathan turned, looked up at Anne, and mouthed, "I love you!' Anne blew him a kiss. Then, he was led outside from the dock.

David Bassington, standing beside Anne, said, "Congratulations Lady Anne. Leo Hiscock is a great barrister. I couldn't be happier for your family. The report going to the times will meet your approval, indeed!"

"Thank you, Mr Bassington. I must go now and give my father a big hug. It must have been a terrifying ordeal for him."

Army Headquarters, Port Elizabeth, South Africa ...

Standing with Sergeant Attwood, Richard Turner discussed the rush of preparations at the garrison. Pack horses were being loaded, and troopers checked their equipment everywhere. Richard estimated that nearly two hundred troopers were readying their kits for departure. He was brushing aside the dust being stirred up by the horses and wagons as they passed when he saw Freddie Sanderson coming towards him.

"Freddie, do you have a minute for a talk?"

"I must make it quick, Richard. There is bad news, and we must head out on patrol. Your departure must be delayed. Settlers are being brought in from outlying stations, and no travel will be allowed past Colchester. We have set up a checkpoint there."

"What has caused this, Freddie?"

"News came in yesterday that Piet Beckhoff had been found dead and mutilated. Also, the three men travelling with him were in the same condition. It seems we have some very nasty natives moving around the country. The army is on full alert, and large patrols are now preparing here, and others from Fort Brown have been requested. We will hunt them down and put an end to the trouble."

"I see!"

Richard recalled what Sarah had said, describing the eastern cape as an explorer country.

"Will this cause a war with the natives?"

"We hope not, but a lot of them will be dead before this is over. It is not only the army that is hunting them. The settlers are in uproar that this could happen so close to Port Elizabeth. They are disturbed that the army has not stopped them from coming over the Fish. But it is a bit critical to blame the army. We only have so many men."

"Right, I will alert the bullock dray people. It's better to be safe than head out. Take care, Freddie, if they send you on patrol!"

"I will. Richard!" Freddie came a little closer and, in a concerned, lowered voice, said, "Richard, while you are in town, purchase several more muskets, at least one of those cartridge-loading ones. Teach Sarah how to load them. I'm unsure what will transpire, but you may need to fend them off."

Richard could see the worry on Freddie's face.

"Yes, I should do that."

"When you arrive in Grahamstown, don't return to your property. Stay at the hotel in town until everything is clear. Would you please ask Sarah to stay with Jane? She is far from her mother, and being with child, she could use some reassurance. Tell her I am out on patrol and safe. I don't want her worrying about what's going on."

"I will as soon as we return, but if they have closed the border at Colchester, you might see her first."

Freddie shook his hand and said, "Thanks, Richard. Your friendship is most appreciated."

Richard replied, "Well, young man. You take care of yourself out there!"

Lieutenant Sanderson walked off and joined his troopers, who were preparing their equipment, ready to head out. As Richard watched, a column of thirty troopers trotted past toward Colchester. He could see they were fully packed for a patrol with several loaded packhorses at the rear.

By the time Richard reached the hotel, he had thought long and hard about the situation. He entered the hotel, nodded to the desk clerk, climbed the stairs, and entered their room.

Sarah looked up as he entered.

"I just spoke with Freddie Sanderson. They found Piet Beckhoff and his men. They are all dead. There are great goings on at the army garrison. A large patrol rode out as I was there. The search for these marauding natives has begun in earnest. The road to Grahamstown has been closed at Colchester, so I may be stuck here for a few more days unless they can provide an escort."

Sarah turned and gazed out the window at the light breeze creating ripples on the ocean swell. There were several ships in port with much traffic at the docks. "You can come with me tomorrow on the boat. Leave all this behind, Richard! Why not come home?"

"No, Sarah. There is too much at stake. We have invested heavily in this property here, and it will commence making money next year. I will work with the army and maintain the peace at Grahamstown. Perhaps by the end of next year, I can take time off and visit you at Ewell."

Sarah turned and commenced repacking her bags.

"At least you can carry my bags to the docks. I must be on board by eight in the morning."

"There is a complication, Sarah. Freddie asked if you could stay with Jane once we return to Grahamstown. He said she is far from her mother and being with child needs reassurance. How long until the baby is due?"

"I think she is at seven months, so it is close."

Richard continued, "Freddie is usually calm and confident. There must be more to this than they are telling us."

Sarah stopped packing and sat on the bed.

She said, "Blast, this complicates everything!"

The Turner Carriage, Crossing the Thames via the Battersea Bridge ...
Soon after lunch, Anne and her father boarded a coach and started the journey to Guildford. They would stop at Ewell tonight.

"Sorry to drag you away so soon, Father, but we must be in Guildford for dinner tomorrow night. Mr Polkinghorne will be joining us. He is a trustee for Clare Petherton, and I thought it would help Ethel."

The carriage suddenly started to lurch to the left violently and then corrected back to the right. The ride became bumpy and uncomfortable.

"I hate this Battersea bridge. It is narrow and old. Why did we come this way?"

"I asked to go this way, Father. It is far shorter, and we will hopefully reach Ewell by seven tonight."

Jonathan seemed stressed and tried to calm himself. "Sorry, Anne. With the trial finishing this morning and no sleep last night, I am probably a bit irritable. Hopefully, Clare and the children will have returned from Fintelton. It would be good for Mr Polkinghorne to see Clare again in a secure home situation. I would not send her back to Cloverdale Chase now she has no family there."

"I agree. The child would be at risk unless a trustee were with her. Did you meet Lady McDermott after the trial? She seems like a lovely person - so different to whoever that imposter in Guildford is. I hope the children enjoyed their stay at Fintelton."

"Anne, did you think about my plans for William?"

"Yes, I also went through the shortlisted applications for the General Manager's Position."

"Given we are alone, can we discuss William first?"

Anne was not keen on this but realised her father must have an answer. She would have difficulty responding as she dearly loved her little brother and felt he would feel abandoned if sent away. However, she must also maintain good relationships with her father and the family, as the businesses were all at critical development points, and the last thing they needed was a quarrel.

"Father, you must decide what is best for William. I am not one of his parents. Given what you have told me, you must discuss this with Ethel. I take it she is unaware of this decision?"

"Yes – I have not discussed it with her as she is not his stepmother yet! I did not wish to worry her."

"Well, I suggest you do that soon; otherwise, she will think you have been secretive and not taken her into your trust – not a good way to treat your intended wife."

Jonathan was uncomfortable with that but thankful for a female word of advice, "I should do that soon. I agree with you."

"In terms of sending him away, I can see advantages and disadvantages. I fear he will feel abandoned, which may destroy your relationship with him forever. While he is here, you will have the opportunity to build a relationship with him. Surely, you could delay this for some years. He is only seven and a half."

Jonathan replied, "I know there are disadvantages, but my problem with rage is not gone. It is controlled, but I always fear that it might happen again. For some reason, William and I do not get on. I feel a separation may be good for both of us. With Sarah and Richard in South Africa, it is the perfect opportunity."

"Father, I have said my piece. If it were my son, I would not even consider it, but I am not you, and you have far more experience with children than I do. I leave it to you and Ethel to decide. When will you announce your engagement to Ethel?"

Jonathan nodded and realised Anne was keen not to take sides in this decision. About his intended engagement, he said, "Not for some time yet – probably just before our holiday at the Isle of Wight."

He quickly changed the subject, "Now, the General Manager position. I thought Mr Harvey Potter seemed the best candidate. He has good experience, and, like Terry, he wants to move to a regional centre. He is the right age at forty-one and a practising Anglican."

Anne agreed, saying, "Yes, the changes he made in his last position were impressive, and he seems to understand what is needed for business development. But I would suggest we interview two others as well. Mr Bray and Mr Fellows appear impressive. It would be best to compare each of them to the others in person. I think personality in a small country business will be important. I would not wish for us to employ anyone who is too aggressive or brash. You never know until you meet them."

"Agreed, I will organise the interviews once we are in Guildford. Now given I did not sleep last night, and we are off that damn bridge, you will excuse me if I try for some sleep. I hope I can doze off for a while."

"I understand, Father."

Anne was keen for some contemplation and sat back and immediately wondered where her husband was.

Fintelton Manor, Outside Petersfield, Sussex ...
At breakfast on Wednesday morning, the children's spirits were lifted when Clare joined them.

Madeline, noticing Clare's sling for her left arm, asked, "How is the arm, Clare?"

"Still very sore – every movement is painful, but fortunately, no bones are broken. The doctor told me to rest it for a few days, and it may recover quickly."

Mrs Jennings asked, "Will you be alright travelling back to Guildford today?"

"Yes, I discussed that with Mrs Nibley, and we agreed that I would survive." She smiled and then took a seat between William and Madeline.

Mrs Nibley entered and said, "I am glad we are all together at breakfast this morning. After breakfast, we must finish packing and place our bags outside the rooms. I will help you, Clare, so you don't need to worry about your arm.

We were going to use different routes for security on the way back, but I have decided, given what transpired yesterday, that it may be better for the coaches to travel in a convoy. So, if anyone wishes to transfer, we will have spare seats on the second coach."

Clementine and Madeline raised their hands.

Ethel said, "That is settled then. We want to be away by nine-thirty, please, so we are home in Guildford for dinner. As they expected us yesterday, I sent a message advising we were delayed. They expect us around five in the afternoon, so please, everyone, have breakfast, and as soon as you are finished, go upstairs and pack."

Ethel took her seat and commenced her breakfast.

As they were eating, Clare sat up straight and turned to Madeline.

She asked, "Would you please stand next to me, Madeline, at the funeral tomorrow?"

Madeline was honoured by the request. "Certainly!"

Then Clare, turning to William, asked, "Would you stand next to me also, William?"

William asked, "Why?"

"I know I will not cry, as I have cried enough since yesterday, but I fear what will happen tomorrow. I must say goodbye to my father, and the trustees may decide that I must attend in London. I don't want that, but there may be nothing I can do about it."

Looking straight at Clare, William said, "Why would they want you to go to London? Guildford is a much better place."

"Will you stand beside me at the funeral, William?"

"Yes, but what if I cry?"

"Then, I will hold your hand and comfort you."

Simeon said, "He is a bit of a baby. But I don't think he will cry."

William, who had taken a mouthful of sausage and bacon, was miffed and about to dispute Simeon's comment when he cried out, "Ooh! Ow." Then he whimpered and said, "I bit my tongue, Ow-ee!"

Ethel said, "Oh dear! You poor old thing, Will."

Simeon commented, "It might keep him quiet for a while!"

As William glared at Sim, Madeline and Clare looked at each other and giggled.

Ethel was glad to see Clare smile, even if it was at William's expense, and said to herself, 'Dear me, Brothers and Sisters!'

Chapter 16

Star of the Seas, Catholic Church, Guildford, England ...

The mourners stood silently, showing respect, as two workmen commenced filling the grave. William and Madeline each held one of Clare Petherton's hands as she watched.

William whispered, "You were very brave, Clare."

Standing rigidly, Clare silently sobbed as she watched. William noticed her grip tighten as she murmured, "Goodbye, Father."

The young eleven-year-old had struggled to believe her father was dead, but the gravesite had returned her to the cold reality of her situation. The time with the Turner children riding at Fintelton had taken her mind away from her father's death. She had never felt such freedom and adventure, but now she saw the coffin of the person closest to her in the world being buried deep below the surface where she would never see him again. What would her future hold? Who would care for her? Who would love her now? It seemed people were struggling to be her guardians, but they may only be interested in the inheritance she would receive. She was confused and suddenly felt sad and tired.

Mrs Ethel Nibley placed her hands on Clare's shoulders, "It is time to go now, Clare – the wake is in the church hall. You can return here later if you wish."

Stephen Polkinghorne stood by Ethel and knelt on one knee, "Clare, your father would be most concerned about this situation. That is why he appointed Mrs McDermott, myself and Mrs Nibley as your guardians. You are safe now, and we will meet soon to discuss where you wish to remain. I have not asked you yet, but I wondered if you had considered this?"

Clare recognised Stephen Polkinghorne from two years ago when he and Mrs McDermott had visited Cloverdale Chase. She moved forward and hugged him.

"Mr Polkinghorne – I remember you from when my father took me to London last year. I want to stay in Guildford near my father. I understand Cloverdale Chase is not possible as I must live with a guardian. It would be good to remain with the Turners as I feel like one of the family. Mrs Nibley has been kind and rescued me from Steadman and Mrs Preston."

Stephen smiled and said, "Well, I am sure staying with the Turners could be arranged. I will have some words with Mr Turner."

"Thank you."

As Stephen approached Jonathan, Mrs McDermott appeared from nowhere and grabbed the child's hand, demanding, "So Clare, you have finally appeared, young lady. I am Mrs McDermott your guardian. You will come with me, as we must travel to London and see your attorneys, Green & Green."

Clare pulled away from the lady, trying to break free, but Mrs Mc-Dermot's grip held as she nudged the girl away.

Clare cried out, "Let me go. I don't know you. You are not Mrs McDermott – she is in London."

Constable Michael Rawlins stood nearby and heard the commotion. He confronted the woman and asked, "Let the child go, Madam! You are causing her distress."

Stephen Polkinghorne quickly returned, asking, "Madam, I am Stephen Polkinghorne, one of Clare's guardians. Would you mind telling me who you are?"

"I am Lady Angela McDermott, Clare's true guardian! So, if you would not mind, Sir, please let me pass with the child."

Stephen stood his ground with Constable Rawlins and the watchman, confronting the woman.

"Well, Lady McDermott, there must be two of you as I visited Lady Angela McDermott in London a few days ago before travelling here. I know her from previous meetings at Mayfair with Mr Petherton. She advised me she could not attend but would meet with me again on my return. Now, Madam, who exactly are you?"

Mrs McDermott exploded in anger, "You are an imposter, Sir! How dare you question my legitimacy? Why, Mr Petherton would be appalled. How Dare you!"

Constable Rawlins stepped forward with his watchman, and they each took one of Lady McDermott's arms, "Come! We have a couple of your friends locked up at the police station who would love to talk with you."

As they walked away, Clare could hear her shouting, "How dare you manhandle me from a funeral. You have no right. What kind of people are you down here? You have not heard the last of this."

As the lady's rants disappeared into the distance, Jonathan Turner said, "Well, Clare, I have spoken with Mr Polkinghorne, and it appears you will be staying and joining us on our holiday to the Isle of Wight. I am sure your father would approve of that. I think Mr Polkinghorne will also join us for a few days."

There were squeals of delight as the children rushed off towards the hall, looking for some food.

Stephen Polkinghorne smiled as he watched them run away, noting how close the children seemed. He commented to Jonathan, "Thank you, Mr Turner, for rescuing her and providing the security she needs at this time."

"It is our pleasure, Stephen. Mind you, my adventure overnight in prison was an eye-opener!" Jonathan smiled, "She is a mature and lovely young girl. She will fit in well."

Stephen felt a slight tap on his shoulder and turned to find the Viscountess and two other well-dressed women beside her. "Lady Leystead, you took me by surprise. Thank you for dinner last night and for introducing me to Mrs Nibley. I am sure that Clare is in good hands now." Stephen noticed that one of the ladies seemed familiar and said, "Perhaps you would introduce me to your friends."

"Good afternoon, Mr Polkinghorne. Let me introduce you to Lady Jane South, the Countess of Fintelton and Lady Fiona Green."

The ladies nodded their recognition of Stephen, and he said, "Lady Fintelton, I am honoured to meet you and must apologise again for the previous embarrassment caused by Lady Clarissa. I tried to contain her, but I understand she imposed herself on you. My apologies."

"Mr Polkinghorne, it is I who should be thanking you. You did your best to protect my home from her. Our butler in London has the highest opinion of you, and we are grateful for your assistance. Sir, I am unsure if you recall, but let me introduce Lady Fiona Green. She was keen to meet you again."

Stephen looked hard at Fiona and said, "Of course, Lady Fiona, I thought you looked familiar. Please excuse me for not recognising you."

Fiona nodded her recognition and said, "I understand from Lady Fintelton the care you provided for my cousin, Clarissa, in London. I apologise for her behaviour when returning from Jamacia. It appears she was suffering from a disease that affected her mind. I understand from Lady Fintelton that you have organised for Mr Stem to show you the grave. I wondered if I might join you tomorrow, Mr Polkinghorne."

"It would be my pleasure, Lady Fiona. I meet with Mr Stem at the cemetery at one in the afternoon. I travel to Petersfield in the morning and stay at the Red Dear."

Lady Fiona smiled and said, "Then we shall visit together, Mr Polkinghorne and pay our respects."

"It would be a pleasure, Lady Fiona."

The countess asked, "Mr Polkinghorne, given Lady Fiona is keen to hear from you, perhaps you would join us at Fintelton for some days – that would allow a reasonable time for discussion."

The warm gesture overcame Stephen, "I would be honoured, Lady Fintelton. That is most kind. I am booked in Petersfield for tomorrow night, but I can cancel that. Perhaps I could arrive tomorrow evening?"

Later, at the funeral reception, Lady Anne asked the countess if they could speak privately.

"Certainly, Anne. We expect you on Saturday for a few days before the memorial service. The Reverend Andrew Taggart and his wife Laura have accepted my offer to stay, so you will know some of the guests."

"I will be there, and possibly my father will be. With my busy life, there has been little time to catch up with Emma, so I look forward to the visit. But before we discuss that matter, I must tell you something more pressing. This may be difficult, but please keep my news confidential for a few weeks."

Lady Jane suddenly looked most concerned, "Are you well, Dear?"

"Yes, I am well, but it is good news. I am with child Lady Jane. You are soon to have a grandchild."

Lady Jane stood there in amazement with her mouth open. Then she said, "Oh Anne, how wonderful. How wonderful! You must come to Fintelton as soon as possible – there is so much to discuss. How will I contain myself? Oh, Anne, you have been such a blessing to this family. May I tell the Earl? He will be so happy."

"You may, in two weeks, but please keep it confidential until then. I am ten weeks pregnant, so after another two weeks, it will be safe to announce it."

The countess was overjoyed, "This is the best news I have received since Hugh went away. My Darling Anne, now, I have something to look forward to." She embraced Anne and would not let her go.

Anne whispered in her ear, "I have written to Robert some weeks ago. He will soon receive the good news. I pray for his safe return."

Lady Jane stood back and said, "Amen to that. Now, I must collect Lady Fiona; we are off to Fintelton. Mr Polkinghorne will stay for a few days as well. If we are lucky, we may make it by seven o'clock."

"Lady Jane, it is too late to leave now. We have plenty of rooms at Porting. You and Lady Fiona are welcome to stay the night. I think it would be far safer to delay your trip until tomorrow. I will ask Emma to join us for dinner, and we can all have an enjoyable girl's talk."

"But I worry about Sir David. He is getting on!"

Anne laughed and said, "Lady Jane, you know, and I know that he could not be in safer hands than with Pike looking after him. I shall expect your arrival soon. I must be off now as some papers are ready for collection at the office."

Port Elizabeth, Eastern Cape, South Africa ...
Richard and Sarah were waiting for their meals at the hotel restaurant. They noticed far more customers tonight as folks from outlying settlements arrived and took accommodation.

"Our booking is only till Thursday morning, Richard. Perhaps you should extend it. Who knows how long this may last."

"Does that mean you will stay, Sarah?" She could see the pleading in his eyes and a slight smile.

Richard's wife knew this would be a turning point in their relationship. She had been churning the question repeatedly in her mind and finally came to a decision.

"Why don't they serve the meals? We have been waiting fifteen minutes now!"

"Sarah, don't avoid the question. I need to know if you have changed your mind. One way or the other, I must plan how we navigate this crisis."

Sarah looked hard at Richard, wondering if the problem was their marriage or the natives who were causing trouble.

"Since you mentioned that Jane needed company, I have reconsidered whether I should leave. She is in Grahamstown, and I am here, Richard. You understood how much I wanted to see the ocean again and the ships. They are my lifeline to our daughter and our sons. I cannot lie to you any longer. Since you mentioned this trip, I have always intended to go home.

I understand how hard it must be for Jane Sanderson, but I am not in Grahamstown and would not be there until after the crisis ended. Freddie would be home then, and she would have his support. I'm also sure the army wives support each other in their close-knit community. They do not need me, Richard, but our daughter, Katherine, does, and I need her!

She is our only daughter, Richard. I will be far more useful to my daughter in England."

Richard frowned as he was aware of what was coming.

His wife continued, "Our lives here consist of you running the cattle and sheep and managing the building of our house. That will take months; in the interim, I must live in tents and half-finished rooms daily in the cold. The lifestyle here suits a man but not a lady. I will not ask you to come home as I understand how much this adventure means to you. But I will not stay, Richard. I need the civilisation of my home and my friends there. I will be waiting for you when you return. You take as much time as you wish, and we can talk again in England. I pray you will be safe here while you remain."

As Sarah finished talking as the meals were served.

"Thank you!"

Richard sat there for a moment and then said, "I understand. It is my fault. It has been rough and hard. It will continue this way, perhaps for the next year. However, let us eat before the food cools."

He picked up his knife and fork and attacked his meal. It had been a long day, and the fact that Sarah had announced she was not coming home rocked him completely. He needed sustenance and time to think. Her decision would have implications. He was tired and needed rest before thinking about the future.

Sarah hesitated and said, "You understand I still love you, Richard. It is not you but this country. I am no expert on politics, but surely, the natives will never give up on wanting their country back. What will happen then? I don't want you fighting the natives and getting yourself killed, Richard. Come with me and leave all this. You can run a pub again and be with your family."

Richard looked up and said, "Eat up before it is cold. They must be low on staff tonight and served it lukewarm. Probably serving others while ours sat in the kitchen."

She commenced her meal and patiently waited as Richard ate some meat.

At last, he said, "Sarah, I have no intention of fighting the natives. I will make friends with them and find ways we can work together. I cannot control the army's actions and will avoid trouble. There is no way I would chance fighting the Xhosa. But I must continue here for some time. I will build the house in case you come back. I have thought deeply about what you said about the other settlers' houses. I will clad the walls in stone and redesign them, taking notice of the fort-like construction others are using here."

Sarah took a break from her meal and said, "Good!"

"I want to be clear with you before you go, Sarah! I love you deeply. There will never be anyone else for me, but I cannot leave here – not at present. I understand your heart is with the children, and I am comforted that you will be with them. But if I leave now, we will lose all the free land granted to us and the investments I have made. These need time to return income. It will happen, Sarah! It will happen; perhaps someday, the natives will own their land again, but it will be long after we are gone. The British have only just started their colonisation of Africa. Our investment will yield ten times what we have put in. Perhaps even fifty times. The sacrifice will be worth it. I will come home and visit once everything is set up and working."

Richard could see that Sarah was becoming emotional.

"Waiter! A bottle of champagne, please."

"What are you doing, Richard?"

"Sarah, this will be our last night together for some time. Let us enjoy ourselves, and if I am in any fit state in the morning, I will carry your bags to the jetty."

Sarah wiped her eyes and put on a brave face.

Porting, Guildford, Surrey ...

The Countess and Lady Fiona accepted Anne's invitation to stay, and Emma joined them for dinner. As they adjourned into the lounge room after dinner, Anne and Emma excused themselves and sat together on the far side. Soon after, they were in deep conversation.

Lady Jane gestured towards the settee facing the fireplace, and she and Fiona settled there.

"Now, Fiona. Tell me about Hugh. I need to know what happened and about his relationship with Lady Clarisa."

Fiona sat back on the chair and made herself comfortable. Despite being a cool night, the fireplace was not alight, and she shuddered slightly.

"Perhaps if we had the fire going and a glass of red wine, this may be easier for me."

"Of course, my Dear. Anne! Please may we have the fire? We are both a little chilly."

Anne instantly rose and called Henry to make up the fire. Anne brought over two glasses of red and placed them on the coffee table in front of the settee.

Taking a sip, Fiona asked, "Where do I start, Lady Fintelton? Where do I start?"

"At the beginning of the voyage across to New York. I think that is where he met Clarissa. But Fiona, please call me Lady Jane. I prefer that."

"Of course. You see, I was Clarissa's travelling companion or chaperone. I was not privy to their discussions, but she spent many nights in Hugh's compartment during the voyage."

Lady Jane said, "I thought as much as I received his letter from New York asking for advice on Lady Clarissa. I think he intended to propose to her."

"Ah! Lady Jane, I must go back further so you can understand Clarissa's character. I tried to warn Sir Hugh, but I am afraid he was entranced."

The conversation went well into the night, long after Anne and Emma had excused themselves and retired.

Turner Household, Guildford, Surrey, England ...

Some days later, Ethel took a long breath and sighed happily. The normal house routine was back in place, and the quiet was rewarding with all the children in bed besides Clemmie. She found the girl sketching at her desk. Wandering over, she picked up some of the designs and considered them. Ethel placed the drawings on Clementine's bed except for the red dress design.

"These are very good, Clemmie! How did you think of all these dress designs? I love the red one – it is particularly attractive."

"Thank you, Ethel. I love drawing, and Victoria Sopwith lent me this book on fashion. It is in French, but so many of the pictures inspire me. I have changed them slightly to a style I enjoy."

"That is so clever." Ethel took the book and quickly skimmed through it. "I can't see you returning to the bakery. You are destined for the Hursts' design department with Victoria and Anne."

"We all love dresses, but I have no sewing knowledge, so I might come up with style but not the knowledge of putting the design and material together. For that matter, I am unsure of materials as well."

Ethel, hearing this, was not going to miss the opportunity.

"Clemmie, I worked as a seamstress with my mother for several years before entering service. Would you like some lessons on sewing and materials?"

Clementine looked up at her with a smile, "That would be so good. But do you have the time, Ethel? You work so hard here, and I hate to take you away from your spare time with Rosalind."

"She can join in with us. We would not want her jealous, would we?"

Clementine nodded in agreement, "Simeon may be interested as well. He is thinking of becoming a tailor. When can we start?"

"Well, as you are recovering quicker than expected, we could start tomorrow, Saturday morning, after morning tea. I will have the other staff hard at work by then, and we can spend a few uninterrupted hours together. What do you think?"

"Yes, please. But we will need some material and a design."

"I will send a note to my mother tonight, and Rosalind can bring a simple design and some material with her. Don't stay up too late, and please put the candles out before you settle down. I must check on Marcia and Jeremy. I am sure Nanny Smithers has them asleep by now."

Ethel placed the book and the design on Clementine's bedside table and left her sketching.

An hour later, Clemmie looked up and saw from her clock on the fireplace mantle that it was nearly eleven o'clock. She hopped up, blew out the candle at the fireplace, and returned to bed. Watching the flickering candle on her bedside table from the comfort of her pillows, Clementine soon felt warm and relaxed. The candle flame produced changing shapes and colours, which she would love to sketch. Her mind drifted into sleep as her eyelids struggled to stay open. Before Clemmie knew it, she was fast asleep.

Katherine shared Clemmie's room but was away with Clare and Madeline at Sophie Watson's home. An avid reader, Kath usually made the final check on the candles. Clemmie stirred, and as she rolled over, her arm nudged the bedside table gently enough to unbalance the candle, which wobbled and then fell on the drawings. At first, the flame spread slowly on the flat paper and edged towards the curtain. It was as if the fire was alive and sensed the combustible material that towered above it to the ceiling. Soon, the wrestling flames ignited the curtains and darted upwards. Smoke was filling the room as the fire increased in intensity.

Ethel Nibley, who had taken over from Nanny Smithers in nursing Jeremy for the night, finally had the baby asleep and in bed. Ethel yawned and watched the child for a few minutes to see if he stirred, but he was comfortably resting. Ethel could smell one of the fireplaces and thought that Jonathan must have lit the fire downstairs in the drawing room. That was strange as it was a warm night, and most of the fires would be out by now.

Standing beside the baby's cot, she could hear Nosey and Ralph barking and whining in the backyard. She thought, 'The dogs were always quiet. She must go down and see what ails them.'

Ethel made sure Jeremy was covered and then left the room, walked past the boys' room to the staircase and casually glanced along the hallway on the first floor. There was still a light coming from Clementine's room, and the smell of smoke was stronger. 'Clemmie must be hard at work, sketching!' She continued down the next flight of stairs to the ground floor and went into the drawing room to check on the fireplace. There was no fire.

But that did not make sense! Where was the smoke coming from? There was no smell of smoke down here!

"My Goodness!"

Ethel rushed up the stairs and burst open the door of Clemmie's room to find smoke from the ceiling, extending halfway down the door and bursting into the hallway. She coughed as she bent down to see into the room where Clementine still lay fast asleep on her bed. Rushing in but on her knees, she reached the bed and carefully pulled the limp girl to the floor.

"Ouch! What are you doing?"

"Clemmie, there is a fire! Come with me, but stay on your knees."

"A fire!" But then Clemmie started to cough as she had already inhaled smoke. Ethel could see the sand bucket near the doorway. There was no use trying to extinguish the fire which had spread across the room. The curtains were ashes on the floor, and the carpet was smouldering. The fire raged on two walls, and the ceiling was now alight.

"Quick, Clemmie! We only have minutes." She put her arm around the girl's waist and dragged her, coughing, across to the doorway and onto the hall floor. Leaving her, she ran to the stairwell and screamed, "Help! Fire." Then she opened Jonathan's bedroom door but found the room empty. He must be in his study with the door closed. There was no time left.

She rushed back to Clementine, pulled her onto her feet, and walked her to the stairwell. Then she rushed over to the guest room. It was empty, 'That's right, Clare is with Madeline at Sophie's house.'

Clemmie was still coughing violently and unsteady. Ethel knew that the boys, Marcia and baby Jeremy, were still on the floor above, and the other staff were in their quarters on the ground floor at the back of the house.

"Clemmie, I must get your father. Make your way downstairs and out the front, and I will be back soon."

She rushed down the stairs and flew through the drawing room to Jonathan's study. Opening the door, she found him hard at work on figures.

"Jonathan, there is a fire upstairs in Clemmie's room. Quick, come and help me!"

He was instantly on his feet as his expression changed from tranquillity to fear. Flying out of his chair and knocking it over, he ran after Ethel. When he reached the stairwell, Ethel was already past a groggy Clemmie, shouting and urging her on. Clemmie slowly slid down the stairs one at a time on her behind.

Jonathan stopped to help her, but Ethel screamed, "No, Jonathan, leave Clemmie! There is no time! The boys, Jeremy and Marcia, are upstairs."

He looked up and could hear the roar of the fire from above.

"My God! Please, help us."

As he rushed up the stairs past the first floor, he could see the flames coming out of the doorway to the bedroom. It was turning into an inferno, and there was no way to put it out.

Upwards, he climbed and could hear Ethel screaming for him. As he reached the end bedroom on the second floor, Ethel threw Marcia into his arms and said, "Go! I will bring Jeremy. You bring the boys!"

"I will wait for you!"

"No, Jonathan, Go! Get the boys - there is no time." She disappeared into the room and gathered the baby in a blanket and some nappies. As she came to the stairwell, she saw flames curving around the landing and leaping up the wall. Jonathan dodged the fire with Marcia in his arms and followed William and Simeon, who called the staff. Ethel followed down the stairs as fast as possible without losing her balance. As she made the first landing, a rush of flames leapt at her, and she dodged by falling to the floor. Biting hard on her lip from the pain, she scrambled on, determined to exit the house. There was no sign of Clemmie as she reached the ground floor, but then a piece of burnt ceiling fell beside her, and the flames leapt outwards. Ethel knew that safety in a fire was keeping as close to the ground as possible. She dropped to her knees as the fire lit the back of her dress. Then Jonathan was with her, wrapping her in a blanket that extinguished the fire.

Quickly lifting Ethel, he led her out the front door with the baby clutched in her arms. Then he sprinted back up the front stairs and into the House to ensure all the staff were safe.

Soon, Nanny Smithers ran from the front door, still fully dressed, and almost fell as she jumped down the last two steps. She joined the housekeeper and took Jeremy.

As Ethel looked up at the outside of the house, she could see the fire had spread completely through the first floor, and flames were racing through the second floor. They needed help.

She told the Nanny to watch the children as she turned and raced for the neighbouring House. Banging on the front door until a sleepy Mr Houghton answered.

"What is it, Mrs Nibley? My goodness, some of your clothes are burnt!"

"Mr Houghton, we need help! The house is on fire, and it might spread to yours."

Earnest Houghton looked in surprise at his neighbour, then walked out onto the street and gazed up at the burning house next door. Jonathan appeared from the side path, leading the remaining staff and the two dogs.

The sound of the fire was roaring, and Mr Houghton shouted, "I will find the constable and bring help."

"Thank you, Earnest!" Jonathan was out of breath and would have said more, but the situation somewhat overcame him. The family and staff huddled together, slowly backing away into the street as the inferno broke through the roof, casting a red glow across the nearby houses.

HMS Shadow, Rounding Cape Angela, Tunisia ...
The formation of three warships made good headway, tacking out from Cape Angela and moving away from the coast. The skies were clear and the westerly strong in the mid-morning.

Captain Sir Robert South stood on the starboard side of the quarter-deck, watching as the sailing teams finished setting the sails high above for a long tack towards the south coast of Sardinia.

"Morning, Captain".

Robert jumped, taken by surprise by the greeting. Admiral Sutherland stood a few steps behind him with Lieutenant Fenton in tow.

"Morning, Admiral. You took me by surprise. I was watching the sailing team on the main. We are making good progress with this westerly. A straight tack to the east of Porto Pino will allow us to turn southeast and down past Palma. The wind is strong and should hold."

The Admiral took a deep breath and sighed, "This fresh air is good for my lungs. Nothing like being at sea for a navy man." He surveyed the quarter and main decks and was impressed with the neat storage and organisation.

"You keep a well-trimmed deck, Captain."

"Thank you, Admiral. It will not stay that way long. We will be commencing gunnery stations in ten minutes."

The Admiral smiled as he cast his eyes across the horizon, "No need for that. The Ottomans are not strong here. Let the men catch up on scrubbing, I say. They will enjoy the water and sunshine."

Robert, in good humour, laughed, "Admiral, that is the first time I have ever heard anyone suggest we avoid gunnery practice. You will enjoy the action. After meeting those Ottoman frigates on my way down here, we need to be well-practised and ready for anything."

The Admiral nodded and scanned the horizon. Sutherland had forgotten that an Admiral at sea should leave the day-to-day organisation to his captain. He wondered if he was losing touch. Moving close so they could speak privately, he said, "My apologies, Robert. I forgot myself. Please have the gunnery practice first."

Robert responded, "Sir, I always appreciate your advice. There is no need for apologies. While you watch the battle stations practice, I will climb the main and scout the horizon. I must be prepared if we meet trouble."

Before replying, the Admiral thought better of asking his captain to remain on the quarter-deck, "I will be on the poop, Captain, taking a look myself."

South smiled and called his first lieutenant, "Fenton, you may commence battle stations and gunnery practice in five minutes. I am ascending the main for a scan of the horizon."

"Aye, Sir."

As Robert jumped to the guard rail and was off up the rigging with the energy of a youth half his age, the Admiral moved across to Lieutenant Fenton.

"Does he often climb the main?"

"Not often, Admiral. But he places a great value on intelligence, Sir. He discovered the Ottoman frigates coming through the morning sun as we neared Malta. The lookout missed it. He has a sense for danger that none of us have – it is unique."

Sutherland nodded, "Thank you, Fenton."

Rental House, Guildford, Surrey ...

Jonathan sat with Simeon and William at the breakfast table with a frown as he considered the major impact this fire would have on their lives.

Ethel said, "It was a good thing you kept the rental, Mr Turner, as we will need it now until you rebuild the house."

William quickly asked, "When will they begin building, father?"

Jonathan was so far away in his thoughts that he missed the comments.

Ethel spoke up, realising Jonathan's mind was far away, "Mr Turner! Would you like more breakfast? There are plenty of sausages here."

Jonathan stirred, "No, thank you, Ethel. I have had sufficient – your cooking is good." He smiled, saying, "I wonder if war has broken out in the kitchen at 'Porting' with Mrs Jennings looking over Mrs Kirby's back."

Ethel replied, "I am sure they will work it out. She will appreciate the help with so many there now."

"I hope so. Now, boys, we have some work to do. I want to go home this morning as some rooms at the back were saved. I hope my study is still intact as there are important documents I would like recovered. You two can miss school today and help me. Ethel, we will meet you at Porting for lunch."

Later, at the house, William and Simeon scampered through the ruins, making their way to the rear of the burnt-out building.

Simeon called, "You were right, father. The back of the study is untouched."

Jonathan came around the side of the house carrying a ladder, placed it near the study, and climbed onto what remained of the ground floor. He walked across and surveyed what was left.

"Good, we may rescue most of my files and documents. That is a relief."

They worked as a team as Jonathan piled documents into bakery baskets, and the boys carried them to a borrowed horse and cart. After two hours, it was close to eleven o'clock, and they decided to take the first load to Porting.

"There are plenty of rooms at Anne's house, and I can place these documents in a secure room with a desk. We will take this load up there, have an early lunch, and then return. Jonathan advised the temporary guards at the front of the burnt-out house, mounted the cart, snapped the reins and said, "Giddy up!" The horses responded, and they proceeded to Porting.

As the cart rumbled down the High Street, Simeon asked, "Father, we are covered in soot and ash. Should we not return to the rental and clean ourselves up before entering Porting."

"Good suggestion, Simeon, but we can wash at Porting. When we arrive, I will find a safe storage room. We can unload the baskets, wash our hands, dust ourselves in the scullery, and eat. We must have a short lunch as there is much more to salvage."

At Porting, a secure storeroom near the servant quarters was allocated to Mr Turner's documents, and the boys started moving baskets to the room. Anne, who had been at the office early, had returned home and discussed interviews for the General Manager with her father.

Jonathan, who had cleaned himself up, was sitting with her in the study, making a point, "We can't delay, Anne. It is more important than ever that we have a General Manager now, as with the house burning down, there is so much more to do."

"But they are all in London! The interviews must be there if this is to be done quickly. Should we postpone for a month? That would give us more time here."

Mr Turner was adamant, "No, with the new bakery opening in a few months, we must act now. The new man can organise the bakery opening. If we hold interviews early next week, we can appoint someone quickly. I want this decision out of the way and someone with us to take over much of the duties. This house disaster will capture my attention for the next few months – an unavoidable diversion I had not planned for.

You set off for London on Monday and organise the interviews. I will be there by Monday week, and we can start then. I recovered the files for each applicant. Take them with you and have the agency set up the interviews. The first thing I must do here is have the house demolished and remove the debris. Once that is complete, we can consider alternatives."

Anne nodded, but before agreeing, she checked her diary.

"Father! Neither of us may go to London as Sir Hugh's memorial service is next Thursday, and we will be in Petersfield. Then the Hyslop-Stern wedding is the week after. If we left on Tuesday the twenty-ninth of May, we could hold the interviews the following Thursday. I am sorry, but because of my pregnancy, I can't be travelling all the time. We can send details to the agency, and they can arrange the interviews. All we need to do is be there on time."

Jonathan rubbed his forehead and said, "I must remember to use my diary more."

"Don't forget, Father, that we must book at Hursts for new clothing. You will need some new suits, so go to Hurts and have Mrs Smith measure you."

Jonathan rubbed his forehead, saying, "You're right, Anne. I forgot about the wedding and new clothes. Please send a message to Mrs Smith saying that I will be there tomorrow morning. I must have lunch with the boys before we return for more records."

William brought another basket into the storage room, and Simeon stood over an open file, holding some papers.

"Hey, will. Come look at this."

William questioned, "What is it?"

"It looks like tickets for a trip to Africa."

As William crawled around the baskets and approached, he said, "Father must be going to visit Uncle Richard."

Simeon seemed disturbed, "No, the tickets are for you and Aggie. The ship is called 'Riptide', and you leave on the eleventh of August."

William took hold of the tickets and read the contents. He looked at Simeon with an open mouth and said, "Father is sending me away!"

Simeon grabbed the documents back and shoved them in the file, 'Quick! He's coming. Don't say anything! We can talk with Ethel later tonight."

They placed the file back where it had been and turned to face their father.

"Come, boys! Have some lunch in the kitchen, and then we must return home and bring back another load of documents."

Simeon and Willian ran off quickly towards the kitchen. Jonathan sat on a stool and looked at the pile of baskets. He sighed, knowing the work required to make some order from this mess. Noticing a rough pile of files on top of one basket, Jonathan picked the files up and straightened them. He saw the travel file among the papers. Checking if anyone was watching, he placed the file under the other documents in the basket.

HMS Shadow, Off Tunisia, Tacking towards Porto Pino, Sardinia...
Robert hoisted himself up and onto the crosstrees at the top of the main. There was no topsail up today, giving him a clear view of the horizon. He glanced to the east in case any Ottoman frigates were behind them. The horizon was clear of sails, but when he turned south, the tip of a white sail emerging above the horizon for a second or two caught his attention. Then it was gone. He waited to see if it appeared again, but there was nothing.

Sitting back, he took a minute to take in the beauty of the deep blue sea and enjoy the cool westerly that was helping their course home. 'Shadow' was flying, making a good ten knots, with the waves crashing against the bow as they burst through the tops of the swells. Robert wondered if Anne was in Guildford or London. She was probably at Hursts ordering new dresses for when they would be living in London at the end of the year. How he wished he was home. He pictured her golden hair floating in the breeze and her bright blue eyes gazing into his as if she sat beside him. She was more beautiful than any woman he had ever met and more important to him than anyone else in the world. How he wished he could hold her close.

"Sails, Sir!"

Jolted by the sudden call, Robert turned quickly to see the face of the lookout stationed below on the tops, who had climbed up to share his view.

"Where, Stanton?"

"South-east, Sir. Three ships, sailing west, coming up on the horizon. Look like frigates."

Robert strained his eyes as he focused on the southeast, where three small white dashes appeared. He took out his telescope, stretched it to full length, and focused on the sails. They were following a course mirroring '*Shadow*'s'. There were no topsails, and they were tacking. He had not expected this, but they were there. If they were Ottoman frigates, how had they known their course? Surely, it must be a coincidence.

"Well done, Jacktar. I missed them. Keep an eye on them and see if they change course towards us. If they do, call down at once."

"Aye, Sir."

Robert commenced climbing down. It had happened again. Three frigates found their position and were closing on them. But this time, '*Shadow*' must reach Gibraltar for reinforcements. Perhaps not – they were sailing with the frigate '*Solange*', which would give them access to French ports. If the Ottomans came too close, this could be his backup plan. He knew the Admiral would not wish to enter any action against the Ottomans.

'Porting', Guildford, Surrey …

Jonathan and the boys had returned by mid-afternoon, and he then set off for the office to catch up on his work. Ethel advised the boys they would be having dinner here tonight and returning to the rental to sleep. After spending much time sowing, the girls were ready for some fun, and the children decided to go through the back fence and visit the fort. Marcia had never seen the fort and asked Clare if she could come.

"We must ask, Ethel, first."

Ethel allowed Marcia to go if Clare and Rosalind remained with her. The girls readily agreed, and the children set off through the Porting back fence and followed the boys who ran ahead.

At the castle, William asked Simeon, "Why would father want to send me to Africa? I like living here!"

"I don't know, Will, but we can ask Ethel tonight if she knows about the tickets. Hey! Let's put the flag up so the gardeners know we are here."

As they raised the flag, William said, "I don't think Father likes me very much. He always beats me first if anything goes wrong."

Simeon, thinking about what William said, was reluctant to answer.

William was focused on the issue and wanted an answer, "Why? Why is it always me?"

Simeon mumbled, "He has that rage problem. Maybe he still has other problems. I don't know what's in his mind. But if he finds out we looked in his files, we will be in trouble, so keep quiet."

The girls were arriving, and the boys stopped talking.

Madeline asked, "Have you two got a secret? You are awfully quiet!"

Simeon said, "No, of course not. Marcia! Come up the steps, and you can stand on the parapet."

Marcia yelled, "Yow-ee!"

It was not long before an enemy ship was approaching, and the small band of soldiers prepared to fend off the invaders. Marcia was given plenty of ammunition that she could throw from the wall. The grin on her face said it all as she revelled in her first outing to the fort as a big girl.

As dinner was being prepared at Porting, Ethel found some spare time to consider the future and how staying in two houses could work. There was a small knock on the door as she sat in the housekeeper's room, jotting down notes. She opened it and called in Simeon and William.

"You are back from the fort?"

Simeon said, "Yes, Marcia was tired and becoming difficult, so the girls wanted to return."

Ethel nodded and asked, "What can I help you boys with?"

William closed the door behind him. Simeon looked at Will and then explained, "You must not tell Father, Ethel, or we will get a belting."

"What have you done?"

William said, "Nothing! Simeon placed a basket of files in the storeroom, and a file fell on the floor. As he picked it up, there were pieces of paper. Some of them were tickets to Africa."

Ethel was interested as she was unaware of any planned trips, "Who were they for?"

Simeon explained, "That is what interested us. One is for William, and the other is for Aggie."

Ethel wanted clarification, "Tickets for Africa on a ship?"

"Yes! But Father has said nothing about it. Why would Father want to send William to Africa, and why is Aggie going?"

Ethel was confused and said, "I am not sure, but I will find out."

The boys had not noticed, but Marcia quietly opened the door behind them and listened to the conversation.

"Now, boys, enough of this. Let me find out what is happening. Given that the house has just burned down, it may take a few days. So leave this with me, and don't tell anyone, please."

Marcia called out, "I won't tell."

They all turned and saw the little one peeking around the door. Simeon held his hand up and rubbed his chin. He was sure they would all get a beating now that Marcia knew."

Simeon said, "I am sorry, Ethel, we thought the door was closed."

"Not to worry, boys, this would have come out anyway. I will talk with Marcia now. Off you go."

The boys rushed out, and Ethel called Marcia across.

"Little one, what did you hear?" Ethel sat Marcia on her knee and waited for Marcia to speak up.

"That William is being sent to Africa with Aggie. Can I go to?"

Ethel smiled and said, "I think you might have misheard. They were talking about going to a zoo and seeing an African lion."

"Really! Where is the Zoo?"

"London. Now you come with me, Marcia. We will do some drawing and have a story before dinner."

Marcia's eyes gleamed, and she shouted, Hooray!"

HMS Shadow, near Sardinia, Italy ...

The breeze strengthened as the sun set in the west, indicating it would blow hard through the night. 'Shadow' had flown towards Sardinia during the day and was now seventy-five miles southeast of Port Pino.

There was a knock, and Fenton entered the captain's cabin where Admiral Sutherland and Commodore Jacobs were dining with Captain South.

"Excuse me, Captain, but the three frigates have changed course and are on an intersecting course. We have plotted their positions, and they may catch us around two in the morning."

Admiral Sutherland asked, "Have they raised every sail to achieve that?"

Fenton answered, "Yes, Admiral."

Captain South said, "I will be on deck in a few minutes, Fenton."

"Aye, Captain," Fenton closed the door, leaving the three senior officers to discuss the situation.

"It appears you were correct, Robert. They are intent on catching us. But why?"

"Admiral, they may be using this as a training exercise and turn away once they are near."

Jacobs commented, "And they may not. However, it will be fully dark in an hour, and the moon does not rise until ten. We could change course and be well out of their way."

Robert said, "They think we will change course soon and head east of Palma. That would give them time to catch us and allow combat if that is their aim. If we continue north of Palma, dodge around the island, and then stay fifty miles off the Spanish coast, we should have lost them by the morning. It will add a day to our journey but keep the diplomats safe."

The Admiral was all for this plan, "Agreed Robert. At all costs, we must keep the diplomats safe. Heaven help us if anything happens to that Russian, Volkov. Get those signals out quickly before it becomes too dark. Otherwise, we must close on '*Restless*' and '*Solange*' and use a loud hailer."

Robert answered, "Aye, Admiral. Of course, if they are still with us by morning we can always head for Marseille or Toulon and wait them out."

Robert excused himself and left the Admiral and Commodore to talk. As he came on deck, he noticed how strong the breeze had become. He climbed up to the poop deck where the First Lieutenant held the watch.

"Almost a gale, Mr Fenton!"

"Aye, Captain. With this breeze, they will not keep all their sails up. We will outrun them to Palma."

"Good! Now come across to Trotters, and we will plot a new course."
They approached Trotters, who was at his charts recalculating the intersection course.

He raised his head and said, "Evening, Captain. We should intersect with them at two thirty in the morning. That is if they can see us."

"Excellent, Trotters. I want you to plot a new course – we go around Palma and cruise down the Spanish coast, around fifty miles out. Brief your lookouts tonight. If they are still with us in the morning, I want to know at first light. Our plan would then be to head for Marseille. Have the yeoman signal '*Solange*' and '*Restless*' now. We need to keep candlelight to a minimum tonight to make it hard for them to see us, but we must also make sure we do not lose contact with our ships. Please close up the formation – say five hundred yards each in line. Make sure they all have a dull light in the aft. We will be the last ship and be the buffer if the Ottomans arrive."

"Aye, Sir."

As Robert walked to the port guardrail, he heard Fenton calling the yeoman. Trotters was busy plotting the new course and getting his men aloft to set the sails for the new tack. The ship was coming to life again, and Robert was impressed at how smoothly and efficiently Fenton now had '*Shadow*' running. The First Officer was ready for promotion, and Robert would recommend him on their arrival at Portsmouth. The captain was looking forward to some time with his wife before he took up his new position of head of security for Prince William and the Admiralty.

Porting, Guildford, Surrey …

Jonathan said Grace and dinner was now being served. The whole family was assembled, including Ethel and Rosalind. Anne was glad she had acquired a large, long table as it barely accommodated them.

"My, Father, this is like being at home again. If only Thomas were here, we would all be together."

Jonathan smiled and took in the sight of the gathered family, "I am glad that no one was injured in the fire. However, it came very close for Ethel. We all owe Ethel a vote of thanks for alerting us to the fire. The outcome might have been far more serious without her raising the alarm."

Clementine said, "But the house still burnt down, Father. I am responsible and sorry for falling asleep without putting the candle out."

Her father, with empathy in his voice, said, "These things happen, Clementine. We are all safe and will either rebuild or purchase a new house. I procured an insurance policy some years ago in case of fire, and it is still current, so there will not be a great financial loss. But we have lost many memories and personal possessions, including clothing. Ethel will be organising new clothing for everyone starting tomorrow."

There was general agreement about new clothes, especially among the girls. Conversations broke out all around the table. Jonathan told Anne, "I must write to your Uncle Richard in Africa and explain the fire in case someone else notifies him. I would not want him worrying about Katherine."

On hearing the word Africa, Marcia dropped her spoon and, in full voice, called out to her father, "Papa! May I go to Africa with William and Aggie? I want to see a lion, too!"

There was a sudden silence all around the table, and Jonathan dropped his cutlery and looked up with an open mouth.

PART 3

'They came from the sea.
Huge men, muscled and tanned
Singing together as brothers
Celebrating their wealth
from the giants of the deep!'

October 1827

Chapter 17

OCTOBER 1827

Asleep On The Beach, West African Coast ...

William felt a hand shaking his shoulder. He could hear a howling wind and raging surf, blurring the calling voice of someone above him.

"Wake up, William! Wake up."

The eight-year-old boy rubbed his eyes, turned onto his back, and stared at the caller. Above him was the shadow of a man blocking out the sun. He rubbed his eyes again and slowly made out the friendly face of First Officer Michael Leahy from the sailship *Riptide*.

Mr Leahy, a handsome, tall, slim man, had taken an interest in Aggie & William soon after the ship departed Southampton. The officer smiled, "I am glad I found you, William. How did you get ashore? I looked for you last night, but there was no trace."

"I'm not sure." William covered his eyes against the sand blown up by the wind. He rubbed them and said, "The last thing I remember was being in the lifeboat that turned upside down."

"Who was in charge of that boat?"

"Mr Kent."

Leahy, kneeling beside the boy, straightened his back and stood. He said, "I have not found him this morning."

William noticed they were on a long beach with low scrub leading off into the distance. It was flat country and very dry. Leahy pulled William up and pointed out the wreckage of their ship resting on a rocky outcrop.

"We were lucky, she was close to shore."

He turned and looked at where the First Officer was pointing. All that was visible was the bow resting on a rocky point and two masts protruding above the water. The surf continued breaking over the wreckage, and the masts slightly moved as if waving to them.

Leahy turned and gazed at the wreckage, "I have not been out there yet, but I fear that everything is lost. I might try it at low tide when the surf has calmed further. There are a few other survivors along the beach." Michael Leahy pointed to where a group sat. "Best if we all stay together. Can you stand up and walk?"

"I think so. Where are we?"

"I am not sure, William, but Captain Norton was trying for shelter at St Helena Bay. So perhaps we are there, but it does not look familiar."

They both continued their watch on *Riptide*.

"Mr Leahy, have you seen Miss Peters anywhere?"

"Not yet. But there may be more survivors along the beach. You go and join the others. There are rations and water, but don't eat or drink too much! I am unsure how long we will be here. Also, this is Africa, so there may be some wild animals."

William stood and surveyed the area around them, noticing the country was dry, flat, and hot. There were low mountains in the distance but no signs of any settlements.

"The captain will know!"

"We have not found the captain! I think he may be on the ship. Off you go and join the others."

William screwed up his eyes as he peered at the wreck again and considered what the First Officer was saying. If the captain was still on the ship, then he was probably dead.

Leahy said nothing further and started walking off along the beach.

"Mr Leahy, how many others have you found?"

"Only seven, William and with you, eight. Go and join the others. I will return shortly. If the sea calms, we can try to reach the wreck. Some supplies may be needed."

Leahy could see bodies further down the beach, face down in the water. From the lack of movement, he was sure they were not survivors. The only hope was others like William, who somehow had been washed ashore and onto the beach at high tide. They were the lucky ones.

William felt the sand between his toes and the strong, westerly wind that blew in his face. Normally, a westerly would feel cold, but the sun was so strong his clothes had dried, and he felt warm. As the lad stood, he shook the sand off and removed the jacket full of cork blocks, which had probably saved his life. He walked off towards the group of survivors about a hundred yards away. Some were sitting, and others stood pointing at the wreck.

He recalled the almighty storm that had hit the *Riptide* yesterday after lunch. The sky had progressively darkened, and the captain had reduced sail as the wind grew. Then, as waves broke across the deck, all passengers were sent below. The storm kept increasing, and William shuddered in Aggie's arms. She reassured him that the ship was built to withstand storms like this, but William was not so sure. Then, with a gigantic noise, the main mast collapsed. Many sailors were brought below with serious injuries, some screaming in pain.

The storm increased in strength, the ship rolling from side to side. This situation continued for hours, but when there were screams from below that the hull had been breached, the First Officer came to each cabin, asking them to secure their cork jackets[36]. William could not believe it when Mr Leahy said they were abandoning the ship. The thought of moving into small lifeboats in a raging sea was beyond belief. Aggie had turned a shade of white, and William could see the fear on her face.

McPherson Brewery, Head Office, Glasgow, Scotland …
Thomas Turner sat at the manager's desk, working through the mail. Having spent most of his life working in a bakery, he felt eight o'clock was late and would prefer to arrive before six. However, when he was expected at meetings starting at five in the afternoon, Thomas realised his sleeping patterns must change. Marion was fast asleep when he left home, and he enjoyed the crisp morning air as the coach delivered him to the McPherson Breweries offices. The administrative duties were like those at the Guildford bakery, except the volume of mail and documents was ten times as much. He stood and stretched as he looked out the window.

---

[36] Cork Jackets (or Life Jackets) were noted in the English Sporting Magazine in 1802. An inflatable life preserver was demonstrated in the Thames below Blackfriars Bridge in 1806. The Life Jacket, we know today, was not widely available until the early 1900s. Wikipedia and JS.

The door opened, and Douglas McPherson asked, "How are you managing today, Thomas? It appears you have discovered the mail."

Thomas turned with a smile and moved across to shake Douglas's hand.

"It is similar to Guildford, but there is much more. I need to find the delegations book before I go any further. I'm not sure which invoices I need to send to you."

"Ha! Good thinking. I forgot to show you that. We will also review the current budget to familiarise you with what is reasonable. My father always ran a tight ship and insisted on careful planning. He should have been an accountant. He was so concerned with money!"

"Well, it is rather important." Thomas grinned.

"You're correct, it is! But our cash flow is strong, and the business prospers, so I am unconcerned about that. I thought it might help if I set aside this morning to work together. We could visit the company shipping line for lunch and discuss its use. Our decision to set up in Ireland will stretch our resources, but first, we must understand the market there. There may be cost benefits in sourcing materials from Ireland, but I am unsure as I have never been there. We have a ship leaving for Cork in a few weeks. It may be a good opportunity to visit James and Isla and see the new baby. The child should have arrived by now."

Although Thomas was aware of the shipping line, he decided to ask for more information, "James mentioned the ships. Why do you need a shipping line?"

"Good question. My father inherited it from his brother. He even had doubts about it in the early days, but now, it is an integral part of the company. We can bring in supplies from France and Spain that are far cheaper than buying locally. We have an exemption from the government but with a cap on imports. The exemption specifies we must purchase a percentage of our requirements locally. It seems fair, but we always make sure we import as much legally as possible.

The shipping line also helps if there is a grain shortage at our English breweries. We can transport supplies there quickly by sea. Occasionally, if we have a ship idle, we can take on general freight and generate some extra income."

"How many ships do you have?"

"Six at the moment, but we may build another two as the demand for freight is increasing."

"I shall look forward to our lunch. If you could spare me ten minutes to discuss these invoices, that would greatly assist me."

Douglas held up the batch of invoices and said, "A pleasure, Thomas. It will mean I am free of them sooner than expected."

They both laughed.

The Bath Hotel[37], *Picadilly, London …*

Anne picked a table towards the side of the dining room, avoiding a high-profile position where she might be noticed. She was not a prominent figure in London society, and Lady Leystead was keen to keep a low profile by sitting at the side of the room. Anne felt it was prudent not to advertise the meeting with Katherine Constance. She sat back and relaxed, enjoying the ambience as she waited.

The waiter approached and asked, "Lady Leystead! May I provide some refreshments – perhaps a glass of white wine?"

"Thank you, but some cold water would be suitable. Perhaps two glasses, one for my guest as well."

"Certainly, Milady."

Although she was tempted, Anne was not keen on dulling her mind with the intoxicating taste of a cool white. She knew it would go straight to her head, and today, of all days, her mind must be clear. Suddenly, a woman's loud voice, coming from behind her, shattered her solitude.

"Why, Anne, I nearly missed you. I mean Lady Leystead." A beaming Marjorie McPherson, accompanied by another lady, stood beside her, demanding attention.

As Anne stood, she replied, "Mrs McPherson! What a pleasant surprise. I take it you are here for lunch?"

"Yes, I am here with Lady Chester. Let me introduce you. Lady Chester, please, may I introduce Lady Leystead, the Viscountess of Leystead."

The lady came forward, nodded, and said, "A pleasure, Lady

---

[37] The Ritz, London, was built on the site which had been first the Old White Horse Cellar, also known as Hatcher's White Horse Cellar. Hatchetts moved across the road facilitating the building of the Bath Hotel on that site. This in turn was sold to the financial backers of the Ritz in 1902. The financial backers of the Ritz felt they had secured one of the prime sites in London for their project. Wikipedia.

Leystead. I was not aware that the Viscount had married. He has caught a beautiful young lady, my Dear."

Anne swallowed, realising Lady Chester was unaware of Hugh's death.

Marjorie McPherson immediately informed her, "No, no, Milady! Sir Hugh unfortunately passed away while he was in Jamacia. Lady Anne married Sir Robert South, who inherited his title from his brother. He is now the heir to the Earl of Fintelton."

Lady Chester was aghast, "My Dear, I apologise! Please forgive me; I was unaware."

"There is no harm done, Lady Chester. Thank you for your kind compliment."

Mrs McPherson, unable to contain herself, asked, "Anne, you are by yourself. Please come and join us at our table for lunch."

"That is very kind of you, Mrs McPherson, but I am entertaining a business associate today and expect her at any moment. I hope you have a lovely lunch. It was wonderful to meet you, Lady Chester."

"But Anne! Bring your guest to our table, and we will make a happy foursome!"

"Thank you, Mrs McPherson, but we will discuss private matters and cannot change our arrangements now."

The waiter approached and announced, "Lady Leystead, your guest has arrived."

"Thank you! Please excuse me, ladies, as I must go. I will call on you again, Mrs McPherson, if I may!"

"But, but ...."

Lady Chester took Majorie McPherson's arm and led her off, saying, "Come now, Marjorie. Leave the child alone. She has important business to deal with."

After giving a beautiful farewell smile, Anne thought, 'Thank you, Lady Chester. You have diverted a disaster.'

Anne waved to Mrs Contance, who acknowledged the wave with a smile and quickly walked over to the table.

"Welcome, Mrs Constance. Thank you for joining me today."

"Lady Anne, I expected the invitation somewhat earlier but am glad it came. I see merit in your suggestion, as this is a far better place for us to discuss our concerns."

Anne smiled and said, "Before we go too deep into conversation, let us order and then we can concentrate on the more important matters."

Mrs Constance sat back and took some time regarding Anne. She smiled and said, "You are not only intelligent but a pretty young thing, Lady Leystead. Robert has found himself a lovely bride. I notice you are with child. Congratulations. The Earl and Countess must be pleased."

"Thank you. Yes, they are pleased, and so am I. Robert has only been back a month from his last mission and is so excited. Now, for today, please call me Anne, and I will call you Katherine."

Katherine Constance looked up and regarded Anne again. She had not expected this level of familiarity. Had she misjudged this woman, or was this a ploy to put her off-guard?

"That is most kind of you, Anne. I was not expecting this kindness."

Anne smiled and said, "Let's order. The food is very good here."

The conversation went well over the next half hour as they ordered and ate their main courses. Anne related her history in Guildford and her courting with Robert. Katherine told Anne about her upbringing and how she wanted more than what her parents could provide or what a bank teller could earn, especially in a man's world. Anne found that the barriers were breaking down, although she knew that Katherine would become as fierce as an injured tiger if challenged.

Anne thought it was time to raise David Constance's situation.

"Katherine, I am here primarily to discuss your son's future. The Earl is aging and has had many scares over the past three years, and despite our hopes for his continued health, we fear the end time may come soon. I have discussed your son's situation with him, and I want you to know that we will do our best to ensure he is assisted in his career. I hope that gives you some relief."

Katherine immediately lost her relaxed poise and became business-like, saying, "Does that mean he will gain recognition?"

"I am afraid not. I understand that you firmly believe David is the Earl's son. The circumstances are such that it is impossible to tell whose son he was."

Katherine sat back and was quiet for several minutes. A sudden attack of dizziness left her unstable and sapped her strength. She bent over, clasping her head with both hands.

Anne became concerned and asked, "Are you well, Katherine?"

She continued sitting there but raised her head and murmured, "Just a dizzy spell. Please excuse me for a minute. I have these issues. It happens when I become stressed. The doctors think my blood levels are out of balance. They use leeches[38] to balance it. You can imagine what it does to my arms. Thank goodness the fashions now include full-length sleeves."

"Oh, no! I hate leeches, and my doctor avoids them if he can."

Anne called the waiter and asked for some more water. As Katherine gathered herself, Lady Leystead realised her suspicions were correct. There was a medical problem, which probably acted as the catalyst for Mrs Constance's legal action. Now, she needed to ascertain the seriousness of the complaint.

Soon, Katherine regained her balance and said, "I am relieved you have extended friendship to me and pledged assistance to David. He is not a deep thinker but is competent in his profession. He will be an honest and good builder. I wonder about Fanny, though! You might have guessed she and David are attached. She can lead him astray sometimes."

"How do you mean astray?"

"She is money-hungry and encourages him to overcharge. He has lost some clients as a result."

"Does she know he will inherit your assets?"

"I know your solicitors have investigated my assets, and you may have guessed my attorney's advice is that I should not continue the action. I am happy to do that now I have your pledge. But, it would be best if I told you more."

Anne nodded and waited.

"I have never told David of my past. He believes I am a lifelong bank worker and that some of my investments have been highly lucrative. He is unaware of the townhouse in London or my other property. He is also unaware of my agreement with the Earl of Fintelton or the other gentlemen mentioned in your evidence.

You are an intelligent girl and will realise that something has triggered my action against the Earl, and it was nothing that you have

---

[38] Manchester royal Infirmary used 50,000 leeches a year in 1831. The prices of leeches varied between one penny and threepence halfpenny each. In 1832 leeches accounted for 4.4% of the total hospital expenditure. The hospital maintained an aquarium for leeches until the 1930s. The use of leeches began to become less widespread towards the end of the 19th century. Wikipedia

done. I realised it must be you who visited my house in Wimbledon. I am not upset about this, as it was inevitable and would come one day. But I had hoped for a few more years yet.

You see, in my line of business, good looks are everything."

She smiled and took a long breath, "I am now forty-one years of age, and my body is ageing. But I am afraid it is more than that – I have contracted an incurable disease. I will say no more than that. Even the effort of coming to lunch today has overcome me, and fatigue has set in."

Katherine Constance took a sip of water and leaned back against her chair. Anne smiled and waited for her to continue.

With a forlorn expression, Katherine said, "I may not be here this time next year. I needed to clarify where my son stood. I want to be sure he has guidance in the future. The world is cruel, and he will perish without money. Given my profession, you may find this strange, but I agree with what is said in Proverbs – 'Plans go wrong for lack of advice, many counsellors bring success[39]."

Surprised, Anne said, "I am not here to judge you, Katherine. I come in goodwill. But surely, David will inherit enough from you to have a fine life."

"That will depend on the woman he marries. Fanny will spend the money as fast as she can get her hands on it."

"In that case, you need to talk with your solicitors and set up a trust which Fanny cannot touch."

Katherine smiled and said, "I think you would be a suitable trustee, Lady Leystead. But I understand that may be difficult for you. So perhaps you might suggest someone at arms-length who you might be in contact with in the future. My mind would be at rest if this were the case."

Anne was astonished by Katherine's suggestion. This woman, who threatened legal action against the Earl, was now asking for help managing a trust for her son. Was this a trap?

"I would need time to consider that."

"Thank you, Anne. I am exhausted now and must return home. Would you ask the waiter to call a carriage for me?"

"Certainly, Katherine. But why not come in my carriage, and I will deliver you home."

---

[39] The Open Bible, New Living Translation, Proverbs 15:22.

Mrs Constance glanced up and looked deeply into Anne's eyes. She could not understand the kindness that this lady was giving her. They had been enemies at their last meeting, and now there was an offer of friendship. She had never experienced that before.

"That may be dangerous for you, Anne, and I would not put that risk upon you. Thank you for the offer, but I will find my way home."

Anne smiled and said, "Let me think about your request. We should meet for lunch again in a month. I will send you a message."

Katherine Constance felt giddy again as her eyes became misty from tears and a pressure rising in her head. She whispered, "Yes, that would be nice. Thank you, Anne."

Lady Anne could see that she was struggling and called for assistance.

"Call my carriage please and have two of your staff assist Mrs Constance. She will be riding with me as soon as the carriage arrives."

"Yes, Milady!"

Katherine was now gripping the table, and Anne could see the whites on her knuckles. It appeared Katherine might collapse at any moment. Moving around the table, Anne knelt beside her and put her arm around her shoulder to steady the woman.

"What is your address, Katherine?"

She whispered again, "Gloucester Place! I shall show you when we approach."

"Does David know how ill you are?"

"No, and please don't tell him."

Soon, they were on their way through the traffic towards Mayfair. Anne had wrapped Katherine in a blanket and sat beside her, ensuring she did not lose balance.

Mrs Constance turned and said, "Now, you know all my secrets, Lady Anne. I am at your mercy."

"I am not your enemy, Katherine. Our Lord told us to be kind and merciful. I know I am not without fault, but I try to follow His ways the best I can. Hopefully, when we meet again, you will have recovered."

Turner Business Offices, Guildford, Surrey ...
"Mr Turner, the builders are here to see you. Also, a letter from your brother, Richard, has arrived. There may be some news about William,

Sir!" Miss Daisy Eltham smiled as she passed Mr Turner the letter, thinking he would be pleased to hear about his son.

"Thank you, Daisy. Please ask them to have a seat – I will be there shortly."

The recently arrived General Manager of Turner Bakeries and Mills, Mr Harvey Potter, knew this would end their meeting. They had spent a productive hour together, with Harvey gaining insights into the organisation. Jonathan Turner, placing the letter in his desk drawer, was becoming tired and wondered how much longer he could keep up this pace.

"Harvey, you must excuse me as I need to confirm the final design for the new house. Since the fire, I have been burning the midnight oil, trying to catch up. Can we meet again tomorrow for morning tea, as there are further issues to discuss? I am so glad you have arrived in Guildford. Was the parting of ways with your old firm difficult?"

"Yes, they were not that understanding, but I made sure I parted on good terms, giving them a month more than required. I believe my replacement will arrive in early November, and I left my forwarding address in case they needed any advice.

Mr Turner, I was hoping Lady Leystead would have returned from London by now. I need to talk with her about the financial reporting. We either need her back full-time, which I understand will not happen, or employ an accountant with the required skills. I am afraid the accounts are behind, and we cannot catch up with our present staffing. Could we ask Mrs Hiscock to come and work for a month or two until the situation stabilises?"

Jonathan was gathering his papers on the desk, "I, too, expected Lady Anne back by now. She must have hit some troubles with the Hursts opening. I am reticent to ask Mrs Hiscock, a married woman, to return to work. Perhaps discuss it with Lady Anne while you are in London for the new bakery inspection. I will write today advising she should expect you soon. There is no need to book accommodation as comfortable rooms are available above the bakery."

"Thank you, Mr Turner."

"I must be off, Harvey. I will see you in the morning."

As Mr Potter nodded and moved to his office, Jonathan rushed to invite the builders upstairs.

On the Beach, West Coast of Africa ...

The wind had dropped during the day, and William noticed that the waves were calming, softening the crashing from the surf. Mr Leahy continued bringing in survivors from up and down the beach through the morning. To William's relief, one of the first was Aggie Peters, asleep on the sand only fifty yards from where he was found.

Ted Jeffries, the bosun, hunted for firewood during the day, and William helped him as best he could. The bosun was a medium-height, red-haired man whom William had found thoughtful and kind. They had many conversations about the ship and working at sea during the voyage. Knowing some of William's background from Aggie, Jeffries had slowly brought William out of the fearful and sullen state his father left him in as they departed Southampton.

Returning from collecting wood and grass, William found Aggie wrapped in blankets and beckoning him.

"Aggie, Mr Leahy found you! I was afraid you had drowned."

Aggie smiled in relief, "I, too, thought I had lost you, William. You don't know how relieved I am to see you."

She opened her arms to him, and he was not backward in giving her a mighty hug. Her shoulder on his cheek was reassuring, and William felt confident for the first time since waking this morning.

"Does anyone know where we are?"

"Mr Leahy said somewhere near St Helena Bay. I think that is up the coast from Cape Town. We seem alone here – I have not seen any locals or houses."

Aggie looked around at the low scrub and the distant hills. She shivered, "I have never seen a beach like this before. It is like a desert meeting the sea. I hope there are no wild animals around."

William had forgotten about the dangers of Africa, and he, too, scanned the land more closely, wondering if any lions were close.

"Where is Mr Leahy?"

"He took two sailors, and they went to the wreck. He said we needed supplies. There they are!" Aggie pointed, "You can see them coming back along the beach."

Later in the afternoon, as they gazed towards the wreck, a shout came from one of the passengers, "Look, two ships."

Everyone stopped and focused on the two sailing ships cruising down the coast. As the vessels approached, many survivors rushed to the water's edge, waving towels and shirts and yelling.

Mr Jeffries called William, "That won't help much. We need to light this fire so they can see us. Come on, Will – I will show you how to light a fire without flints."

The bosun quickly gathered dead, dry grass and piled it over a flat piece of bark. He picked up a stick and, placing its point through the pile and onto the bark, rubbed it quickly between his two hands. After a minute or two, he commenced blowing on the small pile.

"Have you seen this done before, Will?'

"Yes, back in Guildford, we did it at school. Mine never worked; my hands were too small, but I have grown."

"Good lad. Grab some bark and a stick, and place some dead grass on the bark like mine. We need that smoke going up quickly. If those ships miss us, they will sail past and down the coast."

William ran around collecting what he needed, knelt beside Mr Jeffries, and copied his actions. Soon, they had the fire started, and a column of white smoke rose in the light breeze. The boson said, "That's no good; we need to signal with darker smoke."

Quickly, he gathered greener grass and thrust it on the raging fire. Noticing the flames subsiding, Jeffries shouted, "The wind has dropped – it must be changing. Quick, help me blow on the base of the fire." Together, they knelt and blew until they became dizzy. Thankfully, the fire strengthened, and a column of dark smoke rose.

At first, the ship seemed not to notice *Riptide's* wreckage on the rocky point or the smoke signal.

"We need more branches and grass on the fire. Plenty of grass as it makes more smoke!"

William rushed off and started tearing grass from the ground. Throwing a clump on the fire, he steadily continued delivering green grass. Soon, dark smoke appeared, and a pillar of black smoke rose as the air was almost still.

As they watched, the leading ship turned into wind and became stationary. Soon, the other followed, and they could see small boats lowered over the sides. William noticed a strong, pungent smell on the breeze and said, "What is that smell?"

Jeffries replied, "Those ships are whalers. They boil blubber from the whales and scoop the oil off the surface of the try pots. That's the smell of the boiling. You can smell a whaler ten miles downwind when they are coming. The smell is as bad as a slave[40] ship. Don't know how they can stand it."

William was excited, "Do you mean they hunt whales? How big are the whales?"

"Yes. Some sperm whales are more than half the ship's length. They're the biggest sea creatures you will ever see. There must be whales around here if these ships are coming past."

The First Officer joined them and said, "It's the whaling season now. The whales will still be coming back down the coast. Although I thought there were more whales on the east coast."

Soon, the first whaleboats shot through the surf, and the men pulled hard to keep ahead of the waves. The speed of the boats inspired William as they easily landed on the beach. Running beside Mr Leahy, he wanted to stand beside a whaleboat.

"Ahoy, mates!" A crewman with a deep American accent shouted as they approached. "We thought you could use some help." The huge whaleman shook Will's hair and slapped him on the back, almost knocking him over.

"Oops!" he said and helped the boy up.

Mr Leahy, with a great smile on his face, said, "Thanks so much. In that storm last night, we lost our ship, the *Riptide*." He pointed towards the wreck where the ship's bow stood out above the low tide waves.

"Yes, Sir! That storm was dangerous! It gave us some trouble as well. I am Jack Shelford from the ship *Blue Angel*, out of Nantucket, and that other whaler is the *Wind Catcher* from New Bedford." Pointing, he said, "Here's Paul Manson coming now, first mate of *Wind Catcher*."

Manson came to them and held out his hand, saying, "Paul Manson, Sir. From New Bedford."

"Mr Shelford and Mr Manson, I am Oscar Leahy, First Mate of *Riptide*. You, gentlemen, are a welcome sight. We went down last night, and I am afraid we have found eighteen, including four children, drowned, and also the captain who remained on *Riptide* and lost his life."

---

[40] Whaleships and Slave ships were known for their unpleasant smell. The whaleships boiling of blubber to release oil had a lingering pungent smell. Slave ships were renowned for their crowding of slaves below decks and the smell of uncleaned faeces. JS

Shelford said, "How many survivors, Oscar?"

Not used to this familiarity, Leahy grimaced, "Thirty-eight, Mr Shelford. I searched this morning and identified everyone. But three lifeboats are missing with crew and passengers onboard. Forty-three in total. I have no idea what became of them."

"I am afraid we picked up two overturned lifeboats out at sea. They were probably caught up in a rip because you were close to the coast. There were no survivors. Sorry about that. We did not see a third boat." Realising how formal the British were, Shelford continued, "I hope you don't mind using first names, Mr Leahy, but that's what we Americans do most of the time at sea. Of course, we also use nicknames."

Leahy realised he needed to relax, "That's fine, Jack." Turning to Manson, he said, "And you too, Paul."

Manson had a grin on his face and said, "Sure, Oscar. The war is long over now!"

Leahy blushed, "Sorry, friends. You know how stuck up we British are!" He grinned, and then they all roared with laughter. William, sensing the atmosphere of friendship, tugged on Jack's arm, "Mr Shelford, can I have a ride on your whaleboat – it's so fast."

"Sure, fella – what's your name?"

"William, Sir! William Turner from Guildford."

"Hey, you catch on quick, kid! Sammy, come here, take this kid, and show him the whaleboat."

Sammy, an even larger man than Shelford, strolled over and said, "William, right?"

William stood frozen with his mouth open, looking up at this huge black American man.

"Well, William! I'm going to call you, Will. OK!"

William gulped as he said, "Yes, Sir."

"You can call me Sammy."

As William and Sammy walked towards the nearest whaleboat, Shelford said, "Oscar, if you are sure you have everyone accounted for, we can start taking the survivors onboard. What do you say, Paul? We should be able to make Cape Town by tomorrow."

Manson answered, "If the weather holds, no problems. It is about one hundred and twenty miles to Cape Town. If we load everyone before dark, we can have you there tomorrow morning."

"Where are we now? Captain Norton was trying to take shelter at St Helena Bay."

Manson said, "We are around thirty-five miles north of there. So, he nearly made it. Are all the dead buried?"

"All but four. We can do that in an hour if you can spare two men. The soil is soft here."

Shelford agreed, "With pleasure. If we can start taking out passengers now, we can be finished by the time you have completed the burials."

"Agreed. I want to leave here before any wild animals find us. I could hear the baboons during the night. Fortunately, they have left us alone so far today."

Manson passed across a pistol and a pouch of shot and powder, "In case you need it this afternoon!"

Shelford gave Oscar a wink. "If you would inform your people, we will start transporting them out. The surf is calm, so this will be the best time before the wind gets up again."

Porting, Guildford, England ...

Jonathan Turner sat beside Ethel in the drawing room, discussing their day.

"I had a good talk with Harvey Potter today. He is an intelligent man, and I am gaining confidence in him. Anne will be pleased when they meet in London – he has new skills neither of us have."

Ethel asked, "Is he going to London? I thought he just arrived from there."

"I need him to understand our new bakery before we can make any plans. I think he should also visit Bristol to see our building. Potter will be critical to implementing our expansion plans."

Ethel nodded her agreement and suggested, "Perhaps we could invite Mr Potter and his wife to dinner. After all, they are new to Guildford, so she must be lonely. As your new wife, I have not had the opportunity to entertain, so it is time I had some practice."

"A great suggestion, Dear. I am sure Anne would not mind if we entertained here. There is no sign of her returning soon, so why not? I shall ask the Reverend Taggart and his wife to attend. If word spreads that Andrew and Laura attended, it will help the women of this community understand that my beautiful wife should be welcomed. Has anyone visited yet?"

"Only Marjorie Smith! It seemed formal, and she seemed uncomfortable. Perhaps Mayor Rupert instructed her to come because of your position in our society."

"Give it time, Ethel. It has only been a week since we returned from Bournemouth, and people still remember Eleanora. They will adjust in time, and I am sure you will find friends soon. This Sunday in church should be interesting. Let us see if Mervin Webster and his wife appear. I would be surprised if we are not invited to their home soon."

Ethel smiled, sitting back on the settee and yawned. In her new role as Jonathan's wife, she struggled to make the transition. Mrs Gregory, the housekeeper, had settled in far better than Ethel and was driving Norma Kirby mad with many changes to the routine.

Johnathan said, "This will interest you. I had a letter from Richard today. Initially, I was tempted not to tell you, but on second thought, I thought I should. You need to know this news as my wife and your position in the family."

"What is it?"

"Sarah is returning home. She has had enough of South Africa."

"Poor Richard. He will be lost without her. But Jonathan, William must be there by now as the ship sailed two months ago. Who will care for him?"

Jonathan recalled Ethel's attempts to change his mind while staying with the Earl and Countess at the Isle of Wight. She had many good arguments about why he should not be sent but did not understand how great the problem was between William and himself. For several weeks after William had left, Ethel was cool towards Jonathan. It was only by his pleading and committing to bring him home in two years that she reconciled herself to the decision.

"I think you should read the letter. Richard has put forward a considered opinion of what should be done. Here, please, read it." He passed across the letter.

'Ewell Station'
Rathbury Road Via Grahamstown
Eastern Cape Province
South Africa

Mr Johnathan Turner
High Street
Guildford, Surrey
England

21 July 1827

Dear Jonathan

I hope this letter finds you and your family well and that your businesses prosper. I hear little news from England except from Katherine, who writes regularly, informing me of what is happening in Guildford.

By now, you will have heard from Sarah that she has returned to England and will live at our pub in Ewell until she decides what is best for Katherine. My expectations were too great, and towards mid-May, in a surprise move, Sarah decided to return home. I agree with her decision, as the burden of living as a settler in an unfinished house was too much.

I apologise for not writing sooner; however, it has taken some time for me to recover from her departure. I needed to put certain issues in place, like hiring a housekeeper, leaving me free to manage the many tasks required for a large estate. The army also requested that I remain in Port Elizabeth until they stopped the native raiding party's antics. Once the all-clear was given, I slowly returned to Grahamstown with a bullock team carrying more of our house's construction materials. So, some time has passed before I could write.

I have not received any mail from you concerning William. I believe the mail delays are due to bad weather in the Atlantic and the many ships that need shelter from storms. I hope this has not delayed Sarah, as a worrying trip to Southampton will convince her never to return to Africa.

Your last letter advised that William would be accompanied and arrive in the spring. There has been no further news, so I assume his guardian will contact me on their arrival at Port Elizabeth. I have heard nothing since then. Be assured that when he comes, he will be properly housed here and attend the local school in Grahamstown. Given his interest in the outdoors, he will find Africa a wonderful playground. I will ask the person accompanying him to remain until he is fully settled.

I plan to remain here for two years and then visit Guildford. By then, the house should be finished, and the station will be making substantial profits. The failure of many small settler grants has led to me acquiring several parcels of land, and some of the settlers are willing to come and work for me. With the natives looking for work and the displaced settlers, I now have around forty workers on the estate.

The local council here is keen on the Grahamstown area prospering and has encouraged me to continue acquiring land. They are not pleased, but they accept that I have established a native camp beside my property due to recent indigenous troubles. However, the initiative has been productive, and no further cattle have been rustled or butchered since that camp was established. The Xhosa men have become good friends, and I believe this could be a good partnership in the future.

Once William arrives, I will write again and let you know that he is here and safe. I look forward to his company as I have been somewhat lonely. Let me know the news from Guildford, especially about Beth's new arrival – I am guessing it must have taken place by now. Have you considered marrying again, Jonathan? I am sure Sarah will ask about this. It may be a good move, given the tribe you are now looking after.

I will send this letter off today when I visit town. I hope it is not delayed; however, I hear that many ships have layovers in various ports due to the bad weather in the Atlantic. Write when you can, as I am eager to hear news from home. Also, please encourage Oliver and Harry to write. I write to them, but receive few replies.

With great affection for you and the family

Your brother
Richard

Ethel looked up and said, "Jonathan, this letter was written on the twenty-first of July. It is now the seventeenth of October. That was two and a half months ago – surely Sarah must be in England by now. We have heard nothing. I think you must check tomorrow."

"Richard did mention the bad weather in the Atlantic. Perhaps her ship had a layover in Tenerife and was delayed. But I will make inquiries of Oliver and see if he is aware of her arrival time."

"Jonathan! We should also inform him of our marriage and the arrival of Bethany's baby. It appears he knows little of the past few months' events."

"I will write to him today, but it is clear he has enough to keep him busy at his station near Grahamstown. It will be interesting to hear Sarah's story when she arrives!"

Approaching the 'Blue Angel", West Coast, Africa ...
Standing at the front of the whaleboat and gripping the bow eyebolt with one hand and the gunwale with the other, William enjoyed the wind blowing on his face and the acceleration as the five whalemen pulled hard together. The bow split the waves, throwing white, foamy spray into the air, and was whisked away by the breeze towards the boat's stern. A broad smile shone on Will's face each time the massive men of the rowing crew heaved them forward – the feeling of speed lifting his spirits into a new world.

Sitting beside Aggie near the aft of the whaleboat, Ted Jeffries nudged Aggie and pointed at William, "Seems to be enjoying the ride!"

Aggie laughed, so thankful that William's mind had passed the misery of being wrenched away from his family. Despite the tragedy of this shipwreck and losing so many to the sea, it was a new beginning for William as he talked rapidly to Sammy, who rowed in the bow oars' position.

"Thank you for what you have done for William. He has been through a terrible time. During the first few weeks, I thought he would never talk again. He often cried at night."

Jeffries smiled and leaned back, "Not many of the men here come from happy families. But sailors find a way to rise above their past. William will be the same – there is a spirit in that boy that cannot be suppressed. He is strong, that lad. Give him time, and he will be himself again."

Considering Ted's comment, Aggie found herself wishing she was strong. The trip had plunged her into a new environment foreign to anything she had ever experienced. The kind attention from First Officer Leahy had helped her weather the challenges of cramped quarters and poor food. Life at sea was not the romantic vision she first had, but after a long voyage and shipwreck, she knew how blessed she was to be alive.

"He has learnt more about life than most boys his age, and being a good swimmer may have saved him last night. He learnt swimming from a doctor in Guildford at the men's club. The only pool big enough for lessons was at the club. Are you a swimmer, Mr Jeffries?"

"Yes, I taught myself soon after joining *Riptide*. It has come in handy."

William was surprised by the mothership's size as the whaleboat neared. He asked Sammy, "Why is there a fire on board?"

"We caught whales before the storm – there is still blubber to be boiled. They should finish by late tonight, and then you will hear a lot of scrubbing. The captain wants it all cleaned up before we reach Cape Town."

William looked up at the *Blue Angels'* gunwale, where numerous men were ready to haul them on board. Among them stood a well-dressed lady with a girl and boy on each side. They seemed out of place.

"Who is that lady, Sammy?"

"That's Captain Hart's wife and two kids! They live on board – he brought them on the trip this time. Will, come and sit next to me as the whaleboat is hoisted aboard."

To William's surprise, two spars were extended out from the ship, and men lowered various ropes which were fastened to the whaleboat before it was hoisted onboard. Waiting his turn, he was helped down onto the deck.

Aggie called William, and they followed Mr Leahy towards the aft of the ship, where Captain Hart and his wife, Jenny, met them.

"Welcome, passengers of the *Riptide*. Please allow me to explain the arrangements for our overnight trip down to Cape Town. Fortunately, the weather is good, so all the men will be housed on deck under a tarpaulin for shelter, and the women and children will be housed below deck near the main cabin. The '*Blue Angel*' crew will make your stay as comfortable as possible, but please understand that this is a whaling ship, and we are not set up for passengers. Dinner will be served here at six o'clock before sundown."

Tables and chairs were positioned as the captain spoke, and some light refreshments were soon served. Aggie was amazed as the food here was far superior to what they normally had on Riptide.

Mr Leahy came across and joined Aggie and William at a table.

"Miss Peters, we will be in Cape Town tomorrow. Various matters must be dealt with in port, which will only take a few days. It will be some weeks before an official enquiry begins for the shipwreck of *Riptide*. I understand you travel on to Grahamstown."

Aggie agreed, "Yes, as soon as we can find transport."

Leahy frowned, "Travel here can be precarious. May I suggest that if you can wait two or three days, I will accompany you to your destination. It may be safer, and I will not have any pressing engagements until the shipwreck enquiry commences."

Aggie was pleased to hear this, "Certainly, Mr Leahy. That is most kind of you, and we would appreciate your protection."

As Aggie and Mr Leahy talked further, young John Hart approached their table and asked William, "Would you like a game of checkers? I am John Hart, and this is my sister, Mae."

Mae came forward and said, "Hello, what is your name?"

"William Turner! Yes, I would like a game of checkers."

Chapter 18

Onboard 'Blue Angel', entering Table Bay, Cape Town …

As their ship glided towards Table Bay, William, John, and Mae stood at the gunwale, gazing at the high mountains towering above Cape Town. The breeze had changed from the west to a south-westerly, and the temperature was dropping rapidly. Aggie appeared with a small coat in her hand.

"Here, William! Put this on, or you will freeze."

William obediently pulled on the coat and buttoned it up.

Aggie asked John and Mae, "Do you need coats? That southerly is cold."

John said, "I'm used to the cold. You should feel the wind around Cape Horn. When we left Nantucket, we went down the East American coast and rounded the cape. It was freezing."

Mae started walking towards their cabin, shouting above the noise of a sudden gust, "I will get my coat, Miss Peters. I don't like the cold."

Mr Leahy nodded to Mae as he passed and approached Aggie, "Miss Peters! The Captain and Mrs Hart are going ashore for two days before they cast off for Durban. They plan on staying at the Goede Rust Hotel near the port and invite you to join them. Captain Hart has suggested that if your destination is Port Elizabeth, they can offer free passage and accommodation on *Blue Angel* for the trip. He would be pleased to deliver you and William to the port on their way to Durban. I have also been invited and can see you through to Grahamstown."

"That is kind of the Captain, Mr Leahy. I had no idea where to stay and would have consulted you. But this plan solves that issue. Please advise Captain Hart we accept his recommendation for accommodation and travel to Port Elizabeth. I think William will enjoy the extra time with John and Mae."

"Yes, they enjoy each other's company. I will advise the captain, and I am sure Mrs Hart will discuss this with you soon."

Aggie smiled as Mr Leahy walked aft. William tugged her arm and said, "Look at all the sailing ships in the port. There must be more than thirty ships. Many of them are American whalers. John told me how they layover here before going up the coast to Durban or crossing the ocean to Australia[41]. Where is Australia, Aggie?"

"I think they used to call it New Holland. It is to the east of us across the Indian Ocean. If we had an atlas, I could show you. Perhaps, if you remember, we can find an atlas when we reach the hotel."

Porting, Guildford, Surrey ...

Anne sat in bed and looked across at a fast-asleep Robert bedside her. The sun was peeping over the horizon, giving enough light for her to see his brown hair curled down over his eyes and his body resting after a challenging mission to Malta. Unfortunately, Admiral Sutherland had contracted pneumonia after 'Shadow' rounded the tip of Portugal and headed straight for Portsmouth. Despite being so close to home, he succumbed and was buried at sea. Poor Lady Amanda would now be alone for the rest of her life. Anne thought she must write today and give her condolences.

The summer weather had disappeared, and the nights and mornings were cold. Anne hopped out of bed and stoked the fire, placing some kindling and wood on the embers. Soon, it blazed, and she warmed her hands and feet before hopping back into bed.

She smiled and felt her tummy as the baby gave a kick. It was as if this little one was already part of the family. The morning sickness had left her in June, and she felt more energetic than ever. For some reason, she needed to clean anything in sight, rearrange furniture, and consider changing the house's colour scheme. Of course, Robert stopped her when he returned and insisted that she had more rest than

---

[41] The first time that the name Australia appears to have been officially used was in a despatch to Lord Bathurst of 4 April 1817 in which Governor Lachlan Macquarie acknowledges the receipt of Captain Flinders' charts of Australia. On 12 December 1817, Macquarie recommended to the Colonial Office that it be formally adopted. In 1824, the Admiralty agreed that the continent should be known officially as Australia. Wikipedia

was necessary. He was so caring. She wondered how she ever managed to find such a loving husband.

Then she thought of William. So far away and alone, except for Aggie. How could her father do such a thing? 'Please protect him, Lord God. He is still a little boy and is probably feeling lost and deserted. Please give him friends.' Thoughts of William brought a frown to her face as she felt another kick from the baby. Putting both hands on her tummy, she said, "No, I haven't forgotten you!"

A sleepy comment came from Robert, whose eyes were open, "What were you thinking, Anne, that brought that frown?"

"William – so far away."

Robert raised himself on his elbows and fluffed up his pillow. Resting back, he said, "He will be challenged, but I think William will rise above it. That boy is resilient."

Anne snuggled beside him, "Don't leave me again, Robert. You have done your navy service now. Stay home and safe."

"Well, you will have to put up with me for the next three years while I head up security for the Prince and the Admiralty. But we will need to live in London. That will present some problems."

"At Harting?"

"I think so. I am not keen on acquiring another property, and given our new situation, there is no need to do so. I am afraid we will inherit the estate sometime in the future."

"Let's hope that is a long way off. I want our parents to enjoy junior for a while. Ouch – he or she is active this morning."

Robert felt her tummy, and immediately, there was a kick, "He is touchy! Must be practising boxing."

"It may be a girl, Robert."

"No, it is a boy!" He grinned and felt the tummy again and received another kick. "Hmm! It might be a girl!"

Anne giggled, "I want two boys and two girls."

"I don't mind that at all. But first, we must think about today's challenges. I want to talk with our bankers and check the estate's finances. Then we must start packing for London. A break from having your family live with us will help your health. Next week, we visit the Prince at Bushy House in Richmond. Are you well enough for the trip to London, Anne?"

"Of course! Victoria had me measured before I left London. I was unsure if any official engagements were coming up, so I purchased one or two new dresses." She giggled, "You will be amazed when you see the waist size. I have never had a waist so large."

Robert grinned, "In that case, no breakfast for you this morning!"

Anne grabbed a pillow and threw it at him, "Just you try to stop me!"

Robert laughed, putting the pillow aside, "It is so good to be home. I think we will enjoy the next three years. I expect it will take your father at least a year to build the new house, so our moving to London will let him move the boys out of the rental and in here. They will all be together again."

"You mean the boy – don't you? Remember, William was sent to Africa."

Robert stood there thinking, "Sorry, I had forgotten. I should not have done that. Would you like a cup of tea?"

Anne nodded her agreement. Robert was up in a second, pulled on his dressing gown and was off on his mission.

Anne sat there gazing out the window. Would everyone forget William? How long would he be away? She felt her tummy again and felt a slight movement. Anne said to her baby, "Don't worry, little one. I will never leave you or let you go."

Ewell Station, Outside Grahamstown, Eastern Cape Province ...
Richard wiped his brow as the breeze had dropped. The sun was hot on his back despite pulling his collar up as he surveyed the house. The roof and all the bedrooms on the first floor were complete, and the two bathrooms were finished but not painted. He had changed the design and clad the exterior walls with stone, again delaying the construction. Standing back on the scaffolding, he checked the front wall line. It was nowhere near straight, but it would do. No one would notice unless they made a close inspection – not likely out here.

The question that worried him was whether Jonathan received his letter in time and kept William in England. Richard was unsure if Ewell station was the best place for the boy. Not that he would turn William away, but without Sarah here, there would be no maternal help, which would probably be more important for a seven-year-old.

He was sure his housekeeper, Mrs Janssen, would take an interest in the lad, but she was only there from six in the morning until five in the afternoon. It was the night that concerned Richard. That was the time when young children were most insecure.

He imagined Sarah was now reunited with Katherine, Oliver and Harry in England. Little did he know that Sarah's ship had a forced layover of nearly a month for repairs in Tenerife and to avoid the harsh weather in the Atlantic.

Who was accompanying William? Richard wondered if he could convince the lady to stay longer than she had planned.

A call came from below, "Baas, you coming? The land clearing!"

Richard's memory was jigged. He had agreed to go with George and the Mbeki brothers to survey the land to be cleared. The Xhosa's cattle were already wandering onto his land and needed more grazing pasture.

"Yeah, George. Coming."

He would think more about William's care tonight over dinner. With some luck, Jonathan would have received Richard's letter and not sent the boy. Having heard nothing, he worried that William was on his way to the Eastern Cape.

Admiral Bird's Office, Admiralty, London …
Commodore Wendell Wadsworth knocked and entered the Admiral's office.

"A Mrs Stubbington from the Home Office is asking to see you, Admiral. She apologises for having no appointment but insists it is a national security matter. Will you see her, Sir?"

The admiral raised his gaze from the papers on his desk, looked directly at Wadsworth, and said nothing.

"She said it would only take ten minutes. Mrs Stubbington is quite insistent."

"I recall her name from somewhere – she heads up a small unit that gathers information. I think she is becoming a bit too big for her boots. Tell her to make an appointment."

The Commodore swallowed and backed out of the office.

Facing Mrs Stubbington with a humble voice, he said, "I am afraid the Admiral is extremely busy. If you would like an appointment, we can make it for Thursday. Would that be suitable?"

Hearing this, Janet pushed the man aside, saying, "Get out of my way, man. I have not the time for this nonsense."

She walked past him into Admiral Bird's office and closed the door behind her."

The Admiral looked up with a smirk and said, "I was wondering what you would do, Janet."

"Walter, I have no time for your insults. I need your assistance for an urgent operation. It has been approved at the highest level and must commence soon. Many English and Irish lives are at stake, so I need the Admiralty's complete cooperation and secrecy."

"This is all very dramatic, Janet. You understand that we plan our missions carefully, as gathering and training a team takes time. I am afraid I cannot help you. If you would excuse me!"

Janet Stubbington had dealt with Admiral Bird before and was ready for his obstructions. She enjoyed playing the games of these men of high rank and watching them come unstuck.

"The Irish have reestablished their network in Dublin and are planning again for missions against us. But this time, it is different. A counter faction is gaining strength in Boston and may be prepared to deal with us. We have located their leaders and must arrange an urgent meeting. They have previously indicated that negotiation is far preferable to the useless slaughter of their men and ours."

Admiral Bird laughed and said, "So you want a ship to carry your emissaries to Boston and hold this meeting at short notice. The Americans will laugh in our faces. They are far more onside with the Irish than you might think. Your little scheme is doomed to failure. Go away, Janet and play your games elsewhere."

Stubbington enjoyed the Admiral's ire, saying, "There is one complication!"

Admiral Bird angrily said, 'I am sure there are many more complications than you suggest.'

"Only one of our men can identify their leader. So, he must be on the ship on Saturday week. He will need orders from you."

In a raised voice, Sir Walter Bird stood and demanded, "Get out, Janet! I am not writing orders on your command. Get out!" The admiral was turning red with rage.

"It is not on my command, Walter." She passed across a letter.

At first, he did not accept the letter but reluctantly took it and commenced reading. Slowly, he took his seat and looked up.

"You mean the Prime Minister is ordering this!"

"Yes. We are sending some diplomats for a meeting in Boston to brief the Americans on the mission in the eastern Mediterranean. That will be the cover for our man. While that is happening, our man will be meeting with the Irish. He will need at least two or three days to negotiate with them. After that, he will head back with the British diplomats on our ship."

"That is if he is still alive."

"We have great confidence in our man."

Walter Bird asked, "And who is our man?"

"He is a talented officer we have previously worked with, Walter."

"I know exactly who you have in mind. Sir Robert South?"

Janet Stubbington nodded in agreement but said, "There are many lives at risk if we do not proceed. It is not just the Irish who are at risk. Many English sailors and civilians will suffer if this plot is not stopped."

"Damn you, Janet. South has only been home for a month. Now, you want me to send him on a mission to Boston when his wife is about to have a baby. Have you no heart, woman?"

Janet ignored the question and said, "You will not need to tell Sir Robert. The prince will do that next week. You need to have HMS *Shadow* ready in Portsmouth on Saturday week as the Diplomats will arrive on Friday night and board on Saturday morning around ten. We have checked the tides, and they will be correct."

"Today is Tuesday! It can't be ready in a week and a half."

"It is almost finished, Admiral. We have been arranging this for the past couple of weeks. Shadow will only need your final directions when you hand South his orders. Concerning Lady Leystead, please leave that with me. I must be off and leave you to organise Shadow and the writing of Captain South's orders. Always good to have your cooperation, Admiral."

Bird scowled as she left his office. He then called his secretary, "Wadsworth, Come! You have some urgent new tasks to complete."

James McPherson's House, Glasgow, Scotland ...

Douglas McPherson stood beside the coach as Thomas helped a pregnant Marion into the coach. Dark clouds were rushing in from the west, and the occasional rain squalls were hitting the suburbs.

"Do you have plenty of warm clothes and blankets for the trip?"

"Yes, Douglas. We are fully prepared. All going well we should be in Greenwich within a week. The roads are good, but the weather looks ominous. I am sorry about postponing our trip to Cobh."

"That is fine, Thomas! We can easily reschedule. I am more concerned about your trip. The rain should hold off today or be light. The roads should be clear as you head south. If it were November, I would be melancholy as that is when it usually pours."

Marion had composed herself and appeared comfortable, "I am sorry to take Thomas away, Douglas, but I promised Mrs McPherson that we would have the baby at Greenwich."

"Compose yourself, Marion. I will take care of everything while you are away. As you know, Lachlan, Taye, and the children are already there and hopefully settled in. You and Thomas will find it a full house, so enjoy the peacefulness of your trip for the next week. I hope to be in Greenwich in two weeks. If the baby is early, I will be keen to see the little one."

Marion smiled, "I am glad Taye will be there. We have become best friends. Thank you, Douglas."

Thomas tapped the cabin ceiling and waved as the coach commenced the long trip to London. Douglas waved and Marion watched as he quickly returned up the stairs and into the house as a squall blew rain against the coach window."

"Douglas has become a good friend, Thomas! He reminds me much of his father."

"Yes! Without his kind help, I would have been lost up here in Scotland."

Marion smiled, "You have settled into the job well, my Dear. I have been impressed, but now I want us to travel quickly to Greenwich and settle in before the baby arrives."

"Back on the road again, my Darling! I shall make sure you have the best of care."

Marion smiled and hugged Thomas. She wondered if she would reach Greenwich before the baby came.

The North End⁴², Boston, Massachusetts …

The cart slowly made its way along Salem Street and stopped short of Christ Church to let several men off. Slowly gaining their balance, they walked off in different directions, all tired from a long day's work.

"Aiden! Tis still time for fishin tonight. Are you coming, lad?"

"No, Brody. Not tonight – early morning tomorrow. Get some sleep and dinner! We can fish another time. See ya on the cart."

With his bag over his shoulder, Aiden Reid crossed the church entrance, paced along the side, and entered a small lane at the back of the parish grounds. Coming in the other direction was the Reverend Klause, a man he was coming to know, given the Irish were forced to attend Episcopal churches.

"Hard day, Aiden?"

"Yes, Father. Ready for some dinner."

"See you on Sunday. Hey! Tell Biddee that Mrs Riley has had her baby! By the way, it is Reverend, not Father!"

"Sorry, I forgot."

The Reverend Hadley Krause turned and walked on with a smile. Aiden Reid wondered when Catholic Church worship would be allowed again. Probably not soon, as the protestant city elders were a staunch lot here in the North End. However, he liked the friendly Reverend Krause, who cared for everyone, even the poor Irish immigrants. He tramped up a narrow lane with dilapidated three-story buildings on either side where various men relaxed on iron landings enjoying their nightly pipe.

From a gap between two buildings, a well-built man in his early twenties leaned against a wall and ensured his cap was pulled well down over his forehead. He kept in the shadows, making sure he was not noticed. Aiden walked past and bounded up the front stairs of a tenement building, carefully avoiding the children playing on the stairs.

"Hello, Mr Reid!"

---

⁴² A wave of Irish immigration started in the 1820s. The (suburb) North End became a fashionable place to live in the 18ᵗʰ century. Wealthy families shared the neighbourhood with artisans, journeymen, and labourers. In the 19ᵗʰ century successive waves of immigrants came to Boston and settled in the neighbourhood, beginning with the Irish and continuing with Eastern European Jews and Italians. By the late 1840s, living conditions in the crowded North End were among the worst in the city. Wealthy residents of the North End moved to newer, more fashionable neighbourhoods such as Beacon Hill. Wikipedia and JS.

"Hello, kids. What are you playing."

"We have some chalk for drawing pictures."

Aiden could see lines and colours resembling what he thought was a horse, "Nice donkey there, Maisy!"

"It's a seagull, Mr Reid!"

The Irishman looked up. His intuition told him something was wrong, but there was no more than that in his mind. He looked around, checking all the laneways for strangers. There was nothing.

"Hey, kids! Have you seen any strangers going past?" Young eight-year-old Erin said, "Just Tommy Dwyer! He is odd – he keeps pulling my hair."

Aiden smiled but continued surveying the street. There was nothing there. He nodded to the children and entered the front door. Rushing up the six flights of stairs to the third-floor apartment, he closed his door, breathed a sigh of relief, and dumped his bag on the floor. Still worried, Aiden looked at the street from his window.

"Biddie!"

Biddie Reid poked her head around a corner and said, "Late night – must be a lot of work. Come in the kitchen – tea's ready! Michael's already gone."

"I've just got time for a bite before the meeting. Michael will keep the brothers entertained until I get there. How was your day, girl?"

"We'll. I've got a little something to tell you, man! You're going to be a father."

Aiden stood there in disbelief. He could see how overjoyed Biddie was. "You mean it's true!"

"Yes! I'm about six weeks pregnant. Miracles happen, Aiden – after all this time."

Aiden took her in his arms and kissed her hard.

"We can celebrate tomorrow. I'm over the moon, Biddie. We could never have done this back in Ireland. I must eat and get going."

After a good meal, Aiden washed his face, put on his cap, and headed to the Green Pub two streets away. Reid could only think of one thing. He would soon be a father. He was not sure if he was ready for that responsibility. Thank goodness he had been promoted to supervisor – the extra money would be needed.

As he walked towards the pub, thinking of the new baby, he

wondered how he would cope as a new father at his age. Their lifestyle would change forever. He was thankful they were away from Ireland and safe in Boston.

Stubbington knew how alert Reid was and ensured he remained in the shadows, where he could make a deeper retreat if Reid stopped or turned. He trailed him by about seventy-five yards and kept close to the building entrances. Aiden suddenly disappeared down a laneway. Ross darted into the shadows and watched.

Reid was sure there was someone there and decided to go to ground. He waited patiently for ten minutes, but no one emerged. He must have been mistaken. From long years of surveillance experience, he scanned the alleyway, searching for an alternative exit he could use. He spied a gap at the back of the building, wide enough to slide through into an alley to the next street.

The Englishman waited for twenty minutes, knowing he had probably lost Reid. The man was uncanny and had the intuition of a cat. However, he was in no hurry now that he had identified his residence. He waited another ten minutes before emerging and returned the way he had come.

Reid watched from a fifth-floor empty apartment as the lone figure walked away along the empty street. The children had been called to dinner, and most men had finished their pipe sessions. Darkness was flooding the streets, and the outline of the man was blurred, but Reid was convinced that he had seen this man before. Not in Boston, but in Dublin!

The Goode Rust Hotel, Cape Town, Eastern Cape Province …
Mrs Hart waved to Aggie as she and William entered the dining room. Captain Hart and Mr Leahy stood to receive them.

"That is most courteous of you, gentlemen, but I am a servant, so there is no need but thank you for your good manners."

Charles Hart replied, "Miss Peters, as far as we are concerned, you are a lady equal to any of us. We are pleased that you and William can join us."

Oscar Leahy added, "Here, here!"

Aggie blushed, took the seat offered, and found herself gazing into Connie Hart's smile.

"While the men are sorting out all those business matters, I thought we could discuss what we should do for the next few days. Perhaps some shopping tomorrow and the children will enjoy some time on the beach. Will you join us, Miss Peters?"

"We would be honoured, Mrs Hart. I managed to acquire a new dress and some clothes for William this afternoon. All our possessions went down with the *Riptide*. Once we are in Port Elizabeth, I might purchase more."

Mr Leahy asked, "Miss Peters! What about money? Did you lose everything in the shipwreck?"

"I am afraid so, Mr Leahy, except for the money in my purse, which was tied to my belt. We have a few pounds left."

The First Officer of *Riptide* said, "The company will reimburse you for all losses, so keep an account of your expenditures. The insurance covers the total loss. I will speak with Mr Jeffries tomorrow and see if any advances can be made from the company office here. Your tickets were first class, so I am sure there will be something we can do."

"Thank you, Mr Leahy. That would assist our shopping greatly."

Connie said, "It may be prudent to get what you can here as Port Elizabeth may be somewhat limited. We have an old suitcase you can have. Better to stock up here where there is some choice."

Aggie was pleased with this suggestion, "I had not thought of that. Thank you, Mrs Hart."

"Please call me Connie, Miss Peters. I don't mean to be forward, but we Americans are far more relaxed about class than the English are." Connie Hart reached over and took hold of Aggie's hands. "We have all been through a terrible storm in the last few days. I am sure that we will become the best of friends!"

The kindness from the captain's wife stunned Aggie, and she held Connie's hands tight, "Thank you. Please call me Aggie. I have never been to sea before, and this trip has been far more of an experience than I expected. I was thankful to be alive when I woke up on that coastal beach."

William was already talking with John and Mae about the township. While Mae was interested in shopping with her mother, John was keen on swimming at the nearby beach. William remembered that the *Blue Angel* was a whaleship, and someone said whales might be in the bay.

"Captain Hart! Will there be whales in the bay tomorrow? I have never seen a whale before."

Charles Hart considered William's question and laughed, "I am not sure if they will enter Table Bay with all the whaleships anchored here. I must have seen twenty ships this afternoon. There were a lot of British ships as well."

William looked disappointed.

Charles said, "We will see many whales as we cruise to Port Elizabeth. Mind you, Miss Peters, I forgot to mention when we offered you accommodation on board that if we encounter whales sounding along the coast, we will hunt them. I hope that is not an issue for you and William?"

Aggie smiled and said, "No, Captain. Not at all."

William's face lit up, and he asked, "Can I go on a whaleboat and throw the harpoon?'

"I'm afraid not, William. It takes years for a greenhorn to be competent in a whaleboat."

William interjected, "What is a greenhorn?"

"A new crew member, William, without any experience. Chasing whales is dangerous as they are monsters. If a whale's tail drops on a whaleboat, it can tear the boat apart. But you can watch the hunt from the *Blue Angel*. If we catch one, you can stand on the whale once the men bring it alongside. How about that?"

The boy was overjoyed, "Really! Stand on one! Do they float?"

Malone's Irish Pub, North End, Boston …
The room emptied as members finished their last drink and left in ones and twos. Michael Walsh sat next to Aiden Reid at the head of the table.

"A good meeting, Aiden. We are making headway now most of the men have jobs. We should be able to send twenty pounds to Cobh soon. They will need that money with the poor harvest this year."

Michael noticed that Aiden pulled a letter from his pocket and was deep in concentration as he read.

"Bad news?"

Aiden shrugged, "A letter from Braydon Kelly through the network. O'Shannessy gave it to me downstairs. Looks like the brothers in

Dublin have been reformed. He doesn't trust Cahill, who has taken Murphy's position."

"Danny Cahill is bad news!"

Reid tucked the letter away and said, "Don't say anything about it to anyone. For all we know, they may have contacts here. We need to think for a while."

"If the English are involved, they wasted no time helping the brothers reform."

"It would have happened without the English. They would not have stayed in a vacuum."

"Might be time for Braydon to get out and travel here. He could bring his family."

Aiden frowned and stood, "No, we need him there. We all can't leave our homeland if Ireland is to gain independence. At some point, they are going to need help."

Michael was taken aback, "Surely you would not return, Aiden. They would find you and string you up. The English have infiltrated the Brothers. We cannot trust them!"

Reid smiled, "I must be going, Michael. I need to do some planning before work tomorrow. A lot is happening at the docks."

Michael Walsh waved goodnight as he stood and moved to another group still finishing their drinks and talking.

Later, Reid talked with Biddie at home and explained what was decided at the meeting. After she was in bed, he sat beside a candle and read Braydon's message again.

Reid put the letter down and thumbed his chin as he considered the news. It was not clear if the English were involved in the resumption of operations by the brothers. But it looked like many more Irish boys would soon be put at risk. Danny Cahill had always wanted a leadership position but was easily misled by others. It would take time to organise a mission and find a suitable leader. The outcome would indicate if the English were involved.

But who was the man in the alley? Was he following, or was it a coincidence? If the man reappeared, he must somehow follow him and ascertain who he was. Whatever happened, Aiden Reid realised that being in Boston might not be as safe as he had believed.

South Household, Porting, Guildford, Surrey ...
Clementine sat at her desk and penned a letter to William.

Clementine Felicity Turner
C/- Porting
South Hill Road
Guildford, Surrey
England

Master William E Turner
Ewell Station
Via Grahamstown
Eastern Cape Province
Africa

Thursday 18 October 1827

Dear William

As I write this letter, I worry, wondering how you are. I still cannot and probably never will understand why our father sent my little brother so far away. In my heart, I can never forgive him for this, and I pray every day for your safety, and that blessings come to you as you try to understand what has happened.

You will have arrived at Ewell Station and be in Uncle Richard's and Auntie Sarah's safe care. You will be heartened that Katherine remains well and shows little regret for missing her mother and father. I found this strange initially, but I have found her to be a mature young lady and good company for me. As you know, we share a room and are still doing so at Porting. We keep up our sewing and often talk of you during our sessions.

You remember that the High Street house burnt down! Father has contracted builders to construct a new home on land he purchased beyond Porting and more than half a mile out of town. Walking down the High Street will no longer be so convenient, and the new location far from town will feel a little confined and isolated. However, that is what he decided, and so it must be.

Bethany's baby arrived in early September and is over a month old. They were in London for the birth, and I am sure they wished to be near Neville's parents. Father visited soon after with Ethel. It was a fine, healthy boy (called David – how predictable!), and Beth was also doing well. She finds the constant feeding of the baby tiring, but she is devoted to the child and is coping well. I am sure he will be one or two by the time you return.

Here is some news you will not have expected! Yes – Father married Ethel soon after you left for Africa and following our vacation at the Isle of Wight with the Earl and Countess of Fintelton. So you and I have a stepmother now. I am still adjusting, but Ethel is kind and forgiving (characteristics that I seem to lack!). So, pray that I will be charitable and accept her new family role. I think it is good for Marcia as she loves Ethel greatly, and I wonder if she remembers her real mother at all. Excuse me, as I am confused and saddened by the situation here.

Father tells us that he only sent you for two years. Is that what he told you? I am personally determined to keep him to his word. So be of good cheer, William. We are all keen for your return.

Thomas and Marrion will soon arrive in Greenwich as Marion is due with her baby in the first week of November. I will write and tell you of the outcome. Anne is due in the first week of December, so two more babies will join the family in the weeks ahead.

Please write and tell us how you are and what you have seen on your trip. I hope the voyage was uneventful and that you remained well. What is Grahamstown like? Is it as big as Guildford? Are there any native people near your station? Why do they call it a station – surely it is a farm? There is so much I wish to know about Africa.

I have added another page with some comments from Simeon, Madeline, Katherine, Rosalind, Marcia and Clare. I am sure Anne and Bethany will write to you soon. When I see Thomas in Greenwich, I will ask him to write. He is so busy that he probably has not had a spare minute.

Please, little brother, say your prayers each night and try to forgive Father for his actions. I know you are strong, and you will come home a man. I pray each night for your safety and miss you greatly.

Your loving sister
Clemmie

XXXX and many hugs
See attached good wishes from Simeon, Madeline, Katherine, Rosalind, Marcia and Clare.
PS: Jeremy is now walking, and we must put everything up, or he will grab and distribute things everywhere. I look forward to when Father will let me work in London with Victoria.

The Country Squire Pub, Guildford, England ...

Terry Spencer, Ralph Fenn, Peter Swamp and Aaron Hall were in a darts game when Terry decided he needed another drink.

"Drinks, boys?"

Ralph and Aaron declined, but Peter said, "A pint, please, Master."

"You've already had two, Swampy!"

"One more won't hurt, and I can drop you off from the cart on your way home."

"Agreed!"

Terry ducked across to Merryn at the bar, "Two pints please, Love!"

Swampy called, "Terry, your turn!"

With some urgency, Terry said, "I will be right back."

As Merryn pulled the pints, she looked up to find a tall stranger with a scarf around his neck covering his lower face. He stood beside the counter, rubbing his hands as if he was freezing. There was something familiar about the man.

Terry returned, picked up the drinks and glanced at the stranger. He went to walk away when he heard a familiar voice say, "A pint please, Miss!"

Stopping, Terry turned and put the drinks down on the bar. He reached over and pulled down the scarf, which revealed a smiling Leonard Webster.

Terry cried out, "My goodness, the academic is back. Welcome home, son!"

Terry hugged Leonard with a firm grip and said, "Good to see you, lad. I thought you were in Oxford?"

"I was, but I thought better of it. Ha, ha! There is no place like Guildford."

Before he could talk further, Merryn was around the front of the bar, hugging him and attracting the others' attention. They ran over, recognising their tall friend, and the conversation started earnestly.

"I could easily do the studies, but I was not interested. I don't think I am suited to Oxford. I got a room at the Fox and Hound for tonight and will visit the family tomorrow morning. I'm not sure my father will be pleased at all. So I need to think out my strategy tonight."

They all laughed and slapped him on the back. Swampy said, "Well, if he kicks you out, there is plenty of room at my place. You are welcome anytime, Leonard."

The tall young man was slightly overcome by this generous welcome, "Thank you, but I hope it won't come to that. But it is good to be back. Cheers!"

They all lifted their glasses and took a swig as other patrons who had come to know the quiet, tall young man approached to welcome him home.

After a great night of recollections and dart games, Peter and Leonard set off in the Swamp's cart. There was something on Leonard's mind, but he was unsure how to ask. He sat there quietly as Peter, in a jolly voice, accounted for everything that had happened while the lad was away.

"Yes, the house burnt down to the ground. No, that's not right! There were a couple of rooms left at the back. Mr Turner recovered all his important files. He was happy about that. But I can't understand why he sent little William away. Jess was annoyed as she liked the boy. She was unsure if she wanted to work for them anymore, but she stayed and is now happy. She says Mr Turner intends to bring him home in two years."

Leonard said, "He would have been better off keeping him home for two more years until he was nine. They don't take them into the Navy until they are twelve."

"I think they used to take them at eight, but that may have changed. I'm not sure, but William is a good kid. It was a bit of a tragedy, especially for his brother, Simeon. I haven't seen him smile since, and Clementine is the same. They must have been close, eh?"

"I'm sure they were."

Both Leonard and Peter were quiet for a few minutes. Young Mr

Webster was trying to gain the courage to ask, but Swampy decided to start.

"Don't you want to know how Jessica is?"

"Jess. Yes, I do!"

"She is over the Hotspur thing – thank goodness. But I think she is still rather fragile. A thing like that for a girl can be quite shattering. She is another one who has lost her smile and confidence."

Leonard needed time to think about that. He sat there and mulled it over.

Peter could see the worry on his face, "Leonard. I'm Jess's brother, and I have always kept an eye on her. I have seen the way you sometimes look at her."

Leonard immediately sat up straight and coughed a couple of times.

Peter was keen to ask but decided to be as subtle as he could, knowing he did not have the same way with words as Leonard.

"I don't want to intrude or upset you, but can I ask if your return to Guildford has anything to do with Jess?"

Leonard sat there and continued to mull it all over in silence. Peter decided he would wait for an answer. It took nearly two minutes.

"I am a simple kind of person, Swampy, and I haven't ever been interested in girls, but when I met Jess, I could never forget her. So, to answer your question, the answer is yes."

Swampy looked at Leonard, and his face gleamed. He said, "I couldn't be happier if something happened between you two, Leonard. Let me know if I can be of help. Of course, I can keep a secret!"

They were passing the Tunsgate on High Street when someone walked out beside Leonard and said, "What couldn't you be happier about, Peter?"

Beside him stood Jessica Swamp and her mother. Mrs Swamp said, "I am glad you finally got here, Peter. I thought you had forgotten us. We were about to start walking."

Both Peter and Leonard were startled. Peter recovered first, "Just delayed a fraction, Mother. I had to check one of the cartwheels, and Leonard gave me a hand. It's tight now."

Peter grinned at Leonard but saw how rigid his friend had become.

Mrs Swamp complained, "About time I say …" as she noticed Jessica staring up into the face of the man beside Peter on the cart.

He said, "How are you, Jessica."

Jess stood there and said, "Well, thank you. I thought you were in Oxford. Why are you back here, Leonard?"

Peter said, "He missed…!" He looked at Leonard's horrified face and continued, "missed our games of darts."

Jessica smiled and said, "Is there room between you two boys for me?"

Leonard opened his mouth, but nothing came out. Peter quickly replied, "Yes. Leonard, give her a hand up, will you!"

While they talked, poor Mrs Swamp was struggling at the rear of the cart. Peter jumped over the seat and helped her onboard. Jessica snuggled between Peter and Leonard and asked, "Now tell me, why did you return to Guildford?"

Leonard, who had regained his countenance, said, "I decided Oxford was not for me? I need a more hands-on occupation."

"You know we have passed your parent's place. Are you taking a room somewhere else?"

"I haven't told Father yet, and I'm keen not to displease him. He had his heart set on me finishing at Oxford. I took a room at the Fox and Hound and will let my parents know I am back tomorrow morning. The conversation might be a bit uncomfortable."

Jess said, "Better than that, why not come to dinner at our house tomorrow night, and we can discuss what you should say. Peter, Mother and I will help. You need to think this out carefully. Isn't that right, Peter?"

"I couldn't have suggested anything better. We will see you tomorrow night then at six thirty. Farmers eat a bit earlier." Jess smiled, and Leonard hopped out and continued walking with the cart. He said, "Thank you, I would be honoured."

The young man walked along beside the cart as if in a daze. Jess gently said, "Leonard the Fox and Hound is in the other direction."

"Of course. My mistake. Goodnight, all!"

He stopped, watched the cart move off and walked back down the High Street towards the Fox and Hound. After twenty yards, he turned and looked back, finding Jess's smiling eyes meeting his immediately. He waved, and she waved back.

British Army, Grahamstown Barracks, Eastern Cape Province (South Africa) …

Richard Turner opened the door and faced the Sergeant at the desk.

"Good morning, Sergeant Foreman. I was wondering if the mail shipment had arrived from Port Elizabeth?"

"Morning, Mr Turner. It has! But we have changed the delivery. Now, it all goes direct to Mr Kuipers's shop."

"The Ironmonger!"

"Yes, Sir. Mr Kuipers has agreed to set up a Post Office shop next to his. It has not been built yet but should be soon. A special counter is inside his ironmonger's shop until the Post Office is built. Grahamstown will have its first Post Office."

"When did this all commence – it wasn't there the last time I was in."

"No, Sir. Only last week. The Captain and Mr Kuipers have been working on this for some time. He felt distributing the mail through a Post Office was more appropriate."

Captain Hargreaves was passing and said, "Grahamstown is growing, Richard. We needed a Post Office. How is the house building going?"

"Morning, John. Nearly finished. I have most of the stone cladding up, so I should be able to hold off any angry natives if they invade." Richard smiled at his humour.

"Probably a good move. We have heard from Nkosi that the tribes across the Fish are gathering. Because the son of Chief Bhule was a member of that raiding party, anger was growing in the tribe and some of the other tribes. Nkosi thinks they will come south for some revenge. I have a patrol out checking the Fish for anyone coming across and will keep rotating the patrols for the next few months. So, your stone cladding might become important."

Richard scratched behind his ear and said, "Living here is like returning to feudal times. I wonder what the natives would think if they saw a knight in shining armour?"

John Hargraves laughed, "Probably not much. They are not interested in our history. They feel this is still their land. I will send riders out to warn all the settlers if anything is reported."

"Thanks, John. I'm off to Kuipers."

"Richard! We are having some folks over for lunch after church on Sunday, including your neighbours, the Smits. How about coming and joining us for a meal? We will need to support each other if this native backlash develops. Now that Sarah has gone home, you need some company besides yourself."

"Sounds good. I will be there. It will be nice to spend some relaxed time with you and Thelma again."

He waved as he walked back towards the township centre, heading for the ironmonger's shop.

After visiting the new post office desk, Richard headed to Balma's hotel and the dining room. He thought he might have some morning tea while reading the letters he received. Gaining a comfortable chair beside a window, he thumbed through the seven envelopes while waiting for his coffee and cake.

There were several bills, a letter from Katherine, one from Jonathan and the most important was from Sarah. He looked at the postmark and saw it was from Teneriffe. That was strange as he thought she would be in England by now. Opening the letter, he read:

Sarah Turner
Sailing Ship 'Nomad'
Tenerife, Spain

15 September 1827

Dear Richard

I am writing from the Hotel Gran Santa Cruz in Tenerife, where we were given accommodation while the Nomad docked for repairs. As we crossed the Atlantic from Africa to Spain, the weather was awful, with strong winds and damaging high seas. The ship was damaged, and the captain decided repairs were necessary before continuing. The repairs are now completed, and we will board tomorrow before heading for Southampton.

I could have rebooked with another ship but decided against this as the repairs were originally to be completed in two weeks. This was extended by another two weeks, and now we are ready to sail again. I should be at Guildford with our daughter, Katherine, by the time you receive this letter.

I decided to write as you probably expected my arrival in Southampton to be at least a month earlier. I am sure that Jonathan will have sent William by now. The horrible weather has delayed shipping across the Atlantic, and some ships have been wrecked with much loss of life. I am thankful for being spared from a disaster, which also influenced my decision to stay in Tenerife while the weather cleared. We should pray that William and whoever accompanies him have a safe trip.

I miss you, dear Richard, but I feel my decision to return home was for the best, as if I had remained, I would have become most depressed. I look forward to being with our children again and will write soon after I arrive in Guildford.

Tenerife is a delightful city, and the people are warm and friendly. There is much to see, and I have made many friend-ships with some of the other English families. On your return to England, I suggest you plan to break your voyage here for at least a week and enjoy the port and the surrounding country.

It is approaching six o'clock, so I must ready myself for our final dinner ashore. Please give my regards to George and the Mbeki Brothers and their wives. Also, write to me and tell me whether Jane has had her baby yet. Please give my regards to the other settlers and the storekeepers in town.

I will pray for your safety and progress at the station. Keep safe and write to me soon.

Your loving wife
Sarah

Richard sat back, thinking of his wonderful wife. He had not fully appreciated her until she was gone – without her, it was a lonely existence. 'What we English men do to achieve financial security!'

"Richard! Richard, can you hear me?" A yell broke into his thoughts.

Richard turned his face to an over-alert Lieutenant Freddie Sanderson standing above him.

"What is it, Freddie?"

"The natives are on the move. We have heard they crossed the river near Mpeko and are making for the mountains. Estimates put them at more than five hundred warriors."

With Richard sitting there and not answering, Freddie became impatient.

"You must get home, pack your bags and head for Port Elizabeth. Send all your Khoikhoi home and tell the Mbeki boys what is coming. Although I think they will already know! Nkosi will not let these northerners slaughter them."

Richard asked, "Do we know what these men want?"

"Revenge, of course. It is alright for the Xhosa to come across the Fish and murder settlers and steal their cattle. But as soon as they suffer consequences, they feel they must avenge it. They are completely unhinged!"

"I will have a quick lunch and get moving. Is there a party heading out of here tomorrow morning?"

"Yes – be here by ten, and you can join them. I am off to tell everyone else in town to pack and be ready to move tomorrow morning. Take care, Richard."

Freddie did not wait for a response and moved across to a table where the Hoiters were sitting and explained the same message.

Richard took a deep gulp of his coffee and sat back, thinking about what Sarah had said. 'Perhaps Sarah was right. Was there a future here, or was he mad staying where there was a chance of being massacred? But what about William? What if they had arrived in Port Elizabeth? They must be warned before they leave for Ewell Station. Damn, Jonathan, for exposing his young son to this danger. Damn Him!'

Chapter 19

Webster Household, Guildford, Surrey ...

"What do you mean you decided that Oxford was not for you?" Mervin Webster sat there, infuriated by his son's decision. "You know how much I have worked over the years so you and Betty could succeed in life. I thought you might become an attorney or an engineer. What are you going to do?"

"I am not sure yet, father, but I am not interested in remaining at Oxford, where I feel life is passing me by. I want hands-on work, something that takes my interest."

Gwendolen and Betty sat at the breakfast table, not daring to enter the discussion. Mervin Webster was fuming, and Gwendolen wondered if her husband's anger might give rise to another serious health turn.

She plucked up courage and was about to ask when her son spoke first.

"Father, calm yourself. I may return to Oxford one day, but at present, I am not motivated to study. I feel guilty wasting your money when my heart is not in it. I respect your advice and can see your wisdom, but I am a man now and must make my own decisions. Can we not discuss this as friends? When anger becomes involved, wisdom vanishes from the discussion. Now that I have realised what I want in life, I would appreciate your advice on achieving a vocation. I have not set out to anger you."

Gwendolen wasted no time and suggested, "Mervin, I think Leonard is being most reasonable and is trying hard to ensure your father-son relationship is not damaged. He is full of goodwill towards you. Why would you be angry with him when he shows his respect and asks for your advice?"

Mervin sat there and said, "I am not angry!"

Betty smiled, "Good, Father! Now, eat up your porridge and think about what Leonard proposes. I think he is being most sensible. Surely, working for a few years will help his search for fulfilment. There is no substitute for real work."

Mervin glared at his daughter and took another spoonful of porridge. The news from his son at breakfast had ruined his day, and it would take some time for him to digest it. He worked hard so his children could enjoy a privileged position in society. Now, his son wished to join the working classes. What was the point in striving for success?

After several more spoonfulls of porridge, he sat up and said, "Leonard, my reaction was hostile, and I apologise. It is just that I had hoped you would attend Oxford and make us all proud."

Leonard was about to say, 'Are you not proud of me now, Sir?' But he remembered what Jess and her mother had said last night, "Whatever you say to him, make sure it does not agitate him. He will be bitterly disappointed and need time to adjust to your desire." Leonard rephrased what he would say.

"I want you to be proud of me as well, Father. Give me a few weeks, and I will try out some jobs and see what develops. May I move back home, please?"

Mervin readily answered, "Yes, my son. Your old room is ready for you. We shall talk again of this after dinner tonight over a sherry."

"Thank you, Father." He stood and came around the table, knelt and hugged his father.

"There, there, my boy! You have always been welcome here and always will be in the future."

Ewell Station, Outside Grahamstown, Eastern Cape Province ...
Richard Turner woke to George shouting from the verandah. Pulling on his dressing gown, he opened the window and peered out.

"Baas, the Xhosa are all gone!"

Richard replied, "OK, George. I will be right down."

He could not see the far pasture behind the house, so he quickly pulled on his clothes and rushed outside.

"What do you mean about the Xhosa, George?"

"Come, and I show you." George walked off around the house and pointed past the far pasture.

"There is no one there, Baas! The people, the cattle, the goats, the chickens, even the huts are empty. They must have left last night."

As Richard ran, he called George, "Come with me! Come and saddle your horse, George. I am going out to the Xhosa camp. You get some help and take all the men and women back to town. Use the cart and the wagon and take the other horses. They can take all the chickens – they can have them. The Mbeki brothers have let us down – not telling us about a raiding party. The Xhosa must be close if the brothers gave no notice and left last night. You must get the Khoikhoi to safety."

Richard led Maisy across to the homestead and tethered her. He rushed inside and grabbed his hat, pistol, musket and loading pouch. Locking the front door, he mounted Maisy and galloped towards the far pasture and the Xhosa camp. The corral gate was wide open, and there was no sign of any livestock. It was the same story inside the huts. They had taken everything. Walking across to the main fire pit, he felt the black soot and found it cold. So, no fire was lit last night. They were keen that no one saw them go. Were they protecting themselves from the raiding party, who must be close?

Returning to Maisy, Turner mounted and pulled his horse toward the Fish River. He knew if the raiding party was coming, it would be from the north. Digging his spurs in, Richard galloped Maisy towards the northern edge of the station. He thought the Mbeki brothers could not drive their cattle that fast. He may be able to catch them and discuss this.

After a half hour of searching along the property's northern border, there were no signs of the cattle or the tribe's people. Could they have gone south away from the raiding party? That was not advisable as they would need to cross other settlers' land and probably would be blocked. They must have left early last night and headed for the wild country near the Fish. You could hide anywhere there and not be found for weeks.

Richard removed his wide-brimmed hat and wiped the sweat from his forehead. He decided on a ten-minute ride towards the Fish to see if he could find a trace of where the Mbeki had gone. Around a mile past his property's northern border, he came across a large campsite. It was not the Mbeki, as it was too large. There must have been nearly a thousand men to make the track coming to and leading away from the campsite. He counted more than sixty burned-out fire pits across the meadow. Richard dismounted and found the ashes were slightly warm. The native raiding party was near, but where?

Quickly mounting Maisey, he galloped off to the south back to the Ewell Station homestead. There was no sign of any life here at all. George had done a good job, and the men and women were all gone. A gust of wind blew in his face, but he was sure he heard a musket crack pierce the noise of the wind. He stopped his horse and listened again. "Steady, Maisy." There was another crack and then repeatedly. They were shots, and now he could also hear men screaming something like war cries. The natives must be attacking the Smits, his neighbours between here and Grahamstown. He was cut off from the town. Damn – that was all he needed.

He suddenly realised he was sitting on a horse in the wide open. A clear target if any natives were watching. He dug the spurs into Maisy and galloped to the homestead's front verandah. Stripping off her saddle and blanket, he threw them through the front door, untied the horse, and carefully took off the bridle and reins. Now she was free, he slapped her rump and shouted, "Get away from here, girl! Get going!"

The horse seemed to understand and galloped back towards the native's corral.

Richard rushed inside, locked the front door, and took the saddle and other equipment to the mudroom. He collected his guns, climbed the stairs, and tried to focus on the Smits' place through the side window of his bedroom. The musket fire was continuous, and Richard realised that Elias must have his sons with him to protect the property. He could not see the homestead clearly because of some trees but could hear the wild cries from the attackers who must have circled the building.

Richard had never been so alarmed. What Sarah predicted was happening, and he was alone at the homestead and would probably be the next target of this bloodthirsty war party. Taking a couple of deep breaths, Richard calmed himself. What should he do? Work through your defence plan, Stupid! He suddenly remembered the plan for a native uprising. What was the first step? Lock and bar the doors. He raced downstairs to the kitchen storeroom, pulled out all the door bars, locked every external door, and barred them. Shutters next! Running upstairs, he checked each side of the house for signs of natives and saw nothing. Clear! He unlocked the front door and rushed along the verandah, circling the house, closing and baring every shutter. As he worked, he could hear the continuing musket fire and various cries of anger and pain coming from the Smit's property. They were putting up a stubborn fight, but he knew no one could hold off that many natives for long.

Once inside again, he circled the ground floor, closing the inside shutters and locking them. He checked they were all secure before retreating upstairs. He followed the same procedures again, closed all the shutters, and checked the locks. The house was now secure and ready for battle. The problem was he was alone.

Suddenly, the shooting and the native war cries ceased. There was complete silence. Richard decided to crawl up into the ceiling through the access point in the fourth bedroom and take a look from the roof. He had installed a roof hatch in case there was a need for repairs. Shoving his guns and pouch up into the ceiling cavity, he stood on a chair and pulled himself into what might be called an attic. Because the house was large, it required a significantly sloped roof. The ceiling space was spacious and high. Due to the roof's pitch, the hatch was out of reach. He lowered himself back into the bedroom, tied some rope to a chair, secured the rope's end between his teeth and pulled himself up into the ceiling cavity again. Then he pulled the chair up and replaced the ceiling access cover. Balancing on the chair, he unlocked the hatch and opened it slightly enough to see the Smit's house.

Elias was standing in the front yard with a white flag. There were around twenty dead or injured natives around the house, but more than five hundred warriors crouched, ready to attack. A lone native had walked forward and talked with Elias.

From Elias' hand and arm movements, Richard could see that he was telling the natives to leave. Suddenly, a spear was thrown over the head of the native and curved down, piercing through Elias' chest. He fell backwards to the ground, and immediately, the firing recommenced.

The native near Elias fell, but several other natives ran from the side of the house and barged through the front door, followed by thirty to forty others. The firing had ceased, and Richard could hear the cries of victory. A tall native with a long knife bent over Elias and quickly cut through his neck and removed his head. He held it high for all the other natives to see. There was a loud cheer as the native who killed Elias took a bow of honour. Richard felt sick in his stomach, thinking it may be him next.

Then screams started coming from the Smits' house, and he prayed for Elias' wife, Margarete, and their daughter, Trude. After ten minutes, the screams slowly subsided, and the men exited the house. The natives gathered wood and carried it into the house. Once satisfied, some natives gathered kindle, and within ten minutes, the house's interior was covered in flames, the warriors jubilantly dancing, celebrating their victory.

"Have your celebration now, black men, but you won't live much longer once the army arrives." Richard had always been sympathetic towards the indigenous people's plight. He had helped where he could. After seeing firsthand what had happened next door, his generosity turned into rage.

Elias Smits' wife, daughter and five sons were all dead and being burned inside their home. He shuddered at what must have happened to the defenceless women. He could not forgive this. These animals deserved no pity. He would make sure they suffered for this. His only hope now was the army, but where were they? He must plan to remain alive to take revenge on these animals.

Richard gritted his teeth and thought, 'I pray my defence plan works!'

Turner Mill, Guildford, Surrey ...
Terry Spencer lifted his head to answer the call from Jeb Hiscock.

"Hold on, Isaiah! I will be back in a minute." Terry climbed down from the grinder and walked over to Jeb.

The bakery manager stood there with a grim look, "A message from Aaron Hall. His mother is sick again, and he must look after her. With the father gone, there is no one else."

Terry's smile disappeared, "If only there was a daughter or relative, but they have no one."

Jeb nodded, "So I won't be able to lend him to you today, Terry. Sorry!"

"I understand. At lunch, I might duck home and tell Lydia. She can take a basket around. Perhaps cook them a meal for tonight."

"Good idea. I will ask Audrey to arrange for the church women to help with meals. I'm not sure if she will last that long. It is the consumption."

Terry rushed back to Isaiah Linton, who was helping him with a new part he needed moulded out of iron.

Jeb stood there gazing up at the huge machine that continually produced flour. It was the most important cog in the Turner Mill and bakery's processes. Without the Mill, they would once again be at the mercy of the river millers, who would charge twice the price per pound that the Turners charged. Terry needed help to keep the monster grinding. Jeb shuddered at all the job losses if the mill were ever to shut down. He must mention this to Mr Turner.

Porting, Guildford, Surrey ...

Robert carefully took Anne's hand as she climbed into the coach.

"Thank you!"

Robert grinned, "Nothing but the best for my wife. We shall take it slowly and ensure you rest fully at Epsom tonight. I am keen to see how your cousin, Oliver, has developed the hotel there. I hope he has saved us his best room."

"Whatever it is, Robert, it will be sufficient."

Jonathan and Ethel stood nearby, ready to wave goodbye, "We shall take care of the place until you return. Don't stay in London for more than a week. We want the baby born in Guildford."

Anne grinned from the open coach window, "It will depend on Robert. Hopefully, he will not start his new role until after Christmas. Then we can all be together. That would be a change, wouldn't it?"

After a long but pleasant day on the road, Robert and Anne's coach pulled up at the front entrance of the Racing Horse pub at Epsom. Many people were entering and leaving the hotel.

"Looks busy – that's a good sign." Robert was down first and helped an awkward Anne onto the pavement.

"I'm glad they have a smooth pavement at the front of the hotel."

Robert agreed and paid a porter to bring in their luggage. There was a slight wait at the reception desk, so Robert found a quiet space where Anne could sit. He then moved over to the counter and started the registration process.

"Lady Leystead! Fancy meeting you here! It is good to see you looking so well."

A tall, well-dressed gentleman and a beautiful lady stood beside her seat. She focused more and recognised Mr Stephen Polkinghorne and Lady Fiona Green.

"Why, Stephen and Fiona. It is lovely to see you. Excuse me for not standing, but it has been a long day on the coach."

"Are you staying here tonight?"

"Yes. Robert and I are taking a break here and then on to London tomorrow. Here he comes." She pointed to her husband, who was returning from the reception desk. "Let me introduce you."

Robert was surprised by the couple joining them and spoke before Anne could make the introductions, "Hello, I am Robert South."

Anne said, "My husband, Robert. Mr Stephen Polkinghorne and Lady Fiona Green."

Robert shook hands with Stephen and lightly held Lady Fiona's hand as he nodded, "Are you staying here tonight."

Stephen said, "An honour to meet you, Sir Robert. Yes, we were at the races today and decided to stay overnight. Fortunately, the hotel staff found us a couple of rooms, so we can relax here tonight and take our time travelling to London tomorrow."

Robert agreed, "Good, good. Yes, I am about to take Anne upstairs for a rest before dinner. I say! Would you like to dine with us this evening? It would not be a late night as, given Anne's condition, we avoid late nights at present. How about 7.30 in the dining room? I have already made the booking and will change it from two to four."

Stephen, appearing relieved, sighed and said, "Yes, that is a relief. We definitely would!"

Fiona said, "Thank you so much. We tried booking the restaurant earlier, but they were full tonight, so we were about to book elsewhere."

Robert grinned and said, "We had an advantage. Anne's father is a half-owner of the hotel. Her cousin is the manager. If you dine with us, you should have good service tonight."

They all laughed and talked for a few minutes until Anne said, "Enough, everyone. I must lie down for an hour. I look forward to catching up with you at dinner."

Stephen said, "Which floor are you on? Let me assist you, please."

"First floor. Thanks, Stephen."

Anne said, "Oh, I hope Mary has the bed ready for me. Sorry, Stephen and Fiona, but I am so tired. This little junior has been kicking me all day."

They all chuckled as the party moved off up the stairs.

The Country Squire Pub, Guildford, England ...

Terry Spencer walked into the Country Squire an hour after he was expected. The boys playing darts were in a competitive game and hardly noticed his entry.

Peter Swamp turned and saw the exhausted Terry watching as he sipped a pint.

"You look like you have had enough work for one day. Terry. What delayed you?"

"Aaron Hall was meant to assist me today, but his mother is seriously ill. He will be unavailable for some time due to his mother's consumption. I had no one to help me, so I had to do what I could alone. It is still not finished, but I need a break."

Leonard said, "What's not finished?"

"The connection brackets on the grinder. One is loose and needs replacing. It is reducing our productivity. I need to replace it soon, or it might crack. If that happens, the whole mill will stop. Isaiah Linton made me a new one today, but I haven't fitted it yet. "

"I can give you a hand tonight. I am looking for something to do and would like to see the mill."

Terry considered Leonard's offer. He was unsure if the lad understood anything mechanical but was desperate for a helper.

"Have you ever repaired anything mechanical?"

Leonard smiled, "I worked once in a blacksmith's shop and enjoyed my time there. There were a lot of couplings that needed mending."

Terry was desperate and thought he would give Leonard a try. The job was too big for one man and must be finished by early morning.

"OK, I will give you a try. Let me get a meal, and then we can go back to the mill, and you can help. The job might take all night, so I hope you had no other plans."

Leonard was keen. He said, "We can finish the dart's game while you eat!"

Ewell Station, Outside Grahamstown, Eastern Cape Province ...
Richard Turner lay on a thin mattress in full darkness, trying not to move or make a noise. He could hear the natives outside the house trying on each door and window. The dead warriors were now on a cart and taken onto Richard's land and buried beside the dam. The natives stood there for nearly an hour before leaving the burial site.

He had thought through their movements and expected to hear them soon testing the house's defences. They would search for anyone on his farm. His only hope was the army's arrival, but there was no sign of them before he hid. When he saw the complete contingent of warriors walking towards his house, he decided it was time for his last option – the hidden room.

During the homestead's construction, Sarah made clear her fears of staying in Africa. Accepting her advice, he altered the house plans so that the fourth bedroom ceiling was lowered by two feet. He also lowered the hall ceiling on the ground floor by the same amount to disguise the change in ceiling heights. To the untrained eye, it was hard to spot. The lowered bedroom ceiling below the ceiling cavity floor allowed for a small hiding space under the cavity floor at the far end of the house. A large piece of the floor was cut out to be lifted off or pulled into place with wooden slots and blocks for locking within the hiding space. Access to fresh air was obtained from a small hole through the outside wall, which provided a sufficient flow to keep anyone from suffocating.

Richard was now positioned in the hidden room, praying the natives would not find him there!

There was a huge crash at the front door, and he assumed it must have been broken through. After that, he heard many men's footsteps entering the house. Crashes and bangs sounded from below as they rampaged through the house, destroying anything in sight. Then, there were footsteps coming up the stairs to the bedrooms. A silence came over the house as he imagined they were creeping from room to room. Suddenly, there was talking in the room underneath him. The conversation was more like an argument, but the group left, walking along the hall and downstairs, still speaking with raised voices. He had no idea what they were saying as it was a different dialect to the Mbeki Brother's language.

The silence continued for an hour until Richard heard singing from the front yard and the campfire smell. The natives had decided to camp there for the night, singing together in comradeship. It was a soft song with great harmony – almost beautiful if it was not such a frightening occasion. In his hiding place, the Englishman realised the natives were mourning their lost brothers and that he could now sleep for the night. They had not found him, and there was hope that the army would arrive the next day.

Turning on his side, he rested his head on a pillow that was part of the bedding and equipment stored in the hideaway. Soon, Richard realised that his bodily functions needed relief. Reaching for a box, he pulled out a tin and carefully arranged himself so nothing would be spilt. As he passed urine, there was a creaking sound from underneath, and Richard knew someone was in the bedroom below.

Taking care not to make any noise or movement, he froze. The creaking continued but subsided, so he felt the man had moved away. Breathing in relief, he kept still and thanked the good Lord that it was a warm enough night for him not to cramp. Richard smiled. He was amazed that he was praying so much and becoming religious. He questioned himself, 'Only when convenient for me, eh? Sorry, Lord!'

In the morning, he had one eye close to the air vent hole and watched as the dawn turned into full light. He could hear much talking among the natives who must have slept on the verandahs. There had been no sounds below him that he could recall since early yesterday evening. But now there was shouting in the front yard of the homestead, and he could hear the natives running around, possibly waking many of the other men.

The crash of muskets took him by surprise, and Richard knew that the army had arrived. He wondered how the natives had not detected the British army approaching. Turner's hopes rose, wishing the army a quick victory as he was keen to escape this hidden room. The sound of the constant musket fire gave him hope he might survive.

Richard carefully turned over on his side but unfortunately knocked over his can of urine, which spilled across the floor. He was sure it would leak through the ceiling and cursed himself for not using wax to seal any gaps.

A native within the house heard the faint tinkering as the tin fell over. It was the slightest noise but came during a lull in the firing. Sure that the noise came from upstairs, the black man decided to investigate. Creeping up the stairs to the first floor, he glanced carefully into each bedroom. The rooms were empty, and he was about to leave when a drip of urine fell on his cheek. Feeling the moisture with his fingers, he pressed his finger to his lips. Immediately, he knew it was urine. Looking up, he could see a small circle of wetness spreading on the ceiling. There was someone up there.

Suddenly, the muskets stopped firing, and a voice yelled, "This is the commander of the British Army. You are surrounded. Lay down your spears and walk forward and surrender."

A few minutes of silence followed, and then the Major called again, "If you do not surrender, then we will be forced to attack in force. Do you understand?"

A deep African voice replied, "Mr British Officer. Leave our land, or we will kill you all!"

Richard was unaware that the native was below him but was surprised when he heard a man rushing down the stairs. Richard thought, 'He must have either seen the dampness or felt a drip.'

While there was quiet below, he pulled his gun and pistol closer and checked they were primed and ready. He arranged himself so if they levered the floorboards up, he could shoot as soon as they appeared. He would take some of these natives with him to the hereafter!

The musket fire commenced again. There were wild screams from the attacking natives and cries of pain as the British muskets cut them down. Then, a huge canon blast roared, and he could feel grapeshot hitting the homestead's stone-covered walls. Some of the windows shattered, with glass spraying everywhere. Then another canon blast and more grapeshot hit the walls. The shouting voices of natives became cries of distress and sounds of misery as the grapeshot tore them apart. The scrapes and thumps of injured men being dragged into the homestead were audible, and cannon fire continued. During the next ten minutes, as the battle raged, the house was filled with moaning wounded. Richard was amazed to hear native battle cries as the black men sacrificed themselves against a technology far greater than theirs.

Suddenly, Richard heard stamping feet on the floor above him and the shouting of native men intent on finding him. A spear was run through the edge of the floor, and they tried to gemmy it up, but the wood locks held it in place.

Richard said, "My time is up!"

But a mighty blast knocked out half the bedroom wall beside his hiding place, and part of the roof collapsed. Some natives, hit by the roof, were screaming in pain, but the others sounded more determined to find the Englishman. One native fell on the floor above Richard, blood dripping through the floorboards. Richard moved aside from the blood flow and remained ready to shoot if they raised the false floor.

He Heard the order, "Charge!" Then, a wall of infantry swept through the dispersing natives, who were running for their lives. Still, he could hear clashes in the front and back yards. The sound of muskets and pistol fire was soon replaced by the spearing sound of bayonets finishing off the natives. While a growing quiet came from below, the men above Richard continued feverishly to jemmy up the floor.

The noise of infantry boots came up the stairs, and then firing occurred in the bedroom below. Richard could hear nothing until an infantryman put his rifle up through the ceiling access hole and shot one of the natives in the head. The others surrendered. The infantry then poured into the ceiling cavity and pushed the natives face down onto the floor.

Richard called out, "Help! British infantry, I am under the floor. Help me, please."

A familiar voice called, "I say! Mr Turner, is that you?"

"Yes, Freddie. If you could pass me a hammer, I can get these wooden locks out, and you can get the floor up."

"How do we pass it to you?"

"You use your rifle bayonet and gemmy it up."

"Righto!"

Soon, Richard was standing and looking at the smiling faces of his friends.

Freddie said, "My apologies about the damage to your house."

Richard hugged Freddie and said, "I'm alive. Thank God I'm alive!"

Racing Horse Pub, Epsom, Surrey ...

Anne was thrilled to find Lady Fiona accompanying Mr Polkinghorne in Epsom, "Lady Fiona, it is wonderful to meet with you again. I enjoyed your company at Fintelton very much. I have been in contact with Stephen in London, and he did not mention your growing friendship."

Fiona smiled, "We found each other good company and have seen each other occasionally. Stephen, of course, is extremely busy, and we meet when possible. The best times are when we are both in London."

"Well, Robert and I will live in London for the next three years while he is head of security for the Prince and Admiralty. We shall expect your regular company if that is acceptable."

Stephen asked, "No more voyages, Robert. You will become a landlubber for a while. Will you find that difficult?"

"Not at all, Stephen. Since we were engaged and married, the Navy has sent me continually on missions. I had always intended to give it up at some stage, and with the recent death of my elder brother, Hugh, I will inherit the title. Also, becoming a father has other responsibilities, so I may soon become a full-time landlubber."

It was clear that Robert had spent considerable time considering this. Surprised, Anne said, "That is welcome news, Dear."

"I was sorry to leave the Eastern Mediterranean as I was sure there would be action[43]. But on second thoughts, it may have been a blessing. I am home for my wife's support and the birth of our first child."

Fiona said, "A grand gesture indeed."

"Thank you, Fiona."

Anne was happy with these comments from Robert but wished to hear if Stephen had completed the forms sent to him.

"Stephen, if you don't mind me changing the conversation for a minute?"

---

[43] The Battle of Navarino was a naval battle fought on 20 October, 1827, during the Greek War of Independence (1821 – 1829) in Navarino Bay, on the west coast of the Peloponnese peninsula, in the Ionian Sea. Allied forces from Britain, France and Russia decisively defeated Ottoman and Egyptian forces which were trying to suppress the Greeks, thereby making Greek independence much more likely. It was the last major naval battle in history to be fought entirely by sailing ships, although most ships fought at anchor. The Allies victory was achieved through superior firepower and gunnery. Wikipedia

"Not at all, my Lady."

"Did you receive and sign all the forms I sent you on my last visit to London?"

"Yes, they have been signed, witnessed and returned to the attorneys. I fully understand the trustee position and will be honoured to work with you on this project."

"I hope it will only take a few years before a trustee is no longer required. But we must see what comes to play."

Fiona asked, "Who will Stephen be a trustee for?"

Anne swallowed and smiled, "A friend near her deathbed asked if I could recommend an honourable gentleman to be trustee of her estate until her son came of age. Given the size of the estate, she was keen to have her son learn about finances before he took control of the estate."

Fiona said, "I see. I think that is a wise decision. My late husband gambled away almost his complete inheritance except for a provision insisted on by my brother, who was aware of Harrold's deficiencies. I was not keen on living with my brother and his wife, so I am thankful for his wise advice."

Stephen added, "Many men do not have the talent for managing money. It is left to the initiative of the father and the son to listen and understand. Robert! I am sure you will relate to that."

Robert frowned but said, "Yes, I certainly do."

Stephen asked, "Lady Anne, I hope I will measure up to the responsibility placed on me as a trustee. At times, if I may, I will ask for your advice."

Anne smiled and confirmed, "I will be available, Stephen. As I said, I hope this will be a straightforward role."

Robert grinned at Anne and raised his eyebrows before casually glancing into his glass of red wine and then taking a sip.

"What is it, Robert?"

"Nothing, my Dear. We shall talk about it later."

In their room that night, Robert and Anne discussed the dinner conversation.

"Anne, have you briefed Stephen on the complete story about David Constance?"

"No, I saw no need. Stephen is intelligent and will refer anything controversial to me."

Robert sighed, "So he is unaware of David's mother's role and her claim for recognition from the family."

Anne looked straight at Robert, "Why, I thought there was no need to divulge this."

"It is quite possible that his mother has briefed him on the complete story and that if he complains to Stephen, he would be forced to open the whole can of worms again. He needs to understand all the facts before he meets David Constance. I agree with your view of his integrity, but I also can see that the man is just and fair. He may become hostile and support a counteraction if presented with a factual argument. I only say this as I had always hoped we could make a clean break from the matter."

Anne sat on the side of the bed, feeling the baby in her tummy and thinking.

"I see what you mean! This is why I need you with me, my Dear. I am not as strategic as you. I will brief Stephen soon after we reach London. You may attend if you wish."

Blue Angel, Bound for Port Elizabeth, Eastern Cape Province ...
As the ship tacked its way out of Table Bay, Aggie and William found themselves comfortably accommodated in Mr Jack Shelford's cabin for their journey. A hammock on one side of the cabin was strung up for the young lad. Silently, William stood as he took in the hammock's swing and how the canvas was supported at both ends by rope. Finally, he grinned, "This looks like fun."

The First Mate said, "The trick is climbing into the hammock, buddy. I suggest you allow Miss Peters to hold the hammock while climbing aboard. How about we give it a try?"

William assessed the hammock and proudly said, "I can do it myself!"

"Ok, let's give it a go! Show me how you will do it."

William pointed at the wall near the hammock, "I will climb up the wall and jump in."

"Go for it!"

William asked Jack, "What do you mean, 'Go for it'?"

"I mean, show me how you can jump in."

Aggie was watching the interaction and became concerned when

William scaled the wall. She noticed Jack was tense and ready to catch the boy.

As he jumped, Shelford kneeled on one knee and held out his arms, predicting what would happen. William jumped with arms outstretched, hitting the canvas on the side and rolling over. He spun off and landed safely in Jack's arms.

Aggie clapped, breathing a sigh of relief. William was confused by the clapping as he had failed miserably.

Standing the lad up, Shelford said, "Watch this, Will." He stood beside the hammock, put both hands behind himself, pulled the hammock's side below his buttocks and carefully pushed his rear into the canvas. Once in, he gently turned and lay down.

William stood beside him, saying, "But the hammock is too high for me to do that."

"Correct – so we will adjust it."

Shelford hopped out, placed William beside the hammock, and adjusted it to the correct height. The boy quickly imitated Jack's actions and found himself comfortably lying within a few seconds.

Jack told Aggie, "If you need anything, let me know. See you at dinner."

With that, Jack was gone.

Aggie asked, "Are you happy with your hammock, Will?" All she could hear was snoring. They both laughed, which was a turning point for Aggie, as it was the first time they had laughed together since leaving Guildford.

Harting, St James's Square, St James, London …
The coach arrived at around six in the evening, with the light fading quickly. Anne was ushered in by her maid and the Harting staff, assisting her to a first-floor double room.

"But this is the countess's room, Mary! I can't stay in here. What if she arrives unexpectedly?"

Mary replied, "Staines has predicted your protest and advises the countess requested that you and Lord Leystead have these rooms. Staines asked me to show you this message from the countess."

Anne took the note and read quickly, "She says that in my condition, she requires Lady Leystead to remain on the first floor in the rooms she would normally use. It goes on with various other requests. I can see the countess has this all under control."

Mary frowned and asked, "She loves you, my Lady. That is not such a bad thing, is it?"

Later, at dinner, Anne and Robert enjoyed a splendid meal prepared by the cook, Mrs Wapples and the other kitchen staff. They were finally starting to relax after a long day in the coach from Epsom.

"Robert! We are very fortunate to have a home like this and staff to cook our meals. Most people would arrive home and then need to prepare something for dinner if there was food in the house. We are privileged indeed."

"I had never thought of it that way. I have always lived with servants providing for me. Even in the Navy, your meals are prepared for you. We should be more thankful, except we missed church today due to our travel."

"If you miss church, you can still pray and give thanks. We should do that together tonight and pray for our baby."

Robert considered this and replied, "I think we could do that."

Staines entered and passed a message to Anne.

"Thank you, Staines."

She read the message and said, "Mrs Constance is in bad health. She indicates that she is close to death and asks that I come tomorrow at ten o'clock. There are arrangements that she wishes me to be aware of. I would feel more comfortable if you would accompany me, Robert."

"What issues does she wish to discuss with you? Surely, we have done enough. Anyway, I must visit the Admiralty tomorrow morning, so I am afraid I must insist that Staines accompany you. We should have kept Henry Fletcher in our service. He would have been useful for this."

Anne was disappointed that Robert would not come and said, "Staines will do! May I have the carriage?"

"Of course. In your condition, I would not have you travelling around London in a rented carriage. If it is not raining, I will walk to the Admiralty."

Anne was interested, "Why are you needed at the Admiralty? I thought you had time off until after Christmas. I do, but Admiral Bird has matters he wishes to discuss."

"Not another mission, Robert. You must be here for the birth! Please, please don't accept another mission."

"I can assure you, Anne, that if they ask me to take another mission and miss our son or daughter's arrival, I will refuse, and if they force the matter, I will resign. There, let that put an end to it. I remain with you until you and the baby are safe and well."

He stood and walked around to her chair, knelt beside her with his arms around her shoulders and kissed her gently on the lips. A smile flickered on Anne's face, and she whispered, "I wish I were not so big and unattractive."

He whispered back, "My dearest, Anne. I have never found you more attractive than what you are tonight. I love you with all my heart. How about we move out into the parlour, and you can have some tea while sitting beside me? I might have some coffee and liqueur."

Anne extended her arms to him, and he lifted her from the chair. As they walked, Robert kept his arm around her and kissed his wife on the cheek.

Blue Angel, Bound for Port Elizabeth, Eastern Cape Province ...
Around midday on the Monday, William looked up at the call from the lookout, "Thar she blows!"

Immediately, all the crew were focused on the lookout's arm pointing northeast. Some crew climbed halfway up the rigging for a better look.

Captain Hart shouted at his First Mate, "What do you see, Mr Shelford?"

"A pack of about twenty, Captain."

"Any sperm among 'em?"

"We are too far away, Sir. But I suggest we close on them before other whalers see 'em."

"I agree. Mr Cutts, set a course for those whales and tell me when we are close. Mr Shelford, get the men ready for a hunt."

"Aye, Sir."

Standing beside Miss Peters, Oscar Leahy said, "William will see some whaling today. I will be interested as I have never seen the full process before."

Aggie asked, "I hope they don't kill the mother whales with calves.

That would be a shame."

"There are millions of whales out there, Miss Peters. It would be hard ever to eradicate them. However, I am sure they avoid the mother whales." Oscar stood there with a false grin, wondering if that was true.

Men ran and searched for their gear while others in the whaleboats placed equipment strategically. Sammy Flemming rushed past carrying a strange-looking third of a beer keg. William ran after him and asked, "What's that, Sammy?"

Fleming shouted back as he jumped into a whaleboat still held by the davits, "It's a water keg, Will. It gets hot out there, and we share the water around."

Sammy placed the water keg at the rear of the boat, climbed over thwarts to the bow, and checked the latch between the harpoon and whale line was secure. Other men joined him as his whaleboat would be the first to be launched. William ran from the port to the starboard gunrail to see where the whales were. He could see a pod of the mammoths breaking the surface some two hundred yards ahead.

He waved to Aggie, "Come see – they are huge!"

Miss Peters and Mr Leahy were soon beside him, and they wondered how men could secure a whale twice the size of the whaleboats.

The captain had the *Blue Angel* headed into the wind and shouted, "Lower away!"

William ran across to the port, watching Sammy's whaleboat lowered into the water. As it hit the water, the boat header mate, Merve Gates, used a flask to pour seawater into the whale line tubs. Men were hauling up the mast and raising the canvas sail. William was fixated on the activity in Sammy's boat, a sea of preparation, with each man knowing his role.

"Why don't the oarsmen row the boat after the whales?"

Oscar Leahy said, "I think they want to approach as quietly as possible. They can avoid alerting the whales from the splashing of oars."

Quickly, five whaleboats were sailing towards the lolling pod. Shelford called to the captain, "I can see at least two sperms, Captain."

"Aye, Mr Shelford, this could be a great hall." Then, with a grin, he said, "Perhaps young William has brought us luck!" He and Shelford laughed as the whaleboats closed on the whale pod.

Connie Hart and Mae came out with some drinks and cakes for their visitors. "This is a special from the cook. We usually only get cakes while in port. So, Mr Leahy, Aggie and William, you are receiving a treat today." As Connie took some cake, she continued, "Mae and I don't mind joining you."

William took some cake and said, "Thank you! Mrs Hart, how long before the whales come alongside?"

"They must catch them first. I would not expect any alongside until mid-afternoon. As you will see, the whales can fight for a long time before they give in. I have seen some Sperm whales fight for ten to twelve hours, and some never give up, and the headsman must cut the whale line and let it go."

William answered, "I hope they catch some today."

Approaching Glouster Place, Mayfair, London …
As Lady Leystead and her butler, Staines, travelled towards Mrs Constance's house, the butler asked, "My Lady, what exactly is my role in this visit to Mayfair?"

Anne was reluctant to explain fully but understood that Staines required specific directions.

She said, "Your role, Staines, is to protect me. I am unfamiliar with the Constance household and have only met the mistress recently. Your presence will ensure propriety and ensure I have support in case it is needed. I will ask you to wait in the foyer, but keep an ear open if I call you."

"I understand, Ma'am. Sir Robert is aware of your visit here?"

"Yes, Staines."

Anne understood Staines's question. He was attempting to clarify whether this was an approved or discreet visit. She must ensure that the butler knew there was nothing underhand here.

"Staines! I asked you to accompany me because Sir Robert was due at the Admiralty this morning. I also considered you preferable, Staines, as I trust you. It would be best if this visit is not discussed."

"I understand, my Lady."

Arriving at the address, Stained helped Lady Leystead from the carriage and across the pavement to the front door. He used the knocker, and once the door opened, he announced to the maid, "The

Viscountess of Leystead for Mrs Constance."

"Please come in. Mrs Constance is expecting the Viscountess."

Staines stood back and let Anne pass. Then, the maid tried to close the door before Staines could enter.

Anne quickly changed this misunderstanding.

"Excuse me, but if Mr Staines could wait for me in the foyer, that would be appreciated."

"Certainly, Lady Leystead."

Anne quickly surveyed the foyer as Staines entered and sat at the side of the entry room. It was exquisitely decorated with a light creamy wash with fresh flowers adorning a medium-height polished console. Two paintings, one on either side of the room, matched perfectly, giving the room a warm, welcoming feeling. The hallway was well-lit and wide, with several doorways leading into the standard downstairs rooms. It was not overdone but sophisticated and attractive. Anne reflected that the colour scheme and decorations were similar to the estate house at Wimbledon that Mrs Constance was required to live in.

"If you would follow me, please, Lady Leystead."

"Tell me, where will I be meeting Mrs Constance? I need to advise my man here."

The maid smiled and said, "You are in no danger here, Lady Leystead. You will meet Mrs Constance upstairs in her study, which adjoins her bedroom. Her illness has progressed, and she only has the strength to move to the study. Her maid is readying her now. If you would follow me, please."

Anne nodded, and they walked to the stairs.

The maid led Lady Leystead into a tastefully furnished study. Anne could see Katherine's touch again on the colour scheme. She took a seat and enjoyed the room. The door adjoining the bedroom opened, and a feeble-looking Katherine Constance entered with the help of her maid.

"Please don't stand, Anne. I will seat myself, and we can talk. My attorneys advise that Stephen Polkinghorne has signed all the required trustee documents. Thank you for helping me to set this up. It has set my mind at rest that David will not be able to waste his inheritance, at least for the next ten years."

"As I explained at our last meeting, Stephen is a mature, sensible man and will honour his commitment. He has become a good family friend."

"Does he know of my situation?"

"He knows enough to carry out his duties soundly."

"Good! Will you have some tea?"

"Thank you, that would be pleasant."

Katherine rang the bell, and her maid returned. Once the tea was ordered, she gazed at Anne for a few minutes, not saying anything. Anne wondered what she was thinking.

"You will be glad to know that I had a doctor here when I signed the documents for the trustee. I also signed a document that stated I was medically competent. The doctor confirmed this in writing and signed the document. So, if Fanny tries to set aside the trusteeship, she will fail."

"How is your health, Katherine?"

"Not good. I do not venture from the house anymore. You are my first visitor in a week."

"Surely, David visits!"

"No, I have forbidden him to come. He does not know about this place. He thinks I have rooms in Hammersmith. He will know soon enough after I die."

"Would it not be kinder to have him here with you? He will want to see you before you die. You are his mother, and he will have great affection for you."

"No, you do not understand. David has never seen much of me because of my nightly pastime. I have not been like a normal mother. We tolerate each other, and I am sure he feels I neglected him. That is why he is far closer to Fanny than to me. It is best if it is left that way."

Anne said nothing, as she had no idea how to address such a problem. Soon, the maid brought the tea. Anne asked, "Would you mind serving my man a cup of tea, too? Mr Staines is a good man."

"Yes, Ma'am. It will be done."

Katherine asked, "You have returned from Guildford. It must be good to have Robert at home?"

Anne broke out in a smile, "It is wonderful. We have shared so much since he returned. When we are together, we find it hard to stop talking. He has become my window to the world."

Katherine and Anne talked over their tea and enjoyed sharing their experiences of childbearing and being in control of businesses in a man's world. Anne related about the manager of their Woking shop and how she was slowly convincing him about the development of their fashion business. Katherine talked about how she became the confidant of many men's private feelings.

"That is better than the old men I have been escorting over the last fifteen years. They continually bore me to death about their government business and their families. You would shudder at some of the business they tell me about. I am so glad that I have transferred all that elsewhere."

Anne understood her comment and asked, "Where did you transfer the business to?"

"You don't remember what Mr Finchley said at Manifold & Stout?"

"No!"

Katherine looked disappointed, "The building I own at Chelsea! I have a discrete business that runs from there. We only deal with gentlemen well-placed in the government or the Lords. We avoid public and private company men as they are too independent. Government men know that if their liaisons are made public, they will be embarrassed or lose their jobs or seats. It is always wise to have an insurance policy. I will leave the rest to your imagination."

Anne recalled what Mr Finchley had said. Katherine was introducing her to a new world considerably darker than her own. She wished to hear no more about this.

"I see. What will happen to that business once you …. Well, who will inherit that?"

"No one – I have already sold the business. David will inherit the building. I briefed Stephen on it and advised that once I pass away, David should sell the building and the money invested."

"Are the new owners of your business aware of that?"

"Yes. They are already looking for alternative accommodation."

"Your world is far more complex than mine. I have given up most of my business duties for the time being. I will be resting until the baby comes."

Katherine understood, "It is a testing time, Anne. But the baby will arrive before you know it. Make sure you take care of yourself. You will be a far better mother than I ever was. I sometimes look back and feel I should have spent far more time with David. But in my line of work, that was not possible. I hope you will visit again. The doctor gives me, perhaps, three more months in this world. So, as I am becoming tired, I agree it is time for you to go."

Anne stood and thought about her discussion with Katherine. She said, "I will try to come back soon. So don't go downhill too fast."

Katherine laughed and replied, "It will depend on our good Lord!"

As she rode home, Anne contemplated how Katherine could sway a man. She was a good-looking woman who was cultured and a great communicator. In this world run by men, she had been forced into a career where she could succeed. Katherine Constance could have been a great asset to her country.

Blue Angel, Bound for Port Elizabeth, Eastern Cape Province …
Late in the afternoon, the Blue Angel slowly cruised towards the last whaleboat, secured against a dead sperm whale. The crew, who had fought a seven-hour battle with the whale before it finally succumbed, fastened it to the side of '*Blue Angel*'. Aggie and William could see the tired faces of the exhausted men.

Aggie said, "They will be glad to see their bunks tonight."

The First Mate, who stood nearby, said, "Sorry, Miss Peters, but the day has just begun for the crew. This is an unusual but good catch for us near Cape Town – a sperm whale and three large humpbacks are not something we achieve often. The crew will work all night and tomorrow before the whales are flensed and boiled. We should have you in Port Elizabeth by Wednesday evening if we can finish the whales by midday tomorrow."

"Thank you, Mr Shelford. We are thankful for your hospitality. William has enjoyed the day enormously. He will be dreaming about whales tonight."

Shelford smiled and said, "Better than that, the Captain and I have arranged a little surprise for him. Don't worry, as he will be perfectly safe."

The First Mate turned and called, "William, come over here, please."

"Yes, Mr Shelford!"

Jack pointed to a harness being lowered further along the deck. He could also see John Hart secured in a similar harness and nearly ready.

"What is happening?"

"See how John is being fastened into that harness. Here is yours. We will hoist you to starboard and put you on the cutting stage[44] above the whale. Always keep the harness on and hold the line attached to the ship. You can kneel and feel the whales from the cutting stage, then take a few steps on them. Be careful, as there will be plenty of sharks in the water, so stay on the whale nearest the ship. Once you see how slippery it is, you can carefully take a few steps along the whale. But not for long, as we must start the flensing."

"Wow!" William was off in a shot, and Sammy started fastening him up. Aggie was worried but held back and trusted Shelford's advice. She knew William was an excellent swimmer and that if he did fall in, he would stay on top of the water long enough to be saved. She missed hearing the mention of sharks.

Once fastened and fitted with gum boots, the boys were pulled up by lines attached by pulley to two spars. The spars were pushed out by crew above so the children could be lowered to the cutting stage just above the whales floating beside the ship. Men were already working on the closest whale, attaching the chain lines for flensing.

As his feet touched the cutting stage and the harness lines were slackened, William was careful to gain his stability first. He then kneeled, reached, and felt the whale's skin. It was an oily slime and slippery. He decided the sperm whale beneath him was the safest as it was flatter than the humpbacks.

Slowly, he followed John down and onto the whale's back.

"Hey, Will! Watch this."

John, laughing, ran for a few steps, jumped, swung in an arc, and swung back past Will and the cutting stage before returning to where he commenced. William smiled and pushed down with his feet, seeing how hard the skin was. His feet sank in a few inches before it sprang back. Conscious that this was a living creature a few hours ago, William decided to show some respect. He walked back carefully towards the

---

[44] 'Cutting Stage': To facilitate a stable standing platform above the whale's slimy and slippery skin whaleships carried a small rectangular stage between three and five planks wide which was lowered over the starboard side just above the dead whale, secured against the side of the ship. From here the mate could direct operations and the cutting in crew would use their long handled razor sharp spades to cut three foot wide slabs of blubber peeled from around the whales body. JS

cutting stage.

As the crew above tightened William's safety line, a large shark jumped up on the outboard whale and tore a huge mass of blubber from its skin. John was within ten feet of the vicious predator. Captain Hart immediately commanded John to be winched into the cutting stage. William was wide-eyed when he saw the shark and how violently it gashed the whale's side. Standing further along the ship where the guard rail had not been removed, Aggie took a sudden deep breath in horror, and it was all she could do to stop herself from screaming for William to come back on board. The shark ripped and tore at the blubber in a frenzy for five to ten seconds before slithering back down below the surface.

Sammy Fleming scaled down the ship's side, walked along the sperm whale and joined the boys. Aggie could see him pointing out different parts of the whale and explaining their functions. She was tense, wanting them back on deck, but she kept silent, trusting the crew and knowing this was a unique experience for Will.

Finally, both boys were allowed to stand beside Merve Gates on the cutting stage as he made the first cut into the sperm whale. The incision was long and exact, and William asked, "Why such a long slice?" Merve smiled and made a further cut parallel to the first and then a slice across the top. He called for the blubber hooks, lifted the slab end, and attached the hooks. Aggie was impressed as she watched the seaman explain each step in the process. Once finished, Merve signalled above and told the boys they would be lifted aboard. He shook hands with each before they rose above him, back over the guard rail, and down onto the main deck.

William freed himself from the harness, ran over to Aggie, Mae and Mrs Hart, and shouted, "Did you see me? I was on the whale. It is so big and slimy. Wow!"

He could not stop talking about what he had seen. Then he looked over the guard rail and saw the first piece of flensed whale blubber lifted onto the deck and pushed into the blubber store. Several men immediately started chopping the slab into small pieces.

William asked Mr Leahy, "What are they doing now?"

"I'm not completely sure, but I think they are preparing the blubber for boiling."

Connie Hart said, "You're right, Oscar, but you can see all that later, William. It's time to wash up and have dinner. The try-works will be boiling all night and most of tomorrow. So better if we have dinner before the smell gets too bad."

Aggie told William, "I think you need to thank Captain Hart for your adventure."

William nodded in agreement and rushed to Captain Hart, who was discussing matters with several crew members.

"Captain Hart! Thank you for allowing me to walk on a whale. I shall never forget it."

The captain stood up straight and looked down on the small boy.

"One day, William. Perhaps you might become a whaleman and join us. You were well-behaved and a credit to your family. Now, you go and enjoy your dinner."

William smiled, took a last look over the guard rail, and saw Sammy and Merve working hard on another block of blubber. He turned and ran after the others, took Aggie's hand and could not stop talking about standing on the whale.

Aggie was glad she had refrained from screaming when the shark chewed its way onto the whale. William was like the William of old. Suddenly, all his energy had returned, and that contagious smile once again appeared. She was thankful the William she knew had recovered.

Chapter 20

'Blue Angel' Standing Off Port Elizabeth, Eastern Cape Province ...

As the whaleboat pulled away from the Blue Angel, William, standing in the bow, frowned as his newfound place of security grew smaller in the distance. He saw Mrs Hart, John and Mae waving from the whaling ship. Returning the wave, he smiled and moved his arm madly, regretting the loss of his new friends so quickly.

Sammy, the boat header today, shouted to them, "Hold tight! Some waves are coming as we cross the bar. Not too big, but keep hold of the boat until we clear it."

William looked ahead and saw the disturbed water Sammy was talking about. There was no sign of a town yet, but they were coming around a sandy point towards the mouth of a river. Some raised ground with low bushes above the beach blocked their view inland. The waves were small compared to the surf on the western coast at the *Riptide's* shipwreck. As the crew heaved on the oars, the whaleboat's sharp bow cut through the small waves and soon settled in the river's calm waters.

Aggie could see some warehouses alongside the pier and several other craft moored nearby. The wharf was almost deserted except for several natives resting in the shade of a lean-to. She wondered how settled this area was. She quietly said to Oscar, "It seems very quiet for a port! Will we be safe?"

Oscar Leahy grinned and said, "The natives on the pier look like Khoikhoi. They are friendly – it is the Xhosa who cause trouble. This area was Xhosa land until the Dutch settled here. They harbour much resentment, but Mr Turner will explain that better than I can. There is a fort up on the hill over there!" He pointed, "That's Fort Frederick. It was built at the turn of the century to deter the French from annexing this area. The fort houses a rotating garrison of Army troopers from Cape Town. The British Army Headquarters are at the end of the High Street near the fort. They will be able to tell us how to contact Mr Turner. The town is to the north along that ridge."

Aggie said, "I can't see the town!"

"It is only small and is hidden by trees. We should get off at the pier and climb that hill – you will see it from there. The river is the main water supply for Port Elizabeth."

"Oh!"

Oscar could see that Aggie was not impressed.

"Now, now, Aggie – you haven't seen Grahamstown yet. Remember, we are in settler country, and these outposts are in their infancy!"

Putting on a brave face, Aggie smiled, but William was off the whaleboat in a second when Sammy found a space at the pier. Mr Leahy followed William and called, "Hey! Hang on, William. You need to carry your bag."

Jack Shelford, who had accompanied the travellers ashore, assisted Aggie onto the pier and then passed her bag from the boat to Oscar. Jack then climbed up to bid them farewell.

"It's a short walk up to the township. I am glad you accompanied them, Oscar! It is a frontier town, but it should be safe. It is better with a man for protection. All the best, Aggie! William, you look after Aggie! OK!"

William asked Jack, "I thought you would stay for a while."

"Sorry, Will! We need to move on before the tide changes and head for Durban. Plenty of whales should be coming down the coast for us to catch. Then, we sail across the Indian Ocean to Geographe Bay on the west coast of New Holland for replenishment. After that, we go up to Batavia, where there are many sperm whales and humpbacks. Then it is around the horn and home to Nantucket."

"What is replenishment, Mr Shelford?"

"We buy fruit and vegetables, meat, milk and butter. All the American whalers head there as the produce is first class."

William's imagination was fired up, and he asked Aggie, "Can we go to Aggie? I want to catch some more whales?"

"No, William. You will be meeting your Uncle Richard here soon.

He will be expecting us."

William looked back at Jack, "Thank you, Mr Shelford, for helping us. I hope we meet again."

Jack smiled and shook Aggie's hand, saying, "Take care, Miss Peters." Then he was back into the boat, and Sammy had her pulled back and turned around before they headed for the *Blue Angel* at a fast pace.

Suddenly, Aggie was frightened. This place was foreign and uncivilised. She asked Oscar, "Will I get out of here alive, Oscar?"

Oscar grinned again and said, "I will ensure you do, Aggie. But first, we must contact Mr Turner and take rooms at a hotel until he comes."

As he watched the whaleboat speeding away, William said, "I will miss John and Mae. They were good friends, and Captain and Mrs Hart were generous and kind."

"They were good company, but you will make new friends here. Perhaps you might meet John and Mae again one day!"

Oscar said, "When you grow up, Will, I will be a Captain, and you can be my first mate. How about that?"

Bushy House, Teddington, London, England ...

The butler stood at the front of the house with several other staff lined up, ready for Robert and Anne's arrival. As the carriage pulled to a halt, he moved across the apron and opened the door. Robert descended first and let a footman help Anne down.

"Good morning, Lord Leystead. The Prince and Princess are looking forward to your visit. Lady Leystead, welcome! If you would both come this way." The butler indicated the mansion's front door and led them in. The staff bowed as they passed and then followed.

Anne smiled at Robert and whispered, "I feel like a princess, Robert. This experience is exciting. I wonder what Princess Adelaide will be like."

"You will soon know!"

They were shown into a large drawing room. The Prince called, "Robert, you are in time for morning tea!"

As Robert bowed politely and readied himself to shake hands, the Prince brushed past him and kissed Anne's hand.

"Lady Leystead! It has been too long since the Russian embassy. I hope your pregnancy is going well. It must be as you are looking radiant."

Anne curtseyed as best she could in her condition and answered, "The time is very close now, and I am in good health and fine spirits with Robert returning, your Royal Highness."

"Wonderful, Anne. Come and meet Adelaide. She is keen to meet you and display her embroidery. Sorry, Robert, we will talk soon, but first, I must set up the ladies comfortably for their morning tea."

Robert nodded and said, "I agree, your Highness."

He was thankful that the Prince was so forthcoming and welcoming. Princess Adelaide stood and, with a welcoming smile, took Anne's hand, genuinely saying, "My look at you, Lady Leystead. Will this be your first?"

Anne curtseyed again and answered, "Yes, your Royal Highness. I am new to this and thankful for my good health. But I want to be thinner and have a beautiful figure like yours."

The two women laughed, and the Princess offered Anne a seat beside her.

"Do you enjoy embroidery, Anne? It is one of my passions."

Realising this was an invitation to grow their acquaintance, Anne said, "I have always wanted to try, but my business interests have kept me from it. My, that pattern is exceptionally beautiful."

"Yes, it is a dainty old German pattern. I am glad that Lord Leystead is joining the security staff. I will always thank him for saving the prince's life at the Irish Charity Ball. My husband is quite senior in years to me, so I will appreciate each year he is with us. He is far fitter and healthy than his brothers. We are well suited to each other, and this is a happy household. The fact that he knows your husband is competent will reduce his stress levels and mine greatly. You never know what is going to happen during public appearances. He prefers his home life, being with his children, and, of course, entertaining."

Anne nodded and listened intently. Once Princess Adelaide had finished, she said, "I noticed no guards at the gate. Is that normal? The carriage just drove in."

Princess Adelaide called her husband, "William, there are no guards at the gate!"

"Yes, my dear. Robert and I were discussing that very matter. We will attend to it."

"Thank you."

Prince William drew Robert aside as the footmen served tea and said, "I understand you are joining as my Head of Security from the first of January. Colonel Scott will be going to Ireland and will be on the staff of the Viceroy. I think he is in for a torrid time there. Richard Wellesley, you know him? The Duke of Wellington's brother."

Robert nodded.

"There could be fireworks if his brother, Arthur, becomes Prime Minister and does not give him a cabinet position. The Earl of Ripon is having great difficulties holding together the coalition of Torys and Whigs! Mark my words: the Duke will be prime minister by early January. Then I fear we may have problems with Richard. He is nine years older than the Duke, and I hear that Arthur considers Richard too old. Too old, by Jove! Richard is a young sixty-seven with some excellent political skills. Not too old at all, but that is another matter. Ha-ha! Robert, there will be many interesting discussions ahead of us in the new year.

But getting back to your rank, Robert. I have spoken with the Admiralty, and they have appointed me as Lord High Admiral. I expected it would not be until next year, but they brought it forward with Admiral Crouch being out of action. I say that Admiral Bird is a difficult character! I much prefer dealing with Franklin Crouch - a good man!"

The Prince took a breath before continuing. Robert took the opportunity and said, "I agree, your Highness. Admiral Crouch is a fine fellow!"

Looking hard at Robert, the Prince continued, "Now, as I was saying. I spoke with the Admiralty, and you will be promoted to Commodore on the first of January. Birdy had a Commodore as his Secretary, so I was not to have him outdo me with my Head of Security's rank. Admiral Bird will tell you more about your promotion. Let me toast you, Sir! Girls join us in a toast."

The footmen hurriedly passed out glasses of champagne, surprising Adelaide and Anne.

"To Commodore Lord Leystead. Well done, old boy."

"Thank you, your Highness. I am greatly honoured."

Robert was somewhat astonished but pleased. Anne finished her champagne and asked, "I was not aware – congratulations, Darling."

Robert raised his eyebrows with a smile.

Prince William happily said, "I told you, Anne. I would do great things for this young man."

The Prince put his arm around Robert and led him off to the corner of the room.

"Robert, I am glad you are a Navy man. I need an honest answer. What do you think about steam-powered navy ships?"

"We need them quickly, your Highness. I am sure other nations will be already designing them. If we can put them into service first, they will give our navy a strategic advantage. Imagine not being held captive to the wind. It will introduce a completely new type of naval warfare."

"My thought exactly, Robert."

They talked and drank tea for some thirty minutes, settling into comfortable chairs at the end of the room. Robert found the Prince to be intelligent and full of new ideas. He warmed to him and thought his next three years would be most enjoyable.

"Are Robert, time is passing. There is a matter that I must discuss with you before you commence as Head of Security. The Intelligence people want you on another mission. Evidently, they need information from a man who only you can identify. Things are hotting up again with the Irish, and we need to stamp this out quickly. But he is not in Ireland, but Boston! I understand you know something of his movements. They need you to leave this weekend."

Robert sat there with his mouth open. He was committed to being with Anne for the birth of their child. He could not leave her again at such short notice. It would destroy her. Prince William could see the dismay on Robert's face. He turned away and watched Anne as she sat with Adelaide, happily chatting and looking at materials. Thinking to himself, 'the girl must only be nineteen or twenty. She is heavily pregnant, and the baby might come at any time. Understanding from his own experience how much childbirth affected a woman, he decided to delay Robert's departure.'

The Prince said, "My Boy, I can see the position this puts you in. If it were me, I would say no. But you do not have to say anything. I'm sure Birdee would say it is your duty, and you must go. But he is a cold man, that one. I say this man, Reid, as I understand it, can wait!

Once Anne has had the baby and you are sure she is safe, we will send you to Boston. I will tell the Intelligence people and the Admiralty that it will happen, let us say in February next. How say you to that, Commodore?"

Robert had broken into a sweat. He looked across at the prince and said, "I am deeply honoured by your kindness, your Highness. I will serve you with all my heart, Sir. I will not let you down."

"Good! I will settle it all with Birdee and those Intelligence people this afternoon. Mind you, I want the first news when your child is born. Your wife is a delight, and Adelaide and I will visit once the child is a few weeks old. We will pray for a safe delivery. Now, you must be on your way as I will soon have lunch, and then I am off to the Admiralty. "

"Your Highness, might I have a word with your Secretary, please? I must rectify the guard situation."

"Yes. Mr Abercrombie is visiting today. He is down the hall in the study, third door on the right."

"Your Highness, if you would give me three minutes."

"Yes, of course."

Robert darted off down the hall and found Abercrombie's office.

"Mr Abercrombie. I am Captain Robert South, and in January, I will take over as the Prince's Head of Security. I noticed no guards at the gate as we arrived, and upon checking again a few moments ago, there were still none present. Do you realise the government provides an army detachment to protect the Prince? Of course you do! But you are too lazy to check on them and ensure His Highness's safety."

Abercrombie looked up with a frown on his face.

"Mr Abercrombie, I will leave the prince's company and depart in ten minutes. If there are not two guards on that front gate by then, you will not have any balls left between your legs when you go to bed tonight. Do I make myself clear?"

The Secretary looked up wide-eyed and said, "Yes, Captain!" He ran from the room, calling, "Guards."

Robert smiled to himself and rejoined the Prince.

"I think the problem is solved, Your Highness."

Prince William chuckled, "I never knew Bertie could run so fast."

They both laughed, but Robert knew it was a serious situation.

"I shall have a message delivered to Colonel Scott this afternoon,

Sir. That gate must be always guarded, day and night."

As they left Bushy Park, Robert noticed the red-faced guards at the gate. The Secretary had done his job, and Prince William would know that his new Head of Security was astute and would not be trifled with. Captain South was happy, and he sat back and gazed into his beautiful wife's eyes.

"You are beautiful, Anne. I love you more than anything in this world."

"Don't let our Lord hear that, Robert!" She grinned, moved closer and gently kissed him. He loved her fragrance and kept her close.

"Robert!"

"Yes, Darling."

"You recall Mrs Constance."

"Anne, why would you think of her at a time like this?"

"I know it is funny, but when I visited her, she told me about some of her business dealings. It seems she was an escort to many government ministers and bureaucrats."

Robert tried to brush the conversation aside, "Is that important now when we can talk of far more pleasant things."

Anne sat straight up. She loved having Robert close, but this thought of hers could not wait. "They would tell her about their problems at work. They confided in her. Perhaps it made them enjoy her comforts more."

"So, what are you alluding to, Anne?"

"You thought there was a spy network within the government – people who were using the Irish for their means. What if she could tell you names, perhaps, of those involved?"

Robert sat up and looked straight at Anne's beautiful blue eyes, which were gleaming.

"It is possible she knows far more than she has divulged. A man in that situation will often let his guard down. Especially if the woman is indebted to him!"

They sat there for some minutes thinking of what Anne suggested.

Robert asked, "Would she cooperate with us? It is a long shot, but even the slightest lead might help."

"Well, she is still alive, but not for long. Should I visit her again?"

The Local Church, High Street Guildford, Surrey …

Sitting with his mother, father and Betty, Leonard watched the congregation slowly file past their pew and up to communion. He had tried to concentrate on what Jesus's death on the cross meant for him, but his mind wandered knowing that Jessica was here with her brother, Peter. They had arranged a picnic after church, and Leonard had spent much time organising a carriage and Betty the food so they could set off straight after the service ended. They would pick up Merryn on the way.

After the last hymn, the Reverend Taggart stood at the lectern and said, "Before we end the service, could I have your attention for a few minutes? Thank you.

I wanted to let you all know at the same time! You see, I have held the position of Rector here for over twenty years. Laura and I have enjoyed every minute of our ministry in Guildford, but some time ago, I recognised that I was getting on in age and that it may be time for a move to a smaller parish. We have prayed about this for months and received a message recently.

We have decided to move to Petersfield, where I have been generously offered a living. We will move there in the new year, and our last Sunday here will be Sunday, the twentieth of January. We understand you will be surprised by this decision; however, this parish needs new blood and a Rector with a new vision. I am not that person anymore, and I know there will be many applicants for a large church like this."

There was a ripple of shock through the congregation.

The Reverend Taggart continued, "We will be here every Sunday until the twentieth of January. I hope we can talk with you all and keep in contact in the future. You will be welcome to visit us in Petersfield with the proviso that you do not complain about your new minister." He smiled, "I think change is necessary for a church to mature and grow. You can be sure we will keep the church, that being its people, in our prayers forever. Now it is time to end our service and have some morning tea."

Andrew Taggart stood there and looked out over a vast congregation. The church was full, with no empty seats. He could see the look of shock and pain on the faces of many in the congregation. He smiled again and lifted his arms, saying, "Now, May the peace of God, which passeth all understanding, keep your hearts and minds in the knowledge and love of God, and of his Son Jesus Christ our Lord: And the blessing of God Almighty, the Father, the Son, and the Holy Ghost, be amongst you and remain with you always. Amen."[45]

There was a loud response of Amen, and slowly, conversations broke out as the recession passed.

Leonard looked around and saw Jessica was crying. He was somewhat astonished that the news of Taggart's leaving had upset her so much. Then he remembered her difficulties with Philip Hotspur and how Taggart had been instrumental in solving the situation. There was a deep connection between her and this legend of a priest. Somehow, he must comfort her.

Peter hopped up and said, "Good morning, Mr Webster and Mrs Webster. Sad news about the Reverend leaving. We must enjoy having him for the next few weeks."

Mervin Webster replied, "Yes, Peter. He will be a great loss. I have never appreciated a ministry more than Taggarts. A loss indeed! I hear you young folk are going on a picnic. The weather is favourable, but I would take umbrellas if I were you. Your friend Merrin is not here - will she be attending."

Leonard entered the conversation, "Yes, Father. We pick her up on the way. She is still considering church. It is not something she is familiar with."

Mervin listened and said, "Ah, I see. Well, we hope you all have a fine time."

As the families passed the Rector on the way out, Jessica broke into tears again as she met the Reverend Taggart.

"I don't want you to go, Rector. You have been so good to us and saved me from that Hotspur man."

Laura took Jessica and cradled her in her arms. She said, "We will be only twenty miles down the road. You may visit if you like, Jess. It is not the end of the world, Darling."

Noting that Jess was recovering, Leonard said, "Thank you, Reverend Taggart, you have been a good friend. We are having a picnic today up in the hills above Guildford. Would you and Mrs Taggart like to join us?"

---

[45] The Book of Common Prayer, University Printing House, Cambridge.

Andrew Taggart understood how the clever but compassionate young man was crafting the conversation, "Thank you, Leonard, but we have guests coming for lunch. Perhaps another time. Better than that, bring your young friends down to Petersfield when we are settled in."

Leonard smiled, "I will do that, Rector. Thank you again."

Peter and Jessica waved goodbye and followed Leonard and Betty to the carriage. As they climbed in, Jonathan Turner passed and said, "Are you travelling somewhere, Leonard?"

"Yes, to the hills above Guildford. We will have a picnic."

"Enjoy this good weather then." Jonathan waved, and Clemmie and Madeline, who followed their father, smiled as the carriage moved off.

Clemmie complained, "Why didn't Leonard invite me?"

Madeline said, "Perhaps he does not fancy you, Clemmie. But I am sure there will be plenty who do in time."

Clemmie looked at Madeline with a frown and then saw the compliment she was passing.

"That is a good way of understanding his reasons and my future. Thank you, Madeline."

The girls giggled as they followed their father and his wife towards their carriage.

Later in the afternoon, Leonard and Jessica rested on a long, flat rock, taking in the breathtaking view. Leonard said, "Have you recovered from Reverend Taggart's news?"

Jessica turned, surprised that he was considering her feelings, and looked at him, then smiling as she looked away. She said nothing but rested back with her hands behind her on the rock. She sighed, "I am beginning to realise that nothing stays the same forever. Look at poor William Turner – who knows what has happened to him. Why would the father send him away?"

Leonard took an apple from his pocket and took a bite. He chewed, swallowed, and said, "I am told there were huge disagreements between them. I don't know the full story, but Mr Turner must have acted for William's interests. Perhaps it was for the best – I am not sure."

"I would never allow my son to be sent away."

Leonard replied, "I am glad to hear it. I agree with you. Do you want to have children?"

Jessica turned with a question on her face, "Doesn't every girl want to have a son or daughter? It is what families are all about. How about you – do you wish to marry and have children?"

Jessica was unsure where she gained the confidence to ask Leonard such a question. But she hoped he might want to continue the conversation.

Leonard said, "The hour is late, so we should be off soon. But in answer to your question, yes, I would like to marry and have children, but I must have a full-time job before I make any plans."

Jessica laughed, "You are a deep thinker, Leonard. You worry about consequences. I am happy to have my family and my job at the Turners. I am far simpler, but I am mastering reading!"

"That is good, Jessica. You will need that in life. I would like to see more of you, Jess. Do you mind If I call you Jess?"

"Yes, Leonard. I would like that."

"I'm unsure how I can see more of you, Jess. How would we do that?"

"You come to my home and see my father. Ask if we can go walking in the early evenings. I am usually home by half past six. Also, we can meet on Sundays as I don't work then. But what about your parents – they may object if they know you are meeting with me?"

"They don't need to know, although Betty might mention it. I will sort that out."

Jessica smiled. She thought, 'It is a start. A wonderful start. He cares for me!'

Throughout the trip back to Guildford, Jessica Swamp could not keep the smile off her face.

Betty asked, "You are very happy, Jess. Why is that?"

"I have had a lovely day, Betty. Isn't that enough? Thank you for the lunch you prepared. It was beautiful."

Ewell Station, Outside Grahamstown, Eastern Cape Province, South Africa ...
Richard and George, plus a crew of men from town, had worked hard over the last few days restoring what they could of the homestead. At least it was now liveable, and the Army guaranteed the native war party had been destroyed. Richard wondered at the meaningless of the natives' attack. All those healthy young men were lost as the British cut

them to bits with their muskets and cannon fire.

As they sat on the verandah mid-morning, taking a work break and a cool drink, Richard asked, "George, why did those natives attack us? What was the point when they knew the British would retaliate?"

"Me not know, Baas! Maybe what you call payback. It is a point of honour for some of the tribes. I think the Xhosa will learn this time, but there will always be hotheads in the years to come. Is that how you describe them?"

Richard answered, "Yes, hot-headed!"

George continued, "There will always be a new hot-headed chief coming along who has no experience of the past."

"Did the Khoikhoi fight the British?"

"No, Baas! The Dutch. It was before my time, but they learned from the first fight. Better to work with the Dutch than fight."

Richard laughed, "You are right there, George. Much better."

George said, "What's that!" He stood and bent his head as if listening. Trudging off to the end of the verandah, he peered around the corner.

"Baas! The Mbeki are back with all their cattle and people. They are coming into the kraal."

Richard stood and ran, joining George on the side verandah. They watched as the cattle, some carrying packs, moved into the kraal, and the women started unloading belongings into their huts.

"Now we will discover why they did not warn us about the native war party coming." Richard approached the stable for his horse, but George ran after him and shouted, "Baas, not good to disturb them as they unpack. Not good manners – we should wait until they are settled. Maybe tomorrow. But OK, if they see you watching from here."

Richard stopped and turned, "What do you mean good manners?"

"It is the custom, Baas. You don't disturb a chief when they are not ready. They are busy now. Not matter as the raid is over, and we are alive. They are surprised. I can see them looking."

At this stage of life, Richard had learned to take advice. George was the local and could be trusted.

"Tomorrow, you and I will meet them. I want a promise from them that when they hear about a war party, they tell us. Otherwise, we will send them home."

George walked back and sat down, "Baas! Not good idea. Better to talk with Chief Nkosi. He will come and talk to Mbeki brothers. That better – you will see."

As they talked, Richard could hear cavalry approaching. He swung around to see a smiling Lieutenant Frederick Sanderson leading an army patrol. Freddie halted the column and dismounted, "Richard, how go the repairs?"

"Well, Freddie. The men you organised were a great help. Thanks to them, we are back in operation. The bedrooms upstairs are repaired and clean, and the kitchen is coming back together. Starting tomorrow, George and I will paint all the downstairs rooms for a week. I can't repair the wall and roof your canon blasted until more supplies arrive from Port Elizabeth. But I am thankful to be alive."

"Sorry about the canon, but as you say, we found you. Now, quickly, another topic! A man, lady and boy arrived in town yesterday. The boy claims to be your nephew –William Turner."

"William, I must go to town immediately. I have been expecting him for months."

"No need to travel to town. We led them out here. They are in a cart and coming up the driveway now."

"What!"

Freddie pointed, and there were three people in a small cart, one of them being a small boy waving and shouting, "Uncle Richard!"

Richard ran, and William jumped from the cart and rushed to him. Lifting him high in the air, Richard shouted, "My boy – you made it! Welcome to Africa."

William, Thomas, Robert, Anne and Clemmie
will be back in another exciting adventure soon.
Watch out for the next novel in the Turner Series,
Coming in 2026 (hopefully)!

www.vividpublishing.com.au

Acknowledgements

I commenced the Turner Series in 2017, which has been a source of great enjoyment for me since then. The first two books were of epic proportions and required significant research and travel. Turner's Strength is a shorter novel but still needed further research, travel, and building upon the foundation of Turner's Rage and Turner's Awakening.

Along the way, many people have given me advice and information on novel writing, research and time management. My thanks to all these people who have helped in so many ways. Some special people have been with me since I commenced writing in late 2016, and some have joined along the way and deserve special mention.

My wife, Julieanne, has helped with editing but more importantly, put up with me locking myself away researching and writing.

Faye and Trevor Lemke - I would never have been inspired to write these stories without your tome of our family history. Thanks also for all your support along the way.

Cousin Errol Seymour's book, 'The Boy Who Told Stories - The Seymours of Dunsborough', taught me much about my family. Also, thanks, Errol, for allowing me to use material from your book in my author talks.

Bishop David Mulready, a dear friend and fellow writer, provided many inspirational suggestions and has been a supportive editor over the years.

Mrs Christa Robat, a friend, provided documentation on South African history, architecture, topography, and advice on animals (particularly leopards and the Cape hunting dogs) and fauna.

My previous work colleague and supportive boss, Barry Leverton, introduced me to his uncle, Roy Lubke, from Grahamstown, South Africa (now named Makhanda).

Professor Roy A Lubke, Associate Professor Emeritus, Rhodes University, Grahamstown. Thanks for your contributions from your book covering geography and pictorial information of the Grahamstown area and the tribes.

Various family and friends have helped along the way with editing, proofreading and constructive comments. They will know who they are.

Thank you, family and friends.

No book is complete until the publishing process is complete. Thanks so much to Vivid Publishing, an imprint of Fontaine Press, which has been with me from the beginning. Jason Swiney, Publishing Director at Fontaine Press, has always been available, full of great ideas and insightful assistance. The Vivid team and Jason are a pleasure to work with.

www.ingramcontent.com/pod-product-compliance
Lightning Source LLC
Chambersburg PA
CBHW032300020726
47495CB00001B/188